ALSO BY MELANIE BENJAMIN

Alice I Have Been

THE AUTOBIOGRAPHY OF

Mrs. Tom Thumb

THE AUTOBIOGRAPHY OF

Mrs. Tom Thumb

[*A Novel*]

MELANIE BENJAMIN

DELACORTE PRESS / NEW YORK

The Autobiography of Mrs. Tom Thumb is a work of fiction. Any references to historical events; to real people, living or dead; or to real locales are intended only to give the fiction a setting in historical reality. Other names, characters, places, and incidents either are the product of the author's imagination or are used fictitiously, and their resemblance, if any, to real-life counterparts is entirely coincidental.

Published in the United States by Delacorte Press, an imprint of The Random House Publishing Group, a division of Random House, Inc., New York.

DELACORTE PRESS is a registered trademark of Random House, Inc., and the colophon is a trademark of Random House, Inc.

Library of Congress Cataloging-in-Publication Data
Benjamin, Melanie.
The autobiography of Mrs. Tom Thumb: a novel / Melanie Benjamin.
p.   cm.
ISBN 978-0-385-34415-9 (acid-free paper) —
ISBN 978-0-345-52757-8 (eBook)
1. Magri, M. Lavinia (Mercy Lavinia), 1841–1919—Fiction.
2. Women circus performers—United States—Fiction.
3. Dwarfs—United States—Fiction. I. Title.
PS3608.A876A94 2011
813'.6—dc22   2010052863

Printed in the United States of America on acid-free paper

www.bantamdell.com

Frontispiece photograph of Lavinia Warren by Mathew Brady
from the Library of Congress collection

2 4 6 8 9 7 5 3 1

First Edition

Book design by Susan Turner

To Dennis, without whom

From *Harper's New Monthly Magazine,* July 2, 1850

American Vanity

We are not at all surprised at what in this country is most foolishly called the conceit and vanity of the Americans. What people in the world have so fine, so magnificent a country? . . . If ever these magnificent dreams of the American people are realized—and all that is wanted for their realization is that things should only go on as they have been going on for the last two centuries—there will be seated upon that vast continent a population greater than that of all Europe, all speaking the same language, all active-minded, intelligent, and well off.

1885

I SUPPOSE IT WOULD BE FASHIONABLE TO ADMIT TO SOME RESER-
vations as I undertake to write the History of My Life. Popular
memoirs of our time suggest a certain reticence is expected, particularly when the author is a female. We women are timid creatures, after all; we must retire behind a veil of secrecy and allow
others to tell our stories.

To that, I can only reply, "Rubbish!" I have let others—one
other, in particular—tell my story for far too long. Now is the time
to set the record straight, to sort out the humbug from the truth,
and vice versa.

Has any other female of our time been written about as much
as I have? It was not so very long ago when it was impossible to
open a newspaper without reading about my husband or myself!
We even preempted the War Between the States during its very
darkest days. For a solid week, every newspaper in the land was
interested only in our wedding plans—the guest list, the presents
we received, my trousseau, in particular, receiving much press.
President and Mrs. Lincoln were so eager to make our acquaintance that they put aside their own cares, graciously welcoming us
to the White House on our honeymoon journey.

During the elaborate reception in the Blue Room, where
we met a number of dignitaries, including many generals who
would win themselves Glory on the Field of Battle, I permitted

Mr. Lincoln to kiss me. This was not something I allowed strange men to do as a rule, but felt I had to acquiesce to a presidential request. My husband, however, had no reservations of this sort; without even asking, he rose on tiptoe to bestow his usual happy kiss upon Mrs. Lincoln, who twittered and giggled and blushed a rosy red.

"Mr. Lincoln," she exclaimed with surprise. "The General kisses every bit as nicely as you!"

"Well, why shouldn't he, Molly?" Mr. Lincoln asked with a twinkle in his gray eyes. "I reckon he's had much more practice!"

Everyone laughed appreciatively, and none harder than my husband. I could not join in; it was a sore subject between the two of us already, so early in our marriage.

I determined to mention it to him later that night, when we were preparing for slumber. A more immediate problem, however, soon drove the thought from my mind. The enormous four-poster bed, piled high with the downiest of mattresses, pillows, and plush counterpane, was so tall that we despaired of ever reaching the top. Even my wooden steps, which I had carried with me since childhood, were not high enough. With great embarrassment, I had to summon a hotel chambermaid to assist us in attaining our goal. Once ensconced, naturally we were required to put off any thoughts of nighttime ablutions, unless we wanted to sleep the rest of the night on the floor.

The newspapers, naturally, did not recount this particular detail of our visit. This is but one example of why I have decided to write down my own recollections of my life thus far, and I vow I will do my best to keep them free of humbug.

Humbug. I can still hear my mother's gentle voice admonishing me all those years ago. "Oh, Vinnie, my little chick," she said with a worried shake of her head. "If you go with this Barnum you will be just another one of his humbugs. You will be caught up in that man's snare, and however will you escape without losing your soul?"

Looking back, I'm forced to admit that my mother was right; I did lose my soul, and so much more. But I'm not sure that I didn't give it away freely. My mother did not know Mr. Barnum as I did; she did not understand him, nor did the world at large. My intimacy with him is a prize, one that I am not willing to share with anyone. Not even with my own husband, who knew him first.

Not even with Minnie, although she would never have asked this of me; she never asked anything at all of me, except to keep her safe. And in that, I let her down.

This is but one more reason why I am eager to share my life's experiences: because I will finally be able to provide a full account of my beloved sister's all-too-brief time on this earth. My name may be on this volume's cover, as it was on all the handbills, headlines, and invitations, but for once I will not allow Minnie to remain in my shadow, although she was happiest there. I consider it my duty and privilege—even more, my penance—to tell her story, too. She deserves to be remembered; her courage needs to be known—as does the identity of the person, or persons, who killed her.

I have spent the last ten years trying to decide who was most responsible for her death, Mr. Barnum or me. Perhaps by the time I'm finished with this story, I will have figured it out.

Perhaps I won't, for I'm not sure I want to know.

Listen to me! I am putting the exclamation point before the salutation, as Mr. Barnum used to say; I had best dim the lights and commence my story before the audience grows restless. And there is no better way to begin this tale than by revealing, once and for all, my real name.

It is not, in fact—despite the manner in which I have been

introduced to Queens, Presidents, and even Mormons—Mrs. Tom Thumb. It is not even Lavinia Warren, which is how I was first introduced to the public.

No, God saw fit to bestow upon me the lamentable name of Mercy Lavinia Warren *Bump*.

And of the many obstacles He handed me at birth, Reader, I have always believed this to be the biggest.

OVERTURE

From the *Republican Compiler,*
Gettysburg, Pennsylvania, December 13, 1842

RIDING ON AIR

Our readers (says the *New York Express*) may not be generally aware that Railroad Cars are now being constructed to rest on air springs, or in other words, on iron pistons, moving in air-tight cylinders. The effect is wonderful. The cars ride smoothly and comfortably, and one may read or write in them very easily. But this is not all. It has been found a great waste to carry flour in barrels on railroads, in consequence of the jar. This invention is a complete remedy, and flour may now be transported on railways as well as canals.

From the *Brooklyn Daily Eagle,* June 18, 1842

NATURAL CURIOSITY

Can be seen at Shaw's (museum) Hotel, a double pig, having one head, eight legs, four ears, and two bodies.

———◆•••◆———

ONE

My Childhood,
or the Early Life of a Tiny

I WILL BEGIN MY STORY IN THE CONVENTIONAL WAY, WITH my ancestry.

About the unfortunately named Bumps, I have little to say other than they were hardworking people of French descent who somehow felt that shortening "Bonpasse" to "Bump" was an improvement.

With some pride, however, I can trace my pedigree on my mother's side back through Richard Warren of the Mayflower Company, to William, Earl of Warren, who married Gundreda, daughter of William the Conqueror. This is as far back as I have followed my lineage, but I trust it will suffice. Certainly Mr. Barnum, when he first heard it, was quite astonished, and never failed to mention it to the Press!

I was born on 31 October, 1841, on the family farm in Middleborough, Massachusetts, to James and Huldah Bump. Most people cannot contain their surprise when I tell them that I was, in fact, the usual size and weight. Indeed, when the ceremonial weighing of the newborn was completed, I tipped the scales at precisely six pounds!

My entrance into the family was preceded by three siblings, two male and one female, and was followed by another three, two male and one female. All were of ordinary stature except my younger sister, Minnie, born in 1849.

I am told that I grew normally during the first year of my life, then suddenly stopped. My parents didn't notice it at first, but I cannot fault them for that. Who, when having been already blessed with three children, still has the time or interest to pay much attention to the fourth? My dear mother told me that it wasn't until I was nearly two years old that they realized I was still wearing the same clothes—clothes that should already have been outgrown, cleaned and pressed, and laid in the trunk for the next baby. It was only then that my parents grew somewhat alarmed; studying me carefully, they saw that I was maturing in the way of most children—standing, talking, displaying an increased interest in my surroundings. The only thing I was not doing was *growing.*

They took me to a physician, who appraised me, measured me, poked me. "I cannot offer any physical explanation for this," he informed my worried parents. "The child seems to be perfectly normal, except for her size. Keep an eye on her, and come back in a year's time. But be prepared for the possibility that she might be just one example of God's unexplainable whims, or fancies. She may be the only one I've seen, but I've certainly heard of others like her. In fact, there's one over in Rochester I've been meaning to go see. Heard he can play the violin, even. Astounding."

My parents did not share his enthusiasm for the violin-playing, unexplainable Divine whim. They carried me to another physician in the next town over, who, being a less pious man than the previous expert, explained that I represented "an excellent example of Nature's Occasional Mistakes." He assured my increasingly distressed parents that this was not a bad thing, for it made the world a much more interesting place, just as the occasional two-headed toad and one-eyed kitten did.

In despair, my parents whisked me back home, where they prayed and prayed over my tiny body. Yet no plea to the Almighty would induce me to grow; by my tenth birthday I reached only twenty-four inches and weighed twenty pounds. By this time my parents had welcomed my sister Minnie into the world; when she displayed the same reluctance to grow as I had, they did not take her to any physicians. They simply loved her, as they had always loved me.

"Vinnie," my mother was fond of telling me (Lavinia being the name by which I was called, shortened within the family to Vinnie), "it's not that you're too small, my little chick, but rather that the world is too big."

My poor, tenderhearted mother! She thought that she was reassuring me. She was a lovely, pious creature, tall and thin, a clean, starched apron constantly about her waist. She had shining brown hair that I inherited, slightly worried brown eyes, and an ever-patient smile upon her lips. She only wanted me to be happy, to be safe; she wanted to keep me home, where she was certain less harm could come to me. She was trying, in her simple way, to reconcile me to that future, the only future that she—or anyone else—could envision for one my size.

What she didn't understand was that she was only inciting my curiosity about that big world. *Everything* was bigger than me; if the world was so much larger that she had to constantly warn me of it, what wonders did it contain? What marvels? I could not understand why anyone would not want to see them.

My father never tried to fool me in this way. He was not a demonstrative man, but around me, and then around Minnie, who was even smaller, he was extremely reticent. I believe he was terrified he might crush us with his big, work-worn hands, so he did not touch us at all, not a pat or a hug. He never seemed able to understand why God had made Minnie and me so small, and I believe he was slightly ashamed of us. Whenever we were out together as a family, he always kept his head bent; this way, he did not have to look anyone in the eye. I'm not sure he completely understood why he did this, or what he was afraid to encounter in the gaze of his fellow man; perhaps he simply didn't want to see pity for us there—or for himself.

Yet he loved us. And in the way of most men, he reacted by trying to *solve* us, as if we were the one wagon wheel that stubbornly refused to match up with the others, causing the whole contraption to wobble. This took the form of practicality, which, in the end, was much more useful than Mama's clucking and soothing. My first memory was of my father presenting me with a set of wooden steps, lovingly made by his own hands, which were too clumsy for caresses. They had crafted a beautiful set of steps, however, sanded to a honeyed glow so that not a single splinter might puncture a tender, tiny foot. They were lightweight, a miracle of engineering, so that I could easily carry them with me wherever I went.

Later, after the fire, Mr. Barnum gave me a gorgeous set of steps covered in crushed red velvet with my initials embroidered upon them. But they have never been able to take the place of my father's simple gift.

My brothers and sister swooped and ran and carried on like all children, happily including Minnie and me in their play, not worrying very much about whether or not we could keep up. And we could—or rather, I could. Unlike me, Minnie was content with her small corner of the world; she knew she could not easily keep up with the others, so she didn't even try. She found happiness, instead, in what was easily within her reach; no stair steps for her! She spent hours playing with her dolls, sitting on her little stool by the hearth, sewing handkerchiefs or helping Mama prepare meals. She was very shy around others and felt their stares keenly, even though she was as beautiful as a china figurine. Minnie was blessed with impish dark eyes that were such a contrast to her bashful demeanor, black curls, and a smile that revealed one perfect dimple in her left cheek. Only with me, closest to her in size but still larger, able to protect her, did she ever sometimes show curiosity or boldness; once she surprised me by suggesting we creep outside in the middle of the night, to see if there really were fairies living beneath the flowers.

Amused, I took her outside, where we tiptoed, hand in hand, peeking under the forget-me-nots and ferns. While she lifted leaves and petals with dogged optimism, stifling an occasional squeal whenever she happened upon a frog or a startled rabbit, I found my gaze pulled upward. The moon was low and luminous in the night sky; cocking my head, I was just about to make out the face of the man in the moon when Minnie excitedly exclaimed, "Oh, look, Sister! I found one, with green wings!"

She tugged at my sleeve, and I bent down. "It's just a dragonfly," I told her.

"No, it's a fairy, don't you see?"

"I just see a sleepy dragonfly."

"You're not looking at it right, Vinnie. It's as beautiful as a fairy, all green and shimmery. Can't you see it?"

I looked at my sister, her eyes shining brighter than the moon above. Who would have the heart to contradict her?

Growing up, Minnie listened, much more closely than I, to Mama's worries about our safety. Horses were Mama's chief foes;

she feared, as long as she lived, that Minnie or I would be trampled or kicked by a stray hoof.

On our behalf, she also feared wells, rain barrels, unsteady tables, large dogs, poison left out for the rats (even after I had long passed the age where I could reasonably be expected not to eat it), doors that latched, broken window sashes, snowdrifts, and falling fireplace logs.

I never understood her terrors. Safe, to me, was exactly where I was; low to the ground, where I became more acquainted with the bottoms of things than the tops. For example, I grew very adept at judging a woman's character or station in life by the hem of her skirt. Tiny, too-perfect stitches or ornate ruffles of course denoted a woman of high class, although not necessarily one of good character. Sloppy, loose, or haphazard stitches didn't always mean that a woman was slovenly in appearance; more often than not, it simply meant that she had so many children and cares she could not spare the time to attend to her own clothing. Those whose skirts sported tiny handprints or burnt patches resulting from too much time in front of the kitchen fire were always the most kindhearted.

Skirts were not the only things with which I was acquainted. Naturally I was more familiar with flowers and weeds than the tops of trees; furniture legs and the unfinished undersides of tables than framed pictures or mirrors. And that is why I never was fearful, why I could not understand my mother's worries; the things with which I was most familiar were the sturdier, more substantial things in life. The legs of the table, the widest part of the tree trunk, the foundation of the house, the things upon which everything else was dependent, upon which everything else was built. These were my world.

What my mother feared most—even more than tables toppling over on either Minnie or myself—was other *children*.

While she dutifully brought us to church each Sunday, our Christian education ever in her thoughts, my mother was most reluctant to send me to school with my brothers and sister. Fearing merciless teasing, rough play with children who were not accustomed to one my size, she thought it would be best to educate me at home, herself.

I, however, did not share this belief. I'd heard my siblings talk of the wonders of school, of slates and lunch buckets and schoolyard games and the glories of being asked to stay after to wash the blackboard. They came home taunting me with their knowledge, singing multiplication tables and spelling enormous words and pointing to the odd shapes on the globe in the parlor, proudly telling me the names of the continents and oceans.

So when I heard my mother tell my father she thought it best that I stay home with her and the younger children, I stamped my foot with as much authority as a seven-year-old can muster.

"No, Mama, you must allow me to go to school! Aren't I as smart as my brothers and sister? Why shouldn't I go with them, now that I'm old enough? They will look out for me, if that's what you fear."

Mama started to protest, but to my surprise, my father interrupted her.

"Huldah, I am surprised to admit it, but I agree with our Vinnie. She's a sharp little thing, with an intelligence that must be fueled. You could not give her all she needs here. Let her satisfy her curiosity at school, for a life of books is likely all the life she will ever have. It's best we give her that now. She'll have the rest of her days, I'm afraid, to stay home with you."

I was too young to fully understand my father's meaning. I heard only that he wanted me to go to school, and that was all I needed; I threw my arms about him even though I knew he did not appreciate such demonstrations.

"Oh, Papa, I am so very happy! Thank you! I promise I will never make you regret your decision!"

It would be a pretty story, indeed, if I could say that I never did! Yet I have to admit that I was so eager to be allowed my first foray into that large world that I became rather mischievous.

Full of high spirits, so delighted to be where I was, at first I could not be induced to remain in my seat. At the time, you might recall, country school desks were one long table affixed to the perimeter of the room, three-quarters of the way around.

On a dare, I discovered that I was small enough to fit neatly underneath the desk without having to duck my head; basking in the approval of my schoolmates, I took it a step further. Whenever the schoolteacher's back was to us, I would slide off my perch—several large books piled on top of one another—and duck beneath the desk. Then I would run along, barely stifling my giggles as I pinched and poked at my schoolmates' legs: the little girls' sensible woolen pantalets, the boys' worn and patched knees. I was so nimble that they could not catch me; I could run around the entire room and reach the end of the desk almost before the first child had reacted to my lively tugs with a squeak or a squeal.

"Mercy Lavinia Warren Bump," Mr. Dunbar, our teacher, would sputter. "Sit back down immediately!" He would try to catch me, but being the imp that I was, I could elude his grasp easily; he was inclined to heaviness (from the many tarts and pies that the older female students showered upon him), and would flail about, breathing laboriously. By the time he straightened himself up, his face red, his oily hair hanging down upon his forehead, I would be sitting primly in my seat, seemingly oblivious to my classmates' giggles.

"What am I to do with you?" he asked one day; standing over me, he shook his finger angrily in my face, pushed finally beyond his limit. "Shut you up in my overshoe? It's just about the right size for a mite like you; how would you like me to sit you in it?"

To my astonishment, my schoolmates burst into laughter at this. I looked around, scarcely believing what I saw: My friends, who had so admired me just a moment before, were giggling at the notion of me sitting in the teacher's overshoe. They were *laughing* at me; they were laughing at my *size*.

Only my brother Benjamin—just two years older than I— was not laughing; he was hanging his head, unable to look my way. He was, I realized with a sick, hollow feeling in my stomach, ashamed of me. He was ashamed to be my brother. I had never before experienced such guilt and rejection, both.

This, I suddenly understood, was what Mama had so feared: that were I to venture out from the safety of home, I would not be the only one hurt. This realization hit me hard, knocking the very breath from my being; I hung my throbbing head and bit my trembling lip. Up to this point in my life, I had rarely given my size any thought other than for the many inconveniences it caused me—the constant strain at the back of my neck from looking up, even just to talk to my siblings; the extra effort required to do the simplest of tasks, since I had to haul my steps with me everywhere I went; the fear and worry I knew I caused my dear mother, which hurt me only because it hurt her.

Now, however, my size was no longer merely an inconvenience—it was an embarrassment and a weapon. One Mr. Dunbar had seized upon, first thing, in order to shame me into behaving.

Blinking furiously, staring at my slate—for it was the only object I dared look at—I took some comfort in the realization that my sums were just as neat as anyone else's. They, at least, were not remarkable for any reason other than their accuracy. And so, with a great effort, I managed not to cry, for I did not want my tears to wash away this precious evidence.

That day after school, my brother Benjamin walked ahead of me for the very first time. Even though he waited for me to catch up with him after the rest of the children had fallen away, and picked me up and hoisted me upon his back without my asking, knowing that I was tired, for the first time there was a strangeness between us. He had been my closest sibling up until now, the one who would patiently carry me about, hold me up so that I might see the world the way he did. Now, unexpectedly, I didn't know how to breach this frightening new gap between us and I realized, even at such a tender age, that I never would—and that the gap would only widen with time. It grieved me to think that I had shamed him so; I did not stop to think that he might bear some responsibility for his feelings, as well.

From that day on, I devoted myself to study in the classroom, leaving play for the schoolyard or on the long walk home. I realized that one my size could ill afford to play the imp; I resolved to be dignified, always. And indeed, when I first became known to the Public at Large, this was what people remembered most about me; my gentility and deportment were always remarked upon with no little admiration.

Evidently I also impressed Middleborough's elders with my studious, dignified ways. For when I was sixteen, it was decided to divide the school into a primary and a secondary room; soon after, the school committee showed up at my parents' door, asking to speak with me.

"We would like to offer Miss Lavinia the position of schoolteacher of the primary room," the chairman told my parents once we were all seated in the parlor. Mama was justifiably proud of this pretty room, full of her finest china lamps, snowy lace scarves covering the polished wood surfaces. She always kept it neat and scrubbed and ready for unexpected guests.

My parents' surprise, I must say, could not have been greater. Mama gasped. Tears filled her eyes, and Papa colored and ducked his head the way he always did when he was pleased.

"Oh, how wonderful! How kind, how very kind! Vinnie, what do you think?" Mama turned to me with shining eyes, a wondrous smile illuminating her gentle face.

Seated upon my own rocking chair—one of the few pieces of furniture in the house that was made to my scale; Papa had fashioned it himself—I studied my hands, gracefully folded upon my lap. My heart fluttered with excitement, but I waited until it calmed down before finally looking up and fixing the chairman with a steady gaze.

"I accept, naturally, although I do wish to inquire about my pay. How much remuneration per school term are you offering?"

For some reason this amused everyone; the entire party broke into helpless guffaws, the chairman—a large man whose waist could not be contained by his waistcoat—slapping his fleshy knee with such gusto he very nearly toppled one of Mama's prized lamps. Sitting there, my face burning so hotly I thought my cheeks must be very scarlet indeed, at first I failed to understand their laughter. What was so amusing about wishing to know what I would be earning?

Yet I did understand it. For by now I was well aware that some people found it very odd to hear perfectly sensible, rational notions coming from me. This was because of who I was—or, rather, *what* I was.

And what I was, of course, was both small—and *female*.

As a female, not to mention a female with no other prospects, I was supposed simply to accept their kind offer for what, even then, I suspected was likely an act of charity. Yet a *male* teacher would have been expected to inquire about his wages; if he hadn't, he would have been dismissed as a fool and not engaged.

I endured their laughter with flaming cheeks, allowed it to die, yet repeated my question without hesitation; I saw my father open his mouth to say something but then catch my gaze and hastily shut it.

"Miss Bump, I find it unusual, to say the least, that you would so boldly inquire about wages," the committee chairman said after he finally composed himself. "Naturally, I will speak to your father about what we will pay."

"But my father isn't the one teaching, is he?"

"No, but it is customary, of course—"

"As it is customary to engage a schoolteacher who will not be smaller than her pupils. Yet you have chosen to ignore this custom; let us dispense with the other. My wages?"

Perhaps it was because I remained—with great effort, struggling against my anger at the man's obtuseness—so composed that he finally managed to mutter the agreed-upon sum. I nodded in acceptance, to his obvious relief, and the matter was settled. When the committee rose to leave, I made it my business to quickly approach the chairman to shake hands, instead of leaving him to perform this customary ceremony with my father.

"Miss Bump, I declare, I'm mighty glad that I'm not going to be a pupil in your school. I suspect you won't put up with any mischief at all," he remarked as he bent down toward me, a twinkle in his eye.

"No, I assure you right now that I won't," I answered earnestly, for I would not allow him to make this—or me—into a joke. "There will not be a better run classroom in all of Massachusetts; just you see."

And I have to say, without false modesty, that there was not.

On the first day of class I induced Benjamin to drive me to school early, which he did despite his misgivings over this whole enterprise.

"Vinnie, don't you see they're making fun of you? Making you an experiment? How can you let them?"

"If that is true," I replied as we hit a deep rut in the road, causing me to bounce upon the wagon seat as my feet naturally could not reach the floorboards, "I intend to turn the tables upon them. Then we'll see who gets the last laugh."

"I don't understand you, Vinnie. It'd be so much easier for you not to be out as much in public."

"Easier for whom? For I can think of no fate drearier than sitting at home by the hearth for the rest of my life, watching all of you go off one by one."

Benjamin didn't reply, but once we arrived at the school-house, he worked diligently to help me make sure the room was ready. He and I (aided by my indispensable stair steps) soon had the blackboards shining, the chairs smartly lined up, the *McGuffey's Readers* laid out upon the desks. Mama had made me a special cushion for my desk chair, so that I could keep a watchful eye upon my pupils.

I asked Benjamin then to go ring the school bell so that when the first of my students arrived, I was standing calmly in the middle of the room. I did not attempt to hide my size by staying behind my desk or perching upon any kind of platform. I simply stood there, as dignified, as tall, as I could possibly make myself appear.

Mama had made me a new dress, the skirt long and full so that it finally reached the ground, hiding my child's shoes, which were an unfortunate necessity. But I was wearing my first corset; Mama had ordered the smallest one that was carried at the general store, and altered it as best she could. She cut it down, removed several stays, stitched it all back up again, but still it gapped in odd places. Yet I *felt* somehow more correct, more upright, even so. My chestnut hair was secure in a simple, becoming twist; my head felt heavy on top, while my neck felt bare. It was the first time I had not worn my hair in long braids down my back.

Thus, appropriately attired and groomed, I absorbed the unbelieving stares, the nudges and whispers, as the children filed into the room. Many of the pupils, naturally, knew who I was; some did not. Yet even those who knew me seemed taken aback to see the teacher's pointer in my hand.

My heart beat fast, despite my best effort to calm my breathing. I was not afraid, exactly; it was more as if I was standing upon the edge of a table, ready to jump—believing, somehow, that I would fly instead of fall. I felt as if this was the first important moment of my life.

After the singing of the morning hymn, I addressed my young charges in a firm, clear voice; I had practiced my speech the night before.

(Little did I know this would be the first of many, many performances to come!)

"My dear children, I can see you have a number of questions. Let me begin by introducing myself as your teacher, Miss Bump. Some of you I know already; the rest I am eager to get to know. The school committee selected me to run the primary school based on my excellent academic record; only a year ago I was a pupil, just like all of you!"

I smiled at the unbelieving gasps and whispers.

"I say this only to remind you of what is possible if hard work and diligence are applied to your schoolwork. Now, there is the matter of my size."

More gasps, some giggles; holding myself perfectly still, I waited for them to fade away.

"Yes, my size. As you can well see for yourselves, I am of less-than-average height. In fact, I daresay the smallest of you is larger than me. Shall we see? Who is the smallest in the class?" I smiled at the astonished look of merriment that soon appeared on every young face; I knew, then, that this was the best way to approach the subject. The resolve that had first formed in my mind all those years ago, when Mr. Dunbar threatened to shut me up in his over-shoe, now fully took shape: Never would I allow my size to define me. Instead, I would define *it*. My size may have been the first thing people noticed about me but never, I vowed at that moment, would it be the last.

I would repeat this vow so many times in the years to come. I repeat it even to this day. And to this day, I still don't know if I was successful in keeping it.

One small lad was selected by his classmates to stand next to me—Jimmy Morgan, I believe his name was, although my memory cannot be trusted—and he shyly approached, tugging nervously at his red suspenders.

"Come, come, don't dawdle; there's nothing to fear," I said briskly, holding my hand out to him. "See here, my head only comes up to your chin, doesn't it?" I tilted my face up to emphasize the disparity; Jimmy's blue eyes stared down at me, wide and astonished.

He nodded, his cheeks scarlet, as his classmates roared with delight. I motioned for Jimmy to go back to his seat; then I waited for the laughter to fade away.

"Now, you've had your fun, as I've had mine. We will forget about it from this moment forward; I am not your friend, not your doll, not your playmate. I am your teacher and will expect every consideration, every show of respect, that my position demands. You will see that my size has nothing to do with my mind or even my will; I am not afraid to use the whip or the ruler if the situation arises. Now open your readers to the first page, and let us begin."

Without a murmur, every child obeyed my command. And for the rest of the term, I had no trouble at all managing my classroom. The school committee chairman was most impressed, and soon became fond of bringing in other school committees, from neighboring townships, to observe my orderly pupils, their respectful harmony. If this was his idea of sport, I did not give him any satisfaction; I found myself growing more dignified by the minute when under the gaze of astonished onlookers, as if to make up in deportment what I so lacked in height.

Yet to my surprise—for I was still very sensitive, in those days, to remarks about my size—I enjoyed being watched; I basked in the attention, not minding what had prompted it so much as I minded that those who watched left admiring me. And I began to look forward to those days when I had an audience, planning special games and songs for my pupils. The rest of the time seemed dull and ordinary by comparison.

I do admit to having fun with my charges, though; I was still young, of course, and my high spirits could not be contained by my ill-fitting corset. While I refrained from joining them during recess, I did not always walk sedately home at the end of the day. On more than one occasion, stiff from sitting so long at my desk, I joined in footraces and sometimes allowed the biggest children to carry me on their shoulders, which was a privilege much sought after. And when the first snow fell, I was very touched when a contingent of boys appeared at my door with a sled; after I was tucked in with a bearskin, they pulled me merrily to school, sleigh bells jingling around their necks.

At the end of the fall term, when I handed out marks with the knowledge that not one of my pupils had failed, I felt the satisfaction of a job well done. I was seventeen now, an established schoolmarm. My future seemed secure, and it was a future with which my mother, at least, was very content—a decent wage that I could put away for the time when my parents were no longer able to provide for me; useful work to occupy my days and tire me so that my nights were not sleepless with longing; respect within our little community so that I was no longer an oddity but a beloved, vital member, protected and cared for.

Yet there was still a sadness that clung to my mother, despite all this. It was unspoken, but no one ever expected me to marry. No hope chest was begun for me as had been done for my older sister at the same age, no bridal lace set aside.

One day I rounded a corner only to hear my mother whispering to my sister Delia; stifling a giggle, I quickly hid inside a cupboard, rejoicing over the advantage my size gave me in eavesdropping. They were talking about the birds and the bees; I listened eagerly, until I was startled to hear my own name.

"Could Vinnie ever—" Dee began in a strangled voice.

"Oh, it would be dreadful, impossible," Mama replied, muffling a sob. "Don't you remember the little cow on Uncle's farm who . . ." And her voice trailed off.

I did not remember any little cow, but its fate was evident in my sister's sudden horrified exclamation. *That* I never forgot; it made my blood run cold, my heart seize in a nameless fear. I lived on a farm, after all; I knew cows—and horses and goats and sheep. I knew *life*—and how wrenching its beginning could be, even among creatures built far more sturdily than I. Shaking, I stole away from my hiding place wishing I had not been so clever. And for the first time, I looked at myself as Papa did; I felt that there might be something broken within me, after all.

That night I could hear my tenderhearted mother weeping for me, even through the thick plaster walls of the second-floor bedrooms. It was not the first night she had done so.

Did I share in her sorrow? In many ways, I was still too young to be given over to such dire, unhappy thoughts. No one would ever have predicted I would be a schoolteacher, and yet—wasn't that what I had become?

I did have a longing inside me, however, that I could not entirely ignore. I loved my family, loved the farm, loved my work. But contemplating a future only within these confines made me increasingly restless. There was something missing; I could define it only by its absence, but I yearned for it those nights when I heard my mother crying over my lonely, loveless fate.

It was around this time that I went for a walk in the near cow pasture; it was early spring but warm for the season, the weeds already high. They made my progress more difficult, but I didn't mind; pushing through them, I imagined myself in a mysterious forest, like the ones in so many of the fairy tales I read to my young pupils.

Soon, however, I came upon a familiar tree: a tall maple tree with an unusually wide trunk. Upon this trunk, my brothers and sister and I had once scratched our names and ages, according to our height. Craning my neck upward, I could make out *Benjamin, George, Sylvanus,* then *James,* and finally *Delia,* their names plainly visible, high up the tree—

But where was I? Where was my name? I remembered standing against the tree one summer while James took out a pocketknife and carved a line right above my head; he had then scratched my name to the side of it—I could still see his tongue sticking out with the effort as he complained that our names were so devilishly long. . . .

Brushing aside the weeds, I finally located my name; it had been covered up by the tall grasses and the climbing, glossy green tendrils of creeping myrtle, its starlike blue flowers not yet in bloom. I was only an inch or so taller than that line, even though

I was years older. My brothers and sister, however—grown up now, as well—were all much taller than their childish measurements.

I had the queerest feeling; it was as if a shadow had fallen over just me, while the rest of the world remained illuminated by bright sunlight. At that moment I felt hidden from all eyes; looking at my name, covered over by weeds, I saw how easily it could disappear forever. I saw how easily *I* could be forgotten, compared to my brothers and sister, compared to everyone else, everyone who was taller, more noticeable, more visible to the rest of the world.

I did not want to be forgotten. More than that, I wanted, desperately—I fell to my knees and began to tear out the weeds, the vines, by their very roots—to be *remembered*. I wanted my name to be known, beyond this tree, this hill, this pasture, this town.

The weeds were in a pile at the base of the tree; my hands were stained green, my nostrils filled with the pungent, mossy scent of new grass, and my skirt was damp where I had kneeled on it. But my name was now plainly visible; I smiled in satisfaction, brushed my hands off on my skirt, and continued my walk. My fierce desire soon faded away into the twilight; the air grew chilly, and I saw the warm, beckoning lights of home twinkle on, one by one, as Mama began to light the lamps, which shone, at that moment, more brightly than the faint stars on the horizon.

And then I heard Minnie calling, in her surprisingly strong, clear voice, "Vinnie! Where are you? I want to show you the most beautiful four-leaf clover I found!"

I smiled, for I knew she would be standing in the doorway looking for me, clutching that clover in her tiny fist until I came back, no matter how long I might take. So I was content to turn around and return home, content with what I knew was waiting for me there.

So it was that when we broke for vacation that spring of 1858—remember that at the time, country schools were open only during winter and summer, as the children were expected to help with farmwork—I truly had no plans other than to enjoy my time off, sleep in later than usual, and make some new dresses for the upcoming term.

An unexpected knock on our door one afternoon soon revealed that God—not to mention P. T. Barnum—had other plans for me, instead.

INTERMISSION

———◂•••▸———

From *The New York Times,* January 25, 1853

Of domestic news, we have fewer shipwrecks, murders, defalcations
and deaths to record than usual.

———◂•••▸———

From *The New York Times,* March 2, 1853

The construction of a Magnetic Telegraph line to the Pacific Ocean is
only second in importance to the project of a railroad across the continent to its western shore. The subject is before Congress; and even at
this eleventh hour, a united, determined effort of its friends, and a few
minutes of the time now so valuable, will be sufficient to secure the immediate initiative and early consummation of the work.

———◆◆◆———

TWO

Leaving Home, or an Interlude of Heart-Tugging
Music and Recitation

I'VE GOT YOU IN HERE WITH MISS HARDY. SHE'S A TROUPER; she'll show you the ropes," Colonel Wood said as he led me through a narrow, damp passageway. On either side were closed doors to various staterooms. Beneath us was the great engine of the boat, silent for now, as we were still docked. The green carpet in the passageway was dirty and smelled of mildew; the paint on the walls was chipped and dotted with mold. I was perspiring so in the humid, dank air that I could well imagine mold beginning to grow on *me;* my skin felt plastered to my underclothes and uncomfortable corset that still did not fit properly.

"Oh."

"She's simple enough, so don't let her appearance scare you any."

"Oh."

"Now, I know I promised your folks I'd see to you myself, but

I run a mighty big outfit here; I'm a very important man, you'll soon see. So don't come runnin' to me with every little thing. You'll have to stand on your own two feet, as tiny as they are." The Colonel chortled at this.

"Oh."

This one word was all that I had uttered for days; weeks, even, it seemed to me. Ever since I bade my family a tearful farewell just as the fields were ready for plowing. It was late April now, and here in Cincinnati the air was already as balmy as summer, and the wide, muddy Ohio River did not look as if it could ever freeze completely over.

"Here you go—shove on in now, your trunk'll get delivered later." Without even knocking, Colonel Wood opened the door to a stateroom; he held it open for me in one of the few gentlemanly gestures I had observed from him during our brief acquaintance. I arranged my face into a pleasant, welcoming smile, then stepped with assurance across the threshold to meet my new traveling companion, my hand already thrust out in greeting.

"Hello, my name is Miss Lavini—Oh!" I couldn't help myself; I stopped dead in my tracks, all sensible notions drained from my being. My hands, my knees, began to quake, and I would have turned around and run back outside, had Colonel Wood not been immediately behind me, barring any escape.

For slowly rising from a bed—no, two beds, pushed together end to end—was a giantess. An actual giantess, such as I had read about in many a fairy tale, the kind of creature that ate little children who got into mischief or otherwise misbehaved.

The giantess continued to unwind herself, rising slowly—oh, so slowly!—until she had reached her full height, which seemed, from my perspective, to be twenty feet, at the very least! She had to stoop so that her head did not brush the sloping stateroom ceiling.

"Hello, Miss Lavini-o," she said in a basso profundo voice. With a smile, she extended her hand; a hand so massive, so bony, that I fought with every fiber of my being not to recoil from it. As it came near me—again, so excruciatingly slowly—I glanced quickly at the giantess's feet; they were the size of canoes, and I could easily imagine them squishing me into oblivion. I remembered Mama's silly terrors about horses' hooves; how quaint a fear that seemed now!

"M-m-my name is Lavinia," I corrected the giantess as I placed my hand, my tiny, delicate hand, in her enormous one. I winced in anticipation, but to my relief she did not crush me. In fact, she seemed to be as hesitant to touch me as I was to touch her; her hand did not even close completely about mine, and she withdrew it with as much haste as she could muster.

I must confess, right here and now, to making a dreadful assumption. And that assumption was that a person this tall, who moved this slowly, must be very slow of mind and wit as well. All my life, I must admit, I have always associated quickness of mind with smaller people, quicker people, people like me. Large, clumsy creatures, freaks of nature to me—my initial assumption was always that they possessed inferior minds.

So I corrected the giantess, thinking she was not very bright, forgetting that I myself had mispronounced my own name in my initial consternation.

"And my name is Sylvia. Miss Sylvia Hardy, from Maine."

"For the love of Pete, just look at the two of you!"

I spun around, startled to find Colonel Wood still standing behind me; I had forgotten all about him. He stood gaping at the tableau before him, his head swiveling up and down as he took the pair of us in; there was an eager gleam in his eye as he appraised the situation.

"Oh, this is going to be rich! The two of you side by side—

by God, I'm a genius! Barnum who, I ask you? Eh? Colonel John Wood will be the name on everybody's lips, I wager!"

I was too speechless to respond. The giantess, however, was not; she dismissed him with a firmness I could not help but admire as she said, "Goodbye, Colonel Wood. Leave us to get better acquainted, for I imagine Lavinia is tired from her journey."

And despite the rumbling low pitch of her voice—it tickled my eardrums—and the slowness of her speech, I turned to her with gratitude, blinking back sudden tears. I *was* weary; the journey *was* exhausting. The excitement of my very first train trip had long since abandoned me. The exhilarating sense of discovery I had felt as I stared out soot-covered windows while unfamiliar scenery passed so swiftly by; the novelty of eating sandwiches wrapped in paper, bought from enterprising farm boys at various stops; the thrill of rattling over high bridges while far below, unfamiliar rivers ran—all was gone now.

I remembered only the dirt, the barnyard odors of being in such close company with strangers who did not wash regularly, the stiffness of my back from sitting up for so long even in sleep, the impossibility of making myself feel fresh with the dirty water in the lavatory basin. That is, even if I could *reach* the basin; I couldn't, unless I dragged my stair steps with me, but there usually wasn't enough room in those miserable little closets. And often there were no closets at all, just primitive dark corners with buckets full of human waste slopping out with every rattle over a railroad tie.

We changed trains so many times I lost count, always a chaotic affair. I had to submit to countless strangers lifting me up and down, for there was no way to manage the great difference between train and platform myself, and Colonel Wood was always gone somewhere, wrestling with our luggage or arguing with the ticket agent that I should cost him only half a fare because I took up only half a seat.

These dispiriting experiences were all I remembered now; they had left my clothes filthy and stained, my skin covered in a gritty film of dirt, my toes pinched and blistered. My first pair of adult shoes, custom-ordered to fit, had proven to be very uncomfortable for feet used to the soft soles of children's slippers.

I also remembered, suddenly and overwhelmingly, how sad my parents and Minnie had looked when they said goodbye. I had waved at them for as long as I could as I drove away with Colonel Wood in his wagon, all my clothes and mementos and my beloved stair steps packed in a trunk borrowed from my married sister, Delia, as there had been no time to purchase one of my own. I remembered Mama's tears, Minnie's wails, Papa's stoic face, his emotion betrayed only by the working of his Adam's apple.

The memories overwhelmed me, and I could not help it; as soon as the Colonel shut the door and I was left alone with the giantess, my tears could no longer be contained. I sat down on the floor, not caring about my dress, and I put my head in my hands and began to cry. Why, oh why, had I ever decided to leave home? My heart—too large for me all of a sudden, too full of pain and longing for family—felt as if it would break into pieces, so lost, so lonely, so dirty, and yes, so very *small,* did I feel.

Mama had been right all along. The world was too big for me. I would get lost in it, swallowed up or trampled by this giantess—

Who, without a word, without a sound, scooped me up in her arms and carried me to her bed. There she held me on her lap, rocking me as if I were a child, as I turned my head toward her vast, comforting bosom and sobbed my heart out.

A MONTH EARLIER, COLONEL JOHN WOOD HAD SHOWED UP AT our door. It was in March of 1858, during my first vacation from teaching. With a knock, a bow, a presentation of a card, he was ushered inside, where he brought with him the bracing air of a different world. He was dressed not in military clothing, as one might expect (I never did understand how he came by his title), but his costume was no less exciting. He wore a jacket made of red wool; I'd never seen such a thing on a man before! All the men in my life wore sober black, gray, or brown. Complementing his red jacket was an emerald-green vest, which was hung with a bright gold watch fob. His black hat, over graying curls, was shiny and tall, and he carried a polished ebony walking stick. He had a habit, I soon discovered, of pressing two fingers against his mustache—suspiciously black, considering how gray his curls were—whenever he desired to appear thoughtful.

In short, he looked to be quite a man of the world to us Bumps, so insulated in our rural community. I would come to know many men of the world and recognize that the Colonel was not quite the dandy he thought himself to be, but at the time he certainly impressed Mama and me; Papa, however, merely sat and regarded him with a skeptical eye, puffing on his pipe distrustfully.

"Sit down, sit down, and let us figure out our relation," Mama exclaimed as she ushered Colonel Wood into our parlor; he had introduced himself as a cousin, which was all the calling card one needed in Middleborough, Massachusetts.

"Don't mind if I do," Colonel Wood replied, taking the best chair before he was asked. While he addressed Mama, I felt his curious gaze still upon me, as it had been since his arrival. Minnie was off hiding in her room—she always vanished whenever we had visitors—and my three brothers who were still at home, while politely greeted, were given no further notice by our visitor. Colonel Wood seemed fascinated solely with me. His attention was different than what I usually encountered from the few strangers who happened through Middleborough; he did not look as if he was about to ask me if fairies had forgotten to give me my wings (one of the many fanciful sentiments that strangers were inspired to utter when first making my acquaintance).

Instead, I felt his gaze to be more calculated, more appraising, but for what purpose I could not begin to guess.

As Mama and he attempted to sort out their relation—I never did figure it out and later wondered if there really was such a connection—he still managed to throw glances my way, as if he was sizing me up. Whenever I ventured to speak, he listened carefully, and I could sense first his approval and then his excitement as I displayed my usual intelligence in my typical forthright way.

Finally, he admitted he had come here with a specific purpose in mind.

"Have you all ever heard of a fellow named Barnum?"

"Well, yes, Cousin, of course we read the newspaper. Do you think we're so ill informed, just because we're farmers?" Mama answered softly, chidingly; despite our humble abode and plain living, she was very conscious of her heritage as a descendent of one of the Mayflower Compact signers.

"Of course not, of course not," Colonel Wood replied hastily. "Forgive me, I've been so long in the West that I sometimes forget how civilized we are here in New England."

"What does that Barnum have to do with us?" my brother Benjamin asked, regarding Colonel Wood with barely concealed hostility.

"Well, he's had a great deal of success, you know. First with that Tom Thumb fellow, the one that visited England and had tea with the Queen and all. Then with Miss Jenny Lind, the Swedish Nightingale."

At the mention of Tom Thumb, Mama and Papa exchanged glances, careful not to look my way.

"Can't say as I approve of that man," Papa grumbled. "It seems wrong, somehow."

"Wrong? Why, both Jenny Lind and the little man are famous! Millionaires, they say! Living it up, meeting royalty—what's wrong with that? Sounds like a mighty fine life to me!" Colonel Wood was unable to keep up his careful nonchalance; he was now leaning forward, his dark eyes snapping.

"I'd wager it's that Barnum who's getting rich," Papa retorted. "Showing people about like they're *things*, not humans. Humbugging the public, like he did with that Joice Heth, claiming she was a hundred and sixty-one years old! George Washington's nurse, he said she was! George Washington's nurse, my eye. Anyone could tell she was just some old slave woman."

"Oh, but Papa—Miss Jenny Lind is not a thing! She's an artist! And what was the humbug there?" I couldn't help myself; I did not like to contradict my father, but on the subject of Jenny Lind, I could not keep quiet.

I was just a child when Jenny Lind came to America, back in 1850. I never heard her sing; she never came anywhere near Middleborough. But I followed her every move in the newspaper, drinking in every detail of the Swedish Nightingale—what she wore, how she did her hair, what her favorite foods were. And, of course, how she sang: like an angel, the newspapers said. With a voice of such incomparable beauty it made grown men weep, particularly when she ended her concerts with her signature song, "Home Sweet Home." There were Jenny Lind waltzes performed in her honor, Jenny Lind polkas, ballads, clothes, dolls, figurines. I had a china likeness of her that Papa and Mama had given me on my tenth birthday; I kept it on the windowsill in my bedroom.

Mr. P. T. Barnum, the famous promoter, brought her here from Europe; he arranged her concerts and made her a household name, although they parted ways in 1852 and she had since returned to Europe. He told of all this in his recent autobiography, which had caused an uproar, for in it he admitted to several humbugs he had perpetrated upon the public, including the one involving Joice Heth, as well as the one involving General Tom Thumb. Born Charles S. Stratton, the latter had been a lad of only five when Mr. Barnum had first presented him, back in 1843, as "General Tom Thumb, a marvel of miniature perfection, eleven years of age!"

Since then, the tiny general had traveled to Europe and met with Queen Victoria herself. I admit to my curiosity being aroused by the few newspaper illustrations I had seen of him, now a young man, three years my senior. So far in my life, the only other little person I knew was my sister Minnie. The evidence that there were others incited my curiosity and made me feel slightly less alone. Knowing that General Tom Thumb had sung and danced for huge crowds and become celebrated the world over gave me a peculiar sense of pride, I must confess. Also, he was a handsome fellow in the illustrations; boasting large, mischievous eyes and a winning smile, he looked very smart in his various miniature uniforms.

He was no Miss Jenny Lind, of course, but reading about either of them was like reading about royalty, or Presidents; their lives were special, remarkable, not at all like my own or my family's.

"Oh, Papa, you know how I longed to hear Jenny Lind sing! She's the reason I practice so very much on my own music," I reminded my father, who looked at me with a suddenly clenched jaw and narrowing eyes, as if he was trying silently to warn me not to speak further. But I did not heed his warning. "Do you know Mr. Barnum?" I asked Colonel Wood, unable to contain my excitement.

"Why, sure, sure," he answered smoothly, addressing me for the first time. "Naturally! We showmen all know each other."

"Really?" I couldn't help but be impressed. "Did you ever see Miss Jenny Lind?"

"Certainly! Many a time did she sing for me privately, when I was in New York working for Mr. Barnum himself. I take it you sing, Miss Lavinia?"

"Oh, I'm a schoolteacher, but I do love to sing." I returned Mama's fond smile; my songs were much loved not only within the family circle but also in the schoolroom. From an early age, I had enjoyed soothing my classmates with ballads. Mr. Dunbar used to pick me up and place me atop his desk, so that all could hear.

"A schoolteacher?" Colonel Wood seemed momentarily stunned; his face, which had been as smooth as his talk, suddenly creased in thought. "Hmmm. I didn't know that. I thought that you were just—well, just . . . at home. But I guess it don't really matter, at that."

"What doesn't matter?" Mama asked anxiously. Papa remained silent, but I could feel his whole body tense, even though I wasn't seated near him. He appeared as if he was steeling himself for bad news.

"My boat. My floating palace of entertainment. We sail up and down the rivers out west, bringing amusement to the poor, hard-working folks who have no other kind. I have minstrels, jugglers, dancers, and some curiosities—a man who can swallow nails, a tattooed man, a giantess. But what I don't have is a—I mean, as soon as I heard of Miss Lavinia here—and, of course, our cousinly connection—and now that I know she's a true artist, as well—I thought she might be interested in joining me. Singing, of course—just like a certain Miss Jenny Lind? A certain General Tom Thumb?" Colonel Wood winked at me.

You could have heard the proverbial pin drop in that parlor: Nobody moved; everyone looked stunned. Mama could not shut her mouth; had I not been as astonished as she, I would have teased her about catching flies. My three brothers likewise did not say a word. Papa's face turned a dangerous red.

My own heart beat fast. No, no, I couldn't possibly do what the Colonel suggested. An entertainer? On the stage—like Miss Jenny Lind? It was shocking, it was unheard of, it was—

Enticing.

Never before had I imagined leaving home, but that wasn't because of lack of desire, only lack of possibility. All those nights of yearning, of hearing my mother weep for my lonely fate! For a woman in a small town in Massachusetts, naturally, marriage was the only possible way out of anything. It was the only possible way *to* anything, as well; it was the only possibility, period. And I would never marry any of the men here in Middleborough; how could I? The idea seemed grotesque to me, for reasons I could not quite explain. I remembered my mother's and sister's horror that day I had eavesdropped, the lack of a hope chest, the relief my parents had felt when I had been offered the primary classes. This was my fate—to be a spinster schoolteacher. I knew I was supposed to be grateful for it.

Suddenly, however, another possibility had just been revealed; a way out presented itself to me. I could *leave;* I could see the world, that great big world Mama had unknowingly tempted me with for so long. I could see the Mississippi, that Queen of Rivers! I might even see bad men and women, and I admit to an unlady-like thrill as I contemplated this, for there were no bad men and women in Middleborough, except for the peddler who sometimes stole chicken eggs. My yearning, seeking heart began to swell; it was as if a hidden dam of pent-up frustration had burst inside it, flooding me with desire and action. Oh, what else might I find, that I had not even known had been missing? What else might I see, that I had never before suspected was hidden from me?

I looked around at my family; they were beginning to regain

THE AUTOBIOGRAPHY OF MRS. TOM THUMB

their senses. Not one of them glanced my way; they seemed acutely embarrassed by me at that moment. Embarrassed that I had brought such a man into their home and submitted them to such dreadful talk, talk that was not fit for descendents of one of the Mayflower signers. Benjamin was already shaking his head, ready to answer for me.

"I want to do it!" The words flew out of my mouth before I had even decided on them.

"You most certainly do not!" my father thundered, rising in anger, his face so dark the veins on his forehead pulsed. He had never before spoken one harsh word to me; now, he seemed perilously close to an apoplectic attack.

"Pa's right," Benjamin cried. "If Vinnie goes with this man, I'll leave this house forever! I won't be able to bear the shame!"

"What shame?" Colonel Wood asked the company at large, his demeanor suddenly calm in the face of our collected agitation. "What shame is there in bringing joy to people? Becoming rich and famous?"

"The shame of the theater! Of being around actors and dancers and who knows what else! The shame of being displayed before the public like a—it's bad enough with the school, you know, the way people talk, but if she goes out like that, like that Tom Thumb *freak* who—" Benjamin suddenly realized what he had said and sat back down, rumpling his hair until it stood on end. "Sorry, Vinnie! I didn't mean that, not really. But if you parade yourself about on the stage—I just don't see how you can even think about it, the way you are. That's all."

My face was burning, my breast heaving at being the center of such an uproar. I'd never seen my family in such a state; Mama was rocking back and forth in her chair, her arms crossed tight against her chest, making keening sounds as if someone had just died.

"It's my life, it's my future—you needn't be embarrassed by it any longer, Benjamin! You all may be content to stay here on the farm, that's all well and good because you're just like everyone else, but I'm *not*! I'm different, and you all know it, so why not allow me to consider a different fate? And I'm *not* content—I don't think I ever have been!"

"What do you mean?" Mama had stopped rocking; she was staring at me, her gentle brown eyes full of tears and pain. "What do you mean you never have been? Why, Vinnie, my little chick—aren't you happy with us? Don't we take good care of you?"

"Oh, Mama, I didn't mean that, but—we can't continue this way forever! Someday you'll—someday you and Papa won't be able to look out for me. And what will happen then? What will happen to Minnie and me, stuck here on the farm?"

"You'll always have a home with one of us, Vinnie," my brother James, who had been quiet until now, said. "We'll always take care of you, you know that. We don't mind."

"But that's just it!" I leaped off my chair, carried away by my passion. Colonel Wood discreetly rose and left the room; the front door creaked open, and he took a seat on the porch. He had the decency to understand this was a family matter. "That's just it, don't you see? I don't want to be taken care of! I don't want to be hidden away, a burden! I want to make my own way! To have a greater purpose!"

"But you do, you have your school," Benjamin pointed out. Of all of them, even Papa, he was the most distressed, and I was reminded of that day when I was seven, and the teacher had threatened to shut me up in his overshoe. How ashamed Benjamin had been of me then; I knew, now, that he had never really gotten over it.

"That's not what I mean," I said; I ran to him, clasped his big, rough hands in mine, and tried to get him to meet my gaze, but he would not. "Even with the school, I'll always be one of the little Bump girls, the spinster teacher who lives at home, who can expect nothing more than to be invited to the occasional Sunday dinner by those who pity her. If I stay here, don't you see—there's no escaping that fate. But if I leave—why, just think! I'll see things we can only imagine here! I'll experience not just books but life! I'll be *remembered*."

"Why, whatever do you mean, Vinnie?" Mama exclaimed, her face so open and honest and agonized; I hated the pain I was causing her—but hadn't I always caused her distress, just by *being*? She had always worried and agonized over me. "What do you mean you'll be remembered? How could we ever forget you?"

I shook my head. "I mean something *more*, Mama. I can't explain it, but I've felt, for a while now, that if I stay here, I'll just be forgotten somehow. Or worse—never even known in the first place. If I go with Colonel Wood, I'll meet so many people. Why, maybe I'll even meet Miss Jenny Lind! And General Tom Thumb! Wouldn't that be nice, meeting someone like me? Someone else, that is." For I could not forget Minnie, even in my excitement.

And during the lengthy emotional discussion that ensued, my father and my brothers trying desperately to change my mind, which grew more determined with every plea, while my mother wept piteously, I did not forget my sister. Minnie's face was before me always, even as I argued passionately to be allowed to go with Colonel Wood, who remained outside, calmly puffing away on his pipe.

Finally, Papa held his hand up, silencing us all; with a resigned shake of his head, he said, "I've never known what to do with you, Vinnie. I've never understood why God made you the way He did. I can't pretend to know what to do with you now. I'm just a simple man, but you're anything but. So if you're truly set on doing this, I don't see as how I can stop you. For all I know, it might be the very best thing for you. Just don't bring shame to us, daughter. You have the best head on your shoulders of us all—use it."

Benjamin stormed out of the room. Mama burst into a renewed torrent of tears as she ran after him. But all I wanted to do was hurry upstairs and find Minnie.

She was in the room that we shared; sitting on the low bed, made for us by Papa, she cradled her favorite doll in her lap, looking very much like a doll herself. She was so delicate, so winsome; she came up only to my shoulder. Her big dark eyes grew even bigger when she saw me; with a breathless little gasp she asked, "Is that dreadful man gone, Vinnie?"

"No, he's not." I sat down upon the bed next to her; the two of us together hardly made a dent in the feather tick.

"I wish he would go. I don't like him."

"You don't even know him."

"I don't care. I don't like him."

"You don't like anyone." I had to smile, remembering the other day when she had declared the man who bought Mama's eggs and butter "Simply dreadful!"

"No, I don't like anyone but you. And Mama and Papa. And James and Benjamin and everyone." Minnie looked up at me—she was the only person in my life who looked up at me—and smiled, that one dimple showing. She was so trusting, my sister. She smiled innocently at me as if she expected me to tell her a pretty story, a wonderful surprise. She always looked at me like that; my heart, which had been so light at the prospect of my adventure, began to flutter and flail about in my breast, and I had to turn away.

Even though she was now nine, Minnie was still as timid as she had always been; she had not followed the path I had tried to blaze for her. She had no eagerness to go to school; she trembled and clutched at Mama's skirts the first time I broached the subject, even after I assured her that I would be her teacher. So she remained at home, and I had to admit that Mama's limited education was more than enough to school our Minnie. She did not have the curiosity of mind and spirit that I possessed.

School was the only place she would not follow me, however; even when I performed my chores around the farm, she clung to me, holding my skirt or my hand. I reached under the chickens for the eggs; she carried the eggs in a basket. I snipped the lavender from Mama's garden; she tied it up in fragrant little bundles.

Nearly eight years separated us, so that at times it almost felt as if she was my child, not my little sister, so trusting, so dependent she was upon me. When I left the farm in the morning to go to school, she took her seat on a little stool by the kitchen hearth; when I returned in the evening, she was always where I had left her. I had the oddest sensation that her very breath was suspended until I came home.

And at night we slept in the same bed, her little arms encircled about my waist, her head resting upon my shoulder. "Rock me, Sister," she always implored, her curls already tangled around her neck, her eyes already drooping. I would rock her gently, singing some sweet song, often one I made up; before I could finish, Minnie would be fast asleep, a contented smile on her pretty face.

Now, as I began to wonder how she would sleep once I was gone, I realized my heart was not strong enough to withstand such questioning, and so I made myself think of something else.

"Guess what?" I asked my sister.

"What?"

"I'm going to ride on a train!"

"A train? How dreadful! Aren't you scared? I'd be scared, even if you were with me, Vinnie!" Minnie's eyes shone anxiously, reflecting stars that were not there.

"No, I'm not a bit scared. And anyway, Colonel Wood will be with me."

"He will? But why? He's so dreadful! Where will you go—to town? And you'll be home by dinner?"

"No, not to town." I stifled a smile; in Minnie's experience, there was nowhere else to go but to town. That big world that beckoned so brightly to me did not even exist for my sister.

"Then where?"

"To a boat, an enormous boat. On a very famous river. I'm going to take a holiday of sorts, and see some sights, and I promise I'll write to you every day and tell you all about them!" I tried to make it sound like a lark, but my voice did catch in my throat.

"You mean, away? From here—from home?"

"Yes."

"But you'll be back by dinner?" She frowned, struggling to understand; one of her curls escaped its pins and hung down upon her forehead in a perfect question mark, as if to underscore her confusion. In Minnie's entire life, never had I not been home by dinner.

"No, Pumpkin, not by dinner. I will be gone for a long time— I don't exactly know how long, but many months. It's a difficult journey, and I won't be able to come home very often."

"I don't understand, Vinnie! Why do you want to go away?" Tears filled her eyes as she flung her arms about me. The bodice of my dress was soon wet with my sister's tears, and I had a moment of regret and panic; what on earth was I doing? How could I leave her? How selfish was I?

But then I looked around our room, with its gentle, sloping ceiling, and I realized that *everything* here was gentle, everything here was peaceful and safe and designed to protect me and Minnie from—what, exactly? From life; that's what I believed at that moment. My family wanted to protect me from *life*. But it was life that I wanted to experience: a rich, full life, one I could call my own. And there was no possibility I would ever find it on the farm or in Middleborough, with its handful of streets, two general stores, and the occasional wayward peddler.

Maybe the world was too big for me; I expected that I would soon find out. But I also knew with certainty that if I remained in Middleborough, I would grow even smaller than I already was . . . until one day, like my name overgrown with weeds, I would cease to exist altogether.

"Minnie, darling, shhh. Look," I whispered to my little sister, still sobbing on my breast. With a gentle nudge, I pushed her away so that I could cross the room to retrieve something from the windowsill—my beloved figurine of Jenny Lind in a pink dress, with her hands crossed upon her breast, her mouth open in glorious song. I returned to the bed and presented the precious object to Minnie, who had often admired it.

"Here. You keep this for me—you know how much it means to me, don't you?"

Tears still streaming down her face, Minnie took it and nodded anxiously.

"You keep it for me, Pumpkin, until I come back. Because I promise I will—and then I'll take you with me, so you can see the things that I do. I won't leave you all alone here forever. I promise."

"You do?" Sniffling, she turned her wet little heart-shaped face up to me. "You promise, Vinnie?"

"I promise!" And I vowed at that very moment to keep my promise; to do so was the only way I could tell Minnie goodbye. I would not be there to rock her to sleep, but she could, at least, comfort herself at night with the warmth of her sister's promise.

"Then I will take very good care of Miss Jenny Lind until you come back. You can count on me, Vinnie!"

She looked so earnest, her eyes suddenly dry even though her eyelashes were still dewy, her previously trembling mouth set in a firm little line. This was the first thing I had ever asked of her, and she startled me with her eagerness, her readiness to comply. I hugged her to me once more, and smiled as she tried to conceal one last sniff with a very forced hiccup.

That evening passed in a frenzy of packing and organizing; Papa had to sell a milk cow to a neighbor in order to provide me with traveling money. At dawn the next morning, after I had eagerly signed a contract stipulating my employment with Colonel Wood and his exclusive right to exhibit me for three years in exchange for providing me with twenty dollars a week—a fortune!—my family gathered around his wagon. Benjamin was not there; he was too furious to say goodbye. My other brothers heaved my borrowed trunk into the back, and I embraced Mama, who looked suddenly older to me; her forehead was checkered with lines that must have appeared overnight, and her hair was more gray than brown. How long had it been this way? I felt a pang of guilt for not having noticed before, and for the first time I realized she was not the young woman I assumed her to always be.

"Vinnie, my little chick, don't forget us all!" Mama knelt down to my level, her skirt sopping up mud, but she did not notice. "Pray every night and trust in God, and don't talk to bad people if you can help it. Colonel Wood has promised to care for you with a cousinly concern and affection, but, oh! This is still hard!" With a sob, she covered her face with a handkerchief.

Minnie was already crying, her surprising resolve of the night before chased away by the sight of my trunk in the back of the wagon. She was holding on to my hand so tightly I could feel her nails through my gloves. "Vinnie, Vinnie, oh, why must you leave? Why?"

She was nine, but with her tear-stained face and her uncomprehending eyes, I thought she more closely resembled a child of five. My sister, my poor little sister! But I had to go; by now I had convinced myself that the only way I could make a good life for her was by making one first for myself. Then, I could come back and shower her with riches and show her the world, release her from her lonely cell, hidden away by well-meaning family.

This was what I told myself as finally I pried her small hand from mine and let Papa lift me up on the seat next to Colonel Wood. The Colonel was obviously impatient to start; we were traveling to his parents' home in Weedsport, New York—he had a note of welcome from his mother, which he showed Mama and Papa when I signed the contract, helping to ease their minds significantly. There, we would outfit me with an appropriate wardrobe before journeying on to Cincinnati, where his boat had wintered.

Papa settled me in, tucking a bearskin all about me even though it was not cold. But I let him fuss, knowing this was his way of saying goodbye, and that he would sorely miss me.

"Got your money hidden away?" he asked, suddenly very concerned with one corner of the skin that would not stay put.

"Yes, Papa."

"Keep it in case of an emergency. You never know what might come up."

"Yes, Papa."

"Don't let strangers pay for anything, you understand? That's the way to ruin; you pay your own way, if Colonel Wood can't."

"Yes, Papa."

"And don't forget to write. Your mother will surely look forward to a letter now and then."

"I won't forget, Papa, oh, I won't!" And I could not help but throw my arms around his rough and weathered neck; I heard him sniff just once, then he patted my arm and gently pushed me away, muttering something about checking the back wheel of the wagon, as it didn't look "put on right."

Of course it was put on right; Colonel Wood abruptly slapped the reins, and the horses started forward. I twisted around and waved at my family, memorizing their faces, until we rounded the bend in the road and I could see them no longer.

"Not going to cry, are you?" Colonel Wood asked just as I reached for my handkerchief. "I can't stand sniveling females."

"No, not a bit!" I replied, blinking furiously.

"Good. Now, let me tell you about my boat." And he began to spin a yarn of assorted colors and shapes, of minstrel singers and gamblers and cotton bales stacked up at southern docks by slaves dark as night; about the high bluffs of Minnesota, where eagles soared above the river, card games got up after midnight shows, the huge calliope that sang out merry tunes at every port of call; even a man who could spin two dozen plates at once without dropping a one!

And my heart, which had felt as heavy as a roof smothered in January snow, began to thaw, began to soar like the sun that was just beginning to peek through the trees. I felt as big as the sun; no, as big as the sky! The sky was a vast, endless sea in which the sun was just a small orb, the size of a coin. I held my thumb up to it; I blocked it neatly out.

So it was true; the sun was no larger than the tip of my thumb. The notion tickled me, tickled my rib cage until I had to laugh out loud.

I, Mercy Lavinia Warren Bump, was bigger than the sun.

INTERMISSION

―――＊―――

"RIDING ON A RAIL" (1853)

Sung with Unbounded Applause by Ossian's Bards.
(Words—anonymous.) Music by Charlie Crozat Converse.

CHORUS *(sung after each verse)*
Singing thro' the mountain,
Buzzing o'er the vale,
Bless me, this is pleasant,
A riding on a rail.
Singing thro' the mountain,
Buzzing o'er the vale,
Bless me, this is pleasant,
A riding on a rail.

VERSE
Men of different stations,
In the eye of fame,
Here are very quickly
Coming to the same;
High and lowly people,
Birds of every feather,
On a common level,
A travelling together.

―――＊―――

From the Abbeville, South Carolina, *Banner,* November 23, 1854

Ranaway from the owner James SMITH, in Anderson District, a negro boy Bob, about 30 years of age, about 5 feet 10 inches high, black complexion, medium size, weight about 160 pounds. The said negro left on Sunday evening the 14th inst. The owner is now on his way to Texas. Any information concerning said boy will be communicated to Robert SMITH residing near Cokesbury in Abbeville district who will pay charges and take him into custody.

THREE

Life on the Mississippi, or
My Education Truly Begins

Y OU LOOK AS PRETTY AS A CHINA DOLL," SYLVIA PRONOUNCED with an approving smile; it broke slowly as usual across her rough, bony face with its cheekbones the size of large apples, deep hollows, the crooked nose that looked as if it had once been broken. Her smile brought her no beauty, but it did soften her face considerably.

"Do I?" I pretended not to know, but deep down I did; I *was* pretty. As pretty as a china doll.

The gown that Mrs. Wood had made for me was of the shiniest material we could find: a gossamer blue satin that reflected every light in every direction. While I was assured it would look brilliant behind the footlights, it was also of the highest fashion for the present year, 1858; Mrs. Wood had fastened hoops for me that allowed my skirts to sway and swing so that they did not touch my legs at all. She had not been able to send away for a custom corset, however, so she had done what Mama had done: cut down the smallest one she could find. It still gapped uncomfortably at my bosom, and did not cinch my waist as tightly as I naturally desired.

Still, admiring the lace and silk flower festoons that adorned my hem, my pretty new white satin slippers, the silk flowers in my glistening hair, I was happy with my appearance. My brown eyes sparkled almost as vibrantly as Minnie's, and for once I did not fret about my high, wide forehead; Sylvia had arranged my hair in a way that detracted from it.

"Now remember," Sylvia intoned in her considered, deep voice. "Whatever happens, I'll be right there."

" 'Whatever happens'?" I smoothed the bodice of my dress anxiously. "What do you mean? What usually happens?"

"You never know. It's a rough crowd, so you just never know. But you'll be fine, Vinnie; no one would ever want to harm you, as tiny as you are."

"Harm?" I recalled all I had read about Miss Jenny Lind; no newspaper had ever mentioned any kind of harm coming to her, except the threat of being crushed by adoring fans.

"I'm sure it'll be fine," Sylvia repeated as hastily as she possibly could. Rising from two chairs put together, for she could not fit comfortably on one, she had to duck her head in order to clear the ceiling of the private stateroom set aside for performers.

I had been surprised to learn that there were two boats that made up my new home. The one I first boarded, and where my room with Sylvia was located, was a tugboat that towed the larger, flat-bottomed boat when necessary. Both were powered by steam belowdecks, from a great hissing, churning apparatus that gleamed hellishly red at night, and which frightened me more than I was willing to admit. All the living quarters—staterooms, kitchen, and dining room—were on the smaller boat, while the theater, taking up almost the entire length, was on the larger boat. But there were private staterooms for the performers on the large boat, which was where Sylvia and I were, primping for our appearances. Or rather—I primped. Sylvia could hardly be induced to run a comb through her dull hair, and her gown, consisting of so many yards of rough, plain fabric, was not held up by hoops; if it had been, there would have been no space in the stateroom for me.

"Why won't you at least put a flower in your hair?" I asked her.

"Why? They'd never notice it."

"How do you know that? People notice performers' costumes; it's why they go to the theater!"

" 'Theater'?" Sylvia chuckled, so low and throaty that the vibration tickled my ears. "Where do you think we are? Who do you think comes aboard? Why do you think—" But she broke off, and complimented me on my dress again.

After two weeks, I was growing used to the vagaries of life upon a river. While there was something quite soothing about going to bed at night rocked to sleep by the movement of the water, the days were a frenzy of chaos and activity, of men casting off ropes, ramps pulled and lowered, scenery hammered, wood thrown into the boiler. All this activity was very exciting to me, so used to the stultifying sameness of life in Middleborough. While I was in constant peril of being stepped upon or swept overboard by deckhands and performers who had never before encountered anyone my size, I soon learned to shout out my presence whenever I turned a corner or entered a room. There was little privacy and even less decorum, but I enjoyed the easy camaraderie among the company, the way people moved in and out of one another's rooms without knocking, the impromptu "hen parties" that the ladies held late at night while we pinned up our hair and stitched up our stockings, paying no heed to the clinking of glasses just down the hall in one of the gentlemen's rooms. Some of the men even drank spirits on *Sunday*! I found this awfully thrilling, although I did not mention that particular detail in my letters home.

Thrilling as it was, my new life was perhaps not as glamorous as I had imagined. Colonel Wood did not consider things like clean linens and regularly scrubbed chamber pots necessities but rather luxuries, and, as he was fond of reminding me, he was not con-tractually obligated to provide me with any of *those*. And the dampness that I had first noticed soon revealed itself to be all-pervasive, as my clothes never felt completely dry and my hair developed a frizz it had never before exhibited.

Some wayward curls had escaped, I saw, as I took one last glimpse of myself in the cracked hand mirror Sylvia held up for me (a full-length mirror proving to be one of those luxuries Colonel Wood did not feel obligated to provide). But there was nothing to do but pat my curls, as Colonel Wood stuck his head inside the door and bellowed, "The ramp is down, the crowd's a comin'; get your asses down to the stage, for I think we can get in three shows today, at least!"

Sylvia rolled her eyes at him but did not take offense at his language, as I very much did.

"I cannot believe how differently he acts now, compared to when he visited me at home! If he had ever dared talk like that in front of my parents—why, I can't imagine!"

"We've all been wondering why someone like you agreed to come along with the likes of him," Sylvia said with a shake of her head. "That explains it some."

"He was very proper at home." I tried to ignore the growing gnawing feeling in the pit of my stomach that had presented it-self ever since we'd arrived on the *Banjo*. Once he'd crossed the gangplank, Colonel Wood had shown a different—coarser—side to his personality. It was almost as if he were two different people on and off the water.

"Now, Vinnie, don't be nervous," Sylvia reminded me once more as we left the stateroom, which opened to the exterior of the boat. Even as slowly as she walked along the slippery deck, I had to hurry to catch up with her, taking at least five steps to her every one. My head barely reached past her knees, and her skirt was so massive that I was in constant fear of being swept off my feet by it. By now, however, everyone was quite used to the sight of the two of us. As we passed by members of the company—most of whom were either hanging over the railing spitting into the river (the chief occupation of many of the men on the boat) or practicing their acts—none remarked upon the disparity in our heights the way that Colonel Wood still did. "Here come the elephant and the mouse," he often said, snickering, whenever we approached.

"Knock 'em dead, Vinnie," Solomon Taylor, the plate spinner, said with a gallant bow, a stack of plates balanced precariously on one hand.

"Yeah, knock 'em dead," echoed one of the specialty dancers, a thin woman with legs so long they reached past the top of her head when she kicked them. Her smile was desperately gay, but it only deepened the spiderweb of lines around her eyes; she was obviously trying to look younger than her years. Her hair was dyed a vivid yellow not found in nature, and her cheeks were painted bright red. Oh, if Mama could only see her! I had to giggle at the notion. My poor mother would have fainted dead away.

Of course, I had not painted my face, although I did allow Mrs. Billy Birch, the wife of one of the minstrels, to rub a soft chamois cloth over my face "to take the shine off." Despite my excitement and my eagerness to begin my new career, I admit to a few opening-night (or rather, day, as it was only two o'clock in the afternoon) nerves. Singing in front of my schoolmates was one thing; performing in front of a mob of strangers on a floating stage docked in Madison, Indiana, was quite another. Would my voice even carry the length of the boat? Placing my hand upon my diaphragm, I took several deep breaths and reminded myself not to strain on the higher notes.

When we reached the cluttered area in the back of the stage, Billy Birch and his minstrels were in the midst of performing a lively number. I couldn't see them, as they were in front of the curtain, but I heard the banjos strumming gaily, felt the whole stage shudder beneath the stomping of their feet.

Oh! I just come afore you,
To sing a little song;
I plays it on de Banjo,
And dey calls it Lucy Long.

"You ready, Sylvia?" Mr. Lawson, the stage manager, asked my friend. Sylvia nodded, and as soon as the minstrels were done—I heard some scattered applause, a few shouts from the audience, and something hit the stage with a loud thump—Sylvia turned to me.

"Vinnie, I think I should lift you up somewhere. It's awfully dark back here, and you might get hurt."

I looked around; it was quite dark, the only light wafting through rips in the red-velvet stage curtain or spilling in when someone opened the door to the outside. Scattered about were tangled nests of ropes, musical instruments, and heavy pieces of scenery stacked, not very solidly, on top of one another. Stage-hands and performers moved frantically to and fro while the entire floor undulated ever so slightly upon the water. Mama had never seen the backstage of a floating theater, but if she had, she would certainly have added it to her list of things to fear on my behalf.

"I suppose so. How about that trunk?"

Sylvia nodded and carefully picked me up and placed me on top of the trunk. Then she bent down—I still was no higher than her waist—to speak to me. "Now, stay here, and I'll come back for you when I'm done, just like we practiced."

"Sylvia!" I had a sudden panicked thought.

"What?"

"Do you think I should sing the ballad first, instead of 'The Soldier's Wedding'? Which do you think would go over best? I do want to make a good first impression."

"Vinnie, it doesn't matter what you— Whatever you think, dear. Whatever one you like the best."

"I suppose the ballad, then." I smiled up at her, but she only peered at me quizzically, an expression I could not interpret in her sad blue eyes. Then she straightened up, sighed, and moved slowly toward the curtain, as if she were on her way to her own execution. I couldn't understand her reluctance. Why, we were in the show business!

Billy Birch, his face covered in burnt cork (although the back of his neck and his ears remained defiantly pink), winked at me as he made his way offstage, he and his fellow minstrels resplendent in green-and-yellow checked waistcoats and orange pants. "You ain't afraid, are you, Vinnie?"

"No!" I was weary of people asking me this. "Why should I be?"

"No need," piped up the tenor minstrel, his voice high and reedy. "And if anything does happen, we'll all be here watching, so don't worry. We'll get you out in a jiffy."

"What might happen?" My heart was beginning to pound, but Billy only grinned. Frowning, I turned my attention back to Sylvia as she moved through the red-velvet curtain, allowing a sudden sliver of light to pierce the backstage gloom. Without a musical flourish or any introduction, she simply grabbed the curtain and stepped forward. I found this odd, but then again, Sylvia seemed perversely devoted to shattering every notion I'd ever had about life upon the stage. Earlier, when I'd asked to see her notices, she'd stared at me and shrugged, remarking that she'd never thought to keep them.

There was a startled, collective gasp from the audience the moment she pushed her way through the curtain. The gasp was quickly followed by silence, which was soon replaced by whispers that grew louder and louder. I held my breath, waiting for something to happen; the silence onstage seemed ominous.

Finally someone spoke, but it wasn't Sylvia; it was a voice from what I had to assume was the audience. "How tall is she?"

"Seven feet, I wager," someone else replied. And then suddenly Colonel Wood, in his role as master of ceremonies, began to speak in a smooth, practiced patter—yet another side of his personality I'd never before witnessed.

"Gentlemen, gentlemen, come this way! Come stand next to Miss Sylvia Hardy, the Maine Giantess, eight feet tall if she's an inch! Why, Miss Sylvia here used to be the finest nursemaid in all of Wilton, Maine—she could carry an infant quite easily in the palm of her hand!"

I heard gasps; I couldn't contain my curiosity, so I jumped nimbly off the trunk and hurried around to the side of the stage, pushing my way through boxes and crates and furniture. When I got to the edge of the curtain, I peeked around it, safely hidden; onstage, Sylvia was extending her large, meaty hand toward the audience. There was no doubt that a baby could fit within it.

"But what does she do?" I whispered to Billy, who was suddenly kneeling by my side. "What's her act?"

" 'Do'?"

"Yes—what does she *do*? Doesn't she sing? Recite?"

"Sylvia doesn't have to *do* anything. All she has to do is stand. She's not a performer, Vinnie."

"Not like us, you mean?" I didn't look at him; my eyes were still trained on Sylvia, who was now standing with her arms extended horizontally; beneath them, two men stood, with room to spare.

"Well—that is—no." Billy patted me on the shoulder gingerly; most of the members of the company still seemed afraid to touch me, as if I were made of glass. Sylvia, ironically, was the only one who did not display this tendency. "No, not like us. You sure do take the cake, Vinnie, I'll tell you that!"

"So why does she do it, then, if she doesn't want to perform? She looks miserable." And indeed, Sylvia's face reminded me of an illustration of Joan of Arc that I'd once seen in a schoolbook: stoic, unflinching, with upturned eyes that were overflowing with the pain the rest of her homely face could not express.

"Somehow that Barnum fellow found her up in Maine; she didn't have any family living. She's been alone most of her life, they say. I guess that Barnum can persuade a mouse to go after a cat, so he somehow persuaded Sylvia, of all people, to appear at his American Museum. Don't think it went over too well, though. Doesn't seem to have lasted very long, and anyway, she wouldn't be here if it had, would she?"

"Barnum? Sylvia was at the American Museum? Does Colonel Wood know that? I imagine he does, being they're such good friends."

"Wood and Barnum? Friends? Whoever told you that?"

"Why, Colonel Wood did, of course." I turned around and frowned up at Billy; he had an amused look in his light blue eyes, pale against the streaky black of the burnt cork smeared on his face.

"Barnum never heard of our dear Colonel, I'd bet my a——, er, hat on it."

"No, that's not what he told me; he said he'd worked with him in New York!"

"Maybe he swept the street behind the Museum." Billy grunted. "But Wood never worked with Barnum. He must have told you that to make sure you'd sign."

My heart sank; I turned and looked at the stage. Suddenly I saw that the red-velvet curtain, which had looked so glamorous, was patched, the scalloped shades of the footlights were cracked, and the floorboards on the stage itself were warped. Colonel Wood was standing to the side in a bright green jacket with a checkered vest, his curls now as blackened as his mustache, but under the glare of the chipped gaslights, both were beginning to run, inky black streaks appearing on his forehead and around his mouth.

What a fool I was! I'd heard only what I'd wanted to hear and ignored everything else. Why, I knew now he'd never even heard Miss Jenny Lind sing, let alone been given a private performance. At that moment, I had no idea what on earth I, Mercy Lavinia Warren Bump of the Massachusetts Warrens, was doing on this shabby boat, in this shabby dress that had seemed so glamorous, but now I saw that the fabric was as thin and gaudy as cheap wrapping paper.

I had no idea what Sylvia was doing here, either, if it was true she'd once performed at the American Museum. The American Museum! Even in two short weeks on the river, I'd learned that everyone on this boat aspired to appear at the American Museum someday. How odd that Sylvia had never once mentioned she already had!

I tried to look at my friend through different eyes, she who had been nothing but kindness itself. She had comforted me that first awful night, had listened to my weepy recitation of my family's wonderful qualities, had suffered much to make room for me in our cramped stateroom, her giant body perpetually folded up like a retracted telescope. Every morning she helped lace up my corset, which was not easy with her thick, fumbling fingers. And I spent half an hour each evening brushing out her long brown hair, which seemed to soothe her, for she was always in pain; her joints and bones constantly ached, and her feet suffered excruciatingly from carrying about her mammoth weight. All this contributed to her perpetual air of discomfort and sadness.

I loved my new friend dearly. But try as I might, I could not imagine her passive, lugubrious form on the same stage that dainty Miss Jenny Lind and nimble General Tom Thumb had graced.

Sylvia's shoulders slumped as if she was endeavoring to disappear within that ungainly body. She was now concealing an entire newspaper behind her gigantic hands, to *oohs* and *aahs* from the crowd. Colonel Wood was standing onstage, pointing to her and reciting her particulars—height, weight, the color of her eyes—as if she were a slave to be auctioned off.

"Why on earth doesn't she *do* something, so that he doesn't have to resort to such a display?" I whispered to Billy as irritation stirred in my veins, irritation at both myself and Sylvia. Myself for believing Colonel Wood; Sylvia for letting him poke and prod her with his walking stick while she merely stood, obviously humiliated.

A brisk slap of applause startled me; Sylvia was now lurching offstage, pushing through the shabby curtain. My stomach fluttered as I rushed to meet her.

"Are you ready, Vinnie?" A fond smile pushed away the anguish on Sylvia's face.

"Of course." I nodded calmly, as if I wasn't suddenly unable to hear over the roaring in my ears. Then we were walking through the curtain together, and Colonel Wood was introducing me as *"a new sensation, a miniature chanteuse, a living doll—Miss Lavinia Warren Bump!"*

He was only a lime green blur in the corner of my eye; the footlights in front and the gaslights along the sides of the stage were so brilliant and hot that they blinded me. I relied on Sylvia to nudge me with her knee toward what must be the piano, and then she was lifting me up, up, up, until I felt the solid walnut vibrating beneath my feet as the pianist continued to play a flourish.

Blinking, safely above the glare of the flickering footlights, I tried to make out the scene before me. The upper seats, which I'd been told were for the Negroes, I could not distinguish; all was a dusky blur. But I could discern a few faces in the audience, seated on long, hard benches on the main floor. It was mostly made up of men, I realized: a few women, some children, but mostly men, dressed in rough farm clothes. The women at least had hats on, and Sunday cloaks, but the men did not appear to have donned special clothing for the occasion.

This, alone, caused my heart to slow down, the roaring in my ears to fade; I had no fear of these kinds of people, for they were just like my own folks. Even rougher and less schooled, I imagined from the dirt and the faded quality of some of the clothing, the stained spittoons at the end of every row.

Now I could hear the gasps and whispers, the creaking of the benches as people shifted and stood to get a better look at me. Colonel Wood had stopped speaking and was twirling his walking stick as he gestured to me. With a small nod, I turned to the accompanist, Mr. James, and whispered, "I'll start with the ballad."

He smiled and started playing the introduction. I cleared my throat, and the first tremulous notes pushed themselves out of my mouth. *"I dream of Jeannie with the light brown hair,"* I warbled, and knew that my pitch was off, my tone wobbly. But the audience didn't seem to mind; I could hear sounds of *"Shh, shhh,"* and one *"Gol' darn it, shut the hell up!"* as I sensed the individuals lean forward as one, one great, giant ocean wave rushing toward me.

I didn't recoil from it. Instead, I held my hand up, silencing everyone, including Mr. James.

"Excuse me, I'd like to start again," I said. And nodded, as Mr. James played the introduction over.

"I dream of Jeannie with the light brown hair." The words were clearer now, my tone steady, and I felt my throat relax so that every note wasn't pinched. With assurance, I lifted my head so that my voice could carry farther, even as Mr. James softened his accompaniment.

"I see her tripping where the bright streams play." The audience seemed transfixed by my voice; the creaking had stopped now, as no one moved a muscle. In the first row, there was more than one gentleman whose mouth was hanging open, perfectly enraptured.

"Many were the wild notes her merry voice would pour." This was the most difficult part of the song, and I strained a bit to hit the high notes; Mr. Jones, who wore a pained expression as we began that section, relaxed and smiled at me when it was over.

"Oh! I dream of Jeannie with the light brown hair, floating, like a vapor, on the soft summer air." I slowed the last notes, caressing them so they would linger. As the last note trailed off, I took a big breath and bowed my head.

There was a long silence, long enough that I almost looked up to see what was the matter—and then rapturous, thunderous applause! It fell over me like a warm embrace, tingling my skin; it was with some difficulty that I restrained myself from jumping up and down and clapping myself. I was a hit! An immediate success!

Just as Miss Jenny Lind had been when Mr. Barnum first brought her to America. Perhaps, after all, I hadn't been mistaken about Colonel Wood.

Then I started to hear the murmurs—

"She can't be real!"

"She's a doll! A windup toy!"

"I never saw such a thing in my life!"

"Hey, mister, how'd you teach a little *baby* to sing?"

A few people were standing now, making their way toward the stage. Naturally, I recoiled but realized that I was well and truly stuck up on the piano; it was only then that I remembered Billy Birch and Sylvia were backstage, ready in case "something happened." Now I understood what that "something" was.

"It's a doll, one of them puppets, ain't it?" A decidedly rough-looking young man, with a crimson face and boils on his neck, was now at the very foot of the stage, his hands upon it, ready to haul himself up. "Open your mouth, doll baby, and sing me another purty song!"

I was frozen with fear and disgust. I could not move or utter a word. But it didn't matter, as Colonel Wood now swung into his patter and began to talk for me—just as he had done for Sylvia.

"I assure you, Miss Lavinia Warren Bump is not a doll! She's a perfectly formed woman! A marvel of Lilliputian splendor!"

There was a gasp, then someone shouted, "My Myrtle's taller than that, and she's four years old! Go on up! Put her down on the floor so my Myrtle can stand next to her!"

"Yeah—put her down on the floor!"

"Make her walk! Make her sing!"

"Make her talk!"

To my horror, Colonel Wood was walking toward me with outstretched arms; he was about to pick me up and lift me down off the piano, as if I were indeed a doll. I realized, with a sickening twist of my stomach, that he was not going to ask my leave; his eyes simply swept over me as if he was trying to calculate how heavy I was. My fear and disgust melted away to anger as he placed his unwelcome, violating hands about my waist and I slapped him, hard, across the cheek.

"You may not touch me!" I cried, which had the instant effect of silencing the crowd just as Colonel Wood stepped back in surprise.

"Excuse me?" He rubbed his cheek, eyes darkening.

"I said you may not touch me! How dare you, picking me up as if I was a child! I am a lady, and I will not allow such behavior!"

As Colonel Wood's color deepened to a dangerous red, the audience tittered; someone called out, "Hey, Colonel, guess you'd better play nice with your dolly!"

"She ain't a doll!"

"Sure she is!"

"If you ever slap me again, I'll throw you across the stage," Colonel Wood hissed out the corner of his mouth as he faced the voluble audience with a broad smile, raising his hands to calm them. "Don't just stand there, say something to 'em! I could have found me another dwarf who'd be dumb as a rock, just like that dumb giant, but as soon as you said you were a schoolteacher I thought maybe I had something special. Thought maybe I'd found me a meal ticket just like that Tom Thumb. Thought maybe you were one of them special dwarfs."

Stunned, I could only stand there as hurt tears filled my eyes and my stomach churned with disgust. Dwarf? I had never before been called that word, not by any misbehaving schoolchild or exasperated teacher; certainly not by my own loving family, whom I missed more than I thought I could bear. Dwarf? I had read of dwarfs, ancient accounts of comical pets of royalty or grotesque creatures from fairy tales, like Rumpelstiltskin. The word was repulsive and had nothing to do with who I was.

Was that how he had seen me all along? I resolved to take the next train home, back to my family, who had only tried to protect me from people like him. Contract or no contract, I would—

Don't shame us, my father had said; the full weight of his words fell upon my shoulders like a cross to be born.

My body felt icy, separate from my brain. Colonel Wood was openly sneering as he moved again toward me. There were only two things I could do. I could stand there like Sylvia, a thing—a *dwarf*—and let him lift me off the piano—I could almost feel his huge, grasping hands about my waist, my legs dangling helplessly in the air. Or I could take control of the situation and not shame my family.

I will not let my size define me, I had told myself back in my school days. *I will define it.*

"Stop!" I held up my hand, surprising all, including myself. "Stop!" I had to repeat this several times, but after a moment the audience quieted down, although those standing did not return to their seats, and the ugly young man remained ominously close to the stage.

My training as a teacher now came to my rescue. I felt myself expand, perched atop that grand piano; my spine stiffened, my chin tilted, and I willed every molecule, every bit of muscle and flesh and bone and even the hair on my head, to exude *dignity*. I imagined it exploding from the very core of my being; I closed my eyes, picturing myself showering sparks and stars and diamonds of dignity. Then I opened my eyes to survey the audience as an eerie calm fell upon me.

I began to speak, and I was careful to overenunciate my words, as I had often found myself doing when trying to help a confused pupil. The audience was that pupil. So was Colonel Wood. They needed to be educated; they needed to be taught—about me, Mercy Lavinia Warren Bump, descendent of William the Conqueror and Richard Warren of the Mayflower Company.

"I assure you, I am neither a doll nor a windup toy. As Colonel Wood said, my name is Miss Bump, and I hope you enjoyed my song. Now, if you'll permit me, I'd—"

"How tall are you?" the sweaty young man at the footlights interrupted, quite rudely. I had a good mind to ignore him, except that he was echoed by several others repeating the same question.

"Miss Bump is—" Colonel Wood began, but I cut him off with a glare; he returned it but did back away from the piano.

"My height is two feet, eight inches; thank you for inquiring."

"How old are you? Why, you can't be more'n four or five!" another voice rang out.

"While I do not believe it is polite to ask a lady her age, I am not yet eighteen." To my surprise, this was received with a hoot of laughter.

"Almost eighteen, you say? Why, you must have a little fairy beau, then!" someone else exclaimed.

"Unfortunately, Miss Bump has yet to find anyone who measures up," Colonel Wood replied quickly; the audience roared with laughter, while I could do nothing but stand there, the butt of their joke.

"Are those doll clothes you're wearing?" This was from a female voice.

"No, I had them made, just as you do," I replied before Colonel Wood could say something boorish. "Now, I would like to sing another song. Would you allow me?" For I was suddenly weary, unsteady on my feet, although I would not allow myself to show it; my body felt as battered as if I'd been run through a butter churn. I don't know how long I'd been onstage, but it felt like a lifetime.

"You bet, little lady!" someone shouted, and there was a general stirring and creaking as people took their seats. It was a sound I would grow to recognize, the contented sound of an audience settling in, ready to be entertained. But at that moment, I noted it with only exquisite relief, for soon my humiliation would be over.

I nodded at Mr. James, who began the lively military introduction for "The Soldier's Wedding." With clenched fists, I held on to my skirts in an effort to keep myself from toppling over.

"*Give me your hand, my own Jeanette . . .*" I sang with determined force, and soon the audience was clapping along. Somehow I got through the song, I know not how, although Mr. James told me later that I had smiled the entire time. As soon as I was finished, I smoothed my skirts, took a deep breath, and stepped onto the keyboard, then the piano bench, then finally the floor; I couldn't wait to leave that stage.

The roar started; from the back of the audience it came, a deafening sound that made me clasp my hands over my ears. It was applause, my first ovation, and it was a sound I would never forget. Utterly astounded, I somehow found the presence of mind to curtsy, my hand over my heart, as if I was, indeed, Miss Jenny Lind.

A little smile tickled my lips as I turned around to go back through the curtains, passing Colonel Wood. But that dastardly man actually kicked at me as I walked by, laughing to see me jump in fright.

"That's not the last you've heard from me about that slap, little missy. I won't be made a fool of on my own stage, especially not by a dwarf," he hissed, before turning back around to quiet the still roaring audience.

I didn't think I would make it through the curtains; my stomach suddenly seized, and I knew I had to find a chamber pot so I could purge myself of all the humiliation and disgust inside me. I ran, as fast as I could, backstage, past Sylvia and Billy Birch and the Tattooed Man who was preparing to go on, out the door to the deck, where I scooted under the leg of the dancing girl as she practiced her high kicks. I ran and ran, stumbling on the slick boards, but I didn't make it; I turned suddenly and would have hung my head over the side of the boat, but, of course, I couldn't reach the rail.

I fell to my knees in a miserable heap instead, and was sick right there, on the dirty, damp deck littered with tobacco stains and muddy footprints, while behind me people continued to make their way to and from the stage area. It was as if I was invisible to them; it was as if I was too small for anyone to notice.

And at that moment I knew, with another sick heave to my stomach, I was.

NOW THAT MY EYES WERE OPEN, MY EDUCATION TRULY BEGAN. For it was made clear to me—as it must have always been to my family, who had pleaded with me so not to leave—that my value lay only in my unusual size. I could have had a pumpkin head stuck on my tiny body, could have spoken in unintelligible sentences and drooled upon myself—it wouldn't have mattered. People came to see me for my size alone, and naturally this caused me great humiliation and distress, feelings that seemed only to increase with every day. For it transpired that part of my contract— oh, that cursed contract! How stupid I had been not to read it more closely!—stipulated that Colonel Wood could exhibit me in any way he saw fit. And he saw fit to do it in the manner of a gross, disgusting boor with not a shred of consideration for a gentlewoman's propriety.

Now I understood Sylvia's constant pained expression. I also understood that I was not, despite my naïve belief, a performer just like Billy Birch, the minstrels, and the dancing girl.

No, I found myself labeled by Colonel Wood as one of his "oddities," like the Tattooed Man, the knife swallower; like Sylvia. Even though onstage I sang and danced (courtesy of some hasty lessons between shows) as enthusiastically as any of the minstrels, before and after each performance I found, to my disgust, that I was expected to be *displayed*. Like an unusual seashell, or a rock resembling a toad; like the two-headed kitten that long-forgotten doctor had likened me to. It pained me to realize how prescient he had been.

I had to stand upon a table in the galley on the opposite end of the boat from the stage. I had to allow total strangers to gape at me, whisper about me, even attempt to touch and fondle me despite my protestations, my constant reminders that I was not a doll, not a child, but a young lady with all the sense and sensibilities that entailed.

It was the men who persisted in doing this. Children whispered, giggled, but merely stared; women might reach out to finger the fabric of my skirt as women are wont to do. But men wanted to pick me up, put their hands about my waist, even attempt to kiss me without my leave. I could not tell if they thought me a child, despite my desperate attempts at genteel conversation, my blushes, my thoroughly ladylike demeanor—or if they wanted to ascertain that I was, indeed, of a womanly form, only miniaturized.

All I knew is that I had to insist, over and over, that I did not grant permission to be touched; I had to refuse, always, requests for "fairy kisses" upon rough, unshaven cheeks or, worse, lips. I know Colonel Wood did not like it when I was so bold and outspoken to those who paid admission for the privilege of doing so; he loomed over me, glaring, threatening, cursing. But he could

not force me, not in front of customers, and also not in front of the
rest of the company. After that horrible first performance, they
had banded together to protect me; Mrs. Billy Birch had helped me
to clean myself up, make myself presentable for the next show.
Billy and the minstrels had assisted me in coming up with some re-
joinders for the audience, so that Colonel Wood had nothing to
say. Sylvia had seen Colonel Wood kick at me and had since attached herself to my side, particularly whenever he was around.

I greatly appreciated their support. For Colonel Wood had
done what my mother's fears and worries had failed to do; he had
made me understand, for the first time, how physically helpless
my size truly made me. Back home on the farm, I'd never felt this
way; animals I understood and trusted, both in their actions and
in my ability to stay clear of them.

Human beings, I was learning, were much more dangerous
and unpredictable.

"What did you expect?" Sylvia asked me in honest surprise
one day as we departed the boat to walk about the town of Davenport, Iowa.

This was yet another humiliating lesson I had to learn. It was
usual for showboats of this time to parade about some of their
performers—especially the *oddities*—to drum up business for the
shows. Colonel Wood found it amusing to pair Sylvia and me up
for this purpose—"the elephant and the mouse"; obviously we
drew attention because of the disparity in our heights. Every time
we docked in a town, Sylvia and I were sent out to stroll for about
an hour, accompanied by the Tattooed Man (a very stringy individual with ink of fabulous hues covering every inch of his skin,
including inside his ears; I cannot recall his name, as I believe he
gave a different one each time he was asked), and the sword swallower. Mr. Deacon was his given name, but he advertised himself
as "Signor Silvestri, the Great Sword Swallower." He had an oddly

short neck, which struck me as rather a liability in his chosen profession. But he was a very gentle man, the only member of the troupe who said grace before every meal.

Naturally, our "casual" strolls incited curiosity among the townspeople, curiosity that could be satisfied only by the purchase of a five-cent ticket to Colonel Wood's Floating Palace of Curiosities and Entertainment, or so said the flyers that the Tattooed Man passed out to the crowd that inevitably trailed behind us like a cumbersome dress train.

"I have to say, I don't understand why you left your home at all," Sylvia continued as we walked along. Poor Sylvia; she felt, even more keenly, perhaps, than did I, the stares and whispers we inevitably encountered, and so kept up a constant conversation as a way to drown them out. This was the only time she was so talkative; on the boat, she reverted to her usual taciturn habits. "Your family sounds so sweet; you had a respectable situation. With me, it was different. I didn't have anyone left; I felt like a freak of nature regardless, so I thought it wouldn't matter where I went. But you—I don't understand why you're here, Vinnie."

"I don't either." I sighed, avoiding the stares of a group of dockworkers who stopped unloading barrels to gape at us. "I didn't think that—well, I thought I was interesting to the Colonel for other reasons—my singing, for example. I thought I'd be able to sing like Miss Jenny Lind, and be treated with the same respect and dignity. Oh, yes, perhaps I knew, deep down, the Colonel was mainly interested in me because of my size, because of how popular Tom Thumb is, but I thought—I thought I was somehow *more.*" Because I'd always believed I was, I thought but did not say aloud. The notion seemed ridiculous now, as I trudged along a dock accompanied by a giantess, a tattooed man, and a sword swallower. How was it I had ever been a schoolteacher? Despite all that I had taught, I had learned nothing about the world.

"But how could you leave your home and your family?" Sylvia persisted.

I clutched my cloak, which had been made by Mama long ago to wear as I walked to and from school. It felt like the warmth and tenderness of my entire family wrapped about my body, and I nuzzled my cheek against my shoulder and sniffed; it still smelled like home, like the dried lavender Mama always laid in every drawer, the lemon oil she used to polish the good furniture, the warm, yeasty smell of the endless loaves of bread that she baked.

How could I leave home? I tried to remember, for both Sylvia and myself.

"I wanted to see the world," I replied ruefully, then stopped to laugh at myself. We were at the end of the dock; the muddy street before us was utterly disgusting, stacked high with dirty crates and smelly barrels of fish, pungent bundles of animal skins ready to be shipped off to places unknown. The air was filled with the cursing and shouts of dockworkers and bursts of steam from boats about to push out. Very few women were in sight, and of those who were, even fewer could be called ladies. "I wanted to meet new people, see new things," I continued as we crossed the muddy street—I held my skirts up, sinking almost to my knees—and continued uphill, away from the river. "I didn't want to end up a spinster teacher, living only on the kindness and pity of her family. I didn't want to remain in Middleborough all my life."

"I would have loved to remain in Wilton," Sylvia said with a heavy sigh. "But there wasn't anyone left. And then Mr. Barnum came."

"Why did you leave him? What brought you—here?" I gestured about the shabby street, the heads poking out of windows to stare as we continued our progress. Oh, how bitterly I recalled strolling the quiet streets of Middleborough, where everyone knew me and no one thought to exclaim about my size or my fairy voice, where people conversed with me, not *above* me, as if my ears were too small to hear their ridiculous comments.

"Ma, lookit that!" a boy yelled out a window, right above our heads. "That tiny little person—reckon it can talk?"

"Yes, *it* can," I retorted loudly; away from Colonel Wood, I felt free to indulge myself and be rude to those who were rude to me. "And *it* knows better than to say 'reckon.' What year are you at school?"

The boy turned white and ducked his head back inside his house.

"Vinnie, you do beat all!" Sylvia chuckled in admiration. "How you talk! I can never think of anything to say."

"I just get so angry, I can't help myself. So back to Mr. Barnum—why ever did you leave his employ?"

"I didn't want to, but he sold my contract," she replied, slowing so I could catch up. She was patience itself, for shortening her stride was not easy on joints that ached with every movement.

"He sold it? To Colonel Wood? Then the Colonel does know Barnum?"

"No, Mr. Barnum sold it to a Mr. Peabody, who sold it to Colonel Wood."

"They can do that? Buy and sell us? Like slaves?"

"If you sign a long contract like I did, they can."

"Why—why did Mr. Barnum sell your contract?" I asked hesitantly, for I did not wish to cause Sylvia distress.

"He said I bored the audience. He said that's the kiss of death—boredom—and while he wished me every kindness, he had to sell my contract because he found another giantess, one who recited Shakespeare."

"Really? Shakespeare?" I was astonished. Imagine—a giantess reciting Shakespeare! I would pay to see that, myself! "Was he—was he nice to you? Nicer than Colonel Wood?"

"Oh, yes!" Sylvia stopped, and her heavily lidded eyes shone with fondness. "Mr. Barnum was the nicest man I ever met! He treated me like a lady, and nobody had ever done that before. After Mother died, it was like I was invisible, or worse. Mother was the last person to hug me, even touch me, until Mr. Barnum came up to visit. Why, Vinnie, he treated me just as if I was the daintiest little lady—just as dainty as you! He held chairs out for me, he opened doors, he brought me flowers! He's a good man. It's not his fault I'm not cut out for this life."

"No, you're not. I'm not, either. This wasn't the life I thought I'd be living now."

"Oh, yes, you are! Maybe not here on the boat, but Vinnie, the way you talk to people! The way you never forget you're a lady! And the way you light up when you're onstage! You're wonderful. I don't know how you do it. I just know Mr. Barnum will find you someday." My friend's admiration was honest and heartfelt, and I must admit I needed to hear it. I placed my tiny hand in her great one, and we walked along in silence for a bit, studiously ignoring all others. Davenport was a typical river town, something I could now identify with confidence, and I supposed that was one useful thing I'd learned since leaving home. River towns on the Mississippi were all somewhat the same; all had streets leading uphill from the riverfront, churches and schools dotting the ends of the streets highest above the river.

In this town, there were the usual newspaper office, dry goods stores, offices that took care of boating business and trading commodities, and one apothecary shop. Across the street was a candy store; Sylvia tugged at my hand and pointed, and I nodded. The Tattooed Man and Mr. Deacon had already peeled off into a tavern, as was their habit. Unescorted—but not alone, as a sizable contingent was now following us, speculating about us as if we could not hear them; one even speculated I must be Sylvia's child, which made us both smile—we crossed the muddy street. As the crowd followed, Sylvia ducked her head and slumped her shoulders terribly, poor thing, as if she truly believed she could *wish* herself smaller. But she did allow herself a smile; she had a powerful sweet tooth, although I knew that later tonight she would be moaning in her bed with a toothache.

After buying some chocolate drops from an astonished shopkeeper who shouted to his wife to "Come look at these show folks, this giantess and her little friend," we resumed our stroll until we came upon the gleaming storefront hung with a sign proclaiming *Mr. Greene, Fine Practitioner of the Art of Photography, Card Printing & Phrenology.*

The window was papered with photographs—some sepiatoned, others hand-tinted with traces of color—of famous personages. General Tom Thumb was chief among them. The photographs were for sale, twenty-five cents each.

"Did you ever?" I asked Sylvia, astonished.

"Did I ever what?" my dear, literal-minded companion answered.

"Did you ever see such a thing? Paying for someone's photograph! I've never even had my photograph taken, have you?"

"Oh, no! No, how dreadful!"

I had to laugh; despite her deep voice, she sounded just like Minnie. "I don't think it would be dreadful; I think it would be fun," I replied, still looking at the photographs, the one of General Tom Thumb in particular. The caption read *General Tom Thumb in Highland Dress,* and indeed, he was in a traditional Scottish kilt, with a feathered hat, his features rounder, more mature, than I recalled from the few newspaper illustrations I'd seen.

"Do you really think people pay for his photograph? Let's go inside and ask!" I tugged Sylvia's hand, and she reluctantly pushed the door open for me. Inside the hot little room, there was another glass case that contained a few more of these fascinating portraits; I had to stand on tiptoe and lean my forehead against the cool glass, but I could see them. I recognized President Buchanan, and his golden-haired niece, Harriet, who was his pretty hostess in the White House. There were photographs of Queen Victoria; one of the famous actor Edwin Booth, dressed as Hamlet; and another of General Tom Thumb costumed as Napoléon.

There was also one photograph of him standing on a tall table, leaning his hand upon the shoulder of another man, who stood next to him.

"That's Mr. Barnum," Sylvia said, groaning as she knelt down so she could see the images. "The man standing. That's Mr. Barnum."

"Really?" I was surprised and, I confess, a little disappointed; the man in the photograph looked so very . . . *ordinary*. Curly hair parted on the side, a wide forehead, a somewhat bulbous nose, an unremarkable smile. He resembled any man I might have passed in the street; he certainly did not resemble a world-famous impresario. Colonel Wood, I had to admit, looked much more the part than did this man.

"Good God Almighty!"

Sylvia and I both looked up, she rising as hastily as she could, leaning heavily upon the glass case, which shuddered alarmingly beneath her weight. A very surprised young man, with thick spectacles and a pale complexion, stood behind the case. Wiping his hands on a long white apron, he didn't look like a photographer; he looked like a butcher. Except instead of blood on the apron, there were inky black stains.

"Hello," I said with a smile, since he appeared unable to do anything but gape at the two of us. "I was hoping you could help me. What are these?" And I pointed to the photographs behind the case.

"The—the—they're *cartes de visites,*" he finally stammered, pronouncing it *car-tays-vizeetz*. "I got 'em from a supplier in Paris. Folks here are crazy about 'em, but I'm almost plum out. Say, ladies, I'd take your photographs right here on the spot, free of charge, if you'd let me sell them. Whaddya say?"

Sylvia began to tremble, but I answered firmly, "I'm afraid we couldn't do that, not now. But perhaps later. Do you have a card?"

"Would you like to buy one of the little General's? He's our top seller." The man gave me a conspiratorial smile as he handed over his card. "I bet you're sweet on him, ain't you?"

"Why on earth would you think such a thing?" I asked, insulted by his impertinence, and not inclined to hide it.

"Why, because—well, because. He's a mighty handsome little man."

"And I suppose I'm a mighty pretty little lady?"

"Sure! Why, sure you are!"

"And because he's handsome and I'm pretty, we must make a match?"

"No, because you're little and he's little!"

"Really," I said to Sylvia, who was watching me with her usual admiring, openmouthed smile. "The nerve!"

"Well, anyway," the young man said with a shrug. "Take it for free. And come back if you change your mind about being photographed."

"No, really, I couldn't—"

"I'll take it." Sylvia held out her massive gloved hand. "That one." She pointed to the photograph of General Tom Thumb in Highland dress. The young man placed the *carte de visite* into her hand with trembling fingers.

"Gosh" was all he could say as we left the store; a crowd of children, who had been pressed, nose first, against the store window while we were inside, scattered like frightened mice before us.

"I never saw anyone so rude," I muttered as we began to walk back toward the river, the busy hum of activity drawing us like bees to a hive.

"Do you want the picture?" Sylvia asked. I looked up at my friend, in whose shadow I could easily walk; despite the parasols we both carried—each painted with the words *Follow Me to the Show!*—she shielded me from the peculiarly pale sun I had already learned to associate with the West.

"No, you keep it. But thank you." I had no interest in General Tom Thumb beyond his association with Mr. Barnum.

As the *Banjo,* docked in all its desperate jauntiness, came into sight, however, I reconsidered. There it was, the long, flat boat trimmed in peeling shades of red, white, and blue—with a new sign hanging over the ticket office proclaiming, in huge letters, *The One, the Only, Floating Palace of Curiosities Including the Only Dwarf Woman This Side of the Alleghenies.* There I was, my name not of any value, nor my face, nor my talent—only my size and, of much less importance, my gender.

And here was General Tom Thumb, his photograph being sold for twenty-five cents beside those of Queens and Presidents.

·How had this happened? I had not left my family to become the only dwarf woman this side of the Alleghenies, stuck on this miserable boat. I was educated; I was descended from the first Americans; I was gifted with a fine voice, face, and form, not to mention manners and intellect.

As far as I could tell, Charles S. Stratton, General Tom Thumb himself, was not blessed with any of these advantages.

Suddenly I felt a fire burning in my very soul; perhaps it had been tamped down these last few weeks, but it was a fire that had always been there. It had begun as that ember that kept me warm at night while my mother wept for my lonely fate, the same spark that had inflamed me to excel in my job as schoolteacher, even as

I knew it was offered out of pity. It was the fire of ambition, and I knew it was the only thing that would save me from spending the rest of my life a sad curiosity—like Sylvia—or from going back to the farm and hiding from the world, like my beloved Minnie. At that moment, I wasn't sure which of the two fates was the least desirable; I only knew I didn't want either one.

"I'll take that after all," I said to Sylvia, who handed me the photograph of the General. I tucked it carefully into my reticule, then drew up the strings tightly, to keep out the dust.

It may have been only a photograph, but it was necessary fuel to that fire I was determined to nurture or else I would be lost, or else I would be forgotten, just a nameless memory in the minds of some rough folk who lived along a river. "Remember, Ma, remember, Pa," I could imagine them saying to each other years from now. "Remember that dwarf woman we saw? Wasn't she something?"

"She sure was," it would be agreed. And that would be all.

No, I couldn't allow that to happen. And this photograph of General Tom Thumb in an outlandish costume—perhaps it could be my ticket out of here, away from such a sad, anonymous fate.

It could also be my ticket *to* somewhere: to New York, and the Great Barnum himself, who was fast becoming, in my mind, the only person who could repair my dignity and give me the career I so desired. Perhaps he could be persuaded to buy my contract from Colonel Wood.

But first, of course, he would have to know about me. A photograph would be the perfect introduction. And I imagined that I would take a very nice photograph, indeed.

INTERMISSION

From the *Brooklyn Daily Eagle*, September 14, 1855

The Syracuse *Standard* says a healthy lady with four babies, all born at once, passed through that city and took dinner at the St. Charles Hotel yesterday. The children are three boys and one girl, and were born in Tompkins County. They are a trifle over seven weeks old, and are represented to be very hearty and handsome children, and so much alike that it is impossible to tell "t'other from which." They were bound for the Boston Baby Show. Physically, the lady may be healthy, but morally and mentally she cannot be, for no sane or modest lady would make a "show" of herself. To sit in a public place, courting the notoriety of having produced an unusual number of children is neither ennobling nor modest.

From *The New York Times*, November 30, 1859

THE NORTH AND SOUTH

We are in the receipt of numerous communications concerning the Harpers Ferry affair, and the various topics connected with it. They are from all quarters, and on all sides,—some defending the North, assailing Slavery, urging the policy of not hanging John Brown, etc., and others presenting the gloomiest pictures of the state of public feeling at the South, and insisting on the necessity of some immediate step to avert the disastrous political crisis which seems to be impending.

We must decline to publish them all,—simply because we see no possible good which they could accomplish.

———•••———

FOUR

In Which Our Heroine Nearly Comes to Ruin

I NTO EACH LIFE SOME RAIN MUST FALL," MR. LONGFELLOW
wrote, and thus far, I fear I have done an excellent job re-
counting the rain that fell upon my life on the river. It is time to
remember something another great man once said.

"Every crowd has a silver lining," Mr. Barnum told me once
as I recounted to him some woe or another. I laughed, as he intended, but have never forgotten it. Now I shall attempt to recount the silver linings among the clouds—as well as the crowds.

Life on the Mississippi: How romantic it sounds, still, especially to those familiar with the novels of Mr. Twain! Long before
anyone had ever heard of their adventures, I passed by Cairo, Illinois, where Huck and Jim were bound; I saw the sleepy streets of
Hannibal, Missouri, where Tom Sawyer whitewashed his fence; I
passed scores of mysterious islands, any one of which could have
been Injun Joe's hideout.

The scenery truly was thrilling, especially to one reared in the snug, protective hills of New England. The wild islands appearing, as if conjured, in the middle of the widest parts of the river. The high, rocky bluffs in Minnesota, just as Colonel Wood had described, where I saw my first bald eagle, that soaring symbol of our Grand Republic! The bustling docks of St. Louis, rows of boats and barges lined up, like floating dominoes, with exotic names such as *La Belle du Jour* and *El Caballo del Mar*. I was introduced to my first Negro there, a man with skin so dark his eyes popped blinding white; he was as fascinated by me as I was by him, so we shook hands cordially and parted as friends. Then New Orleans, where accents flew as thick and flavorful as the gumbo I tasted for the first time, a mixture of sharp, staccato French and lazy, drawling southern accents, combined with the occasional nasal twang of a Yankee tradesman.

I was presented with a slave once, in New Orleans! A beautiful girl, so graceful and delicate. When I first saw her, accompanying one of her young charges to the show, I was unable to take my eyes off her. Her owner—a smooth southern gentleman, well fed, obviously satisfied with his status as master—noticed and then sent her back aboard the *Banjo* that night as a gift to me. Naturally I could not accept this "gift," but it took me several days to convince the girl to go back to her master.

I had felt morally obligated to refuse her, as no human being should ever be given as chattel! It was the great debate of our time, this decision as to whether or not new states should be allowed in as free or slave-holding, and of course, as a New Englander, I was firmly on the side of the abolitionists like Mr. Garrison and Mrs. Stowe. Yet after the girl left, reluctantly, I felt a surprising wrench; it only then occurred to me that the moral thing would have been to accept her and take her back north, where I could set her free. Even as I realized this, however, I remembered that I was almost as indentured as she; Colonel Wood would not have allowed it. She would have been one more mouth to feed, for obviously a slave could not perform and earn her keep, as the rest of us did.

I dreamed about the girl many nights after; she appeared, silent and reproachful, staring at me before vanishing into a soupy southern mist.

The dangers we faced as our little company cruised up and down the capricious Mississippi were more numerous than any plot from a dime novel! There was the ever-present terror of the boiler exploding, a fate that met many a steamship in those days, causing hundreds of gruesome deaths. We used to read about them in newspapers, exclaiming over the gory details of flesh melting away from bone, of decapitations caused by flying shards of steel. No mere schoolmarm ever faced such thrilling peril!

There were also dangers from the river itself; one never knew if, just around a bend, there might be submerged trees or even wreckage from other boats. Pirates, too, were rumored to be lurking in every hidden cove (although I'm sad to report that we never encountered any). Western storms were a constant threat; the weather in this part of the country was wilder, more electric, than I'd ever experienced back east. Once we came upon a town that had been nearly leveled by a tornado, and we could see the tempest's path from the broken and uprooted trees on either side of the river. It was as if a heavenly foot had stomped through on its ruthless way to somewhere else.

The incessant mosquitoes and flies brought fever, aided by the dank, humid air, so that at one time or another, everyone in our company was felled by the ague. Despite my strong constitution, even I was laid low by it, tended to, with great care, by Sylvia. Soon enough, however, I was up and about, although I cannot say my recovery was aided by the food we were served. Oh, how the thought of one of Mama's layer cakes or delicate pies could bring tears to my eyes, a rumble to my ever-empty stomach! Our cook did not deserve her apron; well-cooked meat was a foreign concept to the woman, and she insisted upon boiling, rather than frying, the fish. A dense, chewy bread was our staple, as apparently she had never learned to put up vegetables or fruit!

Even when we left the boat and ventured onto shore—often in search of a boardinghouse that would serve a decent meal—there were many dangers awaiting our valiant little troupe.

Late at night, after the last show, was a particularly hazardous time. It was not unusual for the male members of the company to want to explore the streets, generally closest to the docks, which were lit up with gaslights, music, and sin. There were often brawls and disturbances; minstrel singers and plate spinners did not blend in well with farmers and fishermen. On more than one occasion we had to beat a hasty retreat late at night, the hands jumping down to the steam engine, many with their nightcaps on, to throw wood in the boilers as Captain Tucker ordered full steam, bullets screeching our way from the docks.

Naturally, I was never part of this kind of mischief. But when bullets were fired toward the boat, they were not particular about their target; I clasped my hands about my ears and ducked, but I heard my share of bullets whistling by my head, anyway. Fortunately, none of us ever came to peril, although once Colonel Wood found a bullet hole squarely in the middle of his silk top hat.

The safest place for any of us was onstage, in front of an eager crowd; that silver lining that Mr. Barnum would one day talk about. To see the joy on plain, work-worn faces as I sang, to hear the delighted laughter when I told a funny story—that was where I felt truly at home, loved, *safe*.

Although my fellow performers did not always feel quite so loved! Western audiences were swift to show boredom or displeasure with an act that did not measure up. Tomatoes, apples, masticated wads of tobacco—all were thrown freely at the stage at one time or another. None, however, were thrown at me.

Why I was never so threatened, I can only ascribe to the peculiar effect I had upon most people, even those who could not refrain from remarking upon my size. Far from wanting to cause me harm, the audience seemed, as one, to desire to shelter me from it. This behavior was so marked, so pronounced, that some of the other acts tried to convince me to appear with them.

"C'mon, Vinnie," the plate spinner, in particular, would beg. "I been hit with so many tomatoes lately I'm turning red! Just step out onstage with me, please? I'll pay you, say, a dollar a week?"

I smiled but declined. I couldn't appear in every act!

There was one person, however, who did not desire to shelter me from harm—one person, in fact, who seemed to go out of his way to cause me grief. And that was Colonel Wood.

"Move your tiny ass, Vinnie—if I catch you being late for an entrance again, I'll boot you from here to kingdom come," he would snarl, kicking at me with his dirty shoe. This was something he became very fond of doing, just as I became very fond of jumping nimbly aside to avoid him.

Or—"I'm sick of your uppity airs, Miss Uptight Yankee. Why don't I just throw you in the boiler; you're so little, I bet nobody would even notice you were missing," he would growl, taking a swig of his jugful of whiskey. "Slap me on my own boat, in front of my own people, the hell you did." That, of course, had been my fatal mistake; on his boat, he claimed his title of "Colonel," placed it on his head like the gaudy hats he wore, and never let anyone forget it. Woe to anyone who challenged him—especially in front of an audience.

"Never thought I'd live to see the day when a dwarf would be the biggest draw on my boat. God Almighty, what idiots these rubes are," he would slobber after he was well and truly in his cups. Once drunk, he had a tendency to fall asleep in the oddest places; you never knew, in the morning, when you might stumble upon his drooling, snoring form sprawled all over a staircase or curled up among a coil of ropes on the deck—or even, more than once, leaning against the door to my stateroom.

The first time I discovered him there, bile rose in my throat until I feared I might contribute to the puddle of vomit in the hallway at his feet. I uttered a swift prayer of thanks for the presence of Sylvia in my room, and couldn't fall asleep that night until she had moved my trunk against the door.

But the fact remained that I made the man money; knowing this, I could not completely believe that he would ever actually harm me. As the months went by, and 1858 passed into 1859 and then 1860, as the *Banjo* drifted up and down the river, its company so oddly detached from the ever-escalating political situation on both shores, my fame grew beyond what the Colonel could have predicted.

After showing him the *carte de visite* of General Tom Thumb, eventually I had persuaded Colonel Wood to have my photograph taken (by stressing the lucrative nature of such an enterprise; he sold the *cartes de visites* for twenty-five cents each, and kept all the profit himself). And over time, these postcards reached people who might otherwise have never visited a floating palace; they reached good people, respectable people. People who clamored only to see me—not anyone else.

The postcards had not, thus far, reached Mr. Barnum, as I had hoped; my fame may have been growing, but only along the Mississippi.

"Get in here, Vinnie," Colonel Wood grumbled to me one morning as I was making my way to the dining room. As usual,

Sylvia was with me; she stopped, gazing down at me with a questioning look. I nodded for her to go ahead, watching as she lumbered down the hall, her shoulders rounded so that her head did not hit the ceiling, and then followed the Colonel into his office. He shut the door; it latched with a terrifying thud, and I realized, a sharp razor of panic cutting itself through my still-sleepy consciousness, that I could not reach the handle myself. I was as good as trapped.

But no, I told myself sternly. It was broad daylight, he appeared sober, and outside I could hear deckhands and members of the troupe bustling about, engaged in their usual morning activity.

"Sit," Colonel Wood barked.

With some effort, I struggled into the only chair available to me, while he took his seat behind his cluttered desk. He did not offer to place a cushion upon my seat, so that I might be on his level; on the contrary, he grinned down at me with ill-concealed delight, while I sat so low I could barely see over the stacks of paper on his desk.

I hid my anger, as I was teaching myself to do, behind an excess of manners. "Yes, Colonel Wood? I'm eager to hear what you wish to discuss."

"Always so damn polite," he muttered. "That tiny mouth always pursed so prim and proper. Think you're above us all out here—you know the rest of the company talks about your airs, don't you?"

This was not the first time he had tried to insinuate himself between my friends and me; I knew enough not to rise to the bait. "Thank you for complimenting me on my manners," I responded with a polite smile. "It is much appreciated."

"Hmmph. Well, keep talking like that, Miss Dainty Dwarf. Because you're going to start doing extra duty. I've had some requests for private audiences for you, from some pretty important folks, and they're willing to pay double the regular price."

"Private audience? What do you mean?"

"Some hoity-toity types, who claim they're above stepping foot on my boat, want to meet you. Privately, they say. Not on-stage."

"But where?" I couldn't conceive of such an idea. I was finally accustomed to being on display in the galley before and after per-formances; I could not say I looked forward to it, but I had learned how to put the onlookers—and myself—at ease. I could not com-pletely avoid being scooped up as if I were a mere child; there were those who would persist in doing so, no matter how much I protested. I had discovered, though, that if I spoke first, about the most normal of topics—the weather, the political situation, the latest fashions—fewer people were inclined to do so.

But always I was surrounded by others—Sylvia, the Tattooed Man, the Bearded Lady who had recently joined our troupe, Billy Birch and his men. The notion of being entirely alone with strangers was vaguely troubling to me.

"I'm going to have to secure some sort of private parlor in hotels, I guess. Most of these towns have one, and I'm sure some arrangement can be made so I won't have to pay—free advertis-ing, something. Up in Galena, there's a Mr. Grant who would like to meet you, so that'll be the first one."

"Alone? This Mr. Grant—he'll be alone?" Uneasiness filled my breast; I shifted in my chair, which was much too big for me. It served only to sharpen my acute awareness—it was almost an electric sensation, my skin tingling and burning—of my physical helplessness.

"How the hell do I know? If he's alone, he's alone. You'll meet Grant, and you'll do whatever he asks you to—none of this holier-than-thou behavior, Missy. You understand? He wants a kiss, you get off your high horse and give him a goddamned kiss." With a leer, Colonel Wood leaned across his desk toward me. His liver-colored lips, beneath his awful mustache still bearing traces of the blackening he used onstage, smacked at me, making disgusting kissing sounds. "You know, you ain't half bad looking in that photograph of yours. Not so bad in person, either. Is *all* of you so pretty and tiny? Might have to check that out someday, what the hell, cousin or not." And he started to laugh again, making those awful kissing sounds.

It was as if a slimy snake had slithered down my spine; I shivered, even though the air was close and hot about me, threatening to cut off my breath. I slid off the chair and ran to the door but could not open it; I could not reach the latch no matter how high I jumped—and jump I did, panic closing in around my throat like a vise, cutting off my breath, my thoughts.

Finally, with a great leap, I did reach the latch, but my hand was so small it was difficult to grasp and pull; my panic did not help matters. My grip kept slipping and slipping until suddenly the door gave way, opened from the outside; I nearly fell into the hallway. The thin dancing girl, Carlotta, was staring down at me in surprise.

"Why, Vinnie, are you all right?"

I nodded. Glancing over my shoulder, I saw that Colonel Wood had not moved a muscle. He remained seated at his desk; he was even going through some papers as if I wasn't there. And I had to wonder if he had actually said the things that I thought he had.

All at once my mind shifted, as if it were a mechanical thing and completely out of my control, toward Minnie, my dear sister. I thought of how small she was, so much smaller than me. How sweet, how innocent. Thank goodness she was still home; had I ever thought to go back for her, to show her that the world was not to be feared? "That dreadful man," she had declared Colonel Wood before she had even seen him. I thought her so simple then; I had laughed at her. Now I wondered how she'd known.

But, of course, she didn't. She was only afraid of the unknown in a way that I was not, at least not until this moment. I took a deep breath and told myself I would not begin to embrace such ideas. Mr. Grant was most likely a perfectly respectable man with a family; why else would he not wish to step foot upon the boat?

As for Colonel Wood—why, I would simply not allow myself to be alone with him again. It was an easy enough thing to accomplish; the boat was always full of people. There was no reason why I ever had to be alone with that man. And I knew I had only to ask and Sylvia would not leave my side.

Calm again, I walked with Carlotta toward the dining room, where I could hear my traveling companions talking, joshing, breaking into bits of song over the clash of silver and china. My heart lightened, for I knew they would be happy to see me. And indeed they were; as soon as I entered the dining room, there were cries of "Vinnie, Vinnie, come sit by me!"

I took a seat next to Mrs. Billy Birch and listened to all the good-natured gossip. Apparently Carlotta, seated by my side and suddenly all blushes and modest glances, was engaged to one of the regulars—the unattached young men who followed our boat up and down the river on their own pathetic rafts or canoes, looking for occasional work or trying to make a living fishing or peddling. Mrs. Billy asked me if I'd like to help make her a decent trousseau.

I nodded, happy for Carlotta. She had no future as a performer, poor dear. Getting married was the wisest thing she could do.

I joined in the congratulations without the slightest twinge of jealousy, and promised to contribute a cotton nightgown.

* * *

GALENA WAS A PRETTY LITTLE RIVER TOWN, LIKE ALL THE others—hilly, with a main thoroughfare lined with shops. I followed Colonel Wood through the bustling street to a handsome building called the DeSoto House; I had never stepped foot in a hotel before and was excited at the prospect. I had no inkling that in the years to come, I would stay in the finest of them all, with the most luxurious accommodations. I would even return to this hotel, occupying the largest suite!

But at the time, I managed not to betray my astonishment at the elegance of this establishment; indeed, I sailed through the door, clad in my most respectable gown, not one I would ever wear onstage but rather one of my church dresses, with matching bonnet, from home. It was a modest blue satin, with a high collar and black-velvet scallops along the hem and sleeves. With my head held high, I managed to give the appearance that I was quite at home in the ornate lobby, wallpapered and carpeted to a fault. Colonel Wood, however, could not maintain his composure. He stopped and gaped, forgetting to remove his hat. He looked cheap and gaudy, totally out of place, and I stared at him through new eyes, secure in my matchless deportment and bearing. Away from the boat, in such genteel surroundings, the unease he stirred in me melted away. He looked exactly what he was—a posturing, insignificant little man. And I felt exactly what I was—an elegant gentlewoman with superior breeding and appearance. A much larger personality, in every way.

Yet as soon as we were led to a little side parlor, where the Colonel left me with an admonition to "Remember, no hoity-toity airs—I'm not paying you to disappoint the customers," that unease crept back. Nervously I paced around, trying to admire the ornately carved woodwork and plush carpeting. The furniture was all large and overstuffed, and I remembered, with a pang of despair, that my stair steps were back on the boat. Locating a footstool, I dragged it over to a chair so that I might be able to climb onto it with some dignity.

Anxious and unsettled, my composure having deserted me, I could not help but recall what Mrs. Billy Birch and Carlotta each had said to me before I left the boat.

Mrs. Billy had tucked a large stone in my hand. "Put this in your reticule," she whispered, as Colonel Wood was hovering nearby. "Don't be afraid to swing it at that Mr. Grant's head if you need to!" I had accepted the unusual gift with gratitude, and tucked it into my reticule, thankful for its sudden heft.

Carlotta had summoned me to her room earlier. I did not usually visit her here; when we females gathered for our nightly gossip, it was generally in Mrs. Billy Birch's room, which was neat and homey, with a spirit lamp for making tea.

Carlotta's room, by contrast, was slovenly, her stockings and petticoats draped over every surface, all in need of repair or washing. I tried not to notice them; obviously she wasn't bothered by the chaos, as she had no blush or apology as she handed me a small envelope. Opening it, I saw that it contained a grayish powdery substance.

"Prevention powders," she said matter-of-factly. "You're so little, Vinnie, I don't know what to tell you to do so that it don't hurt. But you oughtn't to be havin' babies, so use these. Mix 'em with water and then douse yourself with them down there." And she pointed to her—I still blush to recall—womanly parts.

" 'It'? What do you mean 'it'? What might hurt?"

"It. Screwin'. I don't know what the Colonel thinks these men are going to want to do to you in private, and God knows I hope it ain't what I'm thinkin', but just in case. You don't want to have a baby, do you?"

"I—I—I have no earthly idea what to say!" And I didn't; I sat down upon the floor, my legs suddenly giving out, and I stared up at the girl who, I saw, thought she was only being kind.

"I know your ma probably never told you these things. My own ma didn't. But you're such a little thing, and I feel like someone ought. You do know what screwin' is, don't you?" She frowned in concern, her crow's-feet crinkling up; against her sallow skin, bare of the cheap paint she used onstage, her yellow hair appeared even more artificial.

"I, well, yes, I believe so. Copulating, you mean?"

"Listen to you, Vinnie!" She grinned, her pale blue eyes round with admiration. "Always coming up with such fancy words—I plum forget you were a schoolmarm sometimes, and then you go and remind me. Copulating—I swear!" And she repeated it again, as if learning a new word in a new language.

"But why would you give me this?" I held out the envelope, away from my person, as if it might taint me by proximity. I struggled to understand what she was implying.

"So you don't have a baby." She repeated herself patiently, as if I were a child. "Don't you understand? Screwin' is how babies get made."

"I understand that, Carlotta, but what I don't quite see is why I would have need for this kind of—of prevention?"

"Oh, Vinnie! You're such a smart little thing that I forget you don't know much of the world! Why do you think men want to meet you alone? There's only one reason for that, although I have to say it's not right, not for someone your size, but Lord, I've learned it takes all kinds in this world. You have no idea some of the things these river men want—animals, sisters, even other men—"

"Stop!" I was sickened, horrified, by her meaning. Scrambling up from the floor, I felt my face burn, and I couldn't look her in the eyes. "Stop—I don't want to hear this! I have no intention of engaging in—in—what it was you just said. Even Colonel Wood would not—these are respectable people, he said! There is no need for this!" And I thrust the envelope into her hands.

"But, Vinnie, I'm just looking out for you—you have to be prepared!"

"No, I thank you, but—no. There is no need, no need at all!" I hurried out of Carlotta's room, still unable to look her in the face. How did she know of these things? I felt sorry for her, for her life; I felt even sorrier for her fiancé, who must not have any idea of her past. I knew she was only trying to be kind, but I could not help but feel sickened and insulted, all the same.

I refused even to consider the scenario she had so easily conjured up; still, I felt grateful, as I waited nervously in the parlor for Mr. Grant, that Mrs. Billy Birch's rock was securely in my reticule, which was attached to my wrist.

There was a knock on the parlor door; my stomach plummeted to my feet, and I clasped my reticule to my breast. "C-come in," I barely managed to say, through cold, trembling lips.

"Miss Bump?" A short, stocky man with a beard opened the door, hat in hand. His gaze swept the room at his own height; it took him a moment to remember to look down. Finally, he saw me; his eyes widened, and his face creased into a slow grin. "Oh, goodness! Just a moment—" He ducked his head back outside the door, and I heard him say, "Julia! Children! She's in here!"

At the mention of a female name, my entire body, which I had been holding stiff as a corpse, perhaps in anticipation of my imminent doom, relaxed. I reached up to place my reticule upon an end table and turned to receive my visitors.

Mr. Grant ushered in his family: his wife and four children, the youngest a little boy still in skirts, carried by Mrs. Grant. The children shyly hung back while their parents approached me, somewhat timidly, as if I might suddenly attack *them*. They were, I was astonished to realize, almost as frightened of me as I had been of them! This realization made me relax even further; I stepped forward and held my hand out to Mr. Grant, hoping to put him at ease.

"Allow me to introduce myself. I am Miss Bump."

"Thank you for meeting with us, Miss Bump. I am Mr. Grant. This is my wife, Mrs. Grant, and our children. Freddie, Buck, Nellie, and little Jesse."

Mr. Grant bowed stiffly, while Mrs. Grant, a plain woman with small, crossed eyes, shook my hand very timidly and shifted the child in her arms.

"Please, let us sit," I said, and holding my skirts, I stepped upon the stool and climbed, as gracefully as possible, upon the chair I had chosen.

The children could not prevent themselves from giggling at my exertions; I pretended not to notice, and arranged myself and my skirts in my chair, my legs dangling above the stool.

"I thank you much for agreeing to meet us here," Mr. Grant said pleasantly. "But the children did so want to see you, after we saw your photograph in the paper, and I couldn't take them on a boat, you see—you understand."

"Indeed," I said coolly, as if there were no reason to take offense. Then I fell silent, as I could not begin to think what to say. I did not know them, after all. And I was not onstage, I could not break out into song. I had never been bashful in my life, but then nothing had ever prepared me for this; I had a wild impulse to shout that they were all "simply dreadful" and run out of the room. Only the thought of Colonel Wood, who must be hovering outside the door, prevented me from doing so.

"How tall is she, Papa?" one of the boys asked, and while his parents exchanged anxious looks, I was happy to hear his question. At least I could answer that.

"Thirty-two inches, which is how many feet, young man?" I could not help it; my teacher's training came to the fore, and I looked at him sternly—although I had to smile when I saw his face pale and his eyes bulge.

"I—I—I don't know?" He looked desperately at his father, who had an amused glint in his dark eyes.

"Two feet, eight inches," I replied briskly. "You look old enough to know your mathematics!"

"For sure, for sure, son Frederick is lax with his schoolwork," Mr. Grant chortled, slapping his knee. "Well done, Miss Bump! That you should know such a thing yourself!"

I swallowed my anger, continuing to smile politely. "Naturally I know such a thing, as I was a schoolteacher before coming west."

"A schoolteacher!" Mrs. Grant almost dropped her child from her knee. "How can that be?"

"I was an excellent scholar and was asked to take over a classroom."

"Extraordinary! Can you imagine your teacher being smaller than you, Nellie?" Mr. Grant addressed his daughter, for whom he obviously had a great fondness; he had sat with his arm about her shoulders from the moment they took their seats. She was a pretty thing, with long blond curls.

"No, Papa! I can't! You're really old enough to be a schoolteacher? How old are you?"

"Nellie, that's not polite," her mother scolded, and I exchanged a knowing look with her.

"Tell us more about yourself, Miss Bump, for that is why we wanted to meet you, after all." Mr. Grant leaned back and removed a cigar from his pocket; I wrinkled my nose, for I found the smell of cigars distasteful—at home, Papa had smoked a pipe, which I much preferred—but I did not say anything. Instead, I gave a quick recitation of my life thus far; soon we were discussing the weather, the town of Galena, which was as new to the Grants as it was to me. They had recently moved there from St. Louis, I discovered, so that Mr. Grant could take over management of his father's store.

Politics, naturally, were discussed. The presidential election of 1860 was only a few months away.

"I don't really think too much of politics," Mr. Grant admitted, his cigar spattering ash upon his trousers, which he did not notice, although Mrs. Grant did. "But I suppose I have to vote Republican. I can't abide slavery, and I guess that Lincoln's the best man to put an end to it, although at what cost, I don't know."

"Do you think there will be war?" I asked, just to be polite; the increasingly fierce tensions between the North and South did not trouble me and seemed not to affect our troupe as, of course, we moved freely up and down the Mississippi, crossing the Mason-Dixon Line without thought. Even so, I had noticed that more and more, lately, Billy Birch and his minstrels discussed the situation at mealtimes; they were, after all, men.

"If there is war, will you go, like you did before, Papa?" the oldest son said, scratching his nose.

"We won't talk of this now," his mother said hastily, before Mr. Grant could answer.

"Were you in the military?" I asked him.

"Yes, but that was long ago," he replied evasively, stroking his beard. "Don't know that anyone would want me back, anyway. Well, if this fellow Lincoln is elected, there very well may be a war. I don't think the South will stand for him."

"Well, then I hope he won't win!" And with this mutually happy thought, we continued to converse pleasantly. The boys fidgeted and poked at each other but with obvious good nature; Mrs. Grant kept the babe upon her knee the entire time, jostling him gently, while Mr. Grant sat with his arm about his daughter's shoulders. In short, I felt it was a most pleasant afternoon spent with a family similar to my own. My earlier fears and unease were forgotten.

Finally conversation lagged, and we all rose and walked toward the door, the children giggling and asking if they could stand next to me and measure my height, which I agreed to without hesitation. Mrs. Grant once again expressed her surprise that I had ever been a schoolmarm. I imagined my youthful appearance made it very difficult for her to fully comprehend it.

"It's been such a pleasure meeting you all," I said, extending my hand graciously and feeling it clasped with warmth and affection. "I hope we see one another again soon."

"As do we," Mr. Grant said with a smile that crinkled his eyes. And as the Grants left the room, I heard Mrs. Grant remark to her husband, "What a dear little lady! Her manners could not have been nicer."

I smiled, refreshed from this interlude away from the boat, and collected my cloak and reticule. As I walked toward the lobby, where Colonel Wood was saying goodbye to the Grants, they all looked my way, waving; I waved back. They really were very lovely people, such a pleasant family, obviously of good breeding; I did hope we would meet again soon, perhaps for a picnic, or dinner, or—

Mr. Grant reached into his breast pocket and took out a fistful of bills; he handed them to Colonel Wood, who bowed and pocketed the money quickly. The Grants left, and Colonel Wood turned toward me, grinning in almost a friendly way.

"Five dollars! Five dollars, for an hour! What suckers they are! C'mon, we have a show to get back to. But whatever you did in there to charm those folks, Miss Hoity-Toity, remember to do it again. I'm going to put the word out far and wide. Imagine, five dollars! I bet I can charge twice that in a place like St. Louis or New Orleans!"

Colonel Wood held the door open for me, for only the second time in our acquaintance. We found ourselves on the bustling sidewalk of Galena; I saw the Grant family turn into one of the shops, Mr. Grant already reaching into his breast pocket, ready to purchase some new distraction for his family.

As he had just done, back in the DeSoto House.

WAR. DESPITE MY STUDIED INDIFFERENCE TO ITS CAUSES, IT appeared it was coming anyway. Abraham Lincoln was elected President in November of 1860, and immediately secession meetings popped up all over the Deep South—which was where we happened to be, as we were every winter.

"Colonel, I think we ought to think about heading north," Billy Birch announced early one December morning at breakfast. The bright southern light, reflected from the water, shone through one of the narrow windows and illuminated Billy's head, bald as a polished billiard ball (save for the permanent black stain of burnt cork behind his ears). He wore a hat while performing, but other than that was completely unashamed of his naked pate.

"North? During the winter? You know we can't do that—the river might ice over, and besides, what the hell for?" Colonel Wood was hunched over his plate, his graying curls, clumped with traces of blackening, dangling over his greasy eggs. The sight of him eating in the morning was one more reason why I found it difficult to consume the first meal of the day. (The limp toast and runny eggs, fried not in butter but in rancid bacon grease, were another.)

"Haven't you been reading the papers? Here—look at the headline this morning." Billy thrust a copy of the Vicksburg, Mississippi, *Daily Citizen* across the table. **"Secession Meeting TONIGHT! Cowardly Unionists Urged to Leave Town, Declares Mayor. ALL HAIL THE GLORIOUS CAUSE!!!"**

"What's that got to do with us? The box office could be better, I admit, but it'll pick up this evening; not everyone's going to those goddamned Secessionist meetings, you know. It's just a few rabble-rousers." Colonel Wood reached for his coffee cup and drank greedily, his mustache dipping into the cup.

"Colonel, I think you're wrong," Mr. Deacon, the sword swallower, piped up. He was such a mild man; it was unusual for him to speak at the table. "Ever since the election, things have felt different down here. I been performing for years, and I ain't never seen anything like it. These folks are angry, as angry as a hen going after a fox. I don't think they're in the mood for any entertainment."

"And none of us is a southerner," Mrs. Billy Birch said. "What if there is war and we're stuck down here? What will happen to us?"

"I'm not going to be a slave!" Carlotta whimpered. She and her fiancé were still engaged; he was trying to put away some money before their wedding and, to that end, had decided to stay in St. Louis, working at the docks.

"You silly ass, you're not going to be any slave! You have yellow hair, I think—at least it used to be, probably all gray by now underneath that dye." Colonel Wood laughed rudely.

"My great-gran was a Creole girl, they say. Which means I have some nigger blood in me, and I'm not going to be no slave!" Carlotta started to cry.

"Oh, for Christ's sake, shut up. Let a man have his breakfast in peace." Colonel Wood threw a piece of toast at the sobbing girl.

"Colonel, please! She's frightened, poor thing." I couldn't help it; I scolded him in front of everyone even though I knew he detested it. But lately he had let pass a number of my spirited remarks, remarks that he would have mocked me for a year previous.

I slid off my chair and went to comfort Carlotta; ever since she had tried to "help" me with her preventative powders, I had felt a kinship with her. I sensed she needed a good Christian influence; I think she sensed I needed a woman of the world to watch out for me. We probably were both correct.

Colonel Wood glared at me but did not reply; abruptly he rose and shoved his chair back toward the table. "We're not running away from rumors about something that's not going to happen. We have engagements—I have fifty dollars' worth of private audiences for Vinnie in the next week alone, including one tonight, so obviously not everyone is going to the Secesh meeting. And then the boat needs some repairs in New Orleans, where we're heading next. You all have contracts, you just remember that. I don't want to see anyone sneaking out on me—you think Secessionists are angry? Just you see me trying to collect on a broken contract!" And with one last swig of his coffee, he was gone.

We all stared at one another. Billy and the other minstrels, who were our de facto leaders—the performers with the most legitimate experience—scratched their chins and consulted over the newspaper. Mrs. Billy shook her head and poured Carlotta another cup of coffee, her mothering instincts, never far from the surface, coming out in full force.

Sylvia didn't say a word. She seemed sadder than ever, these days. She claimed she had dreams of her dead mother, dreams in which she was told to leave the boat and go back home. So she increasingly longed for Maine yet seemed unable to do anything to get there. It was as if she was paralyzed by her longing; her al-

THE AUTOBIOGRAPHY OF MRS. TOM THUMB

ready agonizing lethargy of movement increased. At times, I thought she was almost asleep onstage, her eyes barely open, as she swayed upon her feet.

The only time she ever seemed motivated to action was if she thought Colonel Wood was being particularly harsh to me. But Colonel Wood lately seemed mollified by the money I was bringing in, the numerous private engagements that continued to line up. He had stopped threatening to kick me, although he did still act strangely toward me, particularly late at night when he had already emptied half a whiskey bottle. The strangeness was in his gaze, more and more; I felt its hot glare burn over my skin as he looked me up and down, as if he was attempting to see me in a different way—a predatory way. At times, I felt almost naked in his presence. It was in the manner with which he studied every inch of my form, as if he was trying to uncover a great secret with only his eyes.

This was when I was most afraid. But Sylvia was my ever-present bodyguard, although she wasn't allowed to accompany me to my private audiences. Those were in hotels, however, that were always filled with people—genteel people, people who could afford luxuries. With only a few exceptions, these audiences were reminiscent of my meeting with the Grants. They consisted mainly of curious families of good breeding who simply didn't want to step foot on a showboat. More and more, my photograph, alone, appeared in the newspaper ahead of our engagements; I saved these notices whenever possible, amassing an impressive collection. I had an idea of what I would do with these once my contract was up.

There had been a few times, however, more recently, when I met with lone gentlemen. I made sure to keep the door open then, my reticule—with that heavy stone in it—clutched in my hand. These meetings had been uncomfortable, for conversation was difficult. These men—great men, some of them men I would hear about later, such as Stephen Douglas of Illinois, Jefferson Davis of Mississippi—were somehow rendered mute by my presence, content to simply stare—or touch. As always, it seemed impossible to persuade these men that I was not a child in women's clothing, eager to be lifted and carried and petted. Usually. the gentleman would turn beet-red at my admonishment and apologize profusely—*after* he had kissed me, his beard and mustache rough against my cheek, so overly fragrant with toilet water that my eyes burned. On such occasions, I was embarrassed for us both.

Once or twice, however, I had noticed a different attitude accompanied by a different look—a look very like the one Colonel Wood sometimes gave me. That voracious, curious look that I had to shut my eyes against, even as I took comfort in the hefty weight of Mrs. Billy Birch's rock in my reticule.

"Vinnie, we think you ought to talk to the Colonel," Billy Birch declared, folding the newspaper and interrupting my reverie. Carlotta was still sobbing some nonsense about being forced to work in a cotton field; I had been patting her arm absently. The other minstrels, backing Billy up as they did onstage, nodded in unison.

"What? Me? Talk to the Colonel?" I went back to my seat, for it was there, upon my special cushion, that I was nearer the height of my companions. And I felt, keenly, the need to be on equal footing at this moment.

"Yes, you. Face it—you're the biggest star on this boat. You're the one who brings in the most money. And that's the only thing the Colonel respects."

"The Colonel does not respect me, I assure you. He tolerates me. But he wouldn't listen to me, Billy, no more than he'll listen to anything but the clink of coins in his pocket."

"Fair enough, but still. You're the best chance we have. We're in danger here, all of us. We're a northern troupe on a northern boat. Why, any moment now someone's going to commandeer this thing if they're thinking about war at all, and where will we be left? Stuck down here, and even the trains are having a hard time getting out."

"They are?" I felt a paralyzing chill in my chest, as if I'd swallowed a block of ice. Why had I no idea the situation was so bad? While once I would have been abreast of the latest political news, more and more, I had to admit, I had been focused only on my career. I scanned the papers not for mentions of the political situation but for mentions of my own name. Just when had I become so self-absorbed? It was a form of self-preservation, I realized now; I had resolved that I could survive Colonel Wood's cruelty if my heart, my mind, had shrunk to a size designed to absorb my own troubles only.

"Yes, they are. Very hard. If any of us tries to leave the boat on our own, that old devil will be after us with bloodhounds, worse than any overseer. We have to make him understand and get us out himself. That's the only way; we have to stay together—and you're the only one he might listen to."

I was silent, thinking. My contract was up in April. I hadn't been home in all this time, and I could scarcely wait until then to see Mama and Papa, and especially Minnie. Her letters arrived as regularly as letters could on the river; they were tear-stained, hardly legible, usually one long, punctuation-free plea: *"Please come home, Sister, Sister, come home I miss you what do you look like now are you still as small as me please come home."* I did not want to be stuck here in the South if war did come. I so longed to see my family, to tell them of my adventures, to assure us all that it had been worthwhile to leave.

I also did not want to be away from the reach of Mr. Barnum, who was most definitely in New York, still running his American Museum.

"All right," I agreed, sipping my cold, weak coffee. "I'll try to talk to him, although I warn you I don't know how much influence I'll have. But I'll do my best to convince him."

"Hurray for Vinnie!" Billy Birch cried out, throwing his knife into the air. Mr. Deacon caught it with an expert flourish and swallowed it neatly, his hand disappearing into his mouth. His throat moved, as if he were truly swallowing it, then he showed us both hands, which were empty. He gulped and dabbed at his mouth with his napkin, then made as if to go; with a sly grin, he turned back to us and produced the knife, which he had neatly hidden up his sleeve.

We all applauded, everyone happy, everyone united. Despite the threat of war, at that moment it felt as if we would remain untouched, in a protective bubble, just a happy little band of performers.

Little did we know that this was the last time we would laugh together like this.

"C'MON, VINNIE, MOVE YOUR ASS. AT LEAST THIS ONE DIDN'T cancel."

I hurriedly grabbed my cloak, leaving Sylvia in our room to read by the sputtering oil lamp. Then I followed Colonel Wood down the hall, in such a hurry that it wasn't until we were off the boat that I remembered I had quite forgotten my reticule.

"Oh, wait!" I called after him, turning to go back and get it.

"Move your ass, I said—we're late!" Without breaking his stride, Colonel Wood grabbed my arm; he practically dragged me through the raucous crowd, much louder, much angrier, than any I had ever seen.

"But I forgot my reticule!"

"Such a goddamned *lady*. 'I forgot my reticule!'" He mimicked me cruelly, while still dragging me so that my slippers skimmed the ground; my arm felt wrenched from its socket. "We're late, and I'm not going to lose a penny of this because you forgot your damn reticule. This has been one hell of a day."

For it turned out Billy Birch was correct: Nobody cared a whit about coming aboard our boat this day. The box office was scarce; the few people in the audience hardly paid any attention to the stage at all, so we did only one show. The rest of the day we stood along the deck, me on my steps so that I could see over the railing, watching the excitement on the shore. People running to and fro, pamphlets being handed out, guns firing up in the air, high-pitched yells that would later become the famous Rebel cry of the Confederacy. Strange flags, flags I'd never seen before, were flying everywhere; they were blue, with a white star in the middle. "Secesh flags," said Billy Birch miserably. "They're going to secede, they're all going to secede, just you wait."

"How?" I didn't completely understand. "How can they do that?"

"They just can. States' rights and all. But Lincoln won't let 'em, he vowed to preserve the Union, and so there'll be bloody hell to pay."

"'Hell to pay'! Imagine, fighting right here in our own country! How horrid!" Yet my pulse raced at all the history I was witnessing. If the South was going to secede and take that first step toward war, how thrilling it was to be there when it happened! I couldn't wait to tell my family all about it when I got home.

But first I had to get there, and the effect of all this excitement and war talk on our situation seemed increasingly ominous. I couldn't help but notice several men pointing to the boat and gesturing excitedly; more than once my ears caught the phrase "bunch of Yankee freaks" as it was hurled toward me and my compatriots. Rumors were flying from boat to boat, all lined up like sitting ducks at the docks, that soon all ships would be commandeered to move war munitions about the South. Not only ships but trains, as well, were rumored to be closed to paying passengers—particularly those with northern accents.

I had dutifully apprised Colonel Wood of the situation, bolstered by Billy Birch. The Colonel cursed and swore but still insisted that we would keep to our schedule and travel downriver; getting to New Orleans by December 12 was of utmost importance to him. "Vinnie has an important engagement then, and I need to get the boat fixed" was all he would say when we asked why. Then he cursed the poor box-office receipt from the morning, and the names of the two of my three private audiences that had sent word they would not be coming.

Hence his agitation as he dragged me through the crowded streets of Vicksburg, which, although there were no gaslights, were amply illuminated this night by torches and burning effigies of Abraham Lincoln, complete with tall stovepipe hat. Although I could barely see them; I was pulled so forcibly through the crowd, concentrating intently upon not tripping or stumbling, that I had little opportunity to look up. I was aware, mainly, only of trouser legs, some creased, some not, and the occasional hoopskirt, hem mud-splattered from the recent rains. It was a measure of how worked up the crowd was that few people stopped to gape down at me as Colonel Wood tugged me along.

Finally, we reached the hotel. Colonel Wood stomped up to the desk and was directed to a parlor off the lobby, which was crowded with men smoking, drinking, and arguing; I followed him, and after being told to "Keep him here as long as possible; maybe I can charge extra," practically shoved inside. There I tried to collect myself. My skirt was not torn, although the soles of my slippers were shredded. I looked about for a mirror, but of course there were none at my level. The only one was stationed above a fireplace, and there was nothing for me to climb upon that I might reach it. So I straightened my bonnet, patted my hair, trying to tuck stray strands back into my chignon, dragged a stool over to a velvet chair, took my seat, and waited.

The room was eerily still and dark; only one oil lamp was lit, so that the corners were hidden and long shadows smudged the carpet. But I could hear the agitation in the streets outside continue to build; shouts of "If South Carolina goes, we go!" and "Damn the Abolitionist Ape going to the White House!" reached my ears through the tightly drawn velvet curtains. These threats were punctuated by the tinkling of shattering glass and muffled thumps. With every sound I jumped, wanting to run to the window and look out at what must have been a tremendous scene. But I made myself stay perfectly still, collecting my composure before my visitor arrived. And as I sat there, so isolated yet also exposed, a curious conviction filled my breast. I felt that whatever happened this night, both in this room and outside on the streets, would be something I would never forget.

I sat for a very long time; I heard the determined tick of a mantel clock piling up whole minutes, and I knew that my audience would not be showing up. I slid off the chair and gathered up my cloak; I was about to go out into the hall and find the Colonel when I felt the building shudder, then heard a thunderous crash, a cascade of breaking glass. My heart was in my throat, my skin prickling with fear and excitement, and I ran toward the window to see what had happened. I was just about to climb, in a very unladylike fashion, atop a small table and pull back the heavy velvet portieres when I heard the *click* of a door handle; whirling around, my heart once again threatening to burst through my bodice, I saw, through the gloom of the parlor, that it was only Colonel Wood.

"Oh! You startled me! What was that sound?"

"Someone threw a log through the lobby window. Turns out the hotel owner is a Yankee, a New Englander. Just like us."

."Heavens!" Now I began to wonder how we'd get back to the boat through the angry crowd.

"Your appointment canceled. These damn Rebels—I don't know how I'm going to get through to New Orleans by the twelfth. I guess I don't think I can now." The Colonel trudged over to the settee, which was illuminated by that one flickering oil lamp. I could see his face more clearly; in the shadows his eyes appeared hollow, his cheekbones sharp and threatening. He plopped down, removed his hat, and wiped his brow with his sleeve.

"Surely we can get out?" Hesitantly, I stepped toward him. For the first time ever, Colonel Wood appeared truly out of options. Beaten. He seemed too stunned to move, staring into the darkness, his bushy brows drawn together over his sharp nose.

"I don't know. We'll have to make it to Kentucky somehow; that's still neutral territory. Then I'll figure out what to do to salvage the rest of the season. Goddamn it, I wish I could get to New Orleans!"

"But the boat will make a trip upriver, won't it? Whatever repairs you were going to get in New Orleans, they can wait?"

"'Repairs'?" He turned to me, a quizzical expression in his eyes. He blinked twice, as if just now registering my presence. "Repairs? Oh—yes. It ain't the repairs I'm talking about. It's that appointment of yours."

"It can't matter, I'm sure whoever it is doesn't care about me at all, not with all this war talk." I tried to soothe him, for some odd reason; I felt responsible for his agitation, as it was my appointment he was worried about. I found myself placing my hand upon his sleeve before I could even think what I was doing.

He looked at my hand, my small, manicured hand, my nails pink and shiny, my fingers small and delicate. He studied it, and then all of a sudden his face split into a terrifying, wolfish grin; I could see all his back teeth, even in the dim light.

"You don't think he *cares*? You know how much I was going to *charge* for that one? Five hundred dollars, that's what!"

"Five hundred dollars?" I was stunned—too stunned to remove my hand. "Whatever for? Who would want to pay five hundred dollars—it wasn't Mr. Barnum, was it?" My heart quickened, and I looked eagerly into Colonel Wood's amused eyes. They widened, then narrowed; their gaze swept me up and down again, lingering upon my bosom.

"Barnum? Ha! No, it ain't no Barnum. I don't know his damn name—an intermediary contacted me. But he wanted to pay to have you, my tiny cousin. Five hundred dollars, to be the first one to touch those sweet little breasts of yours, to take that sweet little c—"

"Don't!" I shrieked, the word tearing itself from my throat. "Don't say that! Don't!" I put my hands over my ears, the searing, animalistic nature of my fear surprising me. Yet I knew it had always been there, always that quivering, fearful understanding of the true nature of man—and my utter helplessness in the face of it. I had buried it under layers of manners and deportment and denial, but I had carried it deep within me, from the first moment I had stepped foot on his riverboat.

"Listen to her shout! My, my, the famously composed Miss Mercy Lavinia Warren Bump, yelling like a whore!" Colonel Wood laughed, amused by my revulsion. "You know, I didn't understand, at first, these men. Oh, I received many such requests, my dear, you can be sure of it. Men who wanted to touch you, feel you, have you. I thought they were queer, at first, figured they were sick. And maybe they are. But I held out for the highest bidder, and over time I started to understand their—curiosity, shall we call it? I mean, look at you." With a leer, Colonel Wood leaned over me; before I could say a word he had picked me up, my legs dangling helplessly, and flung me down upon the sofa.

I lay there, frozen for a moment, unable to register anything but his hot, hungry breath in my face. Then terror claimed me, but I welcomed it. It surged through me like lightning, giving me strength, propelling my legs to kick out at him and my fists to strike him.

But he easily—oh, God, how easily!—trapped my legs with one knee, gathered both my wrists in one hand and held them over my head. His hot, whiskey-soured breath curdled my skin, moving lower and lower until I felt his mustache tickle my neck. The back of my spine began to quiver, turning to liquid; I felt as if I was going to be sick.

"You're perfect, you know. Tiny, but perfectly formed—why, just look at the way you fill out that dress. I've always wanted to touch 'em, feel 'em, see what they looked like." His breath came in rapid pants, like a dog's, as he placed his huge, grasping hand against the curve of my bodice. He spread his fingers out; his little finger reached the top of my waist, the rest of his hand caressed, so delicately I thought I was imagining it, the swell of my breast. His breath grew ragged then, and I shut my eyes, my ears, and willed my mind to take me somewhere else. Desperately, I tried to summon up images from home, of sweetly babbling brooks and the comforting creak of Mama's rocking chair and Papa's workbench in the barn, where he loved to make things for me and Minnie, little toys and chairs and my stair steps. And then

I saw Minnie, her sweet, angelic face with the black curls drooping over her forehead, her innocent, deep blue eyes, and I began to sob and laugh, both. For I was suddenly glad, glad that it was I who had to endure this, instead of her. If this was the price I had to pay to protect her from men like Colonel Wood, from men like that nameless, faceless ogre in New Orleans who wanted to force themselves upon women like me, like Minnie—I began to imagine the size of him, what it would do to me, it would probably split me in two, and then I wasn't glad. I was terrified, and I began to sob even harder as I felt the fragile cloth of my bodice tear beneath his ugly hands, the soft ripping sound it made a scolding, hushed betrayal.

And then I heard a moan. A soft moan, a bleat, like a little lamb. "Oh," Wood said in quiet surprise, and he fell off me, his eyes first open, then closing with a flutter as weak as the cry he had just uttered.

I looked up. Sylvia was standing before me, my reticule in her hand, an expression of utter amazement on her suddenly beautiful face as she gazed down at Colonel Wood, who was grasping his head, eyes still closed. Then she looked at me.

"You forgot this," she said in that deep rumble of hers that always tickled my eardrums. "You forgot your reticule, and I brought it to you. Also, they're taking the boat. Some men."

"Oh." It was all I could say. I felt for my bodice, fingered the torn cloth, and sought to cover it up; my cheeks were hot and sticky with tears, and in that moment I felt as helpless as a baby. Sylvia reached down to scoop me up, and it would have been bliss to allow her to do so, to carry me back to the boat in her arms, and tuck me into my bed, and sing me songs.

But something inside my soul would not allow it; I struggled to hold on to that feeling, that hot little burst of feeling deep within a place that no Colonel Wood could ever touch. I coaxed it, and finally it propelled me out of my stupor. I stepped over Colonel Wood, who still lay upon the carpet, clutching his head, beginning to curse so that I knew he would recover. I tidied myself up, buttoned my cloak, and patted my hair. Then I turned to Sylvia.

"They're taking the boat?"

"Yes, they say we have to leave, we only have an hour to get our things. How will we get home, Vinnie?"

"Don't worry, I'll think of something. Grab him and drag him back with us." I didn't even glance at Colonel Wood, but I did register Sylvia's deep smile of satisfaction as she reached down and hauled him up by his arm, ignoring his curses and moans. It was the happiest I had seen her in a very long time; we looked at each other and almost burst into laughter before mutually deciding against it.

Then I led us out of the parlor, through the crowded hotel lobby, where, despite the excitement of the evening, people stopped to gape at the sight of the dwarf leading the giant, who was dragging a limp man as if he were made of straw. Then we pushed our way through the frenzied, war-crazed streets of Vicksburg, back toward the *Banjo,* where already members of the troupe were carrying trunks and bags and costumes and piling them up on the dock; Mr. Deacon's swords, wrapped in velvet cloth, were piled next to a wooden crate full of the plate spinner's china.

"Vinnie! Colonel Wood! What happened?" The troupe was upon us as we joined them on the dock; strange men with pistols were standing on the upper deck of the boat, staring at Sylvia and me with open mouths.

"Someone should look after him," I said with a dismissive kick at Colonel Wood, who lay crumpled at my feet where Sylvia had deposited him. "What's going on here?" I shouted at Billy over the sizzle of firecrackers popping in the streets, the far-off boom of what sounded like a canon, and that spectral, high-pitched Rebel yell that even bounced off the water, so that it sounded as if we were surrounded on all sides by banshees. Although, from the strutting, military posturing of the men on the boat and in the streets—they all had red scarves tied around their hats and those who had rifles carried them stiff against their shoulders—I knew what was happening.

"They're commandeering the boat," Billy Birch said. "Taking it over to move troops and munitions. We have to find another way back home. There's a steamer coming here any minute that's going north, but they say it's already full."

"Where's the ticket office?" I looked around; gaslights from the boat illuminated the dock, torches flickered a brilliant orange, as if we were at the very gates of Hell—but just past the boat, the Mississippi loomed blacker than the sky above us.

"Up around the corner, but I already been. That's how I learned it was full. But, Vinnie, I bet you can persuade the agent to let us on. As good as you talk, as little as you are—if anyone can do it, you can."

"All right, I'll go. Come with me, Sylvia." And I turned on my heel and began to walk back up the dock, toward the wild streets, where men were drinking openly, singing a new song, one I'd never heard before but it began, *"Oh, I wish I was in the land of cotton . . ."* It was very catchy, I decided, humming a bit of it.

I was without fear at that moment. I had been saved from Colonel Wood; I had been given a second chance. I detested how physically helpless I had been in his presence; the memory of how I had simply closed my eyes and surrendered myself to fate made my mouth taste sour. I would not be so helpless again, I vowed, not even on this unprecedented night. People needed me. I had a duty to them—and to myself.

But I did pause to tug at Sylvia's skirt. "Thank you," I said as she looked down at me. She nodded, unable to speak. And that's all I ever said to her, and she to me, about what had happened that night. Remarkably, soon it faded into just another thread of the tapestry of my life upon the river, just another story remembered. But this one, I told to only one person. And he never repeated it.

It will come as no surprise to the Reader—as it came as no surprise to me—that I succeeded in getting all of us out of Vicksburg. Once at the ticket office, I climbed upon a chair and spoke to the agent face-to-face; I told him of our dilemma, of our desire to get back to our homes, to our families who had been parted from us for so long. I informed him of the many dignitaries—including Jefferson Davis, at that time only a senator from Mississippi—whom I had met in my personal appearances. And just for good measure, I invited him to plant a kiss upon my cheek, the one and only time I ever did so to a strange man, until I met President Lincoln.

But that was to come much, much later, when my life was changed so that had I not still had my beloved stair steps, made by my father's own hand, the tread worn smooth in the middle, I never would have recognized it. For the present I was still the one, the only Dwarf Girl This Side of the Alleghenies, pleading for passage home.

Finally the ticket agent relented, and, with tickets in hand, Sylvia and I went back to the dock, where we spent the night beneath the stars and burning torches, the gunshots and firecrackers only diminishing once the sun came up. The steamer arrived early the next morning, and soon we all—including Colonel Wood, whom I could not simply leave behind, no matter how tempting the thought—were on our way to Louisville. There we disbanded with tearful goodbyes.

Except for Colonel Wood; he slunk off in the confusion of

sorting out our baggage, crying out, "You all still have contracts with me! This ain't no act of God—it's an act of war, and I'm tacking that time onto your contracts!"

"Let 'im try," Billy Birch muttered. "Let 'im try to find me. I'm enlisting first chance I get—do you think that bastard will?" We all laughed at the notion.

Sylvia and I journeyed together as far as Boston. From there, she took one train north, and I another south. When we disembarked from the train, snow was beginning to fall; big, gentle flakes, welcoming me back home.

Sylvia bent to hug me tearfully; she actually fell upon her knees, even though I knew how much that must have hurt her. I asked her what she was going to do.

"I don't know," she said as tears fell, slowly as ever, upon her mammoth cheeks. For once she did not notice the strange looks and whispers we attracted. Her sorrow and uncertainty were too apparent, even though I knew she was relieved to be headed home. "I thought my mother might tell me in a dream, but I haven't slept well these last few nights."

"Who has?" I smiled, patting her on the back. Then a thought occurred to me; I didn't know why I hadn't figured it out sooner. "Sylvia!" I exclaimed, so excitedly that she nearly knocked me over in her surprise. "That's it—I know what you can do and still stay at home in Wilton! You talk so often of seeing your mother in dreams. Why don't you become a spiritualist? You're so sympathetic, I know you'll help any number of people who have lost dear ones."

"A spiritualist? I don't know, Vinnie. . . ."

"Sylvia, you're lonely. This would be good for you, and you'd never have to leave home again. Why, people will come to see you from everywhere! And I promise I'll help, in any way I can. I'll write to all my friends and tell everyone I meet." Little did either of us realize how many, many people I would meet in the coming years—and how happy I would be to learn that Sylvia was able to make a decent living because of them, because of me.

The stationmaster called out that the train to Maine was about to leave.

"Vinnie, you've helped me so much already. You're the only friend I've ever had. Write me, won't you?"

"Of course." Sylvia got up, tears still rolling down those granite cheekbones, but before she walked away, I called out to her.

"Wait! Sylvia, will you do—will you do one thing for me?"

"Anything, Vinnie. Anything you want."

"Will you—will you pick me up and hold me high? I always wanted to see the world the way you see it. I want to see how different your view is from mine."

Sylvia smiled, then picked me up carefully, holding me in her arms so that my feet did not dangle. She lifted me up so that my face was level with hers. And then we turned to look at the world.

I could see roads leading away from the station, snow-blanketed, peaceful ribbons of roads, leading to places unknown. I could see the tops of buildings, the rooflines, the chimneys. I could see over people's heads, so that I was looking down upon them; how insignificant they all looked, how ordinary! The tops of hats were flat and round; the tops of bonnets were thin and worn, catching snowflakes in the creases.

I could see all the way to the end of the train platforms, my view unobstructed by legs and skirts and trunks and poles. From here, the distance between train and platform appeared small and manageable—not the wide, terrifying chasm that I experienced, fearful of missing the platform altogether and rolling onto the track, where I could be crushed.

Yet for all I could see, nothing was as grand as how I'd imagined it. Nothing was as big as my dreams.

"You can put me down now," I told Sylvia, whose blue eyes were full of tears, huge tears—tears as big as her heart. She did, and then she grabbed her two valises, which looked like toys in her hands. I waved as she lumbered along the narrow wooden platform. I knew I would never forget her.

Turning, I made my way to my own platform, after paying a porter to carry my trunk and stand by to lift me onto the train. I was back home by the next morning—dreaming my big dreams in the comfort of my own dear feather bed, my sister's happy, contented face nestled into my shoulder, her arms tight around me, binding me to her. She whispered that I was never to leave her again.

But I knew, even before I drifted off to sleep, the grime of travel still upon me like a second skin, that I would.

INTERMISSION

From *Godey's Lady's Book,* September 1860—Sara J. Hale

This year the **last Thursday in November** falls on the 29th. If all the States and Territories hold their Thanksgiving on that day, there will be a complete moral and social reunion of the **people** of America in 1860. Would not this be a good omen for the perpetual political union of the States? May God grant us not only the omen, but the fulfillment is our dearest wish!

From *Harper's Weekly,* January 19, 1861

SECESSION OF MISSISSIPPI, FLORIDA, AND ALABAMA

The Mississippi State Convention on 8th adopted an ordinance providing for immediate secession from the Union. Reports from Jackson, the capital of Mississippi, confirm this news. On 10th, Florida seceded by 62 to 7. On 11th, Alabama seceded by 61 to 39.

———❖———

FIVE

Another Brief Interlude of Music and Tender Reunion

"VINNIE, WHAT ARE YOU DOING?"

"Nothing!" I whisked the paper off my desk and tucked it inside my apron pocket, placing the pen in the ink bottle so forcibly the ink splattered. Then I massaged my hand; no pen was small or light enough for me to use easily, and my fingers and palm often ached when I wrote long letters. Turning to greet my sister, I smiled broadly. "Just writing to an old friend! What do you want, Pumpkin?"

"Mama said to come down for dinner," Minnie said with a scolding frown; I couldn't help but smile at her. How serious she had grown in my absence! She was now twelve, almost a young woman, although her body had not filled out as much as mine; she still looked quite childish, even in long skirts, and she came up to only my chin. This impression was not helped by the fact that she continued to play with dolls. But her manner was much more serious, even as her deep brown eyes retained their incongruous twinkle. Her thick black brows were often drawn over her nose in a suspicious frown. Papa joked that Minnie was the family inquisitor, judge and jury all wrapped up into one—although her distrust reminded me more of a child's resistance to change.

"Are you sure that was what you were doing?" she asked, folding her arms suspiciously across her flat chest; I decided I ought to introduce her to ruffled corset covers. Carlotta had taught me that trick.

"Absolutely—just writing an old friend!" I slid off the cushions of the chair, pushed it back toward the writing desk, and followed Minnie out of our room.

"Then I don't know why you'd try to hide the letter, Vinnie. Why would you?"

"Why, I didn't! Would you like to read it, if you don't trust me?" I tucked my hand inside my apron, as if to show it to her.

"No, no, I didn't mean that!" Her eyes grew big with remorse as her face paled. "Forgive me, Vinnie! I'm sorry! I do trust you, more than anyone in the world!" And her little rosebud lips trembled as she fought back tears.

I put my arm about her as we made our way down the narrow back stairs—more shallowly spaced than the front stairs, and so the ones that Minnie and I used the most—and into the kitchen. My dear, simple little sister! Every mood so fleeting yet so obvious; there was no mystery to Minnie, none at all. She loved whom she knew, distrusted everyone else, and shared her emotions, her thoughts, as freely as they occurred to her. I remembered how I had promised myself I would come for her and take her with me on my adventures; I knew, now, what a selfish notion that had been. Minnie must not leave home and experience the things I had; this was where she belonged, safe and loved and hidden from people like Colonel Wood. I could not reclaim my own innocence. And so she must keep hers, remaining unspoiled for the both of us.

"What are you sorry about, my chick?" Mama was placing platters of stewed meat, covered in bubbling gravy and topped with airy dumplings, upon the linen tablecloth; my stomach growled in anticipation. I had been home for nearly a year, yet I had not tired of Mama's delicious cooking.

It was December of 1861, and the War that had started so vividly and personally for me was being fought in bloody earnest all across the South. I had spent so much time there, seeing it only as a place where simple people were eager to be entertained, just like their brethren up north, that I had a difficult time thinking of them as the enemy.

But two of my brothers were now in Yankee blue, so I could not be neutral. Benjamin had been the first to enlist, joining up with the Massachusetts Volunteer Militia even before I came home. I missed his presence keenly; I still felt pain at the way we had parted. I needed to know that he was not ashamed of me.

Both he and James, who joined up as soon as the first bullets were fired on Fort Sumter in April, were now in Virginia, so very far away to Mama and Papa—a foreign country, almost! But not to me. I could mentally calculate how quickly I could get there; I knew by heart the train timetables, where you had to get off and take a ferry across the Chesapeake, then get back on the train again. I had spent a good amount of time at the station in Middleborough, poring over the schedules and maps of trains leaving for all destinations. I couldn't help myself. I was drawn to the train station like a fly to a cow patty. I became obsessed in my need to study every method of travel available, to follow the debate in the newspaper about the possibility of building a train clear across our great nation, from Atlantic to Pacific. I had no plans to leave home again, as of yet; I simply hungered to know how easily I could do so. This knowledge gave me peace, where my parents' clucking and soothing did not.

"I'm sorry that I almost made Vinnie show me the letter she was writing," Minnie said with a shy, apologetic smile as she took her seat, piled high with cushions, one more than mine. "Now, Papa, take the best piece for yourself, as you work the hardest!" And Minnie tucked her napkin into her collar and waited patiently to be served.

"Thank you, Miss, I certainly will," Papa said with a serious nod, although his eyes twinkled. "Do you want me to post that letter for you, Vinnie?" he asked as he began to pass around the plates. "I have to go into town tomorrow."

"No—I, that is, thank you. But I thought I might get some exercise and walk into town myself. I can post it then." I took my own seat, across from Minnie.

"I would never walk to town by myself!" She shook her head decidedly. "Think of all those houses and buildings you have to walk past—how dreadful! And people do talk so. You're so brave, Vinnie!"

I wanted to laugh, given what I had endured upon the river. But my sister's admiration was pure and heartfelt, and I never wished to hurt her feelings.

"Minnie's right, it is a long walk for you, Vinnie, and you know how those wagon ruts can trip you up," Mama began, automatically. But when she caught my eye, she stopped.

"You sure you want to go all that way by yourself?" Papa asked, but he did not meet my gaze. Unlike Mama, he asked out of courtesy alone; he knew too well I would make my own mind up and do as I pleased. He did not enjoy knowing this, he did not approve of it, but he allowed it. As he had ever since I returned home.

"Yes, Papa, I do want to go alone. Anyway, I can use the exercise, for Mama's cooking is making my dresses too tight! Soon enough I will look like Mrs. Lincoln, just as people say I do!" I laughed at the joke, happy to deflect interest from my letter. Since the Lincolns had gone to the White House, many people had commented on my likeness to the President's wife.

"Oh, no, Vinnie! You're much more beautiful than that plain Mrs. Lincoln. She has the most awful way of doing her hair, not fashionable at all." Minnie spoke with such disdain that the rest of us couldn't help but laugh. Since when did Minnie concern herself with fashionable coiffures? I tried to imagine my little sister poring over *Godey's Lady's Book,* and failed.

We continued our meal without further inquiries into my letter-writing habits. Although twice I caught Papa looking my way with his eyes scrunched up, as if he was trying to get a good read on me.

He was still trying to figure me out.

THE NEXT MORNING I BUNDLED UP IN A CLOAK AND MITTENS and stout boots. It had been a mild December for Massachusetts; the lanes were not piled high with snow. The sun was shining, and I soon warmed up as I walked the short distance toward town. I enjoyed being alone; ever since I had returned home, I had found myself craving such solitude.

Everything had changed since my return. My family treated me differently, gingerly, as if I might break, or worse—as if I might leave them again. At first they had peppered me with questions, but soon they realized they didn't really know what to ask; they had no comprehension of the details of my life those three eventful years. They knew only that it was very different from theirs. I produced my clippings and told of meeting people like the Grants. I spoke lovingly of Sylvia, and the rest of the troupe. (Carlotta I decided not to mention.)

I did not speak of Colonel Wood. At first they asked all about him, but soon they picked up on my reluctance to mention his name and ceased their questioning.

My family loved me, welcomed me, yet frequently I felt like a guest in my own home. I caught Papa looking at me at times with something close to shyness, as if he did not quite recognize me. And I felt the strangeness myself; the farm was so quiet, my family so loving and good, it all seemed dreamlike, almost. As if I would wake up and find myself back on the river, the hard, pulsing *life* of the river; that felt, now, like the most real time of my life. The bad things that had happened soon receded from memory. I remembered only the excitement, the ever-changing scenery, the cheerful camaraderie of my fellow performers, the elegance of the hotels contrasted with the wildness of the audience—oh, to think of it all made me want to throw my clothes in a valise, grab my cloak, and run out of the house! It made me long to cast off all possessions so that I might always be ready to leave at a moment's notice.

Recalling that life also made me pick up my pen and compose the letter I was determined to post today. The letter was bulky; I had included a number of my press clippings and, of course, my *carte de visite,* which I had inscribed. The address on the outside, which I had copied so carefully from a newspaper article, read as follows:

MR. PHINEAS TAYLOR BARNUM
The American Museum, corner of Ann Street and Broadway
New York, New York

The letter was sealed with a dollop of wax, hard and cold as a button against my thumb. Despite my eagerness to post it, I took my time on this walk; I was in no hurry to get back home, where nothing ever changed. I had no purpose, no task, but to rise early with the family; help Mama with sewing, cleaning, cooking; keep Minnie company and try to improve her mind with reading and conversation; rock her to sleep at night before rolling over to my side of our little bed, where I tried, unsuccessfully, to sleep. But these days sleep did not come easily to me. Try as I might to tire myself with long walks and endless turns at the spinning wheel, I was never as physically exhausted—every joint throbbing, the arches of my feet aching, even my tongue worn out from constant conversation—as I had been after two or three performances a day, not including private audiences.

I couldn't even go back to teaching if I wanted to; the school committee had engaged someone else in my absence.

The trees were bare, the limbs like splayed fingers against the vivid blue sky. It was so quiet, just a few birds rustling in evergreens, a far-off echo of an ax chopping wood. How loud my life on the Mississippi had been! Never was there complete quiet on the steamboat; there was always someone singing a song, laughing at a joke, telling a story. The steady hum of the engines, the constant swish of the river's currents—all had filled my ears for so long that I found the quiet of home jarring. My nerves thrummed in anticipation for some unexpected, unpredictable noise or diversion.

I wandered along the lane, which was crisscrossed with the occasional cow path leading off toward other farms, watching out for the deep wagon ruts, so much trouble for one my size. Too soon did I reach town, where the streets were sparsely populated by people who no longer knew how to think about me.

Since coming home, I had realized that when the school committee appointed me as a schoolteacher years earlier, it wasn't entirely for my welfare. Giving me a title, a job, gave the town a way to look at me that was easy; it meant that they did not have to think about my size, first thing, each time they encountered me. Miss Bump, the teacher, was a much easier thing to consider than Miss Bump, that poor little woman. But I had angered them by rejecting their neat package and leaving to go out west. I had shocked them by performing on a boat. Now I was gazed at, whispered about, more pointedly than I ever had been out west, even when I had paraded around with Sylvia.

Mrs. Putnam, the minister's wife, stopped to observe me as she exited the dry goods store.

"Good morning," I called out pleasantly.

"Oh!" She looked around to see if there was anyone observing us; there was, but she was trapped. "Well, good morning, Miss Bump." She sniffed and looked down her long nose at me. "What a surprise to see you out and about this early."

"A surprise? Why is that?" I smiled up at her; her bonnet was as plain and red as her face. The people of Middleborough looked so *ordinary* to me now. *She could use some of Carlotta's paint,* I thought wickedly, stifling a giggle.

"Why, I'm sure I don't know, I just supposed that you were used to sleeping late back on that showboat of yours. It's a mercy to see you up at a good Christian hour."

"But I saw many a sunrise out west," I protested with a sweet, pious smile.

"You did?"

"Of course! Many a sunrise I saw as I came home after a late night of carousing and unseemly behavior!"

"Why, Lavinia Bump! I never—the wickedness! The shame!" The old woman sputtered and hissed like a cat in heat as she hurried off to be swallowed up by a small band of other churchwomen, all of whom muttered and looked over their shoulders at me.

I tilted my chin and met their collective gaze evenly; they

looked away, still buzzing with disapproval. I didn't care. I was even a bit tickled by my impertinence, although I did hope it wouldn't cause Papa or Mama any grief later. But my spirits were lightened, as well as my step, and soon I was at the post office. It was located at the main intersection of the town, called the Four Corners; the streets that comprised this area housed most of the commerce of the village—dry goods stores, a millinery, lawyer and physician offices, the building where workers toiled at the large shoe manufacturer. Middleborough wasn't a small town, not by New England standards. Yet after the dirty, humid, colorful excitement that was New Orleans or St. Louis, it was so staid and sleepy to me, all the same. Everything here was so stolid; nothing ever changed. Certainly we had no streets dedicated solely to vice!

I knocked politely on the post office door; the handle was too high and heavy for me to reach. Mr. Jones, the clerk, opened the door, peered out over my head for a moment, then looked down. He smiled in recognition. I couldn't help but notice his pants were worn thin at the knees, like those of the good working New England man he was; he would get a new pair for Christmas, just coming up.

"Well, hello, Miss Lavinia. Come on in."

"Thank you," I replied, following him inside; I waited for him to raise the hinged section that allowed him to go behind the counter, although I had to reflect how easily I could have passed beneath it! Then I reached up and handed him my letter, along with thirty cents for postage.

"All the way to New York?" Mr. Jones looked at the address. "Phineas Taylor Barnum? Who's he—not that humbug feller, I hope?"

I sighed. I should have realized that of course Mr. Jones would make it his business to see where my letter was going; of course he would end up telling my parents or my brothers or my married sister or whichever member of my annoyingly large family he might encounter. Which he was sure to do.

"No, of course not," I said with a sniff, as if to indicate I was insulted he might suggest such a thing. "This is about some unfinished business of mine, from out west."

"Oh." Mr. Jones pulled on his chin, lengthening his already sorrowfully long New England face—sharp nose, suspicious eyes, permanently ruddy complexion. "Yes, that business out west of yours. Well, we're glad to have you back here safe and sound. I reckon you're glad to be back, too. Don't like to think of a little lady like you out there consorting with those types of people."

I simply smiled and watched as he took my letter and placed it in the leather mail pouch. Then I asked after his children (who had been students of mine), thanked him, and asked him to open the door for me.

I began my walk back to the farm, after first stopping to purchase a stick of peppermint candy for Minnie, who would be anxious for my return. So would Papa and Mama. They would welcome me home with loving eyes, kind hearts, open—yet stifling—arms.

My thoughts returned to the letter I had just posted. I wished that I could give it wings.

INTERMISSION

From *Harper's Weekly,* March 22,1862

The crisis which the war has reached imparts fresh interest to the war-pictures which are appearing in every number of *Harper's Weekly*. We have now regular Artist Correspondents, to wit:

Mr. A. R. WAUD, with the army of the Potomac; MR. ALEXANDER SIMPLOT, with Gen. Grant's Army; MR. HENRY MOSLER, with Gen. Buell's army; MR. THEO. R. DAVIS, with Gen. Sherman's army; MR. ANGELO WISER, with Gen. Burnside's army; besides a large number of occasional and volunteer correspondents in the Army and Navy at various points. These gentlemen will furnish us faithful sketches of every battle which takes place, and every other event of interest, which will be reproduced in our pages in the best style. People who do not see *Harper's Weekly* will have but a limited comprehension of the momentous events which are occurring.

From *The Defiance Democrat,* Defiance County, Ohio, May 31, 1862

THE NEW MORMON COMPLICATION

Brigham Young has been inaugurated as the Governor of the New State of Desert, and Mr. Ashley's bill for the punishment of polygamy has passed the House of Representatives. Here is a conflict at our doors at once. The Mormons have organized their state government with polygamy as "the corner-stone" just as slavery is the corner-stone of the Confederates. . . . Brigham's wants, like his wives, are many.

———◆◆◆◆◆———

SIX

At Last I Meet the Great Man Himself

O H, GOODNESS!" MAMA EXCLAIMED AS SHE OPENED HER
reticule and removed a clean yellow handkerchief, which
seemed to turn to a sooty gray before our eyes. "The dirt! Vinnie,
my chick, however did you manage on those trains out west with
all this dirt?"

"I didn't," I admitted, bouncing about on the uncomfortable
wooden seat, barely able to see out the window to my right, but
it didn't matter; it was smeared with the same sooty gray as
Mama's handkerchief. "I was filthy when I got to the boat."

"These contraptions are no place for a lady," Mama muttered,
pressing the handkerchief to the inner corner of her eye, trying to
remove some minuscule piece of dirt, although it wouldn't make
a difference; her cheeks had smudges on them, as well.

Papa sat next to me with his eyes squeezed shut; the moment
the train had pulled out of the station in Middleborough, he had

paled. Upon my suggestion that he look at the scenery, beginning
to pass by ever faster, he turned decidedly green. From that moment on, he had refused to open his eyes or move his head; he sat
as straight and stiff as a corpse against the hard back of his seat. I
patted his hand in sympathy; his occasional squeeze was the sole
indication I had that he had not passed on to the Great Beyond.

I was sorry for him, but even that could not dampen my excitement, excitement that had been building ever since that fateful afternoon a month ago when a Mr. Fuller had sent word—by
telegram! We had never seen such a thing!—that, acting on behalf
of Mr. Phineas Taylor Barnum, he, Mr. Fuller, would very much
like to meet me.

Oh, the stir this simple message caused! Mama began cleaning right away, even as she and Papa argued with me about the
obvious intent of the coming visit. Did I have any idea what I
might be getting myself into? Why couldn't I just stay home like
the rest of their children? (Although when I pointed out that two
of their sons were soldiers, they pretended not to hear.) Did I
have no heart in me? Had I so enjoyed being surrounded by
morally depraved show people that I was eager to escape the
bosom of a Christian home to take up with them again? And that
Barnum? That master of humbug! What might he do, in my name,
in the good name of this good family, to dupe the public once
more?

And most frequently asked of all the questions my parents
hurtled at me, when they weren't tidying and scrubbing and con-
soling Minnie, who flew into tears at the thought of another
stranger coming to take me away—

How? How on earth had he heard of me? It had been almost
two years since I had made my escape from the clutches of
Colonel Wood (they made it sound so dramatic, I wondered if
they pictured me running barefoot through a swamp just like Eliza

in *Uncle Tom's Cabin,* pursued by alligators, show folk, and Rebel soldiers) and come back, safe and sound, so they didn't have to worry about me any longer. How had that Barnum (for this was how they began to refer to him, *"that Barnum,"* as if he had no other Christian name) heard of me in that time?

Naturally, I declined to join in this last speculation. For of course I knew: I was the one who had told him. That letter I mailed back in December—that had been my ticket out into the world, I dearly hoped.

And so it would seem to have proved. Mr. Fuller duly arrived; we chatted in the parlor (where I tried very hard to push away the memory of Colonel Wood's fateful visit). I showed him my press clippings, the letters written to me by many a fine citizen of the West. I saved the most distinguished letter for last; in this late summer of 1862, any mention of Mr. Grant, with whom I had passed such a charming hour in Galena, was extremely impressive, indeed. After the Battle of Fort Donelson, when he had demanded "unconditional and immediate surrender" of the Rebel troops, Major General Ulysses S. Grant had become a household name. I could see that Mr. Fuller was very taken by my account of that visit and the letter of thanks, in Mrs. Grant's hand, that had reached me on the boat.

Mr. Fuller departed with no indication of what he felt about me and my clippings, which worried me, even as it enabled Mama and Papa to cease their fretting. But Mr. Fuller must have made a favorable report to Mr. Barnum, for the former was soon back again, armed this time with a contract. At this point Mama and Papa began to protest even more forcibly. In the most polite language—and while simultaneously serving Mr. Fuller some of her most delicate shortbread cookies and tea—Mama made it known that she did not trust Mr. Barnum's reputation for telling lies to the public, as she saw it.

"Perhaps we should meet Mr. Barnum himself," I finally suggested, in desperation. "For I believe only he can put my parents' minds at ease."

Mr. Fuller grumbled and departed again, contract unsigned but still in my possession; days later we received an invitation from Mr. Barnum to visit him in his home in Bridgeport, Connecticut. Thus it was that we three were on the train going west.

There was one more obstacle in the way, one more potentially dire than my parents' objections, and one that I kept to myself: I was still technically under contract to Colonel Wood. After he had crept away in Louisville, I tried to assure myself that I would see him no more. Yet I couldn't trust him, even though, for all I knew, the Colonel might be in the army, or a prisoner of war, or even dead, as thousands were, more and more every day. Although I disliked imagining that evil man clad in the glory of Yankee blue, just like my brothers.

"Do you think that Barnum will meet us at the station?" Mama fretted, patting her graying bun that peeked out of the back of her bonnet, so tightly wound and secured that no amount of train travel could disturb it.

"Mama, please, I beg of you, try to refrain from calling him 'that Barnum.'"

"Mercy Lavinia Warren Bump, you know that I will address him in the most polite manner! Who do you think I am? Is this why you're so eager to leave home again? Are you so ashamed of us?" Mama's eyes began to water and tears rolled down her cheeks, leaving an oily trail of grime.

I sighed and handed her my unspoiled handkerchief. "No, Mama, of course not. I'm sorry—I'm just a trifle nervous, you see. I do so want to make a good impression."

"You have no need to be nervous about that," Mama replied with a sniff. "*He's* the one who should be worried about making a good impression on *us*. He's just a showman. You're a descendent of one of the Mayflower Company!"

"Yes, Mama." I had to smile; my mother's righteous anger at the idea of a man such as *that Barnum* having to impress the Bump family was so powerful that it dried her tears and caused her to sit up so straight, her spine was a good six inches away from the back of the seat.

We passed the rest of the journey mostly in silence, after changing trains in Providence. It was late afternoon before we pulled into the Bridgeport station.

As we disembarked—Papa, his color returning to his usual ruddy hue, gently lifting me off the train onto the platform—a liveried coachman approached. He was clad in a dusky red driving jacket and a tall silk hat; when he reached us, he bowed smartly.

"Miss Bump?" He looked down at me, yet his face betrayed no surprise or amusement at my size.

"Yes?"

"With Mr. Barnum's regards, Miss, I'm to take you and your family to Lindencroft in the carriage. Please come this way." And he turned; we followed him through the crowded station to a waiting open carriage. It was black, polished to a gleam so high that we could see our reflections in it, with brass handles and hinges, a fine pair of chestnut horses, their harnesses also polished and gleaming in the sun. Papa handed me up into the carriage and we all settled in. The coachman climbed atop his perch and coaxed the horses into motion.

"What do you think so far, Mama?" I couldn't help myself, but Mama had been so quiet ever since the coachman had greeted us. I knew she was impressed.

"I think Mr. Barnum affords a lovely carriage" was all she would allow.

Papa nodded, passing his hand over the seat next to him. "Real leather," he said in tones usually reserved for church. "And them horses—a matched pair!"

I smiled and turned my attention to the streets of Bridgeport. We quickly passed through the business section and soon found ourselves on wide streets lined with gracious homes, bigger than any we had back in Middleborough. These were newer, in the more modern architectural style featuring ornately scrolled embellishments, cupolas, wide porches, two and even three stories high, all set back from the street on enormous, beautifully tended lawns. I glimpsed large carriage houses—some larger than our farmhouse!—set far back from the street. Occasionally we passed land set aside as parks, with well-tended gardens, gazebos, and benches.

As we passed so many houses, each one seemingly grander than the one before, I sensed that the coachman was taking us down the most picturesque streets. Mama's constant exclamations of "Oh, my," and Papa's involuntary utterances of "Will you look at that?" were growing wearisome to me; as impressed as I was by the beautiful homes and streets of Bridgeport, they were not the reason I had come.

"That house there, to the right, is the home of Mr. Charles Stratton himself. Or as you may know him, Tom Thumb," the coachman called over his shoulder, slowing the horses down to a stately walk. As this was the one time he had pointed out a home's ownership, I was suddenly very sure that he had driven this way deliberately.

Papa and Mama both twisted in their seats to get a better look. I remained where I was for a moment, impatience to reach our destination rooting me to my seat. But finally I, too, turned to look.

It was a fine home. That was all I would say for it at the moment. It was three stories with a cupola, a wide lawn, an inviting

porch. It was very grand, very big, and if I was meant to be impressed by it and by the implication that if I signed with Mr. Barnum I, too, might one day live on such an estate, I suppose I was.

But I was also annoyed by this transparent sales technique. I
felt it in poor taste. Turning back around, I instructed the driver,
curtly, to please continue to Mr. Barnum's home.

"Yes, Miss," he said apologetically. Then he flicked the reins
and we trotted off again. Ten minutes later we pulled into a gated
circular drive, the coachman saying, with unmistakable pride in
his tone, "Welcome to Lindencroft."

We had driven up to a set of granite stepping-stones so tall, I
could exit the carriage without assistance. Once I alighted, I shook
my skirts out—dust flying everywhere, fine grains captured in
the sunlight—and surveyed my surroundings. The lawn was manicured, with a circular pool embellished with a statue of Posei-
don in the middle. The house itself was grand but not ostentatious;
I'd certainly seen larger, more elaborate homes on the drive over.

It was built of buff-colored stone, three stories high, with ornately carved cornices. A deep porch was framed by columns, and
wide marble steps led up to the imposing front door.

Mama and Papa didn't say a word; none of us had ever been
to a house this fine before, but somehow I felt they looked to me
to take the lead. Both hung back just a little; I felt their country
shyness acutely, and resolved to ease their minds.

"This way," I said with determination. And I walked up the
porch steps—rather steep for me, but I would not falter—and
motioned for Papa to tug the velvet rope hanging to the right of
the door; when he did, a deep gong sounded.

"Well, I never!" He stepped back in alarm, dropping the rope
as if it had scorched his hands.

"It's only a bell to summon the maid," I told my father, although I did not know how I knew that. I simply did.

Sure enough, an aproned and capped young woman opened the door; I gave her our names, and she ushered us inside to the cool interior. We blinked at the sudden change in light; inside the house, all was dark: darkly paneled walls, polished wooden floors, shutters and drapes keeping out the summer heat.

"I'll show you to a room where you can freshen up," the maid whispered to Mama and me; Mama clutched my arm gratefully, for I knew she was worried about her disheveled appearance. After showing Papa into one of the rooms opening up to the main hall, the maid led us up a grand staircase, kindly slowing her steps to accommodate mine; she ushered us into a bedroom where pitchers of water, basins, and the finest of linen towels and cloths were waiting on a shining dressing table arrayed with pins, hairbrushes, and a clothes brush. She withdrew, and Mama and I fell upon the water as if we'd just been rescued from the desert, washing our faces, our hands, tidying up our hair, brushing each other's dresses off. Mama pointed to a stool that had been placed strategically in front of the dressing table so that I could reach everything myself.

"How thoughtful!" she whispered, as if afraid someone might overhear. I tried not to smile at her nervousness, which had the effect of making my own disappear. "Should we tidy the room up?" she asked when we had finished our toilettes. She glanced nervously at the towels, which were no longer snowy white; the water in the basin was now a soupy gray.

"No," I said; once again, I did not know how I knew that. But I did. Ever since we'd stepped foot in that magnificent carriage, I had instinctively known how to behave among such riches. My parents, however, did not; never had I seen them so unsure of themselves. I could not imagine either of them happily living in a mansion; Mama would wear herself out scrubbing all those marble floors, for she would never trust anyone else to clean them!

That did not mean, however, that I could not imagine living in a mansion myself. As we left the room, refreshed and presentable, the maid led us back down the wide carpeted staircase. With each step I felt my spine straighten, my head lift itself upon my neck until my chin was almost pointed straight up to the ceiling. I imagined myself in a Parisian ball gown—in a properly fitting corset!—descending a staircase like this to greet my guests. Despite the huge proportions of this house—the ceilings enormously tall, the woodwork deep, the windowpanes more expansive than any I'd ever seen—I did not feel overwhelmed. Rather, I felt every inch a great lady, expanding to match the generosity of her surroundings.

We were ushered into a library, where Papa was already seated next to a fireplace flanked by bookshelves; the polished grate was empty save for an enormous Oriental fan. He had a cigar in his hand, which he handled as gingerly as if it might suddenly turn into a snake and bite him. As soon as he saw Mama and me, he dropped it—fortunately, it was not lit—and shot from his chair.

"Vinnie!" he cried out in obvious relief; he said my name as if he had given up hope of ever saying it again.

"So this is the famously contrary Miss Bump, who would not sign her contract until she met me herself." Another voice rang out; it was a wry, humorous voice. I heard laughter lurking behind it, kept just barely at bay.

From the depths of a high-backed wing chair, a man rose. He was a tall man; taller than Papa, who was not short. He had large hands, a fleshy nose, high forehead with luxurious graying curls, and bushy eyebrows. His lips were rather thin, held together in a crooked line that gave him a very whimsical look. His eyes, beneath those eyebrows, were piercing gray and alert, the most watchful eyes I'd ever seen. They were kindly, however: observant, wary, yet kindly. I sensed a light behind them, a twinkle that—like the laughter in his voice—was never far from the surface yet held firmly in check.

"I am Miss Bump," I said, crossing toward this man and extending my hand without hesitation. "And am I to believe you are the equally famous Mr. Barnum?"

"That I am, that I am, indeed." He took my hand solemnly, shook it, then suddenly bent down to peer directly into my face. His eyes were level with mine, so close that I could see myself reflected in them, and I had the startling, dizzy impression of a carnival, of colors and sounds and mirrors of every shape and size; of music, joyous, merry music tooted from horns and plucked by fiddles. How one man's gaze could engage so many senses, I had no idea; I only knew his did. It nearly knocked the breath out of me; my heart did a riotous somersault as the back of my neck tickled with excitement, and I fought an undignified urge to giggle.

However, I managed to keep my composure. I looked back at him, meeting him halfway; for a long moment our gazes held. I do not know what he saw in mine, but it appeared to satisfy him; with a businesslike nod, he straightened up, shook hands with my mother, then motioned for us to take a seat. One chair had a footstool placed strategically in front of it; I knew it had been placed there for me.

Once we were all seated, Mr. Barnum rang a silver bell; another maid appeared, and he asked for lemonade and cookies to be served. I felt Mama approved of this, as she smiled in genuine pleasure and relaxed a fraction, just enough so that I did not fear she might break into brittle little pieces if she moved too quickly.

"Did you have a pleasant journey?" Mr. Barnum asked my father.

"Well, I guess. Nothing bad happened, anyway. But I'm not

looking forward to the return home." Papa picked up the dropped cigar and held it, once again, at arm's length. I knew he did not approve of cigars, only pipes.

"This was my parents' first train journey," I explained to Mr. Barnum, who nodded in sympathy.

"Oh, I remember my first trip! Like to have scared the daylights out of me, all the noise and steam and speed. Nothing beats the old horse and buggy, does it, Mr. Bump?"

"No, sirree, not by a long shot!" My father smiled for the first time since we left Middleborough; relaxing, he dropped the cigar in a cut-glass ashtray and left it there.

"But now, why—can't get along without it! I couldn't keep up with my business if I didn't take the train into New York every day!"

"Every day? You take the train every day?" Papa looked at him in horror.

"Can't deny it! Every weekday morning, just about, ol' William—that's the coachman—takes me to the station, and I take the train into New York, then I walk to my museum. I take the train home at night, and William drives me back here. Very efficient—and I don't have to live in the city anymore. I can't imagine living anyplace but Bridgeport now—my wife's health, you know, requires rest and sea air."

"I'm so sorry," Mama murmured automatically, but Mr. Barnum merely waved his hand.

"'Tis nothing new to me; Charity has long been prone to sickness. I tire her out, that's the thing; it takes a lot out of a woman to keep up with me!" And Mr. Barnum laughed, as if it were truly nothing, but behind his eyes that little light wavered a bit.

The maid brought in a tray with tall frosty glasses of lemonade and plates of delicate sugar cookies; she served them all around, then left the tray and silently retired.

"Now, let's get to the point of this. I understand you don't think very highly of me." Mr. Barnum spoke to my father, although I felt as if he was really addressing my mother. He turned to Papa, but his eyes looked at her.

"Oh, my, well, I never intended to be rude!" Mama was very flustered—but she was the one who answered, as Papa chose that moment to conveniently stuff a cookie into his mouth.

"Not rude, just prudent," Mr. Barnum replied cheerfully, with an understanding nod. He sat back in his chair and folded his arms across his chest—an attitude I would soon grow to know very well. It was an attitude of waiting—waiting for someone to give him the answer that he sought. Rarely was he left waiting for long.

"Yes, prudent, of course!" Mama nodded vigorously. "You see, Vinnie—Lavinia—is our eldest daughter left at home, and naturally we worry about her. We are quite an old family, you know—the Warrens from Massachusetts; five of my ancestors came over on the *Mayflower*." Mama smiled in that prim way she had whenever she spoke of her ancestry.

"You don't say?" Mr. Barnum's eyebrows raised and his eyes narrowed intently. He appeared to be filing this information away, for what purpose my mother of course could not suspect—but I did, and I smiled to myself, nibbling daintily at a cookie.

"So naturally we have concerns about her future," Mama continued. "We want only what is proper and dignified for Lavinia and for our family."

"Naturally." Mr. Barnum sat for a second, apparently deep in thought. The room was silent, save for the sound of my father nervously clearing his throat. "Yet you had no qualms about letting her travel about the Mississippi on a rowboat?"

Mama gasped, and Papa, who had been uneasily silent until now, said, "See here!"

Mr. Barnum merely smiled, turning to me for the first time

in this conversation. And then he sat back, his arms still folded across his chest, and waited.

"It was not a rowboat," I replied, struggling not to smile, for I knew he was but toying with us. "It was a floating palace of curiosities, and a very popular one at that."

"Run by a cousin of yours, I understand?"

"Yes, Colonel Wood, a cousin of mine. That was the only reason we let Lavinia go with him," Mama interjected, her forehead wrinkling in concern and puzzlement.

"Cousin." Mr. Barnum snorted dismissively. "Be that as it may, I assure you that what I am offering Miss Bump is much more than a lazy ride up the Mississippi in some rickety boat. But, of course, I'm no cousin. Just a humble farmer's son from Connecticut—no descendent of the *Mayflower*."

"Well, now, I'm a farmer myself." Papa stirred uncomfortably. "I can't fault a man for being that!"

"No, of course not, that's not at all what I meant." Mama, more flustered than I'd ever seen her, frowned down at her hands.

"My poor father died when I was but a lad, and I had to care for my mother and sisters, so I was not able to have the kind of education I'm sure the Warrens of Massachusetts were able to provide for their sons," Mr. Barnum continued, his face so serious but his eyes so close to merry. I was the only one who saw them, however; my parents were too ashamed to meet his gaze.

"Well, it's not as if we were able to send our boys to Harvard, either," Papa said agreeably. "They're farmers, too, the ones who aren't off fighting."

"Fighting for our grand Union?" Mr. Barnum's voice now filled with musical emotion—fifes and drums and "Yankee Doodle." Sitting up straight, he placed his hand over his heart—and I had to look away, biting the inside of my cheek so as not to burst into laughter. He rose and laid his other hand gently upon Mama's arm. "Madam, I cannot begin to convey my gratitude to you, a mother of such brave boys. Your noble sacrifice will never be forgotten."

Mama, her face covered in mortification, simply nodded, still unable to look Mr. Barnum in the eye. He returned to his seat with a loud, dramatic sniff—then turned to give me a brazen wink, which made me gasp out loud.

Mama and Papa looked at me, but I simply shook my head and dabbed my eye, as if contemplating my brothers' courage.

"I do understand your concerns," Mr. Barnum said, his voice still choked with emotion. "I have nothing but the utmost respect for you and your noble family. I'm a father myself, you know—I have three lovely daughters living, and one angel taken from us far too soon."

"Oh, no!" Mama exclaimed.

"So you see, I have no desire to do anything but keep Miss Bump virtuous and safe from harm, while naturally allowing her the opportunity to see a bit of the world in the manner deserving of such a fine lady, from such a fine family. I know I'm merely a farmer's son, a patriot, a father of daughters—but I vow, with all my heart, to protect your daughter. I'd die myself before I would bring shame upon your good name."

During this speech, Mr. Barnum had leaned forward toward my parents in a beseeching attitude, his hands outstretched, his face open and earnest. Mama and Papa listened intently, transfixed.

I leaned forward as well; I did so want my parents' blessing. I could not imagine continuing to live in Middleborough, where I would never fit in, not only because of my size but now because of my reputation. I could imagine no future for me there that did not consist of staying at home with Mama and Papa and Minnie, growing smaller and older with each tick of the kitchen mantel clock, which Mama faithfully wound every day—until I disappeared completely.

I had known Mr. Barnum only a quarter of an hour, but already I felt my wits quicken with every word he spoke, every move he made, as if he were the sharpening stone and I the edge of the knife. It was as if I had at last found someone with a personality, with dreams, as big as my own.

"What I can't understand is how you heard of Lavinia in the first place." Mama shook her head. "She's been back home for almost two years now. I thought that she'd gotten this whole thing out of her system."

"Why, I—" Mr. Barnum happened to turn my way; he caught me shaking my head and he clamped his mouth shut—after first giving me a small, admiring nod. "That is, your daughter's reputation reached my ears from other performers who spoke highly of her; her beauty and grace are known far beyond the Mississippi."

"They are?" Papa looked at me, then scratched his head, as if trying to see these attributes and failing. I smiled fondly; I knew I was just his daughter, just his Vinnie, and I loved him for that. Even though he had never known precisely what to do with me, he had always loved me for no special reason at all, which satisfied my heart more than I could ever tell him.

"Yes, they are. This is quite a daughter you have here." And they all three beamed upon me as if I were an unopened Christmas present.

"We just don't want any deception perpetuated in her name," Mama announced, in an almost apologetic tone. "I'm sure you understand."

"Madam, I assure you. Anything I say in public will be only with Miss Bump's knowledge and approval." Mr. Barnum turned to me, and once again I saw that sparkle flickering behind his gaze.

"Now, Mama, Papa, I would very much like to talk to Mr. Barnum alone," I said decisively. This was my future, after all, and I had sat by, discussed to no end, for long enough. I wanted to talk to the man plainly; I had no desire to bind myself to anyone like Colonel Wood ever again. Even though he was the Great Barnum, I was determined not to let my vanity cloud my judgment this time.

"Really? Do you think that's wise?" Mama asked Papa, as if I wasn't there.

"Yes, I do," I answered for him. Papa looked at me in that odd way again. I nodded gently at him and then waited as he and Mama withdrew outside, at Mr. Barnum's suggestion, to stroll about the grounds and see the stables.

"Now," he said, pulling his chair over to mine and slouching so that we sat, knee to knee, eye to eye. "Let's have it. I perceive you are a most remarkable woman, Miss Bump."

"Why is that, Mr. Barnum?"

"You sent me that letter, didn't you? The one with all your clippings—but you didn't tell your parents?"

"No, I did not."

"And why is that? I have to say, it's very unusual for me to hear from a performer directly in this way; I was surprised to find you weren't already under contract with someone."

I hesitated for only a moment before replying, "Well, I'm not. And I desire only the best for my career, which prompted me to write to you."

"And about that career." Mr. Barnum leaned back a little and lit a cigar, puffing it for a few moments before continuing. "Tell me about it. I know those showboats. I know the West. I know it's a wild and woolly place. How did you survive it?"

Again, I hesitated for only a fraction of a second. "I got out just in time, because the War came. I won't deceive you; it was not easy. I was not pleased with the vulgar manner in which—in which my cousin decided to exhibit me. For that matter, I would like to know your plans before I agree to anything. I think you should know, right off, I have no intention of being a female Tom Thumb."

"You don't?" He raised a bushy eyebrow, and I had a sense of the steely flint that gave that merry light its spark.

"No, I don't, sir. I will not be paraded around in costumes and uniforms; I will not do imitations; I will not be your performing puppet. I think it's not fitting for a woman, and it's certainly not fitting for me."

"You think Charlie Stratton's my puppet? Why, you know nothing of it," Mr. Barnum growled, reminding me of a grumpy bulldog with his round face, round nose, crooked mouth. "He's my good friend, and he bailed me out of a real jam recently, agreeing to go on tour again because I needed the money. He was just a child when he dressed up in those costumes; it worked for him then. Now he's a man—as you're obviously a woman."

"That's precisely my point. I am a woman, not a puppet. I desire respectability in all things. And protection, too, from—from—well, protection that any lady would require from those who would take advantage of her—vulnerability." My voice did falter, as I could not prevent myself from thinking of Colonel Wood's plans for me in New Orleans.

Mr. Barnum fixed me with a bright, hard gaze, searching for the truth I was so obviously unwilling to speak. He found it; I'm sure he did, as he suddenly paled, then growled, the tip of his nose and his ears turning a dangerous red. He squashed his cigar down in the ashtray beside him with a violence I did not expect, then muttered something under his breath.

I hung my head, my face suffused with warmth; at that moment I could not meet his gaze. Yet when he finally spoke, it was with a voice so gentle, so careful, it reminded me of a child cradling a kitten. "Miss Bump, I'm sorry. I appreciate your delicacy in conveying this to me. When I spoke of the showboats being wild, I assure you—I had no idea of something of this nature, particularly happening to one so fine, so ladylike, as you. You have my word that nothing like that will ever happen, as long as you're employed by me. You asked me how I intend to exhibit you—would you like to hear my plans?"

I nodded, still unable to look at him.

"As a lady. As a model lady, a lady of deportment, a lady deserving of every consideration, every finery. Do you remember Miss Jenny Lind?"

"Oh, yes!" I raised my face eagerly. "I do!"

"She was a model of womanhood." He gestured to a painting I hadn't noticed before; it hung on the opposite wall of the fireplace, and it was illuminated by a discreetly placed gaslight. It was of the Swedish Nightingale herself; a glorious portrait of a woman with softly waving brown hair, luminous eyes, in a virginal white dress. Mr. Barnum followed my gaze; I thought I saw a softer light in his eyes as they fell upon this portrait. I wondered at their relationship, and was surprised to feel a small prick of jealousy. I wanted, suddenly, someday, for someone to look at me in that reverent, adoring way.

"Miss Lind was—is—a model of womanhood, and that is how I displayed her—her voice, of course, was without parallel. That was always understood. But there are other fine singers, most of whom you've never heard, Miss Bump. Why is that? Because I decided to play up her modesty, her gentility, her virtue. No singer had ever been promoted in that way. I have something of the same in mind for you. That your size makes you different is not in question; why call attention to it only? But your manner, your intelligence, your family heritage—that makes you just as socially acceptable as Mrs. Astor or Mrs. Belmont. That is how I intend to present you to the public—as a perfect little lady, a gentlewoman, a Society woman. This is what people will remember about you."

Tears stung my eyes as I listened to him; he had put into words what I myself had desired for so long. Yes, my height would be the first thing people noticed about me, but it would not be the last. Colonel Wood had never understood this very fine point; he had been such a rough, despicable man. I hoped never to have to utter his name again.

"Then I agree to work with you," I told Mr. Barnum, holding my hand out to seal the bargain. He leaned forward and shook my hand heartily—not timidly, as most men did—and began to laugh.

"Of course," I interrupted him coolly. "I will require a salary commensurate to a lady of my fine breeding. And a percentage of all souvenirs and *cartes de visites* sold."

Mr. Barnum stopped laughing. He squinted at me with that bright, hard gaze. Then he laughed again, but not joyfully; just one short, rueful bark.

"Five percent is all I'll give."

"Ten."

"Seven."

"Eight, and I want to go to Europe first, to see the Queen, before I perform here. First-class passage, naturally."

"Eight. And I'll consider Europe. It worked for Charlie, back in the day. Our good patriotic citizens never fail to be impressed by a Royal stamp of approval, for some reason."

"Deal," I said, extending my hand once more.

"Deal." Once more, he shook it. Then he leaned even closer to me, suddenly deadly serious. "But there's something we need to settle right away, Miss Bump."

"What is that?" My thoughts raced wildly; did he suspect about Colonel Wood's contract?

"It's the one thing that could doom this whole enterprise." He gazed at me, not blinking; I gazed right back, holding my breath. I waited for him to speak, for a terrifyingly long time; I heard every creak and movement in the house, a muffled door slam, a silvery tinkle of china, so many clocks ticking out of sync. Still, he stared at me, until I was about to blurt out Colonel Wood's name—then, finally, he grinned.

"Now, what are we going to do about your last name? *Bump* will never do."

I drew in my breath sharply, then exhaled. And I began to laugh, out of pure relief and delight. He joined in, and suddenly I felt as if I'd known him all my life. He was no longer the great, revered P. T. Barnum, nor "that Barnum," nor even the Prince of Humbug.

He was my mentor and friend. Mr. Barnum. And that was what he would remain.

Or so we both believed at the time.

INTERMISSION

From the *Brooklyn Daily Eagle,* February 6, 1863

A SURPRISE

Doctor Colton is preparing a surprise for Ladies and Pupils of Schools at the Athenaeum tomorrow afternoon. In addition to the Laughing Gas exhibition, he proposes to condense into half an hour a great variety of experiments, illustrating the properties of the air, with simple explanations—among other things a Balloon, holding thirty gallons of hydrogen gas, is to be sent up with a car full of "little folks." Such a lecture must prove highly instructive, and as the admission is only five cents for children, we trust they will be allowed to attend.

From *Harper's Weekly,* February 14, 1863

THE INEVITABLE QUESTION

The question that every body has seen from the beginning of the war must be answered has at last been asked. Shall there be colored soldiers? It is a question upon which there need be no loss of temper. If a man says that he is willing to see the Government lost rather than maintained by such allies, he must answer the question whether, then, he cares enough for the Government to fight for it.

———•••••———

SEVEN

I Prepare to Make My Grand Entrance

HOW SWIFTLY THINGS HAPPENED AFTER THAT MEETING! Mama and Papa and I returned home, where I spent the next few weeks washing and mending my wardrobe. Minnie helped, even as she valiantly sniffed away her tears, to no avail; every five minutes she dropped something and threw her arms about my waist to cry, "Oh, how can you leave again, Sister? Why don't you like it here with us? I wish I could make you love it here like I do!"

"Oh, Minnie, I do! Of course I do, but you and I are so very— I promise you, things will be different this time. I fully intend to come home often. And maybe even you'll visit me in New York; Mama and Papa might bring you on the train!" I smiled as I said this, but inwardly, my stomach tightened. Mr. Barnum had asked, jokingly, if I had a sister just like me at home—"The more

Bumps, the merrier!" I hastily replied that I did not; perhaps too hastily, as his eyes narrowed suspiciously.

I had no desire ever to inform him of Minnie's existence. Even as I eagerly looked forward to my next adventure, I needed to know that Minnie would remain where she always was—back on the farm, protected by Mama and Papa, waiting for me to return. It was almost as if she were my conscience, my anchor, the one thing tethering me to home, reeling me back in occasionally so that I wouldn't completely lose my way.

"I might want to take the train," she admitted with a reluctant, shy smile. "Mama said it wasn't as dreadful as all that. But now that I think about it, it must be, because it keeps taking you away! What a terrible, nasty old thing it is, carrying people away from their homes so easily. No, I don't want to take it, at that." And she shook her head so vigorously she almost lost her balance.

"Minnie, darling, you don't understand, even though you're thirteen now—imagine! Trains are wonderful things—you'll see, someday. But you have to know that this time, it's going to be so different—I'm going to be so grand!"

"As grand as Jenny Lind?" Minnie looked over at the figurine, back in its place on my bureau; almost the very minute I returned home, she had handed it over to me solemnly, with the assurance that she had dusted it every single day.

"Even grander!" I promised. "And I will bring home beautiful presents for you—dolls and gowns and necklaces, and we'll put them on and have balls right here at home, right in the parlor, just the two of us!" I dropped the frock I was folding and began to waltz my little sister around the floor; she giggled and followed my lead surprisingly well, her tangle of black curls tumbling down over her face.

But when that fateful day arrived and my family drove me to

the station, she sobbed as uncontrollably as she had the first time I left. I, however, had no tears. I bowed regally to some of my fellow townspeople who just *happened* to be at the station that day; to Mrs. Putnam, the minister's wife, I gave a special farewell. I extended my hand to her and said that I hoped that God would be with her and that I wouldn't stop praying for her, not even all the way in New York City, and then Europe. Why, I might even enlist the Queen in my efforts!

She sputtered in horror, but Papa was already lifting me up on the train before she could think of something to retort. Then I was waving to my family, but only for a moment; soon enough I turned around and looked ahead, at the familiar, peaceful buildings and houses and farms that soon fell away as I sped west, toward New York.

The scenery changed, from farmland to coastland; we passed cranberry bogs and fishing villages, and then we found ourselves back in rolling farmland again. Eventually the houses and buildings grew closer and closer together as we went south. Even with the train windows shut tightly, I soon detected a noise, a pulse, I'd never heard before, and I knew we were in New York City. Automatically I clutched my reticule to my bosom, my mother's last-minute warnings still in my ear, but I also couldn't refrain from kneeling up on the seat to see more easily. The train was chugging past what seemed to be a maze of buildings, all perilously close to the track, right on the same level; there were so many people on the sidewalks that I was quite fearful someone would step right into the path of the onrushing train and be killed.

To my great relief, no one did. We continued to chug, slowing down by increments, until we reached a yard full of tracks branching out in every direction. The train stopped, and I waited for everyone else to disembark before I finally ventured forth, looking for a porter to lift me down.

"Where is the station house?" I inquired, after finding myself on the ground, in the middle of all those tracks.

"Are you lost, little girl?" He squinted down at me.

I sighed but decided not to correct him. "No, I'm not lost, I simply want to get to the station, where I'm being met."

"Over there." The porter pointed, across several tracks, to a large wooden building.

"How do I get there?"

"You walk. Across the tracks. Can you do that? I must say, you're a mite of a thing, traveling all alone."

"I'm not—that is—would you mind carrying me?" For despite my eagerness to correct his impression, I heard trains approaching from other directions and I had a momentary fear of being caught on one of the tracks, unable to scramble out of the way in time.

"Sure thing, little lady." And so I found myself being carried across the tracks, much like a sack of potatoes, and deposited unceremoniously upon the station platform. Hastily, I brushed off my skirt and smoothed my shawl. Perhaps it was not the most dignified way to make my entrance into this great metropolis, but it was certainly the safest.

"You must be Miss Warren?" A tall man with a drooping gray mustache and beard approached me.

"No, I'm—Oh, yes! That is, yes, I'm Miss Warren." So flustered was I, I had quite forgotten my new name. Mr. Barnum and I had disposed, once and for all, of the ugly "Bump," and settled on Mama's family name.

"I'm Mr. Bleeker. Mr. Barnum sent me to greet you and get you out of here right away. I'm to take you straight to his daughter's house—do you have any luggage?"

"Yes, a trunk and some wooden steps."

"Give me the ticket, and I'll fetch them. Come—I hate to ask you after your long trip, but do you mind hurrying up a bit? We don't want to cause a stir." Indeed, people were beginning to gather and point at me; I was so accustomed to this that I scarcely noticed it. But this tall man did, and it appeared to cause him great concern; he put his hand upon my head and gave me a little push, even as he apologized for doing so.

It was his kind concern that made me trust him immediately. He was so very solicitous, even as he was obviously anxious to get me to the carriage. So I followed this stranger, so gaunt that his clothes practically hung off him, as if I trusted him with my life. Little did I know that one day, he would repay this trust, abundantly, many times over. But he was no saint, no mythological creature. For in the end, there was one life he would not be able to spare: the life dearest to him, above all others.

At that moment, of course, I could not suspect any of this; I only followed Mr. Bleeker because I had no alternative, and because I trusted Mr. Barnum implicitly. Soon I found myself in a carriage—not as fine as the one back in Bridgeport; this one was coated in dirt, which I immediately discovered was one thing everyone in New York, no matter the class, gender, or heritage, had in common. Dirt. It was the great equalizer.

Dirt covered everything; my white satin slippers were soon coated in it, even before I stepped into the carriage. Dirt covered the buildings, so tall I couldn't see the tops of some of them—four and five stories tall, imagine! Dirt covered the cobblestoned streets, which were also filled with animal filth, garbage, rats, and humans—who were also covered in dirt. Newsboys, lugging great armfuls of papers, their faces streaked with grime and newsprint; men in black coats and top hats, carrying walking sticks, their white gloves sooty gray; women wrapped in shawls and long aprons, pulling along sickly-looking children spattered with mud; vendors pushing carts filled with things I'd never seen before, fruits and vegetables of unknown names, pickles, fish in jars, trinkets—all coated in dirt.

I'd never seen such a kaleidoscope of people, of things, all of so many different colors yet muted with the same grimy gray.

And high above the buildings, in patches, I could glimpse blue sky. And the occasional oasis of green, pastures for horses and even cows and sheep, so oddly out of place in the shadows of the tall buildings.

I was speechless, content to keep looking out the window, again up on my knees, although I knew it was not dignified. Mr. Bleeker simply grinned, saying, "It sure is good to see this place through someone else's eyes."

"I don't see how you could ever get used to it! It looks as if it's always changing!" Just then, a man with long black curls on either side of his head, wearing a funny hat and coat, emerged from a building. He carried an impressive-looking scroll under one arm, a huge fish wrapped in newspaper under the other. I was enthralled.

Mr. Bleeker didn't reply; he seemed to be a man content with silence, much like my father. I liked him already. Although he did say, after I hung my head out the carriage window to get a better look at a man roasting chestnuts in a tin bucket over coals and selling them in paper cones, "Miss Warren, I do wish you'd shut the window, for Mr. Barnum will have my hide if anyone sees you."

I shut the window, not unwillingly; one other aspect of New York—the stinking, rotting smell of human and animal refuse ripening in the sun and stagnant water—had immediately made my eyes water. I sat back down and turned to Mr. Bleeker.

"Why is that? Why does he want no one to see me?"

"Because that's the way he works. He needs to build you up himself, present you in the proper way. And if some newspaper writes about a little lady wandering about town, he won't be able to control the Press. You'll see—Mr. Barnum is a genius." Mr. Bleeker's long face, which had a tendency to look immensely sad when he wasn't talking, lit up considerably as he spoke about his employer.

"Do you like Mr. Barnum very much?"

"Yes, yes, I do."

"How long have you worked for him?"

"Oh, years and years now. Got my start working at the Museum, and now I do pretty much what Mr. Barnum tells me to. I manage some of the acts, did a tour with the General last time he went to Europe—that kind of thing." This lengthy speech appeared to surprise Mr. Bleeker, for he slumped back against his seat and swiped his forehead with a handkerchief.

I left him to his silence and continued to stare out the window, up at the tops of the passing buildings, the only things I could see while seated. At one point we drove by a very long expanse of trees, which Mr. Bleeker kindly pointed out as "the new Central Park; they're always working on it, but it's just as nice as Hyde Park or Versailles."

"Oh." I was very impressed, not only by the park but by the offhand way Mr. Bleeker said "Hyde Park" and "Versailles," as if he was very familiar with them. And I supposed he must be, if he had accompanied General Tom Thumb to Europe. I smiled and shivered in delicious anticipation; soon *I* would be visiting Europe's grand capitals! First Europe, then the American Museum, just as Mr. Barnum had promised. I could hardly wait.

Finally the carriage rumbled to a halt; it had been a rough ride over the cobblestones. Mr. Bleeker unspooled himself from the carriage—he was a very tall man indeed, although not nearly as tall as Sylvia!—and swung me down. Then he helped me up some imposing marble stairs to the front door of a narrow home, which was part of a row of similar homes, all joined together, constructed of a muddy-colored brown stone. I'd never seen so many houses so close together, no grass or trees between them.

"Miss Warren!" A robust-looking young woman greeted us as a maid let us inside. She was obviously Mr. Barnum's daughter, for she shared his same round nose and chin, and curly black hair. "I'm Mrs. Thompson, Mr. Barnum's daughter, but please, call me Caroline. Come, let me show you to your room, for you must be exhausted."

I followed her gratefully up a narrow set of stairs, which were not as shallow as the ones at home, so it took me some effort and time. This was one of the inconveniences I had to put up with as I aged; when I was a child, I had simply scampered up stairs using my hands to propel me. Now, as a proper young lady in a corset, I could not do that. And there were so *many* stairs in this house! We went up two flights until finally Caroline opened a door and showed me to my room; I gathered this was to be my home for the next few weeks.

I thanked Caroline, who discreetly left me alone to freshen up. The bed was tall but not taller than my wooden steps, which were soon deposited in my room along with my trunk. A very pretty Irish maid unpacked that with alarming efficiency, pausing only now and then to exclaim over the diminutive nature of my clothing.

When she was done, I pulled my steps over to the window and looked out; my view was of another row of houses exactly like this one, all in that same dull stone. The street was very narrow, but I saw a procession of nurses with infants in tow strolling along the sidewalks, and the only carriages that turned down it were beautifully maintained. Mr. Barnum's daughter obviously lived in Society.

Beyond the houses, I could not see. But out there was the

great city of New York! I itched to explore every nook of it, the rich parts and the poor parts, both. I wanted to see the immigrants in the Five Points; I wanted to attend a musical performance at the famous Academy of Music, where all the Society people gathered.

Even through the windows, I could hear the rhythm of New York; it was in the constant, staccato punctuation of steel carriage wheels upon cobblestone, a sound that I would soon discover never abated, no matter the time of day or night. Already it was ringing in my ears—I knew I would sleep well tonight; none of that awful, nerve-jangling *quiet* of home!

Most of all, I was eager to see the American Museum, where Miss Jenny Lind had sung, where Charles Stratton, as General Tom Thumb, had performed. Soon, Miss Lavinia Warren would grace the very same stage. Oh! I could scarcely believe it; I had to hug myself, pinch myself, to know it was all real. I was here! It was truly happening! I was going to be famous; my photograph would be sold along with those of Queens and Kings.

For the first time, I really and truly allowed myself to believe that I would not be forgotten after all. No weeds would cover my name; it would be known in every household in the land.

And with this reassuring thought to sing me to sleep, I prepared for bed. I did so want to be refreshed and ready for Mr. Barnum, on the morrow.

THE WEEKS BETWEEN MY ARRIVAL AND MY DEBUT PASSED IN A frenzy of fittings and finery; I was Cinderella, and Mr. Barnum was a most unusual fairy godmother. I would not have been surprised to find out that he could turn a pumpkin into a coach!

Standing patiently, hour after hour, while being fitted for a custom-designed wardrobe was hard work, I soon discovered. Naturally, my proportions gave the designer some difficulty;

Madame Demorest did not have a dressmaker's dummy in anything near the right size, so everything had to be pinned directly upon my person!

In addition to the fittings for my wardrobe, I had numerous appointments with Mr. Charles Tiffany and Messrs. Ball and Black for my jewels; there were endless trips to A. T. Stewart's store for gloves and accessories, most of which had to be custom-ordered. All conducted, per Mr. Barnum's orders, in the utmost secrecy, under cover of night. I did not enter a single building through the front door during the first three weeks I was in New York; I felt rather like a Confederate spy!

During those weeks, I came to know Mr. Barnum's daughters very well: sturdy, reliable Caroline, my hostess; the slightly bad-tempered Helen, also married, whose mouth was always pursed in disapproval of some perceived slight; and the charming Pauline, the only unmarried daughter, obviously her father's favorite. These three fussed over me as if I were a pet or a doll, Pauline pronouncing every single item of my accumulating finery more cunning than the last.

I must pause here to admit to my feeling of utter bliss upon being laced, by Pauline Barnum herself, into my very first custom-made corset. She giggled at my delight; Pauline was always bubbling over with giggles, being only sixteen at the time. But, oh, how that corset felt against the silk undergarment, smooth and cool as a flower petal against my skin! It fit exquisitely, not a gap, not a wrinkle. When I was laced into it, I stood for almost a quarter of an hour before a looking glass, just gazing at myself, at my womanly figure, how my breasts were pushed up perfectly, my waist fashionably narrow, my hips rounded and utterly feminine. The corset itself, in a fine buff silk, the whalebones delicate yet sturdy, was so beautiful I truly hated to cover it up.

Not once during all the time I stayed at her daughter's home did I meet Mrs. Barnum. She remained, indisposed, in Connecticut. Apparently this was not new, as her daughters merely sighed and rolled their eyes at the mention of "Mother's maladies." And I cannot say I mourned her absence, as it enabled my friendship with her husband to blossom in these dazzling weeks with the intensity of a hothouse flower.

For I found, to my great delight, that Mr. Barnum often stayed in New York with Caroline, instead of taking the late train back to Bridgeport. Every evening I would descend the stairs eagerly, looking for his gold-tipped walking stick indicating he was back from the Museum. The two of us often dined alone, as Caroline and her husband usually had a social function to attend. Naturally, we discussed my upcoming debut, all the myriad details of which Mr. Barnum oversaw with the sensitive attention of an artist. No detail was too tiny for his interest; he discussed the placement of a rosette on one of my slippers until even I was weary of the subject!

I began to notice that whenever we were together, he made a point of sitting down. This may appear to be an insignificant detail, but it was one that I greatly appreciated. This was in such contrast with Colonel Wood, who had taken every opportunity to loom over me—he had rarely sat in my presence, never offered me cushions, was fond of standing as close to me as possible so that he could literally look down upon me.

Mr. Barnum did not do this. In fact, he and I soon fell into the habit of sitting knee-to-knee, as we had done that first day, whenever we had something important to discuss. Thus situated in front of a crackling fire, a plate of cookies or walnuts, glasses of lemonade or sometimes fine Madeira, on a table within reach, we would talk for hours and hours. Not only about my plans but about the War, the political situation, his receipts from the Museum; he was soon asking my opinion about other acts and exhibits, and I felt he always weighed my answers very carefully.

Looking back, I believe this was the most satisfying time of my life. I would soon meet public figures, millionaires and monarchs, beyond anything I could have imagined. But it was this time, this sweet, anticipatory time, that I remember most fondly.

I told him all about my life on the river, not varnishing the roughness but, under his eager, hungry gaze that was always on the lookout for an anecdote or unusual story, finding the humor in my memories, as well. I came to believe he was fueled, almost alone, by words and imagination; by a hunger for knowledge and experience that paralleled my own. Never before had I felt such a kinship with anyone, not even Sylvia. It was a meeting of the minds, first and foremost.

The night before my debut, as Mr. Barnum and I sat together in Caroline's snug parlor, I felt a trifle melancholy. My new trunks—made of the finest leather monogrammed with my initials—were packed up in the dear little bedroom that had been my first New York home. On the morrow, I would be moving into the St. Nicholas Hotel, where I would remain while I held my series of grand receptions—invitation-only, highly sought-after, Mr. Barnum reported with glee. Already I missed the warm hospitality of Caroline's home; already I missed these quiet, conspiratorial evenings with my new friend.

"Are you all right, Vinnie?" Mr. Barnum asked as he handed me a glass of wine.

"Yes, I am. Although I admit, I'm a little nervous about tomorrow. You'll make sure no man picks me up or kisses me without my permission, won't you?" This old fear of mine would not leave me. Despite my elegant new wardrobe, I worried that I would be touched and picked up and squeezed as if I were a child. Or worse.

"Mr. Bleeker will be vigilant, I assure you. He's to be considered your bodyguard. You must trust him as you trust me." Mr.

Barnum, a red silk dressing gown covering his shirt and trousers, nodded smartly. His cigar, ever-present, glowed mysteriously in the cozy darkness. Only the light from the fire illuminated us; he did not like to have the gaslights lit at night, for he enjoyed the shadows. He said it reminded him of his childhood, when he would walk long miles back to his home late at night from his grandfather's store, where he first learned to sell things to people who did not know they wanted them.

"Then I am satisfied." I tried to push those worries out of my mind, but others swiftly took their place. "And I'm to meet all the gentlemen of the Press, at once?"

"Yes, but don't think of it that way. People will be introduced to you, one by one, just like any reception. You'll simply stand and shake hands and chat—that's all we need to do at first. And I trust that your charming powers of speech will not desert you." Mr. Barnum winked at me, but behind his smile I detected a stern rejoinder: a reminder that I must not fail him. And I would not, I vowed silently. I would not let him down; the responsibility of this did not fall lightly upon me, but it did not completely bend me, either. I felt myself rising up to shoulder it without complaint.

"Might I not sing a little song?" I asked after a moment, as I tried to imagine what the morrow would be like. "That went over very well on the river."

"I suppose."

"I could sing 'Home Sweet Home,'" I offered. "So everyone will know when to leave."

"No." He shook his head in a very decided way.

"Why not?"

"That was Jenny's song. You must find another."

I bit my lip, my stomach tightening in a curious way. I did not like the way he said "Jenny," as if he had a right. I did not like the gleam that turned his eyes from gray to almost blue when he did so. I did not care for the way he stared into the fire and sighed, as if entangled in a memory.

Most of all, in some soft, womanly part of my heart—a part that I had not, until now, taken the time to explore with any frequency—I did not like the fact that no one had ever said *my* name in that way, that softly proprietary way.

"Fine," I said grudgingly. "Then I'll sing 'Annie of the Vale.' I'm told I sing it exceedingly well."

Mr. Barnum smiled at me, nodding approvingly. "Good girl. I knew you'd come up with something right away. You've got a head on your shoulders, Vinnie. I've not met many your equal."

I smiled back, basking in the glow of his approval, content to be admired for my mind.

For now.

INTERMISSION

———◆◆◆◆———

From the *New York Tribune,* December 23, 1862

Yesterday we saw a very pretty and intelligent little lady at the St. Nicholas Hotel, in this city. This woman in miniature is twenty-one years of age, weighs twenty-nine pounds, thirty-two inches in height. She moves about the drawing-room with the grace and dignity of a queen, and yet she is entirely devoid of affectation, is modest and lady-like in her deportment. Her voice is soft and sweet, and she sings excellently well.

———◆◆◆◆———

From *The New York Times,* December 23, 1862

We attended Miss Warren's reception yesterday at the St. Nicholas. It was a festive gathering. All were paying court to a very beautiful, an exceedingly symmetrical, a remarkably well-developed, and an absolutely choice specimen of feminine humanity, whose silken tresses beautified and adorned a head, the top of which was not quite thirty-two inches from the floor. In other words, we saw a miniature woman—aye, and the queen of them.

———◆•••◆———

EIGHT

Or, A Star Is Born

AND SO IT ALL CULMINATED IN ONE GRAND, GLORIOUS reception, successful beyond anything we could have imagined. Standing upon a small velvet-draped platform in the lovely parlor of the St. Nicholas Hotel, I softly cleared my throat, nodded to the pianist Mr. Barnum had secured for me, and began to sing.

I had shaken many hands, engaged in much conversation, discussed the myriad details of my wardrobe (at least, the details that a lady could discuss in public). I had posed for illustrators eager to sketch my likeness, I had answered questions about my family and ancestors (these, I surmised, were discreetly planted by Mr. Barnum, who was circling the edge of the crowd like a proud parent, careful not to take any attention away from me). All in all, I was an astonishing success. I knew it by the hum of approval in the room, the admiring glances; I knew it by Mr. Barnum's unapologetic smile of pure, boyish glee. There was only one thing left to do, and that was to sing my song.

Fixing my gaze at some spot across the room—in the sudden yellow, flickering glare of the gaslights, which seemed to have been turned up to a blaze, I could not make out anything specific. Then I began to sing. Very softly at first, for it had been a long while since I had sung in public, and my voice was a little rusty and uncertain.

"*The young stars are glowing . . . their clear light bestowing . . . their radiance fills the calm clear Summer night . . .*"

All I could see were smiles around me; smiles from these men, serious professionals, but my singing, I could tell, brought them much pleasure and delight. So I sang even louder, my eyes adjusting to the light now.

"*Come . . . come . . . come love, come . . . come 'ere the night torches pale . . .*"

My vision cleared so that I could make out that spot on the far wall; to my surprise, it was Mr. Barnum to whom I had chosen to sing. It was Mr. Barnum whose face I now saw, a smile upon it as broad as any I had seen. Did I also detect a tear in his eye? I was too far away, but I decided that yes, I did.

"*Oh, come in thy beauty, thou marvel of duty . . . Dear Annie, dear Annie of the vale.*"

I bowed my head after the last note and accepted the applause of the room; it was different from the applause I had heard on the river. This was respectful, from men who were cultured, men who had heard Miss Jenny Lind sing.

But there was only one man whose applause fell sweetly upon my ear, all the way from across the room. It was the one man who heard the Nightingale sing, still, in his memory.

His was the admiration I truly sought. And in that moment, when I knew that I possessed it, I allowed myself to wonder, for the very first time, how it would feel to be known simply as a woman—

And not a woman in miniature.

INTERMISSION

———————

From *The New York Times,* February 26, 1863

A CASE OF FURIOUS DRIVING

Mrs. E. GREEN, residing at No. 22 Watts-street, while crossing Fifth-avenue, near Tenth-street, was knocked down and run over by a horse and sleigh, which was being driven at a furious rate, by LEVI L. HUFF, the colored coachman of Mr. CHARLES GOODHUE, of Madison-avenue. Mrs. GREEN, who was severely injured, was taken to her residence by a policeman. HUFF was arrested and taken before Justice KELLY, who committed him, in default of $300 bail.

———————

From *Harper's Weekly,* March 21, 1863

FOREIGN NEWS—ENGLAND—REVULSION OF PUBLIC SENTIMENT

There was a great demonstration at the amphitheatre in Liverpool on the 19th ult., in support of President Lincoln's Emancipation Proclamation. The *Liverpool Post* says that a more unanimous meeting was never witnessed on any question on which public opinion has been divided. Resolutions applauding the course of Mr. Lincoln on the slavery question, and an address to be provided to him through Mr. Adams were adopted. Some uproar and confusion occurred toward the conclusion of the meeting; but with this exception everything passed off very happily.

—◆◆◆—

NINE

Or, Another Player Makes His Long-Anticipated Entrance

M Y SUCCESS WAS COMPLETE—TOO COMPLETE, PERHAPS. For Mr. Barnum decided I was so popular, it would be prudent to postpone the expensive European tour. We argued, but finally he showed me the projections for the income we could expect if I appeared at his Museum right away.

I had no reply to that—other than to show him that he could add an extra two hundred dollars a week to my salary, as compensation for my understandable disappointment. He swore mildly but in the end did not appear to mind too much as he signed the check.

Indeed, I think he admired me even more.

P. T. Barnum's American Museum! How sad to note how little it is remembered these days! Children of this time have no memory of it. They don't even realize how very much they have missed by not growing up while it was still standing.

I first entered it, accompanied by Mr. Barnum, through a private door that the majority of the public did not even know was there. But later, I insisted upon entering it through the front, just like any member of the public that paid, without grumbling, twenty-five cents each. For nowhere else on earth had there ever been such an assemblage of novelties, animals, music, culture, science, and entertainment all in one place.

You first approached the Museum from the corner of Broadway and Ann Street in Lower Manhattan; it was surrounded by many thriving businesses, including Mr. Mathew Brady's daguerreotype studio, which I would come to know quite well. The street at this intersection was wide enough to accommodate the throngs of people always milling about in case one of the living exhibits might appear for a stroll or a brief, tempting display of his talent. The building itself was five stories of white stone, with the name "Barnum" prominently featured in red letters above the third-floor windows. Panels depicting the various animals and exhibits, including Tom Thumb, were painted gaudily on the face of the stone. Flags flew in a line atop the roof, and the second and third stories each had a wrought-iron fenced balcony stretching their lengths. On one of these balconies, a band in brightly festooned uniforms played; they were singular for their absolutely awful musicianship. Indeed, Mr. Barnum confessed to me that he had hired them expressly for their lack of talent! He wanted the people *inside* the Museum, and if they had to endure a cacophony of out-of-tune instruments, he reasoned, they would not remain long *outside*.

After paying admission, families, immigrants, Society people, farmers in their finest, and a constant parade of newspapermen from all over the world mingled together as they took in the wonders to be seen. And such wonders! On the first floor, there were halls lined with display cases brimming with the most unusual artifacts, exotic animal bones and skins, minerals, the world's largest baby tooth, horrifying medical instruments all gleaming with steel and sharp edges, a part of an asteroid that had once killed a farmer's cow, a thread of the blanket that the Baby Jesus was swaddled in, a real live flea circus, dioramas of all sorts of scenes, even miniature naval battles on real water. There were cases and cages full of preserved animals and skeletons. In one room was the famous "Happy Family," where, in the same cage, a lion, a tiger, a lamb, and assorted birds all lived together in apparent harmony. (Although Mr. Barnum confessed that the exhibit could continue only as long as he had a fresh supply of lambs and birds!)

On the second floor was the waxworks, where mannequins of famous personalities stood milling about companionably, as if at a silent tea party. There was George Washington, Queen Victoria, the Apostles, Napoléon, Joice Heth (the original humbug herself, the old Negro slave whom Mr. Barnum had tried to pass off as George Washington's one-hundred-and-sixty-year-old nursemaid, until she died and was discovered to be only eighty), and Jenny Lind. Naturally, Charles Stratton was represented in this hall as well. In one corner stood a tree trunk upon which Jesus Himself had once sat—or so read the inscription. On this floor too was a picture gallery of astoundingly realistic portraits, some that even appeared to pop out of their frames, so breathtakingly lifelike were they. The famous Feejee mermaid was still on display—the crudely stitched-together torso of a monkey and a fish tail that had been the second great example of Mr. Barnum's ability to whip a gullible public up into a frenzy. This phenomenon was safely behind glass, thank heavens, for I could well imagine how it must smell by now!

And in the middle of the second floor rose the enormous saltwater tank in which a real beluga whale lolled about, alive, but barely. I felt sorry for the poor thing, so confined, so miserable. But it was an extremely popular attraction, indeed. Rare was the person who had ever seen a whale up close, save for Captain Ahab himself!

Strategically placed at intervals were signs that promised *This Way to the Egress!* I bit my lip when I saw people eagerly going in the direction they pointed, and chided Mr. Barnum about it later. "That is an awful trick to play upon people," I scolded him.

"I'm not saying anything deceitful at all. It's not my fault if the educational system in this country is so appalling, no one knows that 'egress' is Latin for 'exit.'"

"And so you sit here and take another twenty-five cents each from these poor people who find themselves locked outside, forced to enter again through the ticket booth!"

"Yes, I do. And I need every extra twenty-five cents I can get so that I can pay your heartlessly negotiated contract, cruel woman! So if there's anyone to blame, it is yourself."

I had to smile at him. I always smiled at him in those days.

Of course, the noise in the place was horrendous; animals and people all chattering, heavy boots and spurs being dragged across wooden floors, the constant importunate cries of the ticket sellers and the men hired to keep the crowds moving. The smell, too, could be overwhelming: so many humans and animals in close quarters, despite the fact that there were fans everywhere, ventilation holes hidden along the walls. Every part of the Museum was illuminated by the new limelight, which was different than gaslight; it shone much brighter, not nearly so yellow, and lit up the stage of the Lecture Hall brilliantly.

The enormous, elegantly appointed Lecture Hall took up almost the entire third floor of the building, its velvet-curtained balconies extending up to the fourth and fifth floors. I know that in these more modern times, it is difficult to conceive of the necessity of calling what was really a theater a "lecture hall." But in those Civil War days, the word "theater" was shocking—not just shocking but amoral. It was considered a sin of the highest consequence to step foot into a "theater."

However, a "lecture hall" was another thing entirely; why, it was a place of learning, of enlightenment! Lectures were given here: scientific lectures, magic lantern shows of foreign lands. That it was also, occasionally, a place where plays were performed, operas sung, and ballets danced was merely convenient, as well as palatable, to the good, upright citizens of this Grand Republic of ours.

January 2, 1863: this was the date I made my debut in the Lecture Hall. On that enormous stage where Miss Jenny Lind had sung and bewitched her listeners, I felt as if I had completed a very long journey. I had finally arrived where I belonged, surely.

I'm certain I went dutifully through my rehearsed program that night. I sang my songs, told more stories, enacted a graceful little dance, answered planted questions from my audience. I was a professional; my body could go through its paces, even if my mind was not fully engaged. And I don't believe it was that night. I remember only the most serene feeling, almost one of complete detachment from this elegantly attired woman standing in the middle of this famous stage, moving about so competently, watched by hundreds of avid eyes. And even as I danced and chatted and sang, I knew, somehow, that I would long remember the details of my humiliation on Colonel Wood's boat much more intensely than I would the details of this evening's triumph.

I wondered why that was. I wondered if this was how it always felt when all your dreams came true. Perhaps, after living with them for so long, did you simply toss them away—and begin to dream about something else?

One of the first evenings I appeared at the Museum, I was

resting in my sitting room—everything in it made to my size, down to the exquisite silver hairbrushes and mirrors on my dressing table—between levees. I had already grown to love this oasis, for I now could not stir one foot in this city without causing a sensation. I had tried to take a stroll through the footpaths of Central Park, but soon found well-meaning citizens too eager to lift me over the snow banks. The first time I entered the grand establishment of A. T. Stewart's through the front door, simply because I wanted to look at the new bonnets, I was immediately surrounded by a crush of people who blocked my progress, some of whom earnestly tried to show me where the children's clothing could be ordered!

And my hand, my delicate, manicured hand, throbbed so at night after shaking so many much larger hands, that I had to soak it in lavender water!

So I was enjoying my respite, intending to finally begin *Lady Audley's Secret,* which I'd heard so much about, when there was a knock on my door.

"Yes?" I called out.

"Miss Warren, it's me. Barnum."

I leaped off the sofa, my book sliding to the floor; opening the door, I smiled and said, teasingly, "What is this 'Miss Warren' business? You're not still angry with me about that extra two hundred a week?"

But Mr. Barnum did not answer; he was not alone. "Miss Warren, it is such a pleasure to meet you," said a little boy, hat in hand, standing in front of Mr. Barnum.

But no. He was no boy. I stared at him in puzzlement, trying to place him, for he looked very familiar. Then the dawn broke upon me, as I remembered the *carte de visite* that I still possessed, somewhere, possibly in an old valise back at the farm, the photograph of an impish young man with light brown hair, merry eyes, clad in a Scottish kilt.

He was bigger now, fleshier, boasting a decided double chin and a mustache, which looked absurd, almost as if it were pasted on. I could not now picture him in a kilt; the idea almost made me giggle. He was immaculately attired, however: a perfectly tailored navy blue suit with snowy white cuffs, gold cuff links. He looked prosperous, well fed, and surprisingly, as I continued to stare, somewhat rudely, at him, extremely nervous.

This was Charles Stratton. Or as he was known to the rest of the world, General Tom Thumb.

"I hope you don't mind, but we thought we'd see if you'd like some company," Mr. Barnum said, following Mr. Stratton into my room. I still hadn't uttered a word; I could only continue gaping, for the two of them aped each other's movements with odd perfection, as if they had spent a lifetime polishing this act. I wasn't sure, at first, who was imitating whom. But as they sat down—Mr. Barnum upon one of the two regular-size chairs I kept for visitors; Mr. Stratton settling happily upon one of my small armchairs—they crossed their legs at the same time, loosened their vests, checked their pocket watches—exactly in unison, as if choreographed.

I very nearly laughed, but there was something in the earnestly dignified expression upon Mr. Stratton's face that stopped me.

"Of course I do not mind. And it is a pleasure for me, as well, Mr. Stratton."

"My friend came up from Connecticut today expressly to see your performance," Mr. Barnum told me with an odd little laugh; I noticed he was twisting his hat about in his hands as if he didn't know what he was doing. If I hadn't known him better, I would have thought he was nervous! But no, the Great Barnum was never nervous.

"Oh? I hope I did not disappoint you, then."

"Oh, no! It was grand! You dance right smart, and sing like an angel!" Mr. Stratton could not contain his enthusiasm; forgetting his practiced dignity, he bounced around in his seat like a jack-in-the-box. "I can't believe you've never performed before! Can you, Phineas?"

Mr. Barnum and I exchanged a quick look; he had taken great pains to present me as his latest discovery, great pains indeed not to mention my previous performing history. I did not mind this omission in the least; in fact, I welcomed it. I suppose it was our very first humbug. But it was a mild one, and it had the added value of somehow convincing me that this might prevent Colonel Wood from making any claim toward my services.

"Thank you, that is very kind, Mr. Stratton. Especially coming from one as experienced in this business as yourself."

Mr. Stratton puffed and preened but looked to Mr. Barnum as if seeking permission to do so. Mr. Barnum, however, did not respond; indeed, his mouth was clamped shut, his eyes bright: He was observing us, keenly, and I did not like it. I managed to hide my uneasiness and continued to listen politely to Mr. Stratton, who could hardly contain himself; conversation poured out of him as if from a bubbling coffeepot.

"I was just saying to Phineas here that I have some business that will keep me in New York for a few days. Gosh, I do want to tell you all about it! I have so many business dealings these days—real estate, insurance, horses, investments. Do you know what investments are, Miss Warren?"

"I do," I replied but immediately regretted it, for his plump face fell; obviously, he had wanted to inform me himself.

"Oh. I'm just learning all about this, for Phineas says I need to di-di—what was the word, old chap?"

"Diversify," Mr. Barnum supplied.

"Diversify! You see, it's best not to limit myself to performing interests. You don't want to put all your eggs in one basket, especially these days!"

I had to smile at Mr. Stratton's enthusiasm, but I could not shake the feeling that he was simply reciting a speech that someone—Mr. Barnum—had taught him.

"How very smart of you," I said warmly.

"Thank you!"

"You know, Charlie here bailed me out of a jam recently, Miss Warren. He really is a true friend," Mr. Barnum interjected as the conversation lulled; apparently, Mr. Stratton had run out of rehearsed topics of discussion.

Again, I found his speech a trifle off. "Miss Warren" sounded odd, given how familiar he and I were by now. I wondered why he was acting so strangely; there was no hint of the intimacy that had grown between us.

"True friends are the best friends," I replied automatically. But Charles Stratton mistook this little aphorism as a compliment; he blushed and shook his head violently.

"No, I was just doing what anyone would do in the same situation. I owe Mr. Barnum everything, and I will never forget it."

For the first time, I decided, Charles Stratton sounded sincere and unrehearsed. I peered at him, attempting to see beyond the obviously calculated appearance—he tried too hard to resemble a gentleman of the world, with his careful grooming (his odd little mustache glistened as if it had been oiled), the cuff links polished to a gleam. Yet despite his earnestly grown-up manner, his brown eyes were appealingly boyish, almost bashful; I found

myself wondering what it had been like to live in the public spotlight since the age of five. It must not have been easy for him; it
was little wonder he had learned to cloak himself in practiced at-
titudes and rehearsed speeches!

Suddenly I felt a tickle along the back of my neck; glancing up,
I observed Mr. Barnum observing me. He was not smiling; he
looked grave, almost concerned.

There was another knock at my door; before I could rise to
open it, I heard a childishly treble voice call out, "May I dare enter
the domain of the lovely and popular Miss Warren?"

I immediately frowned, as did Mr. Barnum and Mr. Stratton.
What was *he* doing there?

He was Commodore Nutt, or as he was better known, "the
Thirty Thousand Dollar Nutt," Mr. Barnum's discovery prior to
me. He was a little taller than me, thirty-six inches, from New
Hampshire; Mr. Barnum had hoped to present him as something
of a copy of General Tom Thumb. So he'd outfitted him, given him
a military title—so popular in those war days—and taught him to
sing and dance a little.

(I will remind the reader that Mr. Barnum had no need to
train me; I came to him with a full complement of talents.)

Commodore Nutt was younger than me by about seven years;
he was closer to Minnie's age. But he acted much older, putting
on airs, smoking endless cigars, consuming whiskey with an efficiency that was alarming. Upon being introduced to me, on my
very first day at the Museum, he pronounced me "the lovely and
popular Miss Warren." He had thus addressed me, ever since. It
was obvious he was enraptured by me, puffed up beyond his years
by an inflated sense of self-importance.

"Ah, the lovely and popular Miss Warren," he said now, as I
opened the door, stifling a sigh; he placed his hand upon his heart
and bowed deeply. I suppressed an urge to pat him on his head

and tell him to run off to play. He was such a *boy,* not unpleasant to look at, with shiny brown hair and eyes, a mischievous, almost elfin little smile. His voice was not as high-pitched as Charles Stratton's, yet I could not think of him as anything but a very nice lad—and one who was not earning nearly as much money as I was.

"Pray sit down, Mr. Nutt." I refused to call him by his military title; his real name was George Washington Morrison Nutt. I felt the tribute to the Father of our Country rather misplaced; there was nothing grand or imposing about this fellow. He capered about the stage like a child on leave from school; for some reason, the audiences enjoyed seeing him cut up so. I could not help but notice, moreover, that his audiences were not quite as big as mine—and he sold far fewer *cartes de visites.* "Of course, you know Mr. Barnum and Mr. Stratton."

"Whatever the lovely and popular Miss Warren desires," he replied, eyeing my other visitors disapprovingly. But then he flashed an expansive smile as he shook hands all around. "Mr. Barnum, as always. And Mr. Stratton, what a pleasure and honor. What brings you out of retirement, old fellow?"

Mr. Stratton did not appear to perceive the insult from the younger man; indeed, he grinned sunnily and exclaimed, "Miss Warren, of course!"

"Indeed!" Mr. Nutt's nostrils flared, and his chest puffed out like a bantam rooster's. "What a tragedy for you. For naturally she and I are in each other's company every day, while you are stuck at home in Connecticut."

"No, I'm not, for I'm to be in New York often, now that I'm in Business!" Mr. Stratton nodded eagerly.

"Oh, really. How fascinating. Ah, beauty, cruel, cruel beauty!" Mr. Nutt whirled and reached for my hand, raising it to his lips, kissing it. "You know not how many hearts you break!"

"Now, see here!" Charles Stratton rose, a faint, puzzled frown almost creasing his face. "I was here first, old chap."

"All's fair in love and war, as the poet says," Nutt retorted, with a grin.

"Ridiculous!" I yanked my hand away, then pointed to an empty chair. "You—sit over there. And you"—I gestured at Mr. Stratton—"just—sit. And you!" I whirled around and glared at Mr. Barnum.

He was watching the three of us pensively, as if we were performers upon a stage, a stage of his own design. His eyebrows drew together, his crooked mouth pursed, and I saw that piercing, all-seeing light in his eyes escape from behind its gray curtain.

If I hadn't known any better, I would have sworn I heard a cash register jingle in his brain. Actually, I did know better. And I knew that I had.

I was disgusted, I was insulted.

I was also, in spite of myself, intrigued.

INTERMISSION

From *The Scientific American,* April 4, 1863

Present Condition of the "Roanoake"

The iron-clad steam battery, *ROANOAKE,* is rapidly approaching completion and it is thought that steam will be applied by 1st of April. The turrets are nearly finished and the pilot-houses are completed. . . . Her armament will be one 15-inch gun and one rifled 200-pound Parrot gun in the forward turret; one 11-inch gun and one 15-inch gun in the midship turret, one 11-inch gun and one rifled 200-pound Parrot gun in the after tower.

From the *Brooklyn Daily Eagle,* May 23, 1863

Politics in Petticoats

The people of Brooklyn in turning out largely last evening to hear a young lady talk politics, and in very warmly applauding the incoherent nonsense which she uttered, gave a marked proof—not of their good sense—but of their chivalric feeling for the sex. Miss Dickinson labored for an hour last evening (the thermometer was at eighty-seven), to show a sweltering crowd the way in which Providence is teaching the nation.

Miss Dickinson came to an abrupt conclusion, and left her audience about as wise as she found it. As the ways of Providence are interpreted by Miss Dickinson, our salvation depends solely upon the darkey. She is not very clear on this or any other point, but as nearly as we can guess at it, this is what she means.

———•••••———

TEN

Two Rivals for One Hand

CHARLES STRATTON WAS BORN IN 1838 NEAR BRIDGEPORT, Connecticut, where Mr. Barnum had not yet made his home but soon would. It was there, in 1842 while visiting his brother, that Mr. Barnum heard of this remarkable child who was barely two feet tall, even though the lad was nearly four years old.

Phineas Taylor Barnum was still in the early stages of his career as a showman; he had already come to some fame by exhibiting Joice Heth and the Feejee mermaid. But he was looking for something even more remarkable, and the moment he discovered this tiny child, he realized he had found it.

Convincing the child's parents—whom I never did like, finding them coarse and vulgar and, worse, stupid—to entrust little Charlie into his care, Mr. Barnum began to teach him how to sing, to dance, and to do popular impressions of the day. ("Yankee Doodle" became his best known.) He clothed him in miniature uniforms, increased his age from five to eleven (in order to play up his diminutive form), and began to exhibit him, to mild acclaim, in the United States as Tom Thumb. However, he soon decided to take little Charlie overseas, where he was an instant sensation and received the best publicity possible by being asked to perform for Queen Victoria. It was the young Queen who gave Charles his title of "General," as well as a miniature blue carriage, matching miniature Shetland ponies, and the right to call himself a Royal favorite.

Mr. Barnum brought his Royal protégée back home, and from that point on General Tom Thumb, as he was now universally called, was a household name, the top performer at the Museum (until Miss Jenny Lind came along), and a true friend of Mr. Barnum's. He was also a miniature adult who had never been a little boy, and that was the part of him that always managed to touch me. The lost, sad part of Charlie, the part that caused him to say, so wistfully, whenever he saw a child absorbed in a toy, "Vinnie, I like to watch them play. You know I never had any childhood, any boy-life."

This poor soul had been taught to take wine at dinner when only five, to smoke at seven, to chew tobacco at nine. Little wonder, then, that by the age of twenty-five, when we met, he was already showing signs of an overly indulgent lifestyle; he was growing portly, short of breath, and was much too fond of wine.

Charles Stratton told me all this about himself, and more; he was soon escorting me out to the lobby after my levees in the Lecture Hall, where he waited patiently and proudly for me to sign my photographs. The public saw this, saw his attention to me, and soon there were whispers and rumors of a romance. Whispers and rumors that Mr. Barnum did not appear to mind in the least. In fact, I suspect he planted more than one anonymous letter to a diminutive Cupid in the newspapers himself.

Commodore Nutt also saw this; he grumbled and tried to

shoo Charles away, as if he were simply a pesky insect, and once the two even came to blows over who would escort me to my dressing room. Commodore Nutt continued to give me pathetic looks, spouting flowery paeans to Love. The public also became aware of this budding rivalry, and I didn't have to wonder who was responsible for informing them.

"I blame you for all this mess," I told Mr. Barnum curtly one evening after Nutt tried to read me a love poem, and Charles threatened to thrash him.

Mr. Barnum had offered to drive me back to my hotel himself, so for once neither of the two "rivals for the exquisitely manicured hand of the Queen of Lilliput," as a newspaper article had tittered, was present. I felt a great relief, as if I had suddenly been released from a stifling, airless room; it was such bliss to speak my mind freely, to sit without fear of being clutched at or mooned over or scrutinized for my every gesture, look, or sigh.

"What mess?"

"Between Nutt and Stratton. Although Nutt is the worst. That boy is so maddening with his looks and sighs."

"So you've made your mind up?"

"What do you mean?"

"Between the two. You've settled on Charles?"

"I've done no such thing!" I turned my head and, perched upon two velvet cushions as if I was an expensive bauble, gazed out the carriage window. We were rumbling over the cobblestones of Fifth Avenue, whose tall, imposing buildings were all dark and looming, while the round streetlights shone bright pools of light upon the clean sidewalks (relatively clean, that is, compared to the sidewalks in less desirable parts of town). The streets were quieter this time of night, but of course they were never completely free of carriages and wagons and carts; the rumbling of wheels upon cobblestones never ceased.

"Ah, Vinnie, what are you waiting for?" Mr. Barnum removed his spectacles and massaged the red indentation on the bridge of his nose; he looked weary, especially in the grainy shadows of the carriage. Weary and older, somehow; he was only in his early fifties, but he had lived more than one lifetime. Successes, bankruptcies, more successes: He had built palaces only to see them burnt to the ground. In the 1850s, he even temporarily lost ownership of his American Museum. It was then that Charles Stratton had volunteered to go out on tour again, bringing in enough money that Mr. Barnum was able to buy it back.

I often forgot this part of his life, this rocky, unsettled business of buying and selling and betting on the taste of the public. He put on such a good face, even to me. But sometimes he dropped that mask to reveal his uncertainty and weariness; those were the moments I most cherished.

I frowned; he did not look at all well. "Are you eating properly? Getting exercise?"

"Yes, m'dear, I am."

"I don't believe you. Is Charity taking care of you? How is she these days?" I still had not met his wife.

"She is as usual. You realize I have three daughters to fuss and fidget over me; I don't need a fourth, Vinnie." He said it kindly, but there was a hint of frost in his voice, in his gaze; it was a warning.

"I assure you, I have no desire to be thought of as one of your daughters," I replied with my own chilly attitude.

There was an uncomfortable pause, which he broke first; he always did. Mr. Barnum could not long stand silence.

"All right, then. Now, about your future—"

"What about it? You're not thinking of kicking me out of the Museum already, are you?"

"Heavens, no—the very idea! Tell me, Vinnie, how old are you? Twenty-one?" Now he sounded very much like a father, and

I did not like it. But I nodded, my cheeks burning, as any lady's would at the mention of her age.

"I know things seem as if they've just begun for you, and of course you want to enjoy them, but you cannot ignore the fact that you have two highly eligible suitors vying for your hand. It's cruel to allow them to go on in this way."

I shook my head, closed my eyes, and sank against the plush cushioned seat; how romantic, how sweet—how very *ordinary*—it sounded when put that way! How unlike my life, the life with which I was so acquainted, the life that Mama had wept over, late at night, as I lay sleeping with my sister.

"They are simply two ridiculous, spoiled boys playing a game, and I happen to be the prize. Yet no one has asked what I want." I opened my eyes, considering Mr. Barnum. He was my confidante, my mentor; he was the person I thought of when I went to bed, and the person I looked forward to seeing when I opened my eyes, eager to begin the day. How quickly he had assumed that place in my life!

"What do you want, Vinnie?" He smiled down at me; in the carriage, we could not sit knee to knee.

"I—I want—" What did I want? Oh, so many things; what *didn't* I want? What didn't I desire? It was because I wanted that I had left home in the first place, shunning the simple life my family so happily led.

Yet there was one thing—one simple, *ordinary* thing—that I did desire; I hadn't known it until recently.

I wanted, to my great astonishment, to be loved. I wanted to be cared for, desired, not desiring; I wanted to be cherished not for my size, not for anything other than for my heart, my mind— just like any woman.

But I wanted these things not from any man; I wanted them from a great man, a man worthy of me. And this was the one thing

I knew that I could never have—a great love. I must settle for something else—*someone* less, in every way. I must settle for a love in miniature. I did not quite know how to do that—settle; it was not a lesson I had ever bothered to learn.

"You've orchestrated this whole thing!" I burst out, tears suddenly in my eyes, my anger at what I could not have lashing out at the one thing I wanted. "*You* brought Charles Stratton to New York, filling his head with that business nonsense! *You* egged on poor Nutt. You've thrown me in the company of these two time and again, encouraged them both, planted items in the paper— oh, don't try to pretend that you haven't! And you've played with us, as if we were your own personal set of marionettes. You know," I said, struggling to sort through my various emotions, all jumbled up like a ball of twine, "I was once nearly sold to a man. In New Orleans. Colonel Wood was offered five hundred dollars to give me to him. So he could do whatever he pleased with me. *Whatever!* It did not matter to him; *I* did not matter! Only the money that he could receive for it mattered to him."

"Vinnie, that's—that's—"

But I would not listen to his protests. "That's what? Appalling? Immoral? Illegal? Yet what you are proposing isn't that very far off, is it? *Is it?*" I wrapped my arms about my shoulders, rocking myself, suddenly desperate for an answer, and not just any answer. The *correct* answer. I needed to know he was not like Colonel Wood, after all.

"Vinnie, excuse me for speaking plainly, but I sometimes forget that you have a heart. Now, don't take offense!" Mr. Barnum raised his hand, anticipating my horrified protest. "I mean that as a compliment. Your mind is so sharp, you're so terrifyingly intelligent and driven—well, you're a lot like me, I like to think, which is why we get along so well. So please accept my apology, for I have no wish to cause you distress or pain; I'm not like that cousin of yours, who ought to be taken out and shot for the scoundrel that he is. We'll not discuss the matter further. I truly believed you were enjoying the situation, the attention."

Sniffing—trying to dab the cursed tears from my eyes, for, perversely, I had an intense desire for him *not* to see me as just another woman—I turned and stared out the window. He did the same thing, and we rode along in silence for a few minutes.

"I've seen it, too, you know," I said at last, my voice thick with swallowed tears—and pride.

"Seen what?"

"I've seen the way people look at me when I'm with those two. I've seen the glances, heard the whispers, the ridiculous romantic sighs. Individually, we will all do well. But matched up, there is the possibility of something beyond what any of us have ever imagined. I'm not wrong, am I?" Finally I turned to face him, once again feeling composed, rational—*just like him.*

Mr. Barnum regarded me levelly. "No, Vinnie, you are not wrong. I'm very glad you understand this. I don't believe either of the other two does, however, and that's not a bad thing. They are both truly smitten with you; please don't forget that—please don't forget that you have a great deal of feminine charm. I may be good at selling, but I have yet to find a way to sell the heart on something it truly doesn't want. I wish to goodness I had," he grumbled, a sudden sadness in his voice. And I knew he was thinking of someone else; I knew, too, whom that someone was. I'd only ever seen him look so appealingly sad at one other person—

Jenny Lind, whose portrait he kept in his library, whose photograph he kept on his desk at the Museum. I turned away, sickened by my insight; oh, what good was a brain like mine if it didn't allow me to have any illusions? For I knew he would never, ever look at me in this way. Yet—

Charles Stratton did.

"Charles and Nutt are smitten with me because neither has ever seen an attractive woman his own size before," I muttered sourly.

"Again, Vinnie, don't disparage yourself. Could it possibly be that they both simply enjoy being with you—as do I?" Mr. Barnum smiled at me, but there was no trace of longing or regret in it, and I decided, right then, never to look for that trace again. I was a busy woman; I had no time to keep looking for something I would never find.

"Very few people marry whom they truly want, do they?" I looked at him levelly. He did not contradict me.

Instead, he asked, "And so you do wish to marry?"

"I can see the benefits of a marriage like this, for a life such as I have chosen. It is a difficult life for a woman alone, even under your management." I thought of how it had felt to have someone beside me as I signed my photographs and met notable strangers; I had felt a measure of safety that I had never experienced before. Also a measure of respectability: I would never again have to fear the likes of the anonymous man in New Orleans, if I were a married woman. "I think I could make it work," I continued boldly, but couldn't bring myself to look at him. "We all have to settle for something—less, eventually. Don't we?"

There was a silence. A long, ponderous silence that told me all I needed to hear.

"So." I cleared my throat and nodded decisively. "We compensate with other things. I will expect the biggest wedding New York has ever seen. And I choose Charles Stratton, for your information. Nutt is a posturing little boy, but that is all."

Mr. Barnum had laughed when I mentioned my ambitions for the wedding, but he turned very serious when he heard my choice. "Vinnie, I feel I must ask if you are at least fond of him. For

Charlie is my friend. I'll not have you hurting him by being cruel or indifferent."

"Have you asked him the same thing about me?"

"No. But Charlie isn't like us; he's all heart, and he needs genuine affection. As smitten as he is with you, I give you my word— I'll not condone this thing if I think, for one moment, that you'll be cruel to him." Mr. Barnum spoke so quietly, so plainly, that I was startled; I hadn't realized how devoted he was to Charles. It touched me; it touched my heart, which was in danger of icing over, so much was I determined to neglect it for other, more practical matters.

"I needed to hear that," I admitted, returning the compliment of honesty. "I needed to be reminded of that. You have my word, I'll be kindness itself. I cannot promise to love him. But I can promise to care for him. I do have that capacity, although I'm not entirely sure you believe me."

"Vinnie, Vinnie, my dear girl. I believe anything you tell me; I believe in *you*. More than I can adequately express."

We smiled at each other, and then he leaned forward and for a moment—oh, such a brief, precious moment—he placed his hand upon my face, gentle as a sigh. It was the first time he had touched me like this; indeed, it was the first time any man had touched me so reverently, tenderly. I shut my eyes, hoping to memorize his touch; I knew it would have to last me a long time. A lifetime.

Then I looked up at him with a bright, capable smile upon my face; continuing to discuss the matter, we both swore we would never repeat our conversation to anyone. We both knew the value of romance as a marketing tool; we also knew we did not want to hurt Charles.

Should you care to read further about the details of my

engagement to Charles Stratton, or General Tom Thumb, Mr. Barnum's autobiography provides a very interesting, entertaining account. It was the story that the world—and Charles himself—came to believe. It was the story that both Mr. Barnum and I told him, individually and together, through our actions and our words; you would be hard-pressed to find better actors than Phineas Taylor Barnum and Lavinia Warren, working together.

It was a story of a bashful maiden reluctant, at first, to all overtures on the part of the dashing, beloved hero, a story of a benevolent friend who slyly arranged to help the hero overcome all obstacles and win the fair maiden's hand.

It was a romantic story, a true fairy tale; Charles always did enjoy those. He never lost his little boy's eagerness for happily-ever-after endings. Neither did Presidents, Queens, newspaper magnates, shopgirls, Vanderbilts, and Astors.

Neither did a world sickened and weary of war, we were all soon to discover.

INTERMISSION

—◆◆◆—

An advertisement in *The New York Times,* January 18, 1863—

BARNUM'S AMERICAN MUSEUM—

Now or Never! The wedding is positively fixed for TUESDAY, Feb. 10th, on which the world-renowned Chas. S. Stratton, known as TOM THUMB, will be married to little MISS LAVINIA WARREN THE QUEEN OF BEAUTY, who has been visited and admired by over TWO HUNDRED THOUSAND PEOPLE, every one of whom pronounced her THE MOST BEAUTIFUL MODEL OF A WOMAN . . . see her NOW OR NEVER as her engagement ends with her NUPTIAL CEREMONY . . .

━━◆◆◆◆━━

ELEVEN

In Which Our Heroine Finds True Love at Last

MY DEAR FRIEND DID NOT HESITATE A MOMENT BEFORE capitalizing on our engagement; as soon as Charles placed the ring upon my finger, the unbelieving grin upon his face thawing my increasingly icy heart a fraction, he was appearing with me at the Museum. Between my levees, we both appeared in the Great Hall, selling our individual *cartes de visites*—and reminding everyone that, soon, there would be photographs of us together to purchase. The crowds were endless, the excitement palpable; never had I experienced anything like it. Policemen had to be called in to keep the crowds at bay as we entered the hall, and to keep the lines for our photographs orderly.

There were moments when I paused and looked around, trying to absorb the scene, the frenzy, trying to make sense of it all. How was it that just a month ago, I was excitedly preparing for my little reception at the St. Nicholas Hotel?

Now everywhere I looked I saw faces, happy shining faces, smiling down at me, calling my name; even in my dreams I saw outstretched hands, all wanting to shake mine, clamoring for my signature, clutching my photograph. The noise, the chatter, was incessant, and at night, when I was blessedly alone in my hotel room, my ears still rang from it. My neck ached alarmingly, as there were simply so many more people to *see*. It was as if Charles and I were one pebble, tossed into a pond, staring up in astonishment at the ever-widening ripples caused by our presence.

I had always looked up, of course; that was my natural position, just as a flamingo stands on one leg or an otter swims on its back. But for the first time, I was so acutely aware of the strain it put on me—my muscles always knotted, both at the base of my skull and where my neck met my shoulders. And my hand, my tiny, delicate hand! I thought it had ached before! Now, so crushed it felt at the end of the day, I finally decided to carry a nosegay, so that my hands might be occupied and thus not available for shaking.

And through it all, through this outpouring of joy and heartfelt wishes for our future—even then, I knew that our union had struck a chord in a nation heartsick of casualty lists—a stranger was by my side. A man who tucked his arm in mine to escort me wherever we went; a man who sat beside me while we signed photos, our elbows often bumping, my skirts often draped over his knee; a man who, in the rare moments we were alone, sighed and whispered my name, brushed his lips against my cheek, held me in a clumsy embrace. Very tentatively, as if he were seeking permission, which he was.

And it was up to me to bestow it; it was up to me to put him at ease, to blushingly return his shy affection, his timid glances. I had to pretend to be thrilled by his trembling, fumbling caresses, so thrilled that I might desire to return them myself, one day. One far-off day, a day I could not yet bring myself to imagine. And because I could not, I concentrated solely on the now; telling myself that at least we had this astonishing experience to bond us together, and hoping that perhaps it would be enough of a foundation to build a believable marriage. Believable to him, to my family, to my public.

For myself, I did not hold out such hope.

Marriage. I truly could not comprehend it. Right now, it was just the curtain that would soon fall upon a very elaborate, precisely plotted play. What happened after the principals retired backstage, I simply could not imagine.

I don't believe Charles could, either, and this somehow gave me courage. He was such a creature of the public; he had grown up knowing no other life. I suspected he viewed everything as a performance, even the act of brushing his teeth or combing his hair. So that his idea of marriage was no more real than mine; we had that, at least, to unite us.

And so I continued my part in this elaborate play and, little by little, day by day, I began to enjoy myself; perhaps, like Charles, I even began to believe it was real. I started each morning hungrily scouring the newspapers for articles and illustrations about us, and I was never disappointed. The Civil War was still raging, but you would not know it by looking at the front pages of the New York newspapers; body counts and war maneuvers were displaced by articles about my upcoming nuptials. When I went to Madame Demorest to be fitted for my wedding gown, I was accompanied by two lady reporters who enthusiastically described my bridal finery. (Oh, it was beautiful; an exquisite concoction of white satin and lace with a flowing train, decorated with pearls and beads!) I also modestly released such details of the rest of my trousseau as Mr. Barnum felt necessary, as well as illustrations of my jewels. Mr. Barnum took care of releasing the details of everything else.

He, of course, oversaw the entire operation; it was his gift to us—and to himself.

"Vinnie, Charlie, now, who are you going to have as your wedding party?" Mr. Barnum asked us one evening, after the Museum had closed. We were in his office, both of us exhausted; Charles was too tired even to hold my hand, as he did, much like Minnie, whenever he was near me. In fact, I was beginning to think of him in much the same way as I did my beloved sister: someone just a little more delicate, just a little more innocent, than I was. Someone in need of my constant protection, perhaps more in need of protection than he was of my love.

Maybe it was because I was thinking of her that her name popped out of my mouth. "Minnie," I said, stifling a yawn. Then I realized what I had said and sat up straight.

"Minnie?" Mr. Barnum looked confused. "Who's Minnie?"

"Why, she's Vinnie's sister!" Charles piped up, even though I shook my head, warningly, at him. But he did not pay any attention. "And say, Phineas, she's just like us! Smaller than Vinnie, even. I met her when I asked Vinnie's parents for her hand. I'm awfully glad to have a sister I don't have to look up to."

"You have a sister?" Mr. Barnum looked at me; there was surprise and hurt, both, in his eyes. "You never mentioned that to me before."

"I never—I just didn't think it necessary, as Minnie's so shy. She's content to stay at home with Papa and Mama."

"What other secrets do you keep from me, Vinnie? I have to say, I'm quite hurt!"

I could not decide if he was joking or not; he had a teasing, crooked grin upon his face, but his eyes glittered, hard.

"None. It's not exactly as if Minnie is a secret, of course, it's just—"

"That you never felt like telling me, your friend, about her?"

"No, it's not that—you don't understand." I shook my head and attempted to undo the damage. "Actually, to get back to the subject, I think Pauline would make a wonderful bridesmaid, and I'd be honored if she would accept."

"And of course you'll be my best man, Phineas." Charles rubbed his eyes sleepily.

"I am much honored," Mr. Barnum replied seriously, patting Charles on the shoulder. "But I can just imagine what the newspapers would say to that—accusing me of hogging the spotlight or some such nonsense. No, I think it would be better if you found someone else. What about Nutt?"

"Old Nutt? Well, he's a jolly old fellow, but he's mad at me, you know. I guess he's still mad about Vinnie."

"I think that he might appreciate it if you ask him, Charles. I wouldn't be surprised if he'd put aside his wounded pride out of happiness for the two of you."

"Well, if you think it's best, Phineas—"

"I do, old fellow. Now, Vinnie, obviously you want your sister to stand up with you—why pretend otherwise?" Mr. Barnum turned to me, again with that hard glitter in his eyes; I could hear the gears in his brain turning now, as well, as he chewed his lip, drummed a pencil against his desk. "I have an idea. Listen to me. We haven't discussed what you'll do after your honeymoon tour—by the way, the Lincolns have definitely invited you two to a reception at the Executive Mansion, and that's a bit of publicity beyond anything I could dream up, bless their Republican souls—but now I'm coming up with a plan. Imagine this: a quartet of the most wonderful, intelligent, and perfectly formed ladies and gentlemen the world ever produced, presented for the first time ever before the public. You two, Nutt, and now—Miss Minnie Warren. What do you think of that?"

"No." I shook my head so vigorously that some of my hair

escaped its pins, falling down and tickling my nose. "No. Not Minnie. She is not cut out for this life, and I've promised that I will keep her safe. And safe, for her, is back home, on the farm, where she belongs."

"Vinnie, Vinnie, what's the danger in the life that you are living now? Surely you don't feel as if you're physically at risk in my beautiful Museum?"

"Of course not." I waved my hand impatiently; Mr. Barnum was being deliberately obtuse, and both he and I knew it. Charles, however, did not.

"Why, Phineas is right, you know, Vinnie. Look at how long I've been with him—the worst thing that ever happened to me was when Queen Victoria's dog almost bit me, remember, Phineas? We were at the palace, you know, and I had my little toy sword that I used onstage, and when that dog came yapping toward me, I waved my sword at it—how everyone laughed! Remember, Phineas?" Charles's eyes gleamed bright, as they always did when he was relating stories of his past successes. I tried to smile patiently; he had told me this story many times before.

"Charles." I placed a gentle hand upon his arm, something I knew soothed and pleased him. "You hardly know my sister. Minnie is the sweetest soul in the world, but simple. Trusting. The type of timid soul who can be wounded by so many things, not just physical ones but a glance, a word, an idea, even."

"No, you're the sweetest soul in the world," my erstwhile lover argued, right on cue. I turned back to Mr. Barnum with a sigh.

"I still say Pauline will be perfect. She was such a help to me when I first came to New York, and she is exquisite—think of how lovely she'll look, how the Press will remark upon the beauty of Mr. Barnum's daughter, such a compliment to you!"

"You can't fool a fooler, Vinnie." Mr. Barnum laughed. "It

won't work. I don't want Pauline, and that's that. I am her father, after all; I can forbid it."

"Is this my wedding or yours?" I retorted.

"That's a fair enough question, isn't it? Which, do you think?" He sounded amused.

"Don't you mean our wedding, Vinnie? Not just yours? It is *our* wedding, isn't it?" Charles looked at me so anxiously that Mr. Barnum and I both colored with shame.

"Yes, absolutely, dear, it's our wedding. Not Mr. Barnum's."

"Absolutely, old chap—I'm throwing you and your lovely bride the biggest shindig this city has ever seen, and actually I wanted to suggest something. We've been bringing in a lot of money, the three of us together, in all of this. We could easily keep it up for at least a month. Why not rethink the date, and I'll throw in fifteen thousand dollars as a nest egg?"

I had to laugh; the man was impossible! Like a child, really. A child obsessed with one toy and one toy alone, who always steered the conversation back around to that one thing, who took it to bed with him at night. Then I had to laugh again; I had an image of Mr. Barnum sleeping with the day's receipts tucked under his pillow. I would not be surprised!

But Charles did not laugh. He puffed out his chest, as he did whenever he felt the need to assert his manliness, and declared, "No! Not for fifty thousand dollars would I wait one more minute to marry Vinnie!"

"Not for one hundred thousand dollars!" I chimed in, just to see the look on Mr. Barnum's face. And I was not disappointed; his mouth dropped open so that his ever-present cigar fell to his lap, burning a hole in his trousers. Cursing mildly, he jumped up and brushed the ash off, hopping about in a very undignified manner.

"Well, if that isn't all—look at the monsters I've created, the heartless creatures! Putting the old man in the poorhouse, all in the name of love!"

"Oh, Phineas, no—I'm not heartless! I would never put you in the poorhouse!" Just as suddenly, Charles's manliness faded away; he was an anxious, repentant child once more.

"Charles, he's exaggerating, as usual." I patted his plump, warm hand. "Just wait—he'll extract something else equally dear, in exchange for the money."

"Commodore Nutt will be bitterly disappointed if he's not your best man." Mr. Barnum turned to Charles, beseechingly. And my heart began to sink.

"Oh, I couldn't do that to him," my tenderhearted fiancé said. "Very well. I'll ask the old chap to stand up for me."

"I think that's best, to keep peace, and help the poor soul get over his disappointment." Mr. Barnum turned to me with a coaxing smile, that barely suppressed glimmer in his eyes. "Come, Vinnie, think of it. The wedding party now consists of you three absolutely perfect, charming people—who do you think best completes such a tableau?"

"Oh, Vinnie, do ask your sister, do!" Charles turned to me as well, grasping my hand. "For your sister naturally will be dear to me as any of my own, and this would be the perfect way for us all to begin. And how convenient, as well—think of the photographs of the bridal party! Why, none of us would have to be seated or standing on a step; we'd all be the same. I've never before had my photograph taken with people all of my same size—imagine!"

Charles looked so eager, so happy; Mr. Barnum did, as well, although his eagerness was more likely caused by the dollar signs he saw at the mention of photographs.

I didn't know what to do. It wasn't just the wedding; it was what would happen after. *That* was what I feared.

"Just the wedding," I decided. "That's all. After that, Minnie goes back home."

"Of course," Mr. Barnum agreed with that admiring, approving look that blinded me so that I did not always see what else was behind it. "Just as you wish, Vinnie. You know I promised your parents I would never do a thing without your approval first."

"I know," I said reluctantly, ruefully. "And that's exactly what I'm afraid of."

"SISTER! SISTER! WE TOOK THE TRAIN AND IT WASN'T DREADFUL at all, although Papa looked awfully sick and kept his eyes closed the whole time even though I know he wasn't sleeping. And then I was hungry but Mama said we'd eat at the next stop but there wasn't any food there, only some dreadful boy selling black bananas. Mama says New York smells awful, doesn't it? And then we saw buildings that almost blocked out the sun, and I ate a piece of ice that was flavored like cherry, in a paper cup, and then we rode in the most beautiful carriage and Mr. Barnum kissed my hand, just like I was a lady, just like I was you! Oh, Sister, I'm *so* glad to see you!" And Minnie finally paused for breath only to fling her arms about me, nearly knocking me over; she squeezed so tightly I thought she might crack one of my stays. I held her close for a moment, laying my cheek against her tangled, glossy black curls, which Mama had tried to put up in a ladylike sweep. But it hadn't survived the trip; those curls had a mind of their own, and obviously they had decided the occasion was much too exciting to remain in so sedate a style.

"Minnie, Pumpkin, let me look at you!" I held her at arm's length, hungrily taking her in as if it had been years since I'd seen her, not just weeks. Even when I came home from the river, I hadn't been this happy to greet her; I think I'd been so numbed from the whole experience. But I wasn't numb now! Something new, something wonderful, seemed to happen every day, and I wanted to share each and every experience with my family.

Minnie smiled, that dimple, that impish sparkle in her eyes, warming my heart. She was wearing the new dress I had sent to her, in the newest fashion—hoops so wide they swayed like the Liberty Bell, tiny waist, brown velvet panels alternating with gold satin. She wore a fur-tipped cloak and gloves and a fur hat (also gifts from me); she looked adorably ladylike.

Mama, too, looked very fine, in a similar dress and cloak, carrying a muff. I had never seen her dressed so handsomely, and it suited her to a remarkable degree. No longer in her comforting apron and homespun dress, she looked every inch a Warren of Massachusetts. Papa, so bashful and cowed, his shoulders pinched, his head bent, did not look so nice in his new suit and coat. A farmer's clothes were all he would ever be comfortable in.

But I didn't mind; I was just happy that they had arrived for my wedding. Mr. Barnum had arranged for a nice suite in the Metropolitan Hotel, on the same floor as mine, where I was newly ensconced in preparation for the festivities. I hooked my arm through Minnie's and led them all down the plush carpeted hall, the ornate wallpaper illuminated by softly flickering gaslights.

"Now, Minnie, once you get settled we'll need to rush right over to the dressmaker's for a fitting. You, too, Mama; I picked out the loveliest gray watered silk for your gown. Now, Mama, you have to remember you're in a hotel. Everything is done for you—you don't have to lift a finger! You don't have to make your own bed or even scrub out the chamber pot; someone will come every morning and do that for you. Mrs. Astor has asked, expressly, to meet you, so she would like very much to throw a reception for us on Monday before the wedding. I still have to do a few levees at the Museum, and I can't wait for Minnie to see the sights! Mr. Barnum has arranged it so that you all can have a private hour or so seeing everything on Saturday. Oh, and Minnie, we're going to have our photograph taken! Can you imagine?"

"My photograph? I don't know—will it hurt very much?"

"No, darling, it doesn't hurt a bit. Mr. Brady is the nicest man, and while it's rather tedious and you have to stand absolutely still, it's over very quickly. Can you do that?"

"Of course, if you're there with me, Vinnie."

"I will be, I promise. I won't let you out of my sight. Here we are!" And I motioned for the porter, who had been following respectfully behind with the luggage, to open the door to their suite. I ran ahead so that I could see their faces as they took it all in; I was so happy, so thrilled, to show them this side of life. Oh, how they deserved the finer things!

"Oh, Vinnie," Mama breathed as she fingered the fine velvet portieres, draped ceiling to floor, covering the windows. "How on earth do they clean them? You can't wash velvet!"

"I don't know, Mama." I laughed, for it had never before occurred to me to wonder. "I'll have to ask someone."

"Vinnie, they don't leave these lights on all the time, do they?" Papa, who had been studying one of the hissing gaslights jutting out from the wall, turned to me with a frown. "Think of the expense! How much do they get for a room like this, anyway? I'm not sure I like that Barnum fellow paying my way, after all. I'd like to give him something for all this—do you think he needs a milk cow for his place in Connecticut?"

"I doubt it, Papa. But I'll ask, just for you."

"Well, I'd appreciate it." And my father went back to studying the gaslight, passing his hand over the top of the globe, checking to see how hot it was.

"Oh, Vinnie, look!" Minnie came running out of her bedroom clutching the beautiful gift that I had placed on her bed. It was a

Jumeau doll, from France, an exquisite creature with a china face, real black curls, and the most sumptuous dress of blue silk, with lace petticoats and pantalets, and even satin slippers. I had chosen it because I thought it looked like Minnie, with those curls; as my sister cradled the doll in her arm reverently, smoothing her ringlets, I was satisfied that I had been right.

"Do you like it, Pumpkin?"

"Oh, more than anything I've ever seen! Even more than my new kitten back home. Thank you so much, Vinnie!"

And the light in my sister's eyes as she sat carefully upon a small stool, cradling the new doll as if it were her own child, made me smile; it made my heart warm and expand so that I felt, in that moment, as full of love as any bride. For it was Charles who had bought the doll for Minnie; he had taken me shopping for it, insisting that he wanted to make her a present, and quite gravely asking my advice on the matter.

"Thank Charles, your new brother. He was the one who bought it. You can thank him tonight, at dinner. We're dining with Mr. Barnum at Delmonico's on East Fourteenth Street—ladies can only dine there in a private room—and oh, just wait until you all see it!" I was Father Christmas at that moment, showering my family with unknown delights. "It's all crystal and marble and the finest silver and china, and waiters who whisk away your plate as soon as you're finished and give you another, full of something else delicious! It's like nothing you've ever seen before—so many dishes! And the wedding reception will be just as grand, I assure you!"

Mama and Papa exchanged an odd glance. Then Mama turned to me, her gentle eyes filling with tears, and she said, "Vinnie, dear, we need to discuss something with you."

"What? What is it—are the boys all right? Benjamin? Nothing happened to them, did it?" Oh, how stupid of me—it was so easy to forget about the War, with all that was happening to me, especially here in New York. Despite it being the most prominent northern town, a great many citizens were very sympathetic to the Confederacy. So much of the commerce and manufacturing had depended upon the cotton from the South, and with the blockades, business was slowing down. And there were so many immigrants; were the slaves truly to be freed, the immigrants were fearful that their jobs would be taken away. And then, of course, there were rumors of an impending military draft, which did not sit well with the Copperheads, the name by which the Rebel sympathizers called themselves.

All that was but a faint, nagging buzzing, like an insect circling about my head, easily swatted away by the more immediate, personal demands upon my time and attention these days. But Mama and Papa, of course, did not have such pleasant distraction; they lived every day in fear for their soldier sons.

"The boys are all right, aren't they?" I repeated, anxiously, when they did not reply.

"Yes, dear, as far as we know, they're fine." Mama tried to reassure me, but the lines around her mouth deepened, as if from the effort of holding in her constant worry.

"Then what is it? Why do you look so strangely at me? Papa?" I turned to my father. He could not meet my gaze; he sidled back to the gaslight, to further inspect its construction.

"Vinnie, dear, it's just that—it's just that we don't feel entirely comfortable with all—this." Mama gestured around at the ornate room. But her suddenly furtive eyes betrayed her; I knew instantly that their accommodations were not what she was talking about.

"What do you mean, 'all this'?"

"I mean, dear, that Papa and I have decided not to stay for the wedding. We came up to bring Minnie, and entrust her to your care. But we have tickets for the train home tomorrow."

"Oh." I decided to examine the portiere nearest me; I pulled it to the side and, standing on tiptoe, surveyed the street below, concentrating on the smallest details—the way the Negro man in front of the hotel doorway stood with his heels pressed together, his feet splayed out in a *V,* like duck feet. I observed how a basket of some kind of fruit—apples, they must be—fell off a wagon as it rounded a corner, and was immediately set upon by a pack of feral children who appeared as if conjured up, for they had not been visible a moment ago. I studied how the filth that gathered between the cobblestones was covered in a filmy sheet of gray ice, and how this dressed it up, made it appear not as it was—a sludge of horse manure, sewage, rotting produce, and who knew what else—but rather like the icing on top of a cinnamon bun.

"You do understand, don't you, Vinnie?" My mother's voice was very gentle, as if she was afraid it might break.

"No," I said, baldly. "I'm afraid I don't."

"It's just that—it's not that we don't believe we won't grow to like Charles, and look at him as our own. It's not that we don't truly believe you know what is best for you, for you always have, and you've never let us down. But this is all so grand—my heavens, Astors and Vanderbilts, you say!—and we're so simple. We're not comfortable with all this, not the way you are, and, well—"

"It's not as if this is just a *performance,* Mama." Finally I turned away from the window, anger doing its best to smother the hurt. "It's not as if Mr. Barnum is selling tickets to my *wedding.*" (I did not reveal that at one point, I was afraid that he was—and had to ask him, flat out, not to. He claimed that it never crossed his mind, but I was not so sure.) "We're getting married in a church, you know, Grace Church, and Reverend Putnam from home is even going to assist. *Mrs.* Putnam will be there, for heaven's sake!" I shuddered, remembering how rude that woman had been to me back home. Now she was swanning about Manhattan, telling all who would listen that she was "the wife of the minister who will be uniting those adorable little sweethearts in Holy Matrimony."

"I know, dearest, and we don't want to hurt you. That's the last thing we want to do."

"But you have, you have, and I don't know *why!*"

To my horror, I began to cry, and Minnie, alarmed, placed her doll carefully down on a chair and ran over to me to pat my hand; she soon had tears running down her own rosy cheeks, although she had no idea why I was crying.

"Vinnie." Papa was suddenly kneeling next to me, carefully pulling up his new trousers so as not to tear them. "Blame this all on me. I'm the one who's a country fool, not your mother. I'm the one who asked to go right back home. Don't blame her— blame me."

"Oh, Papa!" I looked into his sweet, simple brown eyes, those eyes that had never understood me, never known what to do with me—but had never gazed upon me with anything other than pure, unselfish love. And I knew that he was not telling the truth. I knew that it was my mother who had made this decision. A lifetime of worrying about me, about all her children, had made its mark upon her so that now her handsome face was falling, as if under the weight of it all—me, Minnie, my brothers off fighting in a war. She was dear, she was sweet—but she was also far more knowledgeable about the world than Papa was. She had never trusted Mr. Barnum, and now some of that distrust was throwing its shadow across me as well. I did not know what I had to do to win back her trust, and at that moment, frankly, I did not much care to learn. I was simply stunned, my heart pierced by the sting of her rejection.

"It's all right, Papa," I said, stroking his large, weathered hand; my small white one looking like a delicate glove against it. "I understand. I don't want you to be uncomfortable."

"Good," Mama said, clearly relieved that I appeared to believe him. "Now, Vinnie, after the honeymoon I want you and your Charles to come home for a nice long visit. I mean it. Delia and I are planning for it; you're going to get the boys' room, we'll spruce it up, we're already sewing some new curtains, and I'm going to have a lovely at-home to introduce you all to our neighbors. I'm sure that you have plans with Mr. Barnum, but he'll allow you that time with your family, won't he?" Mama looked anxious; I knew she was apologizing in the most meaningful way she knew how— by diving into a cooking and cleaning extravaganza. I had seen her attack a floor with a brush and a bucket of soap as if she were scrubbing the deviltry from Lucifer himself; I suspected she needed to scrub away some of her own demons right now.

"Of course, Mama." I wiped away my tears and smiled at her. "I can't wait. And I'm sure Charles will be pleased as well."

"I'm so glad." Mama nodded, reassuring us both. "Now, you'll take good care of Minnie, won't you? You know we'd never think of leaving her with anyone but you. You're the only one we trust— and you're the only one she trusts, as well!" Mama smoothed Minnie's curls and planted a kiss atop her head.

"Of course! I won't let her out of my sight for a moment! I have so much planned for the two of us, Charles will get very jealous, indeed!" I seized upon this request, fell upon it as a soldier might fall upon his own sword. This was how I could recapture Mama's trust: by caring for Minnie as if she was my daughter, too. Nothing bad would come to her, no harm, no disappointment, no pain or sorrow. Not as long as she was with me.

"And I'll take care of you, too, Vinnie," Minnie assured me solemnly. "So Mama won't have to worry at all!"

"We'll take care of each other," I agreed. "I'll begin by moving you into my suite right away. You can't stay down here by yourself." I rose, happy to begin my rehabilitation. "Come, Pumpkin, and help me! Be careful with your doll—she's made of china, not wax!"

"Vinnie, for goodness' sake! You forget how old I am now! I know how to carry a doll!" Minnie's little nose stuck up in the air as she sighed with disdain; I shared a smile with Mama and Papa. I could do this; I could keep my sister safe and innocent. I could preserve her childlike ways.

If only it had been that easy! For the one thing that I did not realize—and I don't believe my parents did, either—was that my sister was really no longer a child. She was a young woman, despite the fact that none of us was willing to see it. And young women have passions and yearnings that even the most vigilant sister cannot always anticipate or even acknowledge.

Particularly when she hasn't yet experienced them herself.

AND SO WE WERE MARRIED. THERE HAVE BEEN SO MANY ACCOUNTS of that day; I'll simply enclose the following report, which was printed in the Manitou, Wisconsin, *Daily Bugle*.

LILIPUTIAN WEDDING, A FAIRY'S DREAM

This Tuesday last, a ceremony like no other took place in Grace Church in New York City. It was there that that miniature gentleman, Charles Stratton or as he is more popularly known, GENERAL TOM THUMB, at last married his dainty bride-in-miniature, Lavinia Warren.

The bride wore an exquisite gown of white satin and lace, and her hair was arranged à la Empress Eugenie, with a bridal veil held in place by a coronet of orange blossoms. Her little white kid gloves measured from wrist to tip of the finger only four and one-half inches! The bridal bouquet consisted of roses and japonicas, and the jewels adorning the lovely bride were a gift from her dashing little groom, all of dazzling diamonds.

The bride and groom were attended by Commodore Nutt, whose broken heart was much evident, as he had competed for, and lost, the lily-white hand of the tiny Queen of Beauty. However, he was much consoled by the fact that, upon his arm was the tiny bridesmaid, Minnie Warren, younger sister of the bride and even more petite.

The four tiny principals took their places before the chancel, and the ceremony began. The responses of the bride and groom were given in clear, distinct tones, easily heard throughout the packed church where the likes of Vanderbilts, Astors, Generals, Governors and Ambassadors all sat in rapt attention, honored to have been invited to so solemn and heartfelt a ceremony.

After the ceremony, the fairy-like wedding party then entered their tiny carriages and were driven through cheering crowds to the Metropolitan Hotel, where a reception was held for ten thousand guests! The petite party had to be lifted upon a grand piano, from where they greeted their guests, to avoid being crushed by their loyal subjects, all eager to bestow their blessings upon their little King and Queen of Cupid's Arrow.

The hundreds of wedding gifts were displayed, only a few of which will be mentioned, as there is not enough newsprint to list them all:

A MINIATURE SILVER HORSE AND CHARIOT, EYES OF THE HORSE MADE OF GARNETS, THE CHARIOT DECORATED WITH RUBIES, GIVEN BY TIFFANY & COMPANY

A Chinese Firescreen of Gold, Silver, and Pearl, A
Gift of Mrs. Abraham Lincoln

A Set of Gold Charms, All of the Tiniest Size, To Be
Worn by the Bride, a Gift of August Belmont

A Set of Perfectly Matched Pearls, Given by Mrs.
Cornelius Vanderbilt

A Quaint Gift of Embroidered Slippers, Personally
Worked and Given by Mr. Edwin Booth

A Cunning Bird Automaton, Bejeweled and Covered
in Real Feathers, Given by Mr. P. T. Barnum

After the reception, the tiny pair retired to the Honeymoon suite; they were serenaded by the New York Excelsior Band, which prompted the newly minted bridal couple to appear on the balcony where the General addressed the crowd, beginning with the words, "I will make this speech, like myself, short."

The General and his new wife will leave on a bridal tour which will commence in Philadelphia, ending up in Washington where the President and Mrs. Lincoln will give a reception in their honor.

This account is accurate for what it relates. It is also glaring for what it does not.

It makes no mention, for example, of how slowly, almost reluctantly, I walked down the aisle toward my groom, who was very handsome and dignified in full black dress suit. Minnie, in the sweetest white silk, a crown of rosebuds in her hair, smiled so happily at me. I remember blinking at her in surprise; she was so poised, she had so eagerly participated in all the festivities, that I almost didn't recognize her.

The article also does not relate how mechanical, how tinny, my voice sounded to me, despite having rehearsed the responses until I no longer had to think of them, until they were like lines in a play.

It does not describe how proud Mr. Barnum was, like the grandest, most successful parent of them all—like Adam himself. The father of us all. He beamed, he shook hands, he poured champagne at the reception; he slapped Charles on the back and gave me a paternal kiss, the only time he had ever kissed me, and it felt wrong. Awkward, forced—unlike anything that had ever passed between the two of us.

The biggest omission of all, however, is what took place after the reporters left to file their stories, after Charles and I retired to our honeymoon suite. There, we encountered an enormous bed the size of a boat, sprinkled with rose petals. I almost laughed at the absurdity of it; did the Metropolitan not realize whose wedding reception it had hosted? Although a set of velvet steps had been thoughtfully placed beside it—a very nice touch, indeed.

A table had been laid for us, with two slices of our wedding cake, a bottle of champagne, and a lovely roast quail. But the bottle was simply too big and unwieldy for Charles; he tried to pop the cork, huffing and grunting; he suffered not a little loss of pride upon not being able to manage it, and I felt for him. Discreetly, I turned away from him during his exertions but finally summoned a porter to do this chore, reassuring my husband, "A groom should not do anything as ordinary as open a bottle of champagne on his wedding night."

I believe Charles was mollified, for he relaxed over dinner, and we managed to chat about the odd little details that stood out to us after this very long, endlessly ceremonial day—the comical things, such as when the minister called him "Charlie" instead of "Charles"; how Mrs. Astor, in all her diamond-encrusted finery, actually elbowed Mrs. Belmont out of the way in her excitement to greet us first.

As we began to talk, I realized we hadn't truly spoken to each other at all until that moment. How odd, on our wedding day!

Eventually we exhausted trivial conversation, and we both simply stared at each other. Mr. Barnum was not here to wink and cajole and suggest; it was up to us now—alone. Finally my mind—which had been clenched all day, as if holding a line of defense against some onslaught of memory or feeling—relaxed. And a memory did assault me, paralyzing me, leaving me to stare at my new husband in horror.

"*Oh, it would be dreadful, impossible,*" I heard my mother's stricken voice, from long ago. "*Don't you remember the little cow on Uncle's farm who . . .*"

I felt my stomach lurch, my skin turn clammy, beads of moisture pop out along my forehead. The room started to sway, and I had to run to the lavatory, reaching a chamber pot just in time. Wedding cake, quail, it all came up—along with the fear that I had carried with me ever since that day I had eavesdropped upon Mama and Delia, talking about the birds and the bees and the perils of childbirth for little cows. And little women.

A fear that was now terrifyingly real, as was my life; no longer was I playacting. The curtain had fallen at last; the crowds, for the moment, dispersed. Suddenly, I had real decisions to make, decisions that would have consequences not just for me but for the person pounding on the door as I hovered over the pot, my stomach still heaving, asking me what was wrong. The person I must now, and forever more, call my husband.

Just as he was reasonably expecting to call me his wife.

INTERMISSION

From *Harper's Weekly,* July 25, 1863

THE TAKING OF VICKSBURG

We publish on page 465 a new portrait of Major-General Grant, the hero of Vicksburg. Most of the portraits in existence represent him as he was at the commencement of the war, with a flowing beard. He has since trimmed this hirsute appendage, and now looks as he is shown in our picture. For a life of the General we refer to page 365, No. 336, of *Harper's Weekly.* He has just been appointed by the President Major-General in the regular army.

THE DRAFT

The attempt to enforce the draft in the city of New York has led to rioting. Men have been killed and houses burned; worst of all, an orphan asylum—a noble monument of charity for the reception of colored orphans—has been ruthlessly destroyed, and children and nurses have lost every thing they had in the world.

[TWELVE]

———◆···◆———

And So She Is Married

General and Mrs. Charles Stratton are cordially invited to . . .

The pleasure of the company of General and Mrs. Charles Stratton is requested . . .

With kind regards, would General and Mrs. Charles Stratton please accept . . .

So many invitations, so many kind, generous invitations! Mrs. Astor—dear, dear Caroline Astor!—never tired of throwing dinners in honor of we newlyweds, seating us at her enormous dining table so that all might see and converse with us. She even introduced me to her Parisienne dressmaker, and insisted that her hairdresser visit me daily to do my hair in the same fashion as hers.

And Mrs. Hamilton Fish! Sweet, pious Julia, who was so ill-at-ease in society, despite her husband's wealth—even she overcame her shyness to throw an elaborate reception for the General and me, where every guest left with a sterling silver replica of our famous blue carriage, which was such a fixture now, no social event was complete unless our elegant equipage, with its matched pair of Shetland ponies, was seen to be parked outside.

Then there was Mrs. Theodore Roosevelt—beautiful, gentle Mittie; she threw a grand ball in our honor. As we were ushered into her lovely brownstone on East Twentieth Street, I spied two little boys peeking around a corner. The youngest clung to the hand of the oldest and when Charles saw them, he beckoned mischievously, so that they had to come forward.

"Hello, young gentlemen! What are you up to this fine evening?"

"We were waiting for you," the eldest replied. He had spectacles, was painfully thin, and spoke in a wheezy, high-pitched voice. His younger brother had golden hair and the face of an angel. "We wanted to see if you really were as small as Mama said."

"Well, are we?" Charles asked, cocking his head quizzically.

"No! I thought you might be as small as a gopher. But you're not! You're not much smaller than me!"

"Charles." I gently nudged my husband and glanced upstairs, where we could hear the violins tuning up for the ball.

"Can't we stay here a little longer, Vinnie? I'd much rather play with these chaps than parade around a ballroom." Charles looked at me so eagerly—as did the two boys.

I shook my head, feeling every inch the schoolteacher. "No, of course not. Say goodbye to these nice young men."

"Well, goodbye, then—what were your names?" Charles shook hands solemnly with the eldest, but the youngest hung shyly back.

"I'm Theodore Roosevelt the second," the older boy replied with comical gravity. "And this is my brother, Elliott."

"That is a very big name for such a little boy." I smiled as I nudged Charles again. He waved, sadly, as we headed up the massive staircase; so many of these grand homes had very steep stairs!

I understood Charles's reluctance to leave them; the truth was, we were not fond of balls, although it was very kind of our friends to want to give them in our honor. But Charles and I had to dance almost exclusively with each other, all eyes upon us. I attempted to dance with other gentlemen, but it was difficult; they had to take such mincing steps, and my arms ached with the strain of reaching so high up. And for Charles it was impossible to dance with other women, what with the fashions the way they were; those huge, swaying hoops kept him from getting near enough to a woman to grasp her hands.

But, of course, we did not complain in public, as it would have been hurtful to our new friends. And so many of them did I make in those heady days in the late spring of 1863! The General and I were back in New York, back in the St. Nicholas Hotel, once more, after our whirlwind honeymoon tour, the culmination of which—for Mr. Barnum, at least—was our reception at the White House. You can be sure he trumpeted this in all the Press!

While this was, indeed, a once-in-a-lifetime experience (or so I imagined at the time; I've since been to the White House to meet every subsequent president), for me the highlight of our trip was the day after the reception. Mr. Lincoln himself bestowed upon the General and me a pass to drive over "The Long Bridge" that led from the capital out to Arlington Heights, an army camp where one hundred and fifty thousand soldiers were stationed. And among these thousands was my brother Benjamin, whose regiment had arrived from the front just the day before.

I was so nervous that day! Of all the dignitaries and Society people I had met in my new role as the General's wife, no one's approval mattered to me as much as my brother's. I had not seen him since that day five years earlier when I left home with Colonel Wood, that awful day when he had quit our house, as he had promised, simply because I desired something more for myself than he did. I had always keenly felt his embarrassment over my size, yet he was the sibling—other than Minnie—whom I missed the most.

We were given a military carriage and a military escort to drive us through the endless rows of white canvas tents stretching before us as far as the eye could see. We had the windows down despite the cold, and the General and I kneeled on our seats and leaned out, waving at the troops, drawing cheers and enthusiastic shouts as we drove along. It warmed my heart so to see the joy we brought to our brave soldier lads, so many of whom would never come home; it brings a tear to my eye to think of this, even now.

Finally we stopped, and our carriage was mobbed so that some tall soldier had to pick the General and me both up, and set us atop the conveyance. From there, we could better make out each individual face, some of them so young it made my heart constrict; they reminded me of my pupils, when I taught school. These boys should have been thinking of nothing more dangerous than what tree to climb, what hill to sled down. Yet they all carried guns with an ease that I found terrifying.

The General and I were chatting amiably with the crowd, sharing details of our wedding, which, naturally, they had all read about, when suddenly I heard my name. "Vinnie! Vinnie! *Over here!*" Looking out, I spied Benjamin pushing his way through the sea of tattered blue; had he not called my name, I would not have recognized him. For he was a man now, not a boy, a hardened, muscular man with a beard and mustache and a set to his jaw that reminded me so much of Papa's. I burst into tears at the sight of him—and at the joy in his eyes as they lit upon me. The last time we had seen each other, I had found only accusation and pain there.

"Benjamin! Oh, Benjamin!" So overjoyed was I to see him, I tried to stand up, forgetting that I was perched atop a somewhat unstable carriage! A nearby soldier, however, instantly understood the situation and picked me up, placing me neatly on the ground just as Benjamin approached. My brother scooped me up in his arms, twirling me around and around so that my legs flew out and I was afraid the soldiers might see my petticoats. I wrapped my arms around him as best I could—I could not reach all the way around—and I buried my face in his chest. The fabric of his uniform was rough; he smelled like tobacco juice and sweat and smoked meat and some kind of liquor. Then he set me down upon the ground; the soldiers nearest us had respectfully stepped back, so that we were alone inside a circle of dirty, tattered blue legs and muddy black boots.

Benjamin knelt and gripped my shoulders, gazing so piercingly into my face that I felt a moment of foreboding.

"Vinnie, Vinnie—let me have a look at you! Why, how pretty you are, what a fine lady! I can't believe it!"

"And you, Ben—you look fine! Such a soldier—are you well?"

"As well as ol' Bobby Lee lets me be; he keeps us on the run, but we have good generals now, and I think the tide might be turning."

"Oh, that's wonderful! I can't wait to tell Mama and Papa all about you!"

"Are they all fine? The cows—is Papa able to keep up with the cows and all?"

"Yes, yes—everyone's well."

"And Minnie? Is she—is she still at home?"

"She came up to New York for my wedding, but she went home after."

"So she's not traveling with you?"

"No."

He nodded, and I knew he was relieved to hear this. But then he swallowed and said softly, "Vinnie . . . about the way we left things . . . I don't know what to say, still. I never understood how you could go off and——"

"Is this my new brother-in-law?"

Suddenly Charles was next to us, clasping Benjamin's hand. Charles, ever sunny, ever simple, beamed up at Benjamin, completely unaware of any tension between us.

"It's a pleasure to meet you, Sir," Benjamin replied quietly. Then he colored, and seemed suddenly aware that he was kneeling on the ground. Hastily, he rose.

Just then a soldier shouted, "General, I seen you once when I was but a lad, up at that American Museum. It sure is a pleasure to see you again."

Another chimed in, "Me, too. Saw him when I was just a little mite. Never thought I'd see him out here in all this muck."

"We wish you much happiness, General!" another voice called out.

"You sure did make me laugh when I was little, with that tiny sword of yours! I'll never forget that day!"

Charles grinned and trotted over to talk to these soldiers, moving among them with ease, dancing, capering—bringing a smile to faces still filthy with the grime of battle. As he did, I looked up at Benjamin. He was gazing at my husband with an open mouth.

"What do you say to that?" I asked my brother, with a triumphant smile.

"Well, I guess he's pretty popular, that Tom Thumb, isn't he?

I didn't tell anyone in my regiment about you and him, but some-body found out, and you know what, Vinnie? They didn't tease me at all. Matter of fact, I'm supposed to get your autographs for some of the men." He scratched his head, unbelieving, still. "I guess you did all right for yourself after all, Vinnie."

"Do you really think so, Benjamin?"

"I do." He knelt back down and took my hand in his; I looked at his hand, so rough, the nails bitten off, bearing red scars from gunpowder, I assumed. I couldn't begin to imagine all he'd been through, but still I could think of him only as the brother who had carried me to and from school whenever my legs were too tired. "Vinnie, you're my sister and I love you, and I'm sorry I was ever ashamed of you. I was wrong in all that, 'cause look at you now! These fellows sure are happy you came out here. So'm I."

"Me, too!" I embraced my brother once more, my arms about his dirty neck. Then he joined the General and myself in our car-riage as we continued to drive through the camp, the General, in particular, being greeted so warmly by those who had seen him perform. And it seemed to me practically every soldier in the Union army had done so; I was very proud of him at that mo-ment.

How proud I was, as well, to be escorted through that army camp by my brother and my husband; how touched I was to see the joy my husband and I brought our boys in blue, fighting so valiantly to preserve our Union! It was a moment I would never forget, and I was eternally grateful to Charles for making it pos-sible. For I knew I would never have experienced it on my own, as Lavinia Warren Bump.

And then we were back in New York, back in Society, the whirlwind of it all; every morning the silver tray next to our door was piled high with thick white envelopes of invitation. One morning, about two weeks after our return, I spied an envelope that was more ornate than the rest; opening it, I quickly read it, then laughed out loud.

> *The pleasure of the company of the esteemed General Charles Stratton and his very popular wife Lavinia Warren Stratton is requested by their friend Mr. Phineas Taylor Barnum, that is, should the Astors, Belmonts, Depews, and Roosevelts decide they can spare them for a few minutes this afternoon. While Mr. Barnum has nothing to recommend him but his friendship and kind regard (as well as a contract), nevertheless, he would greatly appreciate it if the General and his Lady would deign to come down to a little establishment called the American Museum (perhaps they have heard of it?) to discuss matters that might be mutually beneficial. The visit will not take long and soon enough, the esteemed couple will be back breathing the rarified air of Mt. Olympus—also known as the St. Nicholas Hotel—and cavorting with their fellow gods and goddesses on Fifth Avenue.*
>
> *Sincerely, Citizen Barnum*

"Charles!" I showed the letter to my husband, who was in his bedroom, being fitted for a new suit, as he simply did not have enough to keep up with our social engagements.

"Old Phineas!" Charles read the letter and laughed, which made the tailor—a thin Italian man with a scolding look and ever-flapping hands—drop his tape measure in disgust.

"I suppose we have been neglecting him. I'll send word that we'll be there this afternoon."

"Will we be back in time for dinner with the Vanderbilts?"

"Yes, dear," I said distractedly, as I mentally went through my wardrobe; the pink satin had a tear where someone had stepped upon my train (people were always stepping upon my train); the green silk was clean, but I'd worn it just last week. The gray flow-ered satin with the lace overskirt might do well. And had my new order of gloves arrived? I certainly hoped so, for I could not dine out without gloves, and I simply could not send my maid out to Stewart's to buy some; mine had to be custom-made.

"Make sure that you have a fresh shirt," I reminded my hus-band. "And don't forget that Mr. Vanderbilt likes Cuban cigars; you must bring him some tonight."

"Yes, dear," my husband said absentmindedly, as he began to fuss with the tailor over the fit of his jacket.

And I left him in his bedroom, while I went off to my own.

"I can't believe it, not even with my own eyes. The famous General and Mrs. Tom Thumb—or is it Stratton only, these days?"

"Our friends call us General and Mrs. Stratton. So, too, may you, if you promise not to be vulgar." I nodded regally, bestowing permission.

Mr. Barnum stared at me; then he allowed that twinkle in his eyes to sneak out from behind its gray curtain, and we all laughed.

"What a life you two are living now! Why, Charles, what's this I hear about a yacht?"

"Mr. Belmont suggested I purchase one, and he invited us to race with him on the Sound this summer. I think it's a good busi-ness decision, don't you, Phineas?"

"I don't know about a business decision—those things de-preciate terribly. But it sure will look good, and I can use it in some publicity. So go ahead, enjoy yourself—or rather, selves. For I take it you're not sitting at home while Charles is out smok-ing cigars in smoke-filled rooms, are you, Vinnie?"

"No, I've been so touched by how gracious Society has been to us, how eager they are to befriend us. Of course, being a Warren of Massachusetts does help, you know." I sat up straight, tilted my nose—and caught a glimpse of myself in the reflection from one of the glass-encased bookshelves along Mr. Barnum's office wall. Goodness, but I looked just like my mother! Stifling a cough, I turned away from my reflection.

"Society later, business first. No, actually—remember, I'm just a sentimental old father asking this—any notion of the pitter-patter of little feet? *Very* little feet, that is? You wouldn't believe the letters we get here at the Museum, asking—we've even had baby blankets and toys sent in. Your adoring fans are most eager to see the most popular couple in America become the most popular family."

Charles blushed, and I consulted my hands, folded primly in my lap. I was aware of the intense interest in our family plans. It insulted my sensibility, but I also had to allow it, since we had married in such a public way. Logically, it would follow that we would be expected to present an infant Thumb to the public sooner rather than later.

"Vinnie says—Vinnie says she is unable to—Vinnie says that we should count our blessings and enjoy life, just the two of us," poor Charles sputtered, his face reddening with each heartbeat.

I blushed as well; while I was not surprised that we were having this conversation with Mr. Barnum—nothing surprised me about him any longer—that did not mean I enjoyed it.

"I see. I'm sorry to hear that, Vinnie. You must be devastated," Mr. Barnum murmured.

I could not return his sympathetic gaze. I knew I could not deceive him, as I had managed to deceive my husband.

I had told Charles, that first night, that I would never be able to have children. He was disappointed; he so loved children, and at first I felt much guilt in my deception.

But I could not silence the memory of that horrified gasp of

Delia's as she contemplated the little cow that had died. I also re-membered something, something that was such a part of our family lore that we all ceased to understand the ramifications of it. But I had been a normal-size baby, as had Minnie. We were not fairy creatures at birth; we were healthy-size infants whose growth was not slowed in the womb but long after we had emerged from it. That was the fact I could not forget; that was the realization that had chilled me on our wedding night. I would die in child-birth, I knew it as well as I knew the freckle on the back of my left hand. It was a fact of me, one that was present at my own birth, the one part of me that needed fixing, but how? I simply was not made to bear children without great danger to myself. And so I told my husband that I could not—not that I would not. In my mind, they were one and the same.

As far as the physical aspect of our arrangement, well—I'm afraid I did not ask him how he felt about *that*. I told him that most couples did not share a bed, as they were together so much during the day; I think he believed me. And the times when we did have to share a bed—such as our wedding night, and naturally during our honeymoon tour, when every hotel had ridiculously provided us with the most enormous bed possible—I managed to pat him away after a quick embrace and kiss.

Did he have needs? Again, I did not ask him. Did I? My long-ings were of a more profound nature than simply skin against skin; they were for intimate conversations, long into the night; lazy days spent reading together, debating topics small and large.

They were for a union, but not merely of flesh. A union I would never have, and that was by my own design. But then again, it was not a fate that I had ever thought would be mine in the first place. And so, as time went on, my longing faded. As I hoped any longings that Charles possessed would as well.

"Well, that's that, then." Mr. Barnum sounded disappointed,

as Charles and I exchanged uncomfortable glances. Then—deliberately avoiding my gaze—Mr. Barnum cleared his throat and said, "Charles, I promised Nutt you'd drop by and see how he's doing. Poor fellow has been rather down lately. If I didn't know better, I'd say that he was pining over Miss Minnie—I think he was quite smitten with her when she was up here. But why don't you go see him? Vinnie can stay here and keep me company; it wouldn't do to have her taunt the poor lad with her loveliness."

Charles nodded eagerly and trotted off to seek Commodore Nutt. I watched him go, nervously; then I took a breath, summoning up my courage. I pulled my chair over to Mr. Barnum's, and we sat knee to knee, eye to eye, just like old times.

"What is it? Why did you send Charles away? Is something wrong?"

"Not wrong, not exactly. But Vinnie, I have to say, I never thought I'd see the day when you would lie to me."

" 'Lie'?" I colored; I truly did not wish to have this conversation with him. "Mr. Barnum, please, you must not make me explain. I simply cannot have children, that's all, and I wish you would leave it at that."

"What? Oh, no—no, that's not what I was talking about, no." Mr. Barnum looked as mortified as I was; he even deliberately dropped his tobacco pouch to give himself a moment to collect his bearings. "Vinnie, I am sorry about your, er, situation. Forgive me for not having considered something of that nature before I blundered on. However—well, first things first. No, I'm talking about the fact that you were still under contract to someone else when you signed with me."

"Oh." I sank back into my chair and allowed my feet to dangle, something I generally tried very hard not to do. "Colonel Wood. He contacted you." It was not a question; I knew it was true. I had always known it would be true, someday.

"Yes, he did. Tell me, Vinnie, why didn't you mention it from the first? It would have been no problem at all—I would have paid the scoundrel off with a pittance, and no more would be heard. But now you're famous, you're Society—you're worth so much more. And this Wood, whatever he may be, is no fool."

"No, he's not, although he is an evil, evil man!" I spat the words bitterly, for they were bile in my mouth. All the humiliation, all the times he had kicked at me, threatened to pick me up, throw me across a room—and then the ultimate mortification of trying to *sell* me as if I were a slave—it all came back, washing over me so that I felt my very skin turn grimy and dirty with riverboat muck once more.

"Is he—he is the one who you told me about? Who tried to sell you?" Mr. Barnum's voice was very gentle; I longed to look into his face, knowing that I would see absolution there. But I could not bring myself to. I simply nodded.

"I see. Rest assured, next time I see him I will thrash him with my own cane. However, before I thrash him, I have to pay him off, and he is demanding quite a sum not to go to the papers and complain that the dastardly Barnum has cheated him out of a livelihood—not to mention, he made some ridiculous threat to tell stories about you that would make Mrs. Astor's hair stand up on end. Now I understand what he was alluding to—although no one would ever fault you, of course. Still, talk of it would be damaging. So you see, Vinnie—come, look at me, friend." Mr. Barnum hooked his finger beneath my chin and lifted my face so that I could not look away. His eyes were kindness and understanding, both; I searched and searched, but could not find one hint of accusation or disappointment in them. And so I was able to nod and bravely smile back, ready to follow him into battle.

"What do I have to do?"

"Well, this is going to cost us both, Vinnie, as both our reputations are at stake. Look, I'm willing to pay the man what he asks. But it's a very pretty sum, I don't mind telling you. It's going to take me a while to make it back. This is where you can help."

"How? I'll do anything—absolutely anything, I promise. I give you my word."

"I'm glad to hear that, very glad to hear that. For I want you to convince Minnie to sign with me."

"No." I shook my head violently. I repeated it just in case he didn't understand, as he wasn't used to being contradicted. "No."

"Vinnie, consider the facts. I believe Minnie had a very good time at your wedding, didn't she?"

I didn't reply. Yes, my shy little sister did have a good time at our wedding, much to my surprise. While she had clutched at my hand with every step, she had never been completely overwhelmed; indeed, she accepted it all with an equanimity that surprised me. And at night, she had even stayed up late to talk everything over; that was when her excitement truly could not be contained. During the day she was a model of bashful maidenhood; at night, she bubbled over as she tried to process all the lovely things she was experiencing. And as happy as she was to board the train back home, her letters since had betrayed a thirst for news they never had before. No more were they tear-stained pleas for me to come home; now she asked, in a clear hand, how Charles was, how her good friend Mr. Barnum was, did I have any new gowns made up yet, did I think she might be able to come visit again soon?

But I had promised myself—and more important, I had promised Mama, from whom I still felt somewhat estranged—that I would keep my sister safe. And that did not mean dragging her up onstage with me; indeed, the thought of Minnie onstage was so foreign that I could not comprehend it. What on earth would she do? Hold my hand and clutch her doll?

MELANIE BENJAMIN

"No!" My tongue was almost tired of saying the word; would he not listen to me? "I told you before, this is not the life for her. If you want Nutt to join Charles and me, that's fine, as long as he behaves like a gentleman. But no, Minnie must not. She's much too young."

"She's no younger than Nutt; she's not much younger than you were when you first left home."

"That's entirely different. Minnie is not me. She's not as strong; she's not as—"

"What?" He cocked a bushy eyebrow. "She's not as bright as you? As capable of understanding the world? I don't know if that's true or not, but what you must acknowledge is that she'll have you with her the entire time. You're in a very different position now, and I'm no Colonel Wood. You'll never be in the kind of danger you were then, and you're a married woman, anyhow. You won't be attracting the kind of people who prey on maidens."

"Perhaps not, but—"

"And the four of you, together—now, you must know you will cause a sensation the likes of which this country has never seen. You will be the most famous quartet in America, I'll bet my hat on it. Think of the audience you will reach; think of how many people will see how proper, how intelligent you all are—what joy you will bring! And you miss your sister, I know it. Charles is a good soul, but—I can see that you are lonely, at times."

"Yes, maybe." I was reluctant to admit it, but I was. "But that's not the point. And anyway, I don't believe Mama and Papa would allow it." And I hoped that they wouldn't, but I knew, deep down in my sinking soul, that they would. They were both anxious to repair our breach, and entrusting me with Minnie's care would do that.

"You can talk them into it, I know."

"I can't refuse this, can I?" I was suddenly weary; I had a long

[236]

evening ahead of me. The Vanderbilts' dinner would run well past midnight.

"I don't know why you would want to. Think of the possibilities for us all—and especially for Minnie. Think of the things she will see now! Think of how delighted she will be to join you!"

"I suppose so." She would be happy to be with me; that was the one bright hope I clung to, defeated and deflated as I was—also ashamed, for it was my own actions, after all, that had brought about this situation. "Is there anything else you require of me? Does this repay my debt to you?"

"Now, don't talk like that. There are no debts between friends, are there?"

"No, but between business partners, there often are."

He pursed those crooked lips and looked away; his bushy brows gathered threateningly over his eyes. "Very well. Consider your debt fifty percent repaid. We'll talk about the other fifty percent later."

"I warn you, I do not have any other siblings to offer up as collateral."

"I understand."

"Fine." I rose, and was about to leave when I felt compelled to turn around; I did not like leaving him this way. "I do apologize for not telling you about Colonel Wood. I simply wanted, so much, for you to like me and sign me. I was afraid to bring anything up that might prevent that."

"Vinnie, I liked you from the instant I saw you. I would have done anything to keep you from going off—I would do anything, still, to prevent that. Friends?"

He looked so kindly, so earnest—it always surprised me to see how open and honest his face was. One would expect the Great Barnum to have the best poker face in the world, but he did not. His genius lay not in concealing but in sharing—his enthusiasms, his opinions, his disappointments, even. That he did not always reveal all the facts of the matter was really a small quibble; the great thing about him was that he, himself, believed everything he ever said.

So he believed we were friends—and so did I. He believed he had extracted a reasonable price from me—and for a time, I did, as well. So we shook hands and parted cordially, peace restored.

I would remember that handshake later. And recognize it as the moment that I gave away my sister, as well as my soul.

INTERMISSION

From *Harper's Weekly*, December 24, 1864

SHERMAN

How often, as the alarm of Sherman's march has rung into some neighborhood in Georgia which had before only heard the war afar off, it must have bitterly recalled to mind of some thoughtful Georgian the prophecy of Alexander Stephens four years ago. He foretold ravage and destruction. . . . And now at last, after four years, the prophecy is fulfilled where it was uttered.

From *The American Woman's Home*,
by Catharine E. Beecher and Harriet Beecher Stowe

In the Divine Word it is written, "The wise woman buildeth her house." To be "wise" is to "choose the best means for accomplishing the best end." It has been shown that the best end for a woman to seek is the training of God's children for their eternal home, by guiding them to intelligence, virtue, and true happiness.

------◆------

THIRTEEN

And Baby Makes Three

D o YOU THINK WE'LL LIKE THE NEW BABY?" MINNIE ASKED
anxiously as she sat upon a stool, watching the stewardess
unpack her trunk. We were in our stateroom on the S.S. *City of
Washington*; finally, I was on my way to see Europe!

It was October 1864, and we were now a corporation—
officially known as the General Tom Thumb Company, in partnership with Mr. Barnum. Newly incorporated, we had toured
New England and Canada starting in the fall of 1863, presenting
a "marvelous, miniature quartet of the most perfectly formed men
and women ever seen," just as Mr. Barnum had imagined. Charles
performed his most famous impersonations (unfortunately, he
could no longer fit into the body stocking required for him to im-
itate Hercules, so that was dropped), I sang songs, we both
danced, Commodore Nutt performed some sketches, and Minnie

recited a simple poem as Mr. Bleeker invited the smallest child in the audience to stand next to her, for effect.

Each performance ended with a reenactment of our wedding, all four of us wearing our original clothes—a touching tableau suggested by Mr. Barnum, who soon got wind of an odd phenomenon sweeping our nation: a phenomenon known as the "Tom Thumb wedding."

Newspaper reports began to appear, describing children being dressed up in wedding finery and arranged in pretend weddings, complete with cake and roses and infant minister. It was the nuptial ceremony in miniature, reenacted in our honor. There were hundreds of "Tom Thumb wedding" parties; "Tom Thumb wedding" fundraisers; "Tom Thumb wedding" pageants at schools.

Was I supposed to be touched by this, viewing it as a tribute to our love? Or was I supposed to be offended, seeing it as a mockery, a joke? I never could decide. After all, my own married life still seemed to be pretend. So much of it took place under the microscope of the public eye. At the end of a long day of performing—of waltzing together, singing together, presenting the perfect little married couple, capped by reciting the marriage vows themselves—Charles and I had nothing to talk about, and no house to keep. We took our meals at our hotel in silence and went to our separate bedrooms, exhausted.

I shared my bed with Minnie, just as we had when we were young; I rocked her to sleep every night. Charles did not seem to mind, for he was so very fond of her. In my sister, he'd found the playmate he had been looking for all his life, a partner in mischief and fun. I often came upon the two of them playing a game of marbles upon their knees, or whispering plans to tie Mr. Bleeker's shoelaces together while he and I sat discussing business.

Minnie, now fifteen and maturing into a very pretty young

woman, had settled in with the troupe remarkably well. Her serious nature was now lightened by flashes of humor, and while she was quite shy onstage, offstage she was invariably eager to explore her new surroundings—enjoying museums, taking strolls in hidden parks, and trying on bonnets in millinery stores. I promised Mama and Papa that I would see that she ate well, never walked alone without an escort, and went to church every Sunday. Above all, I promised myself that I would keep her sweet, innocent nature just the way it was. And to that end, I kept her close by me at all times. Much closer than I did my husband.

Our inaugural tour was so immensely successful that Mr. Bleeker felt compelled to write to Mr. Barnum proposing the postponement of our European tour for a year. "Leaving now," he cautioned, "would be throwing away the cream."

To no one's surprise, Mr. Barnum wrote back, "My dear Bleeker, Go on; save the cream. Your returns show it to be cream and not skim milk. Yours, P. T. Barnum." So we continued our travels in the United States, this time heading south. We even crossed enemy lines for one brief, confused moment when Mr. Bleeker couldn't read a map, although to my disappointment, the enemy did not appear to notice. We soon got our bearings and turned around, crossing back into the safety of Kentucky.

It was there, in Louisville, where I saw my old friend General Grant, who was on his way to take command of the Army of the Potomac. The tide of war was turning, ever so slightly; after New York was torn apart by the Draft Riots of 1863 (we were on the last train out, heading north to Canada, before rioters tore up the train tracks leading to and from the city!), the Union was amassing more and more victories. Chattanooga, Spotsylvania, Cold Harbor—these battles had drained the Confederacy of more men than it could afford to lose. And General Sherman was at that time planning his assault on Atlanta.

It was also in Louisville that I exchanged photographs with a handsome young actor staying in our hotel; he introduced himself by reminding us his brother had attended our wedding.

A year later, I tore that photograph up in horror; John Wilkes Booth had just shot the President.

And now, at last, we were turning our sights to Europe. Our company remained the same, including Mr. Bleeker as manager, and his dear wife, Julia, who mothered Minnie and me in the best possible way, proving to be a boon companion and loyal friend as well as an experienced seamstress. We also employed Mr. Kellogg as treasurer (the poor man developed a nervous tic; as there were so few banks in those days, he practically slept with our proceeds under his pillow at night, forever fearful of robbers!); Mr. Davis, who assisted Mr. Bleeker; Mr. Richardson, our pianist; Rodney Nutt, George's brother, who served as footman and groom for our small Shetland ponies; and Mr. Keeler, who did everything else that needed to be done.

There was one member, however, whom we had to leave behind, and whose replacement we would not meet until after we crossed the Atlantic. It was the very smallest person in a troupe of very small people, and it was the person whom Minnie was so eager to meet, as the *City of Washington* steamed its way down the Hudson toward open sea.

"Do you, Vinnie? Do you think we'll like the new baby?" Minnie asked again, as the stewardess left our stateroom with a curtsy and a wish, in a strong Irish brogue, that we "have safe travels, wee that ye are, mind that you don't get swept overboard!"

"I imagine we'll like it. We liked the other one well enough." I shrugged; I had not gotten too attached to the previous infant, regarding it as simply another prop I had to use onstage. However, both Charles and Minnie had become alarmingly attached, and I had warned Mr. Barnum that this would happen.

This, then, was the last thing I owed him, the last price—or so I thought at the time—that I had to pay for my carelessness regarding Colonel Wood: I had to agree to participate in one colossal humbug, the biggest one of them all.

I had to pretend that I was the mother of an infant daughter. I had to allow Mr. Barnum to fill the papers with the news that General Tom Thumb and his wife, Mrs. Stratton, were the proud parents of an infant daughter, as yet unnamed. I had to accept the mountains of cards and letters of congratulations, the acres of miniature blankets and nightgowns that would not cover a chipmunk, let alone an infant, but the public, naturally, assumed our child was of fairylike proportions. Mrs. Astor sent an exquisite miniature cradle; Mrs. Vanderbilt, a tiny christening gown.

We borrowed a baby. How callous that sounds now! But Mr. Barnum persuaded me to pose with a foundling—a very small one—that he had personally selected from a charity hospital. In Mr. Mathew Brady's studio, just across the street from the Museum, I sat holding that infant, who was beribboned and beruffled in borrowed baby finery (for the things given to us were much too small), smiling at Mr. Brady's camera.

The child, I must say, was well behaved, although rather heavy for me; by the time we were done, the crook of my arm ached.

In our last few appearances at the Museum, in preparation for our European tour, we had introduced our "child" to the public. "Miss General Tom Thumb," she was called, as I paraded her about the stage; no one thought to christen her with a first name. Although I suppose this made it easier to return her to the hospital, as if she were a pair of shoes that did not fit, on the eve of our sailing.

Easier for me, at any rate; not for Minnie, and not for Charles, either. They both grew quite fond of the child, who was cared for by a hired nurse when we weren't performing. Charles had so enjoyed playing with her; he dangled his watch chain above her until she gurgled and cooed; he tickled her; he sang her songs.

And Minnie, who loved all children, who still traveled with a doll although she no longer played with it, well—she had cried and cried when we had to give the baby back, kissing the infant until I was alarmed that she might smother her.

She had tears in her eyes now, as she thought of it. "She was such a little thing. I hope someone good takes care of her. It seems so sad to give her up like that."

"I know, but it's much easier to get a new child when we land. Traveling on a boat would not be fun for an infant—and besides, Mr. Barnum felt that that baby was getting too big. Babies will grow, of course."

"But Vinnie, don't you miss her? Don't you want a baby of your own? One you'll never have to give back?"

I stopped in the middle of arranging some flowers that had been sent to our room by General Winfield Scott, conveying his best wishes for a safe voyage. The boat was starting to rock a bit, as we must have been heading out through the Narrows. And although I was a very good sailor, my stomach lurched at that moment, as I contemplated the notion of ever having a baby. It was still the one thing that could make me have nightmares. Always, it was a dream of blood and pain and cries and finally—nothing.

I wanted to cry out, "No! No, I never want a child, and neither do you!" But I knew it would hurt Minnie, who loved children so; I didn't want her to think I was as coldhearted as I really was. So instead I answered, "Of course, Minnie. But wanting a baby isn't the same as actually having one. And you know—I've told you, darling, remember?—that I can't."

"But Charles wants a baby, I know he does. He told me. Oh, poor Charles!"

"Poor Charles will be just fine. And in the meantime, we can all play with the new baby, and care for it, and I imagine it will be a very nice one, at that. Perhaps, since we're getting it in France, it will even cry with an accent!" I smiled, coaxingly, at my sister. She looked so pretty in her new traveling dress, nearly identical to mine, which was black satin while hers was brown. We both had such lovely wardrobes for this trip, smart cloaks and fur caps and muffs, so many pairs of gloves I couldn't imagine ever running out, but of course knew that I would. I always ran out of gloves, at an appalling rate; I simply shook far too many hands. My husband might kiss every lady he met—and he did, much to my annoyance—but I shook the hands of them all, plus their husbands. And my supply of gloves could not keep up.

Minnie's dark eyes twinkled at the thought of a baby crying in French, even as tears still rolled down her cheeks. She laughed, just as I'd hoped she would, her little dimple showing. And I relaxed—for the moment, anyway—and proposed that we dress for dinner.

I have fond memories of that first journey across the ocean. The weather was fine much of the time, and, dragging my steps with me wherever I went, I was able to look over the railing, marveling at the whitecaps, the seagulls that followed us like a noisy white cloud, the occasional whale surfacing perilously close to the boat, so much more thrilling to see than the poor whale in his tub back at the Museum!

In particular, I enjoyed the brisk, salty slap of wind against my face. I timed it so that I would walk out, bareheaded, stairs in hand, toward the prow of the ship just when the winds were fiercest; the sailors at first were amused, but soon enough they ignored me. I would climb my stairs—well away from the rail— and face the wind with gritted teeth and shut eyes, welcoming that first harsh sting against my soft, protected skin that had never been without a hat, bonnet, or veil. Invariably, it brought tears to my eyes—welcome tears.

For I needed to be punished. I needed to atone for what I had done and for what I still must do, as Minnie continued her discussions of the new baby and even knitted a blanket for it. I deserved every slap in the face that the cold North Atlantic winds could give me. I deserved more, even. But I had to content myself with that.

LANDING IN LIVERPOOL, WE SPENT THE NIGHT AT LINN'S WATER-loo Hotel, thinking that we would make a very quiet journey on to London the next day. The next day, however, was Mayor's Day, and the city was thronged with sightseers eager to see the grand parade. So loud were the crowds that we ran to our balconies to see what was happening; in a flash, the crowd had turned toward us and was waving and shouting its welcome.

"Well, if it isn't Tom Thumb and his little bride!"

"Welcome back, General!"

"'Ope you 'ad a safe crossing!"

Soon the street in front of our balcony was thoroughly blocked—and so was the mayor's parade! We retired quickly inside our suite so that the parade could continue, although the cheering for us resounded unabated.

This was just a glimpse of the extraordinary adoration we found waiting for us all through the rest of our trip. I had dreamed and dreamed of this moment, and was not disappointed. To see, with my own eyes, the places I had read of in my history books was an experience I will always cherish.

From Liverpool we journeyed to London. There we were guests of the Prince and Princess of Wales at Marlborough

House. The Prince and Charles shared a touching reunion, as the Prince had been a boy the time Charles visited his mother the Queen in 1847, and remembered him well. He also remembered being sent up to bed much too soon; fancy, the future King of England being sent up to bed just like any boy!

The Princess of Wales, a stunning dark-haired, dark-eyed beauty with the tiniest waist I'd ever seen, did not say a great deal; I felt she was not very confident of her English, since she was of Dutch ancestry. However, she did not have to speak; her beauty was more than enough contribution to our pleasure, Charles's and mine. (Minnie and Commodore Nutt did not join us; they were not always invited where we were, and while Minnie never minded, I'm afraid Commodore Nutt did. His impish, elfin face could scrunch itself up into petulance so swiftly, as if it were made of rubber. Indeed, he threatened, many times, to go off by himself at night and find his own fun. This worried good Mr. Bleeker so that I'm quite sure he spent more than one night camped out before the Commodore's door as a precaution!)

While I truly felt bad for Minnie and the Commodore, my spirits could not be dampened, and at times I had to refrain from pinching myself. Was it possible that I, Mercy Lavinia Warren Bump Stratton, was having tea with the future King and Queen of England? "Mrs. General," they both called me, with all the deference I could wish for; I addressed them as "Your Royal Highness," and returned the favor, curtsying deeply whenever we met.

Oh, if only that sour-faced Mrs. Putnam could see!

After a brief stay in London, we prepared for the first real destination of our tour, Paris. In December of 1864 we took the famous ferry across the channel and landed at Calais, that cold, empty-looking city.

Calais happened to have a charity hospital, though, and upon landing, Mrs. Bleeker went directly there, as instructed by Mr.

Barnum. He had contributed enough money to ensure discretion in the matter. Mrs. Bleeker came back to our hotel with a cherubic infant girl, whom Minnie clasped to her childlike bosom immediately. But the stern English nursemaid we had engaged took the child away, saying grimly, "There's nothing worse for a child than to be coddled and cosseted! Mrs. Stratton, Ma'am, if you please, I think I know what's best."

"I'm sure you do," I replied with relief. After that, I saw the child only during performances, although once more, both Minnie and Charles snuck into the temporary nursery whenever the maid's back was turned.

It was in France that I came to rely upon Charles for the first time in our marriage. So far in our life together, I had felt it natural to assume some kind of position of direction, and indeed, Charles seemed relieved to rely upon my judgment and good sense. He was a seasoned performer, yes—far more seasoned than I. But regarding the ways of the world, I felt my life upon the river equipped me to deal with them in a far more practical way than he could. After all, he had been sheltered by Mr. Barnum from the time he was five until the time of our marriage.

Charles, however, was the only one of our party who spoke French. And so, faced with that slippery language that would not stay upon my tongue no matter how much I tried, I found myself turning, more and more, to him for direction. He made all our travel arrangements to Paris, with the assistance of Mr. Bleeker; he ordered for us all the few times we ventured out into restaurants. Every morning when we gathered for breakfast in Mr. and Mrs. Bleeker's hotel suite, Charles translated out loud all the newspaper accounts of our visit. Some mornings he had to read to us for what seemed like hours, so numerous were our notices! Accounts of my wardrobe, Charles's cigars, our every stroll and dinner—each detail was devoured by our French admirers.

The notices were even more numerous when we were summoned to appear at court, for this was before the Republic; the Emperor Napoléon III and his exquisite wife, the Empress Eugénie, were on the throne. And while I was delighted by the pageantry—the beautiful Worth gowns on every attending lady, the glittering jewels adorning the Empress's scandalously low-cut neckline—all I could do was smile and nod. I had to rely on Charles to speak for me, for the very first time.

I must admit that I was proud of him. The manners and courtliness that he had learned, even before his letters, as a child traveling on the Continent served him well; that mind that had absorbed everything that Mr. Barnum had taught him when only a child of five was on display. Reader, I'll not pretend that I ever felt Charles to be my intellectual equal. I'll even go so far as to admit to some feelings of frustration over my husband's immature ways—his habit of simply repeating what others said while conversing about politics or music or art, rather than forming his own opinion; his eagerness to introduce himself with a full recitation of the places he'd seen and the people he'd met; his gullibility, for my husband would believe every tall tale ever told to him, every pipe dream sold, every pot of gold promised.

But in Paris, I was finally able to find more things to appreciate about him. After our invitation to the palace, our success was assured in that gray city (for that was how I remembered it; we were there in winter, and every building, sidewalk, street, and even the sky all seemed the same gunmetal gray to me). I may not have been able to understand the language, but there was no mistaking the interest in the throngs and throngs that we encountered whenever we attempted to leave our hotel. It grew tiresome; it was much too difficult to navigate the narrow Paris streets hemmed in on every side, ears assaulted by the excitable Gallic language. I was quite accustomed to being stared at and pointed to, but hearing myself discussed in a language I could not understand began to wear on my nerves.

The crowds were so pressing that when we tried to go see Napoléon I's tomb, we had to turn around after just a few blocks and return to our hotel. So it was that Charles and I found ourselves spending long, lonely afternoons together. Minnie was usually with the infant, and Nutt was usually off with one of his conquests—one of his many conquests, if his boasts were to be believed—so it was just the two of us. One of my talents long being an aptitude for fine embroidery, I began to teach Charles. To my surprise, he took it up very quickly and soon proved himself even superior to me—and he did not mind Nutt's teasing about it, or even Mr. Bleeker's gentle jokes. Charles retorted that a man had to occupy himself somehow, and this way he'd have something useful to show for it. And indeed, he embroidered many seat covers and pillows and fireplace screens that I still use to this day.

It touched me to see him so intent upon choosing thread of the right hue or a perfect needle. His head bent over his work, his tongue sticking out between his teeth, he was the very picture of virtuous industry. He tugged at that reluctant heart of mine, almost as if he had embroidered himself to a very small, remote corner of it. I don't believe I ever liked my husband as much as I did during our time in Paris.

Yet most of our marriage was still spent upon the stage; whether or not they could understand us, the enthusiastic Paris audiences always applauded ecstatically. Our act was the same as it had been at home, except that we no longer reenacted our wedding. Our wedding clothes were on display before the performance, but now I ended the show by bringing out the child (whose name I still had not learned), doing my best to smile maternally, while in reality, I trembled with fear.

I may have been able to face down a crowd of Rebels to get passageway home from the South, but when called upon to care for an actual infant, I admit to some cowardice. It, or rather, *she,* proved to be very wiggly indeed; squirming, waving clenched fists in the air, so close to my face they almost hit my nose, blinking her eyes against the bright gaslights. Automatically I tightened my grasp about her; this wriggling, live *thing* in my arms reminding me of the time I had dressed up a baby pig in doll clothes, back when I was a girl. The pig had shot out of my arm like it was greased, landing with a sickening thump on the floor, where it lay for a moment, stunned, before it shook its head and ran squealing off, dragging its clothing behind. I was most afraid the same thing would happen now.

After what seemed an interminable amount of time walking the perimeter of the stage with this fussing child in my arms, holding it up, laying my cheek against it, while the audience *ooh*ed and *ahh*ed, I very gratefully handed it off to Minnie, who was standing in the wings with her arms greedily outstretched. Then Charles joined me onstage and together we danced around to the strains of "The Tom Thumb Polka," one of the many songs that had been written in honor of our marriage.

Finally, the curtain came down; we repeated this at least three times a day.

Our notices were rapturous; we were the *"crème de la crème."* Soon there were dolls, songs, greeting cards featuring "M. et Mme. Tom Pouce" all over the city.

Mr. Barnum sent us huge bouquets and cabled us his congratulations—ending with what almost seemed an afterthought. Queen Victoria had asked, once we returned to London, he wrote, if we would come to tea. The Queen was quite fond of babies, of course; would we mind bringing our precious daughter with us, so that Her Majesty could see her and give her a gift?

I stared at the telegram, paralyzed. When I had agreed to this humbug, it was onstage only—or posing for photographs. I had never imagined that I might have to play the part of mother up close, where others could see how ill equipped, how terrified, I was.

"Minnie! Oh, Minnie, you must help me!" I ran to find my sister; Charles said she was in the child's bedroom while the nursemaid was having her dinner. Then I had to ask him where the child's bedroom was; he pointed down the hall, and I burst into the room. "Minnie, I need your—oh!"

Minnie, who was kneeling on the floor next to the cradle, rocking it gently with a beautiful smile upon her face, looked up. "What is it, Vinnie? What's wrong?"

"I didn't know—why, it's so pretty in here! Who did all this?"

For this room, unlike the other stuffy rooms in our suite, was utterly lovely. Scattered around were dolls—several that I recognized as Minnie's—and watercolors of animals and cherubs. Pastel scarves were draped over the lamps, softening the light. Simple vases of posies graced the tables and mantel, and a stuffed white lamb perched on a rocking chair. The whole effect was one of peace and security—exactly how a nursery should feel. It had never once occurred to me to make sure that the infant had appropriate surroundings; it had never occurred to me to buy any toys for it, or to check to make sure the nurse wasn't harming it in some way.

"I did," replied Minnie. "I hope you don't mind, Vinnie, but Mrs. Bleeker took me shopping one afternoon when you were out, and I picked everything out for Cosette. That's what we named her—Cosette—because the poor thing didn't have a real name. And everyone deserves a name, don't you think?"

Minnie looked at me so anxiously, wanting to be right. And, of course, she was. Everyone deserves a name.

Even a foundling child who was beginning life as a stage prop.

"Yes, darling, of course. And Cosette is a beautiful name. Now, could you help me, please, dear? I need to—that is, I want to—learn how to hold her better, how to care for her, just a little, just enough to pretend—I think it would be good for me to learn, don't you?"

"Oh, yes, Vinnie! You do hold her awfully strangely. You never did play with dolls when you were little, did you?"

"No," I admitted ruefully, gathering up my hoopskirt and joining Minnie on the floor. The fire in the hearth, just behind us, crackled and popped. The room was scented with lavender and powder. The child in the cradle was sleeping peacefully, her little eyes scrunched up; she had long black eyelashes and black curling hair. She could have easily passed for Minnie's child, so identically sweet and untroubled were their countenances.

But that was absurd, of course. My baby sister could not have a baby. I suppressed a laugh at the very idea.

"Now, watch what I do," Minnie instructed me, and then I did have to smile. She had never instructed me in anything before; it was such an odd reversal of roles. I led, she followed; that was the way it had always been. Since when had she become such a serious little grown-up?

Minnie reached into the cradle, placing one tiny hand—much tinier than mine; Minnie was so petite and delicate, her hoopskirts often threatened to swallow her whole—beneath the child's head, the other beneath her back. Then she gently scooped it—her—*Cosette*—up from the cradle, and clasped her, reverently, to her chest. The motion was so fluid, so instinctive, that it looked like part of a dance. The child, small as she was, really was too big for Minnie, but my sister did not appear to notice; she simply rocked the child, easily, naturally, against her chest. As if the weight of the child in her arms had triggered some hidden switch,

Minnie began to sing softly, to murmur words and phrases that I could not completely understand, but they were soothing and melodious, like the echoing fragments of songs long after they were finished.

"How do you do that?" I whispered, truly in awe; it was almost as if I was in church, with a real life Madonna and child before me. Minnie's face, with her halo of tangled curls, was lit up from behind by the glow of the fire, so that the only thing you could see was her cameo profile as she bent her head toward Cosette's.

"I don't know, I just do. I don't even think about it. Oh, Vinnie, can't we keep her? Can't we?" Despite her passion, Minnie's voice never rose above a whisper as she continued to rock the infant.

"Minnie, I just don't see how. I would love to, truly, but arrangements are arrangements, and it's for the best. This is no life for a baby."

"It could be. I'd help, you know! I'd do everything; I wouldn't mind a bit. I don't need to be before the public like you. I'd much prefer to stay behind stage and take care of Cosette—you wouldn't even have to pay the nursemaid!"

"Oh, Minnie." It was not in my nature to deny my sister anything, and I struggled against it, trying to sort out the thorny details. The child had no papers, not with our name on them. But would an actual child of ours? I didn't even know. I supposed there would be a baptismal record at least; I knew that Mama kept all of ours in her family Bible. So that would have to be created, somehow. If we actually adopted it, would someone find that out? Or could Mr. Barnum cover it up? But what about later—when the child grew big? We couldn't use her in the act then, could we? I couldn't imagine how. But then, that wasn't the point; Minnie was talking about real life: raising a child, caring for her, kissing her scraped knees, soothing her cries at night, worrying about her schooling, her future—all the things my own parents had done so well.

I couldn't imagine it. Minnie couldn't do it all by herself; I would have to be involved somehow, and I did not wish to be. That was it, pure and simple; my life was onstage, next to my husband, either reenacting a pretend wedding ceremony or holding a pretend infant.

I had no room for big love, big decisions, big messes, big happiness; not in this miniature life, spent under the magnifying glare of so many eyes, that I had made for myself.

"See how sweetly she's sleeping, Vinnie?" Minnie whispered, bending closer to me; she leaned in to hand me the child, careful not to wake her up.

"No," I said, recoiling, as if the child was a hex or a bad omen—something I did not want to touch for fear of how it might affect my future. Hastily I scrambled up from the floor, hiding my trembling hands behind my skirts. "No, no, I'm sorry but we'll just have to take very good care of Cosette now." I avoided Minnie's surprised, hurt gaze. "And when the time comes, we must return her and trust that she will find a good family who will love her just as much."

Minnie didn't speak at first; she merely bent her head down to Cosette and kissed her on the tip of her snub nose. Then she looked up at me, so that I could not help but see the single tear rolling down her cheek; it continued to fall until it landed upon Cosette's smooth, untroubled brow. "I don't see how," Minnie whispered, careful not to wake the child. "I don't see how anyone can love her just as much as me. I don't see how I can ever love any other baby just as much as Cosette."

I turned away. I detested this whole charade. But I could see no way of ending it without exposing it—and Mr. Barnum, not to mention myself. I left the room with a bitter taste in my mouth and a bitterer stain on my soul, knowing that Minnie felt, in her sweet, susceptible heart, that what she had said was true; she could never love another baby as much as she loved Cosette.

I also knew that she would say the same thing again, in a few weeks, when we went to England. Only instead of Cosette, it would be Isabel. Or Alice, or Beatrice—or whatever she decided to name the next one. My sister's heart was endlessly elastic, but I had to wonder, even then, how long she could go on mourning baby after baby after baby.

I also had to wonder why I, the mother in this particular play written by Mr. P. T. Barnum, never did. I never shed one tear over any of those infants—not until much, much later in my life.

INTERMISSION

From *The New York Times,* December 26, 1865

GENERAL NEWS

The Commissioner of Agriculture has received from the American Legation at Jeddo, Japan, several hundred varieties of fruit and flower seeds indigenous to that country, many of which, the consul believes, may be cultivated to advantage in this country.

One thousand four hundred men are now employed on the Reno, Oil Creek and Pit Hole Railroad. In about two weeks the railroad will be open.

Quite a number of plantations near Augusta, Ga., have changed hands; lately the purchasers are mostly from the North.

Frederick Douglass has written a letter accepting the position of delegate in Washington of the colored men of New York.

From *The Blairsville Press,* Blairsville, Pennsylvania, April 19, 1869

General Sheridan received a few days since the following report from Maj. General Schofield, at Ft. Leavenworth: "General Custer reports from the headwaters of the Washita, March 21st, the successful termination of his expedition. He has rescued the captive white women, Mrs. Morgan and Miss White; made the Indians submit to the Government, and holds three Cheyenne chiefs as security for the fulfillment of his promise. The troops are in good health."

FOURTEEN

Thrills and Chills Guaranteed to Tingle the Spine! (or, Trains, Indians, Runaway Wagons, and Mormons)

OUR DAUGHTER DIED IN SEPTEMBER 1866. MR. BARNUM put out the press release: **"The Infant Daughter of General and Mrs. Tom Thumb Dead of Brain Inflammation."** Even in death, she remained nameless.

I killed her; I demanded her death. But I did not mourn her; that was Minnie's duty, one that she begged to be allowed to perform.

"Let me reply to these letters, Sister. It will give me some pleasure."

"Oh, Minnie, no, darling. You don't have to do that—Mr. Barnum's secretaries will send out a card."

"No, let me, Vinnie. It's odd, but I feel as if I owe that to her—to all the babies entrusted to us these past few years. It will soothe me to do so—and the people are so nice to write like this." Minnie held up a letter for me to read.

Dear Mrs. General Tom Thumb, I am very sorry to here of the loss
of your Fairy Angel who will surely be in Heaven now waiting for
you. We lost a Daughter ourselves to the fever and I trust that
they are both in a better place.

I returned the letter with a shaking hand and shakier conscience; I could not bear to keep reading. As relieved as I was to
end this charade, I did not enjoy knowing that we had played so
upon the emotions of those to whom we had previously given
only joy. But I could not continue the practice of snatching babies
and returning them as they grew too big; too big to complete the
happy tableau that Mr. Barnum was determined to present of perfectly formed miniature father, mother, and child. So I demanded
that we end it; we had made enough money on the European tour
that Mr. Barnum had no choice but to agree with me.

Unfortunately, the only possible way to end the charade was
to "kill" the child that had never really existed, except in the public's mind. And so I was a murderer now.

But the deed was done; the letters and cards would soon subside. We would never have to speak of babies again—or so I
thought.

"All right, you answer them. But, Minnie, promise me, if it
gets too hard for you, you must stop. I know you—I know your
tender heart."

Minnie nodded, picked up her pen, and began to write; her
sweet eyes were full of tears, but she answered every one in my
name, writing as tenderly as if it had been her own child who
died.

This was late September of 1866; we were back from Europe,
resting up in Middleborough—enjoying a nation now at peace.

Mama and Papa were growing older, but they were content,
now that all their children were back home. Safely returned from

combat, Benjamin and James had begun families of their own; indeed, all of Mama and Papa's children were married, with the exception of Minnie. And of course no one ever expected her to wed; she was fully part of my household, as Charles was quite as devoted to her as I was. We made our own little family. Whatever fears I had in taking her away from home and exposing her to the bigger world were forgotten as I relied upon her, more and more, for companionship. With Minnie always with me, I never had to spend much time alone with Charles.

Mama and Papa, however, had come to view my marriage most favorably. Papa especially doted upon Charles. He made him a complete set of miniature hand tools, such as any industrious Middleborough man would need. They were beautiful, hand-carved, and he made an equally handsome miniature toolbox in which to store them.

As disturbed as Mama was by the baby business, she never blamed Charles for it. She took to referring to Mr. Barnum as "that Barnum" once more, and sent back every present he ever gave her until finally he got the message. It bothered him, for he respected my mother immensely, often saying she was of "good, reliable New England stock." But Mama could not forgive him—even if she could not help herself from loving me in spite of my own guilt, and trying, over and over, to find an excuse for my behavior.

"I suppose that man left you no choice," she said one day soon after we returned from Europe. We were in the kitchen, knitting companionably. I was wearing a simple country gown without hoops, and my hair was parted plainly and loosely in the middle, gathered in a knot at the base of my neck. My feet were clad in those flat child's slippers I used to find so tiresome but which now brought me sweet relief. It was such a blessing not to have to dress fashionably, mindful of hoops and trains; not to have my hair done up elaborately, anchored with heavy jeweled combs that caused my head to ache; not to have to converse nonstop with total strangers. Rocking with my mother in her cozy kitchen full of freshly preserved vegetables and fruits, jugs full of orange bitter-sweet branches with their red berries, the scent of apples in the brisk New England autumn air—it was utter bliss.

"I suppose he just put up handbills declaring it a fact, and you could do nothing but go along with him," my mother said with a sniff.

"Mama, it wasn't exactly that way."

"Do you know how many people here in Middleborough wanted to see your daughter after they read about her in the newspapers? Do you know how many times I have had to make excuses to my own neighbors? Vinnie, that Barnum simply doesn't consider other people in anything he does. I don't know why you admire him so."

"There are more sides to this story than you know" was all I could tell my dear mother. But I refused to continue this line of talk about Mr. Barnum; the man had sorrows of his own to bear. For he was still feeling, keenly, the loss of the American Museum in a horrific fire that occurred in 1865.

Oh, to think of that grand building and all that was in it, going up in flames! To imagine the horror, the spectacle, the heart-breaking screams of the animals panicking and running into the street only to be shot by police, fearful for the public's safety; the sickening stench of burning flesh and feathers; the heat of the con-flagration as it spread greedily from floor to floor. Mr. Barnum was not present at the time, thank Providence! But many a brave employee endeavored to save what they could; miraculously, none lost his life.

Mr. Barnum soon opened another museum, farther uptown, but I never thought his heart was fully in it; so much of his own history—as well as mine—had gone up in flames on Ann Street.

"Mr. Barnum has suffered such terrible losses," I reminded my mother. "And his wife is no helpmeet for him."

"Have you ever met her?"

"Once, in Bridgeport, while we were visiting Charles's parents."

"What is she like?"

I laid my knitting down for a moment and frowned, remembering. "She was as I had pictured her—thin, sallow, with graying hair, sunken eyes. A sour set to her mouth. She carried smelling salts with her everywhere she went, and retired at least four times a day to her room to nap. Poor Mr. Barnum!"

"'Poor Mr. Barnum'?" Mama snorted. "It sounds as if he got the kind of woman he deserves. I'm sure he's dragged her to the devil and back many times, that man!"

"Oh, Mama, no. You don't know him, not like I do. You don't—" But I broke off.

Mama did not reply, but she did look at me with a sudden sharpness. I had seen her look at my brothers and sisters like this, as if she could see right through to their hearts—and all the secrets they thought they carried within them. But she had never before looked at me in this piercing, knowing way, as I had always confounded her so.

I attacked my knitting with such dedication, sparks must have flown from my needles; at least I assumed that was what made my face burn with such surprising heat. No more was spoken of Mr. Barnum that day.

Not long after that, however, I was ready to pack my trunk again. Left too long to my own devices, to muse and ponder and dream, left to be truly a wife to my husband in the dull, flickering glow of lantern light instead of footlights, I felt as if I was suffocating. Over and over, I returned to that tree trunk in Papa's cow pasture to pull up the weeds that continued to grow over my name.

What did I fear so, in the warm bosom of those who only loved me? I could not say, as at the time I did not recognize it for the fear it was. I simply felt driven to see, to experience—to give of myself to those whose approval should have meant less than my own husband's but instead meant so much more. I simply knew that I could relax and sleep only on a rocking train or a bobbing boat. I simply realized I needed the warmth of an audience like a plant needs sun.

And I simply understood that the most satisfying moments in my life were spent poring over maps and train routes, discovering new towns that were popping up all over this great country of ours. I could not bear to think that there was somewhere I had never been, someone who might not know my name.

So in late autumn of 1866—after remaining in Middleborough for a suitable period of mourning for our "child"—Mr. Barnum and I decided that the Tom Thumb Company should once again set out, this time to the Deep South, where we had not been able to go during the four bloody years of the War Between the States.

"It will be lonely without a baby," Minnie said softly as we settled into the train for our first leg of the trip. Eastern trains were becoming much more commodious for the traveler; some, like this one, even had upholstered seats if you paid extra to travel in what was called the "first class" section. There were also separate, private water closets for ladies and gentlemen! The modern world was astounding!

Commodore Nutt was once again with us, completing the perfect miniature foursome; across the aisle, he and Charles soon had a lively game of cards going with Mr. Bleeker and the other men of our troupe. While I did not approve of cards, at least the game kept Nutt out of more serious trouble. How a man could have such an appealing, impish presence onstage and be so completely unpleasant off, I could not fathom! Perhaps it was because of our earlier history, or perhaps it was because he sensed my disapproval now—either way, he kept as far away from me as possible. Although Charles, of course, held no grudge; Charles would not recognize a grudge if it came up and bit him on his pug little nose.

"It won't be lonely, dear—think of how many people we will meet!" I patted Minnie's arm excitedly; I had a pleasant, bubbly feeling in my stomach, as if I had swallowed a giggle. I always felt this way at the beginning of a journey.

"But we always have to say goodbye to them." My sister sighed, leaning her curly head against my shoulder. "And that's dreadful."

I smiled and kissed her forehead. "Remember how you used to call everyone 'dreadful'?"

"Did I?" She laughed, shaking her head so that her hair tickled my chin. "I don't remember."

"You did. You even thought Mr. Barnum was dreadful at first."

"How silly of me! I was so little then! I don't think anyone is dreadful now."

"You don't? Not anyone?" I couldn't help myself; I inclined my head toward Nutt, who was slapping down a card and laughing boisterously, causing all the other passengers in the car to look his way.

Minnie followed my gaze. "Oh! Well, yes, I suppose I do think *he* is rather dreadful, at that. I'm so bored by his everlasting sonnets!" Then she closed her eyes and yawned, nestling her body even closer to mine.

I was glad to hear her say this. For I had feared lately that that horrid man had become quite smitten with her. He followed her around and attempted to sit next to her at mealtimes, reciting Shakespeare's sonnets to her—which, kind as she was, she always applauded, complimenting him upon his memory. Several news articles had hinted at a romance or even assumed a marriage between these two—and Mr. Barnum, I knew, would not be displeased if there was.

But I would, for I wanted to keep Minnie to myself. She was the one person in my life whom I could love without guilt or shame or pretense. I was also selfish enough to think that I could fulfill that same role for her, and that she would be content with that. She always had been, after all; there was no reason to believe that we couldn't continue on in this way.

And so, as the train began its comforting sway, back and forth, back and forth, along the rickety railroad ties, I rocked my sister to sleep. Just as I always had, just as I always would. It was a comforting, pleasant thought with which to begin our latest journey together.

IF EASTERN TRAINS WERE BECOMING MORE COMFORTABLE, THEN southern trains were still mired in the past—if they existed at all. For it soon was evident that the only thing left of the South, now that the War was over, was poverty. The scenery that we passed was a smoky nightmare of burnt-out plantations, scorched cotton fields, wrecked locomotives piled up next to railroad tracks. Our travel through these states was disjointed and unpredictable, as so many of the train routes had been broken up by the Union: tracks pulled up, bridges destroyed so that the Rebels could not move their troops easily from one point to the next. And there simply wasn't enough money to rebuild them—so we often had to travel by stage or omnibus, hiring wagons to cart our miniature carriages, in which we always drove about town before our first show.

It was such a pleasure to see the joy on the faces of those poor, noble citizens of the Old South whenever they spied our polished little blue carriage, or Commodore Nutt's walnut-shaped one. Shouts of "Tom Thumb! Ol' Tom Thumb! Mrs. General! Minnie Warren!" would follow us to our hotel, where we would disembark and greet the crowd that had gathered to laugh and applaud. After the hardships they had endured, it was clear they needed entertainment, and we were happy to provide it as we continued the same program we had performed throughout England and France—without the baby, of course.

Charles and I barely glanced at each other while we danced "The Tom Thumb Polka"; watched by so many other eyes, we had no need to look into each other's. Our true intimacy was with the audience. Never did we talk so animatedly as we did with our visitors after the performance, in the little informal levees that we held, where we signed our *cartes de visites*. Charles happily bestowed his kiss upon every female who wanted one, and even those who didn't, and while I still could not approve of such indiscreet behavior, I enjoyed shaking hands with my many admirers. I often thought about how frightened, how ashamed, I had been in my early days upon the river; those dangerous times were like a dream to me. For I was Mrs. General Tom Thumb, beloved and admired, and no one would want to harm me now.

I always made it a point to wave to my new friends as they left clutching my photograph; I turned and greeted the next in line just as I heard the clink of coins rattling in the money box.

While none of our many admirers would ever have harmed us, we did face dangers on the road. We had, by necessity, to travel with great sums of money, Mr. Kellogg's constant nightmare. There was always the danger of being robbed, particularly as our travel arrangements were often detailed in the Press.

One night we stopped at a very desolate hotel in Opelika, Alabama; the stairs leading up from the "lobby"—really just one large, stained spittoon—were merely rough boards loosely nailed to the rail. Our rooms were on the second floor, which was a blessing, as the third floor was reachable only by ladder!

The few inhabitants we had seen on the first floor were of such rough, dissipated appearance that our entire company was happy to gather in one room for the night, especially as Commodore Nutt was feeling poorly, suffering from the quinsy. We passed an uneasy few minutes until we heard a sudden scratching at the door, followed by retreating footsteps.

"Look here," Charles suddenly said, as we all rushed to open the door; on it was freshly chalked the message *11:35*.

"Whatever can it mean?" I wondered, and Rodney Nutt piped up, "It must be a message from the Ku Klux! It must mean someone is going to die at precisely eleven-thirty-five tonight!"

At this, we all froze in fear. The Ku Klux had just started to make its terrible presence felt, swearing vengeance against former slaves and northerners, and the name alone could strike terror in even the stoutest heart. Just as we were absorbing this, we heard the unmistakable report of two pistols fired successively.

"Sylvester!" Mrs. Bleeker cried; Mr. Bleeker had remained outside to settle the horses. She wanted to run downstairs, but we enjoined her to stay; just at that moment, Mr. Bleeker burst into the room, his long face pale, his hair standing on end.

"Get your wraps, there's a 'bus for the station at the door; we need to be on it."

Half the company ran downstairs; the other half remained to bundle up Commodore Nutt, who was carried downstairs in Mr. Bleeker's arms. Just as our half reached the door, we saw the 'bus pull off with the rest of the party, to our dismay.

"It'll be back soon enough," the toothless hotel proprietor

told us as he spat on the floor. "And if it ain't, you can all stay here until the morning, when the train comes."

"No!" Mr. Bleeker said in a strange, strangled voice. "We must get to the station!"

I was surprised by his urgency, for Mr. Bleeker was such a patient, mild man. Minnie held tightly to my hand, and I felt her shivering. Charles, I noticed, was trying very hard to look as brave as Mr. Bleeker, but he could not help but tremble, too.

Finally the omnibus returned, and we all piled in, Mr. Bleeker urging the driver to hurry the horses on as he kept looking over his shoulder. But before we could reach the station, the driver pulled up with a cry.

"Get down!" Mr. Bleeker hissed, pushing Charles down to the floor of the wagon. I pulled Minnie down next to me, and we hid behind the seat in front of us. But I could still see; passing us on the narrow road was a line of horses, all covered in white fabric, with only holes cut out for their eyes and ears. Upon these horses were ghostly figures in white sheets and hoods; they passed us in silence as they rode in the direction of the hotel. Not a breath was exhaled, not a sound was made, from our party or theirs. Even the horses did not whinny. Minnie trembled and clutched at my hand, and Charles shut his eyes, like a child who wishes to believe himself invisible. But I did not blink as I watched those masked men ride by, erect in their saddles, ominous in their number.

Finally they passed, and we proceeded to the station at a breakneck speed; once we joined the rest of our party, Mr. Bleeker finally exhaled, a little color returning to his face.

"Those shots you heard back at the hotel," he began, pausing to take a gulp of whiskey from the Commodore's ever-present flask. "There were two men downstairs who tried to get me to take a drink with them. I said I had to get upstairs to my friends, but they kept insisting, getting meaner by the minute. Finally, I broke away, only to see them exchange a look and run outside. I was curious. So when I got upstairs, I went to take a look out on the landing. In the yard were two figures in white, like the men who just passed us, and they both pointed a pistol at me and fired. They nearly got my hat! I ducked inside, and that's when I found all of you in the room with that message on the door, and I said to myself, *Bleeker, get everybody the heck out of here!* I just know they were planning to rob us, and if we'd stayed there they surely would have, or worse! Why nothing happened when they passed us on the road, I'll never know—maybe they just didn't recognize us."

Mrs. Bleeker paled and nearly fainted upon her husband's shoulder. Charles, too, turned an awful green color, and Minnie laid her head upon my shoulder and shut her eyes.

I remained upright on that cold, hard station bench, unable to stop seeing that ghostly line of horses and riders, pale, almost luminous, against the black of the Alabama forest. I couldn't believe I'd actually seen the Ku Klux with my own eyes. How terrifying!

I couldn't wait to write Mr. Barnum all about it.

OUR TRAVELS CONTINUED, NO LESS ADVENTUROUS—I SAW MY first alligator in Texas while crossing the Red River!—and in May of 1869, while staying in San Antonio, we received the following letter from Mr. Barnum:

My Dear Bleeker:

An idea has occurred to me in which I can see a "Golden Gate" opening for the Gen. Tom Thumb Co. What do you think of a "Tour around the World," including a visit to Australia? The new Pacific Railroad will be finished in a few weeks; you will then be enabled to cross the American Continent to California, thence by steam to Japan, China, British India, etc. I declare, in anticipation, I already envy you the pleasures and opportunities which such a trip will afford.

For the next three days I shall study all the maps I can lay my hands upon and, in imagination, mark you crossing the briny deep to those far-off countries. And as for gold! Tell the General that in Australia alone (don't fail to go to Australia) he will be sure to make more money than a horse can draw.

Decide quickly. If you consent to undertake the journey, prepare to start next month. Love to all,

Truly yours,
P. T. Barnum

"Well, isn't this something," Mr. Bleeker said after he finished reading the letter out loud to us all.

"A world tour," his gentle wife exclaimed, and as usual, I could not detect her own wishes in it; our dear Mrs. Bleeker was a cipher, a genuinely loving, soothing presence who seemed to exist only for us. I could never imagine her in her own home, mending her own clothes, deciding on her own entertainment or enjoyment. She was expressly put upon this earth to live in the service of P. T. Barnum, the General Tom Thumb Company, and her husband—and possibly in that order.

"Australia?" Charles blinked, nervously lighting up a cigar, as Mr. Barnum would have done. "That wild place? Why, has any American ever been there?"

"Which is all the more reason that we should go," I said decidedly; my husband's nervous fears never ceased to challenge me, stirring up a recklessness I did not always know I possessed. "Imagine, to be among the first! And to travel the new Union

Pacific railroad, too—I imagine we'll see buffalo. And Indians, naturally!"

"Indians!" Charles puffed even more nervously, blowing a quick succession of smoke rings into the air.

"Oh, Sister—Indians?" Minnie, seated next to Mrs. Bleeker on a sofa, paled.

"From a distance, I'm sure," I said hastily, although inwardly I did hope to see one or two up close; I had always wondered if their skin was as red as the clay earth they roamed, as was said.

"It's a tremendous opportunity." Mr. Bleeker consulted the letter again, spreading it upon the table as if it were a map. Indeed, we all drew close, to study it. As if Mr. Barnum's expressive handwriting alone could tell us which direction to follow—and I truly believed, at that moment, that it could.

"If we do this," Mr. Bleeker said in his grave, considered manner, "you'll be world famous, for I know of no other troupe that has undertaken such an arduous journey. It's truly unprecedented."

"Then we must do it!" I couldn't contain my excitement; I clasped my hands together and jumped up and down, letting my dignity fall to the floor in a rumpled heap. To think of it all! The exotic scenes—Commodore Perry had returned from Japan only a scant nine years before; even during the Civil War, newspapers had been full of the strange Oriental habits and customs just beginning to be known to the West. Those long sticks they used for utensils, the way they drank their tea in small bowls instead of cups. The way they sat upon the floor to eat! How charming a custom, especially for one my size! I had spent far too many an elaborate dinner perched upon precarious cushions, my feet dangling from my chair like a child's. I couldn't wait to partake of an authentic Japanese meal seated upon the floor, where everyone would be my size.

Australia, I knew nothing about, other than that it was a wild, untamed place, much as our American West had been twenty years ago. Yet I was eager to see it; eager to see the highest mountain peaks on our own continent; eager to see the new railroad, almost finished, that linked the Atlantic to the Pacific; eager to see *everything*. That world that had beckoned to me for so long— it was not bigger than me, after all. I would conquer it by seeing every corner of it; I felt sorry for the women who had to content themselves with gazing at the globe while they dusted it, dutifully, trapped in the houses of their husbands.

"We must do it," I said once more. "Think of how famous we'll be! How much we will impress those who think our bodies are weak simply because they're small!"

"Vinnie has a point there," Mr. Bleeker said, doing his very best to keep his face neutral—he had the best poker face among us, with his drooping mustache and beard, and sad eyes; we often joked that if we found ourselves penniless, we could always send him out to win back our fortune in a saloon game. But I saw that glint in his eyes, the way he quickly licked his lips, as if tasting something tantalizing and sweet. I knew he desired to go, quite as much as I did.

He deferred, however, at least in manner, to Charles; after all, it was my husband's name upon the masthead of our stationery. In theory, Charles was the decision maker of our party.

"Mr. Barnum obviously thinks this is a splendid idea," I reminded him solemnly. He nodded—just as solemnly—and puffed upon his cigar once more. I could not look at Mr. Bleeker, for fear of spoiling the moment; we held our breaths, waiting for my husband's verdict.

"Well, if Phineas thinks it's a good idea," he finally concluded, nodding gravely. And our collective breath was exhaled, glasses raised in a toast to the new adventure. Then we all scattered like mice to write letters, pack trunks, and take the first train back north so we could buy new clothes, mend old ones, and say goodbye to friends and family.

We left New York on June 21, 1869. The newspapers trumpeted the General Tom Thumb Company's "Three Years' Tour Around the World." The company numbered thirteen, which Mama felt boded ill for our safe return. However, Mr. Bleeker quickly pointed out that he always paid full fare for each of the two ponies we brought with us to pull our miniature carriage, so that really there were fifteen in the party. I don't believe this mollified her.

"Vinnie, please take care, and bring yourself and Minnie safely home," Mama said, clinging to both of her daughters before we boarded the train from the New York and Harlem Railroad Station. This was a new, expanded station, very different from the little shack where I had first disembarked in New York, all those years ago. Yet there were rumors that an even grander, more central railroad terminal was to be constructed by Commodore Vanderbilt just a few blocks away. All those trains that came into New York from the north and east, like pins stuck haphazardly in a cushion, would now all end at the same terminus. The new depot was even rumored to have a restaurant inside for waiting passengers!

"Mama, I will, I promise! Try not to worry, and we will write whenever possible." I kissed my dear mother on the cheek and patted Papa fondly on the shoulder; both were kneeling down, although I knew how difficult it was for them, now that they were older. Age had even made Papa less stoic; he had tears in his blue eyes, which he did not even try to hide.

"I'm always saying goodbye to my girls," he said gruffly. "I don't know why that is. I always said I never knew what to do with you, Vinnie, and I have lived to see the truth in it. You never stop surprising me—all the way around the world now! I never imagined I'd leave Middleborough, let alone see my daughters off to Japan!"

"We'll bring you back glorious presents—would you like a samurai's sword? That would be handy for cutting hay!" I laughed, kissing my father lightly; he surprised me by hugging me to him so tightly I could hear his faithful heart beating against my cheek, like the faint but reliable ticking of an old pocket watch. Then he released me with the same urgency, and groaningly pushed himself upright.

Blinking up at him through my own tears, I smiled, then gently pulled Minnie out of Mama's possessive embrace. "Keep her safe," Mama whispered to me, and I nodded, pulling Minnie toward the train, where Mr. Bleeker was waiting to lift us both up the stairs. The engine was already huffing, steam billowing out from the tall chimney. I hesitated only a moment, searching the platform for a particular gold-tipped walking stick. Mr. Barnum had promised he would try to see us off. I did so want to see him once more; three years seemed like such a long time.

He did not come, however, and I could wait no longer as the conductor made his final cry of "All aboard!" I nodded at Mr. Bleeker to lift me up, and then I made my way down the aisle of the train as it lurched away from the station. Stumbling, I nearly fell, headfirst, into the lap of a woman seated on the aisle. Only Mr. Bleeker's ready hand upon my head kept me upright.

"Goodness me!" The woman laughed—and then she pulled me to her in a smothering embrace. "I declare, you are the sweetest little thing, aren't you?"

"Madam, please!" I pushed myself away from her; she smelled strongly of peppermint drops and camphor. "I beg your pardon!"

She didn't take offense; indeed, she kept beaming at me as if I were a precocious child.

"This is Mrs. Charles Stratton," Mr. Bleeker informed her. "She is on her way to tour the West."

"Oh, I knew her right away—I said to my Fred"—she poked the man next to her with her elbow; he grunted and turned away—"I said, 'Fred, that's that little Mrs. Tom Thumb, I just know it!' She looks just like her little picture, yes, she does!" Still the woman beamed, even as she continued to talk above me, as if I wasn't there. Smiling frostily, I bowed and continued down the aisle, shaking off Mr. Bleeker's steadying hand upon my shoulder.

I climbed up into my seat next to Minnie; Mrs. Bleeker had already placed a cushion there for me, so that I might see out the window. As New York fell away, I wondered how many days it would be until we reached Omaha. There, we would board the new Union Pacific railroad, some of the first passengers to do so.

I doubted that vile woman was traveling any farther than Albany; certainly she wasn't going to be shaking the hand of the Emperor of Japan!

Yet for a moment, I couldn't prevent myself from imagining how it would be to travel—even if it was just to Albany—by myself, to climb upon a train unassisted, to carry my own luggage, to take whichever seat I wanted, no cushion or stool necessary.

I imagined what it would be like to be able to walk around freely, anonymously, nothing about me remarkable in any way. Would I like it? Would I trade my fame if it meant that I never had to suffer fools hugging me to them ever again?

I honestly did not know. And I was more than a little relieved that it was a moot point, after all.

THIS BOOK IS NOT INTENDED TO BE A MERE TRAVELOGUE; MY DEAR Mr. Bleeker wrote a very fine account of our journey in *General Tom Thumb's Three Years Tour Around the World,* which I am sure you have read previously, as it was a very popular book and made quite a lot of money.

I cannot pass over this time in my life, however, without wanting to share some of my impressions. Naturally I am proud of what we accomplished, especially in such primitive circumstances compared to the comforts of today. Our planned route involved an average travel of one hundred and ten miles every day, as well as the giving of two entertainments! To those who are used to more modern ways of travel and hospitality, this may not seem much of a feat. However, the last spike had just been driven in the Union Pacific railroad only a little over a month before we embarked upon it. The West was newly open, raw and unforgiving. Cities which today conjure up images of cultured civility—Salt Lake City, Omaha, Reno—were little more than canvas camps at the time, sprouting up along the newly built railway like prairie flowers. Many more of these temporary cities—hotels, restaurants, post offices, even, made of dirty canvas flaps draped over wobbly wooden frames—have now faded from memory, vanished in the dust of the trains that roared on ahead, once the tracks were laid.

We confidently expected to see Indians, and indeed, even as the train was pulling out of Omaha, nervous passengers were looking out the windows for the red man. Mr. Bleeker packed a pistol; so, too, did Charles, although it was a ridiculously tiny one given to him by Queen Victoria, with custom bullets so small they could scarcely hurt a prairie dog, let alone an Indian on a pony. Yet he strutted about, stroking his beard with one hand, patting his breast pocket with the other, just as he saw the other men doing—acting as if he had enough firepower to take out an entire band of ferocious savages.

While sleeper cars were now in use on eastern trains—a platform could be raised to join two facing seats into one bed, while above, a bunk was lowered from the arched roof of the car—those first trains to go west from Omaha were not outfitted in this way. Hence, on extended legs—our longest was twenty-six hours of continuous travel—we had to sleep, to use the word loosely, upright upon the hard seats. Even though they were upholstered in horsehair—an improvement over those hard wooden seats from my first train trip to Cincinnati back in the fifties—they made for very uncomfortable sleeping, indeed. Although for once, we little folk had the advantage of our companions, as we could curl up easier than they could!

As always, it was impossible to keep oneself clean and tidy; even with the windows pushed up, the dust from the prairie and the cinders and grit from the tracks managed to seep inside the cars. Not to mention that it was very hot, as we left Omaha in July of 1869. While there was a dining car on the train, the food was not well prepared or even fresh, and there was never any ice for water. In the primitive water closets, where I had to lug my steps with me so that I could reach the basin, the water in it was already so gray with other people's grime that I never wanted to splash it upon my face. And the smell in that hot, stuffy little cell was intolerable.

But the scenery, as we sped across the great prairie, was always interesting, always majestic; I'd never seen a sky so big, not even upon the sea. The tall, waving grasses, undulating in the wind, were as hypnotic as any ocean waves. Prairie dogs popped up and down like children's toys, and herds of antelope raced along the train, as did immense herds of buffalo. We could see them from a distance; at first, they resembled a swarm of flies moving now away, now toward, the tracks; as we got closer, we could actually feel the thundering of their hooves through the floor of the train. At the first sighting, more than a few passengers decided to use them as target practice; with cries and whoops, men pulled out their pistols or rifles and thrust them through the windows, the ringing from the shots practically piercing my eardrums.

We reached Cheyenne, our first stop, almost exactly twenty-four hours after leaving Omaha and without having seen a single Indian, much to my disappointment. The manager of the theater there met us at the train and helped us load our belongings— trunks of costumes, trinkets and *cartes de visites* that we would sell, scenery and props—into a waiting Wells Fargo wagon; Charles and I climbed into our miniature carriage, while Rodney Nutt harnessed our two little ponies, who were restless from being cooped up, prancing mischievously against the bit. We hadn't a chance to freshen up; my traveling dress was dirty and wrinkled beyond measure, and I felt as wilted as the feather in my bonnet. But straight to the theater we went, Charles and I waving to the townspeople who spied our carriage and followed out of curiosity; Minnie and Nutt accompanying the Bleekers in the wagon. As soon as we reached the theater—really a barn, barely swept, with rows of crude benches and hay bales upon which the audience sat—we tidied ourselves as best we could. Mr. Bleeker and our agent hastily set up their concession and box office, and soon we were onstage in front of an eager audience of prairie folk. We repeated our performance later in the evening, then collapsed in a canvas tent that served as the town's hotel, before getting back on the train the next day.

This became our routine, then. Many of the hotels were merely tents. Other times we stayed in houses, usually the mayor's own, or one of his relatives'. We never ordered a meal to our own choosing; we ate what was given to us in the hotel, boardinghouse, or private dining room. Privacy was at a premium; oftentimes the men were separated from the ladies by only a thin canvas flap.

Charles and I, and Mr. and Mrs. Bleeker, as the two married couples, were sometimes accorded some privacy, but I always made sure that Minnie was with Charles and me, as she was the only other female. I knew she was very homesick on this trip, much more than she had been in Europe when she had the various infants to occupy her time.

"Vinnie, what do you think Mama and Papa are doing right now?" she would ask me several times a day, and it became almost a game; often I would answer nonsense, just to make her laugh.

"I expect Papa is baking a cake right now, wearing Mama's best apron, and Mama is sitting by the fire smoking a pipe," I might say, casually—and be grateful for Minnie's helpless giggles at the notion.

Or—

"It's five o'clock; wouldn't Papa be bringing in the cows from the pasture right now?" Minnie would muse, peeking out the canvas flap of our latest "theater," as if she could see all the way back to Massachusetts.

"No, he's just taking them out now; they like to spend the night outside, not in the barn, don't you remember? So they can look at the stars and wish upon them!"

Minnie laughed at this notion; her dimple deepened, and her merry eyes sparkled under her dark, suspicious brows. She flung her arms around me and whispered, "I'm so glad I'm here with you—I'm so glad that you're not lonely!"

"Lonely?" I laughed, holding her at arm's length, looking into her sweet, sympathetic face. "What do you mean? I wouldn't be lonely—I wouldn't have the time!"

Minnie merely smiled and hugged me again; then she walked away with such a knowing, understanding look, a sudden, sharp blade of guilt knifed itself through my heart. Was it wicked to keep her with me just because I needed her? Just because I was afraid of being left too much alone with my husband?

And did she truly understand that she was the necessary glue that kept Charles and me together, that she alone made us a family? We both clung to her, in different ways. Charles loved her dearly, as she loved him; the two of them played together, lavishing affection upon every stray dog, cat, or even the occasional chicken that wandered into our hotel or theater. Or they made up games of their own device, games that they would not teach anyone else, acting exactly like two school chums who wanted to appear clannish.

With Minnie, the three of us together at table could always find something to chatter about; she loved to listen to Charles's tales, and he was a wonderful storyteller when he had an eager audience, which I must admit I was not. On the rare occasions when it was just Charles and me, we exhausted conversation before the soup was gone.

"We'll be in Utah in the morning. I'm anxious to see how the polygamists live, aren't you? It seems more barbaric than the Indians," I said one evening as we dined alone in our hotel room— a corner of a canvas structure; the proprietor had proudly offered Charles and me "a romantic dinner for two," apart from the communal table set up in the middle of the tent. He had found a small table and two camp stools, and hung up a thin curtain to shield us from the others. Yet we were taunted by the merry dinner talk, the convivial clinking of glasses, on the other side of the curtain.

"Charles? Did you hear me?" I spoke louder, trying to drown out the guffaws accompanying Rodney Nutt as he told a story about a man who once raced a horse the wrong way around a track. "About the polygamists?"

"Oh, I'm—of course, of course, polygamists! Dreadful insects, aren't they—always buzzing around your ears! My dear, did I ever tell you about the time that I swallowed a bug? I was onstage during a sweltering heat, and a fly was buzzing about, and just as I opened my mouth to sing 'Yankee Doodle,' that creature flew into it and down my windpipe! I tell you, I couldn't sing a word after that! I coughed and coughed until . . ."

Smiling tightly, I nodded at Charles as he continued his story, and allowed my mind to wander elsewhere—along railroad tracks, over mountains, across oceans. *Dear God, please don't ever let the world stop expanding, stop sprouting new cities and railroads and passageways for me to visit, for me to dream about*—I almost prayed it out loud.

It was in Ogden, Utah, that I had the opportunity to correct Charles's impression about polygamy. For it was here that I first saw it in practice. Ogden was a town of about two thousand people; compared to the other communities along the Union Pacific, it was a model of cleanliness and order, and we could not help but attribute this to the fact that the Mormon bishop controlled the town. Neat clapboard buildings lined clean streets; there were none of the usual saloons and houses of ill repute that had followed the progression of the railroad in other villages.

The bishop offered us the use of their Tabernacle for our entertainment; I thought this very good of him, indeed, and quite surprising. I could not imagine any Baptist church doing the same! So my initial impression of the Mormons was quite favorable.

He asked that the first two rows be reserved for his family. Over fifty seats in all, and I was amused, thinking, logically, that there were far more seats than could be filled by one brood. Yet in a flash the bishop returned with his brother, followed by seven adult females and forty-two children varying in ages from three to fourteen years; then came three more females and twenty-two children, whom the bishop referred to, casually, as "my family"!

It may have been amusing at first, as we peered out from behind the curtain, sure that at any minute the endless parade of children would stop, but soon I ceased to find it so. During our entertainments, Mr. Bleeker always invited a dozen children, from the ages of three to ten, to stand with Minnie onstage to compare their height to hers. When the invitation was extended on this night, Bishop West immediately turned to his family and beckoned the requisite number to the platform. Mr. Bleeker placed the smallest of them nearest to Minnie and then requested the parents to give their ages. Pointing to the first child, Mr. Bleeker inquired, "What is this child's age?"

"Four years," replied the Bishop with a satisfied smile.

"And this?" Mr. Bleeker pointed to the next.

"Four years," the Bishop answered placidly.

"They're both your children?" Mr. Bleeker could not help himself from asking.

The Bishop nodded. A faint blush mottled his cheeks.

"How old is this one?" Mr. Bleeker pointed to the next largest.

"Four," the Bishop said, his voice becoming a bit strangled.

"Yours, as well?"

The Bishop nodded.

"And this one?"

"Four."

"Yours?"

"Yes."

"And this——?"

"Stop!" I could not help myself; I raced forward to Mr. Bleeker, tugging at the bottom of his coat, imploring him to cease this disgraceful display. Startled, that poor man could do nothing but signal to me to keep quite, and indeed, I did not know what more I could say——I only felt such embarrassment for the children, for the wives, for us all. It was *barbaric,* that's what it was, barbaric that all these children of the same age could be sired by one father in these modern times. I did not want to be here any longer; I could not wait to leave. Yet even when we returned to our hotel, I could not prevent myself from inquiring into the marital status

of the proprietor, and nearly screamed when I was told that he had ten wives!

Ten! Those poor women, having to subject themselves to one man, having to share him with others, having to raise all these other children as their own, having to lie down with him whenever he desired, never able to refuse—

"I trust the pin money won't bankrupt you!" My husband was laughing with the innkeeper, man to man, and I whirled about.

"Charles Stratton, how dare you? How dare you laugh with this man as if—as if—"

The entire company was staring at me, mouths open; they had never seen me act so strangely. I took a breath and tried to calm myself, but I could not dampen the fire of indignation that burned in my breast, searing my skin as if it had been branded from within. Why did these men disgust me so? Why could I not look any of their wives in the eye? I had seen natives by now, brown-skinned people who lived in squalor, whose men drank but whose women carried their children on their backs, proudly erect. I had not been disgusted by them. They were not God-fearing people, and so could live only as their instincts told them, and it was obvious their women were strong, stronger than their men.

But the Mormon women were different; there was something shameful and dejected about them. They did not seem to live in the same sphere as their men, except to serve and—I couldn't prevent a shudder—have relations and bear endless children. It was the same way in Salt Lake City, where we journeyed by wagon, since there was no railroad yet built from Ogden. When we arrived we were treated like dignitaries and introduced to everyone of importance, including Brigham Young. These men were cordial enough, but we met their women only during meal-times when they served at table, their heads bowed in submission. The obsessively clean appearance of the city in general at-tested to a feminine hand, yet it remained hidden, as if behind a curtain—or jail—of masculine design.

I could not get out of Utah fast enough.

Finally, we continued west, to Nevada. Leaving the railroad, we decided to travel by stage to a few places, such as Virginia City; progress upon these mountain roads was perilous, beset as it was by not only unpredictable weather, steep mountain drops, and In-dians, but also highway robbers. Naturally, we attracted much at-tention wherever we went, and my jewels and fine clothes were well known, as was the fact that we had, by necessity, to travel with large amounts of money.

One evening, our last night in Virginia City, two strangers struck up a seemingly pleasant conversation with Mr. Bleeker at the hotel, during which they urged him to take several precau-tions with my jewels, the cash from the box office, and other valu-ables.

"Cut a lining in your hat, Sir; that's always where I carry any gold," one of the fellows said.

"That's a good plan; those highway robbers always check your boots first," said the other.

"Thank you, Sirs, for the excellent advice," Mr. Bleeker said.

"You're leaving on the regular stage, then?" the first man asked as Mr. Bleeker rose to leave.

"Yes, indeed."

"Good thinking, for it has an excellent guard, always."

Mr. Bleeker left these two "gentlemen" to smoke cigars in the lobby of the hotel; he then snuck out the back door and went straight to the Wells Fargo and Company office to arrange for two wagons. We left at seven the next morning, and when we reached Reno, we heard that the regular noon stage had been held up by two masked men who, while methodically relieving all the poor passengers of their valuables, kept muttering, "Tom Thumb! Where's Tom Thumb? He's supposed to be on this stage!"

Finally, we reached San Francisco. It was such a relief to be in a cultured metropolis once more, with paved roads and gaslights and hotels made of wood, not canvas. Triumphantly, Charles and I paraded through the streets in our miniature carriage, our ponies none the worse for the trip. Three times a day we filled Platt's Hall, which held two thousand people, and were able to telegraph Mr. Barnum that the trip had been the "golden opportunity" he had envisioned, indeed.

We left San Francisco for Yokohama, Japan, on November 4, 1869; we would not return to the shores of this great country of ours until June 22, 1872. All in all, we traveled 55,487 miles (31,216 of them by sea) and gave 1,472 entertainments in 587 different cities and towns in all climates of the world without missing a single performance because of accident or illness.

We met the Viceroy of India, King Victor Emmanuele II of Italy, Emperor Franz Joseph of Austria, and assorted Maharajas and Shahs. We ate leechee nuts in China, chewed tea leaves in Ceylon, and consumed octopus in Japan. We saw the Pyramids, pilgrims on their way to Mecca, and sampans in Japan. The heat in Singapore was like being wrapped in a hot woolen blanket and set out in the noonday sun; the cold of the Australian desert at night made your bones cry. We saw women dressed scandalously, in nothing but scarves and jewels, in Madras; we observed entire families bathing together in the nude in Japan. Trains, when we could find them, were primitive: some with benches, with no backs, for seats; others simply cavernous cars in which you sat upon the floor. Ships were steamers, and often they were overcrowded, with poor people practically hanging off the deck rails. Often we would get to a destination with no clear idea how we would then travel on to the next place; maps were crude, unreadable, and unreliable.

Yet even in such places we would sometimes come across a reminder of home; of civilization. Minnie spied an 1862 issue of *Godey's Lady's Book* in a fish market in Bombay, of all places; she eagerly begged the fishmonger to give it to her, instead of using it to wrap up his eels. Somehow he understood, and she carried it with her through the rest of the tour, reading and rereading it although the fashions, of course, were long out of style even before we left home. (Such wide skirts we used to wear! And those ridiculous, enormous-ribboned bonnets!)

And one evening in Ceylon, while I was trying to read by the weak oil light in the hotel parlor (there was no reading in the primitive bedrooms, as everything was encased with thick mosquito netting), Mr. Bleeker presented me with a tattered copy of the *New York Herald Tribune.* "Look at this," he said with a sly grin. He pointed to an article with his bony finger.

"*Barnum's newest sensation,*" I read aloud, and laughed. I checked the date of the paper; it was over a year old. But seeing Mr. Barnum's name in print, so far away from him, after having been gone so long, made my heart leap unexpectedly, almost as if he himself had entered the room. We stayed in communication during the trip, of course, but mainly with telegrams, which were always so businesslike and addressed to the troupe in general, never to me personally. And if telegrams were sporadic in the places we were visiting, letters were even more so. So it was with a hunger I hadn't even been aware was gnawing at me that I read his name.

"The old man has kept himself busy while we're away," Mr. Bleeker said with a chuckle, as he folded his long frame into an absurdly small, lacquered Oriental chair. He lit his pipe and puffed until he could get a good draw on it.

"Yes, it appears he has," I said as I continued to read the article. Mr. Barnum had begun presenting a new discovery, an Admiral Dot. Admiral Dot was "a dwarf more diminutive in stature than General Tom Thumb was when I found him," Mr. Barnum had told the newspaper.

"You've got to admire him. He loses his museum, he builds another. He sends you all off to see the world—"

"And he replaces us with someone else." Crumpling the newspaper, I tossed it on the floor. But Mr. Bleeker didn't notice, as he finally had gotten his pipe burning to his satisfaction, and was stretching his long legs out in front of him.

"He just keeps on going. 'Admiral Dot.' He has a genius for naming things, don't you think?"

"Absolutely. Almost God-like, naming all the animals."

Mr. Bleeker must have finally noticed the sarcasm in my voice, for he peered at me through the pipe smoke, eyebrows raised. Then he saw the newspaper on the ground.

"What's wrong, Vinnie? I thought you'd be happy to know that he's carrying on, as usual."

"Oh, I suppose I am, it's just—never mind." I picked up my book and tried to find my place, but suddenly Mr. Bleeker plucked it out of my hands.

"You're not jealous of that Dot fellow, are you?"

"I have no need to be jealous of another performer—especially one so unproven—thank you very much. Now, will you please return my book?"

"But that's just Barnum's way! You know that! He knows what the public wants, and he gives it to them. Truth is, he usually tells them what they want, before they know it. So the public wants to see another little man. So? That has nothing to do with you. It's not personal with him like that."

"Nothing ever is personal with him." I sniffed, then held my hand out for my book. Mr. Bleeker gave it back to me, but I still felt him staring at me. He even scratched his head, so deep was his puzzlement.

Suddenly, however, he snapped his fingers and smiled; like an eager pupil, he tugged on my sleeve. Not in the mood to hide my impatience, I closed my book with a sigh and looked up.

"But Vinnie, listen! I never did tell you what he told me after your wedding. All that day, he was proud as could be, but I tell you, Vinnie, after the reception was over, he asked me to drive back home with him. And he was sad, Vinnie—the saddest I'd ever seen him."

"He was?"

"He sure was! You know he's sometimes a crier—remember how he sobbed when the Emancipation Proclamation was announced?"

"Yes." And despite myself, I smiled; that was one of my most cherished memories, the January day when we all sat in his office and he read aloud Mr. Lincoln's Proclamation from the newspaper, tears running unchecked down his pink face.

"Well, that day in the carriage, he had tears in his eyes. Sad tears. And he said, 'Bleeker, this has been the happiest day of my life. And the saddest.' And I asked him why, and he said, 'Because I'll never have this great a success again. Those two little people, they've spoiled me. How will I ever top this?' And you know, Vinnie, I don't think he'll ever stop trying, even though he knows, deep in his heart, that he won't. But it's just in him to keep going, that's the thing you have to admire about him. You two, though— Charles and you—you brought him the greatest success he's ever known, and he won't ever forget that. Or you. The two of you, well—you're special."

I stared at Mr. Bleeker for a long moment; he stared back, that anxious, eager smile upon his face. And I couldn't help but nod, as his intentions were so obviously good.

"Yes, of course. I know that. I'm just tired from this heat, that's all."

"I'd give my favorite pipe for a cold bath tonight, but the manager said there isn't any fresh water." Mr. Bleeker nodded in agreement, and he settled back down with his pipe, content to watch an enormous moth that was determined to hurl itself, over and over, toward the oil lamp.

I opened my book again, but I found myself staring at the same page for the longest time, before finally giving up and going upstairs to bed.

As our travels continued, our clothing never seemed to be clean; the dust and dampness of travel was trapped forever within the folds of cotton, silk, and satin. We mended and remended until our fingers were sore; it's difficult to contemplate what to pack for three years' travel, and when clothing ripped or became worn, we could not replace it. For one thing, very few places where we traveled were adept at sewing Western fashions, complete with the new bustles and tight bodices in fashion. Sarongs and kimonos were plentiful, but of courser Minnie, Mrs. Bleeker, and I could not wear those! For another, particular items such as gloves, shoes, bonnets, etc., that had to be custom-made for Minnie and myself were impossible to come by. So we had to continually patch and repair.

In some places, such as Japan and China, where there were few Americans or Europeans, communication was impossible, if not comical; we bowed and scraped a lot. Our size, however, never failed to bring a grin or a smile even to the most dour Chinaman

or round Buddhist matron; this was always our entrée into different cultures, and it always assured us goodwill and hospitality. If
few of the people we met had ever seen an American, they certainly had never seen a very tiny one, and so Charles, Minnie, Nutt,
and myself had to put up with much patting and touching and pet-
ting. Never did I feel there was anything sinister or insulting in it,
though—and, after all, we were just as curious about their strange
costumes and manners as they were about ours. So it was more of
a *mutual* curiosity; we patted and touched and petted right back,
free to do so in a way we were not at home—and we enjoyed it.

So used was I to seeing the world through a maze of table
legs, wagon wheels, ladies' skirts, and men's trousers, I could only
note, with pleasure, how much more colorful it was in these exotic lands. The vivid hues of the Orient were a welcome contrast
to the more sedate—dare I say dull?—wardrobe choices of the
West, such colorful silks in hothouse colors of pinks and oranges
and greens!

When travel became difficult, particularly in Australia, where
we had to journey hundreds of miles in the desert with only a
faint pair of wagon tracks to guide us, the four of us—Minnie,
Nutt, Charles, and myself—trudged through the sand just like
everyone else, to give the horses a rest. The horses sank to their
knees, as did Mr. Bleeker and the others; we did not, although it
was difficult to get our footing, as we never reached solid ground.

Despite all the perils we faced—a typhoon on the way to
Japan, pythons in Ceylon, wild kangaroos in Australia, fearsome
spiders everywhere; despite the marvels we saw—the great Pyramids of Egypt, which inspired Mr. Bleeker to whisper that for
once, he understood how we must feel, as he thought himself to
be only about two feet tall at that moment—only once did I experience, keenly, my size and how vulnerable it made me. And
that was in Nevada, before we even left our own continent.

Minnie, Mrs. Bleeker, and myself were perched in a hired wagon; it had a cover on it, but the sides were wide open to the elements. We had stopped at an inn, where the men and the driver got out to ask for directions. We were on a mountain road with drops so steep as to not be believed; as we waited patiently inside the wagon for the men to return, something startled the horses and they took off, uncontrolled, around the bend.

As the wagon careened faster and faster, the thundering of the horses' panicked hooves ringing, like a blacksmith's hammer, in my ears, Minnie and I bounced around helplessly; soon we were covered in bruises. I feared, desperately, that we would be thrown from the wagon. Our feet could not steady us, as they could not reach the floor, and our hands were too small to grip the rough wooden slats of the seats; at one point I looked down, amazed to see that my palm was cut and bleeding. Then I felt an arm around me; Mrs. Bleeker somehow managed to gather us both in her arms, grasping us tightly. And she began to pray, like the serene creature she was; she told us not to be afraid, even unto death.

Death seemed like a distinct possibility, for we could not know when the horses would stop, and sharp boulders surrounded us on all sides. Had the wagon been smashed, we surely would have perished; as it was, the horses continued their wild ride until they rounded a particularly sharp curve—all three of us were thrown, together in a prayerful heap, down to the floor of the wagon—to a suddenly flat, fenced parcel of land. One of the horses swerved, with a wild whinny, directly into the fence; for one suspenseful minute, we slowed almost to a walk.

"Quick, jump, before they take off again!" I cried, not content to pray. I grabbed Minnie and hugged her to me; closing my eyes, I pushed us both from the wagon, and we landed on a soft patch of grass, rolling over and over. Miraculously, we were mostly un-hurt, as was Mrs. Bleeker, who landed only ten feet away. Gasping and blinking, we sat catching our breath until Mr. Bleeker came running up on his long, loping legs, his beard practically trailing behind him.

"Julia! Vinnie! Minnie! To see you alive—didn't think I would! You've had a providential escape!" He fell to his knees and fiercely embraced his wife.

"I did not really think any of us would be killed," his wife replied, although her lips trembled, as did her hands. "I was so busy holding the little ones so that they wouldn't go flying out, I couldn't be afraid."

"You saved us," I told her, my own limbs shaking. "You kept us inside the wagon."

That was the one time, on the entire trip, Reader, when I truly felt vulnerable. Every other danger had been equal to us all. Indians, robbers, those terrifying sudden thunderstorms in the mountains that could wash away a road in the blink of an eye—any in our party could have perished because of them, regardless of size.

But as that wagon careened down the road, and Minnie and I were utterly helpless, unable to brace our feet against anything to keep us inside, I had felt, for only the first time since my days with Colonel Wood, physically vulnerable. Even more distressing, I had felt unable to protect my sister, despite my promises to Mama and Papa—and to myself.

"Are you all right?" I finally looked at Minnie, who was still in my arms. "Oh, what a terrible blow it would be to Mama and Papa, had we both perished!"

"Yes, I'm fine," Minnie answered, with an unexpected little laugh. "I thought to myself, *Go ahead, horses, do your best; I can ride as fast behind you as you can run.*" She laughed again; I stared at her as she gently but firmly unwound my arms from her shoulders and slid off my lap. She stood up and brushed her torn skirts briskly; my timid little sister did not appear to have been frightened in the least.

"You did, did you?" I asked her, amazed.

"Yes. For you see, Sister," Minnie said with a suddenly wise, ancient look in her eyes, "I am not to be killed so easily."

I laughed, surprise and relief chasing away my terror. And I believed her, all of a sudden. I believed her conviction, her defiance in the face of disaster. Or perhaps I simply *wanted* to believe her. Whatever the case, for the rest of the trip I did not worry at all for my sister's safety, and it was a great burden lifted from my shoulders. No more did I feel guilt and anxiety for keeping her with me; she would be perfectly fine.

How foolish I was! For it wasn't kangaroos or snakes or typhoons or runaway horses that I needed to fear. It was nothing nearly so dramatic as all that.

No, it was simply love, the desire to live a normal life, like any woman. This was what I myself did not have the courage to face. And so I did not think, even for a moment, that my sweet, simple sister did.

But I was wrong.

INTERMISSION

From *The Popular Science Monthly,* February 1877

TALKING BY TELEGRAPH

On Sunday, November 26th, Prof. A. Graham Bell experimented with the "telephone" on the wires of the Eastern Railroad Company between Boston and Salem. . . . According to the account published in the COMMONWEALTH of Boston, conversation was carried on with Mr. Watson at Salem, by all those present, in turn, without any difficulty, even the voices of the speakers being easily recognized.

From *Scribner's Monthly,* October 1877

NEW AND CHEAP ANTISEPTIC

Bisulphide of carbon has been recently reported as possessing remarkable antiseptic and preservative qualities, but the offensive smell and inflammable character of this substance make it both dangerous and troublesome.

FIFTEEN

A Sister Act Breaks Up

VINNIE, I'D LIKE TO SPEAK TO YOU."

"What is it, dear?" I looked up from my writing desk. Minnie was standing in the doorway to my boudoir, a charming little picture in her bustled dress, with her hair done up rather severely, although a few curls could not help but escape. With her matronly hairstyle and sophisticated clothes, she looked like a girl playing dress-up; her solemn face with those incongruously impish eyes still looked so childlike.

"Is this a good time? It's a bit—serious."

"Serious?" I couldn't help but smile. "What's serious, Pumpkin? Oh, I'm sorry—I mean, Mrs. Newell."

I still had a difficult time saying those words—*Mrs. Newell*. It seemed incredible to me that my little sister had actually gone and gotten married. How had that happened? It was almost as if she had done it when I wasn't looking; as if I'd forgotten myself and gone to take a nap only to awake and find my sister had run off somewhere. And now, almost six months later, I still didn't know where to find her.

Yet she had gotten married in a perfectly respectable manner, to a man we met through Mr. Barnum, Edward Newell. He was not as small as we were—he was no "perfectly formed miniature man"—but he was not tall, either. He was a performer, originally from England; he started out with a roller-skating act for Mr. Barnum, and when Commodore Nutt decided to retire—and marry a normal-size woman!—Edward took his place in our troupe.

He was also a perfectly nice man who adored Minnie. I hadn't taken much notice of his affection for her at first. I simply had no expectation of romance for my little sister—even when Nutt had mooned after her, I hadn't really thought it was a possibility, more like another of his pranks. And what did True Love look like? I did not know myself, so how could I recognize it in others?

Soon after Edward joined the troupe, however, Minnie began to withdraw from me, ever so slightly. No more was it our happy threesome; even when she was with us physically, it was obvious her thoughts were elsewhere. And I had to wonder, then, if all those times when Minnie had played with Charles and peppered me with questions about home hadn't been deliberate on her part. Had she been homesick—or had she worried that I was? Had she truly enjoyed playing with Charles—or had she seen that he was lonely?

I honestly couldn't say anymore. My sister was turning into someone I didn't recognize; she was turning into a woman. A woman with sudden blushes, mysterious silences, longing sighs—a woman who did not want her sister's protection any longer. For when Edward and I walked into a room together, it wasn't me to whom Minnie turned. She no longer had any desire to hide behind her older sister; she no longer had any desire to hide, period.

Minnie and Edward had married, quietly, without Astors and Vanderbilts and Presidents, this past summer of 1877; it was now December. While Minnie and Edward made their home with Charles and me in Middleborough, they did not need our presence the way we needed theirs. I watched, both jealous and bewildered, as they took long walks together, immersed in conversation; as they sat quietly in a dark corner after dinner, content simply to be near each other; as they retired to their shared bedroom, to their shared bed, earlier than was strictly necessary. Sighs and smiles and murmurs and glances—they spoke in a language that was more foreign to me than French.

Charles watched them, too. Sometimes, he then turned to look at me, confusion and hurt in his big brown eyes. But he never spoke to me about what he was thinking, to my great relief.

"Vinnie, I have something to tell you," Minnie repeated, drawing up a stool next to me, her earnestness pulling me out of my reverie.

"Yes, something serious, I know." I could not prevent a smile from playing upon my lips; goodness, but her manner was full of portent!

"I'm afraid that I won't be able to go back out on tour, if you were planning anything for this winter. Nor will I be able to go anywhere in the summer, either."

"I have no plans at the moment, but may I ask, dearest, why?" I brushed the back of her hand—so much smaller, even, than mine!—lightly, possessively; I was always reaching for her these days, clutching her hand, tugging at her skirts—trying, perhaps, to keep her from drifting further and further away?

Still smiling, I expected Minnie to answer something innocuous, something adorable, like "We decided to get a puppy" or "Edward has a terrible cold" or "I don't like trains, they're so dreadful."

Instead, her eyes lit up with a soft glow, a glow that I had seen in her once before. I couldn't quite remember when; I knew only that I recognized it, and a troubled, vaguely shameful feeling began to stir within my breast. As I struggled to recall the circumstances—as you do when you're trying to remember a particularly terrible dream in the safe light of day—Minnie said, with a shy duck of her head, "I'm going to have a baby."

I stared at her for a long moment, the words bouncing around in my brain but refusing to fall into place, making absolutely no sense. Then, with frightening finality, they did click into meaning; my nightmare was recalled to me, that whole horrible, dreadful business of the baby, and the way Minnie had looked when she had held the French child—Cosette, wasn't it?—in her arms. That same contented, dreamy look was in her eyes now as she raised them, uncertainly, to meet mine.

"No!" I let go of her hands, as if she were contagious, as if having a baby was a disease that I could catch from her touch. "No! Impossible! No!"

"Not impossible," Minnie said with a brave little laugh. "Entirely possible, I'm quite sure. I've just had the doctor, who confirmed it. I haven't told anyone yet, not even Edward. I wanted you to be the first to know."

"But how? But, Minnie, you—and Edward?" I was shocked, sickened. Yes, my sister was married. But so was I. I knew she and Edward shared a bed, but—didn't she know the dangers of allowing a man to touch her, she who was so delicate, so vulnerable—even more vulnerable than me?

"*Oh, it would be dreadful, impossible,*" I heard my mother's stricken voice from across the ages. "*Don't you remember the little* cow . . ." Didn't Minnie know? Didn't she understand how dangerous it was for her to even consider having a child?

No, she didn't. Because I had never thought to tell her—not even when she married Edward. For so long, my fears were her fears, her fears were mine, and I thought I could protect us both. But Minnie had changed, Minnie had grown—Minnie had become a real woman. Not simply a woman in miniature, like me.

"But, Vinnie, of course it's a perfectly natural thing, and I know how sad you've always been that you couldn't have a child. And just think of it—we won't have to give it back! This will be *our* child—for, of course, she will be just as much yours as she will be mine, as I'm sure I will need your help. She! Isn't that funny, Vinnie? I already think of it as a girl!" And Minnie laughed, all seriousness, all gravity gone from her eyes so that they were the impish—innocent—eyes of the sister I thought I knew.

"Minnie, listen to me." I grabbed her hand again and held it tight; too tight, for she winced. "How far—how far along are you?"

"The doctor said nearly three months, he thought."

"Three months." I searched my memory, my vast storehouse of knowledge gleaned from a life so different from hers; the words *prevention powders* were recalled from some dusty, neglected corner of my brain. Carlotta—Carlotta, that poor girl from Colonel Wood's boat—she had tried to give me those prior to my first private audience. What were they again? How did one use them?

"He also admitted it's hard to tell," Minnie continued, happily unaware of my thoughts. "Of course, Dr. Mills said the child will be tiny—as tiny as me!"

"But, Minnie, you—" I stopped. Minnie looked so unconcerned, so happy—so *well*. She did not appear to recall that she herself had not been a tiny baby, and neither had I. But the doctor? Surely he knew better?

"Yes, of course," I told my sister, still holding her hand. I could not prevent myself from searching her, appraising her, top to bottom, as if she were a new broodmare Papa had decided to purchase; she was so very small, so delicate. As if made from wishes and dreams, not flesh and blood. Then I shut my eyes as a cold wave of terror washed over me: *She must not have this child. She must not.* For her, for me—giving life meant summoning death.

But I did not tell her this now; I simply sat and listened to her talk excitedly about the baby, how happy Charles would be, as he did love children so, how we all would love this child, we would all raise her together, she would be ours forever. And my heart twisted itself about in knots as guilt, recrimination, and fear all fought for possession of it. Neither one winning, but none leaving, either—each parked itself in my heart, setting up housekeeping. I knew they would never leave; I knew I would have to carry them all around forever.

She must not have this baby—the phrase repeated itself over and over, wearing such a sharp groove in my mind, I had to grit my teeth from the pain of it. I needed to talk to someone, I needed to figure this out, for that was what I did—I figured things out. I took action. I made plans. I kept my sister safe. I was all mind, not heart—

And there was only one person who understood that. There was only one person I could turn to.

As the train pulled into Bridgeport, I wondered how many times I had taken this journey. It was hard to keep track, for I had taken so very many journeys by now. Since returning, triumphantly and in a blaze of headlines, from our world tour in 1872, the General Tom Thumb Company had gone back out to revisit this country, telling stories of our travels; this was when

Edward joined us. However, after that tour, Charles finally put his foot down; he was tired of mimicking people onstage and now wanted to mimic our Society friends by living a life of leisure.

So he bought a yacht, and a matching captain's jacket and hat, recommended to him by Mr. Belmont; he bought horses—fast, expensive horses—and built fine stables for them; he bought me jewels, just as his friends Mr. Vanderbilt and Mr. Astor did for their wives; he ordered the finest cigars from Mr. Barnum's man in New York. He built us our grand house in Middleborough, just across from Mama and Papa's old homestead, and furnished it with the most exquisite furniture and carpets and draperies, much of it built specially for us. The stair steps were not steep, the windows were lower to the ground so that we might easily see out of them; there was even a special kitchen built with sinks and a stove only two feet off the ground.

It was all grand; it was all impressive. Middleborough twittered and preened whenever dear Caroline Astor came to visit, and even erected a sign at the town border proclaiming this the *Home of Mr. and Mrs. Charles Stratton, or General and Mrs. Tom Thumb.*

It was also less real to me than the flimsy scenery we carted around whenever we toured. I wasn't the mimic that my husband was; while I could do a fair representation of a satisfied lady of the manor, I had yet to learn how to successfully impersonate a wife offstage. While my sister looked for ways to steal even more time with her husband, I made up excuses to spend less time with mine. A quick weekend up in New York, a jaunt over to Bridgeport; my blood always stirred with excitement even as my nerves relaxed in relief each time I boarded the train out of Middleborough.

Even today; even as I still felt—physically, as if I had been clubbed repeatedly—the blow of Minnie's news. Yet I looked forward to traveling; even more did I look forward to seeing

Mr. Barnum. I reached inside my reticule and took out a piece of pink chamois, rubbing it all over my face to take the shine and dirt off, just as we pulled into the station in Bridgeport.

As I stood on the top of the stairs, my favorite porter beamed in recognition and bustled over to lift me down to the platform. "Good morning, Mrs. General! Here to see Mr. Barnum?"

"Yes." I handed him a nickel.

"I thought so—he's outside in his carriage, waiting for you."

"He is?" Mr. Barnum never came to the station himself. How odd that he had done so today of all days—but then again, perhaps it wasn't. Tears filled my eyes; I had not yet cried, so determined was I to fix Minnie's "problem." But the relief of being able to share this with someone who possessed sense and determination; the relief of being able to share my burden, period, with the one person I desired to share my burdens with—it was so unexpectedly sweet. I reached into my reticule again, this time removing a handkerchief; dabbing my eyes, I blinked away the rest of my tears.

Then I followed the porter outside to the curb, where Mr. Barnum's enclosed carriage was waiting. He was standing next to it, bundled up in a heavy coat with a white fur collar that reached to the bottom of his ears even as his white curls brushed the tops, so that his face—pink as a baby's in the cold—stood out vividly. He was heavier now, more wrinkled, a bit round-shouldered, with a tendency to lean more decidedly upon his walking stick. But his gray eyes were just as lively, just as perceptive, as ever.

"What's wrong?" he barked as soon as he saw me. He threw his cigar upon the pavement, crushed it with his walking stick, and lifted me up into the carriage with such haste that I swallowed my words of greeting before they could reach my lips. And then we were inside, Mr. Barnum rapping his hand upon the outside of the carriage, signaling for the driver to go. "Take the long way," he shouted, sticking his head out the door before he shut it quickly against the cold. We lurched away, the horses soon settling into a smooth, slow trot that caused the carriage to sway gently, the lanterns—lit in the gloom of this depressing January day—to swing to and fro, casting ominous shadows upon us.

"It's Minnie," I said breathlessly, shivering, although there were heated bricks on the floor and hidden in the corners of the seat. Mr. Barnum leaned forward and tucked a buffalo robe about me; it was so heavy that I felt pinned to the seat, unable to move. But I was warm, anyway.

"What is it? Is there trouble with her husband? I always wondered about him; he seemed too darn polite, even for an Englishman."

"No, not that. She's—she's with child." I whispered this, feeling for the first time the indelicacy of the subject.

"She is? Why, that's wonderful!" A great, crooked grin pushed across his face, and he clapped his gloved hands in delight. "How happy you all must be!"

"No!" I shouted it, frustrated that he did not immediately understand the situation. "No, it's not wonderful. It's terrible. Don't you see? She's—we must do something about it. Minnie was not—I was not—we were both normal-size babies. Mama always told us this, don't you remember? I weighed six pounds when I was born. Do you know how much Minnie weighs now? Thirty pounds, at the most. Can you imagine—well, you were born on a farm, you must know! I remember Mama and Delia saying, long ago, how I must never—and now Minnie is, and she can't, she can't, it will kill her, and we must stop it!" Somehow I had flung that oppressive robe off me, kicking it to the floor, and now I was rocking back and forth, my arms clutching my shoulders. I knew I sounded wild, unhinged, but I did not care.

Comprehension dawned upon Mr. Barnum's face; he paled,

then colored, then his eyes narrowed, as if he was squinting at some faraway point, and I took a big, crackling breath and wiped my face with the sleeve of my coat. He was thinking; the wheels in that great, perpetual-motion brain of his were turning, and I was weak with relief. I knew I could depend on him.

"Excuse me, Vinnie, for being so forward, but we must dispense with modesty. How far along is she?"

"She thinks almost three months, but the idiot doctor apparently can't tell. He told her the baby would be tiny, like her—I don't know if he's totally ignorant, or if he told her that so she wouldn't worry. I suspect the former."

"Country doctors." Mr. Barnum snorted. "I'll find the finest New York doctor and send him to Middleborough."

"Yes, that would be a relief." I nodded, hesitating—but then I decided to plunge forward, as time was of the essence. "However, would he be willing to—I know there are things you can do, if the health of the mother is in question. It's probably past the stage of any prevention powders, but—"

"What? Prevention powders?" Mr. Barnum stared at me, aghast; then he blushed. He actually blushed; I had never seen him do that, not even when the wild Circassian girl asked if she could dance bare-bodiced at the Museum. "What on earth do you know about such things?"

I met his gaze levelly. "When I was on the river. A girl—a dancer—once thought I might need something of the kind. She was quite mistaken, I'm glad to say. However, it was the first time I had heard of these things, and now I'm happy that I did, for I can think clearly about Minnie's situation."

"Vinnie, you never cease to amaze me," Mr. Barnum said, grasping my hand. "You are the most remarkable woman I have ever met."

I smiled at him, happy to hear this; it filled my soul with

gratitude and yearning and other unfamiliar emotions that I usually did not have time to miss—except when I was with him. But now was not the time to reflect upon such things.

"We need to consider the option of doing—something—so that Minnie does not carry the child to term."

"But do you think there's the possibility that the child might be tiny, as the doctor says?"

"I don't know. All I know is that Minnie and I were not. Nor was Charles, remember? That's three of us who were born normal-size that I know of—and that's enough for me. I have no idea how we'll be able to convince her, for she is over the moon with happiness—she said she's doing this for me, too." And now I was face-to-face with the hard, unpleasant truth of the matter, the factor I had tried my best to ignore but which would not go away. I looked at him and took a big breath. "All that baby business, back in the sixties. It broke her heart to say goodbye to those infants. She keeps saying how glad she'll be not to have to say goodbye to her child, how happy Charles will be, how happy I must be. She thought I mourned those children just as she did, but I did not. She says she's so glad she can do this for me! So it's all my fault!"

"The one thing you cannot do is blame yourself." Mr. Barnum shook his head. "Believe me, I know. When I lost Pauline last year, I couldn't stop blaming myself, wondering if I could have seen the symptoms earlier."

"But this is different! Pauline died of fever! I have pushed Minnie into making a decision that will cost her her life."

"You don't know that, Vinnie. You don't know if she wouldn't have done this anyway."

"She never would have met Edward if it wasn't for me!"

Mr. Barnum pressed his crooked lips together, as if trying to prevent himself from saying anything further. He did not; I think he understood that I needed to say these things. Instead, he pushed himself off his seat and lurched over to my side of the carriage; he put his arm about me and gathered me close so that I could lean my head against his broad chest. He had never touched me in this way before; always he had been proper, respectful. A kiss upon the cheek in greeting, a fond handshake when embarking upon a new venture, a pat on the back in farewell.

But never had he held me; never had any man held me like this, so completely, as if he had a right to do so. Not even my husband, who would not have attempted to unless I first instructed him how. But I would never have done so; it was not in my nature, so accustomed was I to cringing from a man's touch, fearing the intent behind it, fearing my own helplessness in the face of it. I had never before missed being held.

Until now.

I felt my limbs loosen; no longer did I feel responsible for holding them together within my skin, assembled correctly, upright and proper. At that moment, all my bones and muscles and tissue melted together, melted away, melted *into* someone else, someone strong and caring, someone just as capable as I. Someone who would keep my bones and muscles and tissue from draining away altogether, who would give them back to me, intact, when I needed them again.

But I did not need them right now; I was content to give them away. I was content to simply *be*—with another. With Mr. Barnum.

We sat like that for a long while, as the carriage indeed took the long way around Bridgeport, swaying rhythmically, hypnotically. The clap of the horses' hooves against the hard, frozen streets was muffled by the sound of my own heartbeat, Mr. Barnum's breathing, the faint tick of his pocket watch hidden beneath layers of fur, wool, and understanding. It would be all right, I thought drowsily; Minnie would be all right. I had someone to help me, someone who understood.

Someone who didn't need me to be strong. This was such a novel sensation, I didn't quite know what to do with it. But given time, I thought, as I nestled farther into Mr. Barnum's welcoming arms, I could learn.

I WAITED OUTSIDE MINNIE'S ROOM; DR. FEINWAY WAS THROUGH examining her and had stepped out onto one of the balconies with a cigar. I had held Minnie's hand as she bravely allowed him to measure her abdomen, her hips; as he listened to her heart, felt her pulse, put a strange tubelike contraption against her stomach, which had distended alarmingly in just the last couple of weeks, since my return from Bridgeport.

In that short time she had changed from a slender, delicate reed to a puffy, swollen *thing*. Her ankles and wrists were no longer separate, defined entities but rather ugly extensions of her arms and legs. Her body was already stretching to absorb this child, and to my unpracticed yet worried eyes, it looked as if it couldn't stretch much more.

But she was happy, despite her obvious physical discomfort. She smiled all the time, when she wasn't retching over a chamber pot or falling into a deep, exhausted sleep in the middle of the day.

"Mrs. Stratton." Dr. Feinway beckoned to me from the other end of the hall; I slid off my chair and followed him.

Charles suddenly popped out of his room, blocking my path. He held a stick of wood in one hand, a miniature carving tool in another. "Vinnie, I'm making a spinning top for the baby, do you want to see? Your father showed me how to carve it!"

"Later, dear." I patted his arm. "I'll look at it later. Right now I need to discuss something with the doctor."

"Oh." His face, which had been smooth and happy with his accomplishment, clouded over just a bit, which wasn't much. A lifetime of pleasing the public had ironed out most of the muscles necessary to frown. "Minnie is all right, isn't she?"

"Yes, of course. I'll tell you all about it later." I gently nudged him aside and joined the doctor, leading him down the stairs and into the library, which Charles had designed in almost perfect imitation of Mr. Barnum's own. Once the doors were closed, Dr. Feinway refused my offer of a seat; he was obviously agitated, so I could do nothing but remain standing, looking up at him with my neck at an uncomfortable angle. But he did not appear to notice how awkward this was for me.

"Where is Mr. Newell?" he asked abruptly.

Evading his piercing gaze, I busied myself with straightening a doily upon a table. "He is up in Boston for the day, on business." I did not reveal that I had sent him there; I fully intended to discuss the situation with him after I had all the facts from the doctor. But Edward believed everything Minnie told him—if she had said the sky was yellow, he would have accepted it as fact; his head, not to mention his heart, was not steady enough to hear or speak plainly.

"Well, I would have preferred to have him here. But there is no time, not even for delicacy, so forgive me, Mrs. Stratton. Your sister appears to me to be carrying a normal-size child; according to her calculations, it's still early, but she's already retaining fluid, and her pulse is rapid. There is really only one reason for this. The baby is straining her system."

"Are you sure her—calculations—are correct?" I still could not help thinking of Minnie as that shy shadow that trailed me wherever I went, except to school; surely she had made a mistake.

"It appears she kept a very detailed diary of her—womanly days. She was obviously planning this child, keeping track. So yes, I believe her calculations. She's a little over four months along."

Minnie had been *planning* this? It wasn't just one—singular— unfortunate accident? Unwanted images filled my head, of Edward and Minnie in bed night after night, clinging together, sweating, panting, loving each other as man and woman were supposed to do, but as I had never experienced, never wanted to experience—I was dizzy, nauseated, desperate to sit down so that I would not collapse. But the doctor remained standing. He was a tall, aristocratic man with impeccably shaped, buffed nails. For some reason I could not take my eyes off them; they were obviously a source of pride for him. Could a man be a good doctor and have such vanity? But obviously Mr. Barnum thought he was; I must accept him.

"Then what are we to do?" I asked, tearing my gaze away from his hands. Finally, he appeared to notice the disparity in our heights; his eyes, behind gleaming spectacles, softened, and he looked about for a chair. I gestured to one, and he took it. I had never been so glad to sit down in all my life; once relieved of their duty, my legs began to tremble. I had to press my hands upon my thighs to keep my silk skirt from rustling like aspen leaves in the wind.

"I think the only humane thing is to convince your sister to abort her child. There's no question it will be a normal-size baby if it's taxing her so early on."

"She thinks it will be a tiny, like she is. She doesn't seem to recall that she and I were both normal-size at birth, and so far I haven't had the heart to tell her. I'm afraid—if we tell her, and she refuses to abort the child, then she has to spend the next months in fear, dreadful fear. But if we don't, she won't understand the severity of the situation. I don't know what to do—oh, I don't know what to do!" And I wanted, so desperately, for Mr. Barnum to be here now; I trusted no one else to make this decision for me.

The doctor looked at me in sympathy. Then he removed his spectacles and rubbed the bridge of his nose. Placing those glasses, with his fine, manicured hands, deliberately back upon his face, he said, "There is nothing for you to do. We must tell your sister the facts as we know them, and she must decide."

"But you don't understand, I've looked after her all our lives; she's not as—as—" But I broke off, ashamed of what I was saying. Minnie wasn't as—what? Smart as me? As quick? As perceptive?

As *cowardly*?

"I think your sister is of perfectly sound mind," Dr. Feinway said gently. "But I do hope you can persuade her to see the medical facts. Even the soundest of minds grow soft at the idea of a child."

"If she were to—abort—the child, how is it done?" I was sick, sick to my stomach, sick to my spirit; I had already killed one child, and now I would soon have another on my hands. This irony fell upon me like a particularly ugly, ungainly costume; it turned me into someone else, someone I couldn't recognize in the mirror.

"There is risk in the procedure, I won't lie. The usual way is a flushing out of the uterus with special waters, although I've read about a newer practice involving scraping."

I flinched at the words; my own abdomen tightened, and I felt bile rise up in my throat.

"But if she carries the child to term?"

Dr. Feinway hesitated. "I have been present when a large child was born to a small woman; it's an impossible situation, but sometimes Providence provides a way. But I've never before seen a fully mature woman as small as your sister. There are instruments that can assist—forceps, primarily—but those would be of no use in this case. There are instances when the child can be cut from the womb, but only after—after all hope is gone for the mother."

"She must not be allowed to carry this child!" I balled up my fists, pressing them even harder against my legs. My entire body was filled with a cold, heavy liquid; it had replaced my blood, and I knew, from the bitter taste of it in my mouth, that it was terror. I had never experienced terror before, not even when Colonel Wood had tried to attack me.

Only Minnie could make me feel it; only Minnie could make me feel so many things, love and affection, and now, finally, cold, debilitating terror.

"Do your best to explain the facts, then. And don't neglect to engage her husband," Dr. Feinway said, rising. "Do you happen to have anything to drink? I could use a brandy about now."

I nodded and rose; ringing for the maid, I asked her to show the doctor to the dining room, where we had a small stock of fine whiskey in decanters. Neither Charles nor I drank spirits, but we had some on hand for guests. Although, at the moment, I had a longing to join Dr. Feinway; I had to go to Minnie now, and the temptation to have something strong in me for courage was great.

But I did not; I walked back upstairs, down the hall, past Charles, who asked me, again, to look at his carving. I didn't answer him. Instead I knocked on my sister's door and let myself inside.

"ANNABELLE?"

"No, too silly."

"Amelia?"

"Too serious."

"Sarah?"

"Too plain."

"Guinevere?"

"Too fancy!" Minnie laughed merrily, the shining tinkle of her laugh—like delicate bells—filling the air.

It was the only recognizable thing about her now. Her laugh, the sound of her voice—those things had not changed. Nor had her temperament: by turns serious and trusting, patience itself, always hopeful. She had borne her penance with a peacefulness I knew I could not have, were I in her place. But I could never be in her place; I had made my choice long ago.

Confined to her bed since the day that Dr. Feinway examined her, she had not complained. She had accepted it, not as her fate but rather as her privilege, almost as if receiving a benediction or blessing. So willing was she to obey the doctor's orders, she scarcely moved from her back at all, as if for fear of dislodging the life that was so obviously overtaking hers.

For of course she refused to abort her child. I knew she would, but that hadn't stopped me from dropping to my knees beside her bed and grasping her little hand, my tears punctuating my words.

"Minnie, darling, you don't understand," I began, faltering; I had never wanted to mention Uncle's little cow to my sister, as that was my own personal Gethsemane. I never wanted it to be hers. But then I took a deep breath, squeezed her hand, and looked straight into her eyes.

"The child is not tiny, not like you think," I made myself continue. "The child is most likely normal-size, just as I was—just as you were when you were born. The doctor was very certain that is the case."

Minnie's eyes widened, but she did not flinch. She absorbed the news gravely, her hand going to her abdomen, stroking it, caressing it. She remained silent for so long that I feared she hadn't understood me completely.

"You do—you do understand the way babies are born," I began, blushing. "You do understand how—how—"

"Of course I understand." Minnie's eyes blazed at me. "Honestly, Vinnie, how young do you think I am? I'm a married woman, just like you!"

I bit my lip and looked away. She was right, of course. I could have prevented this by treating her as I had always wanted to be treated myself—as a sensible adult, regardless of my size. But no, I had always wanted to protect her. And I had done my job too well.

Or had I? For after all, I had willingly snatched baby after baby out of her hands, causing her poor, tender heart to break over and over again. I had allowed her to respond to all those condolence letters. I still had them somewhere; I hadn't been able to throw them away, and I hadn't known just why. But now I did; they were portents, weren't they? Harbingers of what lay ahead.

Concentrating on a worn patch of wallpaper next to the headboard, I somehow continued. "Minnie, I—I should have told you, oh, so much! It's all my fault, and I—"

I felt a hand upon my shoulder. Steeling myself against the accusation I knew I would find in her eyes, I took a trembling breath and turned to my sister.

But there was only that now-familiar soft, hopeful light in Minnie's eyes as she smiled and hugged me to her.

"It doesn't matter, Vinnie. I'm glad you told me, but—it doesn't matter. You don't understand, you can never understand, what it is to have life within you! I'm so sorry that you haven't had this chance, but I'm so grateful that I am able to! Even if—but I know that God will find a way. I know that He will see me through this. And I promise, this baby will be yours as well as mine. You're always looking out for me—still! You're always doing things for me. Well, this is the one thing I can do for you, and I would not wish it any other way."

I had to leave the room then, coward that I was, that I now knew I always had been. I couldn't bring myself to witness the bravery in those still incongruously impish eyes, the nobility in that dimple and faint, determined scowl.

All were gone now; she lay, still so patiently, but her body was no longer her own. It was a puffy, stretched, swollen, throbbing vessel for the life within, the life that continued to grow and grow, so obviously not the "fairy child" that we all continued to talk hopefully about, regardless of the facts. Through eyes that were slits, a face too swollen to display a dimple; with hands that were so awkward and puffy, she could barely hold her knitting needles, but still she tried; over an abdomen that stretched her skin as tight as a drum and made it impossible for her to do more than allow an extra pillow beneath her head—my sister prepared for the new life expected.

"What if it's a boy?" I asked her, as I knitted an absurdly tiny cap out of the softest wool; it was all for show, the tiny layette that Mama, Delia, and I were preparing for her, to ease her mind—as well as Edward's. He refused to consider the possibility that the child would be normal-size, and forbade us from discussing it.

"She is not a boy, I know it." Minnie struggled with small knitting needles, trying to maneuver them upon her swollen belly.

"How?"

"Because she is very considerate about when she kicks. A boy would not be so thoughtful."

"What—what does it feel like?" I was hesitant to ask; I talked about the child in theory, allowing her to dream of it. But I did not like to discuss any of the practical—physical—aspects of what my sister was going through. It was almost as if I could wish them away by not giving them voice.

But by the look of relief—of happiness—in Minnie's gaze as she considered my question, I had to wonder who I was protecting in this way. Her? Or me?

"Do you remember the time I swallowed a grasshopper?" she asked me.

"Yes." I laughed; I hadn't thought of that in years. "You said you could feel it hopping about inside you, and then you started to hop, too; you hopped all through dinnertime, until Mama didn't know what to do and was about to send for the doctor."

"Well, it's like that. Only this time, it's real; I do feel something hopping about inside me. As if I've swallowed a very large, very heavy, grasshopper. Oh!" She gasped, and her hand flew to her stomach.

"What is it? Are you all right? Shall I send for the doctor?" I jumped out of my chair, my knitting falling to the floor. I was halfway out the door when I heard my sister's happy laugh beckoning me back inside.

"Vinnie—come, quick! She's kicking right now! Come feel!"

"Oh!" I turned back to her but remained where I was, in the doorway. My hands flew behind my back almost of their own accord.

"Come!" Minnie patted the mattress, one hand still upon her stomach, which twitched, ever so faintly, beneath the sheets. I stared at it in horror.

"No, I don't want to hurt you, dearest—"

"You won't hurt me! I promise—come feel her, Vinnie! Come say hello to your niece!"

"No, can't you listen to me? I said *no!*" I couldn't help it—my voice was rough with anger, and I flinched at the startled look on Minnie's face. "I mean, I will another time. Oh, will you look at that! My yarn rolled beneath the bed!" And I fell to my knees to avoid her hurtful, reproachful gaze; I was grateful for the exertion it took for me to wiggle under the bed and retrieve my knitting.

When I resumed my seat, I felt shyness and guilt, both, envelop me; I concentrated on my knitting with such intensity, the needles came close to poking out my eyes. My sister was a stranger to me now in so many ways; she had outpaced me, she who had always held docilely on to my hand while I led. Suddenly, our roles were reversed. And I knew Minnie wanted only to share her joy; I knew she wanted only to *teach* me the things she was learning with every passing day, every evidence of the child growing within.

But I was as reluctant a pupil now as she once had been. For the lessons my sister wanted to teach me were lessons not of the mind but of the heart.

"So no boys' names, then? Not even one, just in case?" I returned to a safe subject.

Minnie was silent for a moment; she turned her head away from me, staring out her window, but finally, after a soft little sigh, she replied, "No. But I do have an idea for a girl's name. A perfectly lovely girl's name."

"What?"

"Pauline," my sister said quietly.

I dropped my knitting again, tears filling my eyes once more—oh, there was not even ten minutes a day, it seemed lately, that I did not cry!

"Oh, Minnie, that's too—too sweet of you. Mr. Barnum will be so touched."

"Indeed, he will," said a familiar hearty voice. Minnie and I both looked up, startled; there, in the doorway, stood Mr. Barnum himself. A beautiful cradle, adorned with an enormous pink silk bow, was in his arms.

"Mr. Barnum!" Minnie exclaimed; with a very feminine gesture she patted at her hair and smoothed the ribbons on her bed jacket. I ran to her and tried to prop her up a bit upon her pillows, but she was too cumbersome; she smiled and raised her hands helplessly.

I glanced at Mr. Barnum; he was trying, unsuccessfully, to hide his shock at her appearance. His hands shook as he set the cradle down, and his gray eyes were misty with tears.

"We didn't expect you," I told him, rushing over to take his hat, placing my hand upon his arm to steady him. He smiled and kissed me on the cheek; one of his tears fell upon my face, and I pressed my hand to it, absorbing it into my own flesh. Then I turned away, hoping he hadn't seen.

"Would you really like it if I named her Pauline?" Minnie asked him.

"It would mean the world to me. I can think of no greater tribute." Recovering himself, Mr. Barnum pulled up a chair next to Minnie's bed and plopped himself upon it; in his shock, he must not have seen that it was a small chair, made for us. So he sat with his knees up to his chin, his fleshy body spilling over the arms; Minnie and I burst into laughter, and he had no idea why.

"What? What is it?"

"Nothing." I signaled Minnie to keep quiet, and she did, with a look of such delight upon her swollen face that my heart lightened enough so that I was not, for one blessed, fleeting moment, aware of it.

"Well, Miss Minnie, it's good to see you so cheerful, anyway."

"I have our Vinnie to thank for that. She never lets me get bored or anxious. And she tells me wonderful stories every day about all the things she's seen."

"You've accompanied her on all her travels; surely there's not much she can tell you?"

"Oh, but there is! It's almost as if I haven't been in the same places she has, for she remembers things I didn't even know happened! Like the time the Maharaja tried to give her a purse of rubies—I had no idea!"

"You were too shy, Pumpkin. You wanted to remain behind in our rooms and have your dinner with Mrs. Bleeker, remember?"

"I know. That's why I love hearing your stories; I get to live my life all over again, through different eyes!" Minnie smiled at me, and I had to look away; I didn't like to recall how long she had been in my shadow. I didn't like to hear her talk of living her life again, as if she had a premonition about the future.

"Well, I may not be as good a storyteller as your sister, but I'm no slouch," Mr. Barnum said hastily, catching a glimpse of my face as I busied myself with arranging a bowl of forget-me-nots on the windowsill; it was spring now in Middleborough. Life was bursting out all around us: flowers and tender grass and birds singing, newborn calves, foals, the first sprouts of Mama's kitchen garden. Sometimes I felt hopeful; with all the vigor and optimism of the season, how could Minnie not survive her upcoming ordeal? Surely the same pulse, the same spirit that carried the scent of new-mown hay through her window, always open now so that she might hear the birds, would see her through, safe and sound?

Other times, when I heard her moan softly as she sought a comfortable position, as I watched Dr. Feinway's increasingly grave countenance when he left her room (he came every two weeks, arranged by Mr. Barnum), I felt the cruelty of the season. It wasn't fair! Life should not come so easily to the dumb creatures of nature, when my own sister did not have the same chance.

"Have I told you about my elephant?" Mr. Barnum asked Minnie. She shook her head, her curls—dull now, changed like the rest of her—ruffling her pillow. I pulled up a chair on the other side of her; both of our faces turned, like flowers to the sun, to Mr. Barnum as he began his tale.

"Jumbo is his name," he said, shifting about uncomfortably in his tiny chair, still unaware of its proportions. "Well, he's not mine yet—but he will be! He's in a zoo in London now; he was found as a baby in the deepest, darkest jungles of Africa. He's the biggest animal of his kind, I'd swear it! Well, between you and me, I wouldn't exactly swear it in a court of law, but I'm confident the public won't hold me to that. He's really a stunner—his legs are ten feet high! One of my giants could easily pass under him! Yet he's the gentlest animal soul I've ever seen; right smart he is, they say. He can count to three by stomping his foot, and when he does, the whole earth quakes! Minnie, I would love to see you curled up in his trunk; he loves to cradle things. One time at the zoo, one of the monkeys was missing, and finally they found him sleeping in Jumbo's trunk, that elephant rocking him back and forth just like a baby!"

"No!" Minnie exclaimed breathlessly. "Didn't he hurt the poor monkey?"

"Not a bit! Gentlest animal ever—they even let children ride him! Some of those elephants can get pretty ornery, but not Jumbo. Shh, don't tell anyone yet, but I'm planning on buying him and bringing him over here. I can build an entire circus around him. I'll put him in a special train car, bright red with his name in big yellow letters, so that when we come to town he's the first thing folks want to see!"

"Oh, I'd love to see him. Can I? Can we, Vinnie?"

I believe, at that moment, Minnie had forgotten her condition; she was a girl again, about to embark upon a new adventure with me. I was so grateful to Mr. Barnum for giving her that moment of respite, for I knew, despite her cheerfulness, she was worried about her confinement. If I couldn't talk to her about it,

Mama could, at least a little; I overheard Minnie asking her once how much it would hurt. Mama told her only about as much as it hurt to have a tooth out, but that she'd forget about it the moment it was over and she held her baby for the first time. Yet when Mama left the room, she broke down sobbing in my arms, and I heard Minnie crying softly in her bed.

Mr. Barnum proceeded to tell her more stories about Jumbo; he had that same light in his eyes he used to have when he spoke of Jenny Lind, and I smiled to think of how jealous I had once been of her! Now I knew that Mr. Barnum was like a child in his affections: The newest toy was always his favorite. And Jenny Lind was across the ocean, matronly and married; Jumbo was in his zoo. I was right here, and I always had been. As I always would be.

Minnie was growing weary. She slept a lot now; it was painful to recall how she used to move, like quicksilver, such a sprite of a thing. Even when she left her bed to use the chamber pot, she moved so heavily, she reminded me of Sylvia.

I noticed her trying to stifle a yawn.

"Mr. Barnum, it's time for Minnie to rest now," I interposed gently but firmly, for he was not used to having his stories interrupted.

"Oh! Well, listen to me going on and on. I'm sorry, Miss Minnie. You must store up your energy, for when that baby comes, you will surely need it!" He spoke lightly, looking directly at her as he said this. Then he tried to rise from his chair and became stuck; standing, the chair clung to his behind like a burr, and Minnie giggled at the sight.

Finally, after much turning about, he managed to remove it, and so it was with cheerfulness and humor that he and Minnie said their farewells. Just as he bent over her bed to shake her hand, however, Minnie's face grew serious; she tugged upon his sleeve, pulling him closer to her. She tried to whisper, but I could hear her, anyway; didn't she know that I could always hear her? Her voice was ever in my thoughts, ever in my memories.

"Mr. Barnum, please look after Vinnie for me, won't you? Sister worries too much, and I know that you're the only person she'll listen to. Try to amuse her—and just—take care of her, please? She's always taken care of me, but nobody ever takes care of her."

Mr. Barnum's forced smile froze. He looked into my sister's eyes and I suddenly feared what he would say.

"Come, let Minnie get her rest," I said briskly from the doorway, pretending not to have heard—although my voice was suddenly unpredictable; I couldn't quite stop it from quavering. "I'll be back soon, dearest."

Minnie turned her head away from me, but I saw her lips tremble as she nodded.

Resolutely, I led Mr. Barnum out into the hall, as Delia curtsied shyly to him and took my place by Minnie's bed. Together we walked down the stairs; as always, he slowed his pace to match mine, without seeming to think about it.

Still not speaking, we walked through the front door; he didn't have to ask if I wanted some air. We walked until we were far from the house, with all its open windows, and could speak freely. An iron bench, nestled among a patch of daffodils, beckoned, and we sat down upon it. I took in as much air as I could, breathing in greedy gulps, as if I were suffocating. Despite her open windows, Minnie's room was growing unbearably stuffy, the air stagnant, full of sickbed smells; sweat and urine and vomit, and, most pervasive of all, fear.

"You look like something the cat dragged in, chewed up, and then spit back out again," Mr. Barnum finally remarked, and I had to laugh. I had no idea how I looked—me, the perfectly groomed little Queen of Beauty! But it had been ages since I had spent any time dressing my hair, and I couldn't remember the last time I looked in a mirror. I rose every morning, donned whatever dress was handy, did my hair up in a simple knot, and went to Minnie's room. Edward always greeted me with a quick update—usually, she had spent a restless night, unable to lie comfortably, and now bedsores were becoming a worry—before stumbling off to Charles's sitting room, where he might shave and bathe, but more often than not, collapsed on a settee and slept like a dead man. Edward was suffering, too; a good soul, so devoted to Minnie that he appeared unable to think ahead to the outcome of this ordeal. But I could not like him. I was jealous, jealous of his right to spend the nights with her, angry for his inability to keep himself away from her, for giving in to his animalistic urges and putting her in this situation. I knew it wasn't fair to think of him that way—as a heathen who couldn't control himself, just like a *polygamist*—but I did. He was a man, after all. And I knew what men were like.

I patted my hair, knowing that it was in a lifeless knot at the back of my neck, and agreed with Mr. Barnum. "I'm sure I look a fright."

"You should think of yourself some, and take rest whenever you can."

"I've spent my entire life thinking of myself. It's a privilege to spend this time thinking of her," I replied, speaking the truth.

"If you won't think of yourself, then I will—shall I ask Charles to return to Bridgeport with me? I haven't seen him nearly enough, and would enjoy a little bachelor vacation myself. Nancy will be in England visiting her family." Nancy was his second wife; he had remarried following Charity's death in 1873. I was no more fond of his second wife than I was of his first. Nancy was younger than I, vain and cold, interested only in the many material benefits of being Mrs. Phineas Taylor Barnum, for she spent no time with him.

"That would be good of you. I know Charles would enjoy it, for he's been somewhat lost in all this. He's beside himself with worry for Minnie—he spends some time with her each day, reading stories, but mainly he's been left to his own devices."

"I imagine this might lessen your own load a little, too. Charles is my good friend, but I know he requires a fair amount of handling."

"Yes," I admitted, again feeling the blessed relief of plain speaking; it was as if my stays had been loosened, as well as my tongue. I hadn't been able to indulge myself like this in such a long time; for months, we all tiptoed about, not talking about the one thing that was on all our minds. It hovered in the air, unspoken, like smoke lingering from a burnt pot on a stove. And none of us made a move to clear it.

I was so grateful to Mr. Barnum for allowing me to speak what was in my heart; it was the desire to prolong this moment that caused me to blurt out, "She's going to die, you know. It's so obvious, I want to scream, but we all pretend and pretend not to see what we see. This child is not a tiny little fairy sprite. It's a normal flesh-and-blood baby, and Minnie will not be able to survive its birth. We can't *pretend* anymore."

Mr. Barnum, to my everlasting gratitude, did not try to persuade me otherwise. "What will you do if the child lives?"

"I—I don't know," I sputtered, stunned. I had not thought of this possibility. I had not given the thing within my sister any identity or thought beyond its destructive nature. That was the only way I could see it: as the likely cause of Minnie's death. It wasn't a baby to me; it was a poison or a tumor or a fatal condition.

"You should prepare yourself, Vinnie. It's a possible outcome, you know. I don't imagine Edward will be in any position to care for a child alone. You must talk to Minnie and determine what she would wish. Most mothers," he continued gently, seeing the horror upon my face, "give some thought to this, you know, regardless of their condition."

"I can't!" I shook my head; it felt as if the sun had just disappeared behind a cloud, so chilly was my soul. But the sun still shone brightly; I could see our shadows spilling across the lawn at our feet, one long and one short but so close together there was no space between.

"You must try. She might even be hoping that you do. It is my experience that the dying wish us to speak more plainly with them than we think—you heard what she said to me when I left. She's trying to prepare us—she's trying to prepare you."

"No, you're wrong. She's hopeful—" I faltered, remembering the time—*times,* if I was being truthful—I had overheard her crying. But I shook my head, erasing them from my memory. She was not afraid, for the simple reason that I couldn't bear for her to be. "What she said back there, she just meant for the present. She's been knitting for the child, *naming* it—you heard! And you know Minnie. She's always been so simple. She doesn't understand what's truly happening."

"Vinnie, if you've ever done your sister a disservice—and I believe you think you have—it's only in this: that you have persisted in thinking of her as younger and simpler than she really is."

"I don't know what you're talking about." I shifted uncomfortably on the hard bench; suddenly our shadows appeared to me to be too close.

"Your sister is a woman, Vinnie. A woman who has chosen her own fate. You haven't done it for her, no matter what you think. She was more than capable of doing it for herself."

"What do you know of fate? Of choices? You're just a man—

and men never have to pay for their choices like women do." I started to rise, as did my voice, but Mr. Barnum reached for my arm. He continued to speak in a low, soothing tone, which maddened me; I was not a child.

"Vinnie, you can't possibly mean that. We all have to pay for the choices we make—but come, let's not quarrel. There's no need for anger, especially on such a beautiful day."

"Oh, beautiful day be damned." I kicked at a daffodil, to make my point.

"Vinnie!"

"Do I shock you? Well, good. I want to. I want to shock God, too. Can't you see I *am* angry? I'm angry with God—I'm angry with myself," I muttered, still kicking at innocent daffodils, so mocking in their vivid, irrepressible cheer.

"Why on earth? It's simply God's—"

"*Will?* Oh, how sick I am of hearing God talked about in this house! I'm glad He gives Minnie comfort, but I'm not so easily tricked."

"Call it Providence, then—but you're still not responsible."

"Oh, yes, I am! Do you know why? Let me tell you—let me finally tell someone!" Jumping to my feet, my hands clenched, I stood before him as honest as I had ever been with anyone—and as vulnerable. His hand was still upon my arm, but I felt it loosen its grip, recoiling as my confession spilled out of me.

"It's not as if I *couldn't* have children—the truth is I didn't *want* to. I told Charles, I told you, I even told Minnie that I couldn't, when the truth was, I was too terrified to try. So I never explained to Minnie about the dangers of childbirth for the two of us. And now look what's happened!"

"But you—afraid? I don't understand."

"Of course you don't—you never have." I rushed on, desperate to unburden myself—even more desperate, for some reason, to burden *him*. "If you had, you never would have thought up that whole baby business. I'm angry with you, too!" I finally wriggled out of his grasp—or, rather, he let go.

"Me?" Mr. Barnum's expression suddenly became alert and watchful; before my eyes, his soft, uneven features began to harden.

"Yes, you! Oh, if I'd only been honest with you about Colonel Wood! That was my fault, but then you—you *forced* me to bring Minnie along to pay my debt. And then that ridiculous *humbug* about the baby!"

"That baby business made us both a small fortune, if you'll recall. All those *cartes de visites* sold! We made thousands. And you accepted the money, if my memory is to be trusted, without any hair tearing or breast beating." The gray in his eyes turned to steel, and he clutched his walking stick as if he was trying not to use it as a weapon.

"I—well, we needed the money, the way Charles spends, but that's not the point. It hurt people—it hurt Mama, because I'd told her I'd never let you do anything in my name that I didn't approve."

"Then why are you scolding me?"

"Because! Mama feared I'd lose my soul if I went with you, and I told her I wouldn't, but now I have. But I don't care about myself. I'm willing to accept my punishment, but, oh, that it has to be Minnie who pays! That's what I can never forget or forgive, either of us."

"Lavinia Warren Stratton, the conceit in you! I knew you had an ego, m'dear, but I had no idea you thought so much of yourself that you could buy and sell souls." He barked a hard, withering laugh that set my teeth on edge.

"Talk about ego—is there anything in New York or Bridgeport that you haven't plastered your name all over?" My eyes narrowed, considering him. We glared at each other for a long moment; everything else—the flowers, the bees, the lazy neighing of a horse in a nearby pasture—faded away until I was aware of only the rasp of his breathing, the pounding of my wrathful heart.

"Let's not continue this line of discussion," Mr. Barnum said with maddening calm. "Minnie would not be happy to know we were quarreling."

"Oh, you have no idea what Minnie would like," I snapped. I would not be soothed. "You don't know her at all. You only want to make money off her, just like you do with everything and everyone. You know frauds and hokum and cheats and scoundrels—and I include myself in all that!—but you do not know goodness! So don't try to tell me what to do or how to think about my sister. She's mine, she's me—the very best and only true part of me! The only true part I have left! You're a sham, and you expect everyone else to be a sham, too!"

"I don't know *goodness*?" He threw his stick down in disgust. "Or truth? What do you know? Have you ever asked me—I watched my wife suffer all her life, saw two of my daughters die. I know truth from lies, Vinnie, and I see the truth in Minnie and I see the truth in you, although right now you don't want me to—and maybe you never did, at that! For if we're speaking of friendship and goodness, let me ask you this: Why do you only come to me when you need something—money or advice or even, yes, my *name* when it suits your needs? Why do you never visit me, just because? It's always under the pretense of some piece of business. And furthermore, I would like to know something else." He pushed himself off the bench with determination, turning away from me so that I could not see his face. "Why, in all the years we have known each other, have you never once called me by my given name?"

"I—what?" Stunned, I stopped my wild pacing; so unexpected

was his question, his obvious hurt, that for a moment I forgot my anger.

"I have called you Vinnie almost since the first day I met you. Charles calls me Phineas, Bleeker does, all my friends do. But you persist in calling me 'Mr. Barnum.' You always keep me at arm's length, and I would like to know why. Do you only think of me in terms of business, then? Do you have no room for true friendship or affection in your life?"

"'True friendship'? Oh, don't talk to me about what's true!" I resumed my pacing, disgusted by his blatant attempt at manipulation. I'd heard him put that quaver in his voice many times before, usually when he was trying to negotiate the terms of a new contract. "We've only ever been a meal ticket for you. Just like all your other toys and curiosities—*your* giant, *your* elephant, *your* dwarfs. That's all we've ever been to you, and you know it!"

"I do not, and I'm offended you'd even think such a thing!"

"Really?" I spun around. "You're saying we'd be friends even if I wasn't what you persist in calling, in all my advertising and even in your latest autobiography, a *dwarf*?"

"Oh, for heaven's sake, Vinnie! Remember, *you're* the one who first contacted *me*. You sent that note calling my attention to a certain Miss Lavinia Warren Bump, whose dainty height and symmetrical proportions were much admired along the Mississippi. When I sent that first telegram, you answered so fast the wires were still singing! You yourself know that no one would pay a dime to see you, otherwise. And I always admired you for knowing that—I always admired you for your honesty and good sense. But lately, I'm not so sure—"

"*You're* lecturing *me* on honesty? And as far as good sense—"

"Yes, good sense. Look at all your Society friends, all your lavish spending, all the airs—it's almost as if you've forgotten how it all began. But these people, Vinnie—they don't see you! Not really, not beyond being a novelty, and you're going to get hurt if you don't watch yourself. And the thing is, *I* see you—I see beyond the perfect little woman in miniature; I see the real person, but you don't want me to. That's why you always keep me at arm's length—you're afraid of me. You're terrified of what I might see."

"I'm not terrified of anything," I said hotly, even as I knew it wasn't true.

"Yes, you are." Mr. Barnum was reading me, reading my face, as he so avidly read an audience before a show, predicting exactly where they would applaud. I looked about, desperate suddenly for a place to hide, but there was nowhere to go.

"That's it," he continued, circling me, peering at me, *trapping* me, even as I tried to squirm and duck. His eyes were gleaming with an interest that was almost scientific. At that moment, I was more intriguing to him than the biggest elephant in the world; once more, I was his newest discovery. "That's what all this is! You're afraid of what you see in the mirror every day, aren't you? Afraid, and ashamed. And so you've hidden behind it, hidden behind your size, even as you've tried to convince yourself no one sees it but you."

I gasped; it was as if all my clothing had just been torn from me and now I stood, naked and defenseless, beneath his perceptive gaze. Oh, how did he know? How did he always see straight to the heart of me?

"And Minnie—she's different than you, no matter how much you try to convince yourself otherwise. She isn't you, because she's happy. And you're not."

"'Happy'?" Finally, I found my tongue, and it felt strong and supple in my mouth, a weapon I could expertly use against him. "What do you know about happiness? You're just as miserable as you think I am, marrying the wrong woman over and over!"

"By God, if you were a man—" He wheeled and strode away

from me, reaching down to grab his walking stick, swinging it like a scythe as he lopped off the heads of dandelions and daffodils, both. "You are the most extraordinary female I've ever—I knew this day would come. We have usually been on the same side of an issue, but I always knew that there would be trouble between us if ever we were not."

"Trouble? Is that all you think this is? My sister is dying and it's my fault and your fault both, and you call it *trouble*? I can never forgive you for this!"

"If that is what you believe, then you are not the person I thought you were!" He turned. We stood like two warriors at the end of a battle; carnage lay at our feet, but it wasn't bodies we had slain. It was our history.

"No, I'm not. I'm not the person *I* thought I was," I said through a clenched jaw. "No, I'm not brave—not like Minnie. But then, neither are you. The only chance you ever take is with your bank account. The only chance I ever take is with a train schedule. Neither one of us has ever been brave enough to take a chance with his heart."

"And back we come, to the crux of the matter. Because Minnie took risks. Minnie fell in love. Minnie didn't need you, after all."

I opened my mouth to deny it but could think of nothing more to say. He was right. But so was I—oh, none of it mattered. Not now, not with Minnie—

Suddenly, I began to shiver; I was aware of a creeping, numbing chill threatening to overcome me, confusing my thoughts. I realized that I hadn't slept in days, that the back of my neck was gray with dirt and sweat, that my stomach was empty. And I ached all over, not just within my heart. A lifetime of looking up, of climbing stairs too steep for me, of using doorknobs and pens and brushes and utensils, even water glasses, that were too large for my hands—it was just this summer, this summer of dread, that it was beginning to take its toll on my once-elastic body. My right hip was cold and stiff in the mornings; my neck had a permanent kink to it, even while I lay down. The knuckles on my hands were beginning to knot up.

For the first time in a very long time, I felt *small*.

"I want you to leave now," I said, recovering some remnant of rational thinking. "Although if you will allow Minnie to continue in the care of Dr. Feinway, I would appreciate it. But as for me, I would prefer not to be under any further obligation to you."

"You don't mean that," Mr. Barnum said, and I could see, across the chasm between us, the flicker of hurt in his eyes even as he bravely set his mouth in that familiar crooked smile.

"I don't? Why is that—because I'm only a dwarf? A '*novelty*,' as you put it?"

His smile turned into a grimace. "Vinnie, I didn't mean that— you're too tired to know what you're saying."

"Then we're agreed on something." I shrugged. "I am tired. And I don't have time for your showmanship anymore, Mr. Barnum. Now, if you'll excuse me, my sister needs me."

"Vinnie, wait—" He took a step in my direction, but I spun around and began to walk toward the house, to my sister. Away from him.

"Vinnie, don't leave like this," he called, and there was sadness in his voice now, the genuine sadness of an old man, for that was what he was. I didn't usually think of him that way, and I wished I hadn't allowed myself to do so now. I did not want to feel sympathy for him.

So I picked up my skirts and began to run; if I could put enough distance between the two of us, I would never be tempted to go back.

My hair came undone from its bun; it streamed down my

back, heavy and tickling as it hadn't done since I was young. Since Minnie and I were girls, running around the barnyard hand in hand, laughing and searching for hidden treasures, for rocks and eggs and anthills, four-leaf clovers, fairy wings.

Objects that only the two of us, so close together, so close to the ground in a way that no one else was, could see. Objects that Minnie had always found beautiful, and that she had persisted in trying to share with me.

But I never could see them, not then, not now.

I was always too busy looking for the man in the moon, instead.

THE TWENTY-THIRD OF JULY STARTED OUT LIKE ANY OTHER SUM-mer day; it dawned bright and warm, with the promise of midafternoon heat in the pale morning sun. The house seemed airless by eight a.m.; after bringing Minnie her breakfast, which she could not eat except for a little nibble of dry toast, I went outside, hoping to cool off.

Papa's cow pastures were almost all sold off by now, divided up among my brothers, who had built houses of their own. But one pasture remained untouched, just big enough for the small herd he still kept; I headed out there, careful not to step in cow patties or gopher holes. Up ahead, on top of a little hill, was an enormous, leafy tree that was sure to provide nice, cool shade. I was eager to reach that restful spot; I walked faster, as if in a race against time and sun. I knew I could not linger, for Minnie was due any day now. Yet I so wanted to spend a little time sitting against the trunk, maybe even taking off my shoes and stockings to let my feet play in the tall, cool grass; I hadn't done that since I was a child.

Finally, I reached the shade; pausing to collect my breath, I unbuttoned the top of my bodice so that some of the heat, trapped within the folds of my dress, could escape. Then I took a closer look at the tree; it had been so long since I had tramped outdoors, but this tree looked familiar.

Creeping closer to the trunk, I pushed away some of the tall grass, and there it was, like a long-forgotten friend—my name. My name, and the line marking my height, which was still just an inch or two below where I stood now. I looked up, seeing all the other familiar names—*James, Benjamin, Delia* . . .

But where was Minnie? For the first time, I realized her name had not been etched in the rough, gnarled bark. I couldn't remember why that was—had she even been born then? Was she just too timid to romp about that day? Had I abandoned her, as I sometimes did, impatient that she didn't want to run after the others, annoyed that she was so content to sit in the kitchen with Mama, playing with her dolls? I honestly could not recall. However, it wasn't right that her name was not here with the rest of us; how could I have not noticed it before? Anyone looking at this tree would think she hadn't existed at all—

Like a thunderclap, the panic startled me, overcame me; I had to scratch her name right here, right *now*. I had to record my sister's life on this tree this very instant, capture it somehow. And if I did, surely, like a gypsy's charm, everything would be all right. I looked about, but of course there was no handy knife or tool nearby; I grabbed a stick, but it snapped against the rough bark. Finally, I tried to use my fingernail, scraping until my finger bled, but it was no use. There wasn't even a faint outline of her name; I hadn't made a dent.

Breathing heavily, hot and perspiring even under the shade, I sat down for a moment to think. I could run over to Mama's— their house was closer. I needn't tell her why I required a knife; it would only upset her. I could just take one from the rack in the kitchen, slip back outside and run back here before—

"Vinnie! Vinnie!" There was a figure far down the hill, jumping up and down, waving its arms. Standing, I shaded my eyes from the sun with my hand, and recognized it as Charles. "Come quick—Edward sent me to fetch you. Minnie needs you, Vinnie—do you s'pose it's about the baby?"

There was uncertainty in his voice. Uncertainty as well as fear. My legs began to propel me down the hill before I could fully realize what they were doing; I shot past Charles in a blur. I was much faster than he was, as I ran just as I used to as a girl, forgetting about my corset, my train, my straw hat, which flew off my head at some point. Charles must have retrieved it, for later I found it on my bed, crumpled but not torn.

I also forgot about the tree; I remembered only when Dr. Feinway asked me why my fingernails were torn. By then, all the men were banished from the house, sent across to Mama and Papa's; Edward did not want to leave, but Minnie, between gasping and writhing, insisted.

How do I write of what happened next? I've never been able to speak of it: not to Charles, not to Mama, not to anyone. Yet Minnie's story cannot be told without describing the hell of that day, beginning with the sweltering July heat that soon turned the room into a sauna. It was captured in the sheets, in the curtains, within the folds of my clothing, rivulets flowing into rivers of sweat plastering my undergarments to my skin, turning my cotton dress into a velvet shroud, stifling my pores until I felt as if I were being boiled in a covered pot.

When the pains started, Minnie was so hot that she kept tugging at her nightgown, complaining that it was too heavy; by the end, she had lost so much blood that she was shivering uncontrollably, her skin icy to the touch.

The blood! Oh, so much blood, such a defiant crimson, soaking the sheets, sticking to her legs, covering Dr. Feinway's arms, stringing, like ropy spiderwebs, between his fine, tapered fingers. The child simply could not emerge, although nature tried to take over, tearing my sister, wracking her with pain. Her piteous cries pierced the air, pierced my ears so that they still ring with them, all these years later. She started out whimpering, smiling apologetically between the pains; as they came closer and closer, more furious, unrelenting, she stopped apologizing. Her pupils dilated like a wounded animal's as she waited for the next, and then the next, and then the next. Soon her entire body was being wrung with the force of the infant desperate to be born; her limbs flailed, her back arched off the mattress, as the doctor tensely held her legs down. Even as she was in the primitive throes of her torture, he was still able to overpower my diminutive sister. Minnie was helpless against everything, everyone, in that room—except me.

"Can't you give her some ether?" I pleaded with Dr. Feinway, as her eyes glazed over and she bit her lip so hard that now there was blood there, as well.

"Not yet, not while there's still a chance she can expel the child," he barked. He had lost his kind, professional demeanor and was now in his shirtsleeves, spattered with blood, looking more like a butcher than a doctor. He grunted and groaned nearly as much as Minnie, and ran to the window to spit outside and curse his frustration before returning to the bed and the nurse he had brought with him. She was a woman so methodical, so practiced, as to be an automaton. She did not react to Minnie's cries; she did not blanch at all the blood. She merely stood, silent and efficient, waiting to do whatever Dr. Feinway needed.

I hovered near the top of the bed, near the only part of her that was not being torn apart. I mopped her brow but could not do it easily; she had been moved to a guest room, placed upon a regular-size bed so that the doctor could better attend to her. I had to use my wooden steps, standing awkwardly, but by the end I simply crawled into bed with her, holding her to me as she begged me, in the most heartbreaking whisper, to "Rock me, Sister, rock me." And I tried to do just that; I maneuvered my body around hers as best I could, and cradled her shoulders in my arms.

"Little drops of water, little grains of sand," I began, unable to re-call any song but the ones I used to teach in school. All the pop-ular songs I had sung onstage to Kings and Queens escaped my mind at that moment; only the simplest ones, the ones I had taught to children, remained.

But it didn't matter; no angelic smile, no whisper of relief, greeted my singing. I don't think she heard me, and I wondered, later, if she asked only because she knew I needed to do some-thing at that moment.

I remained there, half sitting, half reclining, rocking my sister for the longest time, crooning softly into her tangled mat of hair for hours, it seemed. I was still rocking, still crooning, my voice hoarse and dry, when I felt a hand upon my shoulder. Looking up, it took me a long moment to recognize Dr. Feinway; I was almost surprised to see him there, so fiercely had I tried to block out everything but the blessed weight of my sister in my arms.

But now that weight was motionless, cold. Minnie was no longer moaning or thrashing. Her eyes were shut, her long lashes coal-black against the marble white of her cheeks.

"Vinnie, she's gone," Dr. Feinway said gently but urgently. "The child still might have a chance, but we have to cut it from her. You need to leave now."

"Leave?" I looked at Minnie, lying limply against my arms, peaceful for the first time in such a long while. "Rock me, Sister," she had whispered, and I had. I had rocked her, finally, to sleep.

"Leave," the doctor said, lifting me roughly off the bed so that

I had to release my sister. She fell back, like a marionette whose strings had been cut, against the pillow that was soiled and drenched from her sweat, her blood.

I allowed Dr. Feinway to push me out of the room—until I caught a glimpse of the instruments the impassive nurse was laying out upon a table; there was a knife, with gleaming, sawlike teeth.

"No!" I wailed, wanting to run back in and warn Minnie. But Minnie wasn't there anymore, and Dr. Feinway shut the door in my face; the handle turned until it locked. Then I heard a soft moan behind me. Spinning around, I saw Mama, who had been sitting sentry in the hall the whole time, slide off her chair and onto the floor, where I dropped to my knees just in time to catch her. Not a muscle moved on her kind, careworn face as she uttered only one cry, but it had all the love and worry of a lifetime in it.

"My baby," she moaned, burying her face in my chest—only those two words, but there was no need for more. Then she started to weep, softly, as she clung to me. And I held my mother; I rocked her, too; I sang softly, scraps of songs that Minnie loved. Songs that I knew I would never sing again.

I had no sense of how much time passed, but when Dr. Feinway opened the door and said, "We could not save her daughter," the windows were dark and someone had turned on the gaslights in the hall. I was surprised to see a tear roll down his patrician face; I had imagined him to be above emotion. That my sister had touched him so, in the short time he had known her, moved me beyond words.

"Do you want to see the child?" he asked.

"No! I don't want to see that—that *thing* that killed my sister! Take it away! Take it away from here—"

"Vinnie, please." Mama clutched at my sleeve with trembling hands, her face irrevocably old; I knew that from this moment on, she would look forward only to death, not life. "Please, for me, because I'm not strong enough. But you are."

I hadn't the heart to tell my mother she was wrong. So I gently nudged her off my lap, and rose on unsteady legs, and followed Dr. Feinway into the darkened room, still stuffy, but now a chill wind was blowing in from the window; the heat had broken and the air was cool, fresh, like spring. The nurse was methodically folding bloodstained linens and stuffing them in a wicker basket, the crimson faded to rust; despite the wind, the metallic smell of blood was everywhere. I thought, oddly, that I must replace the carpet and wallpaper in here; the smell would never come out otherwise.

The only light in the room was from two oil lamps on either side of the bed upon which Minnie was lying, her eyes closed, her skin already turning waxen.

"I've never known such courage," Dr. Feinway said softly.

Someone had brushed her curls so that they were no longer tangled and damp; miraculously, they looked like they used to, silky black, no longer that dull, coarse texture of these last months. She almost appeared as if she were sleeping, and perhaps she would to someone who did not know her. But I——who had slept with her so many nights, held her close, watched her dream——knew she was not. I knew it because her red rosebud lips, usually slightly parted, the tip of her pink tongue between them, were blue. Her chest, which always rose and fell so trustingly, was still. Everything about her was so still, so empty; there was no life in this room.

And in her arms was a doll, just as there had been so many times. But it wasn't a doll; it was her child, her daughter—— "Pauline," I said, christening her. She was cleaned up, bathed by the nurse, I presumed, but there were bruises and cuts about her pale, lifeless face; no rosy cheeks and lips, only scrunched-up eyes that had never opened, making her look angry, frustrated. But she had black hair, just like Minnie's.

My little wooden steps—now so worn, so distressed, from being bumped, dragged, and dropped across continents and oceans—were still by her bed. I could have climbed them, had I wished, to touch her, kiss her once more. But I did not. I felt almost in awe. This was not my sister; this was a holy shrine, an icon apart from the horror and pain of the earthly world, the deception, the dishonesty—the sin.

And I wondered, in that moment, if the enormity of my guilt was in inverse proportion to my size. Had I been bigger, would my sins on this earth be less significant—just like my hopes and dreams?

"I imagine so," I whispered, although Minnie could not hear. "I dreamed too big, dearest, for you and me. And you were the one who had to pay. Forgive me, oh, forgive me!"

And then I backed out of the room, unable to look away until I closed the door softly, as if afraid to wake her up. Leaving Mama sobbing quietly in her chair, I ran down the stairs, out the door, and toward the old homestead, pausing in the middle of the road to catch my breath, surprised to feel the night air sweet and refreshing upon my aching brow. Then I gathered up my skirts, as well as my courage, and continued across the road.

I knew I would find Papa in the barn; he didn't turn around as I came in. He simply continued to work, planing a soft pine log, sanding it to the smoothest surface; smooth enough for a cradle, smooth enough for a coffin.

Tears rolled down his craggy face as he began, for the last time, to craft something beautiful, something practical, something that would ease life's journey, for one of his two little girls.

INTERMISSION

A Song and Chorus dedicated to the worldwide friends and admirers of Minnie Warren, entitled "Rock Me Sister," composed by Horatio C. King (published 1878 for voice and piano)

Summer echoes gently stealing Oe'r the meadow, through the grove,
Bore the sighs of loved ones kneeling, By the death bed of their love,
There with face of pearly whiteness, Failing pulse and fainting breath,
With a gaze of heavenly brightness, Minnie Warren smiled on death
(Chorus)
"I am going, rock me, sister," so the little mother sigh'd,
Then as tearfully they kissed her, Fairy Minnie smiled and died.
Set the chimes of elf land ringing, Let each tiny fairy bell,
On the air sweet music flinging,
Whisper gentle Minnie's knell.

From *The Popular Science Monthly,* April 1878

ON EDISON'S TALKING-MACHINE, BY ALFRED M. MAYER

Mr. Thomas A. Edison has recently invented an instrument which is undoubtedly the acoustic marvel of the century. It is called the "Speaking Phonograph," or, adopting the Indian idiom, one may call it "The Sound-Writer who talks."

SIXTEEN

The Curtain Falls, Between Acts

AT FIRST, I DID NOT KNOW HOW I COULD GO ON WITHOUT her.

When Minnie died, part of me died with her. For I had lost not only the sister whom I loved more than anyone else in the world; I also lost the one person in my life who had ever looked up to me. She and I had shared things that no one else could imagine; for so much of our lives, we had shared a chair at table, shared a bed, shared a train seat, shared clothing, even. How often had Mama cut up one of her old dresses and made it over into two smaller ones, just for Minnie and me? There was so much in this world that was too big for one of us alone, but that, together, we could just about fill. Except for hearts, that is; Minnie, alone, was big enough to fill up the hearts of everyone she met. And now my own heart was so empty I decided to put it away for good. There was only one other person who might have had some use for it, but I was no longer speaking to him.

Eventually, however, I did go on, in a fashion, without my sister. For the alternative was to stay home, alone, with my husband.

Edward moved away to New York, although I did not urge him to. Witnessing his grief upon seeing his wife and child lying together in their tiny coffin thoroughly changed my attitude toward him. Perhaps I could not have taken care of Minnie's child, but I found myself softening toward her husband, allowing that he had truly loved her in a way no sister ever could. I was as in awe of his love as I had been of Minnie's.

I was also envious, just as Mr. Barnum had so infuriatingly observed. For now that it was just the two of us, I could not help but look at my own husband through skeptical, disappointed eyes.

Oh, Charles was kindness itself, tiptoeing around me as I fiercely gathered the black veils of that first grief and wrapped myself within them. I would not allow anyone to tell me that I must carry on, that I must be strong, that I must remember that Minnie and her daughter would be waiting for me in Heaven. "I don't care!" I shouted in response. "I want her here! Now!"

Charles did not say such things to me, but it was only because they were not in his repertoire. He had not been taught by Mr. Barnum how to behave with a grieving wife. So he did not recite platitudes and proverbs, and at first I was grateful for that. He was the one person who spoke honestly and plainly about his feelings; possessing none of the stoicism that ran through the male line of my family, he wept along with me. Many nights he crept into my room, climbed into my bed, and slipped his hand in mine as he cried softly into my pillow; I cried into his shoulder. I thought, then, that perhaps we had at last achieved the emotional intimacy of a married couple; perhaps I even allowed myself to wonder if we could achieve physical intimacy, as well.

But my sister's death—the blood, the suffering—was too fresh, too horrible, for me to reach out to my husband in that way. And Charles, ever the devoted pupil, trained first by Mr. Barnum and then by me, had long stopped reaching out to me. My husband fell asleep on my pillow but not in my arms.

Soon, however, I began to be irritated by his tears; it was almost as if he was imitating my grief, although not in a malicious way. I finally acknowledged that my husband had no personality of his own; he was merely an imprint of everyone around him. As soon as I stopped crying, he did; the only time I ever saw him read a book was when I had one in my hands; the only time he went for a stroll was when I proposed one. He went to bed at the same time that I did every night; his favorite foods were mine. The only things he did that I did not were smoke cigars and drink an occasional glass of brandy—the two vices Mr. Barnum enjoyed.

He was so very good at imitation, at mimicry, that I suspected he did have a quick mind. But by now—he was forty—it was rusted over, for the most part unused.

He was also very portly. New clothes were required constantly, and he came to me one day with a tailor's bill in his hand and a worried shadow crossing his usually cloudless eyes.

"Vinnie, dear, do you remember that necklace of yours, the one with the sapphires and diamonds that you hardly ever wear?"

"Yes." I was kneeling next to a trunk, folding some of Minnie's dresses away into it. I hugged one particularly dear white frock to me, remembering how sweet she had looked in it, just like a painting I had seen in France of a little girl carrying flowers in her apron.

"Where is it?"

"The necklace? With the rest of my jewels, in the safe, of

course. Why?" I turned my best schoolteacher's gaze upon my husband; he reddened and hung his head, just like a naughty student.

"I suppose you wouldn't mind selling some of them? It seems that we're a little out of money, at least this month."

"'A *little* out of money'?" I rose, shaking out my skirts. "Be more specific, please."

"Well, the yacht, you know . . . and then the interest on the cottage's mortgage increased, and some of my buildings in Bridgeport are no longer quite as desirable as they once were, and of course I do need some new clothes, you yourself said so the other day."

"You wouldn't need new clothes if you pushed yourself away from the table now and then," I scolded. "I wouldn't mind selling some of my jewels, I suppose—I have so many. But, Charles, you can't let this happen again."

"I know, I won't!" He smiled, so grateful to be let off the hook; he ran back down the hallway to his study, and I went back to my packing. Two weeks later, when the clothes arrived, he showed off the two new top hats he couldn't help himself from adding to the order, and made me a present of a silver fox muff, "to take the place of the jewels!"

Mollified, I did not inquire further into our finances. But I did suggest we consider touring again, not only to bring in more money but because I simply could not bear to be in this house, so empty without Minnie and Edward. I couldn't bear to remain in Middleborough, with all the memories. And I could not bear to be alone with him any longer.

To get back out on the road, with Mr. and Mrs. Bleeker in their old familiar roles, with trains to catch and performances to make, new people to meet, distance to cover every single day— I almost wept at the thought of it! Then I gathered up my train schedules and hotel listings and repaired to my room.

"What about Phineas?" Charles asked me one evening, as I pored over my maps. How easy it was, these days, to plan a tour! So many train routes were now connected, and there were books that listed hotels by city—imagine! I could telegram reservations ahead of time, not take my chance on a letter getting lost or delayed. There were even rumors and rumblings about a new "standardized time" that would organize the country by geographical region; no longer would each individual village or town set its own clock by the sun. How much easier it would be, then, to arrange train schedules!

"What about Mr. Barnum?" I asked, bewildered. I licked the tip of my pencil and raised my arm, hovering over the map before me, ready to draw out a route. "He's no longer our partner—heavens, Charles, don't you remember? He resigned his partnership ages ago, after the world tour."

"I know. I just thought that he could come for a visit and help us plan things. You know how much he enjoys that."

"I'm quite capable of planning it myself. He's very busy with his circus, you know, and that new Madison Square Garden, where he puts on those ridiculous shows. He has no time to visit."

"But he does! He says so in his latest letter!" And Charles's face lit up as he produced this letter; he had obviously been carrying it around in his pocket for all of five minutes. The paper was hardly creased.

"I don't need to read it," I murmured, looking down at my map, wondering if it was up to date. So many new states had joined the Union lately! So many new cities were still sprouting up, cities that had never before greeted General and Mrs. Tom Thumb.

"Vinnie, but he says to tell you, especially, that he could do with a good chat in front of the fire, just like old times."

"How nice for him."

"He said you'd say that! He wrote it, see here? He calls you Mrs. Stratton—why is that, Vinnie? He never did before! But he writes, 'And if Mrs. Stratton says something along the lines of "how interesting" or "how pleasant," tell her that her old *friend*'— and he underlined that, Vinnie; why, do you think?— 'says, "Hogwash," and that she needs to forgive some people, starting with herself.'" Charles looked up from his letter, flush with the success of his reading. "What does he mean by all that, Vinnie?"

"It's nonsense. He doesn't know what he means," I replied, trying to keep my voice even and pleasant, returning to my maps as if I wasn't seething on the inside. Seething and longing, both— how dare he put Charles in the middle of our quarrel! Yet my fingers also itched to tear the letter away from Charles, pick up my pen, and answer it immediately, restoring our friendship, speaking my mind. Perhaps even locating my heart, if I could recall where I had placed it—probably in the trunk with all of Minnie's things.

Minnie. Oh, how could I even think of going back to him, to the way things were before? Minnie might still be here if it wasn't for him, and I knew that were I to be alone with him for just two minutes, he would make me forget that. He would sell me a new memory, for that was what he did. With P. T. Barnum, memories and dreams were available for only a quarter—unless you were smart enough to find your way to the Egress.

I must not have succeeded in hiding my turmoil, for Charles dropped the letter, wringing his hands in worry. "Oh, why are you two quarreling? I don't understand! No one tells me anything, not you, not him! I miss him, Vinnie. Let's go up to Bridgeport tonight and surprise him!"

"You can if you wish, dear." Frowning, I drew a big circle around Middleborough; then I began to trace the rail lines leading away from it. "I'm busy."

"You know I can't go without you," Charles said, pouting. "I don't *want* to go without you!"

I sighed, dropping my pencil upon my desk; I would get nothing done as long as he was standing here. "Do you want me to read to you, then? You're getting agitated. See what Mr. Barnum does to you? That man!"

"Oh, would you read to me?" And just as quickly as a summer storm moving across the countryside, my husband forgot about any quarrel. Together, we walked to one of the small library tables in the study, where he happily echoed the titles that I suggested to him—*Black Beauty, The Water Babies, Through the Looking Glass*. In the end, we settled on *The Adventures of Tom Sawyer*, recently published.

It was such a charming book. It reminded me so much of my days upon the river, when I could wake up every day to a new town. And I was quite fond of the character of Tom, who was such a smooth talker, able to get all the children to whitewash the fence for him—even eavesdropping at his own funeral! I felt I knew him intimately, even if he was just a character in a novel.

MORE JEWELS WERE SOLD, ALONG WITH THE YACHT AND THE cabin, as we told friends that we simply didn't have the time to put them to good use. Yet when we were in New York, we stayed at the finest hotels and dined with our dear friends the Astors, the Vanderbilts, and the Fisks, although sometimes it took them several days to realize we were in town. The newspapers did not always trumpet our appearances as they once did, so often I had to drop a note informing them of our presence.

The younger generation, the children of dear Caroline and dear Julia and dear Mittie, were no longer the admiring little boys and girls who shyly hid from their parents so that they might steal a peek at us. They were now young men and ladies swept up in a new frenzy of balls and parties and dinners, all part of what Mr. Twain had named the Gilded Age. Charles and I were not part of this crowd; rather, I sensed these young people viewed us as relics, odd pets of their parents, leftovers from a simpler, less smart time.

Once I overheard Mrs. Astor's youngest daughter, also called Caroline, whisper to her dinner partner about how "amusing it was when I was a child, when Mother used to dress little Mrs. Stratton up like a miniature Mrs. Astor. She even had her hairdresser give her the same hairstyle! Imagine—how we all laughed!"

I did not let on that I had heard; instead, I smiled brightly at my dining companions and told the story of how Queen Victoria had invited us to tea at Windsor and given us a beautiful grand piano, which we still displayed in our library.

But I remembered that remark; I remembered also that Mr. Belmont had once presented Charles with a nautical jacket and cap identical to his own. Charles had been so pleased, so proud; he had worn it every time the Belmonts invited us onto their yacht.

Finally, I remembered that Mr. Barnum had not liked that jacket; nor had he ever accepted any of our invitations to go sailing with the Belmonts.

I did not drop a note to dear Caroline the next time we came to town.

Naturally, we could not avoid Mr. Barnum altogether. We encountered him at occasional dinner parties, where he and Charles always greeted each other so fondly, I did feel guilty for keeping them apart. I sometimes caught Mr. Barnum looking wistfully at me from across the table, leaning forward, as if he could scarcely contain some thought or idea and was eager to share it. And it wasn't only my grief and loyalty to Minnie that kept me from returning his gaze. I had bared my soul, shared my dark secret and even darker emotions with him—and now I was afraid of who I would see reflected back to me in those glittery, knowing eyes.

And so he would subside, hunching over his cigar. I would stir uncomfortably, and suggest to Charles, far too soon, that we think about going home.

Only when we took our leave would I allow myself to look at him; his shoulders were more stooped with every passing year, and at times I noticed his hands trembled when he lit his cigar. But his mind was as sharp as ever. He was filled with plans for this circus of his, talking boisterously of combining it with others, making it "the greatest show on earth," he told all who would listen, and in fact I was not surprised the day I saw it advertised so in the newspaper.

I was surprised, however, to receive an invitation to join it in 1881. Our finances were at their lowest point; we were discussing letting out the house and moving in with James and his wife. I couldn't exactly say what had happened; we toured, but our audiences were smaller than they once were. We were popular but no longer made headlines. Charles invested but saw little return. Yet we had to keep spending—new wardrobes as the fashions changed, new ponies as the old ones died. Without Mr. Barnum investing in our tours, we had to front the money ourselves, which wasn't always easy.

So it was in desperation that I tore open the letter, the envelope embossed with the seal of "The Barnum and London Circus Company." And I nearly fainted with relief at the amount he was proposing to give us for a season's work; it would more than cover the stack of second notices piling up, alarmingly, on Charles's desk. I telegrammed our acceptance right away; then I dashed off a letter to Mr. and Mrs. Bleeker, asking if they could accompany us.

Then, and only then, did I remember to discuss it with my husband.

INTERMISSION

From *The New York Times,* November 5, 1880

Mrs. Astor Entertains Gen. Grant

Mrs. John Jacob Astor entertained Gen. Grant last evening at her residence, No. 388 Fifth avenue. A dinner was given, and the company, consisting of both ladies and gentlemen, was very select. The occasion was purely a social one. Gen. Grant remained until about 11 o'clock. He was in the best of spirits, and, while making no speech, engaged freely in conversation with those who approached him.

From *The Manufacturer and Builder,* May 1881

Electric Illumination

It is daily becoming more and more evident that the near future will decide the question of the practicability of illumination with electricity in competition with coal gas. Never was there such widespread public opinion manifested in the subject as at the present time. . . . The indefatigable Edison has announced that he has at length solved all the practical difficulties that had hitherto threatened the success of his electric lamps for the household, and has taken the field in person to superintend the work of introducing his system.

———◆◆◆———

SEVENTEEN

Ladies and Gentlemen, in the Center Ring . . .

Aftere the second American Museum burned down in 1868, Mr. Barnum effectively retired from the show business, aside from his partnership in our around-the-world tour and the occasional discovery, such as Admiral Dot. He claimed he chose to concentrate on traveling, politics, and philanthropy. But in 1871 he bought a small circus; then he bought another—and then another. And soon the whole thing had exploded into what he called "P. T. Barnum's Grand Traveling Museum, Menagerie, Caravan & Hippodrome." Now, instead of having the public come to him, Mr. Barnum was back to his roots, when he had first traveled the New England countryside with Joice Heth forty years ago. He was bringing the world of P. T. Barnum to the public.

But true to form, he reinvented what was an already established tradition. He was the first to move his circus by railroad, on his own train—an endless stream of cars all emblazoned on the side with his name, just like the old American Museum. While other circuses had to rely upon unpaved roads and unpredictable ferry crossings, Mr. Barnum's circus chugged steadily along all the new streamlined tracks that linked the country together. In the winter, he parked the show in Bridgeport; in the spring, he launched the new season in New York, in the giant Hippodrome at the Madison Square Garden, which seated thousands.

In 1881, when we joined his circus, he had partnered with so many other circus owners, consolidating everything into one grand show, that I had difficulty keeping them all straight—there was a Mr. Bailey, a Mr. Hutchinson, a Mr. Sanger; the show now was called the Barnum and London Circus. We arrived at the cavernous, roofless Madison Square Garden—formerly a train station until the new Grand Central Station was built, when it became an outdoor arena for spectacles—in the spring. The colossal tents were going up, over the three immense rings of the circus; the place was a madhouse of sawdust and people upon wires and animals forever being exercised and trained. Awed, and not a little intimidated, by the enormity of the operation, Charles and I were overjoyed to see Mr. and Mrs. Bleeker once more; their friendship and familiarity were more welcome than the practical assistance they would provide in helping us navigate the usual difficulties of travel—getting on and off trains, managing luggage, reaching hotel beds, opening windows, etc.

However, from the moment we boarded the vast circus train, after the last performance in New York, I thought we had made a mistake. While our accommodations were, by far, superior to everyone else's, they were far from luxurious. Charles and I did not have a private car, only half a car, to ourselves. An entire circus company is gargantuan; I was reminded of that canvas city of soldiers we had visited just after our marriage. There were stagehands and construction workers and animal handlers; publicity men, ticket takers, popcorn sellers; wardrobe girls, prop men, barkers; an army of men responsible for raising and lowering the tents and packing them up; cooks, laundresses, boys whose jobs were just to take care of the animal waste; wagon drivers. And that's not even counting the performers! Trapeze artists, specialty riding acts, jugglers, dancers, a woman who gyrated upon a pyramid of chairs, gymnasts, wrestlers, high-wire acts, Japanese acrobats who balanced upon their fingertips—not to mention all the animals!

Even though I had grown up on a farm, the overwhelming odor of all those captive creatures made my nostrils close up and my eyes water; I couldn't bear to walk past the animal cars after a long night's trip. Mr. Barnum had to have special cars built for the giraffes, elephants, lions, and tigers; all the rest, the zebras, peacocks, goats, sheep, all the many horses and ponies—some of the most magnificent trained creatures mixed up with dull draft horses that pulled the wagons—managed with regular animal cars. The dogs used in specialty acts traveled with their owners.

Similar acts traveled together. Those in the center ring were closest to the front of the train (the first cars were reserved for the advance men—publicity people, managers in charge of erecting everything); then the other rings were parceled out in cars farther and farther down, with the sideshow acts coming after all the other performers. They were then followed by the band members, then the workers, like the roustabouts and seamstresses and cooks, and then finally the animals and their handlers.

Charles and I, and the Bleekers, were given the best car, right behind the advance men. We had to share it with two European bareback riders, ladies both; they spoke no English, so we communicated with smiles and grunts. I could not complain about our accommodations on the train; we had seats that turned into bunks, and our own washroom, and the walls were freshly painted, the gaslights gleaming. We could retreat there and be somewhat private, apart.

Why did I not enjoy this life? I was on a train again, traveling once more through the night so that I awoke every morning in a new town. Compared to the primitive conditions under which we crossed the continent thirteen years earlier, we were traveling in the most modern manner. No Indians to worry about; no hair-raising wagon rides on treacherous mountain roads; no journeys across a scorching desert, fearful that we might sink into the sand. Not once did we ever have to get out and travel on foot.

But when we were introduced as *"General and Mrs. Tom Thumb, those beloved Lilliputians!"* we were not alone; this was not our show. In the circus parade that began every new engagement (we would hurry off the train each morning at dawn, drive in wagons to the site where the tents were being pitched, then dress in costume and assemble for the parade through town), our miniature carriage, while given a prime spot, was just one in a never-ending line of colorful wagons and rolling calliopes. And at the beginning of each performance, while we were featured in the center ring, we were merely the first of a very long procession of other entertainers who marched around, waving at the audience. We had to be exceedingly careful not to step in animal droppings.

Then we were ushered out of the big top, to a noisy line of tents and booths that made up the sideshows: the acts that were too intimate to be viewed in the vast expanse of the rings. These included many of the kinds of acts I had first encountered on the river—sword swallowers, tattooed ladies, specialty dancers. While our tent was very tastefully decorated, and we performed the kind of dignified entertainment we had given for Presidents, Kings, and Queens, there was no ignoring the somewhat low quality of our surroundings. Just outside, the barkers were always shouting out a patter, the cheap music—usually just a banjo or a trumpet—from the other tents nearby produced a cacophony, and the puppet shows across the way were always eliciting shouts of childish laughter.

Upon our temporary stage, in a tent full of townspeople whose excited eyes, reflecting all the color and sights still to be sampled, could scarcely be induced to linger long upon him, Charles stood, top hat and cane in hand, and began to sing, as he had for years—

"I should like to marry, if only I could find
Any pretty lady, suited to my mind,
I should like her handsome, I should like her good,
With a little money—yes, indeed I should.
Oh! Then I would marry, if I could but find
Any pretty lady, suited to my mind."

I then twirled out to meet him in my beautiful gown, my last few jewels blazing under the oil lamps and torches, which was all the illumination possible in these tents. I curtsied, he bowed, and we began to dance about the rickety stage as our pianist segued into the "Tom Thumb Polka."

But no Kings and Queens smiled and asked us to tea; no natives gaped in awe at the sight of us, so elegantly clad. The audience murmured a bit, clapped politely, and soon hurried on to one of the other attractions. It was an endless, rolling sensation, watching them move in and out of our tent, eagerly but dutifully. There was so much for them to see. They didn't want to waste any time.

One day I left our tent, looking for Charles. He had taken to disappearing between performances, but I knew where he went—the Punch and Judy show, about five tents down from ours. My husband never tired of watching the antics; he laughed heartily whenever the crooked-nosed Punch, in his red jester's cap, hit one of his foes with a stick and a cry of "That's the way to do it!" Charles was also attracted by the children; he watched them wistfully as they held tightly to their parents with one hand, sticks of rock candy in the other.

"Vinnie? Vinnie Bump?" a voice called out behind me. "I thought it was you! See, I told you I knew *her*!"

Turning around, I saw a stout woman standing before me, her hands upon her hips. Next to her were two small women, about my height. But they were not like me—not at all. I glanced uneasily at them, then looked up at the woman who had spoken.

"Excuse me? Are we acquainted?"

"'Are we acquainted?'" the woman mimicked me, then gave a low, admiring whistle. "You haven't changed one bit, except for all the fine clothes! Don't you remember me?"

"I'm sorry . . ." I began to apologize, automatically; I'd met so many people in all my travels. This happened quite often; someone who had shaken my hand on one tour would appear on the next, asking if I remembered him. Usually, I nodded and said I had, and that sufficed. But I did not think it would with this woman, who stood there, smiling so strangely down at me, her bright yellow hair so badly dyed that a line of gray arched above her forehead, like a sad crown.

"Carlotta?" The words flew out of my mouth before my brain had finished identifying her. "Is it you?"

"It sure is! Oh, Vinnie, Vinnie, it's so good to see you!" And she dropped to her knees, holding out her arms; with a smile, I walked into them. I hugged her tightly; it *was* good to see her!

"I can't believe it's you! Did you ever marry your young man on the river?" I stepped back so that I could get a better look; her hair, of course, was the same, a riot of yellow piled atop her head in blowsy curls, but her face was no longer so desperately made up. In fact, she wore no paint at all; with her soft, malleable features, a few missing teeth, and wobbly chin, she looked like any country woman. She was wearing a plain beige dress, homespun but not patched; it was clean and pressed.

"Oh, no. No, he was killed at Chickamauga." Her pale blue eyes blinked, but there were no tears.

"Oh, I'm so sorry!"

"That's all right, it was a long time ago. Lawd, I ain't the only woman who lost her man in the War. So I'm still in the business, same as you!"

"You are?"

"I'm traveling with the company as a seamstress. I always was good with a needle! It's been a spell since I could kick the way I used to—oh, remember, Vinnie? How high I could kick! But I still can't stay in one place, I guess. Same as you!"

"Well, yes, I suppose—did you know I'm married now?"

"Married? For God's sake, do you think I live under a rock? Of course I know all about you and your little General! I been reading about you in the newspapers for years! Look at you, little Vinnie, all dressed up, a married woman! And all them places you've seen! Oh, I'm sorry about your little angel, though. And your sister."

"Thank you." My voice wobbled a little; how ironic that Carlotta, of all people, was offering her condolences for my "child" and my sister. After all, she was the one who had spoken so plainly to me about the dangers of relations with men; I remembered those awful gray "prevention powders" she tried to give me. How long ago it was now!

"Curious, isn't it?" Carlotta mused, pulling me back into the present. She still remained on her knees before me; those eerie women hung back behind her, eyeing me suspiciously. The eager, pushing circus crowd bustled about in both directions, undeterred—ignoring the four of us as if we were ghosts.

"What is?"

"We all thought you were going to be famous, Vinnie, and you are! Do you ever talk to any of the old company?"

"No, not really—I write to Sylvia; she's in Maine. She gives spiritual readings, and seems quite happy. But that's all."

"Me either. Billy's still performing around with his minstrels; I hear of them now and again. Colonel Wood, remember him? What a mean man! I always worried about you and him, Vinnie. I never liked the way he looked at you."

"Yes, well, he was an awful man." And still haunting me, in so many ways, I didn't add. "I need to fetch my husband, Carlotta, as we have a performance. You should come by our car one night, and I'll introduce you to him."

"That's mighty nice of you, Vinnie! I will!" Carlotta—I had such a difficult time reconciling the name with this matronly, staid-looking woman—rose to her knees with some difficulty. "But before you go, I wanted to introduce you to these two. They didn't believe me when I said I knew you, but see?" She turned to them, a triumphant smile creasing her leathery face. "I do! I told you!"

"Oh." I stared at the two women, uncertain how to react to them. For I had seen them before—and done my best to avoid them.

They were part of a troupe of other small people that performed with the clowns. Almost from the first day we joined the circus, I had seen them hanging about wherever we went, trailing Charles and me like shadows, whispering and pointing. But they weren't like us. They had large heads on small, barrel-chested bodies, oddly proportioned arms and legs. They truly looked like the pictures of dwarves in fairy tales—like Rumpelstiltskin, like jesters. They were tossed around by the larger clowns, mute and wild-eyed. They looked simple, in their heads.

They made me uneasy; they made me ashamed, for how the audience howled with laughter whenever they jumped up and down, flapping their grotesque arms, rolling their bulging eyes! I did not wish to make their acquaintance.

"This one here is Miss Humphries, and the other one is Miss Mary," Carlotta told me, nudging them. They each curtsied, still staring at me with round eyes, taking in my silk dress, tightly drawn up over a bustle, in the latest fashion. Both were clad in rough homespun shifts that dropped straight to the ground. Then Miss Humphries extended her hand.

It was odd, ugly, disfigured, with short stumps for fingers and a very fleshy palm. I placed my own delicate, perfectly formed hand—my nails buffed a pretty pink—in hers.

"How—how very nice to make your acquaintance," I said with a smile that I hoped hid my shudder.

"Yes, Ma'am," Miss Humphries said, and stepped back behind Carlotta.

"Have you been with the circus long?"

"All my life, me and my sister both," she said.

"Oh, you're sisters?" They did look alike, upon closer examination. "How nice. I have—I used to travel with my sister, too."

"We know," the younger one piped up. "We've read all about you."

"Oh? Well, isn't that nice! You've *read* about me, you say? Isn't that wonderful!"

"Yes." The older one scowled at me. "We can *read*."

"Of course, of course, I didn't mean—well, naturally!"

"I thought you all might get along." Carlotta beamed down at us, lumping me with those two—two—oddities, to my horror. Did she not see how wrong she was? Did she not see that I was nothing like these two?

And nothing like the others, the other grotesque, misshapen little people who found themselves all under the same sweeping circus tent. I had done my best to ignore their existence. Dressed up like pygmies, some were used in the flame thrower's act; others were dressed up like ugly babies and rolled around in rickety prams as part of another clown routine. They all traveled together in a car far, far down the line from ours. There was no need for me to ever utter one word to any of them, and I hadn't. Until now.

"I really need to find Mr. Stratton," I repeated to Carlotta, desperately; the challenging, slightly resentful yet also envious way the two lumpen girls kept staring at me filled me with unease. "I'm sorry to be rude—"

"Of course, now, you go on and fetch your little husband. But isn't it interesting, Vinnie?"

"What is?"

"Just that—you and I ended up in the same place, after all this time! It just beats all, don't it?" She chuckled, shaking her head, gesturing to the other two. "Here we are, all together, in Mr. P. T. Barnum's circus!"

"Yes, isn't that interesting? Good day, ladies." Pressing my lips tightly together, I turned and hurried off—doing my best not to run, so very much did I want to get away. I pushed along the crowded passageway, hemmed in on all sides by booths and tents and dancers and giants and men in black vests and red-and-white striped pants yelling out, "Come see the *bearded* lady, freshly shaved just yesterday but *already* with a beard *two feet long!*"

And other men in black vests and red-and-white striped pants countered back with "Come see the world-famous General and Mrs. Tom Thumb, those *diminutive darlings* of royalty, those *wee world travelers—intimate* friends of *Mr. P. T. Barnum himself*!"

"We really are!" I wanted to cry out to the crowd, some of whom were pointing to me and smiling—laughing, even—others of whom were simply ignoring me, having already seen their share of oddities—Isaac the Living Skeleton, George the Armless Wonder. I'm sure there was a two-headed kitten around somewhere as well. "We really are world-famous! We really do know Queen Victoria! Mrs. Astor came to our wedding! We're not like the rest of these—"

But I didn't know what to call them. Because I didn't know what to call myself. Dwarf? Tiny? Perfect woman in miniature? None of them, all of them; had I ever been simply Lavinia Warren Stratton? To anyone—even myself?

Oh, good heavens—I was late! We were going to be late—and where was Charles? I pushed my way through the crowds until I spied him. Clad in his top hat and frock coat, Charles was nevertheless upon his knees in front of the Punch and Judy show, playing marbles with a pack of dirty children. I hauled him up by his arm and dragged him back to our tent, brushing the dust off his clothing and scolding him. Five minutes later, we were back onstage; he was singing, I was twirling, we were dancing in front of the restless crowd as the pianist played the "Tom Thumb Polka."

Once, I remembered, closing my eyes as if I could wish myself back in time, this very tune had been played in our honor at Royal Albert Hall. We were the guests of the Prince and Princess of Wales. We rode in the Royal carriage, accompanied by a regiment of palace guards, the Princess of Wales and Minnie both too shy to wave to the crowds.

It really had happened, I whispered to myself fiercely. *It wasn't just a dream.*

"What isn't just a dream, Vinnie?" Charles whispered back. I shook my head and allowed him to lift me up by my waist in time to the music. Someone in the audience clapped; someone else tittered.

When the season was over in November, I wrote a short letter to Mr. Barnum informing him that we would not be returning in the spring.

For once, he did not try to change my mind.

INTERMISSION

From the *Brooklyn Daily Eagle,* May 2, 1882

William Godfrey Krueger, the inventor of a flying machine, and who had spent many years of thought and restless toil over it committed suicide yesterday at his boarding house, No. 186 Forsyth Street, New York. He was out of money and was in daily expectation of getting the first installment of a pension due him from the Government. It came yesterday morning after he had killed himself. Krueger was a native of Prussia, and had been in this country twenty-three years. For fifteen years he has been entirely absorbed in studying out the great problem of his flying machine, and did little more than to write an occasional article for the newspapers. The secret of the flying machine died with him.

From *The Century,* January 1883

WOMEN'S WAGES BY JANET E. RUUTZ-REES

I have been looking for some clue to the unsatisfactory relation of women's work to women's pay. There are, in reality, two distinct classes of women who are in the field of remunerative employment: those who desire to add to an insufficient income, and those who depend upon themselves absolutely for bread. Both classes call for consideration, and yet the fact of their existence is precisely that in which the difficulty we are considering has its rise.

[EIGHTEEN]

—◆◆◆►—

A Terrible Conflagration

O H, WHO IS THAT LITTLE GIRL?" MAMA CRIED, PAUSING IN
her rocking. She leaned forward and peered at me, as if trying to remember my name. "Little girl? I spoke to you—who are
you?"

My heart squeezed up until my entire chest ached, even as I
patted her arm and pushed the rocking chair, lulling her back into
silence. How many times had I been mistaken for a child? But to
hear my own mother do so hurt me beyond reason—even if it
was only the result of a sick, muddled mind.

Charles and I had moved into the old homestead with my
brother James and his family, this December of 1882, after letting out our house. Papa had died in 1880, but Mama was still
alive. Infirm, growing deaf, content to rock in a chair all day, her
hands were now idle, as was her reason. Even as I was glad that she
could no longer remember Minnie, and so could no longer mourn

her, I grieved that she could not recognize me. I was a stranger to my mother, to my entire family, really—and in a way, hadn't I always been? James and his wife were kindness itself, but I felt they were always defensive about the simplicity of their life, comparing it, too often, to what Charles and I had grown accustomed to.

"I don't suppose the Queen served sassafras tea when you all went calling there, did she?" my sister-in-law would say as she prepared for callers.

"No, Mary, but I've always liked sassafras tea," I would reply.

"Well, it's what we're used to around here," she would say, resentment flavoring the tea almost as much as the sassafras.

Or—

"I reckon they take wine with their meals in France," James would remark at dinner, passing around platters of good boiled New England beef.

"They do," Charles would agree.

"Well, we don't go in for that around here, you know," James would scold, mildly—as if we had asked for wine, demanded wine, threatened to lock ourselves in our rooms unless we were served wine.

I don't mean to be ungrateful; my brother and his family did us a great kindness in allowing us to stay with them. But it was uncomfortable, nevertheless. So I did what I always did; I plotted my escape. If my family didn't know what to do with me, my audience did; they smiled, they clapped, and in the spotlight, up on a stage so that all I could see were faces, not legs, I felt big. As big as my dreams.

But never as big as Minnie, who, after all, had been large enough to carry two beating hearts within her. Next to her memory; next to my sister-in-law, with her brood of children and happy domesticity; next to my mother, who, even in her confusion, often caressed the finger upon which her plain gold wedding band still resided—I felt insignificant; I felt small; I felt *less*.

So we were going back out on tour again; this time with just the Bleekers. No more circus trains for us! Just a genteel entertainment, singing, dancing, stories of our travels; we were even introducing a new feature, a stereopticon, to project images of the places we had seen. Mr. Bleeker was quite excited about it; it had been my idea. I couldn't wait to try it out.

"Little girl! Do I know you? Are you Delia's daughter?" Mama stopped rocking again; she was growing agitated, shrugging off her shawl, kicking at her skirt.

"No, Mama," I said, placing her shawl back upon her shoulders. "I'm Vinnie. Remember? Vinnie—your daughter."

"Vinnie?" She tilted her head like a parrot; she was very birdlike these days, the way her hands incessantly plucked at her clothing, and her eyes blinked constantly in any light stronger than a candle. "Vinnie? I used to know a Minnie, once. Whatever happened to her?"

"Minnie died, Mama."

"Died? How?"

"I killed her," I replied. Then I ran upstairs to finish packing.

THE FIRST STOP ON THIS LATEST TOUR WAS MILWAUKEE. WE arrived there on January 9, 1883, a gray, wintry day, although we barely saw it, getting in late, as usual, and driving straight to our hotel. Starting with our circus travels, it seemed to me that we spent less and less time in a particular city, so that I truly had no sense of place. Milwaukee, Minneapolis, Davenport, Sioux City— they all looked the same to me. All had bustling, well-lit train stations, paved streets, new electric wires going up next to all the commercial buildings in the center of the city. Even the smallest towns had tall buildings now, for elevators were becoming commonplace.

Of all the many marvels of the modern age, the elevator was the one that most changed our lives. Maybe others were talking about telephones and electric lights, but Charles and I never tired of gushing about elevators. A lifetime of taking stairs meant for normal-size legs had taken its toll on both of us; Charles was now forty-five, I, forty-one. Our hips ached, as did our backs. Oh, the convenience—the bliss!—of walking into that wonderful little iron cage, watching the lift boy, clad in a smart uniform with a cap, move the handle, and then miraculously rising up, up, up, past all those awful stairs and landings!

Never before had Charles and I ever stayed above the first or second floors of a hotel, until elevators came into vogue. And so we were particularly excited to find that, upon checking into the Newhall House Hotel, we had rooms on the sixth floor— imagine! The very top floor, and we could get to it easily. Surely there would be a very fine view of the city from there!

This somewhat made up for the fact that the Newhall House was not the nicest hotel in Milwaukee. We could no longer afford to stay in the newer gilded palaces of stone and marble; the Newhall House was twenty-five years old, one of the few wooden structures left in that city just north of Chicago, which had suffered the infamous fire twelve years before. But still, the hotel was clean and bright—new electric lights were in every room— and we were happy to see other theatrical folk there, as well.

"Old troupers, all of us," Mr. Bleeker said as he waved at one of the members of the Minnie Palmer Light Opera Company, seated across the lobby. "We'll all die in the harness. It's a sickness."

"Speak for yourself, Sylvester," Mrs. Bleeker said fondly.

We were all four seated in one of the parlors after dinner; it was particularly cozy on this night, as it was frigid outside, but inside, we had the warm familiarity of flocked wallpaper, worn carpet, chipped hotel dinnerware. That was the life we knew, the four of us, and we had shared it for so long. The few times we saw one another out of such surroundings—not on a train, or in a theater or a hotel—it seemed odd; we always acted stiff, uncomfortable, overly formal. *This* was where we belonged—in anonymous hotels, in cities we never saw save from a train window or from a stage door. It may sound depressing, but it was not; rather, the bland anonymity of our surroundings served only to sharpen our identities, making us dear and recognizable to one another— making us a family.

The first stop on a long tour was always particularly full of warmth and laughter, like the first Sunday dinner after a long absence from home. And this night, we were all especially happy, for some reason. Mr. and Mrs. Bleeker sat close together on a plum-colored velvet settee; Mr. Bleeker's lean face relaxed until it almost looked merry. He had his arm around his wife, who nestled her head against his shoulder without her usual reticence. Generally, Mrs. Bleeker conducted herself so modestly as to be ignored by those too busy to observe her gently mocking smile, her soft brown eyes that were quick to notice the most unusual details—the one man whose topcoat wasn't buttoned properly, the one flower that poked its nose up through the grass ahead of the others. But tonight she appeared not to care who might see her playing coquettishly with the buttons on her husband's vest; if I hadn't known her better, I would have thought she had taken wine with dinner!

Charles and I sat close together, as well—the other couple's playfulness seducing Charles into trying something of the same with me. And tonight, for a change, I allowed it; I allowed my husband to hold my hand in his, tucking it under his arm with proud ownership. I even sighed, playing my part, and inched closer to him.

To the casual observer, we were simply two old married couples, happy in one another's presence, perhaps on holiday together. I enjoyed thinking that was how others might see us tonight, this restful, contented night.

"What do you mean, Julia?" Mr. Bleeker looked fondly down upon his wife, who blinked up at him with eyes that crinkled at the edges, like a fine piece of lace.

"I mean, I don't want to spend all the rest of my life on the road. I love you all, but I want a little farm, up in Albany near my family. You may be an old trouper, Sylvester, but I'm not. I only married one."

"You've been talking about that farm for years," Mr. Bleeker scolded, but his eyes kept smiling.

"You've been promising me you'd give it to me for years," his wife retorted.

"You know we could never go on without the two of you," I interposed, but not anxiously; I could not take this talk seriously. Mrs. Bleeker often mentioned that farm but always stood ready, her worn portmanteau in hand, the next time we met at Grand Central Station. "Why, who would ever change my costume so quickly as you? Who would lace me into my corset? And who would keep track of us all?" I turned to Mr. Bleeker. "Remember how calm you were back in sixty-nine, when you outsmarted those bandits in Nevada?"

"Why, sure, don't you remember?" Charles squeezed my hand excitedly. "How you told them we would be on the stage, and then you got us all out of there early?"

"Oh, that was a time!" Mr. Bleeker laughed. "I do wish I'd seen those varmints' faces when they held up the coach and we weren't there!"

"That was a lovely trip," I said, remembering. "All the places we went!"

"It was a tiring trip," Mrs. Bleeker insisted. "I just wanted to get back home safe and sound!"

"But the things we saw—the Pyramids! The temples in Japan!" I closed my eyes, as if I could conjure up those long-ago sights. They were fading from memory, little by little; I could no longer recall the entire settings—I didn't remember how we got to the Pyramids, for example, but I did remember, vividly, how it felt to stand in their ancient shadow. Unreal, almost, as if we were standing in front of a flat backdrop painting of them, instead—until I noticed the clouds moving across the sky, throwing gently changing patterns of light across them, making the rough, uneven surfaces suddenly stand out, almost reaching toward us. Only then did I know they were real.

"Remember, Vinnie, how I said to you that I knew exactly how you must feel, for the first time in my life?" Mr. Bleeker chuckled. "Because I felt about two feet tall next to those things?"

I was about to reply, but to my surprise, Charles answered first. "I do," he declared, decidedly. "I heard you say that to Vinnie, and I wanted to tell you, old fellow, that you couldn't possibly know how we felt. Because none of those desert chaps, the ones working there digging in the sand at the bottom, were pointing to you and laughing."

I was stunned. I remembered that—I remembered thinking *exactly* that. I was nodding to Mr. Bleeker but watching those brown men pointing at our party, holding their hands down to the ground to approximate our size, and doubling over with laughter.

What I didn't remember was that Charles saw them, too—and that he felt the same way. I studied my husband now; he was older, his face so puffy, his beard still rather ridiculous. But there was something in his eyes that I'd never even bothered to look for before—and that I recognized, for I saw it in my own in those rare moments when I paused long enough to stare into a mirror. Hurt and determination, both: That's what it was. Hurt at the cruelties the world sometimes threw at us; determination not to let anyone notice.

Perhaps I had also recognized it in the eyes of those misshapen little women from the circus; perhaps I hadn't wanted to, and so made myself forget I'd seen it. Until now.

I shook my head, even as Charles looked at me with a new, understanding smile. I did not know what to say—so I squeezed his hand and smiled back. For a moment, we were miniature reflections of Mr. and Mrs. Bleeker, seated opposite.

For a moment, it didn't even feel as if we were pretending.

We passed the rest of the evening like this, four friends reminiscing about old times. When the clock struck ten, we all rose and took the elevator up to the sixth floor. Mrs. Bleeker knelt down to give me her usual good-night kiss, and Mr. Bleeker shook Charles's hand. Then we turned and went to our respective rooms—theirs farther down the hall than ours—shutting the doors behind us.

Once Charles and I changed clothes and climbed my steps up to bed, he immediately rolled over to the far side, leaving me the space I always desired. But I did not roll over; I lay upon my back, conscious of his presence in my bed in a way I never had been before. His warm, steadily breathing presence; the way his nightcap got twisted about, even before he closed his eyes; his feet sticking out of his nightshirt, pink and sturdy as a child's but with little tufts of hair upon his toes—like a man.

I had never felt my husband's bare feet against mine. We had never slept that closely; our bodies had never been so entwined. There was always so much distance between us, and I had put it there, from the very beginning. Charles, ever-pleasing, ever-pliable, had not once questioned why I had. Neither had I—until tonight.

Holding my breath, I stretched my right hand toward my husband. Yet I could not reach him; the bed was too big, and I was too small; suddenly, delicately, *femininely* small. Afraid to disturb him, afraid not to, I inched even closer and reached out again.

Sighing with a soft, unexpected snort, Charles rolled over in his sleep and moved tantalizingly closer toward me.

That wasn't what I expected; I snatched my hand back as if he were a hot coal, something dangerous, something that could hurt me. Rolling away onto my own side, my heart racing so that it was pounding in my ears, I held my breath, waiting to see what he would do next. But he did nothing; he simply continued to sleep, unaware of my turmoil on the other side of the deep, linen-covered—and dream-littered—chasm between us. I almost laughed at the absurdity, the feminine timidity, of my behavior—why, I was forty-one! I had been married for twenty years now. I was behaving like a blushing virgin—

Which, of course, I was. I wouldn't have known what to do even if I had touched my husband's shoulder, turned him to me, welcomed him with a smile. Beyond that, I couldn't imagine; my horror of everything that had happened to Minnie would not allow me to think further than an embrace, perhaps maybe a kiss.

I plumped my pillow and told myself, sternly, to get to sleep; we had three performances on the morrow, and we had to get to the theater early to try out the stereopticon. Even though I tossed and turned and couldn't get comfortable, my nightgown unusually hot and heavy against my tingling skin, I did finally go to sleep that night.

And when I did, I later remembered, I was thinking of my husband. For only the first time in our marriage; also, as it turned out, the last.

"VINNIE! VINNIE!"

A hand was upon my shoulder—my husband's hand. I snuggled down into my pillow and smiled; hadn't I just fallen asleep, imagining this, his hand upon me?

"Vinnie! Wake up!" He was shaking me, not tenderly but forcefully. "Wake up! I hear people in the hall! I smell smoke!"

I opened my eyes; Charles was kneeling beside me, his nightcap all twisted about, his eyes, even in the darkness, wide with fear. I yawned—and swallowed a faint trace of smoke.

Then I heard the footsteps in the hall, the confusion. Someone was banging on our door; someone was banging on all the doors in our hallway.

Someone was yelling, *"Fire!"*

I sat straight up, my heart pounding. Charles continued to hover over me, wringing his hands. "Oh, what do we do, Vinnie? What do we do?"

"Get dressed!" I barked, jumping out of bed—forgetting to use the steps, so that I fell with a thud to the floor. Scrambling up, I threw on a dressing gown; Charles did the same. Then I ran to the door and opened it with my usual difficulty, the doorknob large for my hand, and too high; I felt my shoulder strain as I wrenched it open.

The hallway was filled with people, frightened people, their faces still creased from sleep while their eyes were blank with panic. Everyone was in dressing gowns or nightshirts, some with shoes on, most in bare feet. It was utter pandemonium as people ran to and fro like confused mice, simply following their instincts. And their instincts told them to get out—for there was smoke, hazy right now in this part of the hall, but someone shouted, "It's coming up the elevator shaft! The smoke is coming up the elevator shaft! We can't use it!"

And over and over, on everyone's lips, the one word— *"Fire!"*

My instinct was to run to the Bleekers' room: Did they know? Were they awake? But I took one step out of the doorway and was nearly knocked off my feet; there were so many people, now some of them were carrying portmanteaus, or dragging trunks that were much bigger than I was. One almost smashed me even as I stood in the doorway. Everywhere I looked were legs, legs running back and forth, dragging things, holding things—sharp things (umbrellas, walking sticks, even one man with a sword), heavy things. There was no possibility of pushing myself through that stampede without being trampled to death. I couldn't even shout my presence; the din was far too great, as the air was filled with panicked cries and shouts of confused directions: "The elevator must be working!" "No, the flames are coming up the shaft!" "I think the stairs are this way!" "A man said we must be prepared to jump!"

Quickly I leaped back inside our room, banging the door shut behind me. Charles was standing in his dressing gown, uncinched so that it hung loosely, his belly, in his nightshirt, protruding; he was still in his bare feet.

"Put your shoes on!" I told him, as I sprinted to do the same thing. "Gather up anything of value—take my steps, and I'll get my jewel case!" I ran to find the case, but a maid had put it high on top of a bureau, so I could not reach it. Cursing her stupidity, I grabbed the steps out of Charles's hand and dragged them to the bureau; standing up on my very toes, I was able to reach the case.

"Now!" I jumped off the steps and thrust them back to

Charles. "We can't go out in the hall—we'll be trampled to death! We'll either have to wait for people to clear it, or—or—"

"Or what? Get burned to death?" Charles cried. His face was an alarming red; his breathing was labored, and he was shaking from head to toe. He did not look at all well, but I couldn't allow myself to worry about that; first, I had to get us out of this room.

Something was rattling; it sounded like dice being shaken in a cup. I looked down, and it was the jewel case; my hand was trembling so, all my jewelry was bouncing around inside. Later, I realized how ridiculous it was to worry about that case; I had forgotten that everything in it was imitation now.

My entire body was shaking, with fear and energy, both; my heart was racing but only to stir my blood, stir my mind, so that I might come up with a way out. That I would was never in doubt; I knew I could not rely on Charles, and I did not want to die here, consumed by flame and smoke. So it was up to me.

"We can—we can tie bedsheets together!" I looked around, realizing we should probably dampen them first, in case the flames reached our room, but there was no water in the pitcher. "Quick, take the sheets off the bed!"

Charles and I both ran to the bed and began to remove the sheets; it was difficult for us, as they were so heavy and the mattress so huge, the top of it just about level with our eyes; even the pillowcases were cumbersome in our arms, as we could not quite reach all the way about them. In the end, I held on to each pillow while Charles tugged at the cases, both of us falling flat on our bottoms in the effort.

Meanwhile, the commotion outside our door grew even more deafening; the temperature began to rise, and as the early-morning light began to fill our room, we could see that the air was beginning to turn hazy. The smell of smoke stung the inside of my nostrils.

Oh, where was Mr. Bleeker? Why had he not burst into the room to save us, as he always did? But maybe he needed to be saved, for a change; what if they were sleeping, incredibly, through all this? I dropped the sheet I was holding and ran to the door once more—but the hallway was now thick with smoke, with even more people covering their eyes, choking, running, and still crying that one word—*"Fire!"*

I shut the door, knowing I couldn't open it again unless we had no choice but to try to make our way out through that teeming, terrifying hallway. But I couldn't let any more smoke inside our room; while Charles was trying to knot the sheets together, I shoved two of my dresses beneath the doorway to try to keep the smoke out. The Bleekers couldn't save us, and I couldn't save them; we were all on our own, now. I could only pray that we would see one another, safe and sound, when all was over.

"Vinnie, it's so hard—my hands are too small!" Charles protested, massaging his wrist. I ran to help him; it *was* difficult, knotting those heavy hotel sheets together; I didn't know how we'd get them secure enough to hold our weight.

"Here, tug on this," I told him, grabbing one end of two knotted sheets and handing him the other. "Tug hard!"

He did, I did—and the sheets slid apart. We stared at each other; Charles sat down upon the floor, as if he simply had no more will, and began to cry.

"Vinnie, we can't do this! Where's Bleeker? We can't save ourselves! We're too little!"

"Don't say that!" I longed to shake him; I detested his weakness at that moment, for I was too close to giving in to my own.

Kicking at the sheets, I ran to the window, but of course it was too high, the sash far above my head. I needed to stand upon something solid in order to open it, and my steps were too wobbly. "Help me," I yelled at Charles, as I spied a heavy chair next to the bed; we managed to inch it—oh, so excruciatingly slowly!—across the plush carpet, until it was in front of the window. Climbing upon it, throwing all dignity to the wind—my nightgown was now twisted about my waist, exposing my legs—I tried to unhinge the lock on the sash; it was big, slippery in my sweating palms, and at first I didn't think I could move it. But finally it did loosen, and I tugged on it until it released; leaning my shoulder against the sash, I pushed with all my might, praying that it might move. It did, enough so that I could then jump down and put my hands in the opening of the window; Charles joined me, and we were able to push it up enough so that we could lean out.

The scene before us was unreal. The street was full of people, some running, some crying—some lying broken and still. Oh, how wonderful it had seemed yesterday, to be on the very top floor of the hotel! But now it simply meant that we were a very long way from the ground. Smoke rolled out of windows on either side of us, and below, terrifying fingers of flame indicated that the fire must have started on one of the lower floors. I felt the heat rising all around me, as if from the very depths of hell. Horses were neighing, people were sobbing and shouting, bells were clanging—fire bells, from fire wagons; there were many already in the street below, and others coming; you could hear the clatter of horses' hooves, the squeal of careening wagons, echoing between the buildings several streets over.

The hotel was surrounded on all sides by other buildings, but it was also surrounded on all sides by wires. All those new electric wires cities were installing these days—they were like a lethal spiderweb just outside the hotel windows, close enough that a normal-size person could touch them in places. Even as I registered their presence, I saw someone jump from a window on our floor, hit a wire with a sizzling sound, and bounce up and then down to another wire before finally falling to the street below.

I turned away, sickened; there was nowhere to look any longer, no escape to try—all was hopeless. Sliding to the floor, I buried my face in my hands because I couldn't bear to look at Charles. For the first time in my life, I was all out of ideas. Charles slid down next to me and, like a loyal, trusting puppy, laid his head on my lap. Automatically, I began to smooth his brow.

My heart, which had been racing so fast, fueling my fear and desperation, began to slow down, and I was painfully aware of it, wondering how much longer it would continue to beat, wondering what would come first—the smoke, or the flames. Oh! A great cry almost tore my heart open right then; I did not want to die! Not in this way—smoke was beginning to snake in beneath the closed door, despite my wadded-up dresses. But we could not jump—not six floors! That was too high for even a normal-size person; for us, it would be like jumping from an even greater height.

Had Minnie known, just before her heart stopped beating, that it was her last breath? Oh, Minnie! Had she forgiven me? Had she even blamed me, in the first place? Before she died—and she must have known that she was dying; she must have known she could not keep losing so much blood—had she been angry? I was angry now—I was furious! To think that I would die here in this way—why, if there had been someone nearby whom I felt was responsible, I would have yelled, I would have screamed, I would have accused and blamed.

But Minnie hadn't done that, and so, as I strained to see her dear face one more time—but the smoke was so thick it was obscuring my memories as well as my vision—I had to believe that she wasn't angry with me, that she didn't blame me. If only I could forgive myself—

And then my eyes flew open wider as I peered through the smoke, trying to see one last image; my heart, with one final, mighty burst of energy, opened up and flooded my sinking spirits with one last thought. It was of a face; it was of an apology. It was of an acknowledgment that there was one person I would miss—and one person that I hoped would miss me. But that could happen only if I forgave us both.

Charles was coughing, his head still buried in my lap. So was I—my chest was already aching from the effort, although I hadn't realized it. My throat was burning, as were my eyes; perspiration was running down my neck, between my breasts, my thighs.

But I had strength enough left to whisper, "I'm sorry, I was wrong, I forgive us both, I forgive you—" His name was upon my lips; that name I had withheld, for no reason. For every reason.

I was just about to utter it, wondering if it would be the last word I ever spoke, when I heard a voice cut through my fading consciousness.

"Hello?" it said, in a brogue almost as thick as the smoke filling the room. The wall behind my back shuddered, and an enormous thud was heard in the window above my head. "And would there be anyone in here now?"

I leaped up, knocking Charles to the floor; there, in the window, was the tip of a ladder, and a round, beautiful, blessed Irish face, covered in grime and wearing a fireman's hat, staring at me.

"Oh! Thank Providence!" I burst into tears; I couldn't believe that he was real. I climbed upon the chair just so I could touch his face; without a word, he grabbed my arm and started to haul me over the windowsill.

"Wait! I can't—" I gazed down at the ladder; there was no

way I could traverse it, for the rungs were far too widely spaced. "I can't climb down! And my husband is here!"

"Your husband?" The fireman blinked, just as Charles scrambled up on the chair next to me. The three of us stared at one another for an almost comical moment, considering the circumstances. "Ach—you're wee! Both of you!"

"Yes, and we can't climb down the ladder ourselves!"

"Then I'll just have to take you down, then, one at a time. Who's first?"

Charles and I looked at each other; I don't know what he was thinking, but all I could wonder was what if something happened—the ladder collapsed, or the flames broke through, before the man could climb back up? Having just absolved myself of Minnie's death, I could not bear to think of either of us having to live with that burden.

"No, can't you—please, take us *both*?"

"How much do ye weigh?" The man was so calm, standing upon a ladder hundreds of feet above the ground with electrical wires humming not five feet behind him, flames licking below him, people screaming and hanging out of windows on either side.

"Not much—maybe eighty pounds, total?" I tried not to look at my portly husband.

"All right, climb aboard!" The fireman was cheerful about it, as if he was offering us a ride upon his favorite horse. As we hesitated, not sure what to do, he simply reached with one hand and grabbed me about the waist; I was hauled out the window and instructed to climb on his back, which I did, pressing myself tightly against him, trying to make myself even smaller so as not to touch those hissing electrical wires. He yanked Charles out the window by the back of his nightshirt and tucked him under one arm, like a ham. Then he started to climb down, but I called out, "Oh, wait—my steps!"

"Your what?"

"My steps—please, my father made them!"

"Sorry, Miss—no time!" And we began to inch our way down the ladder.

I couldn't look, but I couldn't shut my eyes, either; I wanted to be aware of every moment. I wanted to be able to convince myself I had really survived. So I concentrated on the fireman's back; his heavy coat; the sweat running, in neat little rivers, down the back of his red neck; his matted brown hair curling out from under his black fireman's helmet.

Yet I couldn't shut out all the rest—the bodies that fell on either side of us, landing with the sickening thump of a ripe melon being thrown to the ground; the people hanging out of windows, waving, screaming, holding towels and handkerchiefs up to their faces to block out the smoke, which was boiling out of every window now, thick and black, bits of paper and fabric swirling within it. The air began to cool as we continued down the ladder; I had the oddest thought that Charles must be feeling quite a draft, as the entire lower half of his body was sticking out, uncovered, for all the world to see.

Finally, we reached the ground; the fireman tossed Charles, unceremoniously, to the street and knelt down so that I could slide off his back, muttering, "Eighty pounds, my arse." He then grabbed the ladder and moved it over to the next row of windows, and began to climb back up.

"Charles, Charles!" I bent down, shaking him; I was overcome with joy, with relief—I could have danced a jig, right then and there. "We're safe!"

But to my surprise, my husband was crying. Lying on his side in the street, while people stepped over us, shouting for us to get out of the way, he hid his face in his arms. His shoulders were shaking; he was sobbing more wretchedly than he had at any time during the ordeal.

"What? What's wrong? We're saved!"

"Oh, Vinnie! To have to be lowered down that way, that awful, mortifying way! Like a—like a sack of something—just hauled out like that! It's so humiliating—I couldn't do a thing for myself, I couldn't save you or me, it's so awful!"

I stared at him, unable to believe what I was hearing. I suppose my heart should have softened toward him, for he was a man, after all. And men did have their pride.

But we were alive! I was so grateful for that, I couldn't understand his shame.

I rose; all around us were people sobbing, yelling, running about. There were broken bodies, arms and legs at unnatural angles, littering the street; even as I registered this, another fell just ten feet away from us.

"We need to move away from here," I told Charles, gripping his arm. "Come, let's find a place to stay, and we'll look for the Bleekers."

Sniffing, rubbing his eyes, Charles rose and allowed me to guide him through the carnage, across the street to a bakery that had opened its doors to the survivors. Someone was handing out blankets, and one fell across my shoulders, as if by magic. The warm, homey smell of fresh bread and pastry was an odd counterpoint to the horrible stench—of burning flesh as well as burning wood—outside.

Already there was a coroner's wagon on the scene; stretchers were being removed from it, filled with bodies covered with sheets, and then placed back inside. Hospital wagons were also being loaded with the wounded, and every few minutes the driver would slap the reins as a wagon sped off, full of broken, burned occupants. Mothers were searching for children, crying out their names; children were screaming for parents. Everywhere there were people walking, looking, seeking.

But also, people were simply sitting, on curbs, in the street, still in their nightclothes which were now torn and streaked with ash and dirt; some were dripping wet, as if they'd doused themselves with water to protect against the flames. All were staring at the scene before them, eyes glazed over, as if they simply could not process the carnage, as if they simply could not understand how they had escaped it.

"You stay here. I'll go out and see if I can help, and find the Bleekers," I told Charles, who dutifully nodded and sat down upon an upturned bucket. Someone had placed a blanket around his shoulders, too, but he was shaking, his face still that awful red, his breathing labored. But I couldn't stay inside with him, waiting to be told what to do next; I needed to move, to fill my lungs with air, to remind myself that truly, I was alive.

So I moved among my fellow survivors as the hotel continued to burn; occasionally, there would be a fresh cry as pieces of it came crashing down. But soon there was no one left inside to scream; the flames continued to crackle, the bells to clang, but from within the flames there was only deathly silence.

"Please, let me help." I tugged on the skirt of a woman in a white dress, a blue cape around her shoulders; she carried a basket of blankets and a bucket of clean water with a ladle, and was moving among the survivors, giving them drinks and warmth.

"That would be a blessing." She smiled down at me, not betraying any surprise at my size, and handed me an armful of blankets. The heat from the fire was still blazing hot but only if you were facing it; otherwise, the January air was relentlessly cold. As the sun continued to rise, people's wet garments began to sparkle as if fine diamonds had fallen upon them—but after a closer look, I saw that they were ice crystals. Shuddering in sympathy, I was grateful for the blanket across my shoulders, the warm shoes upon my feet—for many survivors were barefoot.

"Do you know where—is there a place where the wounded are being taken? Where we might be able to meet up with our friends, to see if they survived?"

"I believe there's a man writing down the names of the survivors—over there." She pointed to a man carrying a pad of paper and a pencil, near the largest fire wagon. "You can check with him and give him your name."

"Thank you." I headed that way, handing out blankets; a few people recognized me and smiled weakly, calling out, "Mrs. Tom Thumb! What are you doing here?"

"My husband and I were staying in the hotel," I replied. "We were rescued by a fireman." I scanned the crowd in all directions, searching for the Bleekers—surely Mr. Bleeker, so tall, with his distinctive long gray beard and sad face, would stand out? Surely they escaped, just as we had?

And then I heard my name again—"Vinnie!" But it was a moan; about twenty feet away, I saw Mr. Bleeker kneeling over a broken body in a nightgown.

"Mr. Bleeker!" Picking my way across what now resembled a battlefield, I fell to my knees beside him; he was holding his wife's hand, shaking his head as tears rolled down his face.

Julia Bleeker was still alive; her eyes were closed, and her breathing was shallow. But her face was pale, her nightgown was plastered to her body in bloody patches, and her leg was turned out from the hip at an unnatural angle.

"What happened?" I picked up her other hand; it was cold,

and I was reminded of Minnie. But then she squeezed it, and I had
hope. "Mrs. Bleeker! It's me, Vinnie! Charles and I are fine—we
were rescued from our room."

She didn't reply, although her eyelids fluttered; I looked over
at Mr. Bleeker, who took a big, shuddering breath.

"She jumped—we both jumped from our room to a balcony
about two stories below. I landed just fine, but Julia, she—she hit
the fencing, the iron fencing, and her head—it just hit it. This big
post. I was able to get her down a ladder, but—I don't know, Vinnie. I just don't know."

"Oh!" There was no bruise visible on her face, but it was so
deathly pale.

"I tried to get to you and Charles, I did, but it was impossible." Mr. Bleeker now looked at me anxiously. "Gosh, I'm glad
you got out. I was worried sick; so was Julia. She kept crying,
'Oh, Sylvester, those dear little souls! How frightened they must
be!' But then—" And he couldn't go on.

"I know. Don't think about it."

"That farm," he said, a great tear rolling down his face.

"What?"

"That farm. She always wanted that farm up in Albany.
'Sylvester,' she said, but never in a scolding way—oh, no! 'I surely
would like to have that little farm.' But I never gave it to her. I'm
the one with the show blood in my veins, not her. But she never
once complained, she always followed me, and now—"

"Shhh," I said, for I believed Mrs. Bleeker could hear us, even
if she couldn't speak. "You'll give her that farm, I know it. You'll
have all the time in the world."

"Do you think so, Vinnie?"

I looked at him; his eyes were round with both hope and fear.

"I do," I lied, as all at once, two men and a stretcher made
their way through the crowd toward us. Much too roughly, they

loaded Mrs. Bleeker upon it and trotted off toward a hospital wagon; Mr. Bleeker had to sprint to catch up, shouting, "Where are you taking her?" It all happened so fast, I didn't get to say goodbye—to either of them.

I continued to pass out blankets until the sun rose high in the sky; it must have been noon before I realized I was still in my nightgown. But then, so were many other people. Eventually, policemen rounded everyone up and directed them to other hotels; we were told not to leave Milwaukee for at least two days, as they needed to take down statements from us all.

Somehow, I managed to get Charles more or less upright and moving again, and at my urging, over the next few days we gave two benefit performances for the victims of the fire. And we dedicated each performance to our good friends Julia and Sylvester Bleeker. It was the first time we had performed without them, and it felt wrong; neither of our hearts was in it, but we were happy to help a good many people, a number of whom feared being stranded now that all their money was in ashes.

After the benefits, Charles and I left for home, this time for good; there was no question of continuing the tour. And so, after traveling the globe, crossing the country countless times, traversing up and down and through rivers, deserts, and mountains, the General Tom Thumb Company came to its sad end in the ashes of a hotel in Milwaukee, Wisconsin. Minnie was gone; Nutt had died in 1881 of Bright's disease.

And now, too, was Mrs. Bleeker taken from us; she died twelve days later from her injuries. After staying in Milwaukee to give testimony at one of the inquests, Mr. Bleeker retired to a niece's home in Brooklyn—still agonized because he had not been able to get to Charles and me.

Although, oddly, many news reports and articles began to surface saying that he had—that he had saved Charles and me from the flames himself, depicting him as a grieving, but heroic, husband and friend.

And while I don't know exactly how that rumor began, I could not help but suspect that an old friend of ours might have had something to do with it.

INTERMISSION

From the *Brooklyn Daily Eagle,* June 11, 1883

It is not open to dispute that the Brooklyn Bridge is the most wonderful work of its kind on the globe. . . . There is no instance in the world save that afforded by the Brooklyn Bridge of a span of nearly 1,600 feet sustained entirely by cables.

From *The New York Times,* December 27, 1884

A Brilliant Christmas Tree—How an Electrician Amused His Children

A pretty as well as novel Christmas tree was shown to a few friends by Mr. E. H. Johnson, President of the Edison Company for Electric Lighting, last evening in his residence, No. 189 East Thirty-sixth-street. The tree was lighted by electricity, and children never beheld a brighter tree or one more highly colored than the children of Mr. Johnson when the current was turned and the tree began to revolve. Mr. Johnson has been experimenting with house lighting by electricity for some time past, and he determined that his children should have a novel Christmas tree.

———◆••◆◆———

NINETEEN

Finale, or——the Curtain Comes Down

AND NOW IT WAS JUST THE TWO OF US——GENERAL AND Mrs. Tom Thumb, Mr. and Mrs. Charles Stratton. The perfect couple, a love story in miniature, the sweethearts of a country torn apart by war but united in good wishes for our happiness: we were never supposed to end up like this. Diminished, unnerved, hiding in the house I had been so determined to leave all those years ago.

Quite bluntly, Charles was never the same after the fire. Shaken to the core by his inability to save himself, humiliated by the manner in which he was saved, he refused to ever again appear in front of an audience.

"Charles, you're being ridiculous," I told him, time and again. "Can't you just be grateful that we survived?"

"No." He shook his head, his breathing even more labored these days, his body not merely large but puffy, his skin clammy to the touch. "I can't forget the fireman hauling me down the ladder like that. I couldn't do a thing to help myself, Vinnie! You don't understand. You don't know what that's like!"

I pressed my lips together and shook my head. I did know what that was like—but now our roles were reversed. My husband was not inclined to look into my eyes for understanding or recognition. He was not inclined to look into anyone's eyes, lest they see him for what he believed he was—a coward.

He was only forty-five, but until that night, he had never faced any real physical danger. The worst was probably the time when he was a child and Queen Victoria's dog had tried to bite him, a story he told over and over to anyone who would listen. And his pride had suffered; this was the man who had stomped around with a tiny pistol in the West, confident he could slay any number of Indians with it. He had laughed along with everyone else at the notion, but deep down, I knew that he thought he could. He may have been imitating people all his life, but what made Charles such a gifted mimic was his conviction; he believed in every single role he had ever played—including that of husband.

And now he thought he had failed in that as well; suddenly he could not meet my gaze or even enjoy being in the same room with me. I didn't have the courage to tell him that he was wrong; he had never been given the chance to succeed in that role. For hadn't I made sure of that, long ago?

So he holed himself up in Mama's parlor, where he read over old newspaper clippings and hauled out tarnished medals and yellowing citations, reliving his past instead of facing the future. Charles had been a Mason for years, attending elaborately secret meetings (I knew they were secret because he always made a point of telling me they were); soon after we were married he had been made a Knight Templar in the Bridgeport order. And now I often found him looking over all his various hats and plumes and swords from that organization; it meant a great deal to him these days. I think he felt it bestowed the last measure of dignity he had left.

We both slept badly after the fire; we moved from my old upstairs room to one on the first floor, and could not go to sleep unless one or both of us checked to make sure the windows and doors were unlocked, and there was a bucket of water close at hand.

And never again did I reach for him in bed, as I had that night; my desire had been quenched, along with the flames.

"Charles, I'm taking the train down to New York to see Mr. Bleeker," I told him one morning in July. "Would you like to join me? I'm sure it would do him good to see you."

"No, no." My husband waved a plump hand in the air, as if brushing the very notion away.

"Charles, why won't you see him?" I sat in one of our little chairs; we had moved what pieces of our miniature furniture that we didn't sell into this house when we let out our own. It looked as if there were whole families of furniture living together, mother and father chairs spawning baby chairs.

"I just—I just can't, Vinnie. That's all." Charles, who was seated upon the floor, paging through an old scrapbook, looked up at me; even that small effort seemed to tax him. His breathing was so rapid, I could hear it across the room.

"You don't blame him for the fire, do you?" This suspicion had crossed my mind, as Charles refused to even write a sympathy letter to his old friend.

"No," Charles said, too quickly.

"That's absurd. Mr. Bleeker tried to come to our aid—remember, I told you? But for pity's sake, Charles, he had his own life to save, and that of his wife! We were not Mr. Bleeker's responsibility, you know. Why can't you be glad that we're alive?" Suddenly furious with him—as I was so often these days; I suppose he was not the only one changed by the tragedy—I ran to him and took his hands in mine. "We must get out of this house—we must get back to work! If we don't, we'll—we'll—we'll simply rot! We don't know any other life, the two of us. It's all we have."

"Vinnie, I just can't. I can't face anyone." Charles pulled his hands away; he wouldn't meet my gaze.

I sighed. There was only one other thing I could think of to try; there was only one person I could think of who might be able to talk some sense into him.

"I might stop in Bridgeport on the way back," I said, keeping my voice casual. "To see Mr. Barnum. Wouldn't you like to come with me, then?"

Charles hesitated; I could see the struggle in his once-merry eyes. But then he shook his head violently. "No."

"Well, why don't I stop to see if he would like to come to you, then? It's been such a long time since he's been to Middle-borough."

Again, that hesitation; again, his negative response. "No, no—why won't you leave me alone, Vinnie? For pity's sake, that's all I want—to be left alone, finally! All my life I've been surrounded by people! Leave me in peace, for once!"

I sighed, then rose—stiffly, my right hip uncooperative. "Well, maybe I'll just stop in on my own!"

"Do whatever you want." Charles shrugged. "Take your time. Enjoy yourself."

"I'll give Mr. Bleeker your love. And Mr. Barnum, too—that is, if I do decide to stop in Bridgeport. I haven't made up my mind."

I turned to go, but Charles abruptly cried, "Vinnie!" before I could leave.

"What? What is it?" I spun around in alarm. He had jumped

up, his arm full of clippings, a morose figure in his dressing gown and worn slippers. The shades were drawn, but I could still see the stumps of cigars in every ashtray, the papers and photographs and citations and ribbons and, above all, memories; remnants of memories, threadbare, worn almost to shreds from a lifetime of use, lying in tatters at his feet. The room smelled like sadness, like stale breath and cheap cigars and musty papers that hadn't seen light in decades. It reminded me of a deserted, desolate circus tent long after the crowd had gone.

"You're not mad at me, are you?" He looked so pathetic, his soft brown eyes almost quivering with tears.

How easy it would be to tell him I was not—I considered it, for a tempting moment. My approval was the one thing left that I could bestow upon him without guilt. But then I realized that approval would do him no good this time; indeed, it would probably harm him. He needed to be shocked out of his torpor. He needed to be reminded that he was lucky he wasn't dead, so that he could get back to living.

"Yes, yes, I am," I said briskly—coldly. "I'm quite mad at you, if you want to know the truth."

Then I turned to go, before I could see the effect my words had on him. I didn't want to be late for my train.

THE TELEGRAM ARRIVED AT MR. BLEEKER'S HOUSE THE NEXT morning. We were having breakfast in his niece's narrow dining room; it was odd, just the two of us. I wasn't sure we had ever taken a meal alone together before.

Mr. Bleeker's sad face was even sadder; it was only now, with his wife gone, that it was obvious how much warmth and light she had given him. But he was not like Charles; he did not live in the past. He was doing his best to enjoy life with his niece, who had two small sons, and for the first time, I wondered why he and Mrs. Bleeker had never had children of their own.

"Julia couldn't," he said frankly, over toast and eggs. "I think that's why she enjoyed traveling with you all, even though she did long for that farm. But you and Minnie, especially—you were like daughters to her. You were our family."

"Odd, isn't it?" I sipped my coffee—the cup was large for me, so I had to use two hands.

"What is?"

"We all pretended to have children we didn't, in a way. Except for Minnie. She wasn't like us; she wasn't content just to pretend."

"Yes, except for Minnie. She would have been a wonderful mother."

"I know. It's been five years," I said softly, wonderingly. "Almost exactly—it was July, I remember it so well. Five years, too, since I last spoke—well, five years."

"Vinnie, what happened between you and Barnum?" Mr. Bleeker asked, and I was reminded that no matter how sad his face was, his eyes were ever sharp, ever perceptive. "I've always wondered. Goodness knows plenty of people have fallen out with him over the years, but I never thought you would."

"I—that is, it's hard to put into words. We both said things that hurt, and—that whole baby business." I shook my head. "It was the one thing my parents warned me about when I first met him. They warned me not to get caught up in one of his humbugs. Well, I did, and I brought Minnie along with me, and see what happened? Minnie's gone. I can't forget that."

"Just like I can't stop thinking that I was responsible for Julia," Mr. Bleeker whispered. "How do we live with that? How have you gone on?"

"By being so angry with Mr. Barnum, I sometimes forget to be angry with myself," I replied, smiling ruefully. "But ever since the fire . . ." I stirred my coffee and shrugged.

Ever since the fire, I had not stopped thinking about him.

That horrible moment when I thought I was about to take my last breath and form my last thought—it had been of him. I knew I wanted to see him one more time. I knew I wanted to tell him things—just what, I couldn't say. But inside my soul, in addition to the great burden of guilt I carried with me about Minnie, was a greater burden of things unsaid.

"Ever since the fire?" Mr. Bleeker prompted.

"I've been thinking it would be good to see him again."

"He is in Bridgeport now, I understand," said Mr. Bleeker, ever the organizer, ever the manager.

"I was hoping he was," I replied, wondering if I should wire him that I was going to stop on my way back. Or should I simply surprise him? He always did like surprises. Maybe I could stop into a shop and buy a stuffed elephant to bring him—he would like that; he would laugh, throwing back his head, and then motion for me to pull up a chair and sit with him.

Or maybe I should wire, after all. What was the best way to end a rift like ours? I smiled, thinking that if it were left to him, he probably would take out an ad in *The New York Times* proclaiming his apology and selling tickets to our reunion for twenty-five cents each.

And so it was that I was thinking about someone else, his moods, his quirks; wondering how I might reach out to him again over the morass of all the years, memories, and misunderstandings—

When the telegram arrived informing me of the death of the man whom I constantly had to remind myself to think about. The man whose name I eagerly took but whose heart I had never wanted, in the first place.

* * *

CHARLES STRATTON, BETTER KNOWN AS GENERAL TOM THUMB, died of apoplexy, some said, the inevitable conclusion to a lifetime of cigars and rich foods. Others said he never recovered from the devastation of the Newhall House fire, of witnessing the tragedy of so many unfortunate souls.

They were all mistaken; I knew better. I knew he died of shame. He had played the hero, the leading man—the perfect man in miniature—onstage for as long, literally, as he could remember. The realization that he was not built to be a hero in life was too much for him to bear; he could never play that role again, and so he simply—stopped. Like a child's windup toy, used too often, the spring finally broken.

We buried him in Bridgeport, Connecticut, the town of his birth. Years before he had done a benefit for a brand-new cemetery, and had arranged his own plot at the time; he had even posed for a statue he wanted placed upon his monument—a life-size statue.

Ten thousand people attended his funeral. He would have been so pleased—a packed house! I smiled, safely veiled in my widow's weeds, thinking of how he would have shaken the hand of every man and kissed the cheek of every woman here. Charles did so love to meet people.

Two plumed Knights Templar stood at attention at the foot of his casket; upon the lid was his own small, plumed Knight Templar hat and miniature sword. Among those in attendance were Astors, Vanderbilts, and Bleekers; also the tattooed man he became quite fond of while touring with the circus, and many, many children, which would have touched him immeasurably. Queen Victoria sent a wreath, as did President Chester A. Arthur. The largest floral display of them all said, simply, "Friend"; it was given by Mr. P. T. Barnum, who sat several rows behind me in the church.

Minnie's service had been so small, I remembered, watching the throngs file past Charles's coffin, the reporters scribbling down every detail. Just in Mama and Papa's parlor. How Charles had sobbed! As if she were his own sister, and truly, I knew he thought of her that way. Whatever my husband was or wasn't, there was no denying he was genuinely giving of his love and affection. Charles had no enemies at all; he was the only person I knew of whom I could say that. No, Reader, I take that back. Minnie didn't, either.

And there was genuine grief at his funeral, too; I saw it in the faces that passed me. I heard it in the sob coming from several pews back, the sob of an old friend, the man who had taken a five-year-old boy and turned him into a miniature adult—and together, they had conquered the world. There would have been no P. T. Barnum without Charles Stratton, and there would have been no General Tom Thumb without P. T. Barnum.

I longed to go back there and comfort him, for I alone knew of the genuine affection between the two. Others saw only a business partnership; I saw a friendship. Mr. Barnum's sobs tore at my heart in a way that my own husband's death did not; my tears would not fall, and so I appropriated his. He could cry over Charles, for the both of us, just as I had cried over Minnie.

But I did not go to him. I sat in my pew, upon a cushion so that I would be visible to all, and I adjusted my thick black veil so that it hung with dignity down my back. And I tried to remember the things I loved about Charles. For this day, of all days, I did not want to pretend; I did not want to feel as if my mourning dress was a costume, as my wedding dress had been. I closed my eyes, and I remembered Charles as he was with children: warm, open-hearted, all pretend dignity tossed aside, almost always on his knees, even though he—alone of all adults—did not have to bend down to be on their level.

I remembered Charles as he was with Minnie: the two of them co-conspirators, impish, playing pranks, sharing confidences, sharing a chair, the back turned to the rest of us, as they whispered together.

I remembered Charles as he was the last time I saw him: tear-stained, asking for my approval—because he had given up asking for my love. And I had refused him. It seemed to me I spent our entire married life refusing him, he who asked for so little of me. He had died alone, in our bed; even if I had been there with him, he would have died alone. For I had never allowed love to join us there, and without it, the two of us could not begin to fill up all the empty spaces between us.

His coffin looked so small in this great church, the stained-glass windows looming over it, those tall Knights Templar dwarfing his tiny plumed hat, perched so jauntily upon the top. I thought I should go and stand by him, so he wouldn't be so lonely, as he had always stood by me—

And that's when I realized what I would most miss about him. For I had lost the person who shared my view of the world, the person who had stood by me as I traveled continents, met Queens, shook hands with Presidents. I hadn't stood alone in over twenty years; always I had someone by my side whose eyes saw the world as I did. Through a maze of legs, of wheels, of barriers large and barriers small.

Barriers of hearts, and barriers of minds.

I bowed my head, tears finally trickling down my cheeks. And I found a way to mourn for my husband.

INTERMISSION

From *The Humbugs of the World,* by P. T. Barnum

And whenever the time shall come when men are kind and just and honest; when they only want what is fair and right, judge only on real and true evidence, and take nothing for granted, then there will be no place left for any humbugs, either harmless or hurtful.

TWENTY

One Last Encore

AFTER THE FUNERAL, I WENT BACK TO MIDDLEBOROUGH—back to my family. It was unspoken, but I knew they assumed that I would finally settle down, once and for all, within their bosom. Henceforth, I would be "Aunt Vinnie" to my various nieces and nephews, so numerous I honestly could not remember all their names.

"Aunt Vinnie, who used to be in show business"—I could just imagine how it would be. On Sundays the children would be forced to come into my parlor and visit with me, giving me a dutiful peck on the cheek while I rocked in my widow's weeds and told them stories they would not believe until they were older. It would only be after I was gone that they would believe me, after someone inherited a trunk full of scrapbooks and costumes and handbills—probably intended to be thrown out, but for some reason, someone thought to open it first. Then, imagine the surprise!

Aunt Vinnie had told the truth; she wasn't just a dotty old lady after all. Who would have believed it?

Oh, this was but one of many elaborate scenarios I envisioned for myself as I sat, brooding, in the house of my childhood. Sometimes the trunk was opened by an eager niece who wanted to go into the theater herself; she had always believed me, even though her brothers taunted her. Sometimes the trunk was sold, unopened, only to be discovered at an estate sale a year or two later.

And sometimes the trunk was simply thrown out. And no one remembered me at all, until I died and my will was read, stipulating I was to be buried next to my husband. That little man, that General Something-or-other; hadn't he been famous first?

Yes, he had. And now, without him, with only his name, who was I, anyway? Who would want to come see the widow of General Tom Thumb, all alone? What could she do on her own, other than tell stories that nobody believed anymore? Stories of Kings and Queens and Mormons and old Civil War generals? Who would pay money for that? *I wouldn't,* I thought to myself as I tried, unsuccessfully, to fall asleep in the room I had shared with Minnie as a girl.

Only I was all alone now; Minnie was gone, and even though at times my chest still ached with the memory of her head nestled against it, it had been five years since I had rocked her, finally, to sleep.

And Charles—I had never imagined that I would miss my husband as much as I did. I even missed his solid warmth in bed next to me, even though we never touched. But still, his snoring, his movement in the night, for he was a restless sleeper—I missed it now as I lie, once and for all, alone. Alone in my little bed, the one I used as a girl. The elaborate carved bed I had shared with Charles was gone; I put it in storage, for I could not bear the reminder of my failure as a wife.

And just as I had, so long ago when I heard Mama weeping softly over my lonely fate—how prescient she had been!—I lay in my virginal bed, and tossed and turned, longing for something else, something more. And just like then, I didn't know what it was.

I knew only that at age forty-two, after almost twenty-five years of running—running to catch trains, running to make performances, running to the next city, the next country, the next continent—

Running away, from my husband, from my family, from my name scratched in a tree, destined always to be smaller than everyone else's—

I still hadn't found what I was looking for.

Why was I, alone of everyone I knew, always still seeking? Still searching? Why did everyone else seem content enough, *brave* enough, simply to—live? Minnie, for all her timid ways, her shyness, was braver than I had ever been. She had been brave enough to live the life that I had only pretended to, the life that I had done my best to avoid yet somehow had ended up impersonating all over the world. That of the perfect wife and mother, the embodiment of the feminine ideal—in miniature. Always, in miniature.

There was only one other person I knew who never seemed satisfied. There was only one other person I knew whose dreams were as immense as the ones I had dreamed so long ago. There was only one other person who, though larger than me, had never allowed his shadow to completely obscure my own.

I picked up my pen and wrote another letter. I even walked into town to the post office myself, as I had done all those years ago; I even worried, just a little, about his reply.

But I didn't worry too much. For I knew I had found my way back from the Egress, after all.

* * *

"I WAS GOING TO COME ANYWAY, WHETHER YOU WANTED ME TO OR not," he said grumpily—although he couldn't completely prevent a crooked smile from spreading across his face.

Those lips were thinner now, the bushy eyebrows completely white, along with his curls. He did not use his gold-tipped walking stick as an accessory—punctuating sentences with it, outlining imaginary train routes, twirling it like a magician. Now he leaned heavily upon it, especially when going up stairs.

His voice, so much higher than one would think it should be, was still the same, as was his mind; closing my eyes, I could almost hear it whirring and turning, just as before. And, of course—that barely checked glimmer behind the gray eyes; I knew it was still there, just waiting for the perfect opportunity to mesmerize, beckon, delight.

"You were not, for you are afraid of me," I told him, just as grumpily. I had received him in Mama's parlor, now updated with gaslights instead of oil lamps, although there was a rumor that in the next few years, electricity would be run to all in Middleborough. My sister-in-law had redecorated everything, so that the plain, homespun braided rugs and simply carved furniture were gone, replaced by more ornate, heavy chairs, plush carpets. It looked like every hotel parlor I'd ever visited, but I didn't tell Mary that. She was very proud of this room.

"Afraid? I don't know what you mean," Mr. Barnum replied. "I am afraid of no one."

"You are afraid of women, and you always have been. You were terrified of Jenny Lind, you know. Why else would you let her slip away so soon and go back to Europe? And you're afraid of your wife now. Why else did you leave her in London while you came back home?"

"Why, that—" He began to stir; it had been such a long time

since we had sparred, and I don't believe he quite remembered how. I almost apologized, for I did not want to spoil the visit—but then he relaxed and allowed that glimmer in his eyes to wink at me. "Well, Vinnie, I see your tongue has not dulled with time. No one ever has spoken to me the way you do."

I smiled, pleased. But then an awkwardness fell over us. There was still so much left unsaid, so much I wanted to tell him—too much, in fact. For I didn't know where to begin.

"So why did you ask me here?" Mr. Barnum finally said, pulling his spectacles out of his pocket, putting them on, as he always did when he was preparing to talk business. "I heard—well, dash it, Vinnie, I heard that Charles left you in the lurch and that you're practically destitute. Is that true?"

I hesitated; it felt disloyal to talk about Charles in this way so soon after his death. But finally I nodded. "It's not so bad, though, as you see. I have a home, a roof over my head."

"Not fitting for you," he answered, shaking his head. "I know your family is dear, but Vinnie, you can't be happy living here, can you?"

"No, but that's not why—oh, I don't know. Yes, that's it—that's why I asked you here, to see what you advise for the future. For you always know what to do."

"Oh." Now his eyes hardened. "That's the only reason you asked, then? Because you needed something? I should have known. That's the only reason anyone ever calls for Mr. Barnum."

I looked away. I did not know how to apologize to anyone, let alone him. I was quite sure he didn't, either. The room was so silent, of a sudden, only the sound of his breathing, my sigh; his foot jostling, my skirt rustling. Our hearts, too rusty, both of them, from disuse—but suddenly now I could hear them both pounding, roaring in my ears.

Or was it just mine, alone?

"Minnie," I finally said in a whisper, not looking at him. "Minnie."

"I know," he replied, so gently. I was reminded of his gentleness at other times in my life: when he found out about Colonel Wood, for instance. When he heard of Minnie's plans to name her child after Pauline.

When he said my name, as I left him outside on the lawn, before Minnie died.

"We both—that is, I don't blame you, anymore. We both were equally responsible, for it all—the baby hoax, taking Minnie out, away from here. I wanted her with me, just as much as you wanted her in the troupe. I could have said no—I knew that, for you always listened to me. But I didn't. I can't blame you anymore."

"You shouldn't blame anyone. Vinnie, I've never in my life apologized for anything—not for Joice Heth, not for taking one nickel from the public, not even for the Feejee mermaid. I never made a person do anything he didn't want to. I'm not going to start apologizing now, either. But I am—I do regret—the thing is, Vinnie, dash it, Minnie was *happy*, you know! She could find the beauty in quiet things in a way I never could, and she should be envied for that, not mourned. She was happier than you and I will ever be and ever were, God bless her soul. We just don't have it in us to be content like that—but your sister did." He was excited now; he had inched his chair closer and closer to mine, until, before either of us could fully register it, we were sitting knee to knee.

I looked away, still loyal to Minnie's memory; it was hard to forgive him. It was harder still to forgive myself. I missed her so much, missed her joy, her trust, her touch—

Suddenly I felt my hands being picked up and clasped with warmth and understanding. I couldn't help it; a quick sob escaped my burdened heart and a tear rolled down my cheek. I tried to brush it away, but my hands were held captive.

"She did find beauty here, in this home, and she always tried to open my eyes to it," I whispered. "But I can't be content with it, even now, because you were right. Being content with home would mean being content with myself, just as I am, and I've never been able to be that. Yet I've lived such a little life, compared to my sister."

"Who said such a thing? I'll thrash 'im within an inch of his life!"

"Nobody—just me."

"Well, I'll thrash *you,* then!"

I looked up and smiled. "No, you won't."

"No, I won't," he said agreeably. Still holding my hands, he gave them a stern little shake. "But I won't hear such talk. Mercy Lavinia Warren Bump Stratton—even that name isn't as big as you are! You've traveled the world, met everyone worth knowing! Whatever I said—and who can remember, anymore?—the plain truth is that you were never meant to stay at home on a farm, and it has nothing to do with your size. Imagine you, selling eggs at the kitchen door, or getting excited about baking pies for the church bazaar!"

"I'll have you know, my pies are exceedingly light and delicious," I replied primly.

"Who cares if they are? I can have any kind of pie I want, anytime I want. But if you had decided you were content with that accomplishment only, I would never have had the privilege of your friendship. And that, my dear, would be a tragedy."

"No, it wouldn't. You'd still have Jenny Lind, and Charles, and Jumbo, and your circus. You wouldn't miss me at all."

"Then why am I here, then? Why'd I come all the way from Bridgeport to godforsaken Middleborough, at the first sight of a letter from you? I hardly even opened it before I was packing my bag!"

"I don't know," I mumbled, my tongue tied, for once. I felt as if I were on the edge of a grand discovery, something that would change the world—or, at least, my life.

"Because I missed you, you fool! I was wrong about something just now. I have been content, you know. Would you like me to tell you when?" Mr. Barnum's voice was softer—shy, almost.

I nodded, unable to meet his gaze.

"Remember when you first came to New York? And we used to sit together in Caroline's parlor and talk? Then I thought I was happy. I wasn't used to talking over my plans and schemes with anyone else, but somehow—I just found myself talking them over with you. And I was happy."

"So was I," I whispered.

"And I've missed that, I've missed that so much. So don't go talking about not living a big enough life, for you were big enough for me to miss, terribly. And that's saying a lot, as I own an elephant. Several of them, in fact."

"Me, too—oh, I've missed you, too!"

I couldn't say more; he didn't try. He acted, for the first time in his life, as if words truly were no longer necessary. I simply *felt* his understanding in the way he continued to hold my hands; the warmth of his grasp made its way somehow to my heart—which filled with satisfaction. Looking up, gazing into his eyes, I thought I recognized his heart, too; it was the light that I always saw there, finally revealed, fully, to me. I smiled in its illuminating glow, and the name that I had carried within me, for so long, finally found its way out of my suddenly open heart, and rushed toward that light.

"Phineas," I whispered.

His eyes grew wide; a great, satisfied grin broke crooked

across his face. And in that moment, I found what I had been searching for all my life. I saw happiness; I saw respect.

I saw love.

"So," he said after a moment; he released my hands, and we settled into our respective chairs, knee to knee, eye to eye.

Heart to heart.

"Let me tell you about my latest idea." He took out a cigar from his breast pocket. I reached for the matchbox on the table beside me, struck a match, and lit it for him. He leaned back in the chair and puffed away, satisfied.

"Is there a role in it for me?"

"It's all about you. Opera, that's the thing. Hear me out. A perfect, miniature opera company—what do you think about that?"

"Opera? That would take a lot of people, wouldn't it?"

"It would, indeed. Have you heard of the little women over in New Hampshire? Sisters, they are; genteel, ladylike, although they can't hold a candle to you. But they sing—that's what I hear."

"Opera," I mused, mulling it over. Opera was all the rage now—and, of course, I could sing. I had always been told I had a lovely voice. "Tell me more."

"You'll be the leading lady. But imagine headlining your own troupe! I've even picked out a name, the Lilliputian Opera Company, starring Mrs. General Tom Thumb. What do you think?"

"I like it," I said, nodding, turning it around in my head, waiting for it to click into place, to make sense—to get my heart racing again, wondering where all my train schedules were. Had I packed them away, like everything else? Oh, I certainly hoped not!

"I like it," I repeated, smiling up at him. "I like it a lot, Phineas."

"I knew you would, Vinnie," he said, with a satisfied smile, as he puffed away on his cigar—just like a man. I got up then, pausing to rest my hand upon his shoulder, as I began to walk around the parlor, turning on the lights—just like a woman.

For outside, the dusk was falling.

And I knew we would talk well into the night.

CODA

———•◦◦◦•———

From the *Brooklyn Daily Eagle,* April 7, 1878

Professor Edison, the inventor of the most marvelous instrument of modern times, has already hit upon a scheme in which millions seem to lurk, namely, the publication of a cheap phonographic library, by means of which a five hundred page novel can be sold in electrotype sheets to be adjusted to the phonograph. The instrument will then be adjusted and the novel will be read aloud to the listener by machinery. Fortunately this instrument has only just come into fashion, otherwise we should never have come into possession of that exquisite mine of Oriental fancy the Arabian Nights.

AUTHOR'S NOTE

————◆◆◆————

I first encountered Lavinia Warren Stratton in the pages of one of the masterpieces of historical fiction, E. L. Doctorow's *Ragtime*. She appeared, briefly and near the end of her life, in a scene with Harry Houdini.

She didn't make much of an impression on me then. However, a few months later I was searching for the subject for my next novel, noodling around on the Internet, reading books, histories, lists of notable people—anything that might help me find that one person whose story I just had to tell. On one list, the name "Lavinia Warren Stratton" leapt out at me; I remembered her from Doctorow's novel, did a basic search on her name, and was immediately entranced.

Lavinia—known as Vinnie—was born on October 31, 1841, in Middleborough, Massachusetts, to a family of good standing. All of her siblings, as well as her parents, were normal-size, except for her younger sister, Huldah, called Minnie. Both Minnie and Vinnie had a form of proportionate dwarfism, probably caused by a pituitary disorder; had she been born in more modern times, she would have been given human growth hormones. But at the time, she—and her future husband, Charles Stratton (or General Tom Thumb, as he was more widely known)—were highly prized "curiosities" in an America that was just beginning to be linked. With the advent of the railroad, steamships, photography, and the modern press, people could now experience a world outside their own small villages; most people had never seen, nor really ever heard of, little people. And the fact that Vinnie and Charles and Minnie were "perfectly formed people in miniature" made them palatable and interesting to the public; those who had disproportionate dwarfism were, tragically, considered distasteful, and often used in circuses and sideshows to depict savages or idiots.

Vinnie had a very loving and normal childhood, and was engaged as a schoolteacher in her town. However, a Colonel Wood—purported to be a cousin, although that was never proven—showed up at her door one day with an invitation to appear on his "floating palace of curiosities" out west. To the great shock of her pious New England family, Vinnie leapt at the chance. In her autobiographical writings, she admits to a desire to travel, to see things, to experience a wider world than she could in New England.

She doesn't admit that her fate, were she to remain at home, would likely be a dismal one. A woman in mid-nineteenth-century America had few options; either she married, or she remained dependent upon her relatives for the rest of her life. She could not have a career (beyond that of modest schoolmarm) of her own. It's unlikely Vinnie or her family ever thought, given her size, that she would marry. However, after her cousin's visit she had another option. She could leave Middleborough; she could travel, she could have a career, and she could do this as a single woman precisely *because* of her size. For a man named P. T. Barnum had just introduced the public to General Tom Thumb; suddenly there was great interest in the "curiosities" of the world, and Vinnie was only too quick to take advantage of this opportunity.

After spending almost three years upon the Mississippi—her travels were interrupted by the outbreak of the Civil War—Vinnie returned home to Middleborough. A year or so passed before, somehow, P. T. Barnum "heard" of her, and sent an agent to interview her. Her parents were skeptical; they did not wish to have their daughter caught up in any of Barnum's infamous "humbugs." But somehow, Vinnie and Barnum persuaded her parents to let her go, and it was only a matter of weeks before Vinnie was capturing the hearts of the New York press with her stately levees; she was heralded by all as the "Little Queen of Beauty."

It made sense—not only to Barnum but probably to Vinnie herself—that the Little Queen of Beauty should marry a King, and the perfect candidate happened to be close at hand. Charles Stratton—Barnum's great discovery and greater friend—made her acquaintance; Barnum wasted no time in fanning the flames of love and most important, the press, and in February of 1863, the two were married.

Their marriage was the nineteenth-century equivalent of the wedding between Prince Charles and Lady Diana; every paper in the land covered it, relegating the Civil War, for a few days at least, to the back pages. From that point on, Vinnie and Charles, along with her sister Minnie and another little person, Commodore Nutt, performed as the most famous quartet in the world. They traveled the globe; they met Brigham Young, every president in the White House, Queen Victoria; they were among the first passengers on the new Union Pacific railroad linking the country and among the very first Americans of any size to travel to the new colony of Australia.

In 1878, Vinnie's beloved sister Minnie died in childbirth. Commodore Nutt had already retired from their troupe, and suddenly the most famous quartet in the world stumbled upon hard times. Vinnie and Charles continued to perform, but tastes were changing; the country was more sophisticated, and their venues were becoming smaller. Hard-up financially—for they had believed they had to live the life their society friends could more easily afford—they even traveled with Barnum's great circus for a season, performing as part of the sideshow.

In 1883, Vinnie and Charles were touring once more, staying at the Newhall House in Milwaukee when that hotel caught fire, resulting in one of the worst hotel tragedies in history; Charles apparently never recovered from the shock of that experience and died only six months later. Retreating to her childhood home, her finances in ruin, Lavinia was on the verge of retiring when Barnum encouraged her to keep going, to keep appearing before the public.

Of course, she did. In 1885 she remarried—to another little person, Count Primo Magri of Italy—and formed the Lilliputian Opera Company. She continued to tour, even appearing in vaudeville and early silent pictures; ever short of funds, the couple opened up a roadside stand near their home called "Primo's Pastime," where they entertained anyone who would stop and buy a souvenir. They also spent a sad couple of summers as part of the "Midget City, Dreamland" exhibit at Coney Island.

In researching Lavinia's life, the challenge was always to separate the humbug from the truth. P. T. Barnum looms large over everything written about her. Many articles and even a book or two, written not only at the time but much later, appear to accept

as fact everything that Barnum ever put forth, including the blatant falsehood that Vinnie and Charles were the parents of a daughter who died in infancy.

Even Lavinia's own writings left much to the imagination. She
had hopes of publishing an autobiography in her lifetime, but
didn't; several incomplete chapters were discovered after her
death, however, and edited and published by A. H. Saxon in 1979.
She also published a couple of essays in the *New York Tribune Sunday
Magazine* in 1906 that purported to be part of her autobiography.
But there is so much missing from all of these pages! She never
mentions details of the death of her sister, for instance. She doesn't
discuss the baby hoax. She doesn't discuss much of anything, actually; her writings are really a rather uninspiring travelogue, listing the places she traveled and the people she met. And she freely
borrows from Sylvester Bleeker's published account of their world
tour.

She also doesn't discuss her feelings. She never shares any disappointments, any frustrations about her size, her physical dis-
comforts. She presents a determined, sunny face always. You have
to read very carefully to find the disappointments and frustrations.

For example, she gives her time with Barnum's circus in 1881
only a couple of paragraphs and concludes by saying, "It was not
to our taste." Similarly, while writing about some of the dangers
of her life upon the river with Colonel Wood, she admits, "It cannot be denied that these occurrances (*sic*) were a little disquieting."

And she makes no mention of her "child," the humbug she
and Barnum perpetuated concerning a baby Thumb. Accounts
vary as to whether Lavinia was barren, or she chose not to have
children. I have to think that, as intelligent as she was, she was very
aware of the dangers to one her size. And when Minnie became
pregnant, apparently Barnum's doctors tried to convince her to

have an abortion, which she refused. So obviously, while press accounts of Minnie's death mention her "fairy child," Vinnie was only too aware of the risks.

How she felt, then, having deceived the public into rejoicing over the "birth," and then mourning the "death," of her own child can only be imagined; likewise, the guilt and grief she must have felt in watching her own sister die in childbirth. She discussed the hoax once in public, in an interview given to *Billboard* magazine in 1901, explaining the procedure of obtaining "English babies in England, German babies in Germany." But she also takes pains to say that "Mr. Barnum was a great man."

As I researched Lavinia's history, her great intelligence and drive were the characteristics that spoke to me. There seemed to be only one other person in her life who even came close to matching those characteristics, and that person was, of course, P. T. Barnum himself.

Lavinia's story is so big—there were times when I feared turning her into a nineteenth-century version of Woody Allen's Zelig—that it threatened to get away from me at times. Yet I found that whenever I turned back to Barnum, a story came into focus. I believe that every novel is either a mystery, a tragedy, or a love story—some are all three—and it became clear to me that this is a love story. An unusual love story; an affair of the mind rather than the body. P. T. Barnum was always the light she was seeking; whether, as at first, he was just the means to bring her to a wider audience and take her away from the dangers of working with shadier characters or, ultimately, the companion, the true partner, she could never find in Charles Stratton or even her beloved sister Minnie.

I chose to end my novel, then, a good forty years before Vinnie's death. To me, the story had to end with Barnum; he was the great love of her life, I came to believe, and everything she did began and ended with him. Even in her own autobiographical chapters, Lavinia only devotes four pages to her life after the death of Charles Stratton.

Did Vinnie marry Charles Stratton only for the fame she had to know it would bring her? Most accounts record their marriage as a happy one. Yet he does not loom over her life in the way that Barnum does. It is difficult to imagine that Vinnie wasn't aware of the enormous fame that would result in marrying a fellow little person—the most famous little person in the world, in fact. The novelty of the perfect little couple in miniature was too much to pass up. Most accounts also record Charles Stratton as being somewhat of an innocent, an intellectual weakling—although a very genial man, one who would not have caused Vinnie any grief. He also would not have excited her mind in the way someone like P. T. Barnum would have.

Barnum died in 1891; somewhat like another larger-than-life character, Tom Sawyer, he arranged to have his obituary run a few days prior to his death so that he could read it. His last words were, "How were the receipts today at Madison Square Garden?"

Lavinia died on November 25, 1919; she was buried next to her first husband in Bridgeport, Connecticut. Despite her second marriage, she signed her name, until the end of her life, as "Mrs. General Tom Thumb."

Yet when she was asked, after Charles Stratton's death, if she was preparing his biography, she answered no. However, she assured the questioner, she was confident that "My own autobiography I hope to have published and put out to the public before long."

In some way, I hope I have fulfilled that ambition; I can't help but think Vinnie would be pleased to see her name in print, once more.

ACKNOWLEDGMENTS

———◄••••►———

One of the delights of telling Vinnie's story was learning not only about her life and that of P. T. Barnum, but also about a colorful, exciting period in our nation's history. Some of the most helpful books I read were *The Lives of Dwarfs* by Betty M. Adelson; *The Life of P. T. Barnum* by P. T. Barnum; *P. T. Barnum, the Legend and the Man* by A. H. Saxon; *Freak Show* by Robert Bogdan; *Barnum Presents General Tom Thumb* by Alice Curtis Desmond; *General Tom Thumb's Three Years Tour Around the World* by Sylvester Bleeker; and, of course, *The Autobiography of Mrs. Tom Thumb (Some of My Life Experiences)* by Countess M. Lavinia Magri, formerly Mrs. General Tom Thumb, with the assistance of Sylvester Bleeker, edited by A. H. Saxon.

There is a delightful website called The Lost Museum, which reconstructs Barnum's American Museum in an interactive fashion, and also provides much history about Barnum and his various performers: www.lostmuseum.cuny.edu/intro.html. Another

website, The Disability History Museum (www.disabilitymuseum
.org), introduced me to Lavinia Stratton's autobiographical essays
published in the *New York Tribune Sunday Magazine* in 1906.

Two sites were very helpful in providing color commentary
on the period: www.sonofthesouth.net is a wonderful resource
for *Harper's Weekly* magazines of the Civil War period, and Cornell
University Library's "Making of America" website is a treasure
trove of nineteenth-century periodicals: dlxs2.library.cornell
.edu/m/moa/.

I am indebted, as always, to Laura Langlie for her insight, sup-
port, and savvy. Thanks, of course, to everyone at Random House:
Kate Miciak, my wonderful editor; Gina Centrello, Libby McGuire,
Jane von Mehren; Susan Corcoran and the tireless publicity team;
Sanyu Dillon and the amazing marketing team; Robbin Schiff for
her brilliant cover art; and Denise Cronin, Rachel Kind, and
Donna Duverglas. Much gratitude to Randall Klein for answering
my endless questions, and Loyale Coles.

And as always, I could not have done this without the support of my family, especially Dennis, Alec, and Ben Hauser.

CONTENTS

Acknowledgments / v

Foreword / vii

Introduction / 1

Well, How Did I Get Here? / 4

Chinese Food Always Leaves Me Hungry / 14

When Did You First Know? / 19

Sex Time! / 32

Howard Stern Every Day / 34

Always on Our Toes / 40

Bella's Birthday Blues / 43

What Does Autism Look Like? / 48

A Career Takes Root / 58

It's a Small World. But a Big Hotel / 63

Now Entering the Age of Autism / 72

The Autism Marriage: Soul Mates or Cell Mates? / 82

A Paper Mitten on the Giving Tree / 88

New Word: The Stagtastrophe / 92

The Things We Do for Love / 99

The Little Green House / 107

The Middle Child / 117

Up, Up, and Away / 125

Don't Ask. Don't Tell. / 131

Another Night in the Holiday Inn Express / 139

Does Heroin Feel This Good? / 146

Dr. Wakefield and the Anti-Vaxxers / 151

Mother Superior / 166

Beef: It's What's for Breakfast, Lunch, and Dinner / 173

You've Got to Fertilize the Roses / 178

My Turn / 189

References / 195

Glossary of Terms / 196

Author's Note / 198

ACKNOWLEDGMENTS

MY FIRST FORAY INTO WRITING WAS FICTION. NEVER IN A MILLION YEARS did I think I'd write a "Kimoir." But here I am. My biggest thank-you is for my husband Mark, who has stuck by his girls through thick and thin, thinner, and thinnest. Mia, Gianna, and Bella are the joys of my life, and while I'd change their autism if I had a magic wand, I treasure them just as they are. Thank you, girls, for coming into our life.

My family, the Rossis and the Staglianos, helped us survive our ups and downs. My mother-in-law opened her heart and her checkbook when autism and unemployment wiped us out. My mom and dad opened their hearts and their home, allowing us to move in with them when we had to sell our house in Hudson, Ohio. We were like a three-ring circus setting up shop in their living room.

I can't thank my agent, Eric Myers, enough. He took me on as an unknown writer with a single article on Huffington Post as my entire publishing "oeuvre." Susan Senator, a fellow autism mom and writer, encouraged me back when I first began writing and made me realize I had a shot at being published. David Kirby, a journalist and author, read my first attempt at a novel and laughed along with the story, not at me. His vote of confidence convinced me I could make a go of writing.

J. B. Handley handed me my blogging career on a silver platter. Mark Blaxill and Dan Olmsted turned the silver into platinum inviting me to run Age of Autism.

Jenny McCarthy turned the autism world on its head by bravely speaking out on behalf of our children and remaining in the fight

long after she could have folded her tent and gone home. I can't thank her enough for the foreword.

My editor, Jennifer McCartney, turned my jumbled-up stream-of-consciousness words into proper prose and did so with the TLC an author needs. For Tony Lyons, Publisher at Skyhorse Publishing and fellow parent of a daughter on the spectrum, a big thank-you for taking a leap of faith and turning "You ought to write a book" into reality.

And finally, to all the autism moms and dads out there, this book is for you, really. We need hope and laughter to get through the day. After all, none of us is Mother Teresa, and Lord knows we have all we can handle.

Kim

FOREWORD

Kim Stagliano is one of my favorite Mother Warriors. She's incredibly funny, and her book gives a bird's-eye view into what it's really like to love and raise kids with autism while dealing with the ups and downs of marriage when her husband loses his job . . . three times! Kim is a loud, vocal advocate (sound familiar?) for prevention, treatment, and care for all people with autism. Let me tell you, it's not easy to make readers laugh while talking about controversial subjects like autism, vaccines, and poop. Imagine if Erma Bombeck and David Sedaris got together and had a baby who grew up to be Kim Stagliano, wife, writer, and mom to three gorgeous girls with autism. Now turn the page and read a book called *All I Can Handle: I'm No Mother Teresa.*

Enjoy!
Jenny McCarthy

INTRODUCTION

OH, GOD. NOT ANOTHER BOOK ABOUT AUTISM.

George Bernard Shaw once said, "Youth is wasted on the young."

When I agreed to marry Mark, little did I know that I'd shifted my life from Plan A to Plan X (as in X-files) without having the slightest clue of how different my life would be compared to what I then considered normal.

Just as well I couldn't see what was coming when I said *yes* to Mark.

If a light came down from the clouds right now and a voice (imagine James Earl Jones or Morgan Freeman) told you that in twenty years you, a prep school and college graduate, would not own your own home, would have less money in the bank than you did at age twenty-five, would have three children with autism, and would be happier than you ever thought possible, what would you do? Laugh? Cry? Join a start-up religion in Idaho and wait for the mother ship to take you to Alpha Centauri?

Here's the thing. None of us knows what we'll do or how we'll react when life lobs lemons at us like hand grenades.

Mark and I are no exception.

Throughout our marital and parenting travails, we've kept a stiff upper lip. And we've collapsed like a cheap tent. Mostly, we've navigated the middle ground of perseverance and clung to one another for dear life. Even when clinging meant drawing blood. There's been plenty of that. We're both loud, opinionated,

Italian-Irish, and Boston born, and we agree that any argument worth having should be at a decibel level just above "jackhammer" and include words typically reserved for folks on vessels in the open sea.

Our marriage is a mystery to me. And like any good mystery, there were clues and foreshadowing sprinkled about long before the kids and autism came along and the German company fired him by e-mail, and the boat started rocking, then leaking, then listing. I missed most of the clues that telegraphed, "This is kind of unusual, Kim." And the ones I took note of, I quickly ignored. I guess that's human nature.

Or youth.

This book is an "all right already, I hear you!" to my family and friends, colleagues, autism moms and dads, my literary agent, Eric Myers, and some very smart editors, including Jennifer McCartney at Skyhorse, who, like my agent, took a big leap of faith on a mom sitting at her computer in Connecticut. When you finish *All I Can Handle*, I hope you'll have laughed a lot, cried a bit (don't worry, you won't need Prozac to get through the book), and absorbed a visceral feel for what life is like for the tens of thousands of autism families who face the challenges of that diagnosis, now affecting at least one in 110 kids.

My sector of the autism community has taken a real hit in the media recently. We're the crazy folks who are anti-vaccine (so not true), believe in junk science (*buzzzzzzzzz*—wrong answer, thanks for playing), and spend our waking hours molding fashionable hats out of Reynolds Wrap. I look horrible in silver—no tinfoil hats for me. Just a lot of questions on why autism rates continue to soar, catapulting entire families into emotional, marital, and financial chaos. The current lifetime cost of raising a child with autism is estimated at $3,200,000 according to a 2006 report from the Harvard School of Public Health.

That's not a nest egg; it's an estate in the Hamptons.

All three of my daughters—Mia (12/15/94), Gianna (7/11/96), and Isabella (9/14/00)—have been diagnosed with autism spectrum disorder. The definition of autism from the National Autism Association is *". . . a bio-neurological developmental disability that generally appears before the age of three. Autism impacts the normal development of the brain in the areas of social interaction, communication skills, and cognitive function. Individuals with autism typically have difficulties in verbal and non-verbal communication, social interactions, and leisure or play activities. Individuals with autism often suffer from numerous physical ailments, which may include: allergies, asthma, epilepsy, digestive disorders, persistent viral infections, feeding disorders, sensory integration dysfunction, sleeping disorders, and more. Autism is diagnosed four times more often in boys than girls."*

Given the boy-to-girl ratio, you can see how our family is pretty unique.

If you're not in the autism community, then chances are you or someone close to you has lost a job during the economic crisis of the last several years. Boy, Mark and I know about unemployment, and to call it humiliating and debilitating is an understatement. In short, it can flatten you like a steamroller. After reading about our lives, you're sure to feel better about yourself.

That's promising, isn't it?

WELL, HOW DID
I GET HERE?

Back in the seventies there was a Kodak ad featuring Paul Anka singing, "Times of Your Life."

"Good morning yesterday, you wake up, and time has slipped away."

Kodak moments are meant to be warm and comforting and not moments that make you run for a cocktail. If only life were that simple. Having a child with autism is life changing. When all of your children have autism, that's life *altering*, as if the laws of the universe simply don't apply to you.

★ ★ ★

My girlhood dreams were of the garden-variety sort: I'd go to college, graduate, marry, have three children (boy, girl, girl), and live a charmed life. My dashing husband and I would have plenty of money (that was a given) and we'd take our kids skiing at Killington in Vermont in the winter and swimming in Falmouth on Cape Cod in the summer. The kids would be at the top of their classes in private school. They'd grow up to have straight white teeth and brag-worthy careers. I'd become a mother-in-law and then a grandmom. And when I died, my obit would read, "Damn, she was lucky."

★ ★ ★

"Welcome to US Airways flight 2314 to Cleveland, Ohio. It's a beautiful October day, perfect for flying. Please make sure your luggage fits in the overhead bin."

The older woman in seat 7C smiled at me as I approached, admiring (I imagined) the French manicure and spray of sapphire and diamonds on my left hand. What really caught her eye was the large basket of pink and white roses tied with delicately braided satin ribbon.

"Pretty flowers," she said as I maneuvered the basket in the overhead bin.

"Thank you."

I settled beside her, clicked my seat belt, opened my book, and waited for takeoff. Curiosity got the better of her.

"Were you in a wedding?" she asked.

A bit sheepish, I nodded. "I got married on Saturday. They're my wedding flowers," then I turned back to my book and didn't say another word until we landed.

The meddling matron had looked horrified. Seat 7B was vacant. Where was my new husband?

"Oh honey," she must have thought to herself. "You two don't stand a chance."

★ ★ ★

On October 19, 1991, I married Mark Steven Stagliano in beautiful Hilton Head Island, South Carolina.

Unbeknownst to us when we'd picked the date, Lenox China, where Mark worked, had scheduled their annual sales meeting for October 21 in beautiful (insert eye roll please) Lawrenceville, New Jersey. Uh-oh.

So we got married in a bass-ackward fashion. Instead of taking a honeymoon, we arrived on Hilton Head a week early with our families. Mark golfed with his friends, his dad, the wonderful Mike Stagliano, and his brothers Mike and John. And he golfed. And he golfed. And he golfed.

I tended to wedding details (I'm sorry, Amy, Genny, and Michele, for those monstrous frothy pink bridesmaids' dresses!) and fumed a

bit more each day that Mark was spending so much time golfing. We had a blow-out argument about it, which was really about his lack of attention to me, *the bride*, and we each threatened to call off the wedding forty-eight hours before showtime. I suppose we both chalked the argument up to wedding jitters. We kissed and made up, and I refocused on important issues like finding a bridal salon to steam the wrinkles out of my wedding gown.

The best piece of advice I got for my wedding day came from my dear friend and high school roommate, Laurie. She told me to concentrate on Mark's face during the vows. "Look right into his eyes, Kim. You'll be nervous. Make sure you really look at him." Little did I know that she was going through a painful separation at the time, as her husband, a Navy pilot, had decided to spread his wings elsewhere. I'll never forget how she put aside her troubles to come support me at my own wedding.

Thanks to Laurie's advice, I can still see Mark standing there at the altar atop the ugly gold carpeting at Holy Family Catholic Church— thirty-three years old and tall with black hair—the same handsome guy I'd backed into a corner at Champions Sports Bar and Restaurant in Boston's Marriott Copley Place almost two years prior.

On my wedding day, I was twenty-seven years old, standing in an $1,800 House of Bianchi silk shantung Cinderella gown decorated with pink crystals and Alencon lace. My gown came with a pair of lace "modesty sleeves" that pulled up to the short puffy sleeves of the gown. Once my mother explained what they were I dutifully pulled them on, but I happily tore off these "church sleeves" after the ceremony. Remember, this is in 1991, before wedding gowns turned into strapless columns of plain silk that resemble paper towel rolls.

I tried to listen to Father Chappell (I swear that was his name) as we said our vows. As I listened to him speak the words that were going to bind me to Mark for life, here's what I heard:

"For better or for *blah blah blah*. In *whatwasthat?* and in health. For richer or for *somethingorother*."

Worse? Sickness? Poorer? Hey, Padre, this is my wedding day, and I'll have none of that depressing talk, you hear me?

I'd spent more time concentrating on the limo color (blue not white) and the wedding cake (chocolate cake with raspberry filling) than considering how Mark and I would handle the important details of our life together. "Problems" weren't even a blip on our radar screen, despite our easily ignited tempers, which I chalked up to our Irish/Italian heritage.

Pre-Cana training? The Catholic marriage class did little to break our sense of entitlement to perfection. Why would anything bad happen to us?

On Monday, October 21, Mark flew to his sales meeting in New Jersey. On Tuesday, my family checked out of the house we'd rented for the wedding and I flew home to Ohio *by myself*, toting a large basket of wedding flowers.

★ ★ ★

I'll never forget the look on the face of that woman seated next to me on my flight. I admit that I was a bit kerfuffled at how easily Mark and I separated just days after taking our vows. I'd put on my brave face for the wedding guests. "Of *course* I don't mind. He has to go to work," I chirped as I packed my bags to return to Cleveland alone. I was actually feeling painfully homesick for my home state of Massachusetts, my parents, and my friends, whom I'd known far longer than I'd known my new husband.

★ ★ ★

Even our courtship had been unorthodox.

★ ★ ★

I fell in love with the (first) boy I *thought* I was going to marry in September 1977, my freshman year of high school. I was thirteen

years old—younger than my funny, adorable middle daughter, Gianna, who is now a teenager. Back then, parents didn't hold their children back to allow them to mature. I turned fourteen on December 28, 1977, and graduated from high school at age seventeen. By my oldest daughter Mia's age (she's sixteen as of 2010), I'd kissed a boy and I liked it, to paraphrase singer Katy Perry. When I think of what I was doing at their age I lose my breath—my girls are so beautiful, and yet so impaired by their autism. (I hate writing the word "impaired" as much as you probably disliked reading it.)

Autism does hinder their ability to do a lot of typical teenage girl things. They can't go to the mall alone with friends. They've never had a sleepover. They can't sext naked photos of themselves to a boy—wait, score one for autism there. Sometimes you have to find the sunny side of the street in a weird neighborhood.

One cold fall night in October 1989, my relationship with my high school sweetheart came to an end. "David" and I had dated for nine years. I'd fallen in love with him in ninth grade at Noble and Greenough School in Dedham, Massachusetts. I sat behind him in Mr. Sculco's biology class, ogling his golden-blond curls. I was Bella to his Edward long before the *Twilight* series. David was my first true love. And in time, my first, well, *you know*. I had every intention of marrying him after college.

His intentions lay elsewhere—kind of all over Boston, if you get my meaning. Hey, he was a handsome Dartmouth grad with an impish smile and piercing blue eyes who'd been in a relationship forever—I can't blame him for wanting to play the field. I say that *now*—but back then? I was crushed. I'd been practicing writing "Kimberly Ann Kristin Rossi Daub" for close to a decade. A girl doesn't just toss that kind of commitment aside lightly.

Our split was dramatic. Actually, *I* was dramatic (think Marisa Tomei in *My Cousin Vinny*). He was his usual uber-calm Germanic self.

I always yelled.

He never did.

We were destined to fail.

Fast-forward two weeks from the breakup.

My friend Cathy dragged my heartbroken self to a party at Champions. Their restaurants were like T.G.I. Friday's with different ferns and a sports theme. Banners decorated the bar announcing Champions' first anniversary, and beer and liquor promoters were everywhere. One of them was my client from Miller Brewing. (I sold advertising specialties on commission, and I had no money problems—something I can hardly fathom today.)

I also recall talking to a handsome but obnoxious guy named Miles who sold Corona beer and thinking, "Oh my God, I hate being single and all the men in the world are jerks." Then I noticed this tall, great-looking guy watching the Bruins game on a TV mounted up high on the wall.

Physically, he was the anti-Dave, and that's about all I needed.

He wore a gray suit—looking very corporate and adult. Not like a carousing frat boy. Maybe, I thought, he was even *over thirty.* That was my new benchmark for maturity. (Now we get AARP flyers in the mail.)

I took a sip of my Cape Codder and stepped forward toward this guy.

Another sip. Another step.

One more sip, and I've crept up on him like John Belushi scooting across the darkened campus in *Animal House.* I am pleased with my stealthy approach. I am damn nervous.

"What's the score?" I asked, using the female pickup line equivalent of "You come here often?" I was twenty-four years old, and had been on four dates in my life.

Tall guy looked amused and told me the score.

I searched for the next box in my meet-up checklist:

"So, what's your name?"

"Mark Stagliano." (Italian!)

"I'm Kim Rossi," I told him, hoping the vowels in my last name would make up for my bazillion potential inadequacies. I was wearing a conservative, black, knee-length skirt and a long-sleeved blouse buttoned high (there wasn't much to advertise) with lots of colors on it, as if a rainbow had vomited all over me. After the breakup, I was feeling hideously unattractive and undesirable, plus I've *always* been self-conscious that I have more curls in my hair than curves on my figure.

I think he asked me if I was with a liquor company.

"No, I'm not, are you?"

The hockey game progressed on the TV well over my head.

"Yes," he said, eyes darting from my face to the game, "I'm with Seagram."

Now I'm giddy. He has dark hair and is gainfully employed at a Fortune 500 company? Maybe I can do this dating thing after all. The butterflies in my stomach feel kind of good.

Either the game or the event ended, I can't recall. He asked for my number and if he could walk me to my car.

The butterflies are now flapping furiously.

I nodded, hoping my large, blue eyes weren't bugging out of my head like the Cookie Monster at this attention from a new man.

We walked into the Copley Place parking garage toward my car.

"I'll call you," he said, not offering a kiss but just a smile.

"Great," was all I could manage.

For the first time in weeks, I thought about dating someone new instead of my broken heart. As I drove out the Mass Turnpike to my duplex in Newton my Plan A seemed suddenly a possibility again.

The next day at work, my phone rang.

"Hi, Kim, this is Mark Stagliano, we met last night. I'm going to be setting up displays at Marty's Liquors in Newton. Do you want to meet for lunch?"

Ha!

We began dating steadily (dating is what people did before the phrases "hook up" and "friends with benefits" entered the sexual lexicon). That meant we were exclusive, which was the only way I'd ever date. It was a much bigger deal for Mark, though, who, as a thirty-something guy, had played the field until it was nothing but dirt.

Let's face it—Mark was my rebound relationship. Most people don't even remember theirs. I married mine.

We dated for several months, and even went on a vacation together to our future honeymoon/wedding spot on Hilton Head Island, South Carolina. In umpteen years of dating, Dave had never taken me past South Boston, let alone on a real vacation in a hotel. Boy, was I smitten!

Then came our first test. Mark's job was cut in a huge company-wide layoff at Seagram. My dad was an orthodontist. I knew nothing about how cutthroat and unforgiving the corporate world could be to its employees. This was in 1990, perhaps the beginning of the end for company and employee loyalty.

The second test followed fast when Mark told me, "I'm moving back to Cleveland, Ohio. I don't want to live in Boston anymore."

Thud went my heart. How could he leave me?

"It's a quick plane ride away," he explained.

I sniffled and nodded.

Now I was dating an unemployed thirty-two-year-old living in Cleveland, Ohio.

This was definitely not on my Barbie dream house architectural plan.

Mark went from being my rebound guy to the man I cared enough about to visit all the way in Cleveland freaking Ohio.

I liked Ohio. Perhaps I just liked being far, far away from a lifetime of memories with David. Boston was rife with "remember whens," and many of them were painful.

Eleven months after we met, Mark asked me to marry him.

Perhaps you got engaged at the top of the arch in St. Louis or while spinning slowly over the Dallas landscape on the ferris wheel at the State Fair of Texas. I'll bet he presented you with a diamond ring nestled under a vanilla butter cream in a Godiva chocolate box, or had the waiter in your town's fanciest restaurant bring you a special dessert that hid a sparkling surprise.

Me? Not so much. We were at his apartment in Brecksville, Ohio, a suburb just south of Cleveland. We weren't in the living room. We weren't in the kitchen. Or the bathroom, garage, or laundry room.

Capisce?

A girl wonders. *Did he propose to me in the heat of the moment? Does he even remember?*

The next day I asked him, "Did you propose to me last night?"

"Yes."

"Then are we engaged?"

"I guess we are."

And that was that. Hardly the stuff of a Kodak moment.

Lest you think Mark isn't romantic—he did give me a beautiful engagement ring made from an oval diamond with two oval sapphires on either side. It was a traditional Boston three-stone ring. He handed it to me on December 23 at my parents' house while my dad watched the Nazis lose yet again on the History Channel and my mom baked apricot thumbprint cookies for Christmas.

So maybe the presentation of the engagement ring was a bit unorthodox. So was our wedding, as we opted not to marry in Boston, but on Hilton Head at the Catholic Church and a reception at the Port Royal Golf Club. Mark was an avid (that's a euphemism for addicted) golfer, and it's where we'd vacationed while dating. And it meant we could legitimately not invite our huge extended families. We did it to save money.

Mark and I both come from large Irish-Italian families. During our engagement, my folks were still putting my little brother Richard through college at Catholic University in Washington, D.C. We were

old enough. It didn't seem right to ask our parents to foot the bill. Instead, we shared expenses.

Our wedding day was intimate and perfect.

I wonder if that woman—on the flight I took holding a basket of roses instead of Mark's hand from Hilton Head to Cleveland, Ohio, on October 22, 1991—remembers me.

The flowers are long dead (and in a box in my basement) but hey, we're still married!

CHINESE FOOD ALWAYS
LEAVES ME HUNGRY

HAVING A CHILD WITH AUTISM IS LIKE A GIANT GAME OF CHESS. YOU need to think several moves ahead to ward off potential problems. "If I park close to the store I only have to walk 500 paces with the three girls, but then I'll be too far from the cart return on the way out, and have to navigate the posse through too many cars to be safe."

I wasn't born with a Ouija board for a brain, able to see accidents, mishaps, and embarrassing moments before they take place. It takes years of practice—painful practice—to become autism savvy enough to be able to go out with any sense of confidence or safety for the girls.

Before I really knew what was going on with my first two daughters, Mia and Gianna, I had an incident that, in hindsight, was where I veered off Suburban Mommy Street and onto the Autism Autobahn. Lenox China had transferred Mark from Ohio to Pennsylvania. We were living in Doylestown in the heart of beautiful Bucks County, and our life was comfortable and secure. I was now thirty-four years old with two pretty girls and a handsome husband who looked dapper as he left for work each morning. My girls had playdates, and I shopped in specialty stores that did not have the word "consignment" in their name.

Since our wedding day in 1991, Mark had traveled extensively. One year he had more than ninety nights logged at the Marriott.

While a lot of moms take a break from cooking when their husbands travel, I always had just enough Italian guilt to make me cook for the girls regardless of how many places I was setting at the table. I rarely gave myself the same proper nutritional attention. I have a perverse relationship with food. I'm by no means anorexic, nor do I binge and purge. I just hate to let other people see me eat. I might enjoy a piece of coffee cake—inside my parked car in the garage—and then throw away the wrapper before entering the house. I'm not quite Harley Jane Kozak's character in my favorite movie of all time (*Parenthood*), who stuffed her face with Hostess baked goods in her closet, but I know I have issues with food. I use food to tell people I love them. I bake and cook all the time. I use food to encourage praise: "How does she do it?" And I withhold food to punish people. "You can have a bowl of cereal tonight, Mark." I'll save the food issues for another book.

So. During one of Mark's trips, I was ravenously hungry come dinnertime and, with no adults around to see me eat it, I wanted Chinese food. I'd fed the girls their dinner. I had money in my pocket and a snazzy hunter-green Grand Caravan (that had displaced my kickass hunter-green Maxima after Gianna's birth) at my disposal. I called in my order to Hong Kong Jack's, which was in the same plaza as my grocery store, bundled the girls into the car, and off we drove into town. My stomach was growling, and I could almost smell the eggrolls.

We pulled into the parking lot next to Genuardi's Supermarket. I picked any old spot. Again, this was pre-autism diagnosis. I got three-year-old Mia out of her built-in booster seat in the middle row of the minivan and then tried to get two-year-old Gianna out of hers. She'd have nothing to do with me. She started screaming a shriek of death, pain, dismemberment—she had these toddler meltdowns regularly. To keep Mia from wandering into traffic while I was struggling with Gianna I wrapped my left leg around her, twisting my body into a bizarre ballet pose. Mia seemed to have no

sense of danger (a feature common in people with autism, I was to learn later), but fortunately she only has two speeds: turtle and snail. It's dashed our Special Olympics hopes for sure, but otherwise it's a blessing.

But Gianna was not about to cooperate. I finally got her out of the car seat and set her next to Mia as I went to close the minivan door (this was before all those magic features like doors that close all by themselves, which I firmly believe have brought about the rapid atrophy of my back and shoulder muscles). Gianna threw herself onto the pavement and continued to scream. She had almost no speech at the age of two. Screaming was all the poor kid could do. Most kids her age would have been able to tell their mother, "I want to go home!" or perhaps in Gianna's case, "Get that holy water away from me!" Her behavior was atrocious and overwhelming.

My breathing became rapid, and I felt the blood rush to my face as I approached my own meltdown. I was hungry, and food was just steps away. I didn't own a cell phone, and no one I knew pulled up to rescue me. I wasn't about to ask a stranger to go into the restaurant to pick up my beef with broccoli and steamed rice. We had a neighbor with twins and a sense of entitlement bigger than all get-out—she used to call the Wawa convenience store and tell them to bring a gallon of milk out to her in the parking lot. I wasn't going to emulate her. I was like Hermie the dentist in "Rudolph the Red Nosed Reindeer," *In-dee-pend-dent*. And hungry!

I struggled a bit longer with Gianna. And then I gave up and drove home without my dinner.

Some moms would have left the kids in the car and picked up the food. Not I. I had a strict set of motherhood rules. Never leaving the kids in the car was one of them. (I was also convinced that washing the babies' clothes in anything other than Dreft laundry soap *for babies* would cause leprosy, or worse. My poor mother— she raised three kids quite well, and yet I drove her crazy with all

of my rules. Using fabric softener was like pouring gasoline on the clothing in my mind. I was manic about purity and safety from the day they were born. How'd that work out, Kim? Uh-huh.)

The importance of this particular mom-rule was reinforced some-time later, after an incident in our new home of Hudson, Ohio: I pulled into a diagonal slot on Main Street right next to a frog-green Nissan Quest minivan (oh, yes, I remember that automobile). The day was sunnier than usual for the Cleveland area, and dry. I could see a DVD player showing a Disney movie through the window. How I longed for a built-in DVD player in our own minivan for our long trips to New England, or even a sprint across town. More than the movie caught my eye. There was no adult in the front seat. In the back there were two toddlers and a newborn in a car seat. By new-born, I don't mean a three-month-old. I mean, honey, your umbilical cord is showing. They were alone!

I looked around for the mom, assuming she was nearby. Nope. A few minutes ticked by. I was furious. My inner Bobby Brady cross-ing guard emerged and I flagged down the elderly cop who patrolled the mean streets of Hudson looking for parking viola-tions. "Sir! There's a car here full of children!" He walked over to the car and peeked in. Yes, human life-forms. Unattended. He eyed me suspiciously. In Hudson, Ohio, it was best to mind your own business. There was no Hillary Clinton "it takes a village" talk there.

A harried woman carrying a shopping bag suddenly exited Saywell's—the old-fashioned drugstore with a soda fountain and lunch counter—and approached the Nissan. "Are you the owner of this vehicle, ma'am?" the cop asked. Before she could answer, I ripped into her, "What are you doing leaving your kids in the car? Are you crazy?" The cop turned to me and asked, "Do you want me to arrest you for disorderly conduct?" I held my tongue by some miracle. He asked the mother where she had been. Her answer? Get

this: "I went to buy peanut-butter-and-jelly sandwiches for my kids' lunch."

Hello? You can't freaking make a PB&J sandwich at home? You've never heard of a drive-through? Go for the McNuggets at Mickey D's around the corner! This woman left her toddlers and newborn in the car for a good fifteen minutes while she bought sandwiches for their lunch. Ay-yi-yi.

By then I had two kids with autism and a third who was not on the fast track to Harvard. She was an infant who couldn't sit up and had weird twitches that terrified me. My anger at the idiot in the Nissan was real. It wasn't just about her crappy parenting. It was as much about my disgust and jealousy that she could treat her perfectly healthy, typical kids so callously, knowing her toddlers wouldn't try to get out of the car as I knew my Gianna would have. That she had the luxury of jeopardizing them in any way infuriated me, when every day I was losing my mind trying to tend to my three girls, who were so far from neurotypical, despite my rules, my good parenting, my expectations.

As I drove home from the "Saywell's Incident," I thought back to that evening in Doylestown when I left my dinner in the Chinese restaurant and brought the kids home. Should I have left my girls in the car for a few minutes and treated myself to a meal?

Nope. I'll never be that hungry.

WHEN DID YOU FIRST KNOW?

"When did you and Mark first suspect something was wrong with the girls?"

I hate that question.

I'm a "curebie." That's an autism parent who believes that, in our lifetime, we will be able to bring these kids to a point where they blend in with their peers and can live full, independent lives—through a combination of medical treatment, therapy, schooling, and a rosary that stretches from Connecticut to California. Call it recovery. Call it cure. Call it remission. Call it pasta e fagioli. I don't give a crap what it's called. I'm not going to argue semantics. I just want Mia to be able to live a garden-variety, normal life without needing an adult to keep her safe. (More on that later.) I want a cure for her, damn right. What kind of parent would I be if I didn't? I'm just willing to admit it in public. If people think that means I don't love my kids the way they are, screw them. There. Honest enough?

I know that many things are wrong with Mia, my firstborn. But I loathe ever talking about her as if she were broken. Even though she is broken. It's confusing, isn't it? I write about the trauma and difficulty of autism every day, and yet I hate to bring my kids into the conversation. Too bad, Kimmie. Start talking. . . .

I've had more than a decade to think about this stupid question, "When did you first know?" but I've yet to form a good answer. I'll try.

I'll give you the short version of Mia's birth.

We were in our new condo in Brecksville, Ohio, a stone's throw from our apartment. My mom and dad had come to await the baby's birth and stay for Christmas. It was mid-December. I went into labor at home. And my water broke as I stood naked in my bathroom after a shower (God forbid I should have nubbly legs on the delivery table). By the way, it's not really water that comes out when your water breaks. It's a terrifying spray of the fluid that has kept your baby alive for the last nine months. When it gushes, you're about to give birth. Now, first babies usually take their sweet old time coming down the pike. Not Mia. From the minute my water broke, I went into hard labor.

My mom pulled the half-cooked chicken from the oven and grabbed her purse. Mark bundled me into the car. My dad followed in a daze. The hospital was twenty-five minutes from our house. I was having full grinding contractions every two minutes. My seat was soaked with "water." We were like an episode of "I Love Lucy," with my mom trying to comfort me as I batted her hand away, "Don't touch me!"

When we got to the hospital, my obstetrician and the wonderful woman named Karen we'd hired as our doula (they help you get through natural childbirth and act as a translator with the medical staff) arrived, and less than three hours later, Mia Noel Stagliano was born. (I'm crying as I write that. Does everyone cry when they think of the day their children were born?)

Labor made me autistic. I thought about that many years later, as autism vocabulary words like stimming (repetitive movements) and flapping (picture your hands shaking at the wrist over and over) entered my lexicon. I couldn't bear to be touched. I paced the delivery room. And I swear to God, to get rid of the pain, I flapped!

Years later, my physical reaction to that pain convinced me to pursue medical as well as behavioral treatment for my girls, despite the controversy. Maybe they were in pain, too.

Mia was a gorgeous newborn. She nursed well, slept fine, and was an easy baby.

I had no concerns at her two-week checkup.

I had a question at her two-month checkup.

She'd developed a bump on her plump red lip. The pediatrician assured me it was a "nursing blister." I felt proud that she was nursing so heartily.

At her two-month checkup she also began her routine childhood vaccinations.

She was given her hepatitis-B vaccination (along with a bonus 12.5 micrograms of mercury that I never suspected in a trillion years would be in anything given to babies). Hepatitis B is a sexually and/ or IV-drug-use-transmitted disease. A mother can pass the disease along during childbirth. If the mother is positive. I am not.

She got five more vaccines during this visit as well: polio, diphtheria, tetanus, pertussis (DTaP), and Haemophilus influenzae type b (Hib).

Pediatricians call them "well visits."

Sometime between her two-month and four-month checkup her head had started to take on the shape of a parallelogram (picture a rectangle with the two sides leaning to the right). At her four-month checkup on April 12, 1995, I asked the doctor about her unusual head shape. One ear also seemed larger than the other and looked oddly placed. Today, I realize that she may have had encephalitis—a swelling of the brain that changed her head shape. Back then I was just another overanxious mom. At this visit Mia also received her next round of vaccines: hep B (more mercury), polio, DTaP, and Hib.

At Mia's six-month checkup we had a substitute pediatrician. I wrote down the doctor's instructions and my response in the blue journal I'd been notating at each pediatric visit since her birth: "Watch vision/coordination on left side to see if preference to right is limiting her. Dr. noticed head immediately!"

Her head was perfectly formed at birth. Still round and lovely at her two-month checkup. Something was "off" at four months.

By six months, the shape of her head had alarmed her doctor. While I followed the "back to sleep" protocols religiously by keeping Mia on her back when she slept, the skull change was not affecting the back of her head—so we didn't discuss this as a possible cause. (I even had that special "never flip over" pillow in her crib so she'd remain on her back at all times.)

I wonder if it occurred to him that she was experiencing brain swelling. I have to believe it did—what else would explain a change in head shape? Why didn't Dr. Substitute order an MRI then and there? Instead Mia got another round of DTaP, hep B, and Hib.

I thought I'd done everything right, dammit. I gained *under* thirty pounds during my pregnancy. I had natural childbirth. I had a Peg Perego Roma stroller. I nursed. I bought organic baby food. I vaccinated Mia without question. I read all the baby books and followed them to the letter:

Dr. T. Berry Brazelton? Check.

Dr. Spock? Check.

Penelope Ann Leach (remember her)? Check.

What to Expect When You're Expecting? Check.

I drove my poor mother insane instructing her on the "right" way to take care of an infant. Bless her for holding her tongue and still offering me good advice like, "Never wake a sleeping baby."

I had a $700 Bellini crib, for God's sake!

I was perfect. And so was Mia when she was born.

At her nine-month checkup, I reported that she had developed mysterious flat, uneven spots on her back and torso, as if drawn onto her skin with a Sharpie marker. She didn't get her measles, mumps, and rubella vaccine (MMR) until her fifteen-month checkup. So what were these viral-looking spots and why was my only instruction from the doctor to "alternate Tylenol and Motrin?"

The day after her nine-month checkup, I took her right back to the pediatrician, because suddenly she wasn't sleeping, and she was sobbing in a way I had not heard before, like she was in pain. She was

inconsolable (my exact word on my notes to my doctor). She had stopped smiling and had dark circles under her eyes. Oh God, how did I miss the importance of the dark circles? Worse, how did my doctor?

We had started Mia on solid foods at six months. By nine months she was eating wheat biscuits, soft pasta, and yogurt. Dark under-eye circles are a common sign of food allergies—although I knew nothing of this at the time. Is this when her debilitating food intolerance developed?

I left the doctor's office with nagging questions about Mia's health and no answers. This was to become the norm as she descended into her autism.

One week later, we moved from Brecksville, Ohio, to Doylestown, Pennsylvania.

Imagine this: You've just gotten a promotion and a pay raise. (No, really, use your imagination.) Your company needs you to move to another location. They send people called "packers" to your home to wrap all 42,756,938 things you've amassed in newsprint paper and then place them with care into durable cardboard boxes that cost several dollars each. Your fine china and crystal? Lovingly wrapped and safely boxed. Your clothing and curtains and pillows and towels? Bing, bang, boom, box, seal, stack. Snotty tissues and tampon wrappers in the wastebasket in your bathroom? See you on the other side—you're coming with.

Unfortunately relocation packages are now the mastodon of the corporate world. Long gone.

We settled into a new, four-bedroom Colonial in a young neighborhood, within walking distance to the charming downtown shopping area. (If you've never been to Doylestown, Bucks County, plan a trip. It's an amazing area full of museums, shopping, and antiquing, and it's minutes from the art community of New Hope. It's forty-five minutes from downtown Philly and accessible to New York City, too. It's also near Trenton, home of the fictional Stephanie Plum, so you can

pretend you're about to run into Morelli.) Mark drove into New Jersey to Lenox each day. I worked from home for my Cleveland-based sales promotion company and cared for Mia. I joined my first playgroup and relished meeting other young moms. Life was awfully good.

In October 1995, at ten months, Mia said her first words. One morning, she was lying on her changing table (it was a Bellini knockoff, we weren't rich enough to afford the crib *and* the changing dresser) and she said, "Ober." Her favorite doll was Grover, the blue Muppet from *Sesame Street*. Soon after, she said, "Shhhhhhhooooo" as I put on her shoes and socks. From there her vocabulary grew. My nagging fears left over from her nine-month checkup in Ohio had dissipated (not disappeared) in the hubbub of the move. If the doctor wasn't concerned, I supposed I didn't need to worry—too much.

In November, I was walking through Genuardi's when I spied a disheveled elderly woman pushing an empty cart, shuffling up the aisle ahead of me. She looked homeless and thin and hungry. I burst into tears and handed her a twenty-dollar bill. (I was relieved to learn later that she was a "staple" in the store and that she had a home and got three square meals daily, despite her unkempt appearance.)

By the time I got to the fish counter a lightbulb went on in my head. I bought a pregnancy test, ran home, peed on it, and, sure enough, I was pregnant. Mark and I hadn't discussed family planning. We just knew we'd have two children. Or three. Or four—and when they came, they came. Mia was going to be a big sister!

I had another easy pregnancy with natural labor and delivery. I went into Doylestown Hospital at 6:00 PM. Dr. Scott Dineson broke my water with a twelve-inch crochet hook from hell at 6:45 PM. At 8:36 PM, Gianna Marie was born. Dr. Dineson lived four houses up the street from us. Walking past his house got a bit awkward after my delivery as I thought of where his hands (up to his elbows) had been.

I expected nineteen-month-old Mia to have some issues with her new baby sister. She didn't. It was as if the baby didn't exist.

I learned quickly to keep Gianna in a playpen or her swing, because if she was on the floor, Mia was likely to walk right across her tiny body. Not maliciously. Mia did not seem to realize there was another human in the house. I instinctively knew this wasn't normal. Little girls are supposed to love babies, aren't they? It bothered me.

Mia's disregard for Gianna didn't set off alarm bells.

I *can* credit Gianna for bringing out one of Mia's first sentences. "Baby cry."

Perhaps the crying upset Mia more than the average child. I don't know. After her second birthday, her speech became our main concern. Mia had a large vocabulary, but it wasn't developing into sentences. She could recite her alphabet at twenty-three months, and she could also count to twenty. If we asked her to get a specific book, she'd go to the shelf and find it. Her receptive speech seemed intact.

But she used her words as labels only. Even for Mark and me. Cup. Waffle. Book.

Mom.

Mia never called out to me. She cried. She came to get me. But she never used her voice to attract my attention. Another warning sign I missed.

I know all the "learn the signs" say kids with autism don't point. Mia did. She made eye contact with her amazing blue eyes, another thing children with autism "don't do." Her photographs as a toddler show a beaming girl, happy to flirt with the camera. She also used imaginative play.

At our pediatrician's suggestion, she had a hearing test. I guess this was the best he could offer for a child whose speech was clear but not progressing in its proper usage as communication. I dutifully took Mia to The Children's Hospital of Philadelphia (CHOP) and sat in the audiology chamber.

"Mrs. Stagliano," the audiologist said, leading us into the chamber, "Mia will sit in your lap on this stool. On her left is a monkey with cymbals. On her right is a bird that flaps its wings and chirps. When she responds to a sound from either the left or right, the monkey will clap or the bird will flap to reward her for having turned correctly in the direction of the sound. That's how we'll know if she is hearing. We'll use many tones and volumes. Are you ready?"

Did I have a choice?

The door to the chamber closed. Mia and I sat together. Just the two of us in a creepy box with ratty toys waiting to perform their herky-jerky tricks if, and only if, my child passed the tests.

Mia passed. The results were "normal."

I've since grown to hate normal test results. Every test we've ever run has been normal. MRIs, EEGs, genetics. Normal means *we don't know.*

Then we contacted Early Intervention, also known as "EI," for an evaluation. EI is available across the nation. They offer health care and behavioral services for infants from birth to age three who are not developing properly or who have medical conditions such as cerebral palsy or Down syndrome.

A beautiful woman with flowing blond hair came to our house.

"I'm Dawn, and I'm here to test Mia."

Thud went my heart.

Dawn from EI opened her bag and brought out an assortment of developmental toys.

"Can Mia stack blocks?" she asked me.

"Um, no." I answered.

Mia tried. She stacked just two blocks with hand over hand help.

"Does Mia play with dolls?"

"Sometimes!" I chirped, happy to be able to show off Mia's ability.

Mia did not play with the little plastic doll Dawn handed her. Mia only played with her Elmo doll. I didn't tell that to Dawn.

At the end of the session, Mia's so-called "developmental age" was far enough behind her chronological age that she qualified for services. That's how Early Intervention decides who needs help. There's a checklist of what a child should do and by what age. You know the drill: rolling over, sitting up, crawling, walking, talking. Mia was not developing on time, which was no surprise, since I was the one who'd called Early Intervention to start.

When your child qualifies for help, it's a bittersweet moment. You're grateful for the help, trust me. And it's even better to learn that the services from Early Intervention are free. But in my heart, I wanted Mia to blow the doors off the tests and to be able to tell Dawn "good-bye" so we'd never see her again.

Late in the summer of 1997, Mark and I had the opportunity to travel to Charlotte, North Carolina, for a business trip with a side order of golf. Just before our long weekend, we drove to my parents' house in Massachusetts to drop off Mia and Gianna. My sister Michele was visiting from Texas. Her son Colin was four years old. We only saw each other once or twice a year, so this was her first opportunity to spend time with my girls since the previous summer.

As soon as we arrived at the hotel in Charlotte I called my parent's house to check in on the kids. My sister was hysterical. "Mia has autism," she told me. "How could you not know?"

I listened as she stated the obvious:

"She doesn't speak. She doesn't pay attention to Mom or me. She doesn't want to play with Colin."

How dare she! I was immediately angry at her for ruining my vacation and shattering my carefully built wall of denial.

I realize now it took great love and courage and a healthy dose of Rossi anger for her to drop that bomb on me.

Michele was right. I suddenly knew this wasn't a mere speech delay and that Mia wasn't simply a "thoughtful" child who'd rather stare at P. D. Eastman's classic children's book *Go Dog Go* for hours on end than play with another child.

Mia had autism.

Mark went golfing.

I walked to the mall near our hotel.

I went into Barnes & Noble and skimmed through every book I could find about childhood development. I grabbed books by Penelope Leach, T. Berry Brazelton, and Dr. Spock off the shelf. I'd read most of them already, but this time I was looking for information about autism. I came up short. There was next to nothing about speech delay, let alone autism. I was really on my own.

I stumbled back to the hotel. I kept Michele's diagnosis to myself until we got home. We were there for a nice weekend, and I didn't want to ruin it.

When we got home I scheduled an appointment for Mia with a developmental pediatrician at Children's Seashore House, at CHOP.

Her diagnosis was not autism but "global developmental delay." That sounded like a bad day on Continental Airlines, but it didn't sound like autism. Mark and I breathed a sigh of relief.

We next saw a neurologist at St. Christopher's Hospital. His name was Dr. Grover. I took that as a good omen, since Mia loved her Grover doll so much. He ordered genetic testing for Mia and declared her too smart to have autism.

I had no idea what to do. The development pediatrician at CHOP gave me no direction outside Early Intervention, which I'd already started.

It would be two years before I learned of any programs that would be of much use to Mia. She lost two valuable years as we pursued only therapy.

Years later, I discovered that I'd had an incredible resource right in Bucks County: Dr. Harold Buttram, an original Defeat Autism Now!

doctor, was in the very next town. Defeat Autism Now! doctors treat autism biomedically, as opposed to just recommending genetics testing and external therapy. He would have taken one look at the circles under Mia's eyes and known just what to tell me. I am dead certain our lack of medical care and options allowed her autism to progress to the point where she developed seizures. I had only mainstream medical care—but I had no network. I wasn't part of the autism underground. So I didn't know.

He was just nine miles from my house.

One of the suggestions from EI for Mia was that she enroll in a preschool or day care center to be around typically developing peers. Day care is expensive, so that's easier said than done. I was working from home for my Cleveland-based company, which had been sold to a large corporation in the promotions industry. I wasn't working hard enough to make a living on commission with two young children at my ankles. I had to get a "real job."

Even as Mia met with a home speech therapist and occupational therapist (OT) each week, Gianna began to worry us, too. Her speech wasn't developing at all. She had no words at twelve months. Again I called Early Intervention, while looking for a day care center, while looking for a job.

Fortunately, I found a salaried position in my industry with a terrific company.

In Philadelphia.

Fifty miles from my home in Bucks County.

I had no choice but to take the job. The pay was $36,000 a year, a fortune to me and enough money to pay for day care and some new clothes so I could go back to work.

This was my first taste of the sacrifices to come because of the girls' diagnoses. I didn't want to put them into day care. I sure didn't want to commute ninety minutes each way to an office. I *did* like the paycheck. I started back to work in September 1997 when Gianna was fourteen months old and Mia was almost three. Mark

was a doll and helped me as much as he could. He was still commuting forty-five minutes each way to New Jersey every day. He traveled overnight extensively, but when he was home, he was a huge help around the house and always a good, hands-on father to the girls.

Ah yes, the girls. While juggling the newness of going back to work and a developmentally delayeded child and the stress of putting two kids into child care, I called Early Intervention for Gianna, too.

I missed the signs in Gianna. Her cheeks were papery and red. Her nose ran constantly. Her eyes were always teary. The pediatrician's answer? A surgical tear duct probe to unblock her tear duct.

She had a hearing test that came back (drumroll please) "normal." All that meant was that she could turn toward the sound in the same pediatric hearing test chamber we'd visited for Mia. She was able to turn to the monkey and the bird to hear all of the sounds. Big whoop. She couldn't speak.

Gianna was *not* prone to ear infections, like so many kids on the spectrum, but she had liquid in her ears at every doctor's visit. That isn't normal! Why hadn't the pediatrician been concerned about this? He'd mention it to me as if he were saying, "The sky is blue." The human ear canal is not supposed to resemble Venice, Italy. Even though Gianna passed her hearing test, the fluid in her ears likely made everything sound as if she were underwater. No wonder she wasn't speaking!

Gianna got surgically implanted ear tubes as a precaution to help her speech.

Her speech still did not develop.

Her behavior was atrocious. She spent much of her day screaming and bolting away from me. Where Mia was compliant and passive, Gianna was defiant and overactive. It never occurred to Mark and me that they could have the same "thing."

By the summer of 1999, both of my girls were in Early Intervention and enrolled in The Community Education Center (CEC) preschool.

I was so exhausted by the commute to Philadelphia that I quit my job and went to work at CEC.

In August, we made what I now think was a big mistake. Mark had voluntarily left Lenox before a reorganization, and he was hired by American Greetings (the greeting card people) back in Cleveland, Ohio. Unbeknownst to me, Cleveland was behind the East Coast when it came to developmental delay treatment and education. We enrolled the girls in a developmental preschool within the public school system. The teachers were kind and dedicated, but there wasn't a rigorous autism program. And while they hadn't been formally diagnosed, we were all operating under the assumption that Mia and Gianna each had some form of autistic spectrum disorder.

Those six years in Hudson, Ohio (our suburb outside Cleveland), were the toughest of my life. They began in 1999 with a trip to University Hospitals of Cleveland, where Mia and Gianna were formally diagnosed with autism. They ended in 2005 with us having to sell our home because Mark had been out of work for almost two years.

SEX TIME!

MOST FOLKS WILL TELL YOU THAT KIDS PUT A DAMPER ON A COUPLE'S SEX life. The sleep deprivation, little ears across the hall, and life's daily vagaries can all hinder one's natural impulse to have some fun in the sack.

Add autism to the mix. Then splash on a goodly dose of unemployment and the financial stresses that follow.

Are you picturing a long-sleeved, high-necked, flannel nightgown *under* a Snuggie? A magnum of Viagra?

I thought about this chapter for a long time. Should I write it? My priest is going to read this book. So are my parents and someday, my kids, I hope.

Mark and I have three children—it took quite a few more tries than three to produce them. We practiced for years, carefully preparing.

I can write this chapter. I can. Here I go. Okay. Turn the page.

HOWARD STERN
EVERY DAY

MARK AND I LIKE TO JOKE THAT, IN MANY WAYS, HE AND I HAVE reversed our X and Y chromosomes. For an Italian-Irish guy, Mark is enlightened, and almost always eager to pitch in and get a job done no matter whose "role" it is. This fluidity has served us well over the years in terms of who brings in the bacon, cares for the kids, cooks, cleans, and manages the ins and outs of a marriage and family. Some of his willingness to take on new jobs in the house was the result of being laid off from work. It's hard to say you won't clean a bathroom when you've been on unemployment for several months, unless you want your wife to stick the Scrubbing Bubbles up your backside. Know what I mean?

When I tell friends that Mark does his own laundry and can cook as well as I can (although he can't touch my baking, ha!), they usually respond with, "Oh, you've trained him well!" Not quite. He's a man, not a seal. He was thirty-three years old when he got married and hadn't had a mommy to fold his panties for over a decade. He's picky and likes his clothing and personal grooming to be just so. Go out with Mark and you never have to worry if he's dressed like a reject from a *Star Wars* convention. He always looks like he stepped out of *GQ*.

Mark is the better shopper by far. Back when we had money, he could walk into Nordstrom and, an hour later, emerge with several matching outfits, enough skin care products to care for half of Holly-

wood, and the newest men's fragrance. Me? If you handed me a thousand dollars and turned me loose in a mall, I'd buy a gallon of coffee and a candy bar and then wander around the bookstore, assuming the mall hadn't replaced the bookstore with another nail salon. At the end of the day I'd hand you $973.45 change and hope never to return.

Mark has a hair stylist he sees every four to six weeks like clockwork. She trims his hair, and they kibbitz about life. He loves going to see Penny. I started cutting my own hair several years ago when Mark was first out of work. After years of bad haircuts costing anywhere from $25 at Best Cuts to $125 at fancy salons, I realized my hair rarely looked any different, regardless of cut price. Every stylist cut my hair into a triangle, even when I pantomimed "not this shape," gesturing a pyramid from the top of my head to my shoulders. I'd leave the salon a good deal poorer and looking like Pythagoras' sister Isoceles.

I read somewhere that if you put your hair in a high ponytail on the top of your head, and cut across the top, when you took the hair down, you'd have a Jane Fonda shag cut. I tried it when we were down to our last month of savings. Lo and behold, because my hair is curly and forgiving, the cut didn't look half bad. Of course, it didn't look half good, either. Color? I don't have a lot of gray hair yet—no idea why—but I have a bottle of Nice 'N Lazy in my bathroom ready to go when the time comes. I'll probably look like I dumped a bottle of shoe polish on my head, but I'll be content to have spent only seven dollars.

Given the girls' situation, I'm blessed that Mark is so willing and able to bend his gender. Find me another man who can tell the front from the back of his daughters' extra-absorbency, Stealth bomber–winged, skateboard-sized maxi-pad. Mark can fly into CVS to pick up his Old Spice deodorant, contact lens solution, and a pack of Poise pee pads without ruffling a single (well-coiffed) hair on his head. All while working, looking for work, or most recently, creating his own company to support us.

He makes a damn good wife, which makes him an incredible husband.

One area where our gender swapping has caused a divide is our broadcast listening habits. Mark likes politics, and I like Howard Stern.

I first heard Howard Stern in 1993, when he was a newcomer to WNCX radio in Cleveland, Ohio. Mark? He'd sooner listen to a broadcast from the labor and delivery department at Bridgeport Hospital.

Mark was a Don Imus listener before Imus left MSNBC and went to that rural channel no one outside the Corn Belt had heard of. Recently Imus joined Fox Business, and Mark tunes in when a guest is interesting, or he watches *Morning Joe* on MSNBC. Mostly he listens to his iPod, which at last count had more than 8,000 songs on it.

I became a Don Imus fan when he brought on author David Kirby in 2005, the year *Evidence of Harm* was published. Imus allowed the taboo subject of vaccines and autism to hit the mainstream media. That genie has yet to go back in the bottle, despite the best efforts of the American Academy of Pediatrics, pharma, and several medical shills who are hell-bent on convincing Americans that vaccines are entirely safe, even as myriad other drugs are pulled from the shelves on a regular basis. Don's wife Deirdre is a champion for kids' health, running the Deirdre Imus Center for Pediatric Oncology at Hackensack University Medical Center in New Jersey. Her "Greening the Cleaning" nontoxic cleaning products are taking root across the country in schools, homes, and institutions such as hospitals. Plus, Deirdre is on the board of the National Autism Association and The Coalition for SafeMinds, two groups that are near and dear to my heart.

I still listened to Howard Stern at every opportunity.

There's a strange confluence of pride and shame that makes me feel slightly edgy, as a middle-aged mom who listens to Howard Stern. I shrug my shoulders when I tell people I'm a fan, as if to say,

"What can I tell you? I like him. But even I don't know how I can manage it." Hint: I manage it because my humor level is on the Stern wavelength and I need the release of an easy laugh.

When we lived in Doylestown I had a ninety-minute commute to my office in downtown Philadelphia. I had a cassette tape Walkman (remember those?) and tuned into Howard Stern on WYSP. One day, they ran the now iconic "Cookie Puss" bit, where Fred Norris had bought his mother a Carvel ice cream cake called Cookie Puss for Mother's Day. Cookie Puss is a hideous cake that is supposed to be an outer-space character with a bulbous ice cream cone nose, bulging eyes, and a high-pitched computer-generated voice in the commercials that rivaled Tom Carvel's easily identifiable rasp for its sheer power to annoy.

Fred Norris is a writer and runs the sound effects for the program. He's been with Howard Stern longer than anyone else on the program, dating back to Stern's WCCC radio days in Hartford, Connecticut, in the late 1970s (according to the ever-accurate Wikipedia).

Howard, his longtime cohost Robin Quivers, writer and on-air personality Jackie Martling, and producer Gary Dell'Abate skewered the prickly Fred for several minutes about how cheap he was and what a horrible gift he'd given his mother. Howard changed his voice on his microphone, quickly becoming Cookie Puss and peppering Fred with shaming questions. Once Fudgie the Whale (the traditional Father's Day cake) got into the bit, I lost it and couldn't hold back my laughter. Tears were streaming down my face as I sat on the train.

Listening to Howard Stern reminded me of our Cleveland days, before the girls were born, when I was financially secure and had no children to fill my mind with worry.

Maybe that's why I've stuck with him all these years. Howard Stern makes me feel free.

On December 16, 2005, Stern made his last broadcast from terrestrial radio. I sat in my Catholic sports car (the ubiquitous Dodge Grand Caravan) in the parking lot of the Stop & Shop in Mansfield, Massachusetts, and listened until I was late picking up Isabella at preschool. It felt like being part of a club. "We" were leaving the confines of the radio dial with all of the rules and regulations and the FCC crackdowns. "We" were rebels and iconoclasts sticking our fists in the air and snubbing the mainstream.

In many ways, that's exactly how I feel inside the autism world. Our family doesn't belong among the neurotypical. And with the financial hits we've taken, we don't fit into traditional suburbia any longer, either. We barely belong in our own families. Autism has pushed us into a topsy-turvy world where nothing is as we expected it to be—or how we would have chosen for ourselves or our kids.

Howard Stern symbolizes being an outcast for me. And yet, he makes me feel like I'm in on the joke and somehow a little better than the people who slam him. If they don't get the humor, clearly there's something wrong with them, not with me.

About a year into his contract with Sirius, Stern got his old tapes from CBS after a legal battle, and was able to replay his most famous bits. On Friday, September 6, 2006, they aired a special called, "Howard Stern's Top Ten Moments Hosted by Donald Trump." I immediately thought of Cookie Puss and longed to hear it again, to bring back that memory of such laughter.

I had my Sirius radio in my kitchen on the fridge in the dingy, yellow house on Reservoir Avenue. I should point out that I didn't listen if the kids were around. Well, sometimes I did, but I kept the volume pretty low.

Do you know why?

My kids have autism. Autism equals echolalia. I did not want Mia or Gianna to echo Howard Stern, since they might say a lot more than the funny name given to producer Gary Dell'Abate that has

become a Howard Stern catchphrase, "Bababooey!" Nor did I want Bella's first words to be, "Are those real or implants?"

I listened to as much as I could of the Top Ten Moments throughout the weekend, hoping to hear Cookie Puss. When it wasn't number two my hopes soared. Sure enough, the number one bit was Cookie Puss, and it was just as funny as I'd recalled. I found myself lying in the middle of my kitchen floor with the tears again streaming down my face. God, it feels good to laugh that hard.

I e-mailed the show to tell them how much I appreciated the bit. "I'm a mom with three kids with autism and I was on my floor with tears . . ." Fred Norris himself read that e-mail on air. And he said, "Wow. Three kids with autism." I was really touched.

I've always said that I harbored a fifteen-year-old boy somewhere in my brain. I like fart jokes and raunchy humor and quick wit. Howard Stern delivers them all on a silver plate, along with rapid-fire topical humor and a clubhouse camaraderie.

Sure, there are times when I dislike his guests or topic. I can change the dial when he brings on porn stars who've had sex with garden tools. ("Hoe hoes?") I will always click over to the "Siriusly Sinatra" channel when he goes into any "retard" bit.

But when he and his crew are "on," there's no one faster, funnier, or more engaging.

Our minivan has Sirius in it.

If you see a woman in a minivan with a really bad haircut laughing hysterically while at the stoplight, roll down your window and holler, "Bababooey!"

It's probably me.

ALWAYS ON OUR TOES

AUTISM HAS A WAY OF KEEPING YOU ON YOUR TOES, MUCH LIKE HOT coals or ballet shoes permanently sewn onto your feet. While most people are working *for* the weekend, Mark and I are working *through* the weekend. We live *en pointe* and *en garde* in order to keep the kids happy, healthy, and safe.

It's not as easy to outthink a child with autism as you'd excpect.

Fourth of July, 2000, we were invited to a cookout at our neighbor's house. We'd lived in Ohio for just under a year, and I was seven months pregnant with Isabella, which made me only marginally nimble. The neighbors Janet and Dennis were also newcomers to the Cleveland area. Better yet, Janet was from Massachusetts, and Dennis was from New York, so we had a lot of East Coast experiences in common. I'd never been completely comfortable in the Midwest. The second move to Cleveland did little to ease my sense of being an outsider. Bringing two children who were in special ed only isolated me even more, at least in my mind. Fortunately, Janet and Dennis were funny and easygoing and took Mia and Gianna's unusual behavior in stride, which was a real blessing. In fact, all of our neighbors were terrifically patient and kind to the girls. Not everyone is charmed by "quirky" kids, trust me.

We'd moved into the sort of homogenous neighborhood that has sprung up on former farms from Connecticut to California where two or three builders put up 300 houses using small variations to create a semblence of nonconformity: using a mansard versus hip roof, dormer windows versus bay windows, and varying exterior

paint colors. I called it a Stepford neighborhood. Our homes were spacious, well appointed, and a steal compared to housing prices back East.

Janet and Dennis's house was almost identical to ours inside. Mia and Gianna were at ease there because of its familiarity. Unfortunately, so were Mark and I.

We had not perfected the divide-and-conquer life we now lead. There was an "I" in team, as in Mark saying, "I didn't think of that." That's a nice-ish way of saying he was still living in male la-la land and didn't tend to the kids unless I wrote down instructions on a Post-it and slapped it onto his forehead.

While at the cookout my radar pinged that all my kids weren't in sight. I saw Mia sitting on the floor holding her Grover monster doll. I scanned the kitchen and family room like the *Finding Nemo* Aqua-Scum machine scanned the fish tank for algae. Uh-oh.

No Gianna.

I strode into the foyer.

No Gianna!

I checked the bathroom.

No Gianna!!

I asked our hostess, Janet, if I could look upstairs.

No Gianna!!!

I ran into the yard.

No Gianna!!!!

The baby in my belly thinks I've just snorted a thick ribbon of cocaine as my heart rate rises.

"Mark! I can't find Gianna!" I yelled to him and our friends. "Help me find her!"

Now the entire party is headed into the street hollering, "Gianna! Where are you?"

I felt like an idiot. A big, fat, pregnant idiot.

The role of the bad mother who has lost her child in plain sight will now be played by Kim Stagliano. She was born to play this part.

I knew Gianna wouldn't answer us, but there was a chance she'd come running up the street in her little pink stretch pants, blond curls bobbing up and down.

No Gianna. We fanned out up and down the street, still calling her name.

Finally, I heard, "Excuse me! Is this your child?"

I looked up and saw a stranger holding my three-year-old's hand, walking toward us.

Gianna!

Whomp! My heart rate took one last leap and then slowed down as the moment of panic had passed. The baby in my belly wonders when the roller coaster ride will end.

I took Gianna's hand, willing myself not to squeeze it to death, and said to this neighbor I'd never met, "Thank you so much. Where was she?"

I'd have been happier not knowing the answer.

"Our front door was open. She was jumping on the bed in our guest room." I assumed her guest room was the small bedroom in the front of the house. In our house, that was Gianna's room. Of course Gianna went straight to it.

Mortified, I apologized. "Gianna has autism, and she tends to bolt. We didn't see her leave the house. Thank you."

"Oh, *I'm* sorry," was her response.

That was one of the many times someone has apologized to me for the girls' autism. I hated it then. I hate it today. I know she meant well though, and I was grateful she wasn't screaming at me. She handled the intrustion with grace, thank goodness.

With that, I slunk back to the Independence Day party feeling anything but festive, or independent. There's nothing like the thought that your child is dead to deflate your mood.

BELLA'S BIRTHDAY BLUES

I'M NO OCTOMOM, ALTHOUGH MARK AND I WOULD HAVE LIKED TO have four or even five children. Just not all at once. I think I'd have been a really good regular mom. A cross between Carol Brady and Roseanne. I guess I'll never know.

Mia and Gianna were diagnosed with autism in November 1999. In December, we took them to a neurodevelopmental consultant in Massachusetts named Sarge Goodchild. As a child, Sarge was severely impaired with seizures and developmental delays. His parents were told to institutionalize him. His mom refused and worked an intense home-based program based on "patterning," which are movements that simulate a baby crawling on the floor, and ultimately recovered her son, who went into the same business of helping neurodevelopmentally injured clients. He now runs Active Healing on the North Shore in Massachusetts, and I'm honored to be on his board.

Mark and I had a long talk with Sarge about the prospect of having another child. We wanted another baby. But with two girls recently diagnosed with autism and just learning how much work we were going to have to do to help them, was it wise to bring a third child into the family?

I knew in my heart I wasn't finished having children after Gianna was born. There was another StagBaby out there, waiting to join our family. *After* Bella was born? Hell, I'd have shoved Play-Doh into my tubes right then and there in the delivery room. I waited three months and then closed the factory for good. I knew without a doubt I was *d-o-n-e*.

★ ★ ★

Mark was more pragmatic. He thought having a third child would mean we'd have someone who could help Mia and Gianna throughout their lives. Talk about a heavy burden. I never liked the idea that if we had a typical child, he or she would assume the yoke of caregiver. I'm sure Mark also wanted a son. So did I. Anthony Augustus Stagliano needed to come home to us. That was my name choice. Mark spent my eventual pregnancy talking about Rocco.

Hey, I'm a proud *paisana,* but Rocco Stagliano?

I had discussed a third child with our pediatrician, who recommended genetic counseling. So, of course, we went to genetic counseling. What a waste of time. For the hundreds of millions of dollars spent on autism research, geneticists had no solid evidence as to whether another baby would be likely to have autism. Geneticists don't ask about our family history of allergies, metal burden, immune dysfunction, diet, environment. Nothing. After much thought, Mark and I agreed that a third baby wasn't a smart idea. No Anthony. No Rocco. No more babies.

I blame our neighbors for what happened next.

Joe and Kim lived right next to us. They were a fun couple, with two boys Mia and Gianna's age. We got along very well and enjoyed their company. They had a New Year's Eve party. We reveled. We partied like it was 1999. (It was December 31, 1999.) We stumbled home just a little bit drunk and ushered in the new millennium. Nine months later we welcomed Isabella Michelle to the family. So much for rethinking that third child!

The kids' birthdays are bittersweet as the number of candles on their cakes grows faster than their developmental age. As I'm writing this, it's Bella's ninth birthday.

Some years I'm happy as can be when the birthdays arrive—like when Gianna turned five and we had a big party in the backyard with a rented inflatable moon bounce just like you see at carnivals and a homemade cake so carefully decorated that it *looked*

store-bought—I pulled out all the stops that year. Unfortunately, Mia had seizures all day, so our joy was tempered with tending to a very sick child on the sofa while the party proceeded in the backyard. That's still one of our best birthdays, despite the seizures—which gives you an idea of the quality of birthdays around here.

Mia's fourth birthday, on December 15, 1998, was also one of our best ever—at least in terms of being the most "typical" and likely to impress other moms. You don't think there's birthday competition among moms? Of course there is, don't be silly. Store-bought cakes may be impressive, but homemade cakes score points for "love." Home-based parties are old-fashioned and retro, but can they compare to two hours at the local gymnastics school where Lexi and Lulu get to show off their impressive tumbling skills?

In 1998, the gap between Mia and her three-year-old peers wasn't very large yet.

When Mia and Gianna were toddlers, Mark and I were at the top of our game. Mark was still at Lenox, which paid for most of our health insurance, and we had a low deductible. We had a company car—an old perk most people barely remember today. There were sales contests and trips where you could bring along the wife and all sorts of corporate goodies to savor. Plus we got gorgeous Lenox China at cost.

Those were the days.

Our 401(k) was growing nicely and Lenox matched our contribution. Can you even imagine such largesse in this world? We were able to contribute the maximum amount every year and pay our bills. We had extra money! Hang on, I have to screw my head back on, it's spinning after remembering all those things that made our life easy.

Mia's December birthday meant I could take advantage of the holiday theme. I hired the gentleman who played Santa at the mall to come to our house as a surprise guest. I had all the guests write a

Christmas wish list, and then I corralled them all to the foyer and asked them to sit on the staircase.

"We have a *big* surprise coming."

The kids wiggled and fidgeted with excitement. On cue, the doorbell rang and Santa walked into the house with a "Ho, ho, ho!" The crowd went wild. Each child left the party with a Polaroid (A Polaroid, remember those?) of them sitting on Santa's lap.

Top that, ladies! Stagmom has Santa in the house!

As I said, I'm writing this chapter on Isabella's ninth birthday. I went to bed last night sad. I woke up sad. That feels so wrong on what should be an exciting, happy day. The last day of single digits. (Remember how cool it was to just *think* about turning ten?)

Poor Bella has never had a moment of carefree living. Not even in the womb, where I worried every day about her sisters and her, too. She was born into a tumultuous household, where autism had just taken hold of us, and financial problems were about to turn every part of life inside out. For crying out loud, the poor kid has lived in five houses in nine years, and Dad is not in the military.

At five months she had the ambulance ride alongside Mia as her oldest sister was in the throes of her first of hundreds of seizures. I stroked Mia's head with one hand while nursing Bella in my other arm. The idiots at Akron Children's Hospital asked me why I hadn't left Bella at home. Because she's five months old and she can't reach the fridge?

She's a beautiful girl, Bella. Perhaps our prettiest child—and Mia and Gianna are no slouches in the looks department.

Mark and I have never heard Bella speak a sentence. She's said a few words, and has a couple she can repeat. "Mama." "Bella." "Hello." "More." If you say "hi" to Bella, she will return the greeting. She uses "muh muh muh muh" as if she is speaking. We're working on finding a device she can use to communicate now. First she has to learn how to point her index finger. That's the complexity of autism, friends. You have to teach all the way back to the most basic skills.

Imagine nine years and you've never heard your child speak even a short sentence. It stings.

Happy birthday, Miss Bella Michelle Stagliano. I'd like to wrap up recovery for you, honey. Speech first. I'm still working on it. And I won't give up.

WHAT DOES AUTISM LOOK LIKE?

MIA IS OUR MOST AFFECTED CHILD. IF YOU WERE TO MEET HER, YOU'D first notice her great beauty. You would not be surprised to learn she has autism. She speaks in short phrases, mostly to make her needs known. "Can. I. Have. Food. Please." She's content to play alone. You can usually find her at her computer or watching *Sesame Street* or *Blue's Clues*. She turned sixteen in 2010.

Gianna's autism moments are usually like bolts of lightning. They strike and then disappear, like when she wandered away from us at the Fourth of July party.

Mia's heart-stopping autism moment lasted almost four years.

After months on antibiotics for recurrent sinus infections, Mia, at the age of six, looked pale, tired, and thoroughly sick. However, I did not notice this. How? Call it newbornitis. Bella was five months old. I was really tired.

At three o'clock in the morning on February 1st, 2001, I awoke with a start. Had I heard Bella? Nope. The baby monitor was not flashing its red *get out of bed* lights. I went into Mia and Gianna's room. Mia was half awake. Her pillow was soaked with drool. I couldn't seem to rouse her.

The pit in my stomach told me that she'd just had a seizure.

I'd never seen a seizure, but somehow I knew. I also knew that I couldn't handle seizures and a newborn and autism. I told my stomach to bugger off. Then I kissed Mia and went back to bed.

At 11:10 AM, Mia and Gianna were in the living room where we'd set up a computer for them to play *Sesame Street* and *Blue's Clues* DVDs. Mia had taken to the computer like a duck to water.

I heard a thump and ran into the room.

Mia had fallen to the floor and was seizing in front of me when I got there. A full grand mal seizure, with eyes rolled back, tongue biting, fists clenched, arms and legs contorted.

I grabbed the phone and dialed 911.

Mark was in Massachusetts, hundreds of miles away, with his dad, who was in a nursing home, dying of cancer.

I didn't know what to do first. I was going to have to go to the hospital. I stayed with Mia until the ambulance came.

While the paramedics attended to Mia, I scooped up Gianna and ran across the street to my neighbor Ruba's house. I didn't know Ruba very well, but she was kind, had two children of her own, and her husband was an OB/Gyn. Somehow that made me feel that she was capable. And I didn't know what else to do. I'd have left Gianna with Freddy Krueger if he'd answered the door. I had to take Mia to the hospital. Ruba took Gianna for me. I bundled up five-month-old Bella and got into the ambulance.

Because we lived between Cleveland and Akron, the ambulance did not take us to University Hospitals in Cleveland where our neurologist was, but instead to Akron Children's Hospital just down Route 8 to the south.

The ambulance ride was a blur, as I suppose they always are. I was scared shitless, to be blunt. Seizures are terrifying to watch, and a foreign, mocking voice in your head tells you that your child is dying in front of your eyes, and there isn't a damn thing you can do about it. Seizures are about a lack of control for the parent as much as the patient. I tried to answer the EMS team's questions.

"Does Mia have low blood sugar?"

"No."

"Does she have a history of seizures?"

"No. But she has autism," I told them.

I should have kept my big fat mouth *shut*. Once I said "autism," the game changed. I didn't know it at the time, but most medical professionals think autism and seizures go together like Hansel and Gretel or peanut butter and jelly. They lose their sense of alarm, their medical training reverts to, "Oh, it's just a kid with autism. They have seizures so it's not so bad."

I didn't learn this ugly fact until much later and by hard experience. I sure wish someone had told me never to mention autism to the response team.

Mia had another seizure in the emergency room. I tried to remain with her as Bella nursed and dozed and cried in my arms. I could barely breathe from the stress. I wanted Mark to be with us, but he was facing his own devastating loss as his dad eked out his final days. Of course I had to call him.

"Mark, it's me. I'm at Akron Children's Hospital with Mia. She had a seizure."

He tried to take in the information. He had a hundred questions, like any good father.

"I have no idea, Mark. She just fell over and starting shaking. It was horrible. Gianna is at Ruba's. Bella is with me here in the hospital. I have no car here and no way to get home and you're on Cape Cod and . . ." I had to stop before I threw up.

"I'm just boarding the plane in Boston, I'll be there as fast as I can."

Several hours later, Mark rushed into the hospital looking to me like Superman, Batman, and Ward Cleaver rolled into one very tired husband. He spent the night with Mia in the hospital while I took Bella home and retrieved Gianna from Ruba's house.

The next day, after what was called a "twenty-four-hour observation," Mia was released, and Mark and I were told to see our neurologist at University Hospitals, Dr. K.

Then we were to "wait and see" if another seizure happened.

On February 28, 2001, at 3:20 in the afternoon, she had another seizure.

I remember this seizure clearly for a couple of reasons. I had implemented a therapy program in our house. It was a combination of occupational therapy and other work that we conducted with the help of volunteers. Lauren, a freshman in high school, had just arrived at our house with her mom Mary to work with the girls when Mia dropped and seized.

Mary drove us to University Hospitals in Cleveland.

Again I called Mark, who was at the office.

It was during this visit that I learned how children with autism fall down a rabbit hole of inadequate medical care because of their diagnosis.

As Mia seized on the exam table, Dr. S., the head of pediatric neurology, tended to her. I begged, "*Why* is she having these seizures?" I was sobbing. And kind of screaming.

His answer was calm, cool, collected, and useless: "She has autism. She has different circuitry."

That was it? Seizures are her destiny because she has autism?

Bullpoop.

Because Mia had more than one episode of seizures, the neurologist recommended medication. As much as I hated the thought of meds, we had no choice. In my ignorance, I allowed them to prescribe an old standby med called Dilantin. Worse, because she didn't swallow pills, they gave her the oral suspension, which I later learned was the less desirable option because it can separate, and its efficacy can become spotty. Sometimes the old drugs are the best. New doesn't always mean better, except when it comes to pharma patents and profits. But Dilantin was a real dinosaur in terms of anti-epileptic drugs and had the lovely side effects of excess hair and gum tissue overgrowth. Terrific, let's just add medication-induced physical deformities to Mia's list of challenges. That's just what a young girl

struggling with autism needs, right? Mia's seizures grew stronger and more frequent, despite the medication. She began to slur her words, and her somewhat clumsy gait became even less steady.

Dilantin was an epic fail.

I started doing my homework on seizure treatments. I consulted with an adult neurology resident who was a friend of my brother's from college named Dr. Mike. He was wonderful and gave me a list of tests he'd recommend for Mia, none of which had been ordered in Cleveland or Akron. Finally! I prepared a letter with these suggestions for our neurologist.

I was polite. I knew enough not to be confrontational and say, "Gee, Dr. K, you folks have done jack squat for Mia . How about pretending she's a real, live, human child with potential and not just an 'autistic' and looking at these test options?"

Below is the letter that I sent to Dr. K. at University Hospitals of Cleveland after I scheduled a follow-up appointment to talk about Mia's situation. I've saved it in my computer files all these years, because it upset me so and serves as a reminder of why I work so hard in the autism community.

Here are the topics and my questions that I'd like to discuss on Tuesday as we plan for Mia's care.

1) *My goal is to get Mia off the drugs before 18 months to 2 years.*

2) *I was dissatisfied with Dr. S.'s answer to my question, "Why is this happening?" His response: "Kids with autism have different circuitry."*

3) *Why didn't Mia have a CT and then spinal tap and the MRI during her stay? Because her fever was low to normal? What blood tests were done and with what results?*

4) *I'd like to see a detailed reading of the three EEGs she has had.*

5) *A family friend is a neurologist at UCLA medical center. He recommended the following tests because of her PDD diagnosis and that*

six is at the end of the spectrum for febrile seizures (as you told me): metabolic screening including amino acids, organic acids, lactate, pyruvate, and basic lab work.

6) *I have located a lab in Nevada that does this type of screening with high-quality medical research reporting. They need to work with the attending physician. I will bring their file, which includes "Protocols, detailed explanations, and pricing for testing of Autistic Spectrum Disorder for Children and Adults." The president of the company's daughter has a seizure disorder. He was very helpful to me over the phone in discussing the tests and treatments that helped her. Company is CellMate Wellness Systems.*

7) *How comfortable are you going into this research direction? I also work with Dr. W. in Akron, allergist/immunologist who has helped us with diet/supplement issues.*

8) *Mia was on antibiotics three times since November, plus a thirty-day course of Augmentin started on March 12. 11/12: Cedax, 12/27: Zithromax, 2/28: Omnicef, 3/12: Augmentin. Dr. V. at UCLA indicates that some antibiotics can lower seizure threshold in those with the tendency, especially the penicillins. I have a gnawing feeling that by changing Mia's "gut" with the antibiotics, that I started this process into motion. I know it's not medical or scientific, but it's the only thing different in her life. And it makes me question a yeast connection.*

Dr. K., I can't just put her onto drugs and forget about this for a year and a half. I've worked so hard over the last 18 months to clean up her diet, address food allergies, and provide intense at-home therapy. Her improvement is my fulltime job and I have taken this "stumbling block" called epilepsy quite personally. See you Tuesday at nine o'clock.

★ ★ ★

Her answer when I requested the tests that were *de rigueur* in Los Angeles? "We're not aggressive with autism, Kim." She wasn't even apologetic. It was a simple fact that she, an MD with a PhD on top,

was not going to pursue answers for my child. That to me is the antithesis of medicine, science, and simple human curiosity.

That's when I knew beyond a shadow of a doubt that my kids' care was going to fall to me, and me alone.

I kept a seizure log for the first fifteen months, hoping to find a pattern, something, anything to grab hold of to help my child. In the meantime, Bella was moving into toddlerhood with her own set of issues in terms of lack of development. She wasn't crawling, sitting up, or even reaching properly. And Gianna was nowhere near under control. Mark's and my life became a blur of preposterously extreme parenting with the single goal of getting through the day.

According to my seizure log, in 2001 Mia had at least one and up to seven grand mal seizures on 2/1/01, 2/28, 3/22, 4/16, 4/27, 5/18, 6/15, 7/10 (Gianna's fifth birthday party), 7/15, 8/20, 8/27, 9/25, 10/7, three dates torn out of the log, and then in 2002 on 3/20, 4/22, and 5/11.

Poor Mia's body was racked with exhaustion after a seizure. I had no idea what they were doing to her brain, and, frankly, the medical community just clucked its tongue and turned its back on her.

I walked away from neurology and traditional medicine to seek my own answers.

Fast-forward almost four years. Through diet, supplements, intense chiropractic care (we flew in a doctor from Oklahoma City to Cleveland to work with us and we went to her clinic, called Oklahaven), and enough novenas to clog the lines to heaven for a week, Mia had her last seizure on November 25, 2004.

I flip the bird at University Hospitals of Cleveland every time I hear their name. The joy I associated with that hospital as the birthplace of two of my daughters is erased. They refused to care for my sick child because of her autism diagnosis. That's not uncommon. Autism is viewed (promoted even) as untreatable.

Miss Bella's heart stopper wasn't as drawn out as Mia's, but it served as a stark reminder of why I fight to help the girls every day.

In June 2006, we left my parents' house in Massachusetts and moved to Connecticut. It had been close to a year since we'd left Ohio. Our belongings had been in storage. The Bekins moving truck appeared in our driveway and, at long last, I felt like we were going to get back on track. Mark was working in New York. We were together as a family again, after many months of him living in a hotel in New York during the week.

With great joy, I watched our stuff roll off the truck. If you can't afford a new wardrobe, just put a lot of your stuff into storage for ten months and wear the same suitcase full of clothes day in and day out. When the movers bring your five-year-old Lands' End sweaters and Wal-Mart "Faded Glory" jeans into your house, you feel like you just had a shopping spree on Rodeo Drive.

I unpacked, looking forward to Mark's and my first night alone in our own bed in ages. The bed in my mother's house was the noisiest bed ever created. Our sex life in Massachusetts was paralyzed. It was like having sex via telepathy—no one moved.

The kids were thrilled to see their beds, quilts, toys. Bella especially.

While upstairs, I heard the squeak, squeak of a child jumping on the bed. I went into Mia and Gianna's room to admonish whoever was the jumping culprit, just in time to see Bella sail off the bed and onto the floor.

She let out a howl of pain. I grabbed her and checked her eyes, afraid she'd had a concussion. She seemed okay. I knew she was both exhausted after a long day and confused by the new surroundings. I tucked her into bed with a kiss, assuming she'd stop crying and settle herself to sleep.

Nope.

The cries continued. Angry, tired, I went into her room. I sat down and wrapped my arm around her shoulder feeling one, two, *three* elbows!

She'd broken her arm.

I'd just won the world's worst mother award. I put my five-year-old to bed with a broken arm.

Poor Mark was halfway into the shower after a day of unpacking when he heard my wailing.

I didn't know where the nearest hospital was. I had only my Ohio cell phone. Would it reach the local 911? There was a fire station at the end of our street, less than a quarter of a mile away.

I threw on jeans and a T-shirt and together with Mark got Bella, whimpering, into her car seat. He went back into the house to stay with Mia and Bella as I drove down to the fire station, thinking that was faster than calling EMS. But the station was dark. I pounded on the door, sobbing.

"My daughter has broken her arm and I need an ambulance!"

EMS is not located in the fire stations in our town. Just my luck.

A young volunteer firefighter called 911.

The ambulance came and took Bella to Bridgeport Hospital, where they set Bella's bones and gave her a splint to hold us until we got to an orthopedic surgeon. I'm forever grateful to Shirley, the EMS technician who took care of Bella as I followed behind in my minivan, wondering why my windshield wipers would not clear my vision.

I don't know about your city or town, but in Bridgeport, Connecticut, the hospital is in a fairly rough section of the city. The city I'd moved next to twelve hours earlier. They released us around one o'clock in the morning.

"Excuse me," I told the nurse who was discharging us. "I raced here in a blind panic following an ambulance. It's one in the morning. I don't know where I parked. I don't know how to get home. I have a forty-pound child with autism and a broken arm to carry. Do you think someone could escort us out please?" (Demanding, aren't I?) They paired me up with a nurse who looked like the last doll in a set of Russian nesting dolls. But she got me to my car.

I called Mark and he talked me home like an air traffic controller.

Bella couldn't tell me her arm was broken. She was five years old.

That was another reminder of why I fight for treatments and improvements in care and will never stop.

I've had a daughter wander into a stranger's home. A daughter whose seizures nearly killed her. And a third who injured herself and could not ask for help.

Ain't autism grand?

A CAREER TAKES ROOT

THREE KIDS WITH AUTISM AND BORED? YES. I MISSED THE SENSE OF achievement and positive reinforcement that work brings. Raising special needs children (any children for that matter) isn't known for providing much in the way of attaboys.

I sat down and began to write a novel.

I'm not sure when I realized I was writing a book, but I know how I got started. A high school classmate had introduced me to a writer and autism mom in Boston named Susan Senator. We began e-mailing back and forth. She was writing a book called *Making Peace with Autism,* and I'd just put a few words on paper for the first time.

I sent my early writing to Susan, and she encouraged me. I'll never forget that. Here was a woman whose column had appeared in the *Washington Post* and who had a real book coming out, and she said my writing was pretty good! I was hooked.

Susan and I have much in common. We each love writing, have a strong sense of family and loyalty, and, as autism moms, know that parenthood can be a miserable slog, despite our love for our kids.

We also have great differences.

I am a member of "Team Curebie." I think autism is treatable, that kids can recover, and that some/much/all of it was caused by an environmental insult to a genetically susceptible brain. Susan is a member of "Team NeuroDiversity." She believes her son's autism was present at birth, that families should take educational and

behavioral (traditional) steps to help their children, and teach acceptance. She's a great mom, and I would entrust my daughters to her care without a second thought. And I'd welcome her handsome son Nat into our home in a heartbeat.

Since we are both grown-ups, Susan and I have learned from each other, and we respect our differences. Respect can be hard to come by in much of the autism world, but that's another story. And a rather boring one, at that, so I won't go into it further.

You're welcome.

Susan's kindness got me to screw up my courage and dig into writing. When we moved back to Massachusetts, one of the first things I did was meet Susan in person. She grew up in Fairfield County, Connecticut, and moved to Boston. I grew up in Boston and ended up in Fairfield County, Connecticut. We remain friends and writing colleagues, and I value her input and encouragement still. One morning, after several months of typing before the kids awoke and after they went to bed, I typed the magic words: *the end.* My heart skipped a beat. It was the most amazing feeling.

Not so fast, Stagliano. What I had was a completely unpublishable manuscript.

No one sits down and writes a publishable work of fiction from scratch. Thank God I knew absolutely nothing about publishing when I started, or I'd never have begun.

I joined an online writing community. I read agent blogs and began the querying process, whereby you prostrate yourself in front of literary agents who then send you form rejections that read like "Dear John" letters.

I was having a blast, and I no longer felt adrift.

I wrote a short story and sent it to *The New Yorker,* which is akin to my putting on a football helmet and trying to get a walk-on position on the Ohio State football team. I was having such fun writing, it never occurred to me *not* to submit to *The New Yorker.* Really, it wasn't hubris, just ignorance.

In November 2007, I had my first taste of publishing success. Arianna Huffington had just published her book called *Fearless Voices* and begun a section by the same name on her online site, The Huffington Post. *Hey, I have a fearless voice!* I thought to myself. And I sat down and wrote a post. And HuffPo published it!

Here's "The Fearless Voice of the Autism Mom."

George Bush should have appointed an autism mom to plan out the strategy for the Iraq War. From this I know. I have three beautiful daughters with autism—and have racked up over 243,300 cumulative hours in the autism world. I'm guessing that's more experience than Donald Rumsfeld had in executing wars. Unlike our Secretary of Defense, I knew instinctively, as both mother and general of my own little autism army, that my first job was to keep my troops safe.

The autism mom must plan several moves ahead, just to get through the day. A simple trip to the grocery store requires the preparation of a military invasion. Hiding in every aisle lurks the potential for a meltdown. The lights are too bright and emit a faint buzz, perceptible only to dogs and to kids with autism. The Koala Krisp cereal has been moved from its usual shelf to an endcap, a blatant insult to my children, who have memorized where the cereal is supposed to be, down to the exact aisle, shelf, and section. I shop on high alert, intent on defusing problems before they hit us, zigzagging through the minefield of melons, marshmallows, and meat. One eye on the kids, one eye on the door.

What's the worst part of grocery shopping for an autism mom? The clueless nitwits who assault you out of the blue with "the look." The supermarket snipers. If your own toddler has ever become unruly in a store, you've seen "the look." Women glancing sideways at you, whose nostrils flare as if sniffing a shoeful of manure, forehead furrowed in disdain. Fortunately,

my girls might not be able to read your expression, but I can. Believe me, lady, I can. Do you want me to roll up *The New York Times* so you can use it to hit me across my bottom while you say, "Bad mom, very bad mom!"?

Guess what, Mrs. Mother of the Year? I realize that my eleven-year-old daughter is sucking her thumb. That's how she calms herself as she navigates the store with me. Maybe you shove a cigarette into your mouth for the same reason? I don't need a breaking news bulletin to know that my ten-year-old has told me that it's Tuesday eight times in a row in a singsong voice that's just a bit too loud for proper society. And yes, I'm aware that my six-year-old looks a tad awkward in the cart, her legs now so long that if I put her into rollerblades her feet would glide along the floor. God only gave me two hands, and I need both to corral my older girls, so Miss Peanut stays in the cart until I can no longer lift her up and over the handle.

We autism moms learn fast how to plan out every part of our day while leaving ourselves wiggle room for the inevitable glitches that tip the proverbial applecart right over. But the main reason George Bush should have asked an autism mom to help plan out the war in Iraq? We always have an exit strategy.

Published on HuffingtonPost.com, November 1, 2006.

★ ★ ★

By a stroke of fate or luck, our twisted road from being broke and selling our house in Ohio, to my folks' house in Massachusetts, and finally to the run-down rental in Connecticut had put me within striking distance of New York City: the publishing mecca of America.

With Mark's blessing, I scraped together the money to attend the Backspace agent/author seminar, at the time held at the Algonquin Hotel, where Dorothy Parker and the literary illuminati of the 1920s sat at the round table and made history. The seminar boasted a chance

to meet several big-name agents, and some I'd never heard of. Of course, I wanted a big name.

The day before the seminar, I got an e-mail from The Huffington Post telling me that my George Bush/Fearless Voice post had been published.

Once at the seminar, I realized that the big-name agents I'd thought I wanted to represent me weren't actually my cup of tea, but there was an agent on the panel who struck me immediately. He was a bit older than the twenty-something hotshots, and reminded me of Clark Gable with his dashing good looks and thin mustache. He was thoughtful, his critique style was helpful, and he felt like a pat of melted butter on a pancake to me.

At one point, each attendee was allowed to line up in front of an agent and make his or her pitch. I marched up to the line in front of Eric Myers clutching my printed Huffington Post piece from the day before as tightly as Charlie Bucket held on to his Golden Ticket to Willy Wonka's factory.

I ferflubbled my way through an introduction; "Hi, my name is Kim Stagliano and I have three kids with autism and I've written a funny murder mystery about autism and look yesterday I was published on The Huffington Post!"

Deeeeeeeep inhale.

I can still remember his words to me, "Oh! We like The Huffington Post. Why don't you send me your first three chapters?"

Jackpot!

Four months and several rewrites later, Eric signed me. Fifteen months later we sold a book. It wasn't my fiction, it was this book.

Few things in my life have turned out the way I'd expected, or even dreamt. And yet, everything seems to turn out A-OK.

IT'S A SMALL WORLD.
BUT A BIG HOTEL

KIM STAGLIANO, YOU HAVE 300,000 MARRIOTT POINTS SAVED UP because you and your husband never go anywhere! What are you going to do now? *We're finally dragging the kids to Disney World, even if it kills us!*

Sounds easy enough, doesn't it? Let's take a trip to Disney World with the kids. That all-American vacation. By 2007, we felt like the only family in the country who hadn't made the pilgrimage to Orlando. I knew people who went *every* year. "There's always a new hotel to try!" they'd say, all tan and happy and wearing the latest in mouse couture. Sure, neighbor, rub it in. My older sister had taken her son there at least three times. Not that I was competing with her or anything. My little brother and his partner had been to Disney, and they don't even have kids!

I barely remember my first trip to the Magic Kingdom. I was five years old and my family went to Disneyland in California with my beloved Uncle Eddie, Auntie Ana Mae, and my impossibly grown-up cousins: Eddie (my first crush), Toni (my first idol), and Joanne (sorry Joanne, I just liked you). Most of my memories of that trip are from looking at photographs.

My second trip was when my mom took my brother Richard and me back in 1977. We stayed at the Contemporary Resort, that giant silver and glass hotel that in the seventies really did look contemporary. Today it looks like a prop from *Lost in Space*. We stayed for several

days and then rented a car (a Chrysler Cordoba, I can still smell the rich Corinthian leather) and drove to Miami to visit my Auntie Rosie and Uncle Jerry. My mom had no fear when we were kids. She took us everywhere, often without my dad, who was too busy straightening teeth.

In 1979, we re-created that early childhood trip, returning to California with my aunt and uncle. I was fifteen and in high school. My crushes turned from my cousins (thank goodness!) to every California boy who walked within twenty feet of me at Disneyland.

Mark and I spent our honeymoon at Disney World. Well, it wasn't technically a honeymoon. I'm pretty sure an actual honeymoon has to take place immediately following the wedding, right? If you recall, Mark flew to his sales meetings two days after our wedding in Hilton Head, and I returned to Cleveland.

I felt like Mark and I were strong enough as a couple to not *need* a honeymoon. He had a job to do and so I let him do it. That willingness to give up expectations and roll with the punches has served me well.

I wish we'd had a real honeymoon anyway.

Mark won "Rookie of the Year" and then "District Manager of the Year" back to back. He was the first, and probably the only, person at Lenox to achieve that honor. With these honors came a trip— anywhere we wanted. I chose Disney World.

We stayed at the Grand Floridian hotel, where I lived out my Victorian fantasies from the moment I opened my eyes to minute I closed them, safely ensconced in Mark's arms. We didn't have a care in the world. I get teary when I think of that time in my life. Did I ever really have no cares?

My fifth Disney trip came in October 1995. Mark had a conference in Orlando. My parents came to watch Mia, who was ten months old and a dream baby. She was happy, always smiling, and she'd said her first words, "Ober" for her favorite *Sesame Street* pal Grover, and "shoe."

We stayed at The Marriott World Center Resort.

I went to The Magic Kingdom while Mark was working. I had three days to fill, and I'm not a spa-girl. Call me tactile defensive, but I cannot tolerate a massage. I feel supremely uncomfortable with any sort of physical attention from a stranger—even under the guise of pampering. I can manage a manicure, though it's been years since I treated myself to one. Now it seems like a selfish luxury that would take money away from the kids. Autism resets your priorities and your budget whether you like it or not.

So, did I mind going to Disney World all by myself? Are you kidding? Remember, I'm the girl who flew home from her wedding sans husband. If I close my eyes I'm back sitting on Main Street USA, watching the parade go by, munching on a soft chocolate chip cookie. I got to see every attraction I wanted to exactly when I chose. I didn't have to see the stupid Country Bear Jamboree because my little brother wanted to. I could scream as loud as I wanted inside Space Mountain without my older sister laughing at me.

The best part of that trip was the souvenir I brought home though. No, not a Mickey Mouse plush toy or a Donald Duck T-shirt. I left Orlando with the glimmer of Miss Gianna Marie Stagliano in my belly.

Mark and I had talked about taking the girls to Disney for years. Mark would log on to the Disney site, look at the prices for the hotels that interested us (the three closest to the Magic Kingdom), and log off with a sigh. We couldn't afford Disney.

Finally, in 2007, we decided we were ready for the big trip. We were settled into Connecticut. Mark's job was going well enough, but we still couldn't afford a Disney resort, not even the "cheap" ones. Mark had traveled throughout his career. And one of his perks was earning a slew of Marriott points. Since it was virtually impossible for us to go anywhere alone, those points had really added up over the years. We had enough for two rooms at The Marriott World Center! I liked everything about going back there except the getting pregnant part. Not this time.

Mark booked our rooms and flights in May. Then he was finished with the planning until it was time to pack his clothes. He told Gianna about the trip as soon as he booked it. Big mistake. He and Gianna circled the date on the calendar and so began the daily, often hourly countdown to the trip in October, some five months away.

"Yes, Gianna, my love. I know" (gritting teeth) "we're going to Mickey World."

That's when my work began planning the myriad details of the trip. The first thing I did was to invite my mom to join us. We needed another set of hands so we'd have man-to-man coverage. Divide and conquer—that's how we survive. The October date made it the perfect birthday gift (forty-nine again, Mom?) from us to her.

Now I had to think about feeding the kids while away. They don't eat gluten (the protein found in wheat, oats, and rye) or casein (the protein found in dairy). That rules out pretty much every food that comes in a paper bag or on a paper plate. It makes traveling difficult. I knew I could pack a suitcase full of nonperishable snacks. What about those three pesky meals known as breakfast, lunch, and dinner? I consulted with the hotel, and they came through with flying colors. In this world of celiac disease, lactose intolerance, and nut allergies, chefs are well rounded in making all sorts of dishes. Chef Mark was my savior. We e-mailed several times, and he put together a menu for the girls. I was assured we'd have fresh bread each day plus waffles, muffins, and milk-free eggs at any time.

I was also worried about getting separated from the girls in a giant theme park. Mia and Gianna speak pretty well, but they don't often answer questions. Bella can say her name, but that's not enough were she to get lost. I printed up stickers with the each girl's name, our cell phone numbers, and the sentence I hate to type, I HAVE AUTISM. I'd sneak the sticker on the back of their shirts when we left the hotel.

And I made up bio sheets for them with their physical stats and a photo, in case I had to give it to Disney security or, heaven forbid, a police officer.

The departure date approached. It was time for me to pack. Mark travels a lot and he's very organized. I'm lucky to leave my driveway a few times a week. I am the poster child for adult ADHD. I am not organized. Packing is a real problem for me. First off, I start too early. So I'm adding and subtracting clothing for days, and by the time I'm done I have half of what we need and twice as much of nonessentials. Second, I follow the kitchen-sink method of packing. You never know when a cold snap could grip Orlando, after all, so in went the turtlenecks next to the swimsuits. By the time we left, I knew I had everything the girls would need. There was every reason to believe I'd arrive without a single pair of panties for myself, but that's a mother's lot in life. Kids first.

Finally, October 6 arrived! Gianna was thrilled. I was exhausted. Time to load up the car and head to Newark Liberty Airport. This was my third flight with all three girls. I'd flown once from Ohio to Providence alone with the girls when Bella was an infant. Never again. And we flew the same route when my father-in-law died. The stress didn't seem to matter on that trip.

Thanks to Mark's grueling travel schedule, he's a member of most of the airline presidents' clubs. We were able to hunker down in one while we waited for our flight. It was more relaxing than being in the large, noisy terminal. The flight itself was a breeze. The girls were happy and well behaved. I felt triumphant when we landed.

We checked into the magnificent hotel. Bella was in her glory at the sight of a waterfall. Mia was entranced by the glass elevators going up and down. Gianna was awestruck by absolutely everything. Mark and I spied the Starbucks and grinned. Vacation!

Our first glitch was when Gianna realized she didn't have her lovey with her, a mangy plush manatee. "Where's Manatee? Where's

Manatee!?" she asked with mounting panic. I'd packed Bella's blankie. I know we had Manatee when we left Connecticut, but not on the flight. We realized that Manatee was sitting in the minivan a thousand miles away. This was not good. I thought fast. We were in Orlando, home to SeaWorld and a large manatee exhibit. Maybe....

Sure enough, we went for a tour of the hotel, and SeaWorld had a small gift shop that included stuffed manatees very similar to (albeit much cleaner than) Gianna's pal. "Marriott the Manatee" joined our family, and Gianna was assuaged. I was proud of her for accepting a new friend for the week, knowing her "real" Manatee was waiting for her back home.

We planned to alternate what we did each day to avoid overtiring the kids, spending a day by the pool and then a day at a theme park. Day one was a pool day. We awoke, ate breakfast—Chef Mark came through and served a delicious gluten-free breakfast for the girls. He even baked bread and packed a picnic lunch for us. Back in our rooms I was organizing our things in one room, Mark was watching sports news, and my mom was in the adjoining room on the phone calling my brother to thank him for the fruit plate he'd sent to welcome us to our vacation.

Her back was to the door.

Mia slipped out of her room.

And Bella followed her.

I operate like Mad-Eye Moody, the character from the Harry Potter books. His catchphrase is "constant vigilance!" That's what's required to keep the girls safe. You cannot take your eyes off them, even for a moment. As good as my mom is with the kids, she wasn't accustomed to having to keep them in her sight no matter what she was doing. Not her fault. I walked into the next room and saw that Mia and Bella were gone.

I ran out the door. Bella was in the hallway. I shoved her into the room.

"Mark! Check the hallways! I'm going to the lobby!"

My poor mother was crushed with guilt, but I didn't have time to worry about her. My child was missing in a 2,000-room hotel on 200 acres.

I raced up to hotel security near the door. Panting, "She's missing! My daughter is missing! She has autism. You have to find her!" Of course, I forgot my bio sheet I'd prepared for exactly this moment. If the kids were going to get lost it was at Disney World, not our hotel! I was able to give a description of Mia to the guard, who alerted his staff from his earpiece right away. Then I took off to find her myself. I started by the pool. Oh God, the pool! It's amazing how fast your sense of embarrassment disappears when you need help. I shouted to everyone I passed, "I'm looking for my daughter. Her name is Mia. She has autism. She looks a lot like me and is wearing a blue T-shirt." Guests were very kind. Some stood up to start looking.

My panic was turning to fear. I thought about that little girl who disappeared in Portugal. I thought about Adam Walsh and beautiful Polly Klaas. My mind was a blur of bad endings.

I bounded back into the hotel and heard a voice: "We have her! She's here!" And there was my Mia with the security guard. I'd held back most of my tears until that point. What relief. Who found her? Where was she?

Mia had gone exploring. Those elevators were too interesting for her to pass up. And she didn't have the speech to tell Mark and me that she was twelve years old, bored in the hotel room, and wanted to take an excursion. She left our room, found her way to the lobby, and started riding the glass elevators twenty-two stories up and twenty-two stories down. Exactly what I'd done at age five at Disneyland in California, with my sister and cousins. She was counting the floors as she went. If you can believe it, a woman in the elevator had a grandson with autism, and she recognized Mia's mannerisms immediately. Mia's voice is rather flat, and the slight

inflections she does have are common to autism, but odd to the untrained ear. This kind grandma guided Mia back to the lobby, where security took over. Carol the travel agent from Missouri, I'll never forget you.

My mom felt terrible. And I struggled to rein in my anger. Constant vigilance is a requirement. There's no room for error with autism. We pulled ourselves together and had an uneventful (autism-wise that is) vacation. No one got lost again. Until we returned home.

The week was exhausting for me. Sure, it was a vacation and a beautiful one at that. But it's hard work to take care of the kids 24/7 in a new place. There was almost no downtime for Mark, my mom, or me. It's not like I could lie by the pool with a piña colada and watch the kids swim. I had to be in the pool with them, even though Mia and Gianna can swim. Meals are hectic whether at home or in a hotel, while I cut up food and wipe faces and grab glasses before they get knocked over.

I didn't even get to ride Space Mountain.

By the time we landed in New Jersey, I was ready to get into my own house, where the kids could do whatever they wanted without my having to stay on top of them. Newark Liberty Airport is gigantic. And confusing. We had to board an elevator up to a tram out to the parking lot. But we weren't certain where to go. Mark asked me to zip up an escalator to make sure we were going in the right direction. That was easier than all six of us traipsing into the elevator with our luggage only to find we were in the wrong location. Off I went. I saw that we were in the right spot. I went down to gather the crew. My head swiveled.

"Where's Mia?"

She'd slipped off again, and neither Mark nor my mom had noticed she wasn't with them.

Getting lost in a luxury hotel where the staff is paid to cater to your every whim is bad. Getting lost in Newark Liberty International

Airport where there's a train within twenty feet of you that whisks you to another terminal is beyond this mother's ability to comprehend. I lost it.

"How the hell did you lose her? *You are useless!*" I was scared to death.

I sent Mark up the elevator to find Mia. I ordered my mom to stay put with Bella and Gianna and took off to find a security guard. This wasn't possible!

Mia's guardian angel was still on duty; Mark found Mia upstairs near the train.

I was shaking with anger when we got to the car.

When Gianna suddenly saw her Manatee waiting for her in the backseat, right where she'd left him, she said one of my all-time favorite lines, "Manatee! You're back!"

All was right in the world for Gianna.

I smiled in spite of myself. My breathing slowed down and my heart stopped racing. I let my anger go. Well, most of it. Mark is a fantastic father. He'd never let anything happen to the girls. My mom is the best grandmother the girls could hope for. In time, I might even forgive myself for not keeping Mia safe.

This is life with autism. Constant vigilance is the order of the day. I rely on family, friends, and total strangers to keep my girls safe and sound. Those guardian angels come in handy, too.

NOW ENTERING THE AGE OF AUTISM

E-MAIL MESSAGE: MARCH 2007

From: J. B. Handley: "Hi, Kim. Would you call me please? (503) 555–1234."

I stared at the screen. Say what? J. B. Handley, a successful West Coast businessman and co-founder of Generation Rescue, an organization devoted to preventing and curing autism, wants to talk to me, a mom sitting in Connecticut?

My curiosity piqued, I called him. (Trust me, you don't ignore J. B. Handley.) Our conversation went something like this:

J.B.: "Hi, Kim. I'd like to start a news site for the autism treatment community, and I'd like you to design, launch, and run it for me. What do you think?"

Kim: "Me?"

J.B.: "Yes, you. I want three things. One: original content, two: links to news the mainstream media isn't covering, and three: to be indexed by Google News. Talk it over with your husband and let me know."

I hung up and sat down on my bed, stunned. J.B. Handley, the leader of the *autism is treatable* world, had just called to offer me a very cool job.

We were living in one of the most expensive counties in America, and our finances were still tight. I'd looked into becoming a para-professional within the school district. With one child on a middle

school schedule and two on an elementary school schedule, I couldn't start at 7:35 AM or work until 3:20 PM without one or two of my kids needing child care. Same went for becoming a substitute teacher; the schedule wasn't workable.

J.B.'s call was a lifesaver.

Now, how the heck was I supposed to create a new site for autism with zero computer programming skills, no staff, no journalism experience, and three children with autism zooming around the house?

I had no idea, but I was determined to do it.

I realized quickly that we needed a blog platform, as opposed to a static Web site, so that we could have daily updated content and readers' comments to make the site interactive. I wanted to create a community. Autism can make for a lonely life. I remember how I felt when the girls were first diagnosed and how much I would have loved a place to go to ask questions and learn from other parents. Not to mention how much time and money I could have saved.

On June 18, 2007, I launched "The Rescue Post" with this introduction:

> *Welcome to The Rescue Post, an interactive site devoted to news, views, and opinions from inside the autism community where you, the reader, can contribute to the conversation. Brought to you by Generation Rescue, we will discuss all aspects of autism, from the perspective that autism is treatable and that the mainstream media rarely provides the full story to the public.*
>
> *We welcome your comments. We encourage submissions from experts inside the autism community who believe autism is treatable, and that the current media environment does not offer the full story.*

We ran 187 posts and garnered just over 500 comments during our first three months in business. Not great, not terrible.

The Rescue Post didn't last long.

I got another call from J.B. in September.

J.B.: "Kim, how would you feel about changing the name of 'The Rescue Post' to 'Age of Autism' and working with Dan Olmsted (OMG. Dan Olmsted, the journalist from United Press International [UPI] I'd just seen on C-Span?) and Mark Blaxill (Are you kidding me? Mark Blaxill, board member for the environmental safety group The Coalition for SafeMinds?)?"

Kim: "Really? Heck yes!"

On November 7, 2007, The Rescue Post became Age of Autism. True to J.B.'s goals, our original content exploded thanks to Dan, Mark, and other well-known names in the autism and journalism world, including David Kirby, author of *Animal Factory* and *The New York Times* best seller *Evidence of Harm*, and Katie Wright, whose parents founded the mega-autism organization called Autism Speaks. And we were indexed on Google News, much to the chagrin of those who'd sooner see us drop dead than continue to publish.

Snap!

We cover the news the mainstream media ignores or butchers or outright distorts. The biggest example is that we include a lot of information about vaccine injury. We take the most criticism for this topic. It seems vaccines have become as much a religion as a science. And according to business reports, they are the cash cow for pharmaceutical companies. There's a reason for that:

I recently met with an attorney following a car accident. We started talking about vaccines and autism. I always tread lightly on the topic with someone I don't know well. But I did ask him, "Did you know there is a special court for vaccine injuries? That a claimant cannot sue for product liability as they can when a crib or even a drug causes injury?"

"I didn't know that," he said.

He didn't know that back in the 1980s, following a scare with the safety of the DPT vaccine, the Carter administration created the

"Vaccine Court" to protect pharmaceutical companies who feared that they would be sued to kingdom come and to ensure that they would continue to produce vaccines for public health. Here's the description from Wikipedia:

> *Vaccine court is the popular term which refers to the Office of Special Masters of the U.S. Court of Federal Claims, which administers a no-fault system for litigating vaccine injury claims. These claims against vaccine manufacturers cannot normally be filed in state or federal civil courts, but instead must be heard in the Court of Claims, sitting without a jury. The program was established by the 1986 National Childhood Vaccine Injury Act (NCVIA), passed by the United States Congress in response to a threat to the vaccine supply due to a 1980s scare over the DPT vaccine. Despite the belief of most public health officials that claims of side effects were unfounded, large jury awards had been given to some plaintiffs, most DPT vaccine makers had ceased production, and officials feared the loss of herd immunity.*

The result of the vaccine court is that it did exactly what every corporation dreams of—it immunized (pardon the pun) the Mercks and Sanofis of the world from product liability.

If a child dies from measles or whooping cough in America, you can bet that every newspaper will run a story on it. But did you know that there have been more than 1,300 legal awards to families whose children were found to have been diagnosed with encephalopathy or seizure disorder? It turns out that the children in many of these cases feature symptoms of autism, "aspects of autism," and even "autism-like symptoms."

On June 29, 2010, *The New York Times,* a newspaper that typically champions the use of vaccines, wrote this about a study linking administration of the MMR and chicken pox inoculation in a vaccine called ProQuad from Merck:

Toddlers who get a vaccine that combines the measles-mumps-rubella and chickenpox immunizations are at twice the usual risk for fevers that lead to convulsions, a new study reports.

The risk for a so-called febrile seizure after any measles vaccination is less than 1 seizure per 1,000 vaccinations; but among children who received the combined vaccine, there is 1 additional seizure for every 2,300 vaccinated, said Dr. Nicola Klein, the study's lead investigator and director of the Kaiser Permanente Vaccine Study Center.

The reactions, which occur a week to 10 days after vaccination, are not life-threatening and usually resolve on their own. The fever-related convulsions can be frightening, but they are brief and not linked to any long-term complications or seizure disorders.

"Frightening" is an understatement. "Usually" resolve on their own doesn't mean "safe." It means sometimes your child has just drawn a lottery ticket to epilepsy.

My Mia's first seizure was called "febrile." How the heck do doctors know if that first convulsion has no impact or is going to become the gateway to an epilepsy diagnosis?

They don't.

★ ★ ★

Of course, none of us wants to see a child die. For crying out loud, that's a no-brainer. Because we report on the thousands of families whose kids have fallen into autism following a vaccine injury, the people at Age of Autism are portrayed as "pro-disease."

Hello? Pro-disease? It's laughable. Wait. I should be honest. There is a small grain of truth to the label. Most of us whose kids have severe autism would take three weeks of scratchy, scabby chicken pox or a month of measles over a lifetime of autism. I just shake my head when the pundits say, "Do you want to die of a vaccine-preventable illness?" It's such an insulting and condescending question.

The "vaccine apologists," as I call them, meaning those for whom vaccines can do no harm, love to holler about "herd immunity." That means that unless a certain percentage of the population is immunized, a disease can spread. That's all well and good in theory. But when it's your little calf who falls, herd immunity doesn't sound too good.

A child born in 2010 will receive forty-eight vaccinations from birth through age six if they follow The Centers for Disease Control (CDC) vaccination schedule. Since a lot of folks won't believe me on that, I'll list them for you.

Birth: hepatitis B

Two months: hepatitis B, rotavirus, diphtheria, tetanus, pertussis, Haemophilus influenza, pneumococcal, polio

Four months: rotavirus, diphtheria, tetanus, pertussis, Haemophilus influenza, pneumococcal, polio

Six months: hepatitis B, rotavirus, diphtheria, tetanus, pertussis, Haemophilus influenza, pneumococcal, seasonal flu

Twelve–fifteen months: diphtheria, tetanus, pertussis, Haemophilus influenza, pneumococcal, polio, measles, mumps, rubella, hepatitis A, chicken pox

Two years: seasonal flu, hepatitis A

Three years: seasonal flu

Four years: seasonal flu, diphtheria, tetanus, pertussis, polio, measles, mumps, rubella, chicken pox

Five years: seasonal flu

The first shot comes on the day a baby is born, when he is inoculated for hepatitis B, which is a disease transmitted sexually or through IV drug use. Not even the craziest rock star's kids are shooting up or having sex in the nursery. There's a Web site called www.iansvoice. org. Ian suffered a rare—but real—allergic reaction to an ingredient in his birth hepatitis B vaccination. He swelled up like a Macy's

Thanksgiving Day parade balloon and the blessed child never recovered. He died at forty-seven days of age.

In the spring of 2010, I received an e-mail from a woman who had just been awarded six figures by the vaccine court because she had been neurologically injured by a common seasonal flu vaccine. She lost four years of her health. Thank God she recovered.

You can get a flu shot in the grocery store every fall and winter, administered by a poorly paid health aide who the month before might have been bagging your groceries for you.

Vaccine safety and informed parental consent is one of our hottest topics at Age of Autism in that it draws the most critics, to which I say, "Bring it on."

It is my great responsibility and honor to sound the alarm bells about the autism epidemic every day. Believe it or not, there are people (some with autism, some just lacking in empathy, others trying to save their own political, professional, and economic arses) who want the general public to think autism has always been with us in these numbers. If so, please look under your bed, chances are there is a gaggle of fifty-year-old autistic men hiding there. Some people claim it's just *better diagnosis* and/or what's called diagnostic substitution, meaning people who would have been called mentally retarded in 1965 are being labeled autistic today. Not even the last loser in the class at Tick Tock Tech Medical School could fail to recognize autism in the children I see every day. It doesn't look like cognitive challenges or Down syndrome. It looks like autism. From *Medical News Today*: "A study by researchers at University of California Doug's M.I.N.D. Institute has found that the seven- to eight-fold increase in the number of children born in California with autism since 1990 cannot be explained by either changes in how the condition is diagnosed or counted—and the trend shows no sign of abating."

I admit to using less precise methods of deduction. I looked at my three kids versus the rest of my family tree for the last three generations. I asked my childhood babysitter, who was a special education teacher in Massachusetts in the early 1970s, how many students with autism she had in her self-contained classroom. "None."

There are bloggers and advocates within the autism community who preach that autism is a set of nifty special traits, like a Swiss Army knife for life. *Oy vey.* The media loves to pick up the odd story about the autistic boy who scored twenty points in the last three minutes of a basketball game. What about the rest of the child's life and his prospects for the future? Do they cover that?

I've spent enough time with high-functioning adults with autism and Asperger's to realize that while the skills their diagnosis might bring in terms of memory, focus, or talents in a specific area—the depression, lack of ability to find and hold a job, difficulty in forming romantic relationships, and sense of detachment from the world can be very painful.

I met a wonderful woman with Asperger's in my town. She worked at the grocery store. She was fired because she couldn't stop talking to customers about certain products they were buying—like pregnancy tests. Not everyone who buys a preggers kit is thrilled with the prospect of pregnancy, and hardly anyone wants to chat about it with the checkout clerk. This gal could not stop asking inappropriate questions, despite requests from her supervisors. I know that she's a warm, giving woman, very smart (working on a graduate degree) and capable.

She lost her job at a grocery store.

Our work at Age of Autism is disliked by many people because we shine a light on the autism crisis. I think that's great. I don't ever want to be a scoop of vanilla ice cream melting in a white bowl of obscurity. What's the point in playing it safe all the time?

I once accused an autism blogger of wearing Kevlar pantyhose because she straddled the fence so consistently, never offering a strong opinion. That's just not my way.

At the end of the day, if we can move awareness beyond the ads featuring bright-eyed, healthy-looking kids with a voice-over saying, "Your child has a better chance of being diagnosed with autism than playing major league baseball" and into the harsher realities of autism, we'll help people at both ends of the spectrum.

Advertising 101: Fear and ugly images sell charity. Sally Struthers didn't hold a plump, well-fed child to encourage donations to Save the Children. Heck, even the dogs and cats in the animal charity ads look forlorn.

Here's my idea for an ad: How about a photo of a bedroom with the walls smeared with poop, mattress on the floor, and a twelve-year-old boy punching holes into the walls as his parents (mom with a bloody lip) try to calm him.

That's autism in a lot of households.

It's not politically correct to mention the dirty, smelly, poopy, angry, screaming, fear-inducing side of autism.

Which is exactly why I make sure we do that on Age of Autism and in my writing on Huffington Post and elsewhere.

In 2009, an eighteen-year-old boy named Sky Walker allegedly beat his mother, Trudy Steuernagel, a professor at Kent State University in Kent, Ohio, to death in their kitchen. He spent months in a jail cell. And he now lives in an institution. I wrote about Sky—his story is a cautionary tale. Little boys with autism grow up into grown men with autism. Sky's mother wrote a letter to her family to be read in the event of her death. She predicted her son would kill her.

Where's the alarm over autism, the escalating numbers, the future?

We just spent six months and billions of dollars panicking the American public about the H1N1 virus. Epidemiologists predicted death on a massive scale, and the pharmaceutical companies whipped

out the vaccine version of a microwave cake. People who wouldn't buy a car in its first model year lined up for this shot, complete with twenty-five micrograms of mercury in every dose. Madonn'.

We know how many mistresses Tiger Woods bedded and how much Botox was injected into OctoMom's face. We followed the balloon boy on Twitter and the nightly news (guilty) and lamented the time slot NBC would eventually give Jay Leno, but we can't get experts to wake up and smell the autism epidemic that's churning behind us. The CDC announced the latest increase in autism prevalence, 1 in 150 is now 1 in 110, on the Friday *before Christmas*—the blackest of the media black holes. Friday afternoon is when organizations traditionally release information that they would rather have disappear into the weekend without much media attention.

It seems no one in our government is willing to declare autism an emergency, even though it is an epidemic that continues to grow year after year and is likely to have a huge impact on our Social Security system. Lord, when H1N1 hit our shores, you'd have thought it was raining anthrax and Ebola the way the media hyped up every sneeze and sniffle from Portland to San Diego. But autism on the rise? Crickets chirped.

So at Age of Autism we wrote about the numbers and Tweeted them to death for over two weeks.

David beat Goliath, this I know. For the Bible tells me so.

Age of Autism is our slingshot.

THE AUTISM MARRIAGE: SOUL MATES OR CELL MATES?

"Eighty percent of autism marriages end in divorce." This statement on the difficulty of having an autistic child is bandied about frequently, though I'm not sure there are stats to prove it. As far as I can see, most of my friends who have an autistic child have remained married.

"One hundred percent of autism marriages have an inordinate amount of stress" is pretty much dead-on accurate. I made that stat up myself having lived it for the last fifteen-plus years.

Mark and I never imagined we'd face autism and unemployment and a global economic collapse when we got married. Nostradamus couldn't have predicted the crap we've had to deal with day in and day out.

To the fly on the wall, Mark and I might appear to have a dreadful marriage. We yell a lot. We shake our heads and gesture with our arms like crazy people. We cruise around the house picking up messes, checking to see if bathroom doors are locked, and shuttling yet another load of laundry to the washing machine. I'm on my computer off and on from 6:00 AM to 9:00 PM writing and managing Age of Autism. Mark is at his desk writing orders, following up with vendors, and Tweeting his politics. (I love his sense of justice, honed by our difficulties over the years.) We've gone through periods when sex is like Halley's Comet, an infrequent visitor.

Like all married couples, Mark and I share an unspoken language. "Did you . . ." comes out of his mouth, and I know he's going to ask if I took Bella to the bathroom within the hour. I'll say, "Can you . . ." and he empties the trash can or the dishwasher.

We began our marriage as two independent people. We've never been attached at the hip. Now, almost twenty years later, we're a pretty well-oiled machine, and I feel like we're as secure in our marriage as a couple can be. However, that wasn't always the case. If it hadn't been for our Catholic sense of duty to each other, and our kids, we might well have ended up a statistic, too.

When we were first married, and before the kids arrived, Mark had joined a country club in Aurora, Ohio. We had enough money back then for a country club! I'd learned to accept his golf, albeit begrudgingly. Heck, we were married at a golf resort. He did what he wanted and so did I.

During the summer of 2000, I was in my last trimester with Bella. Mia and Gianna were proving to be anything but typical, while Mark was playing the role of a typical, corporate spouse. Circa 1965. I was overwhelmed by the kids, with a gigantic house to clean, and I was pregnant.

My pre-marriage ideal of the company-man husband was backfiring badly. He bragged that he'd played 100 rounds of golf in a single season. In dreary, rainy, cold Cleveland, Ohio, that's quite an achievement. A round of golf took him away from the family for at least five hours, usually seven or eight on weekends. That adds up to approximately thirty days a year spent at the country club instead of with us.

One Saturday afternoon when Mark had been gone for several hours, and I'd been lumbering around the house pregnant, trying to care for two children with autism, five-year-old Mia had an accident in her bedroom. She stepped out of her soiled pants, took the blob of poop in her hands, squished it, dropped it, stepped in it, and then walked up and down the upstairs hallway, with her hands on the walls.

The sight stopped me in my tracks. The walls and carpeting were covered in poop. Mia was filthy, standing in the hallway and looking at me with her big blue eyes. Gianna was traipsing through the poop, oblivious to the mess.

I lost it.

I yelled. I screamed. I sobbed. I didn't know where to begin. The walls? The carpet? The children? The liquor cabinet?

The smell nauseated me. The view made me see red.

I cleaned up as much as I could, and then I sat on the stairs and cried. I was so angry at Mark. Where the hell was he when I needed him? At the goddamned golf course.

Things didn't improve from there. We grew further apart.

Mark left American Greetings and became General Manager for a German housewares company called Leifheit. The new job came with a sizable salary increase. We needed every penny to meet our rising bills. Assuming we kept to a budget.

And what did Mark do?

He cruised into our driveway in a black BMW 330xi.

I tried to hate that car. But, Lord, it was sweet! I *did* hate that Mark didn't tell me he was going to lease it. He'd had a company car at American Greetings and a car allowance with Leifheit. He spent the monthly allowance and then some at BMW.

Like a four-year-old trying to convince his mom why he absolutely had to have that second piece of cake, Mark's explanation for the BMW was that he was now working for a German company, so the German car made sense. To which I answered, "Sure, how about a $25,000 Volkswagen Jetta?"

Fast-forward to a sunny Saturday in July. We awoke to Mia's horrible sucking sounds that signaled a seizure. I knew she was in for a day of grand mal seizures, and that I would have to be at her side. Bella was nine months old. Gianna was five and still pretty nutty.

Being Saturday, Mark had a round of golf lined up. I looked at him like he was crazy as he got up to shower.

"Are you going to the club?"

"I promised Mike I'd play with him. I'll be home early."

How about an early grave? He was going to leave me for the day because of a promise he'd made to his brother about a round of golf!

Bitterness became the flavor of the week.

He went golfing.

Mark's dad had passed away in February 2001, and his mother generously gave each of her children a monetary gift. Mark could plainly see that I was cracking under the stress of the children. His answer? Hire someone to do the work he didn't want to do so that his lifestyle wouldn't have to change. We used the money to pay for autism treatments and to hire live-in help.

In September 2001, we welcomed an au pair from South Africa named Cindy J. into our home. She was a godsend, and we enjoyed having her live with us for almost three years. Our house had a large finished basement so we were able to create a suite for Cindy. Having her around meant I could leave the house alone— joy!

One trip that I was able to make alone wasn't so joyful. Call it my Elin Woods moment without the other woman.

My anger at Mark had been bubbling up since he'd left the hose at 7:00 AM to, yes, go golfing. It was 3:30 PM, and he hadn't come home. I don't remember what set me off. I think we had a date planned and he was late. I was consumed with anger and frustration. I told Cindy I was going out, and I raced over to the golf course.

I flounced into the grill room and saw Mark sitting at the bar. I grabbed his arm and said, "Come outside with me right now!" The guys at that bar looked aghast.

We stood in front of the clubhouse, and I announced to Mark, "I spend all of my time with the kids. You're always here. I'm thirty-eight years old, and I AM LONELY! I don't love you anymore, and I want a divorce!"

I was not using my indoor voice.

Mark tried to calm me down. Fat chance. I stomped back to my minivan as he walked toward the pro shop, nothing resolved. I shot out of the parking lot, put down my window, and gave him (and everyone on the practice putting green) the finger.

It wasn't just the golf that ticked me off. Mark had changed. At least I thought he had. When we returned to Ohio, I was no longer working, I had two kids who did not fit into the surburban mold of dancing classes (note, never take a child with noise issues to tap-dancing class) and T-ball and tea parties. My time was spent looking for size-six Pampers for two kids who had no interest in toilet training. I was approaching forty and feeling anything but fabulous.

I pretended everything was fine as we paraded around town in his black BMW listening to the *Sopranos* soundtrack thinking we were a couple of big swinging dicks.

As I look back, everything *was* fine. He was working, we had a lovely house, our three beautiful kids were making progress, and we'd accepted their challenges with purpose and grace. What was I such a bitch about? Golf? He wasn't sexting other women, or gambling, or drinking away his paycheck.

Things could have been much worse.

And so, they got much worse.

Mark and I were in a period of calm and relative happiness. It was autumn of 2003, and the golf season was drawing to a close. Amen! Mark received an invitation to a grand opening for Legacy Village—one of those destination shopping centers that look like they were designed by Walt Disney. Cindy watched the kids; Mark and I hopped into the Beemer and off we went to this invitation-only shopping event.

Oh, we shopped! Mark bought me several outfits at one of the snazzy stores. By snazzy, I mean the sort of store that lets you *keep* the hanger, and might even give you a gift box. It was a lovely night. And the last night of life as we knew it.

The next morning Mark received an e-mail from Germany, firing him from his job with Leifheit.

Just like that, we joined the ranks of the unemployed. Mark was stunned. Sales were up—the products were in prestigious retailers and fancy catalogs.

They never called him. He didn't hear from a soul in Germany again. That day, I drove back to Legacy Village and returned the clothes we'd bought the night before. Everything had changed.

Including Mark and me. Suddenly he saw what our household was really like. He didn't have a job to distract him from the circus we called Chez Stagliano. I realized that golf was the least of my worries.

And so we navigated the new world of unemployment. We didn't expect to get citizenship, though.

A PAPER MITTEN ON
THE GIVING TREE

YOU HAVEN'T LIVED UNTIL YOU'VE BEEN A NAME ON A PAPER MITTEN on the church giving tree. Twice.

In December 2004, Mark had been out of work for fourteen months. Our severance pay was long gone. We'd ripped through our savings like toilet paper on your first night in Mexico. And Mark's mother had started to support us financially. I call that the Trifecta of Depression.

The year before, the Rossi family (my folks, my sister, her husband and son, my brother and his partner) had come to Hudson, Ohio, to spend the holiday in our idyllic Currier and Ives town. Hudson personifies charming at the holidays—from the brick clock tower with the giant Hickory Dickory Dock mouse running down it, to the New England–style town green festooned with wreaths and lights, to the Main Street that still boasted an old-fashioned drugstore with a soda fountain and lunch counter.

Mark had been out of work since October, but I had no sense of panic, yet. It never occurred to me that Mark wouldn't find another good-paying job quickly. I understood we'd probably have to leave Hudson, but that didn't faze me in the least. I liked Ohio well enough, but it wasn't "home," and I knew the girls could do better elsewhere as far as special education in the schools went.

I secured a three-bedroom bed-and-breakfast for the family in a Victorian house one gingerbread cut from being a cliché. I decked

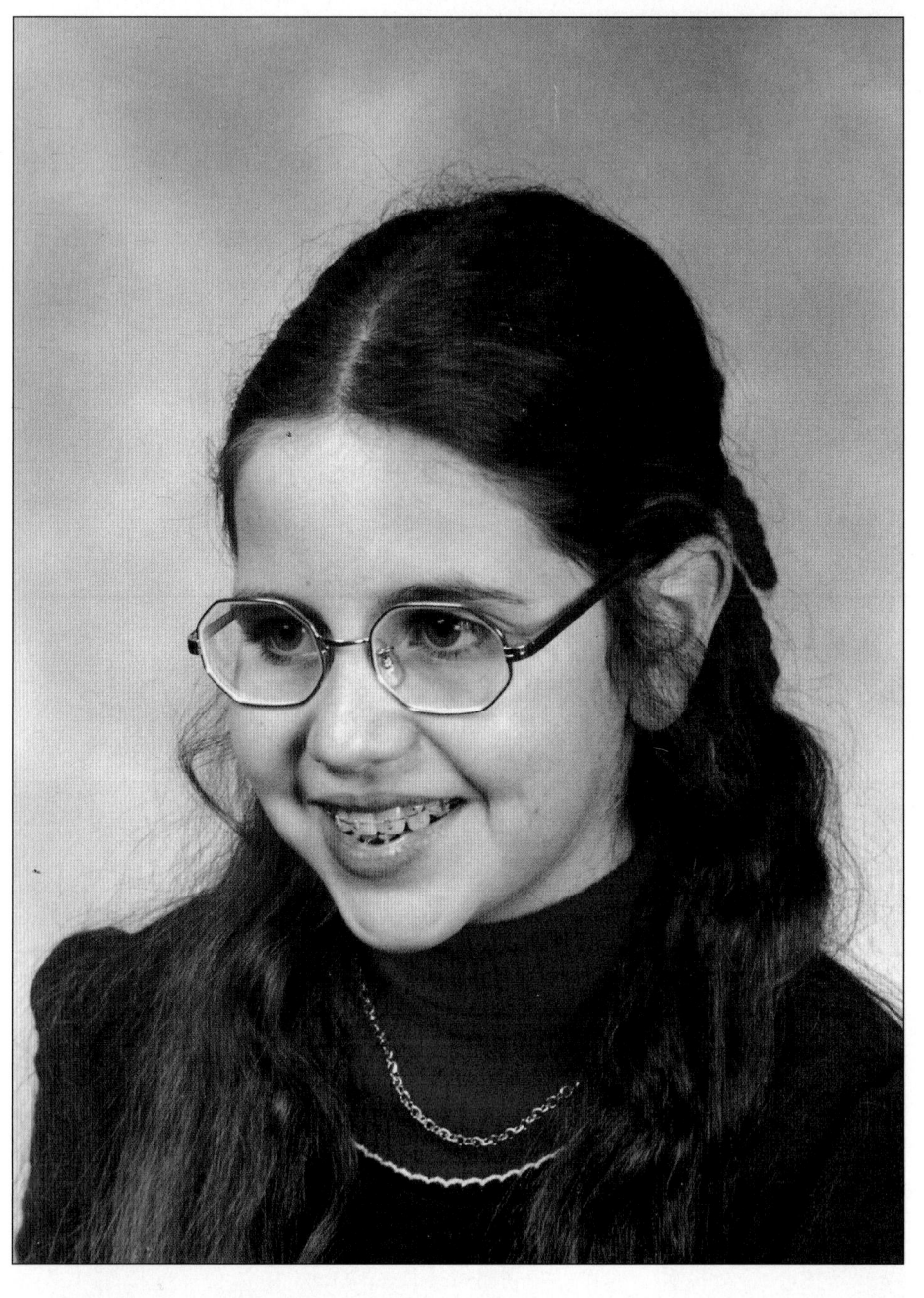

Kim in sixth grade at Dominican Academy

Mark in third grade at St. John
the Evangelist, Rochester, NY

Mark and Kim, 1990,
Hilton Head, SC

Mark and Kim's wedding day, October 19, 1991, Hilton Head, SC

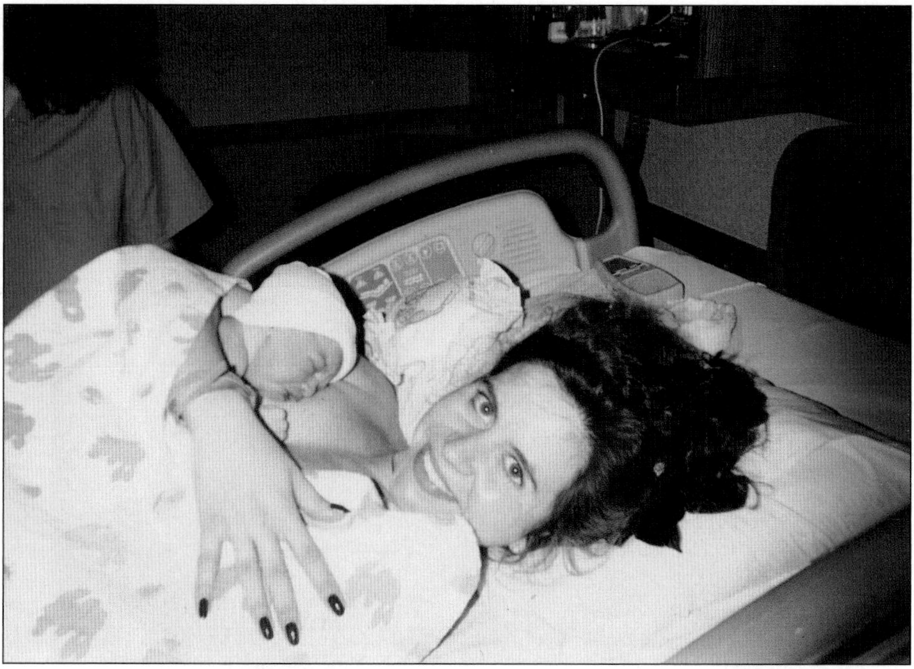

Mia's birth day, December 15, 1994

Mia showing off her social play skills before her diagnosis

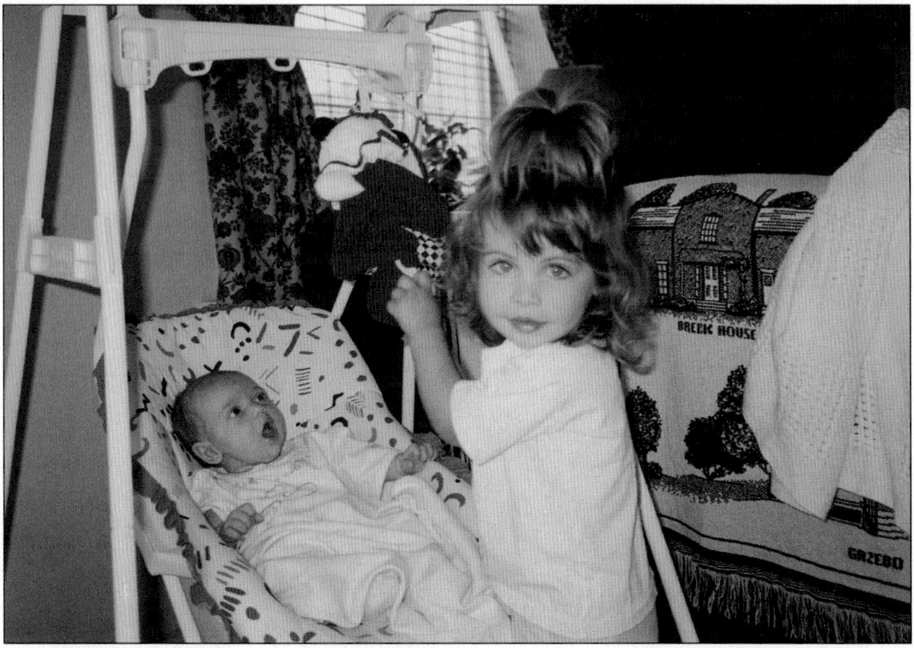

Baby Gianna with Mia

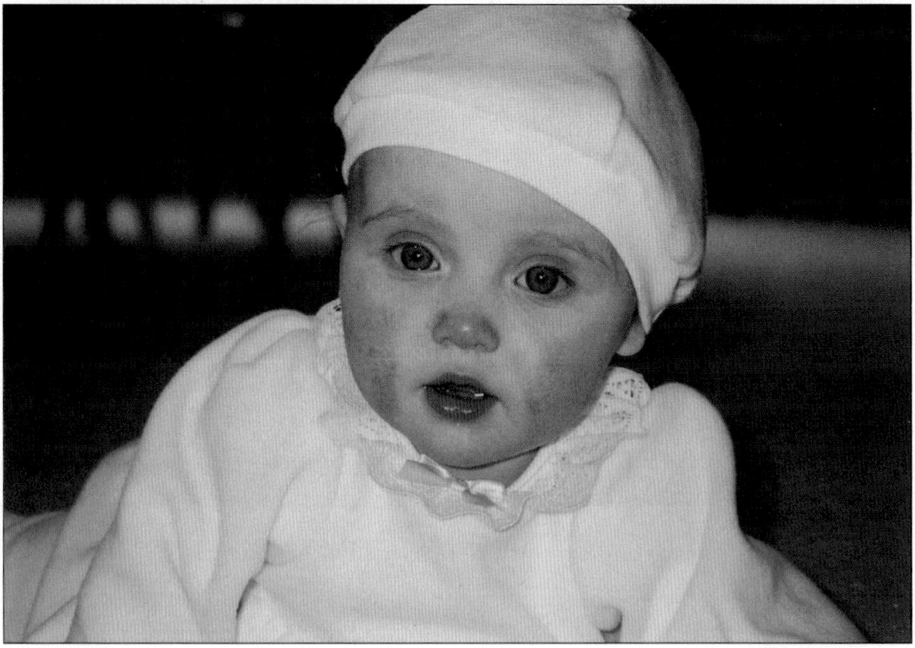

Gianna with rheumy eyes and red, papery cheeks

Mia's fourth birthday party, December 1998, Doylestown, PA

Mia and Gianna potty training

The Sesame Street Kitchen after the famous crapisode. Note the extra button.

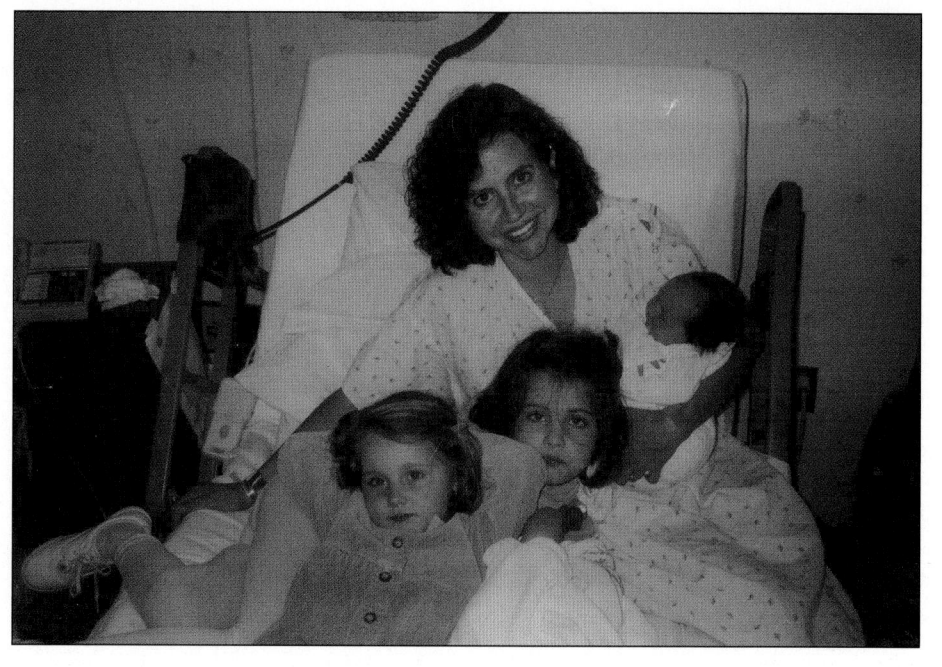

Kim with Gianna, Mia, and newborn Bella, September 15, 2000

Mia, Gianna, Kim, and Bella, Halloween 2001

Bella, four years old, Hudson, Ohio, fall 2004

Mia, looking grim before a seizure episode

Mark, Gianna, Mia, Bella (in stroller), and my mom, Elena Rossi,
at Disney World, October 2007

Mia, Kim, and Bella at Disney World, October 2007

The grounds at Marriott World Center hotel in Orlando where we lost Mia

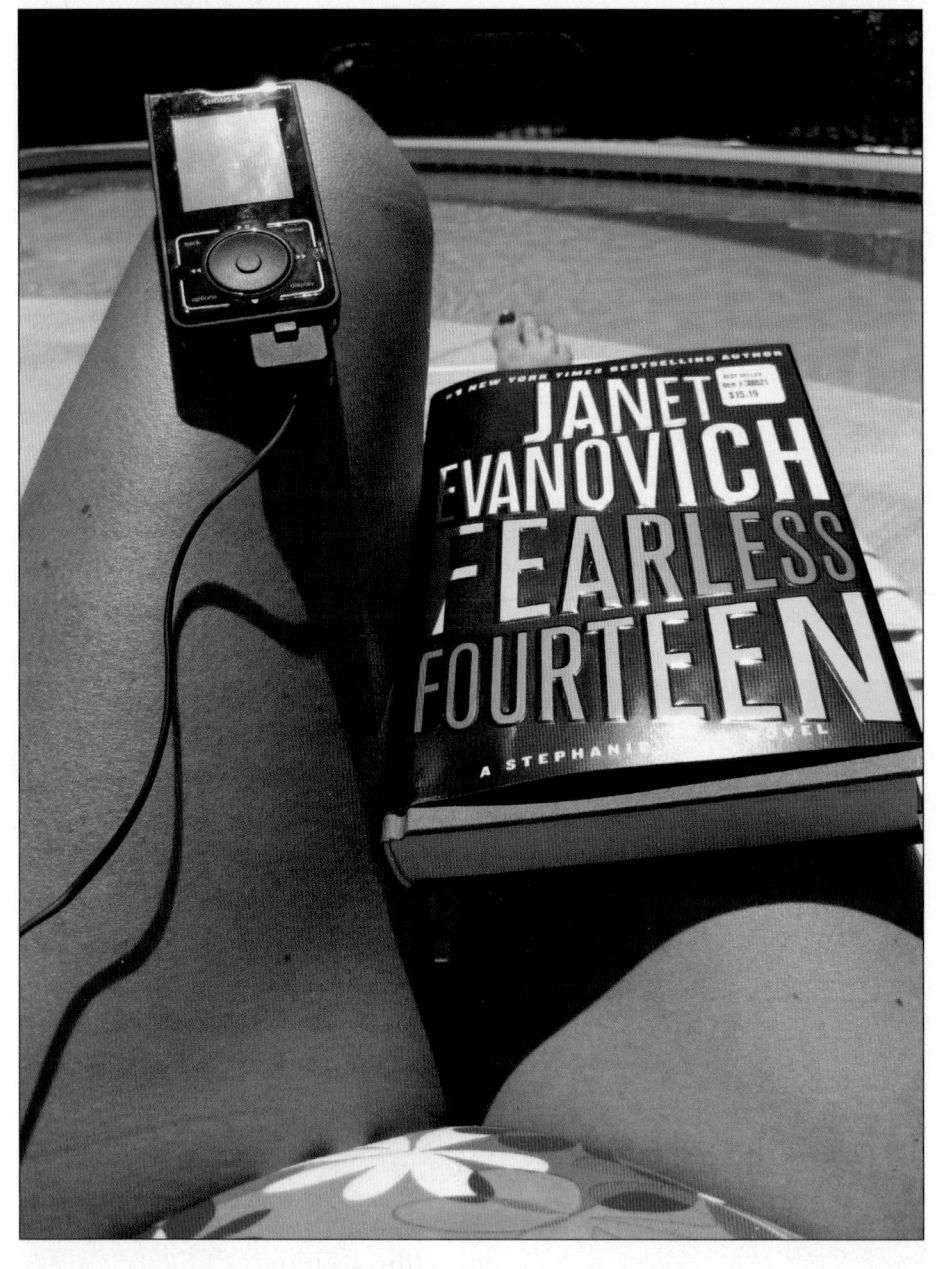

Look! I'm relaxing! July 2008, at the little green house.

The flood in the little green house. See the water swirling under the chair.

Gianna, Bella, Kim, Mia, and Mark at First Holy Communion, spring 2008

Bella's ninth birthday cake, GFCF
of course, September 14, 2009

Bella with Reverend Michael L.
Dunn at First Holy Communion,
spring 2010

Mia's "Stepping Forth" ceremony from eighth grade to high school, June 2010!

the halls and filled the fridge with store-bought goodies from Heinen's, the gourmet grocery store. We even threw a holiday party, inviting dozens of friends to join us in a celebration. Beer, wine, hard liquor, good food—we had it all!

I was so freaking stupid. And naïve.

By Christmas 2004, I had no more delusions about our future. It looked really grim. We had no money of our own. No jobs. No immediate prospects for work. I still wanted to cobble together a nice holiday for the girls. And I did. Well, it wasn't me—it was the generous parishioners of St. Mary's Church who came through.

Mark and I were placed on a paper mitten on the church Giving Tree by an anonymous holiday elf.

I got a call from a powerhouse of a woman named Kelly in early December. It went like this: "Hi, Kim. This is Kelly. I want you to know that we have your name here at church, and on Saturday you need to come and pick up your holiday gifts."

Me: "What?"

Kelly: "Come to St. Mary's Saturday before 1:00 PM."

Me: "No, Kelly. I mean we're okay." (We weren't.) "Give the stuff to another family."

Kelly: "No way, Kim. You either show up or I'm coming to your house with everything."

By now, I'm starting to cry. Mark and I had dropped off gifts for the Giving Tree every year since we'd been married. We're on the giving team! Not the receiving team!

Holy water, we'd become a name on a paper mitten.

What had happened to us?

I traveled back in time imagining the years of placing a gift for a poor family under the trees at church with the smug (yes, I think I was smug) feeling of a do-gooder.

"Kim, do you hear me? You need this. Do this for your kids." Kelly said.

I mumbled something vaguely affirmative to get Kelly off the phone and hung up wondering if she had just returned from boot camp at Parris Island. As a drill instructor.

Saturday arrived. I had no intention of going to St. Mary's in my $33,000 minivan to pick up charitable gifts to bring home to my 3,200-square-foot, four-bedroom, four-bathroom Georgian Colonial for my family.

Ah, pride goes before the call.

The phone rang. Of course.

"Kim, it's Kelly. *Where are you?*"

Panicking, I looked around my kitchen and at our Christmas tree. My decorations were up, but there were no gifts wrapped and hidden in an upstairs closet.

Kelly's words, "do it for the kids," came back to me.

"I'll be right there, Kelly."

I drove to St. Mary's, praying I wouldn't see anyone I knew. We didn't go to church often, so that wasn't an issue. I walked into the large room where the Giving Tree gifts were stashed.

Holy cow.

There, in a corner, was a pile of gifts, a box of household supplies like laundry soap, a beautiful fresh wreath—so much stuff I could barely fit it in the van. Feeling embarrassed gave way to feeling grateful and excited. Gifts for the girls! I can do just about anything if it's for my kids.

I hugged Kelly and thanked her.

I hadn't told Mark what I was doing, so when I got home and asked him to help me unload the car, he was surprised. We were blown away by the volume of items and the generosity. Together we went through the stuff. There were wrapped gifts for the children, hats, mittens, and scarves, gift cards to local restaurants, an envelope with *cash* in it (must have been from another Italian), movie tickets, household supplies, and the one item that made Mark and me laugh like hell: thirty-six bars of Zest soap.

Did you know that rich people think poor people don't bathe? Neither did I. We may have been down on our luck, but we were Zestfully clean, that's for sure. That soap lasted for over a year, and by the time it was gone, Mark was working. We had a little ceremony as the thirty-sixth empty box hit the trash can. We might even have gotten a little dirty.

NEW WORD: THE STAGTASTROPHE

I WAS A BIG FAN OF DEPECHE MODE, THE 1980S BRITISH NEW WAVE group whose songs were not quite as morose as Morrissey's but a far cry from the bubblegum pop of the Material Girl. One of my favorite songs was titled "Blasphemous Rumours." The lyric was, *"I don't want to start any blasphemous rumours but I think that God's got a sick sense of humor, and when I die I expect to find him laughing."*

That sounds about right to me.

We've had so much happen to us since the children were born, I coined a new word, "The Stagtastrophe." We make Murphy look like the luckiest man alive.

I've no idea why I've had so many roadblocks placed in the way of the happy-go-lucky marriage, motherhood, and life I'd imagined for myself as a young woman. Remember those wedding vows?

I'd ordered better, richer, and a side dish of health from the menu of life. We've been served worse, poorer, and sickness at an all-you-can-eat buffet, and frankly, I'm stuffed to the gills and in no mood to tip the waitress.

I take solace in a little delusion I've crafted for myself: "Bad things happen in threes." Well they do, right? Two wizened celebs die a week apart, and the world feigns shock when another 1950s screen star passes away. "See, bad things happen in threes," we tell ourselves, as if to stave off another death. And then—whoops!—there goes another one . . .

The year 2008 was another year of transition for the Staglianos. Finally settled into the rickety yellow house with no front walk and a deck that looked like it was made from timber from the *Mayflower,* we welcomed the New Year with cautious optimism. Mark's job was going well, though there were rumors that financial troubles lurked. His company, NCE Gifts, was the largest wholesaler of decorative flags and had dozens of giftware lines that sold at gift shops, large retailers like Kohl's, and garden centers throughout the United States and Canada. He worked from home, and it was a huge help to me to have an extra set of well-trained (and free) hands available.

Mia was happy in her second year of middle school with Miss Esposito, the difficulty of a new school behind her. Gianna was kicking butt in fifth grade, thanks to Mrs. Windsor and Miss Badowski, two teachers who truly believe that all children are educable if you find the right motivators. Bella was safely ensconced in Miss Saad's first grade, where she was well loved and far more settled in than her kindergarten year. I don't mean to imply that the girls' teachers in Ohio didn't give them 100 percent of their time and affection. They did. But I found that in New England, the curriculum for autism was more specific to the diagnosis. For instance, they used Applied Behavior Analysis (ABA) as a matter of course in school. I should also point out that the teachers in Connecticut were in their twenties, and autism was included in their college training. Plus, they chose to teach the autism population, whereas older teachers simply saw their classrooms transform into autism rooms as the special-ed population grew along with the epidemic of kids diagnosed. It's harder to catch up with the training than to have learned it as a matter of course during your recent schooling.

Even my own career was cruising along—much to my happy surprise. The Age of Autism site was gaining readers every day. We'd made the Google News index, which meant anyone with an alert for the word "autism" got our posts. This was a pretty big deal as it meant our posts appeared in searches alongside an article from

The New York Times or the *Boston Globe*. It expanded our reach, and that's just what we wanted.

I continued to write pieces for the Huffington Post that showcased the travails of autism.

The tranquility lasted for about ten minutes. If you've given birth, think of those moments between contractions. That blessed relief from the pain when you caught your breath and thought that it really wasn't so bad after alllll—here comes another one! That.

I was on the phone with my close friend and confidant Maureen in the midst of our daily (sometimes twice) Verizon to Verizon neighborly chat. She lives in Pittsburgh. Mark came to the bottom of the stairs, looked up, and said, "I just lost my job." My stomach bounced up into my mouth as if I'd jumped over the railing and down to the foyer. Tempting . . .

The Lord giveth to the Staglianos, and the Lord yanketh the rug out from under us. The winter of 2008 was no exception.

Maureen's husband had lost his job in 2006. And she'd helped me through our move when we had to sell our house in Ohio in 2005. She also has a son with autism. She's one of the few people in my circle who "gets" what we've been through from all sides.

I squeaked out, "Oh my God, Mark lost his job. I have to go."

When it comes to sheer terror, practice does not make perfect.

Having been through a twenty-three-month period of unemployment, I was so frightened when I learned Mark had lost this job, I plunged into despair. *That* scared the bejimminies out of me. Kimmy doesn't *do* depressed. Although depression and anxiety are frequent visitors throughout my side of the family. I don't have time for it.

My kids don't care if I'm feeling happy, sad, or am about to take a naked stroll on Route 95 while waving a roll of toilet paper at the traffic. Their needs do not take a break—and neither can I.

I didn't take that stroll on the highway. I drove to church, parked the car, and as I was walking toward the entrance I saw Father Dunn, one of the down-to-earth priests who'd made St. Theresa's such a haven for our family.

"How are you?" he asked.

(Insert flood of tears here.)

He gave me a hug and offered to send up numerous prayers on our behalf. I went inside to ask Mary for help—mother to mother. Then I asked Joseph for help. Father protecting his family. Then I looked up at Jesus on the cross.

"You!"

Yeah. I yelled at Jesus. Then I flounced past the confessional, not remotely remorseful for having called out the Son of God for his shoddy attention to my family's needs and drove home.

I guess you could say I was angry. Fuming. Vesuvian even. How many dues was I going to have to pay in this life?

And I was scared.

If I have one weakness (and I know that I have many) it's that when I'm scared, I become nasty. By nasty I don't mean ten-day-old milk curdled in the carton. Think cornered, rabid dog.

Mark: "I know this is a tough time for us, honey. But it's Valentine's Day next week. What would you like for Valentine's Day, Toonces?"

Angry Kim: "Oh, how about a Whitman's Sampler and a job for you that lasts more than the lifespan of the fruit fly?"

That kind of mean.

Guess what? In six weeks, Mark had a new and wonderful job! You see, when you're good at what you do (and he is, remember that Rookie of the Year award from Lenox China?) people notice. And I assumed that Jesus, Mary, and Joseph and Father Dunn had contributed to our luck.

Mark had been in the wholesale houseware, tabletop, and giftware business since we'd gotten married. He always worked for the vendor, meaning the company that makes (or these days imports) the products. Mark's job was to sell the products directly to retailers like Bed

Bath & Beyond, Williams-Sonoma, and HomeGoods, and also to manage sale representatives from a large national rep group based in Dallas, called One Coast.

The One Coast sales rep in New York had just tendered her resignation to care for her mother, who had Alzheimer's. One Coast had been pleased with Mark's service and professionalism and offered him the rep job with a decent salary. Decent is relative. It was $20,000 less than what he had been making, and still less than what he'd earned way back when in Ohio, but we were grateful. And there was a quarterly sales bonus. Not Wall Street–sized, more like Sesame Street. But we'd take it!

I felt like we'd dodged a torpedo-sized bullet with that job offer.

In our Russian-roulette life, the chambers are never empty.

Our landlord was a woman who had moved to China to work for a major U.S. fast food chain. I'll call her "Cathy." She didn't understand why we thought having a stove with four working burners, a dryer that turned itself off, or a dishwasher that didn't try to rinse the floor every time you ran it was a priority. The house had been a pit when we'd moved in, but a few coats of paint and basic repairs had made it livable if not a showplace.

We were sending her what most Americans would consider a sizable mortgage payment every month. On time. Wired right into her banking account. We'd cleaned her filthy walls, painted rooms, replaced dirt and weeds with flower gardens, and added curb appeal to a house that looked like Cinderella long before the makeover.

All she cared about was the money—as was her right. She'd lived for years in the dirty, broken-down house without a care. Different strokes, right?

After the angst of Mark's job situation had faded, I got a call from Cathy. We'd been cordial enough, communicating by e-mail from China to the United States.

She was returning to the United States with a new job that came with a corporate relocation package. She needed to sell her

house in order to buy a new house. She told us we'd have to move when our lease expired on June 30. Oh my God, is there anything worse than moving? Okay, maybe moving into a final resting place in the cemetery is worse. But at least I won't have to pack for that one.

One afternoon, I received a rare, chummy phone call from her.

"Hi, Kim, it's Cathy. How are you?"

"Hi, Cathy. I'm fine. What's up?"

"I need to ask you a favor. If a realtor comes to the door, would you please tell her we are relatives?"

Did I mention that Cathy is Chinese?

"Cathy, we don't look like sisters," I said half in jest, fully knowing where she was headed. You see, when you get a corporate relocation package, the company agrees to pay for you to move from your residence. Cathy's residence was in China. Her house in Connecticut stopped being her primary residence and became a rental property the day we signed a lease with her in 2006. I figured the IRS wasn't aware of our lease or the tens of thousands of dollars we'd paid to Cathy. Nor was the company offering the relocation.

No realtor ever came to the door, thank goodness. I'm a terrible liar, and my round blue eyes, curly brown hair, and the distinct lack of photos featuring a single Asian family member would have tipped off a blind man anyway.

I still get steamed when I think of her asking me to lie, and how easily she came by tens of thousands of dollars in relocation payments by her error of omission.

The spring passed quickly. We were into May, still without a new house and a lease that expired in just seven weeks. I was getting nervous.

I called on St. Joseph again, retrieving the statue I'd used to sell our house in Ohio. "Please, St. Joseph, the carpenter who found shelter for Mary when she was about to deliver the baby Jesus, please help us find a house. That's clean. And on a nice street. And in

Trumbull. And under $3,000 a month." I buried St. Joseph upside down in our yard.

And our realtor, Jay, found us a snug, three-bedroom ranch in a basic neighborhood of older homes right off Main Street.

Mark hated the house. I liked it a lot. It had a 1960s retro charm although it was fully updated with a gorgeous kitchen and a master bedroom that felt like a suite at the Ritz compared to the grungy yellow one we were sleeping in. Our belongings would fit right in, which is a real plus when you're renting. You have to shoehorn your life into someone else's house. Our mid-nineties Ivy League–colored furniture (navy, hunter, burgundy) would have looked like hell in a house with a more contemporary color scheme. Most of the rooms were soft yellows and creams, and the kids' bedrooms were pink and white.

The best feature was an in-ground pool with a built-in hot tub in the backyard, with a locking safety fence that cost more than my first car.

Mark walked through the house finding fault everywhere. He hated leaving our 3,200-square-foot house in Ohio (of course, he never had to clean it). It seemed that every house we looked at got a bit smaller and less impressive. But since our next stop was likely to be a tent in someone's yard or my folks' house, I thought the little, green ranch was perfect.

I skittered along behind Mark trying to exude optimism, "But honey, look at this ceiling fan and this pantry!"

I think Mark knew I was at a breaking point. He'd had to stitch his head back onto his shoulders far too many times after I'd bitten it off. The homeowner was renting the house following a divorce. The lack of women's clothing in the closet didn't escape Mark's notice. I'm not sure if that depressed him or gave him hope.

"When could we sign a lease?" he asked.

I winked at the realtor.

Thank you, St. Joseph. And thank you, Mark.

THE THINGS WE DO FOR LOVE

I HAVE A STRONG SENSE OF CATHOLIC GUILT. AT MY CORE, I'M HONEST—someone who tries to make the right choice when presented with a quandary. Sometimes autism and caring for the girls stands in the way of quality decision making. It happens. It's like a man robbing the Piggly Wiggly. When you learn that he's out of work and was stealing diapers for his son, you give him a pass, don't you? (I'm waiting!)

I hope you'll give me a pass.

I've never been arrested, although as the autism world heats up, I think there might be a protest or two in my future that could land me in the clink. Once, I was chastised by the Main Street traffic cop in Hudson, Ohio, for mouthing off to him about a parking situation. Hardly the stuff of *Lockdown*. I don't even park in the "pregnant customers only" spot at the local plaza. I'm waiting for the "customers with an autistic child" spots to appear. I could walk perfectly well, even at nine months pregnant. Navigating my three darlings into a store can be treacherous, though. My friend Connie and I snuck into a firehouse in South Boston and slid down the pole after too many cocktails about a million years ago. Was that illegal?

My brushes with the law were always Lucy and Ethel, not Bonnie and Clyde. Until the summer of 2008, when I broke a Commandment, and not even one of the fun ones.

I was sitting in the yellow house at my computer—just a few weeks before we were to move into the little, green ranch.

★ ★ ★

The kids were upstairs or in their rooms. I think. They weren't under my feet. Mark was out. I was reseaching moving companies online. We were moving across town in a matter of weeks. I was stressed out about the move, worried about how to pay for it, and generally in a bad mood.

A sound caught my attention.

"Plink! Plink! Plink!"

I looked around, glanced at the floor, shrugged my shoulders and went back to work.

Plink! Plink! Plink! Shshshshshshsh!!!!!!

My eyes went up to the kitchen ceiling. Water was gushing out of the ceiling fan (the light was on!) over the movable granite island in the center of the room.

Bella.

OhmyGodOhmyGodOhmyGod, I thought as I raced up the stairs two at time.

Bella had stuffed a Poise pee pad into the toilet. (We used those to prevent embarrassing accidents at school.) The pad had dutifully expanded from a small strip to a bloated, gel-filled pontoon that stopped up the toilet completely. As she flushed several times, the water had poured out of the bowl. How did I know this? It wasn't the first time this had happened. It was just the worst time. The water was now gushing onto the floor, across the bathroom, and had soaked several feet of the hallway carpet. It was at least three inches deep.

Sink or swim, Kim?

I turned off the water at the bottom of the toilet, then splashed to the hall closet to grab every towel and blanket we owned. I could have used a bail bucket. I sopped up as much as I could until we ran out of dry towels, so I began to wring them out in the tub and reuse them. The carpet was destroyed. The baseboards were soaked. Time for damage control. We were moving out, and while I had no love lost for the landlady, I didn't want to trash her house. Always with the guilt.

Mark came home to the catastrophe and just looked at me.

"What the hell are we going to do?"

I'm sure he was imagining a lawsuit or worse. We contemplated for a moment.

"We need a Shop-Vac," he suggested.

"We don't own one, and we can't afford to buy one."

"What the hell are we going to do, Kim?"

Fear not! An autism mom has more badges than an Eagle Scout, and more household hints than Heloise herself.

"I know! I can run up to the Stop & Shop to rent a Rug Doctor carpet cleaning machine. If I use it backward, it will suck up the water."

"You're crazy," Mark responded.

"You got a better idea, pal?" I yelled, as I changed into dry shorts and a fresh T-shirt.

"Lock the bathroom door, I'll be right back. And *don't* kill Isabella!"

I flew up Church Hill Road to the Stop & Shop plaza, slammed the minivan into park, and raced into the store. My cell phone rang and Mark said, "Toonces, get a box fan while you're there to dry the carpet."

Ten-four.

★ ★ ★

I grabbed a cart and whooshed over to the *everything but the kitchen sink* aisle that looks like an Ace Hardware–Staples–Walmart hybrid.

Please let them sell box fans, please God let them sell box— *jackpot!*

I grabbed the biggest fan off the shelf and a small one too, for good measure. I careened over to the self-checkout.

Scan. *Beep!* Scan. *Beep!*

Cash or credit?

I swipe my card.

"Cannot accept card."

Crap. Swipe again.

"Cannot accept card."

★ ★ ★

By now I'm hopping back and forth on one foot like I have to pee the mother of all pees. My ceiling is falling down, my drywall is disintegrating, and my carpet is busy sprouting into a lung-choking strip of death. I do not have time to dawdle. I need to buy the damn fans and go rent a carpet machine. I find a teenage employee.

"What's wrong with this machine? It won't take my credit card."

The kid drawls, "Oh, the card readers aren't working. You'll have to use cash."

Cash? What the f*ck is cash? I haven't seen cash since Ohio, for God's sake.

By now, my armpits are soaked with sweat. I'm doing that thing that my dad does when he's pissed off. It's a sucky sound you make while your tongue rolls around as if you're trying to dislodge caramel from every single tooth in your head. In Rossi parlance it means, "About to blow a gasket, please stand back."

Then the lights dim.

"Attention shoppers. We apologize for the inconvenience, but we have lost power and will have to close the store. Please find the nearest exit."

Now I'm eyeing the Drano in the aisle behind me, and wondering how much I'd have to drink to kill myself right then and there.

No way. I'm not going down. I need the carpet cleaner. I need the box fans. Now.

Move over Lucy, here comes Bonnie.

I rolled my cart, with the two fans inside, over to the Rug Doctor equipment. Drat, it's chained to the display. Off to customer service

I go. I recognize the kid working the cash register. He looks like he's in a heavy metal band. His hair is long, his knuckles tattooed, and he has a smile like Antonio Sabato.

"Hi Craig," I say, reading his name tag. "I have an emergency at home, and I really need to rent a Rug Doctor, right now."

"We can't take any money now, there's no power," he says.

God almighty, hasn't this kid ever seen *Little House on the Prairie*? He has a pen and paper, right?

"Craig, I'm in a bind here. Could you maybe write down my credit card information and enter it when I return the machine tomorrow?" I asked in a sweet, slightly strained voice.

"Yeah, I guess I could do that," he said.

Thank God, metal boy has a brain.

He wrote up my order for the machine, I gave him my card info and headed for the door.

The store was in chaos, people still trying to check out, take their groceries, leave their groceries.

I put my head down and sailed out of there as fast as I could.

With my items in the trunk, I eased out of the parking lot and headed home.

Oh no.

I haven't paid for the two box fans.

I pulled into our driveway and schlepped the Rug Doctor from the car to the front door. The house was a New England "garage under," which means it's built into a hill with the garage on basement level. I was not bumping the machine up two flights of stairs. Mark opened the door for me.

"I stole two fans. They're in the car. Go get them."

"You what?"

"It's a long story. Now let's go clean the carpet," I said.

We did manage to repair the house fully. I called an electrician who said the light would be fine—to aim a fan at it for a couple of days and then spray the ceiling with something called KILZ paint.

Sure enough, the light and the fan worked. The ceiling got a fresh blast of paint and the carpet dried out just fine.

No harm. No foul.

Except that I'd stolen the fans. I didn't know if I could go back to the store and tell them. I ended up putting fifty dollars into the Salvation Army's red kettle outside the door as soon as it appeared during the holidays. I told God (because we know how closely attuned he is to my prayers) that I was sorry for stealing them. A few weeks later we had a major flood in our new house, so I'm not sure if God forgave me.

Now you know I've stolen for love. How about public indecency?

★ ★ ★

Our family was in church, and a little boy was seated behind us. I'd visited his family's place for a yard sale last summer (I bought a pumpkin decoration and some manatee books). He was a cute child, well behaved, and maybe four years old. He sneezed. His mom handed him a tissue, and he blew his nose like Louis Armstrong on the trumpet.

Hooooonnnnnnkkkk.

My girls cannot blow their noses. I hate those reminders of how hard it is to teach skills to my girls.

We were once at Mass when Mia had a terrible cold. She hasn't figured out how to blow her nose. I haven't figured out how to teach her. I'm usually pretty good at coming up with some way to relay what she needs to do, but nose blowing had eluded us.

She sneezed, and when I turned to say "bless you, honey," she had the snot equivalent of a bright green eel hanging out of her nostril. I grabbed a tissue and wiped her nose, hoping the other parishioners weren't vomiting in the pews around us. Maybe I'd refrain from shaking hands during the sign of peace? Good plan.

As we left church, I told Mark that I was going to take Mia to the urgent care center, as it was obvious that her cold had turned into a sinus infection.

The waiting room was busy on a late Sunday morning. Mia and I sat down and waited for her turn. She was quite patient. Up to a point.

"Bathroom?" she said to me.

When any of my kids indicates the need for the toilet, I drop everything and take her. I put down the clipboard and took Mia to the restroom. She didn't go.

★ ★ ★

Back in the waiting area, she said it again, "Bathroom?" Up we jumped, only this time, I noticed a small wet stain on the back of her jeans. My heart sunk. I didn't want her to be embarrassed. When my girls get sick, they can't always feel when they have to go in time. This was one of those times. We went into the bathroom.

"Wet!" she said to me.

Mia, like any of us, doesn't like the feeling of wet clothing. You and I don't strip off our clothes, however. If she became agitated she might want to undress in the waiting room. I looked at her. She was so beautiful, with her dark hair and big eyes. I felt so sad.

"Wet!" she said again, kicking off her shoes and starting to undress. Oh boy, I had to think fast. Mia needed dry underwear.

Lightbulb!

"Hang on, Mia. Mama will fix it." I told her.

In a jiffy, I'd slipped off my own shoes, wriggled out of my jeans, and pulled off my underwear. It felt like being in the mile-high club, except the toilet water wasn't blue, and I wasn't having any fun.

★ ★ ★

"Here, put these on," I said, as I held my underwear down by her feet. She stepped into them and got dressed. I grabbed my jeans,

thanking God I hadn't worn my favorite white Levi's, and carefully slid them on, zipped them up, and ran a mirror check.

Together, we went back into the waiting room. Mia was snug and dry. Me? I was going commando.

A good friend will give you the shirt off her back. A good mom will give her child her underwear.

THE LITTLE GREEN HOUSE

WE MOVED INTO THE DARLING RANCH HOUSE ACROSS TOWN ON
July 1, 2008.

Gianna was turning twelve on July 11. She'd made friends for
the first time in her life in the Trumbull schools. I invited ten
little girls from her regular-ed fifth-grade classroom to a pool
party.

I also broke down and bought Costco cupcakes loaded with gluten
and topped with colored sprinkles. Gianna's eyes nearly popped out
of her head.

"Wow. Giant cakes for Gianna! I love it!" she said.

The party was the first in our new house. I loved the kitchen,
which had a green granite countertop, stainless-steel applicances
made in Germany, and a "beverage" fridge with plenty of room for
wine and beer.

And the pool? Wow. Once they were in the water, my girls' differences just melted away. Mia and Gianna can swim thanks to "drown-
proofing" goals on their school plan, which ensures they get
swimming lessons once per week. Bella can't swim yet, but she can
float like a demon in a safety ring.

You'd never know my girls were autistic while they splish-splashed
away an afternoon. I have a great photo of Mia and Gianna with several typical kids, holding hands, about to jump in the water.

I even took a self-portrait lying by the pool with the newest Janet
Evanovich "Stephanie Plum" book on my lap (covering my middle-
aged, three-kid stomach) just to have proof that I'd actually relaxed

during daylight hours. (Sometimes I look at that photo like it's a relic from an archaeological dig.)

It's nearly impossible to take the three girls to a public pool. Mia is our indoor cat, and she's anxious to go home within half an hour of our arrival. Bella loves the water and will sit and splash at the water's edge for hours. Gianna will either swim or pace around the pool, asking if her friends from school are coming. Inevitably someone has a meltdown. Bathing suits get yanked off, in public. Screaming is not out of the question.

When Coppertone makes SPF Invisible, we'll be much better off.

Having a private pool was beyond decadent.

★ ★ ★

Then a harbinger of new problems appeared at our front door.

Have you ever seen a "dunning letter"? Neither had I. Despite our financial ups and downs, Mark and I have always paid our bills on time. For poor people, we have really good credit scores. (We can thank his mom for helping us out financially during that long bout of unemployment.)

Tucked between the screen and front door of our little green house was a letter from a bank, requesting that the homeowner contact them immediately. I knew enough to realize this did not mean there was a shiny new toaster waiting for our landlord, whom I'll call "Angelo."

A few days letter, I opened a piece of junk mail without checking the name on the envelope:

BANKRUPTCY DOESN'T HAVE TO MEAN YOU CAN'T HAVE A NEW CAR!

Oh. My. God.

Our new landlord was late on his mortgage and bankrupt to boot?

This stuff could only happen to us.

We knew the house was part of a divorce situation. But in our naïveté, it hadn't occurred to us to run a credit check on the landlord.

I Googled "bankruptcy Connecticut" and found an automated phone system that provides basic details on bankruptcy filings. Bankruptcies, like foreclosures, are public record. I called the number, punched in Angelo's name, and sure enough, the son of a bitch had filed for bankruptcy on *Gianna's birthday!*

Then *another* bank left a notice in our mailbox. Two mortgages!

I asked him about the bankruptcy.

"Don't worry," he told me. "It's just my ex-wife's credit card debt." Sure. Did she shop at The Men's Wearhouse and buy thousands of dollars' worth of landscaping equipment for *his* failed business? (Those were just two of the creditors on his bankruptcy filing. You can check all that stuff at the courthouse.)

Did he think I'd just fallen off the zucchini truck? I'd been hearing horror stories on the news about marshals showing up on doorsteps and evicting unsuspecting tenants throughout the country! Can you imagine if that happened to us with three autistic kids?

When I saw that first dunning letter, I worried. And then I set aside Angelo's money woes and went for a swim. *Que será será.*

Fall came, and the little green house demonstrated another fine feature. We could sit in the front room and watch the bus approach through our front window, then let the girls skedaddle down our own brick walkway to the waiting bus. (The yellow house didn't have a front walk—just grass.)

Mia and Gianna started boarding the bus by themselves. A new skill.

As the holidays approached, I started to feel at home for the first time in more years than I could remember. I hadn't realized just how homesick I'd been for New England until I'd returned.

President Obama had won the election, and optimism was in the air. In a nod to my newfound (and much appreciated) sense of security, I unpacked my Lenox china for the first time in almost five years. It brought back so many memories, mostly good. The hope and optimism of our wedding day. Serving our first married Christ-

mas dinner. The Christmas I didn't eat a morsel because Mia was having seizures all day. I said mostly . . .

Do you recall that torpedo that missed us when Mark found a new job? Well, it struck us broadside in a direct hit.

It was early November, and I was planning my Thanksgiving dinner. I, like every other American woman who is not an acolyte of Paula Deen (fry it) or Martha Stewart (hatch it, raise it, slaughter it yourself in the backyard), "plan" a basic roasted turkey with traditional fixings.

I was seated at my desk, when I heard Mark snap his fingers behind me.

I turned.

He had his phone to his ear, his face was chalk white, and he simply made a cutting motion across his throat.

Holy freaking moly, he'd just been fired. Again.

I think the right word for the sound that came out of my mouth is "keening."

I dropped to my knees and sobbed.

He hung up the phone, and said the worst words I'd ever heard from him.

"I'm so sorry, Kim. I've let you down. I'm so sorry."

And he wept.

My heart broke. I knew what a good job he'd done for the company, but retail sales had dried up as gas prices skyrocketed and the economy went into a death spiral. His accounts had simply stopped writing purchase orders.

We were financially at the end of our rope. We'd saved some money, but then used it earlier in the year for the couple of weeks he was unemployed and to pay for our move (which cost more than $2,000—moving our kids quickly and with as little disruption as possible necessitated the cost.)

We clung to each other for a moment.

"Don't you dare apologize to me," I begged him.

Within hours Mark had his résumé out to several headhunters and was making those agonizing phone calls he'd made only months earlier: "I'm out of work. If you hear of anything . . ."

I sent an e-mail to my family and closest friends. *Mark lost his job. Economy tanked. Half of sales force let go. Don't call me yet. I can't talk to anyone.*

Dozens of colleagues rallied around Mark. A testament to his reputation.

We got through Thanksgiving and marched toward Christmas. This marked our third holiday season in five years with Mark out of work. You'll laugh, but I was sort of grateful that the girls' autism prevented them from asking for age-appropriate gifts. It would have broken my heart to tell them, "No, we can't afford a Wii" almost as much as it hurt to keep supporting the Sesame Workshop by wrapping yet another Elmo toy every year.

I both started and finished my Christmas shopping in the Stop & Shop: broccoli, Tide, plastic Elmo cell phone. I kid you not. I spent less than a hundred dollars on the three girls. I told my extended family I'd send them millions of holiday wishes but not much else.

December 2008 was a cold month.

And wet.

I usually start my weekdays at 5:30 AM I make coffee, log on to my computer to check overnight comments on Age of Autism, prepare three gluten-free breakfasts and lunches, and get the girls ready for school.

On the morning of December 12, Mark helped me and then headed to his office in the basement. Down the stairs he went.

One, two, three, four, five, six, *splash!*

"Oh my God, Kim! We have a flood!" he hollered up the stairs.

I ran to the door and peered down the six steps into the basement. Clear water was running across Mark's feet on the basement floor. A monster storm had hit the night before, and, while

we were sleeping, the sump pump had decided it was time to die.

Mark climbed back up the stairs. We stood on the top step looking at the swishy swirly water. He shook his head.

"We're effed."

"How are you not dead?" I asked him finally, aghast. "The lights are still on, and everything is underwater . . ." my voice trailed off. I'm no fainting Freida, but I felt woozy at the thought of how close Mark had come to electrocution.

My husband had stepped into several inches of water in a room where submerged power strips were loaded with the electrical cords of a humming office. If any reader is an electrical engineer (or a priest?) and can tell me why Mark wasn't electrocuted when he stepped into the water, drop me a line. I call it a miracle.

I thought I'd gotten past caring about "stuff." I hadn't. Despite being grateful that I was planning a cleanup, and not Mark's funeral—my framed portraits of the girls, our wedding pictures, my in-laws on their wedding day, my grandparents, everything, everything, everything we'd kept in boxes down there was ruined! Not to mention hundreds of dollars' worth of empty boxes we use for moving. Clothing. Books from my childhood. All destroyed.

Even Mark's golf clubs (tee hee!).

My brother Rich and his partner Ed had splurged and sent the girls an expensive *Sesame Street* kitchen for Christmas. That kitchen had become a galley—on the *Titanic*. I saw the water swirling around the white box from Amazon and lost it. My kids had one good Christmas gift, and now it was gone.

But, like most Stagtastrophes, this one passed, and we managed to count the very big blessing that Mark had not been injured. Angelo immediately replaced the sump pump, and the water drained away, leaving behind muck and our soaking-wet belongings.

One of those "like it never even happened except your stuff is gone" companies came and dried out the entire basement, carting

away hundreds of pounds of sopping-wet boxes. Our insurance agent had included sump-pump coverage on our renter's policy. (Thank you, Doug!) It covered $5,000 of the estimated $8,500 we lost.

Christmas approached and with it a renewed hope in the goodness of people. The autism community reached out to us from all directions. A dear friend and mom of three kids on the spectrum (one of whom lost his diagnosis due to her hard work), the fabulous Michelle Iallonardi, took up a collection and sent us a check for more than $1,000 and a scarf her mom had knit. The National Autism Association called to offer us a Helping Hand grant of $1,500 to help pay for the girls' supplements. A Yahoo group for old-timers in the autism world sent me a box of all sorts of goodies. An anonymous donor from New York City sent us a thousand-dollar American Express gift card! It bought our groceries for months.

I was overwhelmed with gratitude. How did so many people love us?

We were even a paper mitten on the giving tree for the second time.

One night close to Christmas, our doorbell rang, and when I looked outside, Santa's elves had left a large gift bag loaded with goodies for our family.

There was a box in the package labeled "for Mom." In it was a gold bracelet with diamonds and sapphires (to match my engagement ring). I wear it every day to remind me that we are never alone.

It's humbling to accept help with grace.

I've learned to say thank you, swallow my pride, and remember that every gift is sent with love and concern.

★ ★ ★

The year 2009 arrived. I'd turned a year older just before New Year's Eve. We settled in for a long winter's ... work. We don't get many naps

here. January brought the excitement of the inauguration of President Barack Obama, whom both Mark and I had supported. It also brought continued reports of the worst economy since the Great Depression.

Mark had been on a couple of job interviews. But for all intents and purposes, the job market in his industry (and every other) was stone-cold dead. We had enough money to last until April. Just a few months away.

I was back to feeling scared. And that meant I was back to feeling angry.

At one time I'd had a plaque with that saying from Mother Teresa: "I know God will only give me what I can handle. I just wish God didn't trust me so much." (I'm pretty sure I sold it at a garage sale.)

I was starting to wish that God would just forget about me for a while and concentrate on something else, like a plague of locusts, or maybe a famine.

Mark had continued to receive calls from vendors and colleagues in his industry. First one, then two, then three vendors asked if he'd continue to represent their product lines. Before he knew it, he had a company. It was strange. It was improbable. He'd always been with a corporation, and I'd liked it that way. We needed the benefits for the family. But as everyone knows, benefits are nonexistent today. No 401(k) and we still had to pay $998 a month for our "company-sponsored" health insurance.

Mark discovered he *had* a job. He was self-employed.

I liked to say that the only person who could fire him now was *me*. Not that I'd ever get rid of the rock that anchors our family.

April came and went. We limped along financially. My generous sister and brother stepped up to the plate and helped us meet some of our expenses. My eighty-six-year-old father pulled me aside at Easter and told me we always had a home with him and my mom—who had a habit of tucking "a little something" into a card of encouragement on a regular basis.

I was getting excited to open the pool and enjoy another summer by it.

Angelo the bankrupt landlord had other plans.

One day in spring he called and told us that an appraiser was coming to the house. Oh boy. Again I asked, "Are we okay here? Is the house okay?"

I saved his voice mail: "My attorney is on top of it. You have nothing to worry about." Right-o, Angelo!

The appraiser came. I introduced myself as Kim Stagliano. I could see the mental lightbulb go on.

"Are you a tenant?"

"Yes," I answered. "And I know that the landlord is bankrupt. If he's appraising the house, does this mean he's about to lose it?"

The appraiser was circumspect and shared no information. If only I'd been in my bikini when he'd answered the door. Of course, then he might have run away.

I knew that having him at the house didn't bode well for our being able to remain as tenants. And I loved that little green house.

Lo and behold, in early May, Angelo alerted Mark that he would not be renewing our lease at the end of June.

I called him. I was furious.

"Angelo! We talked about staying on here for at *least* two years when we signed the lease!"

"I know, Kim, but I need to move back in so my girls can go to school in Trumbull. My ex-wife is leaving town."

Off went my bullshit meter. *Whatever* the reason, Angelo needed to move back into the house. Oh God, how were we going to manage another move, two in one year! My mind began the checklist of dread: Get new boxes, pack, try to prepare the kids and keep their anxiety levels below code red, call moving companies, cable, electric, gas, fill out more change-of-address cards, and on went the list. I was

exhausted on top of being really angry at Angelo, whom I felt had really snowed us.

I went into action. What else could I do?

"Hi, Jay?" (our realtor at Coldwell Banker.) "It's Kim."

God bless Jay. Realtors make no money on rentals. But Jay called us every day with listings and showed us several houses at the drop of a hat. He's a doll.

★ ★ ★

Mark and I walked into a lovely Dutch Colonial and smiled at each other. It was a mile from the middle school, walking distance to Starbucks, and the rent was equal to what we were paying Angelo. Within a week we'd signed a two-year lease *and* learned that the house was paid for—no landlord worries!

Because of the December flood we had far less stuff to move. How's that for a very pale silver lining?

We try to take each tumble off the horse as it comes. We've climbed back into the saddle more times than I can count. Sometimes I land on my backside, but I've never landed on my head. I'm always okay. My kids are happy. My husband is by my side.

And that is what I call "Stagtastic."

THE MIDDLE CHILD

MY PERSONALITY HAS HELPED MY ABILITY TO COPE WITH THIS CRAZY life. I didn't go from a shy girl who never raised her hand in class to a thinner version of Roseanne just because of autism.

In kindergarten I can remember making fun of a girl named Shirley for wearing baby shoes—they were white sandals with a covered heel. They were a safe, appropriate shoe for a five-year-old. I told her she looked stupid in them.

In first grade, to avoid drinking my ice-filled half pint of milk (can you stand ice in your milk?), I'd lie to Mrs. C., "I'm going to upchuck. May I be excused?" Then I'd dawdle in the hallway until an eighth grader would spy me, haul me into the bathroom, and make me do my notorious Fat Albert imitation, "Hey, Hey, Hey!"

Sister Barbara nicknamed me "Hot Seat" in third grade because I could-not-would-not-did-not sit still. I'd race through my work and then bounce up to find something more interesting than my desk. If I were a kid today, a doctor would have me on meds for ADHD. I'm still pretty willy-nilly. That's a major frustration for my über-organized husband.

My nickname in fourth grade was "Bossy Rossi." In seventh grade I wrote an advice column called "Ask Kim." We printed it on the mimeograph machine (I'll give you a second to remember the smell of the chemicals that clung to the damp copies that thing churned out, if you're old enough).

For some reason, I was voted class president in eighth grade, as a newcomer to the school. I'm still not sure if that was a joke or if I'd

made an impression on the class in two short months. Maybe they elected me to spite another student.

Even as a kid, I had "leadership" qualities. But the autism world has some deep rifts. And not everyone thinks I'm the cat's pajamas.

For instance, there's a group of self-advocating young adults and adults with autism (many of whom are self-diagnosed) who dislike the autism treatment community because we want to change our kids' autism. Hello? My girls can't cross the street safely. These folks can blog their hatred of me and talk about me all night on chat groups and blogs. I'd hardly say they share my kids' problems, although I've no illusion that any form of autism or Asperger's is a walk in the park. With the unusual abilities and talents often trumpeted come depression, isolation, employment problems, and sometimes an inability to live independently. And, boy, some of them are pissed off about the seach for an autism "cure."

The irony is that their own autism prevents them from empathizing with what my girls deal with every day. I can deal with these folks because I always imagine how happy I'd feel if my girls were *able* to start nasty blogs and devote all their time to dissing some mom in Connecticut and her peers.

Then there are the skeptics who attach themselves to autism like barnacles. Skeptics are the folks devoted to debunking what they see as myths, including the autism-vaccine connection. I've no idea why this is so important to them. To me, it's like attacking the folks at Mothers Against Drunk Driving for wanting to prevent drunk-driving-related deaths. Stupid.

But boy they are a busy little group of bees. They hide behind online pseudonyms or use the fourty-fourth–fifty-second digits from Pi as their screen name and then they comment over and over and over and over and over and over (feel the perseveration?) on posts about autism and vaccines. There's one dingbat on Huffington Post with 30,000 comments who claims to be a mom in the Midwest. Honey, if you've had time to comment 30,000 times on a blog,

someone had better call child services, because your kids must be really hungry. I suspect they are financed by pharma. Others just want to deny what may have happened to their own children. The anger is way over the top and the nonstop assault they put up is absurd. They never comment on my softer "mom" Huffington Post pieces. I guess they don't get paid for that.

★ ★ ★

The most nefarious are the autism "experts" who are hell-bent on making certain that autism is not viewed as an epidemic, and who advocate the position that it is not treatable, let alone curable. At the risk of sounding like that tinfoil-hat model, I have to wonder if the lack of medical attention to autism outside of genetics and a handful of frightening psychiatric drugs stems from the realization that *all treatment roads* would lead to an eventual determination of cause. The cause *could* include vaccines.

The December CDC announcement that was so underreported stated that the autism prevalence for eight-year-olds has increased again to one in 110 children. That's almost one percent of children! The numbers have jumped from one in 500, to one in 250, to one in 166, to one in 150 and now to one in 110 in just a decade. And that 110 estimate uses data a couple of years old. We could be at one in *under 100 kids.*

At what point should we panic about autism? In my house, the panic train left the station a long time ago.

One of the so-called experts in autism is Dr. Fred Volkmar from the Yale Child Study Center, which is about fifteen miles away from my home. He had the audacity to claim that media awareness is behind the increase in autism. Check out this bit of an interview in Medscape:

Medscape: Do you think the increase in autism is mainly due to the expanded definition?

Dr. Volkmar: It's a couple of things. First of all, there's more public awareness. The fact that we're having a discussion like this, twenty years

ago nobody would have ever called me to talk about autism. It's partly the media and it's organizations like Autism Speaks and other things for good or bad. Even on the Internet, if you type in autism into Google, you will get 15,000,000 hits. The trouble is, only about 100 of those are worth anything and of that 100, about one third are quite problematic. There's more information, there's more media attention, there's more public awareness. We now get referrals from day care providers, who in the past wouldn't even know what the word meant. It's much more in the public conscientiousness.

Is he completely bananas? The reason no one talked about autism is that they weren't affected by it. I'll bet that my eighty-eight-year-old Uncle Mortimer didn't jabber on about prostate issues when he was thirty. Does Dr. Volkmar really think parents whose kids can't speak or provide the most basic self-care only got noticed recently because Autism Speaks ran some public service ads telling parents that their kids had a better chance of having autism than playing for the New York Yankees?

Fred Volkmar blames the increase on the media and the autism organizations that have cropped up in a desperate effort to help families. Got it. Right. Okay. He's the expert, after all—Yale, you know. Big doings there! Lots of funding. Well spent, don't you agree?

When you have an autism leader saying an increase is in doubt, even as school resources are being overwhelmed trying to manage and educate the autism population, I get very, very angry. Then I start writing. And then get I those icky Google alerts.

A thick skin doesn't grow nearly as fast as you'd think. I'm still working on mine.

Perhaps more than others, I need to be liked by people.

Ah yes, the middle-child syndrome. I blame it for my incessant desire for attention. I credit it for my sense of humor and ability to make people laugh. I was a classic class clown.

★ ★ ★

A bit about my sister and brother:

My older sister Michele was beautiful (still is) and the object of everyone's attention. She looks like an exotic Snow White. With my oversized eyes and round cheeks, I looked more like Dopey. She's four years older—which feels a lot better in my forties than it did when I was four. We had a good relationship as kids. She left for boarding school when I was in seventh grade. I followed her to the same school the year after she graduated.

When I was a freshman (called IV class in prep parlance, and yes, the Roman numeral makes a difference, much like adding the suffix "pe" to "shoppe" inflates the bric-a-brac prices), I was sitting at a carrel in the library, and there scratched into the desk were the words MICHELE ROSSI IS BEAUTIFUL. It was my very own Jan Brady "Marcia, Marcia, Marcia" moment. I used my left hand to scribble "All Rossi's are great," assuming no one would know that it was my own (ridiculous) comment. Was I a loser or what?

I can barely describe how unattractive I was when I began high school at the age of thirteen. My brown hair turned from wavy to American Standard Poodle overnight. I wore a thin cloth headband with the little grosgrain ribbon on top. In 1977, it made me feel like I fit in with the preppy crowd. Today you'd be ridiculed for placing it on your Chihuahua.

I wore giant glasses with blue plastic frames and blue-tinted lenses that hid my best feature, my blue eyes. And they had a gold letter K sticker on one lens. Hey, Laverne looked great with an L on her sweater, why couldn't I have a golden initial sticker on my eyeglasses? Because a thirteen-year-old's eyeglasses are not the same as a busty adult woman's chest, perhaps? That part was lost on me. Speaking of busty, I was thin and flat chested. Aw heck, I might as well share this little fact: I used to wear turtleneck dickies—the quasi-shirt that goes over your head and covers your chest and back with two flaps. I figured out that I could increase my bustline by tucking the front material up and under my Sears bra. I've no idea what the boys might have

thought come spring when I shed layers and a cup size. I'm pretty sure no one noticed at all.

Upon graduation, I followed my sister to Tufts University. By age seventeen, I appreciated her popularity more than I envied it. Plus, having blossomed to a full A cup and having learned to straighten my hair, I was less competitive with her. I even joined her sorority house.

Twenty-eight years later, I remain a Chi Omega pledge. I never formalized my membership in the sisterhood, having hightailed it out of Tufts for Boston College my sophomore year, allegedly to study business.

In reality, I wanted to be on the Green Line of the MBTA transit system, which offered me a straight shot to Arlington Street station around the corner from where I caught the Vermont Transit bus to visit my boyfriend Dave at Dartmouth. At Tufts I had to ride a bus into Harvard Square in Cambridge, take the Red Line to Park Street, and then transfer on the Green Line to Arlington Street. Not exactly a well-thought-out reason for changing colleges, I admit. Have teen decisions ever been well thought out? I only thank God and Jesus I didn't have a camera phone back then. Enough said. My mom and my priest are going to read this.

I loved Boston College, though, and graduated in 1985 along with a famous autism dad named Doug Flutie.

Back to the middle-child angst.

My brother Richard is the youngest and the only son. He was born on Valentine's Day, 1970.

I spent the next twelve years tormenting him for having the audacity to join our family. Buried in a family photo album is a snapshot of little Richie dressed in the white pantaloons and floral pinafore worn by my three-foot-tall Raggedy Ann doll. Michele and I painted his face with green eye shadow and turned him into a Martian once, too. He was adorable with his sandy-blond hair and chubby cheeks. I can still picture him sitting on the Pawleys Island

hammock near our house taking his first sip of the drink that I, his loving big sister, had offered him on a hot summer day. The cup was filled with pickle juice.

Despite my initial jealousy of his existence, I grew to love him, even though I'd gone off to boarding school when he was seven years old and didn't see him daily. Lucky for him, right?

When Richard graduated from The Catholic University of America in Washington, D.C., he came out to my mom during a walk to the lake down the street from our childhood home. Soon after, he called me on the phone to tell me he was gay. I was standing in the spare bedroom of Mark's and my apartment on Cross Creek Trail in Brecksville, Ohio. I can't imagine how hard that call must have been for him. I wasn't shocked. It was good to know for certain, though, after having the idea nibble around the edges of my consciousness for a few years for the usual reasons. He'd had no dates or amorous mentions of girls. And he went dancing to techno music at the clubs on Lansdowne Street in Boston while wearing rubber shoes.

★ ★ ★

I finally knew for sure that Rich's roommate Ed Wood was more than just a roommate. Nineteen years later, Rich and Ed are still together, and in my mind are every bit as married as Mark and I, or Shelly and her husband, Mike, or my parents, despite the discrimination they face regarding marriage.

My dad, who was born in nineteen hundred and twenty-two (that's how he says it), accepted my brother and Ed. I will always respect and admire my dad for that. My mom's main concern was always for Richard's well-being. She worried about AIDS. She worried about discrimination. She grieved the loss of having a daughter-in-law and grandchildren "the traditional way." She never expressed worry to me about how having a gay son would reflect on her and my father.

My mom and dad taught me how to be a parent. They've been married for over fifty years. My parents' example of love and acceptance is why I've been able to cope with our challenges and remain married to Mark. I've no idea what keeps him with me except the bitter realization that being in your fifties, financially starting over, and having three kids with autism isn't the trophy wife magnet a man might think.

Whether it's the blessing of my middle-child syndrome or not, most people seem to appreciate my ability to add humor to a pretty grim topic. They seem to appreciate that I'm an outspoken mom, willing to put myself (and my family for better or worse) in the public eye. Even those who don't agree with my autism causation and treatment opinions will tell you I'm a "good mom." I try to reach out to others and build bridges where I can, despite disagreements. Sometimes I'm good at it. Sometimes I fail. Sometimes I'm in a snit and I don't bother to try at all—preferring to lob a grenade on Huffington Post or Age of Autism. The results of these grenades can be found all over the Internet: "Kim Stagliano's writing is pathetic" pops up on an obscure blog, and my stomach clenches. I've been called a bitch, a disgrace to journalism (I'm not a journalist and have never claimed to be), a rotten mother, and more. Nice, huh?

I won't stop chronicling life with three gorgeous girls with autism, even if I never get used to the criticism.

Luckily, I have my family to support me.

I wonder if my brother is up for a visit anytime soon? I'd better check to see if I have any pickles.

UP, UP, AND AWAY

ON OCTOBER 5, 2009, THE AMERICAN ACADEMY OF PEDIATRICS journal *Pediatrics* confirmed that the autism rate is now one in 110 children. Flags are not at half staff. The military is not in the streets. The mainstream media is showing signs of Xanax overdose in their reporting. No worry. Not a hint of panic. No hard questions as to why so many kids are neurologically impaired.

However, just a month before the *Pediatrics* study was published, a study came out from the National Health Service Information Centre in the United Kingdom that claimed the rate of autism among adults, according to their calculations is—drumroll please— one in 100 *adults*. That dovetails with the new American numbers better than the drawers in a Stickley dresser, doesn't it?

If you can convince the public that there are one in 100 *adults* on the spectrum, perhaps that's *always* been the rate of occurrence, even in America. Then you don't have an epidemic of a severe neurological disorder—you have better counting.

It appears that our doctors, mainly pediatricians, have simply gotten much better at recognizing and diagnosing youngsters who cannot speak correctly or at all. Who have socialization problems. Who would sooner look at the pattern in the floor tiles than their own mother. Brilliant, these doctors, aren't they?

Let me tell you—my childhood pediatrician, Dr. Germain, would not have missed autism in me or my siblings. *Dr. Doolittle* couldn't have missed autism.

★ ★ ★

Ah, Dr. Germain. I can still see his crew-cut hair and quick smile. I can feel his chilly hands. He terrified me, of course. I don't think doctors felt compelled to be terribly friendly in the 1960s, Marcus Welby notwithstanding. Dr. Germain demanded, and commanded respect. He had a paddle over the entrance to the examination rooms. On it was a painting of a boy and a girl bent over at the waist, with the words, "Board of Education." What's more shocking is that there wasn't even a Pfizer logo on it! Ah, good times seeing the pediatrician in 1969. He was forthright, direct, and smart. He would not have missed autism, even if he doubted what he was seeing due to its rarity at the time. And he wouldn't have been afraid to break the bad news, an excuse I hear often today about our pediatricians.

While I'm not quite in AARP territory, I'm no youngster. In fact, there was a song written to celebrate my birth, "Late December 1963 (Oh, What a Night)." All right, it was about some other special lady, but I was born on December 28, 1963, and the song made me smile as a kid—even though that special "night" would have been about nine months earlier for my parents.

I'm trying to remember which of my peers in my school, neighborhood, town had autism, or even Asperger's. I'm quite familiar with how those diagnoses look. I'm pretty sure I'm as good as a pediatrician at recognizing the signs. You can go grab a cup of coffee while I calculate the vast numbers of kids from my childhood who were affected.

Back so soon? I'd barely reached my eighth-grade classmates at Mercy Mount Country Day School in Cumberland, Rhode Island.

★ ★ ★

I remember Lonny Kane, who was a young adult with cognitive disabilities in my town. Lonny would have been labeled "multiple handicapped" in a school system today. I would guess that he had cerebral palsy and cognitive challenges. The kids at school made fun of him. Including me and my tap and jazz dancing pals

from The Young Sophisticates School of Dance (we were as sophisticated as kids could be eating Funny Bones, drinking Fresca, and dancing to the theme from *Rocky* in a town called Plainville, Massachusetts.)

I happen to be a stellar voice impersonator. I had Lonny's tone and cadence down to a science. I even squinted my eyes, bucked out my teeth, and contorted my posture. Ha! I had the full Lonny!

God, I was a mean kid. Worse, I was a mean kid with leadership qualities. And I didn't give a rat's patootey about authority. A charming combination. And yet, it's worked to my advantage as an adult struggling to help three children with autism. Go figure.

How rotten was I as a kid? How's this for being no Mother Teresa?

★ ★ ★

I always had to be the first to complete a test, to win the race around our small Catholic elementary school building, to do things better than my friends. I was better at getting in trouble, that's for sure.

In sixth grade (I was all of ten years old, having started first grade at five) my "boyfriend" Jack and I went on a field trip to the John Hynes auditorium in Boston for the Whole World Celebration. Whole World? We stuck with Russia and Cuba—he had packed a flask of vodka and cherry cigars. Of course, a Sister noticed my booze breath on the bus home and called my parents immediately. I was suspended from Dominican Academy for a few days.

Can you imagine what my parents thought of me? They must have been terrified I was on the fast track to Skid Row. Well, Mark and I did end up homeless, so maybe that wasn't a stretch.

As you can see, I'm not prone to shame—in fact I'm rather immune to it by now, having had enough autism moments with the girls to hold my head high under the most alarming circumstances.

I am ashamed that I made fun of Lonny. He didn't choose his lot in life. And I didn't do anything wonderful to end up neurotypical.

His parents were loving and kind and at his side every time I saw him. My mom told me Lonny's mom died, and his dad still takes care of him. Mr. K. must be quite elderly by now. It foreshadows my girls' future.

I have a second cousin about my age named Dawn who has profound cerebral palsy. She is a twin. I saw her sister Debbie several years ago at a family reunion. It pains me now, as an adult, that I didn't know her better or make an effort to understand what she was going through. I wonder if this is how my own children's cousins will feel about my kids? It's difficult to get to know my girls—due to geographic separation and the family quibbles and general life issues that distract us all. I worry that I should be training these boys and girls, my nieces and nephews, to love and look out for their cousins who did not dodge the autism bullet as deftly as they did.

Up the street from us lived Steve Welsh, who had Down syndrome. Always quick to grin, Steve now lives in a gorgeous Nantucket-style group home his mom had built on her own property. My mom still sees him in the area and he's doing well. His mom doesn't realize it, but she's a beacon of hope for me—I worry greatly about what will happen to Mia, Gianna, and Bella as Mark and I age. Seeing that Mrs. W. built a home for her son (and others) quite literally in her side yard gives me hope that we'll find creative, safe, and loving living options for our girls.

So that's three people with disabilities in the first twenty-one years of my life; none of them had autism. None of my friends had a sister or brother who was "institutionalized" as often happened back then.

When I graduated from Boston College in 1985, I went to work as an Assistant Account Executive at Hill, Holliday, Connors, and Cosmopoulos Advertising in Boston. I rode the bus from Newton Corner to the John Hancock Tower in the Back Bay. There was a man on that bus whom I believe had autism. He was about 5′7″and had dark hair with bangs that fell down his forehead. He was a bit chubby and walked with a rolling gait. He could see, but his head moved

around like Stevie Wonder's and his eyes usually looked upward. He had a man with him, perhaps an aide or another sort of paid helper. I remember thinking that the helper was a terrific guy for hanging with this poor soul. At the time I was a twenty-one-year-old YIT (yuppie in training) wearing Belle France dresses to work and dining on turkey and Boursin herb cheese sandwiches at Au Bon Pain each day. I looked at this man as a tragic figure—but not much more.

A few years ago, when I learned that there were people questioning the idea of an autism epidemic, who believed we simply had better diagnosis, the image of this man on the bus whose name I never knew burst into my memory. The only words I ever heard him utter were, "It's Wednesday! It's Wednesday! It's Wednesday!"

★ ★ ★

Calendars can be a source of fascination, perseveration, and perhaps routine comfort for people on the spectrum. My daughter Gianna is very in tune with the calendar. I can ask her on any given day, "Gi, what day is it?" and she'll tell me.

By the age of twenty-one I had come into contact with a person somewhat older than myself who had autism. One person. Not one of my friends in grammar school, junior high, or prep school had a sibling with autism.

One of my dear friends is Ginny G., who, as a teenager, was my babysitter. I'd told her boyfriend at the time that he was ugly. What an angel I was. Ginny attended teachers' college and went into special education. I've had long talks with Ginny about her career and what she knew about autism back in the early seventies. In a nutshell, she was taught that autism was rare. And she saw only a handful of students with the diagnosis.

Ginny is now a grandmother of three little girls and a grandson. One her granddaughters has an autism diagnosis, Pervasive Developmental Disorder—Not Otherwise Specified (PDD-NOS). Another has some sensory issues.

Ask any special education teacher over the age of forty-five how many kids with autism they had in their classrooms, whether in public school or the old state school systems back before inclusion was an option, and they're going to tell you, "One. Two. None." Now go ask a special education teacher who's been teaching for five years the same question and then stand back.

I recently struck up a conversation with two women while seated at the bar waiting for a table at a restaurant on Cape Cod. Mia had sort of gotten in their faces with her greeting, which can startle people. She rubs her hands and puts her face close to yours and makes a humming noise. The two women were very kind to her. When we were seated, I thanked them for being nice to Mia and explained she has autism. Their response, "Oh, we knew, we're former teachers." I seized the opportunity to ask them if they'd seen many students with autism during their careers. "One," said the first. "No," offered her friend.

When Autism Speaks came onto the scene in 2005, the rate used by CDC was one in 166, recently up from one in 250. That was a huge jump from the numbers in the 1970s and 1980s. Then in 2007 the number increased to one in 150. Now, in 2009, the number is a confirmed one in 110.

Today, we have entire schools devoted to teaching children on the spectrum. Tomorrow we're going to need high-rise apartments to provide safe residences for many of them. I'm hopeful that a good number will recover and lose their diagnosis, going on to lead full, independent lives, get jobs, and pay taxes. It seems the young kids who are being diagnosed today are responding well to intense therapy and treatment. That's a bit of hope in an otherwise depressing circumstance.

We become immune to numbers. Five soldiers killed in Iraq. (I'd like a Venti latte). Another child was beaten to death by a peer in Chicago. (Did you watch *Mad Men* last night?) One in 110 American children has autism.

Do you care?

DON'T ASK. DON'T TELL.

A COUPLE OF YEARS AGO, I WAS ON A PANEL AT ELMS COLLEGE IN Chicopee, Massachusetts. John Elder Robison, who wrote *Look Me in the Eye* about his life with undiagnosed Asperger's growing up in the same household as his brother Augusten Burroughs (who wrote *Running with Scissors*), was the headliner. I was in the chorus, and just happy to share the stage with him. He's one of my favorite people, and my first adult friend with Asperger's.

How I survived forty-three years without running into a whole lot of Aspergians is beyond me, considering the drumbeat in the media and some research circles to convince the world that autism, in its myriad presentations from low functioning to Aspergian savant has always been with us at the current rate. Autism can include a person who doesn't speak and appears to be severely mentally challenged, living in his or her own world, rocking back and forth, and someone like John Elder Robison, who has had several successful careers, is articulate, is probably a genius, and who lives what most of us would call an enviably comfortable, "normal" life.

Heck, I worked for one of the geekiest high-technology companies in America and cannot recall anyone on the spectrum there. That company was Bolt Beranek and Newman, in Cambridge, Massachusetts. With apologies to Al Gore, BBN is the company that really did help create the Internet; they designed the "Arpanet" for the United States Army in the sixties.

I'd just been fired from my position as an Assistant Account Executive at Hill Holliday Connors & Cosmopulos, purportedly

due to budget cuts on one of my accounts. I think it was because I screwed up a media insertion and ran a full-page major product announcement ad for Lotus Development (remember Lotus 1-2-3 software?) in the *Wall Street Journal* on the *wrong day.* Ouch.

I wish they'd been straight up with me about why I was fired; I could have learned something other than humiliation and how to apply for unemployment. I now know that firings rarely come with explanations. I sure didn't ask them for details. I just trudged home, shell-shocked.

Anyway, my friend's mom needed a new assistant at BNN. Her old one had just left to work at Boston Technology making some pie-in-the-sky new product called "voice mail," which no one was ever going to use, what with the ubiquity of the pretty young receptionist in every corporate lobby in America. I had high-tech marketing experience and so she hired me. After working at Boston's largest ad agency, joining BBN Software was akin to being in charge of watching paint dry for Sherwin-Williams.

BBN Software made a product called RS1, a number cruncher for manufacturers. Their glitzy product was ClinTrial, which ran statistical analyses on pharmaceutical company clinical trials. The place should have been crawling with autistics, eyes averted, mumbling about trains, and lining up the peas on the cafeteria trays.

I can remember the product manager who used to sit/stand/mount the edge of his desk, posing in a manner he might have thought was provocative. The young female marketing team thought he was repulsive. I can see the face of the VP of marketing, who later lost his job and appeared on a national program about the difficulty of finding a new job when you're over fifty. I got to know his pain all too well twenty years later. And I'll never forget the wonderful, larger-than-life gal whose water broke in the bathroom—turning me into an instant midwife as I escorted her down to a waiting ambulance. ("God, please don't let her get that stuff on my new shoes!")

I can't recall a single employee with autism. And my memory is very good. That doesn't mean they weren't there, so don't go sending me hate mail. Perhaps they were not in visible positions.

Today, when I go out, I often find that other family with an autistic child. It's like having gaydar for autism. Do I ask them about their child? Do I tell them about my own?

I hesitate to do more than make eye contact with the parent, smile, and nod. You never know if the child has a diagnosis or not, and I'm sure not going to spill the beans to a mom or dad who hasn't heard the fateful words yet. For starters, I'm not qualified. Am I accurate? You bet. Most of us in the autism world can spot another child from across the mall.

You just know by the walk, the face, and the way the parents act around the child. Sometimes the smile and knowing nod leads to a conversation. Kind of like a foot shove under the stalls in the men's bathroom. Except not quite so intimate.

While the autism epidemic took off in the 1990s, there *are* older people with autism. I don't want to imply that I believe otherwise. That's disrespectful to the parents who've come before me and fought like heck so that my girls can attend school and have services.

Last summer, Mark and I had taken the girls to Sunny Dae's ice cream in our town. We brought our dairy-free ice cream for Bella and digestive enzymes for Mia and Gianna, ready to enjoy as typical an outing as is possible. Taking the kids into any public location is like herding cats, but we manage, and the familiarity of Sunny Dae's is easier than trying someplace new.

I sat down with Mia and Bella, while Mark and Gianna went to place our order. At the next table was a beautiful woman, with patrician cheekbones, a sweep of dark hair, and an elegant count-enance. Next to her was an equally beautiful younger woman who instantly reminded me of Mia. How can I describe what tipped me off? Well, she was at one with her ice cream. I don't mean that she was messy or inappropriate, she simply was concentrating on her

treat to the exclusion of her mom seating next to her. She just had "the look." A bell went off in my head; *Whoop! Whoop!* Autism at twelve o'clock!

★ ★ ★

The woman and I made eye contact and smiled at each other. The dance began. She spotted autism in my girls as fast I recognized autism in her own. At that point, it's a matter of who leaves the gate first. I did. Of course.

"Hi, this is Mia and Bella. Mia reminds me of your daughter. Does she have ..." I try not to label my kids or others in public where they can hear me. The mom knew what I meant.

"Yes, she does," she answered, with a European accent.

"My name is Kim Stagliano, it's nice to meet you."

"My name is Sophia Moldavi."

"I know you, Sophia, we've e-mailed each other many times!"

Sophia runs an organization in Greenwich, Connecticut, and is creating a farm for adults with autism, like her own beautiful daughter. She gives me hope and scares the hell out of me at the same time. Her daughter is approaching forty. I can barely think to when Mia turns twenty.

That brings me to a question I've been asked: "If you suspect a child has undiagnosed autism, do you tell the mom or dad?" I've already given you my short answer. "No." But that's not completely accurate. I did once tell a parent.

★ ★ ★

I was at a Silpada Jewelry party at my neighbor's house in Hudson. The night before, Matt G., the handsomest dad in the neighborhood (next to Mark, of course), was walking while pulling his young son in a Little Tikes wagon. I was in the driveway when he walked past our house. I heard him say, "Use your words, Jay!" in a stern, exasperated voice.

My heart dropped.

I knew the family and that the boy was having difficulty with behavior. His dad just told me that the boy also had autism.

I flashed back to a park in Doylestown when Mia was maybe seventeen months old. She loved to swing, like most toddlers. I'd give her a push while saying, "Push, Mia!" with a big smile on my face—willing Mia to talk to me, not just at me. I'd let the swing stop, hoping Mia would tell me to push her again. She could speak. She had words. I knew that she could say "push."

But she wouldn't utter a sound. She just stared at me. Her eyes that so closely matched my own, were blank, as if telepathy was enough for her.

That was one of my first warning signs that all was not well for Mia. And I'd used the exact words with her that I'd heard Mike say to his son: "Use your words, Mia!"

★ ★ ★

Mike's wife, Cheryl, was at the Silpada party. She was a special education teacher and a damn good one. But like the doctor who smokes, sometimes when a situation hits so close to home, it's hard to see. Cheryl is a beautiful woman, with sleek, blond, coiffed hair and perfectly applied makeup. At that party, her face looked pinched and her eyes tired.

Should I tell her? What would happen to our friendship if I shared my concerns? What would happen to the child if I did not?

I quietly approached her and said, "I heard Mike walk by with Jay last night. He sounded really frustrated. I wanted to ask you if you've considered maybe having him tested for an autism diagnosis?"

Then I waited. Would I get a glass of white wine thrown at me? Would she slap my face? Storm off in a huff?

"You know, Kim. I have. And I'm so glad you mentioned it. . . ."

Wow. From there we had a really good talk. Cheryl is a great mom to Jay. And Jay is doing well. He has Asperger's Syndrome, is a funny

kid, earnest to a fault, smart as a whip—and getting the services he needs.

★ ★ ★

Today, in my position as a writer and blogger, I get e-mails from strangers, "My grandson isn't talking, and he's almost two. The pediatrician says it's because he's a boy, but I'm concerned." I want to bang my head on my desk when I read that tired response from doctors.

On one hand, experts tell us better diagnosis is behind the rising autism rates. On the other hand, I'm still hearing from parents and loved ones of kids who are clearly not developing properly that they struggle to get a diagnosis.

I try to answer as gently as I can, without instilling false hope. "Trust your gut," is my usual answer. "Don't jump to conclusions, call Early Intervention, check out the GFCF diet for GI issues," rounds out my suggestion.

Sometimes the call or e-mail is not from a stranger. Those especially make my heart sink. Like the twenty-seven-year-old woman whose wedding Mark and I had celebrated just a few years ago, who e-mailed me a laundry list of issues in her seven-month-old that made my knuckles turn white on the computer mouse and my heart drop. The child had severe reflux, could not eat, had not learned to sit up or roll over, and was not babbling.

"What do you think, Kim?"

First off, I admired the mom for having the balls to ask me. That's a good sign, for the child most of all. Mom isn't hiding and is taking her daughter's health into her own hands.

But honestly, how do you answer when someone you care about says, "What do you think?" Am I supposed to be honest and say: I think the child is on the bullet train to Autismland? I could never say that to a young parent. Hope is too important. Not denial—hope. There's a difference.

★ ★ ★

Autism is a frog-in-the-pot diagnosis. The water heats up around you and then starts to burn. It's not my place to plunge mom into that pot. With enough intervention, a child can fight off or lose the diagnosis. I'd rather get Mom started on progress than simply scare her to death.

We don't know what medical advances there might be in just a year or two. I want Mom to get cracking and feel productive, not despondent.

I suggest Web sites like the National Autism Association and Talk About Curing Autism (that alone gives Mom some idea of what I'm thinking) and I try to point her to some experts in her area including Early Intervention. My goal is to help, not to horrify. I know that by the time a young parent has asked me for my opinion, she's already aware of a problem. But every developmentally delayed child does not have autism. Although, when I hear about severe GI problems along with gross motor and speech delays, I see a red flag the size of a football field.

In addition to better diagnosis, we're told autism is genetic. In fact, I'm often held up as the "poster child" for the genetics of autism, because all three girls are considered on the spectrum. Let's take a look at the Rossi Stagliano genetics. Mark's siblings have four boys and two girls between them. My sister has one son. There's no autism, even in the boys. There have been some scares—a seizure disorder in one, a strange fainting syncope in another, some weight issues for a couple—but I'm grateful none of the Stagliano sibs or my sister has to go through what their brother and I and their nieces live with every day. All of these kids are smart as whips and excellent students. I know my girls are smart, too—I just don't know why they fell to autism.

I realize that ten kids do not make a proper statistical sample (see, my time at BBN Software paid off) but even when I expand up the branches of our family trees, there's no autism in sight. My dad is one of nine children. I have over twenty Rossi cousins. No autism.

My mom's mother, my Grandma Yoli (short for Yolanda), was one of ten children. My grandmother was alive when Mia and Gianna were diagnosed, and while she was not well educated, she was sharp and bright and never had a single story of an "odd" relative who may have been sent away to a home like the Kennedy child named Rosemary. My mom is one of four children who collectively have six children of their own. No autism. Even among the second cousins, there is no autism to be found. On Mark's side of the family there are also dozens of cousins, both Staglianos and Mackeys. No autism.

Genetics only? Better diagnosis only? No way. That's nothing more than a patronizing pat on the head.

★ ★ ★

I'm going to ask *Why, What, How,* and *Who* until my voice is raspy and my fingertips bloodied from pounding the keyboard. What caused my girls to become autistic? Why is no one else in our family affected?

"Don't ask, don't tell" doesn't work for the U.S. military. And it sure doesn't work for autism.

ANOTHER NIGHT IN THE HOLIDAY INN EXPRESS

I WISH THIS WERE A CHAPTER ABOUT TAKING VACATION. IF IT were, then I'd make another wish—that it was about staying at a fancy Ritz-Carlton or Four Seasons hotel, no offense intended to the Holiday Inn Express chain. And as long as I was wrapping myself in champagne wishes and caviar (yuck, make that choco-late) dreams, just Mark and I would be at this luxury hotel, looking out the window of our suite at the Eiffel Tower, lit from top to bottom on a clear Paris night. Of course, if any of that were true, I'd be reading someone else's book, not writing my own.

With an autism diagnosis, every day is another day in the Holiday Inn Express, where you have to become the expert whether you have a GED or a PhD.

In 1999, when Mia and Gianna were diagnosed in Cleveland, Ohio, we didn't get a treatment plan of any sort. We were told to continue with the public schools, because the girls were three and four years of age. We did that, and the girls got some benefit from being among other children and receiving an hour or two of speech and occupa-tional therapy a week. I had never heard of Applied Behavior Analysis (ABA) therapy for autism. And the folks at University Hospitals of Cleveland were handing out autism articles a decade old, so they weren't exactly a go-to resource for current treatment. Our wealthy suburban school district, like many, was just waking up to the need for autism programming in their system, and they didn't offer ABA.

Because of this, for many years I didn't think ABA was very valuable. In fact, I shunned it. Had my girls been diagnosed in California, ABA would have been built into their school program without my having to ask. And they would have made more progress and learned more skills before entering kindergarten. I'm not big on regrets, but I can admit to mistakes. I should have pursued ABA for them.

I didn't do much better with Bella. Early Intervention in Summit County, Ohio, was sketchy, and my growing mistrust of medical and school services stood in the way of taking advantage of the programs they offered. The kind woman who did our intake mentioned that Bella might have mild cerebral palsy. That nearly stopped my heart. I could handle developmental delay. I knew autism. CP? No.

I was an idiot.

I should have let Early Intervention give any and every service to Bella, if only to engage her and keep her little body limber. Mia was in the throes of her seizure disorder, and I left Bella to her own devices (motherly euphemism for I ignored her) far too often.

There's a wonderful writer/journalist named Karl Taro Greenfeld. His older brother Noah has classic autism, and his father, Josh Greenfeld, wrote three books about Noah in the 1970s and 1980s. In 2009, Kart wrote a follow-up book called *Boy Alone* about what it was like to grow up with a sibling who was profoundly disabled by a disease that was virtually unknown at the time.

I had the pleasure of meeting with Karl for a few hours one morning in New York as he was writing his book. I read his dad's three books before our meeting.

★ ★ ★

I was blown away by the fact that so little had changed within the autism world since Noah had been diagnosed. Close to forty years had passed, and I, upon getting my girls' diagnosis, was in the same position that Karl's parents had faced decades earlier.

No treatment plan.

No hope.

No cure.

Karl's parents took matters into their own hands, finding every treatment they could for Noah. If you've read *Boy Alone* (and you should), you know that Noah remains within his profound autism despite the intense treatment and the love of his parents, who I consider the very first Parent Warriors. Karl faced the decision that thousands of Americans will confront in the next decades as caretaker for an adult sibling with autism along with aging parents.

He moved his family from New York to California to care for his brother, in an act of unselfishness few will be able to match.

Into the new millennium, I and countless other parents had to do the same thing as Josh and Foumi Greenfeld—blaze a path for our kids using whatever tools we could find or afford.

The young parents I meet online and at conferences have more access to information thanks to the computer. Jenny McCarthy calls it "attending the University of Google." But that doesn't necessarily make life any easier, as it's nearly impossible to sift through the treatment choices, analyze them, figure out which ones might work best for your child and how you can pay for them—all while taking care of a child who is likely a difficult toddler.

There are books galore on every sort of therapy and treatment. Most of the options are expensive. Few are covered by insurance. Even as states add insurance mandates, I'm not hopeful they'll stick. Once Aetna and United Healthcare and Kaiser realize they have to spend $50,000-plus per year for a child with autism, I fear they'll find a way to unload our kids from their plans. Diagnoses will likely slow down as doctors are told to put the brakes on the financial strain of autism on the insurance system. Kids will suffer.

★ ★ ★

To muddy matters further, the treatment communities themselves are at odds with each other. The ABA-only folks cling to the "scientifically proven" label like a life preserver, despite studies that show ABA is not a panacea. The biomedical treatment folks (my crowd) has its own share of zealots, some touting treatments that make even a veteran like me roll my eyes as I imagine dollars swirling down a drain.

A diagnosing doctor will probably tell you that your two-year-old needs twenty-plus hours of ABA a week, because of that "scientifically proven" label. Good luck obtaining that level of service in any strapped Early Intervention program, or finding and funding it yourself. A couple of years ago, when Mark was actively looking for a job, I spent a lot of time on Monster.com trying to help him. I ran across a job in Massachusetts that depressed the heck out of me. A family was advertising for a full-time ABA therapist for their youngster with autism, and the salary was $50,000 a year. Can you imagine paying $50,000 a year out of pocket?!

★ ★ ★

Let's say a parent chooses to see a doctor who specializes in the medical treatment of autism—a doctor from Defeat Autism Now!, part of the Autism Research Institute in California that was founded by Dr. Bernard Rimland, who also was a cofounder of the Autism Society of America. (Generation Rescue also has a list of doctors who are treating autism.) You'll walk into the office full of hope, as these doctors are treating the medical conditions that accompany autism, and some of their patients are dropping the diagnosis. You'll walk out of the office a couple of thousand dollars lighter when you account for the visit, lab work, and prescriptions and supplements you'll need. Can you afford to spend that kind of money? Your child's future is at stake. Can you afford *not* to?

Back in the days of home equity loans, easy credit, and padded 401(k) accounts, these decisions were a bit easier because you could

find the money to pay for the options you selected. When the economy tanked and so many Americans lost jobs, those cash sources turned off like wells gone dry. This has only added to parents' frustration.

I'm sure parents whose kids have other serious diagnoses, like cancer, muscular dystrophy, or cystic fibrosis, also have to make a whole lot of agonizing decisions on behalf of their child. Some of those may involve life and death. As much as I worry about my kids, I know that they are basically healthy and well. I can kiss them goodnight, every night, and know that the next day, they will awaken. I don't take that for granted.

★ ★ ★

On the flip side, I think there's less tolerance, understanding, and sympathy for my kids and for the autism community in general. We don't have a Ronald McDonald House or Make-A-Wish Foundation. When was the last time your church or synagogue organized a fund-raiser for a child who was just diagnosed with autism?

When I gave birth to Bella, Mark and I ate like a king and his queen for two straight weeks with hot dishes appearing magically at the door nightly at five o'clock. Five months later, when Mia's seizures began and I was struggling with two youngsters with autism and a newborn, the phone never rang, the doorbell was silent. Playgroup moms do not sign up to make a month of homemade dinners so that mother of a newly diagnosed child can have a break.

As a parent, I want the public to know how tough autism is for the entire family, most of all for the kids. I want Autism Speaks to stop running ads showing towheaded boys in Abercrombie outfits looking sad because they will never play baseball for the New York Yankees while standing alone on a cul-de-sac in New Canaan, Connecticut. I want to see a twelve-year-old boy in the middle of a rage. I want the world to see the mom who has a fat lip from her daughter who lashed out during a sensory meltdown. I know far too many people who clean feces off their walls every single day and whose children

sleep on a plain mattress on the floor, not in a bedroom that looks like a page from the Pottery Barn Kids catalog.

This is the reality of autism for thousands of families.

★ ★ ★

To their credit, Autism Speaks has shown the underbelly of autism, in the movie *Autism Every Day*. And they took heat from many high-functioning folks with autism who were offended by the portrayal of parents struggling with their kids.

On the flip side, I don't want people to hear "autism" and either fear or hate our kids. There has been a spate of newspaper reports of crimes and arrests where the word autism is thrown into the headline like chum into the water. Autism is not synonymous with violence. Autism does not mean "danger to society." Soon after Seung Hui Cho, the angry student who strafed the Virginia Tech campus with bullets, killing thirty-two people, the rumblings began, "Did he have Asperger's?" I immediately wrote a Huffington Post piece decrying the quick assumption among so many.

I've made a cancer analogy in the past and have taken heat for it. I don't give a crap. Autism is like cancer. Not literally, but in terms of *perception*. Let's say your father calls you on the phone and says, "I found out today that I have early stage prostate cancer." Now imagine if he said, "I found out today that I have pancreatic cancer." Those two sentences invoke a different set of assumptions. Prostate cancer is treatable. You hang up the phone and worry. Pancreatic cancer is a death sentence. You hang up the phone and vomit.

How do we walk that tightrope of wanting the public to understand the good, the bad, and yes, the ugliness of autism, while maintaining respect and dignity for our loved ones? They need help, not hatred. God, I'm starting to sound like a bumper sticker.

★ ★ ★

Autism has become a blanket term for every inch of the spectrum from the most severely affected to the highest functioning success story with Asperger's. I think that's a mistake. It denies the gravity of diagnosis for many, and could paint someone like my friend John Robison with the wrong brush.

Welcome to the Holiday Inn Express known as an autism diagnosis. Don't forget to tip your maid. Checkout time is at . . .

DOES HEROIN FEEL
THIS GOOD?

TODAY IS JANUARY 4, 2010, THE FIRST DAY OF SCHOOL AFTER THE interminable holiday break. Yes, interminable. As in, "Mommy loves you, but, my God, are you children still here and where *is* that school bus?" I cannot fill ten days of break with meaningful, engaging play-time or work time for three children with autism. I cry uncle!

Because God really does have a sick sense of humor, we had a 90-minute delay for cold weather today. Cold weather? We live in Connecticut, not North Carolina. Twenty-degree weather and blue skies on the Monday we finally, finally, finally get the kids back to school does not say, "Oh stay home for another hour and a half, kids!" to me. However, I don't make those decisions. Perhaps the superintendent got a Snuggie for Christmas and simply couldn't bear to un-Snug himself at five thirty this morning.

Telling my girls that we have a school opening delay means nothing to them. When they wake up, they wake up. There's no settling back down into the bed for another hour. For any of us.

I don't blame them for being eager to go back to school. School is much more fun than home. Mia kept saying, "Time for Miss Jianine. Time for Miss Laura." Gianna was gearing up for her after-school Connections Club and for swimming class on Tuesday where she could play the new game she made up. "The drowning game." Yeah, Gianna is using her imagination, which is a huge leap forward for a child on the spectrum. She invented a game where she drowns

and her friend Vicky has to save her. She spent weeks last Fall saying, "Vicky! Vicky! Help! Gianna is stuck!" before I finally asked her teacher what on earth had happened in the pool. Hey, she was alive. She had not drowned. I wasn't that concerned. With autism you have to choose your worries with care. The report back from school was, "It's a game she made up. She pretends to get stuck and Vicky frees her." That's fabulous progress. But really, couldn't the next game be something a little less Addams Family and a bit more Cleaver? Nah, not in our household.

Bella, meanwhile, my sweet little Bella, spent much of the vacation heaving her purple Land's End backpack at me, which was every bit as effective as saying, "Ma! Get me back in school!" Hint taken. I'd put the backpack into the front hall closet. She'd retrieve it and hurl it at me. Ah, good times, holiday break.

By 9:27 this morning (but who's keeping track?) all three girls were safely on their buses on their way to school.

A-freaking-men.

"This must be what heroin feels like," I thought to myself as I closed the front door and made a beeline for the coffeepot to see if there was any left. It was a new year, and things were good.

On December 15, 2009, Mark got a commission check that would choke a horse. A small horse. Okay, more of a pony than a horse really. For us, anything bigger than an unemployment check looked damn good. It meant we'd survived the worst financial year we'd ever faced. And the pipeline, now opened, was going to flow freely with steady income.

We had the best Christmas I can recall in years. And not just because we had a few shekels to buy presents. My sister's stepsons, Mac and Sean, decided to spend Christmas with Grandma and Grandpa in New England and flew in from Texas. This meant that for the first time, we were all together in my childhood home. Mark, the girls and me, Shelly and Mike and their son Colin, plus Mac and Sean, Rich and Ed, and my parents. My dad is in his late

eighties. It was such a blessing to be together at the end of what had been a really tough year. My folks couldn't stop smiling.

Christmas morning arrived. Mark handed me a jewelry box. I hadn't seen one of those since our ninth wedding anniversary in 2000. (I can't count the paper mitten bracelet given to me by the church angels in 2008.)

Inside was a pair of diamond earrings in a design called The Everlon Knot. *"The Everlon Knot is the strength of love forged in an endless unfailing knot. It is a symbol that even in the toughest of times— especially in the toughest of times—the strength of your love will never waver."*

Perfect.

The Everlon Knot is a marketing ploy, of course, created to convince men it's okay to buy jewelry even in a bad economy. I'd considered myself impervious to ad campaigns for jewelry, like those silly right-hand diamond ring ads, *"For me."* But those Knot ads got me. What woman wouldn't fall for this after the years Mark and I had weathered?

I placed the earrings into my ears and admired the sparkle in the mirror, thinking that Mother Teresa was right. God will only give you what you can handle.

But it's really nice when your husband gives you diamonds.

I'm wearing the earrings now as I'm listening to Howard Stern and wondering where Artie Lange has gone. Most of us fans assumed rehab, since there was no death announcement, and he's an admitted heroin addict. I guess that's why I have heroin on my mind this morning. I don't do heroin, in case you're wondering or my mother is reading this. Never have. The only white powders in my house are Johnson and Johnson Lavender, Bob's Red Mill Arrowroot, and Clabber Girl cornstarch. Promise.

I wonder what I'll do with my kid-free morning. Maybe read a book. I read several memoirs over the last year or two. I wanted to channel some of the magic into my own book. (Of course, I've

written a Kimoir, not a memoir. Isn't that catchy? It makes me feel less old. You can roll your eyes if you'd like.)

I avoided depressing memoirs and stuck with memoirs by comedians, to see how they balanced the funny and the heartfelt. I never wanted this book to be maudlin, or as my dad would say, a "Me poor lady" book. I want understanding, mostly for my kids. I want help, entirely for my kids. I do not want pity. My life may be different from what I'd expected, and my kids' issues are severe, I get that. But I'm happy. Genuinely happy. I wouldn't trade my girls for three little Olympians or *American Idol* wannabees, or the smarty pants kids who get those letters saying that because of their stellar performance on the state tests, they've been invited by the Abe Lincoln Foundation to travel to Australia to study the habitat of the Aboriginal Boola Boola bird if I'll please just send in a $3,000 deposit. Don't laugh. Mia has gotten that letter every year since fifth grade because the schools modify the state test for her. One of these years, I'm packing her bag and sending her to the airport just to see what the tour guides will do. I smell a civil rights lawsuit!

Sarah Palin's *Going Rogue* was not on my list of "must read" books, despite its popularity. I prefer to laugh *with*, not *at*. I read Kathy Griffin's *My Life on the D List,* Howie Mandel's *Here's the Deal: Don't Touch Me.* Neither made me want to pop Prozac like Certs, which struck me as a very good thing. Both made me laugh out loud.

I could hang with Kathy Griffin. And she'd like me, because even though she is older than I am (meow) she looks a lot youn—well, maybe not younger, but a lot more plasticky than I do, and that implies youth, which is good enough for many women.

Later that January I was in Trader Joe's shopping for groceries. A little boy who resembled that itty-bitty chicken hawk kid in the Looney Tunes cartoons (big head, short, glasses) looked up at me as I pawed around for gluten-free waffles and said, "Hi. I'm four years old, and my name is Noah."

(Kids who do not have autism boggle my mind.)

I looked straight at him and said, "Hi, I'm forty-six years old, and my name is Kim. Happy New Year, Noah."

Not sure if his parents were tickled pink at their son's precocious introduction or horrified that I answered him. They hightailed it over to the organic yak milk.

DR. WAKEFIELD AND
THE ANTI-VAXXERS

(Good name for a chapter about the autism/vaccine controversy.
Bad name for a Motown band circa 1968.)

LATELY, MY "KIM STAGLIANO" GOOGLE SEARCHES TURN UP THE phrases, "anti-vaccine" and "anti-vaxxer." Despite the fact that I vaccinated my two older girls fully when they were younger and have never told a parent, "Do not ever vaccinate your child," I have been branded with the "anti-vaccine" label.

It's a great label if you want to make a quick point and box me into a mythical category for a sound bite. "Oh, Kim Stagliano? She's that anti-vaxxer lady who runs that 'anti-vaccine' Web site called Age of Autism." It's the equivalent of calling those who are pro-choice "pro-abortion baby killers," even though many folks who are pro-choice, like me, are personally pro-life. As long as we're going down Controversy Street, let's take a left turn into Abortion Alley for a second.

Mark and I had one of our favorite priests over for dinner on a Friday night. As I stood at the stove, I felt like Carmela Soprano, who used to cook for her priest to compete with the other ladies from church. I prepared eggplant and veal parmagiana and baked a chocolate pistachio cake, Mark's favorite.

I had never invited a priest into my home. He arrived at our front door wearing a pair of jeans and a sweater. No collar. He's a regular guy with a quick wit. That he can perform the Last Rites in case you

keel over in front of him is a plus, too. He blessed our house and gave the girls three beautiful pink crosses that now hang on our walls.

Because I am incapable of normal conversation, I managed to weave abortion into our dinner conversation. Thank God Mark knows the Heimlich maneuver. (Kidding, Father Dunn is used to my blunt talk and even managed to swallow a bite of veal and a very large swig of wine as I was talking.)

Here's my abortion story: The doctor who delivered Isabella also delivered Mia six years earlier, when we first lived in Cleveland, Ohio, prior to moving to Bucks County, Pennsylvania. We had an excellent relationship, which is to say that I had a monstrous crush on him. He was handsome, charming, South African (oh, the accent), and partially responsible for ending the agony of labor and making sure all my parts were back in their right place after delivering Mia. What's not to love?

Dr. P. had a son with severe ADHD. I had two very young girls newly diagnosed with autism, which I told him about at my first prenatal visit. He had firsthand knowledge of the difficulty of raising a child with neuro issues. In fact, he knew far more than I did about what I was facing. At that visit, he said, "You know, Kim. You have choices for this pregnancy."

Whoa. I cocked my head, unsure of what I'd heard. Choices? Oh, right—"choices."

Of course, he was telling me that if I didn't think I could handle a third child, because of the difficult road I faced with Mia and Gianna, I could terminate my pregnancy.

"No, Dr. P., I appreciate your concern and your medical information," (he was not pressuring or counseling me in any way, just informing me) "but I'll have this baby regardless of our circumstances with Mia and Gigi."

Bella bounced into the dining room as we were eating—the perfect exclamation point to my "so, Father, let me tell you about the day I was offered an abortion" story.

The good father smiled at Bella and said I had a beautiful pro-life story. And I suppose I do. I know of a woman who became pregnant with triplets via in vitro fertilization, but who aborted one of the fetuses, preferring to have only twins. That shocked me, and still does. But I know that there are instances when a woman might have to make the choice for less selfish reasons. I also know a certain mother who might have to make that choice for her daughters.

If Mia, Gianna, and/or Bella were, well, you know, imagine what could happen to a beautiful woman with a communication disorder—in the care of God knows who throughout her fertile years. I would not require my daughters to bear a child. I think the topic is supremely personal and unless faced with the choice, most women don't even know what they would do, despite what you might imagine beforehand. It's easy to say, "I'd never!" and I believe that never is best. But I don't live in a black-and-white world.

I feel the same way about vaccination. Every parent has to do their own homework and consult with their pediatrician to determine family history, possible allergies to ingredients (the flu vaccine is grown on a chicken egg), and other contraindications that might necessitate altering the pediatric vaccine schedule. Does that sound like crazy talk to you? I sure don't think so. How is "look before you leap" unsound advice?

Mainstream pediatricians have counseled parents on how to best alter the vaccine schedule to their children's needs. Dr. Bob Sears wrote a book called *The Vaccine Book* that helps parents to learn if, when, and how to revise the current vaccination schedule for their own child's health. He's hardly a zealot or fringe physician.

We've moved often enough that the girls have had at least five pediatricians since their autism diagnosis, and none has ever rejected us because of my views on vaccination. I always approach the topic from a position of informed choice and medical history. All three of my girls have autism and have had at least one seizure. Based on that

information, I share that I am uncomfortable vaccinating Gianna and Mia beyond the shots they'd gotten from birth to ages three and four respectively and that I understand the gravity of my decision. I do everything but kneel down on the floor and beg for their forgiveness. A little humility goes a long way. My New York City cabdriver whose cab I took one day had a little sign on his glove box that read, A HOSTILE ATTITUDE PROVOKES A HOSTILE RESPONSE. I try to remember that phrase, and while I fail miserably at times, when it comes to my kids, I can bite my tongue.

When the H1N1 virus hit America in the spring of 2009, I was very concerned that this new virus could severely sicken my children—young children were thought to be the most vulnerable. I did not rule out the possibility of giving them the vaccination. I was genuinely concerned when the outbreak first hit our shores.

America's parents were exposed to a media frenzy of fear that suggested the flu would kill our kids. The vaccine hit the scene faster than McDonald's can pump out hamburgers. People who wouldn't buy an iPhone in its first model year rolled up their sleeves and their kids' sleeves, too.

We did not give the girls the H1N1 vaccination, nor (fortunately) did they become ill. I know several families whose kids were thought to have contracted the H1N1 flu (there was no formal testing), but they had mild to moderate symptoms and, fortunately, all recovered just fine.

My best friend in the world gave her daughter Gardasil (so much for my incredible negative influence on parents). I did not, having been contacted by numerous mothers whose daughters have had severe reactions, including death. Now young men are starting to feel the adverse side effects as this "cervical cancer" vaccine is re-marketed to boys, who, if you recall your seventh-grade health class, do not have cervixes.

What do you do if you don't feel it's safe to give your infant or child all of the vaccines at once but you still want the child to go to day care and then school? There are religious, philosophical, and medical exemptions that vary from state to state. My kids have been in public school in three states without being fully vaccinated for their age group, and with no problems. I agree that if there is an outbreak of an infectious disease, I will remove my children from school. Voilà. You can go to the National Vaccine Information Center (www.nvic.org) to find out the available exemptions in your state.

We have vaccine exemptions for a reason. Not every human on earth can handle every vaccine in existence without any risk of side effects. We've grown to think of vaccines as innocuous jabs that protect us without question. Criminy, you can get a flu jab at the Giant Eagle grocery store from a twelve-dollar-an-hour nurse's aide while you run in to pick up milk and bread. What happens if you have an adverse reaction at home? Are you going to scoot back into the store and ask the checkout clerk for help? The butcher? The baby formula and sinus medication are sold behind the counter, but vaccines are dosed like water.

It's something to think about.

Schools are paid per shot administered when they become vaccine clinics, too, and that especially galls me. A girl can't bring in a Midol pill for cramps without being suspended for a drug infraction, but a clinic can be set up in the cafeteria where kids are jabbed bing bang boom without Mom and Dad nearby. Again, what if there's an adverse reaction? A seizure or even just fainting? I think vaccines are best left to real doctors in offices where medical care is handy instead of being dosed willy-nilly around town.

I might as well get all the controversy out at once. Let's talk about mercury.

I don't believe it's wise to inject mercury into humans. And Thimerosal, the mercury-based medical preservative, is still in some vaccines given to children, despite the claims that it is not.

Seasonal flu, H1N1, and tetanus booster each contain twenty-five micrograms of mercury. There are pediatric versions of the flu shots, but they can be hard to find and are only recommended for children under age three. I'm not sure what happens to a kid at three that suddenly mercury is no longer dangerous. Mercury is also used in the manufacturing process of other vaccinations, and it is extracted to extremely low levels before the final product is complete. Some kids with peanut allergies go into anaphylaxis with just a sniff, so "extremely low" or "trace" levels of any potential allergen or neurotoxin isn't all that comforting to me.

For that reason, if anyone asked me about giving their child a flu shot, I would answer, "Well, there is mercury in the vaccine, and that troubles me. If your child has a preexisiting condition that makes flu a deadly threat, talk to your doctor about your options. I do not give my children seasonal or H1N1 vaccines."

And then I'd let the parent decide. That's called being pro–informed choice, not anti-vaccine. The person frequently blamed for starting the "anti-vaccine" movement is Dr. Andrew Wakefield, a gastroenterologist from England who touched off a decade-plus-long firestorm of controversy about the MMR (measles, mumps, rubella) vaccine.

In February 1998, The British Medical Journal *The Lancet* published a paper authored by Dr. Wakefield. His article suggested a *possible but yet unproven* connection between bowel disease and the MMR vaccine. His article focused on a case study of twelve children with neuropsychiatric disorders and bowel disease. At a press conference highlighting the release of his article, Dr. Wakefield suggested breaking up the Measles, Mumps, and Rubella (MMR) vaccine into three separate injections for safety reasons. After that suggestion, MMR vaccination rates dropped in Great Britain, causing great concern to public health officials.

Dr. Wakefield's original study never stated that the MMR vaccine caused autism. The following is taken straight from his original study:

We did not prove an association between measles, mumps, and rubella vaccine and the syndrome (autistic enterocolitis) described.

We have identified a chronic enterocolitis in children that may be related to neuropsychiatric dysfunction. In most cases, onset of symptoms was after measles, mumps, and rubella immunisation. Further investigations are needed to examine this syndrome and its possible relation to this vaccine.

Unfortunately for Dr. Wakefield, the MMR vaccine had been called into question just a few years earlier, when the mumps component was shown to cause febrile seizures in a small percentage of recipients. Ultimately, the formulation was changed to a different strain of mumps, and a new vaccine was released. Dr. Wakefield's paper raised further concerns among the already uneasy public. And the media, in an effort to protect the integrity of public health programs and corporate interests alike, pilloried Dr. Wakefield and his colleagues.

On January 28, 2010, Dr. Wakefield was found to have "failed in his duties as a responsible consultant" and went against the interests of children in his care in conducting research. On May 24, the General Medical Council revoked Dr. Wakefield's medical license, which in the UK is called "being erased from the medical register." It was a stunning, although not unexpected, blow:

Accordingly the Panel has determined that Dr. Wakefield's name should be erased from the medical register. The Panel concluded that it is the only sanction that is appropriate to protect patients and is in the wider public interest, including the maintenance of public trust and confidence in the profession and is proportionate to the serious and wide-ranging findings made against him.

The effect of the foregoing direction is that, unless Dr. Wakefield exercises his right of appeal, his name will be erased from the Medical

Register 28 days from when formal notice has been deemed to be served upon him by letter to his registered address.

Meanwhile, I can tell you that Dr. Wakefield appears at virtually every autism conference and speaks to parents about how they can address their children's terrible gut dysfunction. To some in the autism community, he is a hero and a martyr. To others, including the mainstream media, pharmaceutical companies, and public health officials (for whom vaccination is as much about sheer numbers and herd immunity as it is a medical procedure that affects individuals) he is a demon and scoundrel.

I highly recommend that you read his book *Callous Disregard* (which was the term the General Medical Council used to describe his work with children) and learn how his scientific studies led Dr. Wakefield into the snake pit that awaits vaccine questioners. You can draw your own conclusions about his work.

In a world where we mistrust pretty much every industry and corporation, including pharma, whose drugs are often recalled and given black-box warnings for their severe side effects, it strikes me as curious that the public is willing to assume that vaccines are safe for everyone at all times and that those of us who question their safety are the kooks.

It's the autism community that has been the most vocal about vaccine safety. So we're an easy target. The doctor leading the charge against the autism/vaccine safety community went so far as to write a book called *Autism's False Prophets* in which he "debunks" various treatments for the disorder. (I agree with him in some instances. Where there are desperate parents, abandoned by mainstream medicine, charlatans are sure to follow with miracle cures.) And then he launched an autism foundation to study (I kid you not) everything except vaccines as a potential trigger for autism. His name is Paul Offit.

Dr. Offit is coinventor of one of the more recent additions to the pediatric vaccine schedule. The vaccine is called RotaTeq from Merck. It makes sense that a vaccinologist and infectious disease expert would help create a new vaccine. There's nothing untoward about that at all. In the third world, rotavirus causes diarrhea and can be deadly. However, in America, with access to clean water, medical care, and electrolyte beverages, it's not a serious threat to our children's health. And yet it's on the American Academy of Pediatrics schedule in three orally administered doses.

Vaccines are big pharma business today. They keep pediatricians' offices busy (did your mom take you to the doctor for those nine "well" visits before the age of two?). The days of creating a medicine for the greater good are long gone. Jonas Salk, inventor of the polio vaccine, did not even patent his creation. From Wikipedia:

He had no desire to profit personally from the discovery, but merely wished to see the vaccine disseminated as widely as possible. When he was asked in a televised interview who owned the patent to the vaccine, Salk replied: "There is no patent. Could you patent the sun?""

Today, it looks like you can patent the sun and then claim it doesn't cause skin cancer.

Here's part of the "Who We Are" from his organization, called Autism Science Foundation (www.autismsciencefoundation.org):

Vaccines save lives; they do not cause autism. Numerous studies have failed to show a causal link between vaccines and autism. Vaccine safety research should continue to be conducted by the public health system in order to ensure vaccine safety and maintain confidence in our national vaccine program, but further investment of limited autism research dollars is not warranted at this time.

However, in May 2008, Dr. Bernadine Healy, former head of the National Institutes of Health and the American Red Cross, made the bold statement that the vaccine autism link has not been "debunked," in a filmed interview with Sharyl Attkisson on CBS News:

Dr. Bernadine Healy is the former head of the National Institutes of Health, and the most well-known medical voice yet to break with her colleagues on the vaccine-autism question.

In an exclusive interview with CBS News, Healy said the question is still open.

"I think that the public health officials have been too quick to dismiss the hypothesis as irrational," Healy said.

"But public health officials have been saying they know, they've been implying to the public there's enough evidence and they know it's not causal," Attkisson said.

"I think you can't say that," Healy said. "You can't say that."

Healy goes on to say public health officials have intentionally avoided researching whether subsets of children are "susceptible" to vaccine side effects—afraid the answer will scare the public.

"You're saying that public health officials have turned their back on a viable area of research largely because they're afraid of what might be found?" Attkisson asked.

Healy said: "There is a completely expressed concern that they don't want to pursue a hypothesis because that hypothesis could be damaging to the public health community at large by scaring people . . . First of all," Healy said, "I think the public's smarter than that. The public values vaccines. But more importantly, I don't think you should ever turn your back on any scientific hypothesis because you're afraid of what it might show."

Upton Sinclair, who wrote *The Jungle* in 1906 about the meat-packing industry and the working class, said it best: "It is difficult to

get a man to understand something when his salary depends upon his not understanding it."

Heck, cigarette manufacturers sat in front of Congress day after day declaring that their products did not cause cancer. Some probably even believed their own words. Doctors used to promote "healthy" cigarettes. Times change. Knowledge changes. And times are changing despite Dr. Offit's best efforts to scream like young Kevin Bacon in *Animal House, "All is calm!"* as the parade churned out of control before him.

All is not calm.

Educated, informed parents, most of whom are not in the autism world, are choosing to alter the pediatric vaccinations schedule, as reported by ABC News in May 2010:

> *The percentage of parents who refused or delayed vaccinations for their children rose sharply in the past decade, a study presented at a medical conference today showed.*
>
> *Refusal or delay of vaccines jumped from 22 to 39 percent between '03 and '08. Thirty-nine percent of parents refused or delayed vaccinations for their kids in 2008, up from 22 percent in 2003, according to the study by the Centers for Disease Control and Prevention, the University of Rochester, and the National Opinion Research Center.*
>
> *Parents refused or delayed vaccinations for various reasons, including the health of the child, the belief that recommended vaccines were excessive, questions about their effectiveness and concerns about possible side effects such as autism—although there's no scientific link.*

J. B. Handley, who continues to grace Age of Autism with his sharp wit and resourceful journalism, called The Children's Hospital of Philadelphia to see if he could secure an appointment with pediatrican Dr. Offit for "his child." He wrote about the call on October 26, 2009:

Given Offit's developing "expertise," I placed a phone call last week to his office in Philadelphia. While I knew the answer, it was still shocking to have the conversation, which went like this, with me ("JB") talking to Offit's assistant ("OA"):

JB: Hi, I have a child with autism, and I'd like to make an appointment to see Dr. Offit.

OA: He doesn't see patients.

JB: My son, he has autism, he needs help. My understanding is Dr. Offit is an expert on autism, he wrote a book, I'd really like to see him.

OA: He doesn't see patients in a clinical outpatient setting.

JB: Well, is there some other way for me to see him? Please, my son, he needs help, can't Dr. Offit make an exception?

OA: He doesn't see patients at all. I'm sorry.

Imagine if the dude who invented a new cigarette filter had written a book debunking lung cancer treatments and then gone on to found a group dedicated to finding the cause of lung cancer, and would look at everything except for cigarettes. Would your eyebrows be up around your hairline?

Unlike drugs, vaccines are exempt from medical liability, and have their own court system called the "Vaccine Court." If you or your child is injured by a drug or a physician's medical error, you can go to a trial by a jury of your peers. Not so with vaccines. You go before the Office of the Special Masters in a *no-fault* system that does not include a jury.

Vaccines are mandated for school attendance and in some instances, for employment. And when the government adds a vaccine to the pediatric schedule, it's a sales bonanza.

If ten people in California get sick from E. coli, the government seems to be able to track down the exact spinach plants responsible as well as the bird that flew overhead and pooped on them.

Tens of thousands of parents over the course of two decades have reported adverse reactions to vaccinations and a resultant autism diagnosis. And yet still we have no answers as to cause or prevention from the CDC. But "everyone knows" it's *not* vaccines.

Here's an excerpt about the vaccine market from an Associated Press article dated November 2009 that might help explain why vaccines are off the hook:

Vaccines are no longer a sleepy, low-profit niche in a booming drug industry. Today, they're starting to give ailing pharmaceutical makers a shot in the arm.

The lure of big profits, advances in technology, and growing government support has been drawing in new companies, from nascent biotechs to Johnson & Johnson. That means recent remarkable strides in overcoming dreaded diseases and annoying afflictions likely will continue.

"Even if a small portion of everything that's going on now is successful in the next ten years, you put that together with the last ten years (and) it's going to be characterized as a golden era," says Emilio Emini, Pfizer Inc.'s head of vaccine research.

Vaccines now are viewed as a crucial path to growth, as drugmakers look for ways to bolster slowing prescription medicine sales amid intensifying generic competition and government pressure to cut down prices under the federal health overhaul.

Unlike medicines that treat diseases, vaccines help prevent infections by revving up the body's natural immune defenses against invaders. They are made from viruses, bacteria, or parts of them that

have been killed or weakened so they generally can't cause an infection.

Investment in partnerships and other deals to develop and manufacture vaccines has been on a tear—and accelerating since the swine flu pandemic began. Billions in government grants are bringing better, faster ways to develop and manufacture vaccines. Rising worldwide emphasis on preventive health care, plus the advent of the first multibillion-dollar vaccines, have further boosted their appeal.

While prescription drug sales are forecast to rise by a third in five years, vaccine sales should double, from $19 billion last year to $39 billion in 2013, according to market research firm Kalorama Information. That's five times the $8 billion in vaccine sales in 2004.

"What was essentially 25 years ago a rounding error now has become real money," says Robin Robertson, director of the U.S. Biomedical Advanced Research Development Authority.

That jump is due to a couple of new blockbuster vaccines and rising use of existing ones. The government's list of recommended vaccines for children since has more than doubled since 1985 to 17. It now also calls for a half-dozen vaccines for everyone over 18 and up to four more for some adults.

Parents of kids with autism are going broke. Doctors like Andrew Wakefield have spent their life's savings defending themselves against legal recrimination for having dared to even suggest that a vaccine could pose a problem. Meanwhile, school districts from Alaska to Maine are groaning under the weight of an ever-increasing enrollment of kids who need special education. And soon, that slew of kids born in the early 1990s, the leading edge of the epidemic, will be "aging out" of school by turning twenty-two. Is there a group home on your street yet?

Now, if Ebola comes to town, or anthrax or smallpox hits the air in a terror attack, I will be lined up to get my family vaccinated. I'm

not stupid—contrary to what you'll read about me around the Internet.

As soon as medicine comes out with vaccines against some of the real threats my girls will face as women with autism—oh, things like physical and sexual abuse, employment discrimination, loneliness, housing crises—I'll roll up their sleeves myself.

MOTHER SUPERIOR

OH, THAT KIM STAGLIANO HAS THREE, THREE(!) CHILDREN WITH AUTISM. I don't know how she does it!

* * *

If I had a nickel for every time I've heard those words from some well-intentioned mouth I'd have enough change to choke the CoinStar machine at the grocery store. (The CoinStar machine is a great way to entertain a child with autism, what with all the clinking and clanking and such. Sometimes you simply need to kill some time, what can I say?)

"How does she do it?" ranks right up there with "I'm sorry" in my lexicon of things people say to me or about me and my kids.

My usual answer is, "Well, they're kids, not appliances. They didn't come with guarantees, a warranty, or a return policy." It's a bit of a flippant response, but seems more motherly than, "I have no idea."

Was there some check-the-box quiz that I missed during pregnancy that would have ensured us three typical kids?

The fact is—what choice do I have? My girls have autism. Their father and I love them, and it is our duty and pleasure to care for them. Even when there's a whole lot of doody and very little pleasure.

Recently, however, at least two mothers on this planet decided they could no longer "do it," meaning care for their autistic child.

And so they murdered their severely autistic sons, each in a grue-some fashion.

The first story broke in New York City, as Gigi Jordan, referred to as a "socialite," although I don't know what that means circa 2010, stuffed her son full of pills while surrounded by luxury at the Peninsula Hotel in Manhattan.

The report in the *New York Daily News* read:

A multimillionaire mom fed her eight-year-old son a fatal dose of pills, then spent the night with his body inside a ritzy midtown hotel before a failed suicide try, police said.

Gigi Jordan was "babbling incoherently" after police kicked in the door of her $2,300-a-night suite at the Peninsula Hotel to find her son Jude faceup on the bed and foaming at the mouth, police sources said.

Jordan, 49, was surrounded Friday by hundreds of prescription drug pills and a rambling note expressing her love for the small boy who police say died at his mother's hands.

"I can tell you the only true happy moment in my life was when Jude was born," she wrote. "He was all the love I ever had in my life.

"He was the only thing that made me feel life was something of beauty, ever."

A police source said Jordan used a sofa to block the suite's bathroom door.

I'll give you a second to swallow the bile that just rose to your throat before telling you about the second murder, which took place in the United Kingdom. Ready? This report came from Damien Pearse of Sky News:

A mum has been charged with murdering her twelve-year-old autistic son by pouring bleach down his throat. The fourty-four-year-old woman, who has not been named, was arrested after police called at her home in Barking, East London.

The boy was taken by ambulance to hospital, but confirmed dead a short time later.

A post-mortem examination confirmed the cause of the boy's death as "ingestion of caustic liquid."

Police are investigating reports the dead child was given bleach after his mother said it was medicine.

The suspect was assessed by doctors before being handed back to police.

Neighbours said the boy was "severely autistic" and that his mother had been struggling to cope.

His eleven-year-old brother was placed in the care of social services.

Barking and Dagenham Council said: "This is a tragic incident. Our thoughts are with the family. A number of agencies have had involvement with them over several years, including the police, the NHS, and other local authorities.

"We are leading a serious case review as required by the Government to look into all details of this tragedy. A police inquiry is also currently under way."

Officers from the Metropolitan Police's Child Abuse Major Investigation Team are heading the inquiry.

The victim's mother will appear at Barking Magistrates Court this morning.

A distraught mother, at the end of her rope, poured bleach down her son's throat. That's not just murder. That's punishment, torture, the inflicting of intentional pain on her child. What dark hell was she in before commiting such an atrocity?

I wish I could tell you these murders are unusual. They are not. In 2006, a physician named Dr. Karen McCarron murdered her autistic three-year-old daughter. She put a plastic bag over her child's head and watched her suffocate to death. I Googled the question *how long does it take to suffocate?* and came up with anywhere from three to five minutes. I can't wait three minutes for water to boil on the stove.

Dr. McCarron held a bag tightly around her child's head for at least that. The child's name was Katie. Dr. McCarron is now serving a thirty-six-year sentence in an Illinois prison. As a physician, surely Dr. McCarron had access to a more human method to "euthanize" her child? It's the anger and brutality of the act that horrifies me almost as much as the killing itself.

I can't wrap my head around the cruelty of these murders. My maternal instinct rejects the notion entirely. And I abhor that these mothers can kill their children while sparing their own lives. Oh, Gigi Jordan "tried" to commit suicide but failed. She was a pharmaceutical executive who planned her son's murder by overdose carefully enough to book a luxury hotel room, to obtain and pack the pills (gee, do you use the Fendi valise or perhaps the Louis Vuitton?), and to then block the door with a sofa. Clearly she was sane enough to be able to think the murder through. So how come she's still alive?

Kids with autism are not without thoughts or feelings. Each child had to know what was happening to him or her. I'm sure they knew they were dying. It's almost too much for me to write the words.

Lest you think it's only the moms who crack, it happens to fathers too. In 2009, a father in Edmonton, Alberta, killed his eleven-year-old son and then committed suicide. Somehow, the suicide makes me feel a little better. Isn't that a sick admission? After reading that this boy had been in a group home and institutionalized, I can muster up a scintilla of empathy (not sympathy, there's a difference). From the CBC Web site:

> *The deaths of a man and his eleven-year-old autistic son on Sunday were the result of a murder-suicide, Edmonton police said Tuesday, after receiving confirmation from the Edmonton Medical Examiner's Office.*
>
> *On Sunday, police found the bodies of the man, thirty-nine, and the boy in a home in northeast Edmonton, after they received a call from the man's common-law wife.*

She was worried because she couldn't get in touch with him.

When officers arrived at the home around 12:42 PM, they found the man and the boy dead in the basement.

Police said they will not be releasing the names of deceased in order to protect the privacy of the family and to protect the identity of other children in the family. They will also not be releasing the cause of death.

The boy was autistic and had been living at a group home.

The family had become desperate for help because the little boy had become difficult for the family to manage, said Karen Phillips, who works with the Autism Society of Edmonton Area.

Phillips had worked with the family and said the mother asked her to share their story.

"The dad just felt he couldn't do it any longer and he just didn't think he could get the help he needed," she said, as her eyes welled up with tears.

At one point, the family took the boy to the emergency department of an Edmonton hospital, where he was later admitted to the psychiatric unit, Phillips said. But the staff there weren't equipped to help a child with autism.

Eventually, a place was found for the boy in a group home, but that search was a struggle, because many group homes are not set up to deal with autistic children with extreme behavourial problems.

The case highlights a lack of emergency services to help the families of autistic children, Phillips said.

"There is no emergency service. So parents are stuck at home with their children in situations that, if the general public knew, they'd be appalled," she said.

"They would think, 'None of us could cope with that.' But it's an everyday occurrence for families who have . . . behaviourally out-of-control children with autism."

Families are told to call police who in turn will take the child to the psychiatric unit of a hospital, but the staff there don't have the kind of training required to help the child, Phillips said.

"They're very good. They try their best, but they're not trained in autism and the doctors there will say clearly, this is not the place for children with autism."

The government was working on emergency respite services for families, but recent cutbacks mean the plans have been put on hold, she said.

The comment threads on the article are interesting. Most folks eviscerated Gigi Jordan, in part because of her wealth and the suggestion of mental instability over the years. The British mom was instantly branded a monster. However, some commenters with either an intimate or tangential link to autism talked about how they feel sympathy for each of these women or men, who were clearly deranged by their anger, loathing, grief, fear, frustration, exhaustion, loneliness, and the absolute drudgery of caring for an autistic child. My comment?

Fuck sympathy.

Yes, it's often sheer drudgery to care for an autistic child. From this I know. And I've felt every single one of those emotions in my years of caring for my daughters.

I've hauled one of my girls into the garage at three in the morning and put her into the minivan, shut and locked the doors while I walked back into the house to calm myself, get control of my anger, and escape the screaming fit that threatened to wake the entire house.

I've sobbed in a steaming hot shower to escape the smell of a crapisode and the resulting mountain of laundry waiting.

I've locked myself in my bedroom, sat on the edge of my bed, and lowered my head between my knees, willing myself to calm down while gasping for breath.

I sure as heck don't own a gun. Between my temper and Mark's, one of us would end up in a pine box.

The deaths of these children betray the growing tragedy that is autism. Yes, tragedy. Countless kids (literally countless, since the CDC can't seem to pinpoint exact numbers even as they can track down

the single pig in Iowa that transmitted some rare disease) are suffering from autism, and so are their families. For most families, autism is a slog. It is 100 decathlons stacked on top of a thousand climbs to the top of Mt. Everest. You get to the top of the mountain and then another mountain appears in front of you. At the summit, when you die, is nothing but worry for the adult children you'll leave behind.

Bob Wright, cofounder of Autism Speaks, addressed the trauma on television a few years back, "Even if you're rich (which he is) autism leaves you broke." It sure can. Mark and I have learned that lesson all too well. We're digging out from a mountain of debt amassed courtesy of autism and unemployment.

I suppose that when you add the financial stress of autism to the emotional toll it takes, some folks will snap. Even people you'd expect to have their you-know-what together.

There was a wide-reaching controversy in the autism world in 2006, as Alison Tepper Singer, then Executive Director of Autism Speaks, made a startling admission in the documentary *Autism Every Day* by Lauren Thierry. She confessed that she'd thought about driving off of a bridge with her autistic daughter. A minority in the community voiced support for her honesty—that autism can indeed drive a parent to consider the unthinkable. Most felt the acknowledgment showed a stunning lack of hope and branded our children with autism as nothing more than a burden.

My children are not a burden. I carried them in my body and will carry them as long as they need me.

That doesn't make me a mother superior. Just a good mother.

BEEF: IT'S WHAT'S FOR BREAKFAST, LUNCH, AND DINNER

I FIRST LEARNED THAT DIET COULD AFFECT MY KIDS WHEN I MET SARGE Goodchild, a neurodevelopmental consultant in Massachusetts. He suggested that Gianna's red papery cheeks, runny nose, rheumy eyes, and less-than-angelic behaviors could be the result of consuming both wheat and dairy.

To tell you I was stunned is an understatement. Get rid of dairy? Never. Quit wheat? What on earth would they eat?

I'd fed my girls healthy foods since birth. I nursed Mia and Gianna for three and six months, respectively, and then I bought organic baby food and what I thought were healthy choices as they grew to be toddlers.

I reviewed Mia's eating habits. Eggo waffles, Annie's Macaroni and Cheese, goldfish crackers, pasta, and at least five or six sippy cups of milk per day. Uh-oh. Mia was on the white-foods-only autism diet track.

Of course, I didn't realize at the time that her eating habits could be indicative of a digestive problem related to her autism.

I ignored Sarge's advice for several months. Gianna's behavior worsened at preschool. She was bolting out of the classroom. Mia was becoming more lethargic and sluggish. Neither child was thriving.

With Sarge's help, I learned about the Defeat Autism Now! doctors who treat kids with autism. I booked an appointment in the spring of 2000.

Dr. Frank Waickman was about to retire. He had the kindly mien found in old-fashioned doctors. He was practicing for the love of his vocation, and it showed. He was the first doctor to ever ask me, "And how are you doing, Kim? How are you and your husband? Do you get out?" Mia and Gianna were young, and I was just starting to show with my pregnancy for Bella. I'll never forget that small bit of personal attention and kindness from him.

He tested the girls for food allergies (standard practice for many Defeat Autism Now! doctors) using sublingual (under-the-tongue) drops. If I hadn't seen the tests with my own two eyes, I'd never have believed any mom who told me that the tests could be so revealing. Remember, this was in 2000, long before I became an "anti-vaxxer crazy woman treating her kids with dangerous and untested products." Go ahead and roll your eyes with me, please? In fact, just three years earlier, I'd laughed out loud at a mom who was taking her son to a chiropractor for his ear infections. I was an allopathic-only idiot.

The girls were tested in a small room. The nurse placed three drops of a liquid under their tongues and waited for a reaction if there was one. I did not know what each test was for while the testing was in progress.

Within seconds of receiving the first drops, Mia's coloring went from straight lines to scribbles, then she dropped her crayon and slumped to the floor like a jellyfish. She was awake but completely stoned. I half expected her to demand a bag of Doritos and a cigarette. Antidote drops brought her back. That was her reaction to wheat.

Gianna had a series of drops that turned her into a fleeing, angry mess. She literally scaled over the children's gate to get out of the room. Her cheeks were flaming red, and she was belligerent. That was her reaction to dairy.

It was like the girls were puppets on strings and the various drops elicited a different performance. None terribly charming or worthy of an encore. I had to remove wheat and dairy from their diets.

Oh. My. God.

I have a cousin who developed or was diagnosed with celiac as an adult. Mark had had terrible digestive issues for much of his life, as had his siblings. And while I didn't have gastrointestinal (GI) problems, I was very much addicted to milk. As a small child I'd wake up in the night asking for milk. My parents joked that they'd considered putting a fridge on the second floor to save trips up and down the long staircase. I still love an ice-cold glass of milk before bed. I can feel myself calming down. The opiate effect. Gluten is the protein in wheat, rye, and barley. Casein is the protein in milk. People who have celiac disease cannot digest gluten. Those who are lactose intolerant and who avoid milk aren't necessarily intolerant of or allergic to milk protein. They are affected by lactose, which is milk sugar.

★ ★ ★

There's very little that's *free* about the gluten-free casein-free diet (GFCF). It's an expensive way to eat. Crummy, processed foods are always cheap. Adding healthier specialty foods to our diet meant shopping in mom-and-pop stores where the prices were sky-high. A big part of our autism expense was the girls' diet.

No matter what your food allergy or intolerance, the net result is *agita,* which is Italian for "pass the Alka Seltzer." And at first, the GFCF diet is a bellyache too. But not for long.

★ ★ ★

When I finally made the decision to go gluten-free and dairy-free, our first breakfast was orange juice and potato chips. I was lost. We began to eat an awful lot of meat. I knew that wasn't healthy for the girls.

So I started baking from scratch. I bought *Special Diets for Special Kids* by Lisa Lewis, PhD. That became my bible. I loaded up my pantry with weird flours and played crazy chemist daily. The kids adjusted really well. In fact, within the first week of dropping gluten, Mia ate a plate of veggies for the first time. We saw nothing but benefits from the diet. And continue to do so.

A favorite, kid-friendly meal is mock mac and cheese. I buy Trader Joes organic rice pasta and a bag of their frozen, organic mixed veggies and a box of Imagine-brand organic potato leek soup. Just boil the pasta until al dente (slightly undercooked for my non-Italian friends) and mix the soup, frozen veggies and pasta together in the pan after you've drained the macaroni. Pour the mixture into a greased casserole dish and top with the ultimate in comfort food toppings, crushed-up Ruffles potato chips. Bake at 350 degrees for about forty-five minutes. It feeds my three kids two hot meals, is cheap to make, and tastes good. Try it!

Today, there are dozens of great cookbooks, Web sites, and products dedicated to the GFCF diets. Companies have realized the size of the celiac and food intolerance market and responded to the demand with delicious, easy-to-use mixes and better labeling. In 2009, even Betty Crocker jumped on the gluten-free bandwagon with cake, cookie, and brownie mixes that are just delicious.

Simple substitutions, like using crushed rice cereal sprinkled with seasonings to make Italian breadcrumbs instead of a can of Progresso wheat-based crumbs, allow me to make cutlets and meatballs for the entire family.

There is emerging science about the GFCF diet for autism. Two studies came out concurrently last spring; one said there is a benefit, the other said there was not. It annoys me to no end that doctors who will prescribe a serious psychiatric drug to tamp down behavior will tell parents that the GFCF diet isn't safe or tested—"There's no science."

Are you kidding me? Tens of thousands of parents have seen results. Trust me, our kids aren't faking their tummy troubles. There's no placebo effect in autism. If your child suddenly stopped having daily acidic diarrhea that made his bottom bleed or BMs the size of a grapefruit that required an epidural to pass, would you say, "Aw, but there's no science, so I won't continue"? Not likely.

Have you got a beef with that?

YOU'VE GOT TO
FERTILIZE THE ROSES

IN 2007, I COINED A TERM THAT IS NOW IN THE URBAN DICTIONARY: the crapisode. It's not quite "Where's the beef?" or "Show me the money!" but it's my small contribution to the pop culture lexicon. I wrote a piece for The Huffington Post called, "The Crappy Life of the Autism Mom." If you've read this far into my book, you know that I do not genuinely believe that I have a crappy life. I'm pretty darn content overall and mostly cheerful, despite what the worry lines on my forehead tell you. My former career in advertising and promotions has taught me that headlines pull in readers. It doesn't matter if the headline intrigues or infuriates, the point is to grab attention when the reader has dozens of story choices on his or her screen at the moment. It's all about the clicks. If no one reads my posts, they can be as finely written as Shakespeare's plays, and I'll have accomplished much ado about nothing.

Bowel movements (BMs). Poop. Crap. The process of elimination has taken up an inordinate amount of my mothering skills thanks to autism. All parents have to deal with toilet training. And while the average age of having a fully trained child is creeping upward (Pampers came out with size-six diapers many years ago, and Pull Ups may soon be adding Penthouse Pet designs to their Dora the Explorer and Go, Diego, Go offerings), most families achieve the goal long before kindergarten.

Not us. Not most families in the autism world. Toilet training can be one of the toughest challenges when you have a child on the spectrum, with kids remaining in Pull Ups or adult diapers well into their elementary school years and beyond. Often the children have sensory issues that can impede their ability to feel when they have to pee or poop.

I started toilet training Mia and Gianna when they were three and four years old. I optimistically bought a book called *Toilet Training in Less Than a Day,* which, after two weeks of mopping up puddles on my floor, I renamed *Big Fat Crock of You Know What.*

I had charts, rewards, potty seats, a teddy bear that sung "I'm Super Duper Pooper," an Elmo doll that could pee in the toilet, and several books. One was called *Toilet Training for Individuals with Autism,* by Maria Wheeler, who explains in her introduction how difficult it is to train this population. I got nowhere with the girls using her technique and became so frustrated that I tracked down Maria Wheeler herself and begged her to come to Cleveland to train the girls. Mark and I spent hundreds of dollars with a psychologist to try and get them trained. All she did was sit them on a potty seat and have them push the button on a kiddie book that made a flushing sound. Man, those PhDs come in handy, don't they?

Gianna was finally trained by Mrs. D., the paraprofessional in her preschool. She sat Gianna down, ignored her frantic little screams of protest, and waited the child out. Plink plink poop! Once Gianna had gone a couple of times, she was on her own. She got it!

Mia took a bit longer—Mark and I used to joke morbidly that we'd be changing period pads and poop at the same time. It wasn't quite so funny when it came true. But Mia also mastered her bathroom skills. You'd think my experience would have made training Bella easier. Not at all. Because as the saying goes, "If you've met one person with autism, you've met one person with autism." Bella responded beautifully to a program I learned from a dynamo of a

woman named Brenda Batts out of Dallas who I talked to at the National Autism Association Conference. She recently published *Ready, Set, Potty!* I was skeptical of her suggestions, the first of which required me to find silky panties for Bella. "What? Silky panties for my baby? Is Victoria's Secret that she pees in her pants?" Two and a half years after we tried Brenda's program, Bella is moving away from a toilet schedule where we take her every couple of hours to independence, where she seeks out the bathroom on her own.

Sometimes the poop is merely the medium. I know families whose kids smear theirs on the walls. One amazing dad created a "poop suit" for his teen son to wear to bed so that he could not have a BM at night and then destroy, er, *decorate* his bedroom, leaving his parents to attempt a daily cleaning ritual worthy of an operating room. I get e-mails from moms explaining that they put their son's pjs on backward so he can't work the zipper. Their Van Gogh brown period is not malicious, at least I don't think so. When we've had poop issues, they've usually been a result of one of our daughters wanting to change herself. In some ways, taking a blob of *you-know-what* out of the pants is progress. It means she's aware she has soiled her pants and wants relief. Okay, so that usually happens with a neurotypical kid when they're around two years old. It's funky when your child is eight or ten or twelve. But with autism, beggars can't be choosers, and when it happens in our household, I always try to chalk it up to forward movement, if you'll pardon a bad pun.

We had a "Mommy, I kinda sorta changed myself" incident a while back that made me laugh, cry, and then laugh again. One of the girls changed herself in her room. That means the pants come down and whatever is in them comes out, got it? Thanks to lots of bananas and proper nutrition, the movement is usually intact. As I walked upstairs, I smelled a little something that was more "oh my God" than eau-de-cologne.

Sure enough, there had been a *self-care* event. I cleaned up the situation and steam-cleaned the bedroom carpet. Honestly, given the

ever-rising autism rates, consider giving a steam cleaner as a wedding gift, as chances are the bride and groom will need it when the kids come along. I checked under the bed and the baseboard heating units, around the closet, anywhere that things could have rolled. All clear.

The next day, I noticed "that smell" in the room. I did a poop check. Nothing. I took the laundry downstairs, thinking maybe that's what I was smelling.

Nope.

The next day, I did another poop check. Still nothing. I looked at the ceiling, just in case. I washed the sheets and comforter.

Nope.

The next day, I noticed something.

There, on the *Sesame Street* kitchen (remember the one that got trashed in the flood? I found it on sale that Christmas Eve and bought it) next to the closet, was a stove knob with Ernie's photo on it. Twist the knob and Ernie hollers, "Turn it up!" There, on the *Sesame Street* kitchen was a stove knob with Bert's photo on it. Twist it and Bert hollers, "Turn it down!" And there, between the two stove knobs, was a giant piece of old, dried-out poop. "Get the Lysol!" I screamed. I snapped a photo with my cell phone just to prove it had happened.

★ ★ ★

Poop is a real issue in the autism world, though one you don't often hear about. I don't mind talking about yucky. I wrote "The Crappy Life of the Autism Mom" to accomplish two goals. One, to show how different life is inside an autism household. And two, to explain to the non-autism world how I felt about a trend toward not respecting the needs of parents to treat their children's autism courtesy of the "neurodiversity" community. Neurodiversity can mean simple acceptance of different ways of thinking. And that's a great message. I want my kids to be accepted. Kind of a no-brainer, right? However,

the message was hijacked by angry parents who've given up on their kids or who never had hope to begin with, medical skeptics with more time on their hands than compassion, and even high-functioning people with Asperger's or autism who advocate against treatment, hope, and recovery. Most of the negative Google alerts on my name come from the hardcore ND world.

Sometimes you have to stir the pot up a bit to make people outside the autism universe know just how absurd our lives are thanks to the nitwits who preach against helping our kids. Here's "The Crappy Life of the Autism Mom."

> Well, that should set off alarm bells in the neurodiversity world.

> Autism is like a box of Bertie Bott's Every Flavor Beans (from the Harry Potter books). Some autistics got the raspberry cream or root beer flavor. They can speak eloquently, write blogs, move out on their own, marry, have children, and manage their autistic traits. Others with autism, like my three girls, got the ear wax/vomit/dog poop flavor. They need help 24/7 to navigate the world. When I talk about autism, I mean the version that my three girls have. I'm not talking about the sort of autism that encompasses quirky kids with some social deficits who are otherwise brilliant.

> The ND community tells me and tens of thousands of other parents that we are disrespecting our kids by trying to help them. The ND blogs berate us as wanting to change our kids because we don't accept them. Here's a "taste" of what autism looks like in the Stagliano household. Would you want something better for your kids?

> Twice last month, we had a "crapisode." What is a crapisode? (This is where you might want to stop eating and put down your beverage.) My ten-year-old (No. 2, appropriately, for the purposes of this entry) pooped in the toilet. That is reason to

cheer, believe me. Toilet training is a major issue in my section of the autism community. Our kids can wear diapers into their teens and beyond. So Miss G. pooped. Hooray! But Miss G. forgets to flush. And she rarely closes the lid. Not hooray.

Miss Peanut, my six-year-old, seems to believe that being a Virgo means she simply MUST swim in any puddle larger than spit. The toilet is like an Olympic-sized pool to her. So Peanut goes into the toilet after Miss G. has had her, ah, success. Peanut flings kaka everywhere and gets it all over herself, the floor, the walls, the tub, the baseboards, and the window. Wes Craven could not film anything scarier than what I saw that school morning, thirty-five minutes before the bus was due to arrive. That's a "crapisode." It happens in the blink of an eye while I'm washing dishes or doing laundry. I'm alerted by a splashing sound that drops a brick into my stomach. Miss G. doesn't understand to flush and close the lid. Miss Peanut doesn't realize that a face full of feces is rarely considered a way to amuse oneself outside the fetish community.

I will never stop trying to help my girls recover from their autism. I cannot tell you what recovery means. It varies by kid and according to God's grace. If recovery means only that Peanut understands she should sit on the toilet, not play in the toilet, I'll take it.

Recovering your kids doesn't mean denying their value as people. To the contrary, it means we are willing to devote our lives, our savings, our sanity to their improved health, development, and well-being.

Maybe we need an expanded vocabulary. The NDs can keep the word "autism," and my kids get a new label. Fine by me. Just don't tell me to give up on my girls and accept their version of autism (remember the Bertie Bott's beans) as simply a different type of personality. Because THAT'S a load of crap.

Published on HuffingtonPost.com, January 3, 2007.

★ ★ ★

The piece has traveled farther and wider than I ever get to go. Then again, I'm an autism mom times three, so I don't get out much. "Crappy Life" has been picked apart and scrutinized more than a specimen in a Great Plains Laboratory comprehensive stool analysis test.

With "Crappy Life" I did what many writers strive for—I struck a nerve. Many parents have thanked me for sharing the difficulties of trying to help a child with autism navigate day-to-day life. Others have berated me for embarrassing my children. Please. Embarrassment is my birthright. Ask anyone in my family about the little gifts my Grandma Yoli had to deal with after my diaper pooped out (literally) at the Farmer's Daughter gift barn in St. Johnsbury, Vermont, in the mid-sixties. They still tease me about "losing my marbles in Vermont" four decades later. The day my kids can read my writing and complain to me that I hurt their feelings will be the proudest day of my life. I will apologize to them and hope they understand that I was fighting for them through my words.

★ ★ ★

The neurodiversity situation shines a light on the fact that autism, as a spectrum disorder, has numerous "factions" for lack of a better word. Autism can look very different from one person to the next. Even my three girls present differently from each other, though each has an autism diagnosis. And the mainstream media, which is so adept at telling you when Brad Pitt has gone pee without getting Angelina's blessing, is woefully ignorant about autism. They use autism and Asperger's interchangeably, for instance. The two diagnoses are not the same, and there's much debate about that.

In 2010, the debate got more heated. There's a book published by the American Psychiatry Association (a.k.a. A Pill for All) called the *Diagnostic and Statistical Manual of Mental Disorders*. Yes, mental disorders. Autism is in there as a diagnosis. I do not think my kids are mentally ill for one minute. I think they have some sort of brain injury or difference that was created in them and that has upset, tipped over, and crushed the apple cart of their neurology.

In the fifth edition of *DSM-V* (yes, the Roman Numerals are to make the psychiatrists look much smarter than the rest of us) Asperger's will lose its own diagnosis code and become part of the autism code.

What does this mean?

A lot of folks in the Asperger's world do not care to be lumped into the autism spectrum. They do not relate to the challenges of full-blown autism. I can certainly respect that they do not want to be included in a group that includes the mentally challenged, or as I have read, "adults in diapers." Ouch.

Meanwhile, many parents of children and young adults with Asperger's support the revised definition since, traditionally, services and school support have been far lower for kids with Asperger's. Their impairments are not as glaring as a lack of speech. They can do the schoolwork, so they don't get services. They often falter socially and academically.

Asperger's is not without its own major challenges. While Aspergians are often thought of as occupying the "top" of some kind of pyramid scale, there are a lot of families with kids whose lives are very difficult because of Asperger's. I met a woman at church whose thirty-year-old cannot find a job. A good friend worries her son will threaten to bring a knife to school and be expelled. Asperger's is not Autism Lite.

The at-a-glance difference between an Asperger's diagnosis and autism is the communication deficit. Asperger's kids can speak, in fact are often hyperverbal, but are lacking in the social skills most of

us take for granted, like being able to read emotions in faces, or understanding when a conversation has steered elsewhere and being able to adapt.

There is good news on the horizon for everyone with autism. After starting a chapter with poop, I want to finish up with the fresh scent of a rose. And thanks to John Robison, I can do that.

There is a study underway at Beth Israel Deaconess Hospital and Harvard Medical School in which people with Asperger's (like my friend and author John Robison, the first test subject) are altering the plasticity of their brains and ameliorating the negative symptoms of their Asperger's. That's a hoity-toity way of saying, "They are getting better!" This therapy is called TMS, short for Transcranial Magnetic Stimulation, and is part of a major study at Harvard under Dr. Alvaro Pascual Leone.

Here's a description of the therapy from the Berenson-Allen Center for Non-Invasive Brain Stimulation in Boston:

> Transcranial magnetic stimulation or TMS is a neurophysiological technique that allows the induction of a current in the brain using a magnetic field to pass the scalp and the skull safely and painlessly. In TMS, a current passes through a coil of copper wire that is encased in plastic and held over the subject's head. This coil resembles a paddle or a large spoon and is held in place either by the investigator or by a mechanical fixation device similar to a microphone pole. As the current passes through the coil, it generates a magnetic field that can penetrate the subject's scalp and skull, and in turn induce a current in the subject's brain. TMS is used in clinical neurophysiology to study the nerve fibers that carry the information about movements from the brain cortex to the spinal cord and the muscles.
>
> Repetitive TMS (rTMS) can be used to study how the brain organizes different functions such as language, memory,

vision, or attention. In addition, rTMS seems capable of changing the activity in a brain area, even beyond the duration of the rTMS application itself. In other words, it seems possible to make a given brain area work more or less for a period of minutes, or even weeks when rTMS is applied repeatedly several days in a row. This has opened up the possibility of using rTMS for therapy of some illnesses in neurology, rehabilitation, and psychiatry.

John Elder Robison also writes about TMS on his blog, which I suggest you read to learn more. In it he says, "*Shirley and Alvaro developed a theory that some parts of the autistic mind are overactive, and those overactive parts sort of overwhelm the other parts. By 'slowing down' the over-active areas they hoped to bring about an improvement in overall function.*"

Imagine not being able to read facial expressions and how tough that would make your life. Like if Jane at work is terribly sad and instead of acknowledging her teary eyes and quivering lips, you were to say, "Isn't the sunshine beautiful today, Jane?" She might think you were a jerk. You are not a jerk, but you cannot read her expression, so you say the wrong thing. And this happens to you over and over and over so that your life becomes a never-ending chain of social gaffes and failures, right from childhood. That's how John describes Asperger's. That's hardly Autism Lite.

My phone rang during the spring of 2008. It was John Robison. John isn't one to pick up the phone for chitchatty girl talk, as you can imagine. I'd never heard him so animated, and I'll not soon forget what he told me about his first changes from the TMS therapy trial, "Kim! I can read people's minds!"

Being a neurotypical female, my first thought was, "You can work for the psychic hotline and make a fortune!" This is not what John meant by reading minds. He meant that for the first time in his life, he understood emotions via facial expressions. Just imagine the veil

of uncertainty that lifted for him. Jane wouldn't think he was a jerk, because he'd know to cluck cluck and maybe even pat her shoulder, rather than expound upon the lovely day.

As the months progressed and he continued the therapy, he experienced a number of positive changes: *"I can sum up what's it's done for me very succinctly. TMS has been the lever that allowed me to roll the boulder of autistic social disability out of my path. Today, thanks to Alvaro and his team, my world is brighter, more colorful, and more alive than anything I knew before. And best of all, I am fully engaged. I'm no longer an outsider. I have gone from feeling like a social outcast to feeling like I can talk to anyone, most any time. It's a magical thing."* John has tracked his progress with great honesty on his blog and continues to do so.

"Let me know when my girls can participate," I told him from the first time I heard about the therapy. TMS is noninvasive and all one has to do is sit there. I want to try every possible therapy I can for my kids. This one is particularly appealing because of the safety net of Harvard and John's assurances. I was born at Beth Israel in Boston. It would be pretty cool to get help for my kids there.

So a couple of nights ago, my phone rang during dinner. It was John. Again, he was not calling for girl talk. "Kim, the TMS therapy is going so well for Aspergians that we're going to begin trying it on lower-functioning kids. We've been able to affect speech, to bring it out. Your oldest daughter can participate." (Fifteen is the youngest age they will accept right now for ethical reasons.)

When the study starts, my Mia Noel will be on the list of subjects. We might be able to tweak her brain and help get rid of one of the most insidious aspects of her autism.

My Mia might speak.

Holy crap.

MY TURN

Most of my newer friendships have been born out of the shared experience of having a child with autism. Jane Doe will hear that Sally Smith is moving to town and send me an e-mail, "Hey, this mom has a son with autism. You should call her."

I usually make the call, because autism can make for an isolated life for us parents. I know I hate feeling alone. Although the Internet is a great connector, it's not a replacement for genuine friendship, despite the thousands of friends and followers you might have on Facebook or Twitter.

One of these friendships started several years ago, while we lived in Hudson.

I got a call that a woman named Sheila was moving to town with her teenaged daughter and husband in the hope of finding better schooling for her child.

Sheila had her hands full with her daughter, who had numerous diagnoses, one of which was autism. Sheila was a fantastic advocate for her daughter, and she pushed our school district to its limits, finally getting better programming than most of us ever imagined, including ABA therapy managed by the Cleveland Clinic school. At the same time, her husband's family-owned retail store was struggling. She and I were like two peas in a pod, sharing child issues and financial worries. I won't say misery loves company, because I've never been truly miserable with my life. But we did have a unique bond because of our circumstances.

One day, Sheila and I were having coffee and she asked a question that blew me away: "When is it going to be my turn?"

The years of caring for her aging parents and tending to her daughter had taken their toll. She was over fifty and perhaps the retrospection that comes with age brought her life into sharp focus. I was busy with a newborn, hadn't hit forty, and still had the doe-eyed hope that I'd "fix" my kids in a couple of years and then get on with my life. Hardy har har.

Here I am, many years after she asked me that unanswerable question. My kids still struggle mightily. We've been through three bouts of unemployment. Our last three homes have been little more than bivouacs as we've traipsed about New England.

And yet I have never once asked, "When is it my turn?"

This *is* my turn.

I love my life. That doesn't mean I wouldn't change the autism part for the girls. If I had a magic wand I'd wipe the autism right out of their lives like peeling off the skin of an orange. I know there is sweet fruit hidden under the bitter pith and the rough skin.

How many people can honestly say they wouldn't change anything about their lives?

Have you ever sat in church and prayed for something very specific? I didn't used to. It seemed presumptuous to make demands of God. I preferred to do what most women do—assume our men are telepathic and that they understand a quick snort of breath is actually our way of saying, "Could you please take out the trash?" I'm guilty of that every day. Poor Mark! My language is different from his. He's direct and I'm oblique.

One Sunday during Mass, our pastor said something that struck me during the homily. (Yes, Father, I do pay attention!) He told us we have to be very specific in our prayers to God. I was taken aback. It feels supremely presumptuous, to talk to God like I'm ordering from a takeout menu.

"Yeah, God? Gimme a No. 7, the executive job for my husband with a supersized salary, and a side order of cure for my kids' autism." I can feel the earth opening up and swallowing me whole just thinking that directly in terms of prayer. And yet, I'm learning to do just that. And (wait, let me toss salt over my shoulder here to ward off the devil) it's working.

I used to pray big thoughts like, "Please let me get married," when I was dating my high school sweetheart. I didn't mention the potential groom by name because I assumed that God knew who I meant.

God sure knew better than I did.

At the risk of sounding like a slogan on a bumper sticker, I know that I am not living in some sort of dress rehearsal. It's showtime every morning I wake up. Some days I'm living in a comedy, others a tragedy, and once in a blue moon, a romance. I just can't think of myself on "hold" until some sweeping change affects me.

I've wondered what kind of mom I'd have been if my girls had the luxury of being neurotypical. With my pushy personality, maybe I'd have become an intolerable stage mother, pushing a breathtaking toddler named Mia into dancing school recitals. I could have been a soccer team sideliner screaming at Gianna to run faster, to score more goals, and to tug the hair of the defense person covering her. Maybe I'd have Bella at the skating rink at five in the morning seven days a week practicing her figure eights and jumps until her bottom was bruised from the falls.

I'll never know.

And I don't much care.

Don't misunderstand me, I'd love to worry to death about sixteen-year-old Mia on her first date with a boy I thought was too mature for her. It would be sublime to hear Gianna tell me she hates me and slam her door in a fourteen-year-old's classic huff. If only Bella could roll her eyes at me in disgust for reminding her to brush her teeth

for the umpteenth time—instead of having to brush her teeth myself.

Sometimes I have to fight the pain of going down the "what if . . ." path. If I start thinking about all of the losses the kids experience—and Mark and me, too—my breathing gets too shallow to be healthy. My heart beats too fast. I have to remind myself: This *is* my turn.

I get reminders every day of the differences in my kids. Every afternoon, Bella returns from school on a small school bus. The driver's daughter, just two years old, rides along in her car seat. The other day, she looked right at me, waved and said, "Hi!" My own daughter was staring out the window. Yes, that hurts.

★ ★ ★

On the flip side, Mark and I have the great honor of tiny, sometimes daily moments of heroics in the girls. When you're truly hungry, a simple meal is as good as a feast. The other day, Mia awoke and told me, "Tuesday. Swimming." It reminds me that even in her relative silence, Mia is aware of her world and engaged in school. I felt proud of her.

Gianna has always had a lovey she carried. As a toddler it was a teddy bear that somehow got lost between Pennsylvania and Ohio. She had her blankey for many years until it wore down to mere scraps (that I've saved). In Ohio, we had a carbon monoxide scare, and she was given her manatee plush toy by the responding firefighter. Manatee was by her side for four years. I had to perform countless surgeries on the poor thing as he continued to fall apart. In sixth grade she read a picture book about emotions called *The Way I Feel*, and connected (that's a kinder way of saying became obsessed) with the page that described the feeling "excited." Despite my limited sewing skills, I was able to create a Halloween costume for her and she became "Excited" straight from the book. She was thrilled.

She lost interest in Manatee (don't tell her, but he's hidden in my closet) and started carrying that book around every waking minute for close to two years. She even slept on it. It fell apart despite yards of clear tape covering the spine and curling pages, and Mark would always order another copy online. We might be responsible for its latest printing.

We took a family photo during the 2009 holidays, and I'm proud to say *The Way I Feel* has been replaced with a photocopy of our family photo. Gianna carries it everywhere (except school) and sleeps with it covering her face. It's a form of autistic perseveration, I realize that. But it's important to her and fills a need. I can't deny her that. That the loveys have evolved from a toddler's toy to a family photo shows emotional growth. I'm proud of Gianna.

Bella, my quiet one, delights us in her own way. One night, after years of tucking her in, kissing her forehead, and waving good-bye as I closed her door, she looked right at me and waved back! She waved back! Tears came to my eyes. (Darn it, even now my screen is getting blurry as I write this, remembering her very real communication.)

Mark and I take nothing for granted. It's an intense, emotional, joyful way to live, even if the big picture sometimes looks bleak. I like it.

God's plan for our financial picture has also been so different from what I'd expected. Please, we're the coiners of the "Stagtastrophe," why would I ever have thought it would be otherwise?

I married in part for corporate security. At the end of my dad's career as an orthodontist, there was no gold watch, no pension, no 401(k), no retirement benefits beyond social security and Medicare. I craved the safety and buttoned-down conformity of the corporate life. I married a corporate man with a corporate father.

Nineteen years and seven jobs later, five of which ended not by choice, my husband is now self-employed. He runs the Stagliano Group, and is an independent sales rep for a handpicked selection of vendors. He has created a pot of gold. Gold smells a lot better than

the chamber pots we'd been clawing out of for so long. He said to me one day with a wicked grin, "This is like having a license to print money." God knows we need plenty of it to get out of debt and squirrel away a fortune for the girls.

He's a success because he's respected and trusted. His company is growing every day. There's now money in my bank account on the thirty-first of the month. (Where's that saltshaker? I feel jinxed even mentioning Mark's success.)

As our married life and our financial life become more stable, I feel hopeful that my sometimes paralyzing fears about the girls' futures will subside as we help them build happy, safe, adult lives. Will they live under our roof until we're old? Will they find a shared community home with support?

I don't know.

But I'm learning to trust in God that I'll find the right answers because God *has* answered many of my prayers.

This *is* my turn.

I'm not going to waste it.

REFERENCES

IF YOU, A FAMILY MEMBER, OR A FRIEND HAVE A LOVED ONE DIAGNOSED with autism, this list of resources will provide useful and actionable information on a wide range of topics.

Active Healing: *www.activehealing.org*
Age of Autism: *www.ageofautism.com*
Ask Dr. Sears: *www.askdrsears.com*
Autism diet info: *www.nourishinghope.org*
Autism File Magazine: *www.autismfile.com*
Autism Research Institute: *www.autism.com*
Autism One: *www.autismone.org*
Autism Speaks: *www.autismspeaks.org*
Autism Society of America: *www.autism-society.org*
Center for Autism and Related Disorders: *www.centerforautism.com*
Dr. Andrew Wakefield's book: *www.callous-disregard.com*
Everlon Diamonds (Hey, why not? A girl can dream):
   www.adiamondisforever.com
Generation Rescue: *www.generationrescue.org*
John Robison: *www.johnrobison.com*
Lovaas Center for Applied Behavior Analysis: *www.lovaas.com*
National Autism Association: *www.nationalautismassociation.org*
National Vaccine Information Center: *www.nvic.org*
Pediatric Vaccination Schedules: *www.cdc.gov/vaccines/recs/schedules
   /child-schedule.htm*
Spectrum Magazine: *www.spectrumpublications.com*
Talk About Curing Autism: *www.talkaboutcuringautism.org*
The Coalition for SafeMinds: *www.safeminds.org*

GLOSSARY OF TERMS

APPLIED Behavior Analysis (ABA): Applied behavior analysis is the process of systematically applying interventions based upon the principles of learning theory to improve socially significant behaviors to a meaningful degree, and to demonstrate that the interventions employed are responsible for the improvement in behavior (Baer, Wolf & Risley, 1968; Sulzer-Azaroff & Mayer, 1991).

"Socially significant behaviors" include reading, academics, social skills, communication, and adaptive living skills. Adaptive living skills include gross and fine motor skills, eating and food preparation, toileting, dressing, personal self-care, domestic skills, time and punctuality, money and value, home and community orientation, and work skills.

Autism: From the National Autism Association Web site: Autism is a bio-neurological developmental disability that generally appears before the age of three. Autism impacts the normal development of the brain in the areas of social interaction, communication skills, and cognitive function. Individuals with autism typically have difficulties in verbal and non-verbal communication, social interactions, and leisure or play activities. Individuals with autism often suffer from numerous physical ailments, which may include: allergies, asthma, epilepsy, digestive disorders, persistent viral infections, feeding disorders, sensory integration dysfunction, sleeping disorders, and more. Autism is diagnosed four times more often in boys than girls. Its prevalence is not affected by race, region, or socio-economic status. Since autism was first diagnosed in the U.S., the occurrence has

climbed to an alarming one in 150 people across the country. Autism does not affect life expectancy. Currently there is no cure for autism, though with early intervention and treatment, the diverse symptoms related to autism can be greatly improved.

Bella: Means beautiful in Italian. (Thank goodness our Bella is a beauty. That would have been a tragic irony the child did not need.)

Biomedical Treatment: Autism treatments that include the use of prescription and nonprescription medications, supplements, diet, and other alternative methods to treat the physical manifestations of autism spectrum disorder with the assumption that addressing the physical issues will lead to an improvement in the behavioral and psychological symptoms.

Casein: The protein found in milk.

Crapisode: (From the Urban Dictionary. Really, go look!) An autism-related event involving a child, poop, and typically the walls, carpeting, and often the child him/herself. First used in this context by a mom of three kids with autism who also happens to write. (Guess who?)

Gianna: Female Italian given name, a form of Giovanna meaning "God's grace."

Gluten: The protein found in wheat, oats, and rye.

Mia: Means "mine" in Italian.

Neurodiversity: Neurodiversity is the concept that atypical neurological development is a normal human difference and not what many would call a "brain injury" or disability.

Patterning: A series of movements that mirrors basics of a baby crawling and creeping.

Stagliano: "They stand out" according to the Babel Fish English to Italian translator. That sounds about right.

AUTHOR'S NOTE

IN THE SPRING OF 2010, A TRINITY OF EVENTS TOOK PLACE THAT SQUIRED my family through most of the Trumbull Police Department. On March 1, I was seated at my desk in my home office when I heard the sound of breaking glass.

I stood, startled, and quietly moved toward the front kitchen window and peered into the driveway.

There was a dark green sedan backed up to my garage door.

Holy sh★t, someone is invading the house.

My guardian angel, or maybe my reptilian brain, took over. We have very poor cell phone reception in our neighborhood so I grabbed the portable phone off the kitchen counter and hightailed it out my front door, just as the marauders (how often do you get to use that in context?) snuck in the garage entrance just behind the desk where I'd been working seconds ago.

I crouched down under the bushes in my front yard and called 911.

"I'm being robbed!"

I was shaking, staring back at my own house, wondering what was happening inside. I knew it wasn't a tea party.

Within ninety seconds a cruiser pulled across my driveway. I pointed toward the garage. The policeman drew his gun and entered the house.

Moments later two men burst out of my front door wearing ski masks. One ran across the street, the other tried to steal the police

car. It was locked. So he ran across the street, too. They disappeared into the narrow riverbed that winds through our neighborhood.

Long story short, the police caught one guy and he is now in prison. The other was never found. The car they left in my driveway was loaded with loot (again, who uses that word for real?). Mark and I lost a few pieces of valuable jewelry that were never recovered, but I was safe.

The local paper proclaimed, MOM OF THREE BUSTS CRIME RING! I even reenacted my part in the drama on the local Fox news channel.

That's how we met the detective in the Robbery Division.

In June, Bella and I were driving home from a trip to the bank on a clear Friday evening when our car was rear-ended, giving both of us whiplash. An eighteen-year-old had taken his eyes off the road and slammed into us. Poor Bella was scared to death. I was mostly pissed off.

That's how we met the officers in the Traffic Division.

The third contact with the police is hard to talk about. It's harder to put it onto paper.

In 2010, Bella presented four different times with an ugly, black-and-blue bruise on the top of her hand, between her thumb and Mr. Pointer. I took Bella to the pediatrician. We got X-rays. We tested for a clotting disorder. The injury was a mystery. Neither her teachers nor I could recall any incident that would create such havoc on her hand. Then, a friend who is a sports physical therapist examined the last of the four injuries and told us it was a sprain. The kind of injury that requires real force.

Through a process of elimination, we determined the one place it could be happening. We were able to watch audio/video tapes that showed an adult making contact with Bella, and we could hear Bella screaming, her body obscured behind her abuser.

There was a series of attacks over the course of two months, all recorded on security tapes.

Watching those tapes made me sick to my stomach. When Mark saw them, he said very quietly, "I've never felt such rage in my life."

That's how we met the detective in the Juvenile Division.

Bella does not speak—yet. She weighs 63 pounds soaking wet. She is passive.

She is my baby.

Her abuse is another reason I will never stop fighting for research into autism's cause, for better treatments and for therapy, and very soon I'll be focusing on adult issues with the same intensity.

I'm no Mother Teresa. But I am a Mother Warrior.

Take care.
Kim

ABOUT THE TYPE

This book was set in Perpetua, a typeface designed by the English artist Eric Gill, and cut by the Monotype Corporation between 1928 and 1930. Perpetua is a contemporary face of original design, without any direct historical antecedents. The shapes of the roman letters are derived from the techniques of stonecutting. The larger display sizes are extremely elegant and form a most distinguished series of inscriptional letters.

ABOUT THE AUTHOR

MELANIE BENJAMIN is a pseudonym for Melanie Hauser, who has written two contemporary novels. *Alice I Have Been* was her first work of historical fiction and her first under this name. Benjamin lives in Chicago.